BLACKWOOD INSTITUTE

THE COMPLETE TRILOGY

J ROSE

WILTED ROSE PUBLISHING

Dear Reader,

Thank you for following Brooklyn
and her heathens on this wild
Journey. I'm dedicating this
omnibus to you — the reader.
These stories are for you.
Thank you for your support.
Stay wild,

JRose

xx

J ROSE SHARED UNIVERSE

All of J Rose's contemporary, dark romance books are set in the same shared universe. From the walls of Blackwood Institute and Harrowdean Manor, to Sabre Security's HQ and the small town of Briar Valley, all of the characters inhabit the same world and feature in Easter egg cameos in each other's books.

You can read these books in any order, dipping in and out of different series and stories, but here is the recommended order for the full effect of the shared universe and the ties between the books.

For more information:
www.jroseauthor.com/readingorder

TWISTED HEATHENS

BLACKWOOD INSTITUTE #1

Blackwood Institute

TRIGGER WARNING

Twisted Heathens is a why choose, reverse harem romance, so the main character will have multiple love interests that she will not have to choose between.

This book is very dark and contains scenes that may be triggering for some readers. This includes self-harm, suicide, drug use and mental health themes—including psychosis, graphic violence, child abuse and sexual assault.

There is also explicit language throughout and sexual scenes involving blood play, breath play, dubious consent, mutual self-harming and light BDSM.

If you are easily offended or triggered by any of this content, please do not read this book. This is dark romance, and therefore not for the faint of heart. Additionally, this book is written for entertainment and is not intended to accurately represent the treatment of mental health issues.

PROLOGUE

BROOKLYN

"BROOKLYN?" Nurse Jackie shouts. "I've been calling you for ten minutes."

Rolling onto my side, I frown at the drooling guy stretched out on the sofa across from me. Fucking newbie. He just swallowed the pills and passed out. What a damn waste.

"And I've been ignoring you for ten minutes," I drone.

She stops at the end of the sofa and glares down at me, her patience spent. "You can't continue to treat this place like a bloody joke, Brooklyn. Get up. Now."

"Why should I?"

"The doctor is expecting you."

I flip onto my back. "It's not my therapy day."

Nurse Jackie crosses her arms. "Do I look like I care, missy? Don't give me that attitude. Get your butt up or it's another weekend in solitary."

Terror runs down my spine. I drag myself up and follow her, fearing the consequences. I can't go back there after last time. Death is fucking preferable. She guides me to the nearby shrink's office and lets me in, where I take my usual seat.

The office chair spins to reveal Doctor Zimmerman, finishing up his telephone call. "Yes, I understand. Thank you, Augustus. I'll be in touch."

The phone is returned to its cradle. Zimmerman stares down his nose at me, sliding his ugly spectacles down to give me his full, unwavering attention. Man, I want to crush those glasses under my boot.

His lips move, but nothing comes out. Ringing fills my ears as I stare at the wall behind him, where thick, treacle-like shadows are dripping down and pooling on the ground. They whisper at me, and my hands tremble in my lap.

Fucking Zimmerman, he's a son of a bitch.

Take the paperweight and smash his head in.

"Brooklyn? Are you even listening to me?"

My eyes snap up and the shadows are suddenly gone, leaving nothing but a clean, bright-white wall.

"Brooklyn! I've given you time to think. I need your answer."

I glance away and focus my gaze out of the barred window. My eyes track the path of the falling raindrops. When was the last time I felt rain on my face? Or wind in my hair? I lick my lips. Breathe. Blink. Fidget. Anything not to reply to this asshole.

"Your attitude isn't necessary. We're on the same side here."

The need to laugh bubbles up inside of me. Smirking, I turn my attention to my hands. My nails are bloody and chewed down, and my knuckles are bruised and scarred. There's an obvious tremble that comes with my heavy dose of medication.

"You aren't leaving the room until we discuss this offer. Take your time."

So be it. I can sit here all goddamn day in silence.

Zimmerman sighs, gently placing the pen down and lacing his fingers together. He refuses to look away from me or take no for an answer. Why can't he just give up on me already? I'm a lost cause. I want to scream in his face, tell him to stop trying to fix me.

"You are going to rot in here for the rest of your life if you don't accept the board of directors' offer. I cannot stress enough how precious this chance is. Don't waste it."

Chewing my ragged nails, I savour the bite of pain and coppery tang of blood. "Why shouldn't I waste it?"

Zimmerman shakes his head, clearly exasperated. "Because you have potential. Don't allow the past to control your future."

"I don't have a future. That's what the court said when they sent me to you," I point out.

"That was nearly ten months ago. We aren't progressing here, so maybe you need to be in a different environment. This place isn't right for you. That's why you need to seriously consider what we discussed yesterday."

I scoff, an amused smile tugging at my lips. "I'm with the rest of the crazies, aren't I? Exactly where I belong."

"No. The people here will never leave. Many won't even get better. With the right treatment and management, you can still have a life. You're only twenty-one."

I finally meet his eyes. Brows furrowed, the wrinkles around his face are even more pronounced than usual. He's tired. Weary. Fed up with our pointless therapy sessions.

"And what about my sentence?"

"If you complete three years at Blackwood and prove that you're rehabilitated enough to pose no threat, then you'll be free to go," Zimmerman explains. "The order has already been signed off on by the authorities. Do you understand the opportunity you've been given?"

Opportunity. I don't deserve it. I don't deserve anything, not even to live. If I take the transfer, I'll finally be free from the weight of nurses watching me. It won't be hard to find some rope, and I know how to tie a noose. Or I'll stash my pills, and without them checking under my tongue each day, it won't take long to build up enough to overdose.

With a tempting plan forming, I attempt my best obedient voice, wiping away any trace of bitterness. He can't know what I'm planning, not if I am going to succeed.

"What will I study there?" I ask, feigning interest.

That's it, keep smiling. Nod your head.

Play the good girl and then you can die.

"Anything you want. Blackwood is the first of its kind—cutting-edge experimental treatment blended with education. The recovery rate is phenomenal. You can live there comfortably and learn whatever takes your fancy. Build a life for yourself. Doesn't that sound good?"

"Well, I would like to feel normal again," I offer innocently.

Did I say that right? Convincing enough? I don't know how to cooperate. I've never done it before. If he were a half-decent doctor, he'd know that I'm lying anyway. I've never known normality. Not for a second. Why would I want it now?

"Exactly. I'm so pleased that you're interested. I really believe that you can thrive there."

Zimmerman slides the clipboard over, uncapping his pen for me to take. Glancing over the paperwork, I take in the ornate crest in the upper-right corner. The words *Ex Malo Bonum* are woven through the image in curling script.

"Just there." He points to the dotted line waiting for my signature.

I hover the pen over the page, considering. If I sign this, I'll be transferred next week. That's seven more days in this hellhole. Then, freedom. An image pops up in my brain of a memory that haunts my every moment.

Blood spewed from his mouth as I slashed his throat, stabbing at his insistent fingers to release their crushing grip. My movements were panicked as pained sobs echoed around me, closing the walls in with the weight of my crimes.

Who knew that death was so loud and messy?

Finishing writing my name, I triumphantly place the pen down. My fate is signed away to this mysterious place, for now. The facilities and programs hold no appeal to me.

I stuff the brochures in my pocket without looking. I don't intend to stick around for long. I'll end my pathetic existence the first chance I get.

"I'm proud that you've taken this step. You have a bright future ahead." Zimmerman beams. "This is the start of a whole new journey for you."

CHAPTER 1
BROOKLYN

PHOBIA - NOTHING BUT THIEVES

"LET'S get this show on the road. It's a long drive to Wales."

I tune out the guards' voices, and the mindless chatter is quickly replaced by the sputtering of the van's engine. This piece of shit has been on its last legs since the day I arrived.

Budget constraints prevent them from replacing it, I suppose. The government always has money for bombs and wars, but never for the places that actually need it.

As we pull away, I glance back through the rear window. Clearview Psychiatric Unit grows smaller in the distance, eventually disappearing into thick, London smog. I breathe a sigh of relief.

I never thought I'd see the back of that place. The only way to leave is in a body bag which, despite my best efforts, never happened. After ten months of failure, it seems like the board has finally given up.

Now, I'm Blackwood's problem.

Resting my head against the cool glass, I curl up into a more comfortable position. Bloody Nylah was screaming all night, keeping me awake. When the nurses finally dragged her away, a round of applause sounded in the unit. She loves to make a scene, especially when they threaten the feeding tube. The rest of us just want to fucking sleep.

I wonder what it'll be like in this place. Zimmerman made it sound swanky, all privately funded and shit. This institute is the shining jewel of the psychiatric community. The words *revolutionary* and *progressive* have been tossed in my face all week.

Why do I care what these people think they're doing? It's still a prison cell, no matter how it's dressed up. But it doesn't matter either way. If they hadn't arrested me in November, I would have succeeded in killing myself then.

That was the next stage of my plan. The only reason I'm still alive is those damn nosy nurses in Clearview who insisted on strict supervision after the last incident.

My fingers automatically crawl up my sleeve. The scar is thick and gnarly beneath my touch, stretching right down my forearm. I stroke the skin, breathing in the reassurance.

No one can stop me this time.

I refuse to live for a second longer than I'm made to.

The hours pass painfully slow as we drive through the countryside. I completely zone out for most of the trip. That happens a lot. It's hard to stay focused when you're drugged up to your tits on more medication than I can even keep track of.

Much later, I hear doors slamming, so I force my eyes open. I'm greeted by dark shadows filling the back of the van, and I listen as the two guards snicker while they stretch their bodies.

"Let's drop this bitch off and hit the pub for a quick one."

"I could use a drink for the drive back. This place gives me the creeps. Especially with all those dead eyes watching you. Reminds me of a graveyard, not a fucking hospital."

"Don't shit your pants, mate. The crazy bastards are locked up here for a reason."

Paul, aka Dickhead One, opens the side door and jerks his head, beckoning me outside. I hop down from the van and he flaunts a pair of familiar handcuffs.

"Really?" I huff.

"Shut up, Brooke. You know the policy."

"You weren't too bothered about policy when my lips were wrapped around your cock last week. And don't fucking call me Brooke. How many times have I told you not to use that name?"

He snaps the cuffs on unnecessarily tight as his eyes narrow. "You keep your pretty little mouth shut about that or I'll have to tell on you. Popping pills is a serious offence. Maybe it'll even increase your sentence."

"You're the one who gave them to me, wanker," I spit back.

He roughly drags me through the car park with his buddy, Dickhead Two, bringing up the rear. Both of them seem desperate to get rid of me. I've always had a way of pissing off the guards, especially since none of them ever appreciated my smart mouth.

"Don't forget my bag!" I bellow.

"I've got it, stupid bitch. Man, I hope I never see you again."

"Trust me, the feeling is mutual, you ugly old bastard."

Any further argument quickly dries up as we exit the car park and head up a cobbled street engulfed in thick mist. The temperature's dropped significantly between here and London, and heavy storm clouds hang low in the sky.

"Man, I hate the countryside," Paul complains.

I roll my eyes. "Drop me off and you can fuck off back then."

He shoves me, his fingers digging into my wrists as they escort me through the grounds. We reach a huge set of menacing wrought-iron gates that hide the gothic monstrosity ahead of us.

Paul shifts on his feet, punching the intercom button for attention. "Clearview transfer here for drop off."

There's a buzz in response, followed by a heavy clank as the gates swing open.

"Jesus," I whisper under my breath.

"Welcome to paradise, sweetheart," Paul goads.

Blackwood Institute is an imposing sight. It's somewhere between a lavish cathedral and an ancient university with its spiralling towers, vibrant stained glass and polished black stone.

Willow trees dot the landscape, and their branches sway in the wind. The quickly descending mist adds to the spookiness, obscuring much of the scenery. An uncomfortable sensation creeps down my spine, immediately setting me on edge.

There's something about this place, an inexplicable feeling, that sets off mental alarm bells. I glance around for the source of my unease, but come up empty. Maybe I'm just losing it. I'm hardly a poster girl for sanity.

After winding up the pathway, we pass beneath a grand archway. The familiar, ornate crest is displayed at the apex, proudly announcing the institute and its date of establishment. Just in case people didn't know that unstable delinquents lie ahead.

There are two grey-faced guards in booths on either side, guarding the main entrance. As we step up, I notice the vast selection of CCTV cameras that are placed at all angles. Dead black eyes blink as our presence is recorded.

A short exchange of information later, we're scanned with wand detectors and finally permitted inside. They don't even spare me a cursory glance while checking that I'm carrying no weapons and scanning my luggage. Apparently, the staff are a little too used to seeing arrivals late at night in handcuffs.

What the hell is this place?

The approaching building casts light across the manicured lawns. Once our passes are checked, we're guided to a warm reception area. The ceiling stretches upwards endlessly, with glimmering chandeliers adding to the luxury. I lose count of the paintings dotted around, along with stupid sculptures and other artefacts. Everything screams wealth and antiquity.

Is this a university, a prison or a fucking museum?

Paul smashes on the desk bell, sneering as he glances around the room. "It's like a five-star hotel in here. Hardly fit for a criminal like yourself, Brooke."

"Don't worry. If you weren't dropping me off, your shit-poor ass would never see a place like this," I quip back. "Enjoy it while you can."

Sparing a quick look around, Paul tugs on the cuffs to bring me closer. When his hand cups my ass and squeezes, I fight the urge to shiver. He doesn't deserve the satisfaction.

"No need to be rude. We might not see each other again, which is a shame. Even though you're a drugged-up skank"—his lips brush my ear, along with his sticky breath—"you've still got a tight little pussy going for you."

Hands clap together, startling him. I manage to pull my gaze from the ground despite my cheeks flaming from the public humiliation.

"Is there a problem here, gentlemen?"

The receptionist looks between us, his deep-hazel eyes questioning. My gaze travels over his neatly styled blonde hair, crisp shirt with a matching blue tie and stylish black glasses.

"Nope," Paul replies smugly. "Just dropping off this troublemaker for you."

"I'm sure you can do that without touching her."

Muttering under his breath, Paul takes a step back and reluctantly unlocks the painful cuffs. I rub my wrists, then tilt my chin up in defiance.

"Bye then. Don't let the door hit your ass on the way out."

A chuckle is smothered from behind the desk, but I don't tear my eyes away from the guards. Not yet. Paul needs to remember me with my head held high, not trampled down by his need to break me. Nobody gets away with that anymore.

"See you in Hell, sweetheart," he spits.

Quickly signing the transfer papers, both men stride back out into the night without a second glance. Good fucking riddance.

The receptionist laughs. "Well, that was unpleasant to say the least."

My attention turns back to him, standing there with a darn cute smile on his face. He's cute in a boy-next-door kind of way. A little geeky for my tastes, but there's something attractive about someone defending you, even when you don't need the help. It'll take a lot more than that to get a matching smile out of me though. I don't do *friendly* very well.

"He's like that," I offer with a shrug.

"Sure. Guards tend to have a superiority complex. It comes with the authority." He adjusts his glasses. "Anyway, you got a name?"

Staring wordlessly, it takes me a minute to realise what he's asking for. *Oh, right.* Receptionist. Stop checking out how tight his shirt is.

"It's Brooklyn West. Transferring from Clearview," I mutter.

He raises a pale-blonde eyebrow as his fingers fly across the keyboard. "Huh, not many people come from there. How'd you swing that?"

"Is it any of your business?"

"I guess not," he concedes. "Hang on, I need to get the deputy warden to come and check you over. He's been expecting you. I'll be right back."

He disappears into the back office, leaving me to look around. I spot several guards standing in each corner. Their beady eyes are fixed on me, and their hands rest on discreetly placed batons.

It's unnerving, but frankly, I wouldn't expect anything less from a place like this. We're just criminals to them. A faceless horde to boss around.

The receptionist shortly returns with an older man in tow. He's dressed in an ugly suit, with his greying hair slicked back and a portly belly hanging over his belt. I spy his ID badge and note the name *Mike Tramwell* next to a very unflattering picture.

"Brooklyn?" he asks tonelessly.

"In the flesh."

"You're late. We were expecting you this afternoon."

"Don't look at me, I just go when I'm told." I shrug as he frowns at me. "Those idiots from Clearview were the ones in charge of my transfer."

"Damn hospitals have no respect for timing." Mike shuffles through papers and slides me a stack. "Sign and let's get this over with. I'm late for dinner. The rest of the formalities will have to wait for tomorrow when the shrinks are back in."

Flipping through the forms, I sign without bothering to read them. I don't give a damn about his dinner, nor do I care what I'm signing. I have no intention of sticking around for long, so paperwork hardly matters.

At least my lateness has saved me from facing anyone else tonight. Doctors and I don't exactly get on, especially not when I'm tired and running low on fucks to give.

Mike files away the signed forms before clicking his fingers at one of the guards. "Check her over, and be quick about it."

"Seriously?" I groan, taking a step back. "I just came from a place like this. You really think I have anything on me?"

If they touch me, there'll be hell to pay.

"Standard procedure. We gonna have a problem?"

One of the guards snatches up my bag, swiftly unzipping it and depositing the contents on the reception desk. I watch with gritted teeth as he rifles through my meagre possessions, regardless of any semblance of privacy that I have left. The other marches towards me, preparing to do a pat down.

"Don't fucking touch me," I warn.

My resistance proves futile as I'm shoved into the desk, my face pressed against the wood. It's humiliating to have hands patting me down and searching my pockets, all while the cute receptionist watches in distaste.

"Shoes off," the guard grunts.

"Piss off," I reply shortly.

After a short tussle that has my cheeks burning, he tosses my battered Chucks back at me and declares that I'm all clear. I curse under my breath while lacing them, and a hand appears to help me up. Those hazel eyes stare down at me, waiting expectantly for me to accept the offer of help.

"I'm Kade. Welcome to Blackwood."

Some fucking welcome that was.

I ignore him while repacking my bag, glaring at the confiscated toiletries dumped in a rubbish bin. The remaining items are simply left on the side for me to sort. My fingers graze the stitching at the bottom that conceals the stuff that I actually care about. Thankfully, they didn't notice anything off.

"She's in Oakridge dorms. Here's the temporary pass until she gets her ID." Mike slides a key card over to Kade. "Can you sort out the rest of the arrangements in the morning?"

"I'll take her up now before I clock off," Kade replies. "It's too late for a tour, but I'll do it with the other stuff tomorrow during my free period."

Mike disappears into the office, but the guards still watch me closely. I shuffle my feet, waiting for Kade to gather some booklets and his jacket. He meets me on the other side of the desk.

"Ready? Let's go."

Anxious sweat coats my palms as we head towards the exit, and my head begins to buzz with the rising panic of the unknown. It took me so long to adjust to life at Clearview. Now, I'm stuck in the vicious cycle of doing it all over again. I cannot wait to be free of it all, no longer beholden to the laws and control of others.

Kade leads the way, leaving me to trail behind. "You're over in Oakridge. Same as me."

I shove my fear aside and focus on him, eyes locked on his tall, lithe body and trim waistline. They certainly don't look like that where I've just come from, that's for sure. He's in good shape. That stupid shirt and tie are definitely hiding a firm chest.

Then I catch on to his words. "Wait, same as you?"

"You thought I worked here, didn't you?"

Well, fuck me sideways. Preppy's a patient? Or more accurately, a prisoner. This place looks impressive, but there's enough CCTV cameras dotted around to tell me otherwise. We're being watched closely with every step we take.

"Don't worry, most people do. I just volunteer a few hours in the office each week. Keeps me busy and in the good books with management. It's fun to help out."

"Sure," I reply sarcastically.

Fun? Really?

What kind of secure unit lets their detainees work for them? I'm given no further explanation as he scans his ID at the door, then guides me out into the dark night. I automatically tighten my jacket against the chill. I think it's autumn, but who can tell? Time loses all meaning when you're separated from reality.

"What date is it?"

Kade gives me an odd look. "Uh, September tenth."

Fuck. Where did all that time go? Nearly a year of my life has vanished into thin air. It's like I stopped living overnight and became a ghost to the world. The anniversary is close—a little over two months away. I can't live to see that day. No matter what it takes, I've got to be dead before November.

"It'll be easier to see in the daylight, but this is the quad," Kade continues. "It's the centre of the institute. Everything else surrounds this."

Gesturing around at the expanse of grass and perfect gardens, it's peppered with picnic tables and old-school streetlamps that cast an orange glow. More cobbled pathways snake outwards, leading to further dated buildings in the distance. It feels like we've stepped back in time a few hundred years. I almost expect a horse and carriage to appear at any moment.

"What about the rest of it?" I ask wearily.

"I'll show you around first thing in the morning. You must be tired."

I nod, biting my lip. Why am I interested in seeing it anyway? Nothing could possibly keep me here for a second longer. It doesn't matter how nice this place appears to be.

Kade clears his throat. "So, what brings you to Blackwood?"

We walk down the central path, heading towards a glowing building in the distance. Towers twist around the roof, with arched windows and more accentuated brick. The gothic-noir theme seems to be a permanent feature around here.

"Brooklyn?" he presses.

I didn't answer for a reason, smartass.

With another sigh, he continues regardless. "Well, hopefully you'll like it here. The teaching is decent, and there's plenty to do. Your three years will fly by, I'm sure."

Does this guy ever stop fucking talking? I couldn't care less about the teaching. I certainly won't survive three years. His honey-smooth voice is managing to grate on me. I'm conditioned to silence now rather than casual conversation.

"I've been here for eighteen months. It's not bad really."

"Look," I interrupt. "As much as I appreciate the thought, can we not talk? Clearview sucked, and this place will too. Your guards have already humiliated me enough for one night. There's nothing else to say, so just show me to my room and fuck off, yeah?"

Hold it in.

You can lose it in private. Keep breathing.

"Sure," he mutters as we climb the steps to the dorms.

Upon entering the building, we're blasted with warmth. Polished chequered floors, rich panelled walls and more ugly paintings surround me.

Admittedly, it's rather nice; kind of like a stately home or something. It's a far cry from the white walls and linoleum floors of my last prison—*I mean hospital.*

Kade pauses to inspect the paperwork. "Looks like you're on the fourth floor. Room twenty."

"Key card?" I stick out my palm.

Hazel eyes resembling pools of molten caramel flecked with green stare back at me. Eventually, Kade surrenders the key card and a collection of information booklets.

"You need a photo taken for your ID badge."

"Tomorrow, right? I'll be there," I assure him.

My skin is tight and prickly, a sure warning sign that I need to be alone. I've had more interaction today than in my ten months at Clearview. My brain can't deal with it all. The need to hide increases, causing my fingers to spasm.

"You don't have any questions? Nothing?"

"Nope. Night, Kade."

Turning my back in dismissal, I grab my single bag and hightail it up the nearby stairs, taking them two at a time. Faster, move it. Don't let him see you crumble. That's private, nobody is allowed to see your vulnerability. Weakness equals exploitation in places like this.

By the time I round the corner, Kade's annoyed face has disappeared. Relief loosens my chest and breathing comes a little easier. I continue to sprint upwards, shuffling through the paperwork as I go. Room twenty. Single occupancy, thank fuck. Having a roommate will only complicate matters if I'm going to succeed in my plans.

I'm panting by the time I reach my door, glancing down the corridor lit by traditional sconces on dark-brocade wallpaper. Somewhere in the distance, angry rap music blares. There's shouting coming from behind one of the doors, followed by a heavy bang.

"Get the fuck out, now!" a deep voice roars.

When a half-naked blonde is shoved out of the room, the door is quickly slammed shut in her face.

"You're a sick bastard, Hudson!" she screeches, kicking the wood in frustration.

I fumble with the key card, trying to unlock the door. It takes too long, and I can feel her eyes on me as she turns, gathering the clothes tossed at her feet. Glancing up is a mistake. The scowl thrown my way burns like acid.

"What the fuck are you looking at? Freak."

Normally I'd stay and piss her off for some entertainment, but the shake in my hands is worsening. I'm running out of time.

Click. Finally getting the door open, I slip inside without another word. My forehead falls to the wood, and my eyes slide shut. Heartbeat hammering in my ears, I allow the sob to finally tear free from my mouth.

Red flashes behind my lids, pools of blood quickly gathering as the image forms. No matter how hard I shake my head, I can't get rid of it—the nightmare that follows me around.

I see the lampshade broken and upended on the floor. A smashed beer bottle in shards around us. Cool steel is clenched in my hand as I slide through rivulets of blood. The shadows wrapped around me that day, steeling my spine and adding fuel to my rage.

They whispered their deadly commands.

Killing is easy, Brooklyn.

You've just got to have the guts.

I open my bag, slumping against the door without even bothering to turn the light on. Moonlight illuminates enough of the room for me to see what I'm doing. My finger glides along the stitching at the bottom until I find my secret stash, fingering the edge of a hidden blade.

Sucking off Paul had its perks. A girl has to do what's necessary to survive. He was good for some things at least. The pills he snuck in for me and this precious contraband were worth the degradation. That's what I tell myself, anyway.

Shucking off my jacket and rolling up the sleeve of my sweater, I stroke the pale skin of my arm. Pearlescent scars meet my fingertips, the bumpy ridges immortalising my sins. It's all about punishment. Nobody should get away with what I did.

As razor meets flesh, hot pain grants me instant satisfaction. I press down hard and bite my lip, savouring the resultant burn. Wetness spreads, running down to my elbow.

I sneak a peek, and the sight of dark trails makes my heart thump harder as my mouth waters. So fucking beautiful. Three jagged cuts, and I'm done.

Only three. Control is necessary; if you do too many, the thrill is lessened. Pleasure comes with precision, not desperation.

I wasn't always this way. Most blame others for their demons. We're all victims one way or another, right? But not me. There's no one else to blame. I got this way all on my own.

I'm the fucking monster in this story.

CHAPTER 2
KADE

JAWS - SLEEP TOKEN

WATCHING her dash up the stairs, I stand frozen. My mouth slackens with shock and outrage. I should be used to the rudeness in this place—manners and mental health really don't mix. It serves me right for being Mr Nice Guy. Not everyone wants to be helped.

Shaking my head, I make my own way up to the fourth floor. My chest burns with every step, and the indignation I feel makes my jaw clench. She's a nobody. Just another lost cause for this hellhole to claim.

I've made it halfway through the program and only have another eighteen months to go. I can't wait to get out of here and never look back. Unlocking the door, I'm greeted by my hollering roommate playing computer games like a hooligan.

I stroll in, setting my coat and key card down. "Dude, it's been seven hours. You're still playing that stupid game?"

Phoenix jerks his chin, refusing to tear his eyes from the screen. "It's Sunday. Get off my back, Kade."

"Exactly. You've got a paper due tomorrow, right?"

He shrugs nonchalantly, gesturing towards the other bed.

"Got it covered."

I glance at my own bed. Eli is tucked away in the corner with an oversized hoodie covering his wild brown curls and blocking out the world. I can see his hands working overtime from here, smashing out the essay without stopping for air. The guy's like a machine when it comes to academia. There must be an incredible mind buried in there somewhere.

"Eli can't do all your homework for you," I berate.

"Why not? He likes doing it."

"Is that why you switched to the history class? Just because he is doing it too?"

A confident smirk crosses Phoenix's face. "You bet. My grades have never been higher."

Gotcha. He's only four years younger than me, but he behaves more like a twelve-year-old than a grown man of nineteen. I slump on my bed with a defeated sigh. Eli shifts, a pale hand reaching out to stroke my hair.

It's his way of welcoming me home without saying a word. I savour the contact with my eyes shut. For better or for worse, these two are my family; our bond runs deeper than blood ever could.

"You're particularly grumpy today. What's got you all in a twist?" Phoenix asks.

The girl flickers through my mind again. *Brooklyn.* Long legs, pin-straight blonde hair and wide, dead eyes. What is it about her that sets me on edge so badly? I normally don't give a shit about anyone beyond the guys.

"We got a new arrival. She gave quite the impression."

The sounds of gunfire and racing engines halt as Phoenix abruptly pauses the game. "A girl? Is she hot?"

"I guess. From some place called Clearview."

The hand tangled in my hair suddenly freezes. I meet Eli's widened eyes. Crap. That's where I've heard that name before. Naturally, I checked these guys' files when we became friends. I'm a control freak sometimes. Well, all of the time.

"Sorry, man," I apologise.

Shaking his head, Eli's hand retreats and returns to the essay. He burrows deeper into the hoodie to escape. I put my foot right in it there like a complete moron.

Phoenix smirks. "You don't normally notice things like that."

"Like what?"

"Whether a girl is hot or not."

Rolling my eyes, I loosen my tie and pop a few shirt buttons. "Shut up, Nix. It's just an observation."

"Sounds like you observed her very… *enthusiastically.*"

After removing one of my shoes, I launch it across the room. The resultant yelp of pain makes me smile.

"She's nothing. Let's talk about something else, yeah?"

Phoenix grumbles in agreement, tossing the shoe aside and rubbing his head. I slide my phone from my pocket and check to see if Hudson has returned my calls yet. But, of course, he has not.

"You seen Hudson today?"

"Last I saw him, he was off to screw Britt again."

What the hell is he playing at? Just the idea of that bitch touching me is revolting. There isn't a guy in Blackwood that she hasn't tried it on with at least once.

"Fine. I'm going to take a shower."

"Don't take too long," Phoenix quips back. "We're playing football with Rio in half an hour."

"Do we have to? He's a dick."

"Agreed, but I owe him for those beers and cigarettes. We've got to play."

Heading to the shared bathroom, I slam the door. I can't stand Rio and his idiotic entourage. All those assholes drive me insane, like it's somehow a requirement to be an air-headed son of a bitch. It doesn't take much to be a decent human being these days.

Ditching my glasses and clothing, I step into the shower and turn the heat up to max. Tension thrums beneath my skin. Brooklyn's snark is what put me in this foul mood.

No one talks to me like that around here, and most view me as untouchable. I'm the only one who is allowed to work in the office, and the position grants me a level of respect and immunity.

The way she breezed straight past that... fuck if it didn't turn me on a little. I've got to get a grip. No attachments, no distractions. That was the deal. I'm here for one reason and one reason only, and nothing is allowed to distract me from that.

However, her empty, lifeless eyes enter my mind again. The look of ashamed anger on her face as that creep had his hands all over her had my blood heating with anger. Despite the tell-tale tremble in her body, though, her sharp tongue hit right back.

Goddammit, that was a pretty sight to behold.

My hand wraps around my hard cock. I don't get crushes like some lovesick teenager, yet all I want is to bang on her door until she answers, take her in my arms and steal away the look of despair that is so clearly cemented in her eyes.

Resting my other hand against the wall, I work my shaft almost angrily, frustrated by my own irrational desire. Imagining the baggy sweater falling from her body to reveal creamy-white skin, I kiss my way up her stomach, chest and neck. Lips meeting, she's gasping into my mouth as I touch her where she wants it.

It's not long before I'm groaning out my release. She's just the newbie. That's all this is. I'll soon forget about her, and she'll melt into the background like the rest of the screw-ups in this place. Insignificant and unimportant. Nobody holds my attention for long, not around here.

Eighteen more months.

Damn, it can't go quick enough.

CHAPTER 3
BROOKLYN

I WANT OUT - LOWBORN

SUNLIGHT BATHES ME IN WARMTH. Streaks of orange, pink and red paint the sky as the darkness of night abates. I let my gritty eyes sink shut, savouring the strange feeling. It's been too long since I've watched a sunrise that wasn't from behind metal bars.

My mum used to drag me out of bed to do it with her when I was a kid. No matter the weather, she insisted we watch, and it became a daily ritual for most of my childhood. Even when she was in the depths of her sickness and responsible for the bruises that stained my skin, it was the one constant I could count on.

Come on, Brooke.

Put yourself in the way of beauty.

Another yawn rips free from my mouth. I'm exhausted. By the time I'd swept my hand over every inch of the tiny room assigned to me, it was past midnight. But you always have to check; I learnt that quickly in Clearview.

When the clinicians at Clearview had put me in solitary for the first time, I'd discovered a stash of pills in a cracked brick. Based on the coma-like state they'd left me in after I overdosed, they were someone's meds that had been fake-swallowed and saved for a rainy day.

No such gifts were left for me here.

I'll have to do it myself.

Nearby, footsteps break my precious solitude. I look around, and my eyes land on an early-morning jogger. It seems I'm not the only one who can't sleep.

He's gangly, all long limbs and skinny skater-boy vibes. Even from here, I can see the dense curls sticking out of his cap. My attention focuses on the hard muscles of his calves. He's shredded in a way that suggests this is a regular exercise routine.

He doesn't notice my presence and keeps on running, which suits me just fine since I'm really not up for conversation. I was awake all night, tossing and turning as the walls laughed at me.

Just the thought of my upcoming morning tour leaves my mouth dry. That preppy geek, Kade, is supposed to be taking me. I don't need a tour. Once I see the shrink, I can get the ball rolling.

It won't take long to build up a nice little cocktail of drugs—enough to stop my heart and choke me to death. It's not a pretty way to go, but beggars can't be choosers. The level of privacy I have in this place is incredible.

They make you shit with the door open in Clearview, so this is a fucking dream to me. Doc was right about what an opportunity Blackwood is, and it's one that I fully intend to embrace.

I take off through the quad, intent on avoiding the crowds. I'll just be fresh meat for them to pick apart and bully. I still remember my first day in Clearview. The guards had marched me into the recreation room and sat me amongst the other lifers. They were exchanging diagnoses like it was a slumber party, all competing with one another. Fuck that.

I'm floored when the entrance door to the dorms refuses to open. Not even a bit. Cursing, I kick the stupid thing. When it still doesn't budge, I slam my body into it and relish the resultant pain. Of course. I don't have a fucking ID badge yet. I came in with Kade last night using the temporary pass.

There's a high-pitched beep and it swings open, causing me to stumble. My back hits something hard, but it's too warm and nice smelling to be a wall.

I turn my head and meet the bright-green eyes of the jogger. He's staring at me blankly, looking almost shocked. His hands grip my arms to prevent me from falling.

"Uh, th-thanks," I stammer.

He continues to look straight at me, his emerald orbs teeming with intelligence. Not a word passes his lips as he studies me before eventually releasing his iron-like grip.

I watch as he disappears inside the building, leaving me staring at his back like an idiot. Clearly, it's not just me who dislikes small talk. But with a tight ass like that, he doesn't really need to say a word.

Back in my small bedroom, I prepare for the day. It's not that bad here. With a surprisingly comfortable bed, white sheets and fluffy pillows, it's better than the lumpy cot I had previously.

The room features grey walls and a built-in mahogany desk, along with matching curtains that hide a heavily barred window. Not too shabby. I guess the private sponsors for this experimental program pay well.

Heaving my bag up, I find that everything is a mess inside after the search last night. My belongings are meagre. Four t-shirts, two sweaters, one leather jacket and two pairs of jeans.

I have a journal that hides some old photographs inside and two pairs of shoes —my dirty Chucks and a pair of ancient Doc Martens. Beneath the stitching, there's a half-empty carton of cigarettes, a lighter and two more razor blades that are all tucked into a secret pocket.

I don't own much. By the time the police caught up to me, the contents of this bag were my entire life. I'm lucky that I've managed to hold on to everything. Especially the creased, dog-eared polaroids. I'd intended to throw myself in front of the train while holding them but was arrested instead.

Choosing my favourite acid-wash jeans and worn *Nirvana* shirt, I dress in silence. My mind ticks away anxiously, even as I lace up my neon-pink Doc Martens. I wonder what will happen to the bag when I'm gone.

Will they throw it away? My shit is worthless. I should get rid of the journal myself though. Someone will only enjoy reading it and feigning insight into why I took my life. Fuck that. That moment would be mine to own. I'll be dying on my terms, in my way and when I choose to.

Not like he did. You took that from him, a voice whispers from across the room. My head snaps up as I search around, but I find myself alone without even a shadow taunting me. Someone knocks on my door, bringing me back to reality as I force air back into my constricted lungs.

"Brooklyn? You in?"

Sliding my best blank expression into place, I grab my pack of cigarettes and leather jacket before opening the door.

"Good morning," Kade greets.

He's dressed to the nines again in a pale-blue shirt with a navy tie. With his black-rimmed glasses and slick, blonde hair, he's probably the fantasy of many female patients around here.

"Uh-huh," I mutter.

Not going to fool me with that megawatt smile, pretty boy.

"Good sleep?" he enquires while leading the way downstairs.

"Sure."

We head outside, and I keep my hair loose around my face to shield me from unwanted attention. If anyone tries to befriend me, I'll just punch them in the face. That should ward off any further attempts at interaction.

"Let's get the rest of the boring stuff sorted and then I'll show you around, yeah?" Kade offers.

"Whatever. You're the boss."

I can feel him looking at me, but I don't react.

He'll learn soon enough.

The quad is a little busier, with a few patients milling about. By the time we get back to the main building, at least three people have greeted Kade. Seems like Mr Popular over here has a lot of friends. I definitely need to get rid of him.

Kade logs in to the computer at the reception desk, leaving me to linger awkwardly. He just walks in like he owns the place and doesn't even bat an eye. Who the hell is this guy? He doesn't act like a patient whatsoever.

"Right," he begins cheerfully. "So there are a bunch of other forms that you need to fill out and return. Sorry, I'm sure you know how complicated all this transfer stuff is."

Kade attempts to roll his eyes, but I refuse to laugh. He stares at me for a long second before looking away.

"It looks like you're booked in with Doctor Ashley at three o'clock today for your psych eval and orientation." He gathers the necessary paperwork. "Give it all to her, and she can return it to the office."

"Got it."

"Now we just need to take your ID picture and we're good to go. Did you get a chance to read everything last night to submit your choices?"

"My… choices?"

Kade pins me with an exasperated look. "The subjects you want to study? In the booklets I gave you?"

Oh, the ones I discarded without a second glance.

"Not so much, no."

"Well, what do you enjoy?"

I stare at him blankly. "What do I enjoy?"

The frown I receive in response does nothing to improve my mood. Fists clenching, I glance away. After glaring at the wall for a second, I then look at my shoes. Enjoy? Focus? Studying? It's like he's speaking a whole different language.

"Come on, there must be something. What did you do in school?"

Drank too much and fucked the hot teaching assistant for a gram of weed. I press my lips together, holding back the truth. That's a little too embarrassing to share out loud.

"Brooklyn?"

His voice sounds far away as I begin to spiral, panic taking hold. I don't know. There's no answer. I don't fucking enjoy anything, and I haven't for a long time. When was the last time I did something for fun? Not since the sickness inside of me took root and ruined my entire life.

"N-Nothing. I did nothing."

"Why won't you tell me?"

Breathing in sharply, I slam my hands on the welcome desk. A pencil pot goes flying and crashes to the floor. Kade flinches back, his eyes wide with surprise.

"Are you fucking deaf? I don't enjoy anything," I yell at him. "I don't want to study anything. And I don't want to be here or talk to you. Capiche, asshole?"

We glower at each other, neither of us willing to back down. I briefly consider reaching over to grab his tie to strangle him with. The temptation is so strong that it makes my fingers twitch.

"I'll just sign you up for a taster," Kade concludes.

"What?" I frown at him.

"You'll do a bunch of different classes for a couple of days to get a feel for things."

My teeth snap together. Breaking his perfectly straight nose isn't the best idea, no matter how tempting the thought is. I can almost hear the bone cracking beneath my fist.

"Fine. Taster it is."

After more keyboard tapping and paperwork, I'm given a schedule that begins tomorrow and lasts for two days. The variety of subjects makes me cringe. This is going to be torture. Hell if they think I'm doing sports though.

"Right, picture time."

Kade disappears to a back office, returning a minute later with a digital camera. I stand straight and manage a tiny, forced smile. The act physically pains me. He raises the camera, ready to snap the picture, but hesitates.

"Hang on…"

Before I can move or smack his hand away, Kade comes close and tucks some stray hair behind my ear. His fingers brush my cheek, causing my heart to stutter. Perceptive eyes watch me, and he looks like he wants to say more, but then retreats.

"Perfect."

The lens snaps as a few shots are taken, and then his back turns. I don't let out my held breath until he retreats to the back office once more. Did I just imagine that? When Kade reappears, I force myself to act unaffected.

"Your ID should be ready in a few hours. You'll be able to access buildings and register your attendance then," he explains.

"Understood."

"It's for the cafeteria as well. Three meals a day and snacks are all provided for you. Unless you're one of the anorexics—they have a different arrangement."

"Yeah, I'm not."

"Good to know. Let's go, I don't have all day."

CHAPTER 4
ELI

SAIL - AWOLNATION

"FUCKING HOTHEAD NEARLY BROKE MY ANKLE!" Phoenix complains, stabbing his eggs. "What happened to playing for fun and blowing off steam?"

I lift one shoulder and drop it in a half-assed shrug.

"I guess you're right. No point dwelling on it," he adds.

Gesturing to his half-full plate, I bob my head.

"Chill, Eli. I hate Monday morning classes. It's too early."

I hate every second of the day, week and month. But you don't see me bitching about it. Hell, you don't see me speaking at all. Not when my brain is full of flavours and confusion. Just functioning is hard enough.

My tongue was stolen a long time ago. Words only pass my lips once in a blue moon because I'm too busy dealing with the constant sensory overload. Speaking only worsens my synaesthesia. Every word and emotion brings new flavours or scents, and it's just too much.

"Earth to Eli. You're gonna want to see this."

He's nodding at something behind me. Tilting my head, my eyes track across the room as I scan familiar, numb faces, some more alive than others.

We're a cacophony of failures here. Some are worse than others, but we're all fucking broken. We are the rejects of society, stuck in a broken system all in the name of experimentation.

Kade parts the crowd as he strides in. More heads turn when they realise he isn't alone. Everything stops as my eyes land on the familiar face following him, one that took me by complete surprise after my jog this morning.

Stomping into the room in her bright-pink boots with her hands scrunched into balls, I can see her temper clearly hasn't changed. Even from here I notice that her angled jaw is clenched and her perfect pixie face is marred by a fierce grimace. Her rage tastes like burned toast, acrid and bitter on my palate.

"Do you reckon that's her?"

I nod in response.

Brooklyn. Her name is scored into my memory. I've already met the ghost that's riled Kade up so badly before I came to Blackwood, but I never expected to see her again. She looks even worse than before with protruding bones, pale skin and that damned blank face, like she doesn't know how to smile.

"She's hot, but the poor girl looks half dead."

The glare I throw at Phoenix comes easily. His big mouth will get him into serious trouble one day. I feel like I'm chewing ashes as anger wells up inside of me. Breathing deep, I clear my mind and wash the flavour away. It's not real.

"They're coming this way," Phoenix whispers.

My heart pounds. I may already know Brooklyn, but we've never been formally introduced. I always preferred to watch from afar, unable to ever speak to her. What if she remembers me? What if she realises who I am?

"Morning, gents," Kade greets.

He places his breakfast down on my left, leaving the seat opposite vacant. Fucking hell. Why did he do that? Burned waffles. Roaring fire. Cigarette ash. *Calm down and get a grip, Eli.* It's not bloody real.

"Take a seat. We don't bite," Phoenix invites.

I can feel Brooklyn hesitating, lingering just behind me. There's an audible sigh that makes me want to chuckle. I feel like that as well. She eventually shuffles past, plonking an apple and a bottle of water down. The first thing I recognise is her frayed band shirt. It's the same one she wore in Clearview.

"Guys, this is Brooklyn. She's new here."

Phoenix immediately shifts closer. "I'm Phoenix."

He sticks his hand out expectantly. She eyes him distrustfully, refusing to shake.

"Hi," she deadpans.

He quickly recovers, his hand retreating and sweeping through his midnight-blue hair instead. Smooth Talker here isn't used to being dismissed. Our eyes connect and he scowls, making my lips twitch into a tiny smile. Serves him right.

Candyfloss and full-fat coke.

Amusement is a good taste.

"Brooklyn is doing a two-day taster from tomorrow. Maybe you can both show her to history class in the morning?" Kade suggests.

He's frustrated. I can see it easily. That tastes like spoiled, sour milk. Negativity in others is never pleasant, hence my avoidance of pretty much everyone but the guys. Talking is completely off the table though, even with those I trust.

"It'll be nice to have some company other than this chatterbox," Phoenix says.

I flip him off automatically, gaining Brooklyn's attention. Her gaze burns, eviscerating me until I'm looking up and making rare eye contact. Pale-grey puddles stare back, framed by long lashes.

Her nose is small and pert, and her lips are chapped and red from excessive chewing. She recognises me from this morning when I nearly fell over with shock from realising it was her.

"This is Eli. He doesn't talk much," Kade explains.

I hate being noticed and judged, hate being *seen*. Invisibility is my friend and protector. Her mind must be working overtime, wondering why I don't introduce myself.

Flipping up my hood, I burrow into the protective bubble of my *Bring Me The Horizon* hoodie. Drop eye contact. Tuck my chin downwards. Anything to escape.

"Nice to meet you," she murmurs, so low I almost miss it.

Brooklyn sees more of me than I'm comfortable with. She sees me far too easily. Far too deeply. Panic floods my mind, sharp and sour like tart grapefruit, so strong it's almost painful.

"So, what are you planning to study here?" Phoenix interjects.

"She doesn't know yet," Kade responds.

"She can answer for herself, thank you very much."

Her voice is gravelly and low, not like the overbearing whine of other girls. It's music to my ears. I hate the screechers; they overwhelm me the most. Hudson often attracts such female interest, and it drives me mad. So many emotions on display to fuck my head with.

Kade clears his throat. "Be my guest."

"I'm not sure yet. That's all," she mutters.

"Well, there's plenty of space in the history course," Phoenix rambles, desperately needing to fill the silence. "It's boring as fuck, and the reading is long, but there's worse things to be doing. Maths? Science?"

"No maths," Brooklyn snaps.

"Science?"

"Nope."

"Err, English?"

No immediate response. He's got her attention now.

"It's a popular choice," Kade clarifies.

I can practically feel her nervous energy from here. It's thick, like that awful cough syrup you were given as a kid. Other people's anxiety is a real issue for me. I've got enough of my own to manage.

"I don't know. How many times do I have to say it? Just back off."

Her voice is high and defensive, and it pushes me over the edge. I lower my head to the table, fighting back the rush of sensations. She's a ball of anger and hatred. It's making me sick to my stomach. Too many feelings, too many tastes. All I want is to be left alone. I can't deal with this.

Kade gently rubs my back, offering comfort. He's the only one that helps calm me. Cool and composed, he's like a soothing balm on burned skin. My favourite kind of person. The other two are more difficult to be around, especially when Phoenix has a manic episode. Brooklyn's an unstable element in this recipe for disaster. It's unhinging me already.

"It's okay, bud. We'll drop it now. Just breathe," Kade encourages.

"Is he okay?" Brooklyn asks.

"It's kind of hard to explain. Eli?"

I bob my head, issuing my consent. Once she knows, it'll be easier. She'll run in fear and that'll be it. I can slink back into the background where I belong, and quietly watch her just like before. She'll never even know.

"Eli has a rare condition called lexical-gustatory synaesthesia," Kade begins. "Essentially, it means that he can... taste emotions."

"Taste emotions?" she repeats.

"Particularly strong ones. They create sensations in him that he can't control. It's overwhelming and frightening. We try not to disagree or argue around him for this reason."

Cue the disgust and judgement.

"I see."

Something touches my hood, then my hand. It's her fingers, brushing tentatively. I raise my head, daring to sneak a glance. She isn't frowning or laughing, and there's no cruel taunt or joke. This is something else. Cool and refreshing, like a glass of iced water on a hot day.

"I'm sorry. I didn't know."

She's apologising? Is that... a smile?

"Having a quirky brain isn't always a bad thing, Eli."

With that she looks away, picking up her apple to bite into. The others are staring too, shocked by her reaction. No one treats me like that outside of the group. I'm a freak to them all, the butt of many jokes. But she's just rolling with it regardless.

Licking my lips, I force the exotic taste of surprise from my mouth. Preparing. Gathering strength. Mustering courage. *Come on, Eli. Fucking get it out already. The girl's waiting.* But no words come, just like usual. They're lodged in my throat, refusing to surface as fear wraps around my vocal cords.

Instead, I manage a tiny smile, hoping to convey my gratitude. On her lips, she wears a matching smile that takes my breath away. She's beautiful when she's like that. Goddammit, I need to see that smile again. It tastes fucking good. Rare happiness. Like freshly cut grass or a recent rainfall.

We lapse into silence, other than the crunching of her eating the apple. The other two are having some kind of wordless conversation with glances and looks.

A heckling voice interrupts the peace. "Yo, Nix. You really sucked last night, man."

Phoenix pouts. "Fuck off, Rio. You play dirty, and it's not fair."

The overbearing dickhead and his trio of assholes circle the table. I look away. They're far too boisterous for me to deal with. Rio runs shit around here among the patients, so he's often trying to screw with me. I can see Brooklyn watching, and I tense knowing that she can see through me even better now. It's uncomfortable as hell.

"Who's this? Been a while since we've had some new pussy in this place," Rio jeers, scooting up close to her.

My blood boils just seeing her shiver, and the awful taste of smoke back in my mouth as I swallow ashes. *Leave her alone, asshole.* If only I could scream it in his face or actually do something. I'm sitting here like a scared kid, unable to mount any defence on her behalf.

"Hey there, hotness. Name's Rio. Room thirty-seven, if you're interested."

"I'm not."

Her voice lashes like a bolt of lightning. Unwavering with fury, she's got strength beneath that weak, trembling exterior. I like that.

"No need to be so rude. I'm just being friendly," Rio sneers. "You'll learn that

I'm kind of a big deal around here, so better cut it out with the attitude. Besides, you look out of place with these misfits. Especially this one."

He jerks a finger in my direction. I'd love to cut it off and shove it down his throat until he chokes to death. What a tempting thought.

"Come join us at our table and we'll show you a good time, yeah?"

"Nope," Brooklyn replies.

"Excuse me?"

Rio is a prick, but he's not someone to be messed with. Places like this run on respect and favours—the code of fellow imprisoned patients. Phoenix and Hudson have proven that with many black eyes in the past. But Brooklyn doesn't care, turning her cold expression on him.

"I said no, fuckface. Get lost before I become less friendly."

Rio's laugh is amused, like he's enjoying the fight. I get the appeal; she's a ballbuster and nobody really stands up to him anymore. He's scared everyone into submission.

"I said come and sit with us. What part of that don't you understand?"

When his fingers tighten on her chin, I see red. Before I can launch myself across the table and punch his goddamn lights out, Brooklyn takes matters into her own hands. There's the blur of her fist sailing through the air, then an echoing crack.

She's got a mean right hook. Rather embarrassingly, it's a huge turn on, seeing the way she's leaning over Rio, dominating the space and humiliating him in front of the whole cafeteria.

"Learn how to take no for an answer, you piece of shit," Brooklyn spits at him. "Now, get out of here before I embarrass you further. God knows your reputation can't take another hit like that."

Rio manages to stand, a hand clasped over his bleeding face. "You're a fucking psychopath! What the hell? Dumb bitch."

Brooklyn grins. It's nothing like the shy smile I received. This one is dark and threatening, with her eyes pinched and pupils darkened. Someone else entirely stands before us now, a side of her I've never seen.

"You bet. Don't forget it. Annoy me again, and I'll break your fucking leg."

Rio and his backup scramble before the guards catch wind of what happened and punish us all. The whole cafeteria is staring, but she doesn't cower or back down. This girl is something else. She has a brutal alter-ego beneath the vulnerable surface. I'm beyond intrigued, and hard, just watching her.

"The hell are you all looking at?" Brooklyn bellows.

Gazes are averted, and she keeps her head high until conversation resumes. I shift uncomfortably, my dick aching from within its denim prison. The fire in her eyes and steel in her spine is incredible.

"Fuck, I think you might be my new favourite," Phoenix gasps.

She laughs, returning to her half-eaten apple like nothing happened. We're in for trouble with this one.

CHAPTER 5
BROOKLYN

I FALL APART - POST MALONE

"ALONG THE HALL, second door on the left."

I nod my thanks to the receptionist, heading in that direction while mentally preparing for the torture ahead. I hate shrinks. They're pretentious, overbearing assholes. I've never met one who didn't act like a pompous twat, using certificates and qualifications to tell me that I'm mentally fucked.

Thanks, like I didn't already know that.

How kind of them to highlight my failures.

I reach the second door at the end of the thickly carpeted hallway and run my finger over the engraved name tag. Doctor Mariam Ashley. *Remember, play along. You know the lines.*

Yes, Doctor, I want to improve.

No, I don't want to die.

Yes, I'm taking my medication.

Weight loss? Just my metabolism.

I'm committed to my recovery, you know.

A voice calls for me to enter, and I slip inside. It's a spacious room, all tall bookshelves and soft lighting. There's the standard sofa, with two armchairs and a coffee table. Tissues are front and centre, of course. I don't need to look at the wall to confirm the rows of framed degrees.

The blink of a CCTV camera in the corner surprises me. I keep seeing them everywhere, discreetly tucked away but watching nonetheless. Dozens are in every room, even more than the few they had in Clearview.

"Ah, you must be Brooklyn. Please, take a seat."

Doctor Ashley stands, circling the desk to join me. She has slightly greying hair and wears a practical suit with bright-red glasses. I'd say she's middle-aged but ageing gracefully. There's no criticising the enthusiastic smile that's spread across her face, even if she looks mildly unhinged. No one is that happy.

"Hi. Yeah, that's me," I force out.

I bypass the sofa, taking one of the armchairs instead. She takes the other, folding her legs gracefully while flourishing a pen and notepad.

"Right then. It's a pleasure to meet you. Please call me Mariam. We like to keep things nice and relaxed here. I want you to feel comfortable with me."

I stare in disbelief. Relaxed? Comfortable? It's different from the sedatives and padded rooms of the last ten months, and that scares me. I like to know the status quo, and this place is defying all expectations so far. Experimental doesn't even begin to cover it.

"I've been informed by Doctor Zimmerman about your history and treatment. I agree with his assessment that this place could be beneficial for you."

"You do?"

"As much respect as I have for his tenure, some find themselves lost in the system at Clearview, and they never step outside ever again."

"Maybe there's a reason for that," I comment.

"And what's that?"

She sits back, eyeing me expectantly.

"I'm hardly innocent."

"Do you think that you deserve to be punished?"

I dig my nails into my palms. "Don't you?"

Sighing, Mariam removes her glasses. "Brooklyn, you were in the depths of a psychotic episode when you committed your crime. Schizophrenia is a debilitating illness when not managed properly. Your sentence was passed with that in mind. You have a disease."

Insanity. I hate that word for implying that I was ever sane to begin with.

"Why am I here then? Why am I not locked up?" I ask defiantly. "*Dangerously unhinged and vicious*, is what the judge called me. You know that, right? I'm sure it's in my fucking file."

"Yes, it is. The answer is simple. We are the best facility equipped to deal with a young adult, such as yourself, who has found her life turned upside down by mental illness."

She makes it sound so innocent, like the sickness thrumming through my veins isn't responsible for all the blood I've shed.

"The ethos of our experimental program centres on rehabilitation, not punishment," she continues. "This isn't a prison, it's a treatment facility. You are a patient here, not a prisoner."

"I can leave?" I chip in.

And go jump off a bridge, something whispers mentally.

"No. You've been transferred here, not admitted on a voluntary basis as some are," she answers firmly.

My heart sinks in my chest. "Right."

"You are still sectioned by law until you are stable. Finish the program, and then you can transition back into the community. Where you will still be supervised, I might add."

Her fancy fucking language isn't fooling me. This place is just another prison, dressed up to look more appealing to the world.

"Look, I'm going to level with you," Mariam begins.

I shrug, inviting her to continue.

"You're a tough nut to crack. Am I right?"

I open my mouth slightly before clicking it shut.

"Your history is complex and extensive," she clarifies. "This isn't going to be an easy process. Clearview didn't work, so we're the other option."

"You sound confident."

"I have faith in the unique system we've built here with education, therapy and rehabilitation in equal measure. You cannot achieve recovery without all three to help you along the way. Frankly, if this place can't stabilise you, then nowhere can."

"What are you suggesting?" I grit out.

This obedience thing is killing me.

"Individual therapy with me twice a week. We also run a group session that I'd like you to attend. I want to change your medication too."

That peaks my interest. "Oh?"

"There are some avenues for managing your condition that haven't yet been explored. We'll add in some new experimental drugs to see if that gets things moving along."

This must be what winning feels like. More drugs? Yes, Doctor. More fucking ammo for me to use. What a goddamn victory. I gloss right over the other shit. It doesn't matter much to me anyway. I've gotten what I wanted.

"That sounds good. I really want to get better."

Fuck, I'm good. I almost believe myself.

"Another thing I want you to work on is embracing the system here," Mariam instructs. "We run a tight ship with a rigid schedule, but sometimes that's the best thing for you."

I smile innocently. "What do you want me to do?"

"Pick a subject to study, and then throw yourself into a routine. Maybe even make a few friends. It'll be good for you to experience some normality and discipline."

"I can do that," I lie easily.

She fiddles with her glasses, offering me a smile. "No more hospital life for you. Think of it as a fresh start for you to move on from the past."

I have to remind my heart that this isn't real. The initial blossoms of hope are pointless. Quickly crushed. I can never have a normal life, no matter how confident she is otherwise. That's not how things work. The world doesn't just forgive and forget. I deserve my punishment. I deserve to die alone.

"Sounds like a plan," I concede.

Mariam writes aggressively for a few seconds while nodding to herself. "Fabulous. I'll get all the relevant information to you. I'm looking forward to seeing you for our individual session. Now, there was one other thing…"

She returns to the desk and begins digging through stacks of paper. My fingers drum on my crossed leg as my impatience returns. *Just give me the prescription and let me go already*, I want to yell. Her whole enthusiastic demeanour is tiresome.

"Ah, here. Doctor Zimmerman sent these for you. There seems to be a bunch of letters here, backdated by several months. He apparently made the executive decision not to share them with you while your recovery was so fragile."

Who would write to me? And what kind of fascist bastard keeps personal correspondence from a patient? The questions mount as my emotions spiral out of control. I'm shaking with anger, barely containing it as my hands clench into fists.

"Why?" I manage to say.

Mariam shakes her head. "Like I said, we're not Clearview. I do things differently around here. You should be in control of your own communication, regardless of your mental state."

She offers me a conciliatory smile as she hands me the bundle, but I don't return it. The letters are heavy in my hand, and the burden instantly weighs me down. I have no one, literally no one. Where did all these unanswered letters come from?

"I'll let you go early so you can dive right in. Someone's probably waiting impatiently for your reply."

She sounds so eager, it's infuriating.

"Family, perhaps?" she prompts. "You should let them know how you're getting on."

"Uh-huh. Maybe."

I don't fucking have any family, but I'll say anything to get out of here. Once I've handed over the paperwork, I'm finally free. Meds are served after dinner apparently, so the rest of the afternoon is mine.

I finger the worn envelopes as my eyes flick over the scrawled writing. Pulling the first letter free from the bundle, I flip it to search for a return address. The back of the envelope features more rushed penmanship, naming the sender.

Allison Brunel.

A chill washes over me, flooding every inch of my body as uncontrollable trembling begins. No. No. Not happening. There has to be dozens of letters here. Are they all from her? Fuck me. I can't do this.

You did this. Now you will pay the price.

I never knew a voice could hold that much venom until the day she said that. Shaking my head, I try to push the sickening memory away of the accusations that were tossed at me; of the cruel insults and vicious words that I carry with me every damn day. It's too raw, too real. All I feel is guilt.

My fingers twitch with the need to cut. To release. I have to get it out, and this is the only way I know how. Fuck the therapy, it doesn't do shit anyway. Only one thing helps. I don't deserve any better. Only pain.

Tucking the dreaded bundle into my pocket, I take off down the corridor. Counting each step in my head, I breathe in time to the rhythm. Meds tonight. That's three doses. Within a week or two, I should have enough.

No mistakes this time.

No second chances or repeats.

No waking up in a hospital bed.

I have to fucking die.

CHAPTER 6
PHOENIX

KISS - LIL PEEP

I RAM my cock deep into his throat, and my eyes roll back with pleasure. Tyler always takes it deep. His skilled mouth almost makes his unbearable personality worth it. Almost.

Grasping his hair, I thrust faster. Harder. Rougher. I pour all my frustration and arousal into the movements. He continues without complaint, not even the bat of an eye.

That's the thing about fucking guys.

It's so much simpler. Less hassle.

There's one girl that has caught my attention. One particular beauty with enough sass and ferocity to intrigue even me. Being bisexual isn't always linear. It's not equal in terms of attraction.

I just go where the wind takes me and don't pay much attention. But lately, nothing's gotten me even remotely hard. Screwing Tyler is just a means to an end to release my manic energy before it destroys me.

I've been all worked up since she drew blood yesterday, owning Rio's ass without stopping for a breath. Months of boredom ended in that moment. All I wanted to do was lean in and lick the blood from her bruised knuckles, then fuck her so hard she wouldn't be able to walk straight for a week.

Groaning, I dump my load in Tyler's throat. He slows, obediently swallowing. Dammit, imagine Brooklyn on her knees down there with her pert lips wrapped around my shaft and my hand fisted in her long hair.

I'd love to tie her up and make her submit to me, all while knowing the fierce woman that lies beneath the surface. That'd make her surrender even sweeter.

"Nix?"

Tyler's staring up at me expectantly, but all I feel is revulsion. Why am I such an asshole? Using people isn't cool. I know that, yet I can't seem to help myself.

"Yeah, thanks."

I zip up my ripped, black jeans, then turn my back to him.

"That's it?"

"What else do you want from me?"

Tyler grabs my shoulders. "I want you to fucking care. To act like you actually give a shit about me for once."

Not likely. Feelings aren't really my jam.

"It's not going to happen. You know we're not about that," I reply emotionlessly. "We agreed on no strings attached."

Tears fill his eyes. Jeez, great. Another meltdown.

"You're a bastard, you know that?"

I shrug. "Yep, I'm aware."

"Goddamn junkie, that's what you are. A screwed-up, unstable addict. I'm just another fix to you, right? You can't get any precious drugs to kill yourself with, so you fuck with people instead."

Tyler turns to leave, angrily wiping the moisture from his red face, but I can't find it in myself to care. Not really. I'm aware of how shitty that is. But truthfully, he means nothing to me. This is all superficial.

Yep, I'm a fucking junkie. He got that right. Addicted to ruining others for my own amusement.

"I'm done, Nix. You've pushed me too far this time."

I gesture to the door. "Fine, fuck off then. Don't come back."

His jaw drops, and hands ball into fists. "How can you treat me like this?"

I clasp his face, tilting it up to assert my dominance. The sight of fear and shame swirling in his eyes makes me smile. That's right, I hope it fucking hurts. This is the real me.

Beneath the smiles and banter, there's something a hell of a lot darker. I'm good at playing the joker and cracking wise in public. But in private? Not so much.

"Listen up, Tyler. You're nothing more than a piece of ass to me. You got that? As of right now, you have outlived your purpose. I'm bored. So, when I tell you to leave"—I bite his bottom lip hard enough to draw blood—"I fucking mean it."

Licking my lips for good measure, I shove him away. There's no hesitation from him this time, and he's out the door without another word. I'm not ashamed to admit that his heartbreak thrills me. Tyler's a good fuck, but screwing him over is even better.

Slumping onto the bed, I dislodge a loose chunk of plaster in the wall and grab one of my stashed meds, swallowing it dry.

I can feel the hysteria bubbling up in my mind. I'm in no mood to stay up for three days until it burns out. My last episode ended badly for everyone.

I scroll aimlessly on my phone to distract myself. Shit, I'd love Brooklyn's phone number. She's stuck in my head like nothing else ever has been. I wonder what she's doing right now.

Kade stormed off when she skipped dinner. That guy's got a serious saviour complex. He's always worried about others, even when they don't give two shits about him. That's why he stopped caring, focusing solely on our little screwed-up family. We look after our own. This Brooklyn chick? She'd steamroll him in a second if she knew how possessive he is.

Groaning, I toss the phone aside. I picture her splayed out on my bed, her legs spread wide and secured to the frame with one of Kade's ties. I'd eat her cunt while she screams and spank her until she bleeds. The door slams open, bouncing off the wall with a resounding *crack*.

"No answer. The hell is she playing at?" Kade storms in.

I watch as he rips his loosened tie off, tossing it in anger at the wall. My mouth goes dry as I consider the item, forcing my filthy fantasy aside. My eyes track down Kade's body. Yeah, we're best friends and roommates, but that doesn't mean I can't appreciate him. Especially when he's all riled up and aggressive.

"Chill out, man. Why do you even care? She's been here for two days."

"Because!" he exclaims.

Raising an eyebrow, I let my cocky smile piss him off further. "Care to finish that sentence?"

"Because it's my job," Kade groans.

"Yeah, right. Whatever you say."

"Fuck off, Nix. Where's Tyler anyway?"

"He's gone. I got bored of the constant whining."

Kade nods thoughtfully, running a hand through his slick, blonde locks. "In that case, come help me find Hudson? He's avoiding me again."

"Jesus. What is it with you and finding people today?"

I'm rewarded with an annoyed glare as Kade runs out of patience. He's always running around after Hudson for one reason or another. That is, when they aren't arguing or trying to kill each other. It's a love-hate relationship at best, but that doesn't stop Kade from caring.

"You know what he gets like. He seemed to be doing better for a while, but the last few weeks have been tough," Kade worries. "We're losing him again."

"I don't know... he doesn't exactly like you spying on him."

Cursing under his breath, he turns to leave. "Again, it's my job."

"Doesn't have to be!" I call after him.

The resounding slam of the door answers me. That's the thing about Kade—he's relentlessly stubborn. When he becomes invested in someone, it's damn near impossible to sway him. That's what happened with me, and then Eli. We were both brought into the family through his need to control and protect.

Hudson is a whole other story altogether.

Picking up my phone once again, I type Brooklyn's name in on a whim. I have to do something to satisfy the fantasist inside of me. I'm disappointed when it yields no results on any social media platforms.

There's nothing.

Not a single profile or photo.

She's a fucking ghost. It's almost like she's been wiped from every inch of the internet. There's no way she's gone her whole life without making any accounts. Someone must have systematically deleted everything.

Growing frustrated, I turn to Google. This time, I'm not disappointed. A whole slew of news stories appear, the headlines viciously blazoned for the world to see. I scroll through, a heavy weight growing in my gut with every word.

Something's telling me to look away, but morbid curiosity beats my conscience.

No one here is fucking innocent. You don't end up in a place like this without some kind of damage. But this girl?

She's earned her place alright.

Goddammit, I should be running in the opposite direction. My record here is damn near spotless. I've worked my ass off to get clean and avoid further rehab.

The guys supported me through it all when I arrived. Sure, I fuck like a degenerate and disregard any sign of commitment or emotional attachment. Still, it's better than heroin, right?

This girl is grade A fucked. No two ways about it. We should all be steering clear for our own protection. But hell, I like a challenge.

CHAPTER 7
BROOKLYN

GASOLINE - HALSEY

IT'S the first day of class, and I'm over it already.

It feels like I'm starting school all over again, back when I was in foster care and had to attend in a borrowed uniform. The memory of those days is fucking toxic, and I push it aside.

I'm twenty-one years old, for fuck's sake. I've done my time in education. Yet, here I am searching for a t-shirt that isn't worn and threadbare, worrying over the rips in my jeans that I hope others will mistake for a fashion choice rather than the sad truth.

You know what? Screw them.

My blonde hair lies tangled and limp, the ashen strands spilling down my back. I didn't bother to wash it after my early morning run. It's not like I have anyone to impress around here, so half-assed messy bun it is.

I ran the perimeter of the institute as the sun rose this morning, figuring it's time I have an escape plan in case everything goes to hell. The looming security fence and cameras were an intimidating sight. Blackwood's luxury and spacious grounds trick you into thinking this is freedom, but there are still precautions.

Nothing about this place is normal.

Security is posted at every entrance and exit, and all buildings are only accessible by ID card. There's also a stupidly complicated procedure for booking visitation or leave, although it's not like I'll be doing that any time soon. It's clever, how they give you just enough independence to create a sense of normality, but it's all an illusion. We aren't free at all; someone's always watching.

That's probably a good thing.

Monsters like me are not fit for society.

"Brooklyn, time to wake up!"

A round of enthusiastic knocking makes me jump. I swing the door open, prepared to punch whoever it is that's disturbing my peace. I'm startled by the blue-haired ball of energy waiting. Phoenix looks far too happy for this early in the morning. Eli stands behind him, cocooned in another dark hoodie that hides his face.

"Mornin', hotness. You ready?"

Phoenix breezes straight past me, inviting himself into my room without a care in the world. I'm left gaping as he begins to poke around in my meagre wardrobe, seemingly at home. He seriously has no boundaries.

Eli moves next, giving me a tentative nod in greeting. No words, of course, just his signature silence and penetrating gaze. Luminous green eyes meet mine, and the tiny smile on his face almost weakens my annoyance. Godfuckingdammit, he's cute in a misunderstood, emo sort of way that makes my thighs clench.

"You need to go shopping," Phoenix announces.

I gape at him as he dangles a faded bra, grinning broadly. Motherfucker. I snatch the offending item away, glowering at his antics. The bastard is laughing at me and enjoying my embarrassment far too much.

"There's nothing wrong with my clothes," I argue.

"Sure. You'd look better without them on, anyway."

I eye him incredulously. "Does that usually work on girls?"

"Every damn time."

Clearly, he's never met a girl like me.

"As tempting as your pathetic flirting is, mind telling me what the hell you're doing in my room at eight o'clock?" I challenge.

His resultant grin is satisfied. The asshole clearly enjoys getting under my skin. "Almighty Kade has given us custody of you for the day. It's your taster."

I glower at him. "I don't need babysitting."

"Doesn't look like you get a choice. What Kade wants, he usually gets. So, it looks like you're stuck with us today. Don't worry, we'll be gentle with you." He proceeds to wink and give me a dirty grin. "For now, at least."

You want to play, joker? I can give as good as I get. May as well have some fun while I'm still fucking here. I saunter over, adding some sway into my hips as I invade his space. His eyes widen when I brush my fingers down his muscled arm and peek through my lashes.

I brush my lips against his ear. "What makes you think that I like it gentle, hmm?" Before he can respond, I bite down on his velvety lobe, ensuring it hurts him. The groan from his parted lips sends tingles straight down my spine.

"Damn, Brooklyn. Where've you been all this time?"

With a quick lick, I meet his eyes and offer a dark look of my own. "You still want to play with me, Nix? You might get hurt."

"You're goddamn right I do, sweetness."

He tries to grab my hand, but I dance back, putting distance between us again. Grabbing my sweater, cigarettes and ID badge, I stride from the room with my head held high. Sometimes being alive is fun, but only occasionally. I can't be making a habit of this playfulness.

The door clicks shut behind them as both guys follow hot on my heels. By the time we get outside, I'm sandwiched between them. Phoenix is sticking a little too close for my liking, with silent Eli trailing at a more reasonable distance.

Pulling a cigarette from my pack, I light up and breathe in deep. I can't see any guards nearby, so I savour each drag. I only have a few left, so I'll need to investigate who is in charge of contraband here. There's always someone—a resident pimp who supplies us delinquents with the necessary substances.

Eli's eyes fix on the glowing stub of my cigarette. The hunger is plain to see in his transfixed gaze. I shock myself by offering it to him. He looks equally uncertain, but finally takes it with a grateful nod.

Phoenix spends the walk across the quad talking incessantly, skipping from one topic to another at random. He's borderline frenzied. By the time we reach a towering building, I'm close to backing out and spending the day alone. A headache is already threatening.

"Maybe you should take a leaf out of Eli's book. It's too early to be this chatty," I complain, causing him to rumble with laughter.

"No way. You'd miss my sparkling conversation."

I stifle my own chuckle. "Not likely."

After scanning our IDs, we head down additional thickly carpeted corridors lined with fine landscape paintings. I'd love to meet whoever designed this place and call them a stuck-up dickhead to their face. That'd be a fun time.

We reach a busy classroom with many lifeless, drugged-up patients taking their seats. I immediately freeze in place as venomous panic rushes in. There are so many of them. What if someone recognises me? I can imagine them whispering already, their hateful stares on me, heavy with disgust.

Maybe they'll take pictures and sell them to the press. Or they'll campaign to get me kicked out and sent back to the Clearview hellhole. Worse still, I could get locked up in prison this time, where my criminal ass really belongs.

A growing black presence billows in the corner of the room, conjured by my panic. My spiralling paranoia steals any remaining courage as I slowly back away, watching the imaginary shadows grow. It won't be long before the voices begin to speak. My hallucinations are always the same.

"Brooklyn? You good?"

Phoenix stands in front of me, his fingers sliding under my chin and raising my lowered head. He blocks out the nightmare behind him. I stare, desperately hoping that he does something. Anything. He nods and mutters to Eli, who heads in to save our seats. Grabbing my hand, he links our fingers together.

"Come with me."

Rather than flinching away from the contact, I allow him to drag me into an empty classroom nearby. There's not a single shadow in sight as we sneak inside. Phoenix flicks the lights on and shuts the door, turning to me.

"What's up?"

Wringing my hands together, I look away. This is so embarrassing. The voice of irrationality is too goddamn loud. That's the thing about delusions, they're so fucking believable that discerning reality from fiction is impossible.

"It's just… there's a lot of them."

"What, patients?"

I hum a response, gnawing on my abused lip.

"Well, I think you'll find that in every class, to be fair."

I roll my eyes. "Thanks. That's really helpful."

Arms crossed and biceps bulging, Phoenix pins me with a serious look. "They are patients, just like you and me. You don't need to be scared of them."

Scared of them? Is he for real?

"I'm not scared of them," I whisper.

His brows furrow. "You're not?"

Shaking my head, I swallow the truth. He can never know what I did, or the demons that I carry with me to this day. It's a secret that I'll take to my unhallowed grave.

"Then what is it?"

Keep it in. Keep it in.

Fucking keep it in.

Phoenix comes closer, his hand stroking along my jaw. I squeeze my eyes shut, trying hard not to enjoy his touch. This was not part of the plan. No attachments or distractions from my goal, that's the deal. What the hell am I doing here with him?

"Tell me," he demands softly.

"No."

Phoenix's breath tickles my face. He's far too close for comfort, yet I can't pull away. "You will tell me, Brooklyn," he orders.

"No."

My eyes remain closed, so when his lips brush against mine for a tantalising second, it's a complete shock. Featherlight and coaxing, the kiss lingers for a moment before he pulls away. It leaves me trembling and urgently wanting more.

"Change your mind yet?"

I shake my head, managing to peek up at him. There's frustration marked across his features, but he tries for a reassuring smile, playing the good guy.

"You can trust me."

"Not with this," I hiss.

But there's something else he might be useful for.

Latching on to the distraction, I push him against the wall, trapping him with my body. This is insane. Neither of us really knows the other. But I don't give a damn. I'm on a one-way trip to the afterlife. This is just some in-flight entertainment.

"Hang on," Phoenix begins to protest.

Silencing him with my lips, my arms wrap around his neck. My body is flush against his, and within seconds he reciprocates, kissing me with sudden urgency. His hands land on my hips, squeezing so tight I wince involuntarily.

More. I need more.

The thoughts are still too loud.

Reaching down his chiselled body, I find his hard cock straining against his jeans. Someone's pleased to see me, and it makes me excited. I'd forgotten the thrill of fooling around with another person.

Phoenix moans against my mouth. His teeth bite down on my chewed lip, breaking skin and causing blood to flow between our clasped lips. I'm so fucking turned on, everything else fades into insignificance.

The tight grip of hysteria silently releases its hold on me and slinks back. His tongue flicks across the seam of my mouth, and I relent instantly. The kiss deepens, and the cool metal of a piercing sweeps through my mouth. Fuck, that feels incredible.

It'd feel even better elsewhere.

There's a bang from outside, followed by high-pitched laughter and shouting. The moment is shattered as reality sneaks back in. We're complete strangers in a classroom going at it like horny kids. What is wrong with me? Phoenix gradually pulls away, offering me a smirk. Dickhead.

"I've wanted to do that since you decked Rio in the cafeteria."

Almost like he can't resist, he leans in and sucks on my bottom lip, where blood still trickles freely. Stealing it for himself, his eyes are hooded with unashamed desire. His finger swipes at the corner of my mouth to remove any evidence.

"Don't think that I won't be back to finish the job another time," he warns darkly. "You're playing a dangerous game."

The grin that pulls at my lips is unfamiliar. What is this feeling? Satisfaction? Relief? My body feels light, like those blissful seconds after slicing my skin and watching the crimson river flow. It's euphoric, like a fucking drug, and I'm already longing for another dose.

"Will you come to class now?" Phoenix asks.

The immediate refusal halts on my tongue. I no longer want to run. There's no desire to hide back in my room and play with my blades until I can think clearly again. Something else has taken place here. An exchange of mutual darkness.

A different answer slips out instead.

"Yeah, I will. Lead the way."

CHAPTER 8
HUDSON

SEROTONIN - CALL ME KARIZMA

I SHOVE a gangly kid out of the way. "Move."

Fucking hell. This place is packed. I told Kade that I wasn't in the mood, but the persistent bastard refused to leave my room until I promised to come down for dinner.

He literally stood there and stared at me, demanding my attendance like some kind of parole officer. Four-eyed fucker. He'll give up one day. Until then, he's a pain in the ass.

I grab some of the crappy-looking food and a bottle of water. I may as well fuel up while I'm here, because the gym is calling me. I have a regular, supervised slot as part of my anger management. Right now, I need to beat the shit out of something. Apparently, violence isn't a healthy coping mechanism.

Thanks, Mariam.

Fucking thanks.

People wonder why some individuals ridicule those who do therapy. It's hardly surprising. The entire thing is a joke. The biggest waste of three hours a week. It's time that could be spent pounding a boxing bag or some sweet pussy. I wonder if Britt is still mad at me, because I could use a round or two.

"Hudson!"

Kade waves me over, looking more relieved than I'm comfortable with. How does he keep that act up twenty-four seven? It's exhausting just watching him. Mr Perfect, with the shirt and manners, swanning around and cosying up to management.

Doesn't anyone else see through it? All the fake bullshit? It makes me sick.

I avoid his hopeful eyes. "Yeah, I'm here."

He settles down, clearly trying to contain himself. Let's face it, I know that I'm awful to him. It's more than he deserves, but he isn't obligated to stick around. Not anymore. I take no responsibility for hurting his stupid little feelings until he finally leaves.

"Thanks for coming," he offers.

I inwardly recoil. His words are just more emotional manipulation, making me feel like the worst person in the world. Which obviously, I am. Why else would I be trapped in this shithole for another eighteen months?

"Maybe you'll get off my goddamn back already."

"I'm just looking out for you, Hud."

Not fucking likely.

"How many times has she called this week?" I demand.

He glances away. "Mum cares about you. We all do."

"Is that so? I'm not sure your father would agree."

"Come on, lay off," Kade snaps. "I don't want to talk about him."

I'm tempted to smash my fist into his face. Beyond tempted. But if I get any more strikes on my record, the warden threatened to send me to the hole. Even I have enough sense to avoid that. My head is fucked enough.

I've seen the kids that come out of the basement level, shaking like a leaf and muttering shit that doesn't make sense. They aren't the same people that went in.

"What do you want, Kade? I have nothing to say to you."

Kade drops his fork with a clatter, slumping back in the seat. "Seriously? We're still playing this stupid game?"

"What game?" I feign ignorance.

His hazel eyes burn across my skin, loaded with contempt. The hope has been utterly extinguished from him. When he first arrived, it was burning bright. I've snuffed it out for good. I prefer it when he hates me.

It's easier this way, rather than him constantly trying to save me. I'm on a path to self-destruction and I fucking love it. Beyond redemption, baby. To hell with them all.

"Well, you should know that a lawyer is coming to see you next week. You won't leave here until you start making progress."

"Not necessary. Cancel it."

Kade rubs his face, breathing deeply. "You're impossible."

I finish my drink, crunching the plastic bottle in one hand without even blinking. "You're the one being stubborn as shit, big brother. As usual."

Unfortunately, it's true. This clean-shirt bastard is my fucking brother. Who would've thought it? We're as different as night and day. Yet, here we are. Stuck together, for better or worse. And it's all his bloody fault. I was supposed to rot in here alone.

There's an awkward silence that's filled with all the words we can't say. If I were a good person, I would fill it with promises and heartfelt platitudes; thank him for putting up with me all these years, or promising to clean my act up so we can both go home. But that's never going to happen. The sooner he realises that, the better. For all of us.

"I'm trying to protect you," Kade says evenly.

I can tell by the way his angular lips are pressed together that he wants to say more. Hell, he probably wants to hit me too. Scream in my face. Punish me for abandoning our family and ruining the perfect life I'd been given. Anger isn't his default, but I know it's eating him up inside regardless.

I have to make him let me go. Kade needs to stop caring about me and the waste of space that I am. He's stuck here, chasing after me and trying to clear up messes that don't belong to him. He's the success story. The good kid that grew into a great man. Hurting him is the only way to set him free.

"It's not your job to protect me. It never was," I state coldly, watching him flinch. "We're not family. We're not brothers. We're not even friends. Get that into your head, before it's too late."

He stares at me with wide, pain-filled eyes. I fight the urge to rub my chest. Just saying those horrible things out loud hurts, and that's the worst part.

I'm not that kind of person. Not deep down. Yeah, I'm an asshole, but Kade and his mum are the best things that ever happened to me. His dad can go fuck himself with a cactus.

"I was... once."

Kade's voice is a harsh whisper, choked with emotion. I stand abruptly, tossing the crushed water bottle down and storming away. I can't look back at him, can't see the broken look on his face. A look that I put there. It'll finish me off.

I'm out the door and nearly running when two familiar faces slow my steps. Fucking hell, there's no escaping it tonight. These guys are everywhere, showing up to pile on more guilt for my shitty behaviour of late. Goddammit.

"Hud! Hold up!" Phoenix hollers.

He's entering the building with Eli in tow, both of them seemingly surprised to see me. I run a hand through my thick, black hair, scrambling for an excuse to avoid them. I feel like shit. They're my friends, but I just can't do it tonight. Not after that conversation.

"Hey," I answer reluctantly.

"Where are you off to? We've got someone for you to meet."

"Not tonight. I'm... I've got work to do."

Phoenix frowns, and even Eli looks suspicious. They know me too well sometimes. I've never cared about Blackwood's pointless education program. Most of the patients don't. It's just an excuse to keep us busy and out of trouble.

"You sure? Trust me, you don't want to miss this. She's a breath of fresh air."

I begin to inch away. "Nope, I'm good. Catch up with you later."

Phoenix shrugs, turning his back to me. Eli smiles weakly and follows suit. My excuses are transparent, but they're good enough not to press further. Unlike Kade, who can't take no for an answer.

I jog away, my mind set on one destination. Out in the drizzling rain, I run through the dark night and into another building protected by stony-faced guards. Britt has a project due, so the art room is a good place to start. I'm right, of course, but as soon as I stride into the room, her face hardens.

"Seriously, Hudson, fuck off. Not today."

"Come on, Britt. I'm sorry for being a douchebag," I lie easily.

"Are you?" she challenges, slamming the paintbrush down.

I know just what to say, it's like a routine at this point. We fuck, fight, argue, then fuck some more. Truthfully, I hate it. Britt's using me as much as I'm using her.

There's nothing deep about it, but when she tries to demand more from me, we run into difficulties. Last time, I literally threw her out. I couldn't stand the sight of her for a second longer than necessary.

"I am, baby. Forgive me?" I squeeze the words out.

I'm abandoning my morals once more in pursuit of a temporary fix. I don't suppose I deserve anything better than this. Not after the things I've said and done. This misery is all I'm allowed, and nothing more. It's my death sentence.

Britt hops up onto the workbench, quickly spreading her legs. I launch across the room without hesitating. Positioning myself above her, I shove the stupid flowery dress up to her waist and yank the thong down her thin legs. I should be worried about hurting her one day, but again, it's not my problem. I don't care if I break her. It might actually be fun.

"Oh, by the way…"

I free my rock-hard dick. "Do you have to talk right now?"

"No need to be an ass. I was going to tell you about the new girl."

Wrapping my hand around her throat, I squeeze hard enough to shut her up. "I don't give a fuck about the new girl. Got that?"

Britt manages a timid nod. I release my grip, grabbing her hips instead. Before any more pointless conversation can resume, I slam into her, relishing the yelp that escapes her mouth.

Britt acts all innocent, but she's fucking soaked. She loves it hard and rough. It's more of a punishment than anything romantic. She thrives on this toxic arrangement, just like me. Just like all of us.

"Oh, Hudson," she moans.

I tune her out, disconnecting completely with each brutal thrust. Pumping in and out of her without a care is a particularly sick form of self-torture. I'm fucking a girl that I literally despise rather than giving myself the chance of something more.

Mariam would have a field day if she heard about this shit. She's probably watching right now. It's not like there aren't cameras everywhere. The guards outside don't give a damn what we're up to either. I have no idea how we get away with half the shit that goes on in this place.

I grunt through my climax, uncaring about whether Britt's satisfied or not. Distantly, I wonder what it would be like to feel loved. To share something with someone special. I had that once, a lifetime ago. Brief and fleeting, a whirlwind love affair that ended as explosively as it began. It's always the same with me.

I ruin any good that comes into my life.

I may not deserve it, but I'd do anything to feel that again.

CHAPTER 9
BROOKLYN

LET ME BE SAD - I PREVAIL

I OFFER Phoenix and Eli a half-hearted wave from the entrance, watching as they walk to their class with reluctance. They can't trail after me all the time. I'm a big girl and more than capable of handling this bullshit alone.

The morning's class is some science crap. Straightening my back, I follow the flow of traffic to the classroom, where there are work benches and stools scattered around. Hesitating, I glance around for a suitable seat. Everyone seems to have places already. Coming here was truly a mistake. I've never felt so on edge.

The memory of Phoenix's teeth breaking skin sizzles through my mind. Damn, that was one hot mistake. I have to stifle the tingling that threatens when I think about that encounter.

What the hell is getting into me? He's just another asshole looking for a quick fix. I shouldn't lower myself to his level, no matter how alive it makes me feel.

There's an empty seat in the back corner, right next to a girl who's laying with her head on the table. The headphones on her head seal the deal. Hopefully, I can go a couple of hours without having to dodge conversing or small talk.

Plonking myself down, I do a quick survey of the room. There are a few familiar faces who I've seen about, mostly in the cafeteria or quad. A couple from my dorms too. From what I've gathered, there are two housing blocks in this place: Oakridge and Pinehill. Each contains fifty patients, who are all enrolled in this so-called experimental treatment.

It's a huge operation, nothing like the close-knit ward of ten that I came from, where everyone knew your name and diagnosis. I hated that—people sticking their noses in my business, wanting to share and talk like some kind of group therapy shit. Luckily, most of them were terrified of me when they figured out my identity.

"Hey there."

It's the girl, her headphones removed.

"Hi."

"You're new?" she asks.

"Yeah, I arrived a few days ago."

Her eyes appraise me openly. I take a moment to give her a once-over. She's cute, but her rounded features are hardened by her dyed red hair, painted black lips and shining nose ring. The scruffy *Nickelback* t-shirt she's wearing earns my approval almost instantly. She has good taste.

"You sure you want to sit here?" she asks uncertainly.

"Pretty sure. Why not?"

Her eyebrows lift as she shrugs, giving me a crooked smile. "People tend to avoid me. I stress them out."

"Why is that?" I ask casually.

"You really want to know?"

I nod in agreement. Not much scares me off.

"Well, for starters, I get here an hour early every day to move all the desks to sit at a perfect ninety-degree angle. All the stools have to be turned four times before anyone can sit on them. Unless you want to get hit by a car tomorrow. And if I don't lock and unlock the windows precisely seven times, my brother will get sick and die. So, I won't be offended if you move."

Fidgeting nervously, she picks at the scabbed skin around her black-painted fingernails while waiting for my response. I stare back at her for a wordless second, until an easy smile finds its way to my lips. Fuck, I'm going soft.

"What's your name?"

"It's Teegan. Yours?"

"Brooklyn. I'm good sitting here, thanks."

She matches my smile enthusiastically, a blush creeping up her neck. The class's attention turns to the teacher as he calls everyone to order, launching into a lecture that has my eyes drooping. His voice literally drills into my head. It probably doesn't help that I had another night of tossing and turning in sweaty sheets to a chorus of hissing voices before jogging without eating first.

I'm slowly fading with each passing day.

What would happen if I just stopped?

If I didn't eat, sleep or drink, would I slip away piece by piece? Or go insane from hunger, my mind giving in just before my body does? Maybe I'd fall back into the grip of psychosis. That thought leaves a sour taste in my mouth as I swallow hard. I'd fling myself off a roof before going through that again.

"Hey, why's the assistant staring at you?"

I quickly look up, following Teegan's line of sight. Sure enough, a pair of hazel eyes stare back at me from behind familiar black glasses, contrasting his crisp, white shirt.

Kade looks rough, unlike his usual perfect self. His sandy-blonde hair is tousled rather than neatly combed, while his collar is undone and his sleeves are rolled up to reveal tanned, muscular forearms.

"He's the assistant?" I whisper back.

"Yeah, he actually goes here too. He helps out in the lower level classes and with the office stuff. It's weird."

How convenient. What's with all the leeway that Kade's been given? He's treated more like a guest than a patient. It doesn't make sense. This is supposed to be a maximum-security treatment program, not some free-for-all hippy-haven where we all sing hakuna fucking matata while holding hands in a circle.

"Any idea what he's in for?" I prod.

"Nope. His brother's a right loose cannon though."

Brother? He kept that quiet, and the other two idiots did as well. What are the odds of two brothers ending up in here? We're far from civilisation and normal society, so it's not fucking likely. Unless being a headcase runs in the family—in which case, ditto.

What exactly are you playing at, Kade?

The pointless class passes in a blur, with Teegan leaning over to copy my answers and beguiling me with more of her compulsions. When she walks the perimeter of the room three times before handing our sheets in, no one even bats an eye. She soon laughs it off.

By lunchtime, I'm feeling rather protective of her. All the cruel nicknames tossed around seem to upset me more than her. Teegan's conditioned to the bullying, whereas I'm contemplating kicking all these motherfuckers' asses to teach them a lesson about respect.

This is hardly the right place to judge others for their problems. I mean, come on. None of us are functioning adults, or else we wouldn't be here. This whole institute is a cesspit of failure and dysfunction.

"Brooklyn, can we talk?"

Kade trails over as we pack up our stuff, which mostly consists of me standing awkwardly. My eyes are on Teegan's smart backpack and stationery supplies. The embarrassment and envy are familiar feelings. I spent most of my years in education being jealous of others, with their shiny, new phones and hole-free clothing.

I fold my arms as we face off. "About what?"

"Just to catch up. It's been a couple of days."

His eyes are wide, almost pleading.

"I'm busy, Kade."

"Please, it'll only take a second."

Sighing, I give Teegan a nod of reassurance. She's antsy, shifting about while trying not to eye Kade too obviously. We say an awkward goodbye, and then she shuffles off, touching each seat in turn as she passes. I can see her anxiety reducing as she does so. The classroom slowly empties until it's just us.

"What's this about?" I sigh heavily.

"I wanted to make sure that you are settling in okay."

Kade seems to genuinely care, yet I can't help but doubt his intentions anyway. Trust doesn't exactly come easily to me, especially not when it involves the opposite sex. I've learned to not trust any guy, even the sweet ones. They will burn you just the same in the end.

"Yeah, I'm fine."

"Chosen a subject to focus on yet?" he probes.

I shrug, dodging the question. "Not quite."

Kade seems to ponder this, running a hand through his messy hair.

"Are you okay?" I blurt. *Where the hell did that come from?*

"Me? Oh, sure. I'm good," he mutters, but his response is pretty lacklustre. "Just some stuff going on. You know how it is."

"Sure, whatever."

Why am I even standing here?

Kade clears his throat. "Phoenix said that you enjoyed history?"

He's fishing, scrambling to change the conversation. I don't suppose I should reveal that I only enjoyed it because I'd been fooling around with his best friend beforehand, without whom I would have fallen into a complete breakdown.

"It was okay. I don't mind it."

He nods absently, studying his watch. "Well, you'll need to make a decision by tomorrow. Just let me know, and I can take care of the paperwork for you."

"Uh, okay. Thanks."

His fingers tap the desk for a moment as his apprehensive eyes flick over me. I swallow, standing my ground. There's this feeling between us, like I should be saying something more.

What does he want from me? Does he just trail around after all the strays in this place? It must be exhausting.

"Right, I'll be going then. See you."

Kade turns to leave, his broad shoulders slumped. I feel guilty, but this is for his own good. The more people I interact with, the more they will be affected by my death. I don't want to be remembered.

Written off, forgotten before my files are shredded—that's my aim. People always preach about not being another statistic, but I can't wait until my life is reduced to nothing more than a number. Then, I'll be free.

"Unless you want to get lunch together?" Kade suggests.

He's lingering in the doorway, peering at me through those sexy glasses and a charming smile on his face. Why can't he be a shitty person? It would make this so much easier, and it doesn't help that I'm attracted to him either. I'm not blind.

"I don't know…" I say awkwardly.

"Come on, it's only half an hour. You look like you could use some company."

Right on cue, my stomach decides to growl loudly. Fucking traitor. I know Kade hears it. His quirked eyebrow and knowing grin leave me with no choice but to accept his offer.

"Fine. But if you pester me anymore about choosing a subject, you'll be eating alone. Deal?"

Kade nods. "Deal."

CHAPTER 10
ELI

FOLLOW YOU - BRING ME THE HORIZON

STEALING PHOENIX'S HEADPHONES, I slip them in my ears and lift my hood back up. He's got a shit taste in music, so I search for some *Bring Me The Horizon* that I know he downloaded just for me. I'm quickly immersed in the heavy beat.

Music is a good coping mechanism because it drowns out the rest of my senses. The louder and angrier it is, the better. Nothing else gets through when my brain is occupied with sound.

I'm huddled in the corner of the football pitch, watching Phoenix and Kade kick a ball about listlessly. They both seem distracted, occupied by their own thoughts. I don't want to play, preferring to bury my nose in a book.

Running is my thing, but alone. It's my time to peacefully experience the world while everyone else sleeps. There are no voices or flavours to overwhelm me at the break of dawn.

There's a blur of movement on the neighbouring pitch. The mandatory gym session is in full swing, despite the freezing weather. Most of the patients are hopping about for warmth, huddled together and moaning. I scan through the bodies, searching for familiar glossy-blonde hair.

My rising heart rate slows when I finally locate Brooklyn standing near the back, entirely alone. She doesn't even seem to care. With her arms folded and hip popped to the side, she looks beyond bored. Dammit, how does she do it? Most newbies would be crying or sulking over being singled out that way. But she's standing there like she owns the whole damn world.

What a sight that is.

I refocus on my essay, trying to keep my eyes from straying. Having her so close to me is a distraction. Already, I've become unhealthily attached. My mind has latched on to her commanding presence. No one's ever looked at me the way she did during lunch on her first day.

It was with such fucking purity and respect rather than treating me like some kind of lab experiment gone wrong. Realistically, there's a reason why I'm becoming obsessed. It's because I've been through this before.

In the hellhole that is Clearview Psychiatric Unit, watching Brooklyn became my obsession. I was fascinated by her. The day she arrived, kicking and screaming in handcuffs that the police had slapped on, years of boredom ended.

She was a spark of interest in the dull landscape of my life. I never said a single word to her face, just studied her from afar. If she ever realises, she'll probably think I'm some kind of sick stalker.

The ball rolls up next to me, disturbing my stack of organised papers and sending sheets flying. Phoenix gives me a devious grin. *Asshole.* It's his homework I'm doing here. He's a lazy son of a bitch who loves to exploit my soft spot for him.

Tossing the ball back, I sneak another glance to the side. While the other girls begin to head inside to get dressed, Brooklyn's being yelled at for standing and refusing to participate. The hapless teacher is a stickler for getting patients involved, but Brooklyn is taking none of it, instead giving one of her classic shrugs.

"Eli! You coming in?"

I yank the headphones out, nodding to the guys.

"Reckon you can hijack movie night? Play something decent?"

Phoenix is cajoling Kade, who looks suitably unimpressed by the suggestion. "Nix, I can't just do that. You want to get me fired? I happen to like my job."

"Come on, man. It's a fucking movie, hardly the peak of criminality."

He won't get anywhere. Kade is a straight flyer, through and through. He lives by the book and never, ever bends the rules. It's one of the things I admire most about him. There isn't a bad bone in his body.

He really doesn't belong here.

The rest of us sold our souls to the devil long ago.

Joining the others, I watch as Brooklyn is assigned to collect all the balls. She's muttering to herself, probably cursing with that potty mouth of hers. It's fucking hot if you ask me. I'd love to make her cuss and scream.

A group of girls hang back, still holding their balls. I recognise Britt among them. She's Hudson's slimy fuck buddy, and the ringleader of a group of girls who spend their days picking on other patients for fun.

"What's taking you so long? Hurry up, I'm freezing my bollocks off." Phoenix pulls me into a side hug. "Did you get my homework done? Crawley will kill me if it's late again. I'll make it well worth your time, don't worry."

I'm not paying attention to his flirting because I'm too focused on the unfolding situation. Brooklyn's trying to collect the balls while being heckled by the pack of hyenas. It's a scene I've watched countless times. They always find a target to focus their hatred on.

Usually, it's the newbie. Girls can be so goddamn cruel, particularly in this place.

I almost shout out loud when the first punch sails her way. The need to warn Brooklyn bubbles up inside of me. She doesn't stand a chance. The girl's fist connects with her jaw and sends her reeling back in shock.

"Seriously, what's up with you?" Phoenix demands.

I point frantically. Rather than running or cowering as I expected, Brooklyn is flying straight back at the girls without a glimmer of fear. She takes two down with brutal blows, and their high-pitched screams reach us even from afar.

"We've got to stop this!" Kade shouts, taking off.

Phoenix remains still, his arm wrapping around my narrow waist. He's watching with a kind of morbid fascination for this brilliantly violent girl who's giving as good as she gets. I know he's a sick fuck like me. He's probably hard at the sight of her bloody nose and scraped knuckles. We think in similar depraved ways.

"Damn, she knows how to put up a fight," he mutters.

Britt's standing back from the fight, letting her lackeys scratch and claw. They're no match for Brooklyn though. She rolls with the countless punches, taking the punishment while dishing out her own.

By the time Kade alerts several nearby guards, who break up the fight, I'm having to readjust my jeans because they're feeling a little snug. Phoenix offers me a sultry grin, reaching out to run his thumb over my bottom lip. I resist the urge to stick my tongue out and lick it.

"Don't know about you, but I wouldn't mind spending some quality time with our cute newbie. With or without your company, although I'd prefer with. It worked for us before."

I feel my cheeks flush.

It certainly did work. Pretty fucking well.

We eventually join Kade on the other pitch. The three of us watch as Taggert and Jackson, two of the scariest guards, plant themselves between the brawling group. They separate a roughed-up girl and Brooklyn.

She's visibly seething as blood leaks down her face and chin. One eye has already swollen up. Who on earth jumps someone over a handful of balls? Brooklyn was outnumbered five to one.

Welcome to the madhouse.

"Are you okay? What the hell happened?" Kade barks.

Waving him off, Brooklyn wipes her face on her sleeve, successfully smearing more blood around. "Yeah, fine. Just broke some cunt's nose, so that's my day made."

After a round of inappropriate high-fives from Phoenix, we're fleeing the pitch and heading back across the quad. Brooklyn is limping, but trying to conceal her pain. We make a beeline for the dorms.

In my periphery, I can see Kade trying to offer her an arm, but he's shoved away with a grunted *fuck right off* from Brooklyn. We get into the dorms without further incident and follow Brooklyn up to the fourth floor.

All of us take a right rather than heading to our own rooms. She's fumbling with her key card and muttering before she realises that we're all still here.

"Um, what are you guys doing?"

"Making sure you're okay," Kade answers.

"You might need some help cleaning up," Phoenix adds suggestively.

Brooklyn's grey eyes meet mine, and I shrug in response. She puts her bloodstained hands on her hips, looking fierce as fuck with her eyebrows pinched in a frown and crimson trails running down her furious face.

"You're not coming in."

"We are," Kade deadpans.

"You're not."

"Brooklyn—"

"Not a fucking chance!"

Her and Kade stare off for several tense seconds. They're both equally stubborn, so to simplify matters, I quickly swipe her key card and open the door, then toss it back over my shoulder for her to catch.

"Bunch of persistent assholes," Brooklyn hisses.

Once inside, I'm astounded by the sheer emptiness of her room. There's nothing personal. Not a scrap. No photos or clutter, nor any cushions, blankets or fairy lights like the other girls have. There's a single black bag sticking out slightly from under the bed. A quick peek in the wardrobe reveals even less clothing than I own.

Phoenix casts me a loaded look before sprawling out on the unmade bed, kicking his feet up like he owns the place. He studies the room closely, cataloguing the sheer lack of personality. I can see his brows furrowing with concern.

"Make yourself at home, why don't you."

Brooklyn glares at him, paying no attention to Kade. He's making his own assessment of her belongings, and he also takes a subtle glance in the wardrobe. A matching frown etches itself across his face at what he finds.

"Will do, sweetness," Phoenix chirps back.

Kade passes me and takes a seat in the desk chair. His eyes are still assessing with his professional mask firmly in place. I can see how uncomfortable Brooklyn is with our presence. She's glancing around anxiously as we invade her privacy.

With a final exasperated eye roll, she eventually disappears into the bathroom to clean up. As soon as the door clicks shut, Phoenix sits upright, his playfulness long forgotten. It's weird to see him looking so serious and uptight.

"The fuck is going on? Didn't you sort out her arrival?"

"Of course! She snatched the damn key card and let herself in," Kade answers gruffly. "I didn't know she's been living like this or that she didn't have anything."

"What happened to 'it's my job,' huh? This is bullshit."

"She's a grown adult. I'm hardly responsible for looking after her!"

"You work for Blackwood," Phoenix seethes. "Don't give me that crap."

"I volunteer! I have enough to worry about with you three!" Kade growls back, clearly infuriated with Phoenix's accusations.

Their argument rumbles on. I turn away from them, unwilling to get in the middle. Raised voices immediately trigger my senses to work overtime. I've got to escape before I have a panic attack. I creep over to the bathroom door, peering in through the gap to check on Brooklyn.

The sight of her standing over the sink, her hands clenched on the ceramic as she silently sobs, shatters whatever pathetic pieces are left of my heart. Thick tears trail down her cheeks, mixing with flecks of blood. She angrily scrubs them away, silently cursing herself for being stupid.

What is she doing to me?

How do I make it stop?

Feelings are toxic to me. Numbness is my preferred state of being. But in the handful of days since she breezed in without any fucks to give, I've been more oversensitised than ever. My flimsy control has completely gone already.

She's broken in a way that is plain as day to me, calling out to my own greedy demons. I've always loved breaking things, and she's teetering on the edge of destruction. I want nothing more than to shove her off the precipice and follow her all the way down to the depths of Hell.

Gently easing the door open, I slip inside the cramped room. She startles, flinching back and scrubbing at the pink tears streaming down her face.

"Eli, what the—"

Social skills aren't exactly my forte. I'm a fucking mute, I struggle with this kind of shit. But I'm going with what feels right. My palm connects with her stained cheek, and my thumb traces the line of her jaw.

I brush her rapidly swelling eye that is already bruising around the socket. I love the way her skin tarnishes, blossoming in shades of black and purple. I'd love to mark her myself.

I gravitate down to her split lip as Brooklyn visibly winces in pain. She's reluctant to display weakness, but unable to hold it in. I can't help myself, pressing the bloody cut and making her flinch some more.

There's something fascinating about her pain. I desperately want to hurt her, but something stops me. I can't be that person with her. It's not normal.

Instead, I stuff the twisted desires down and resolve to fix something for once. Her eyes meet mine, silvery storm clouds punctuated by the lightest streaks of blue that are barely noticeable unless up close.

My hand rests on her skin and she unconsciously leans in, relishing my touch without even realising it. I grab a hand towel and silently offer to help.

"Okay," she relents.

Sinking to rest on the toilet lid, she looks at me expectantly. What am I getting myself into here? I'm no saint. Just seeing her covered in fresh blood has my heart hammering against the ribcage and my cock twitching. She looks like a beautiful fucking disaster, one that I can't wait to see unfold.

Soaking the towel with warm water, I sink to my knees and begin to clean her face. Broad strokes wipe the dark splatters away, revealing pale, translucent skin beneath the mess. Working in loaded silence, the intensity of the moment has my hand shaking.

She refuses to look away, and it's killing me. Is this what it feels like to be seen? Most of the time, I feel like I'm already dead. No one sees me anymore because I've been invisible for so long. Even the guys fall into the habit of ignoring me.

I don't blame them; it's easily done. I'm just there, plodding along in the background. Forever alone. I finish up, turning my back. A hand catches my wrist, demanding attention.

"Eli…"

There's no way to describe the taste of this emotion. I've never experienced it before.

"If you want to talk to me, you can. Just so you know."

Brooklyn releases her hold. Immediately, I miss the pressure of her fingers wrapped around my wrist. I want nothing more than to shove her against the wall and make her feel the pain that I do.

Pull her hair, bruise her skin, drag her down into the depths of Hell with me, no matter how much it'll kill her inside. Life fucking hurts, and I want her to experience it with me. For the first time, I don't want to be alone. Not one bit.

With a perfunctory nod, I walk away.

Bad, Elijah.

You've got the devil in you.

She's already damaged. I'd ruin her.

CHAPTER 11
BROOKLYN
I'M NOT WELL - BLACK FOXXES

"DO you want to tell me what happened in gym class?"

Mariam pins me with an authoritative look. Her pen taps against the notepad as the seconds crawl by, forcing me to respond and break the silence.

"Nope. Not really."

With a sigh, she scribbles something down. What the hell is so noteworthy about that? I want to grab the paper and make her fucking choke on it. Maybe she'd scream and beg for mercy, finally understanding what it feels like to have someone control you.

"Brooklyn. If someone is bothering you, I need to know."

"I said I'm fine," I repeat.

I'm no snitch. Besides, I'm the one who broke bones. Two, to be precise. Those girls' noses shattered with blood-tinged satisfaction. Stupid assholes. They should have heeded my warning before coming at me. I specifically told them I didn't want any trouble, but anything for some drama, right? That's what girls do.

"Violence is never the answer. It doesn't solve anything."

Jesus, she's on her high horse today, and I have little patience for it. I want to scream, *read my file, bitch!* Violence is my middle name.

"I can't make you tell me, but I'm here if you wish to discuss it."

I don't answer, instead staring out of the window at the late afternoon sun. The last few days have passed in a blur without any boring classes. I've mostly spent it hiding under my duvet, stashing meds and pretending I don't exist. No one came to bother me after my taster ended, and I needed to be alone.

"Did you submit your subject choice? I noticed your taster is over. You have to attend classes, Brooke. It's important for your recovery."

She's literally the female version of Kade. He probably wouldn't appreciate that comparison, no matter how hilariously accurate it is.

"Not yet," I grit out.

There's now a whole bunch of pills in my stockpile that I slipped under my tongue instead of swallowing when they were given to me. How much more of this can I take? Each second spent breathing, thinking, feeling... it's agony. Even speaking takes effort.

My lips are numb, and my brain is detached. More and more, I'm hearing whispers that I can't run from. Stockpiling meds is starting to take a toll on my sanity.

"Clock's ticking, Brooklyn. You need to choose something."

Death. I choose fucking death. If she bangs on for a second longer, I'll bring her along with me. I glance up at the blinking CCTV camera. Are they watching right now? Whoever *they* are. I've yet to find a single room without any cameras, except the bedrooms. There must be thousands of hours of surveillance.

What happens to it all?

Who's watching our lives play out?

If I were to kill Mariam right now, they'd take one look at the video and throw me in a maximum-security prison. Technically speaking, it's where I should have ended up anyway, if the prosecutors are to be believed.

My defence lawyer argued otherwise, given the circumstances around my... *crime.* Throw the word insanity in there, and everything changes.

"Why don't you try a couple of classes?" she suggests. "That gives you some flexibility."

"Do I seriously have to attend classes?"

"Yes, or you cannot stay in this institute," Mariam replies sternly.

Fuck. I can't go back to Clearview now.

"English and history." I latch on to my first thought.

Those were the two least objectionable classes out of all the boredom. I just want her to leave me alone again. At least one of them features some entertainment. I recall the way Eli's eyes tracked over me, his green irises darkening with desire as he pressed on my wound. He was fascinated by my pain. Fuck, I relished that sting, despite it not coming from my own hand.

Mariam claps enthusiastically. "Excellent! Good choices."

Nodding, I try to play along even when every fibre in my body is screaming otherwise. By this time next week, I should have a stash of pills large enough to send me into cardiac arrest.

I need to remain focused for just a little bit longer without distracting myself with these guys and their tempting sins. It's fun while it lasts, but nothing can sway me from my goal. Nobody is worth sticking around and enduring this sickness.

Remember what happened to the last person you fell in love with. You're poison, Brooklyn. Deadly.

Abruptly standing, I almost knock the coffee table over in the process. Anxiety grips me as I grasp at my tight chest, fighting to breathe. The voice whispers through the room, sounding far too real.

"What did you just say to me?" I yell.

Mariam flinches back, her mouth opening in shock. "Just... well done for choosing. Are you quite alright?"

Swivelling my head, my eyes scour the room. Nothing. There's nobody. Just us two.

"Sorry. My bad."

I sink back down into my seat, deflating quickly. The voice… it was so real. Not an inner chatter, but actually audible. And my biggest mistake? Reacting. She's looking at me with bemusement, like I'm a ticking time bomb about to explode and decimate us all.

"Are you hearing voices, Brooklyn?"

I swallow hard. "Not since before Clearview. I just misheard you."

What a stupid mistake. Never react—that's the trick. Stuff it all down. Have I screwed everything up? What if she doesn't let me out or puts me in solitary? Fuck, I need to fix this. I scramble to make up something convincing, even if it's bullshit.

"I'm excited to start learning. I really want to turn my life around."

I put on my best optimistic voice and force a bright smile onto my face. Meanwhile, my nails are cutting into my palms.

"Well, that's good."

She's still eyeing me cautiously.

"So… I have reading I should be getting on with," I prompt.

"Of course. I won't keep you any longer."

I bolt for the door. Nothing will remedy this, and I need to escape before I get myself in any more shit. It's not surprising really. I've had all the other symptoms of abusing my medication: the sickness, cold sweats, insomnia. The voices were bound to come back too once I stopped taking it.

Just breathe.

Only one more week.

It'll all be over soon.

I manage to get outside before I double over, gasping for any available air. That was close. Too close. I have to keep going and maintain the image of wanting to get better. I'm so close to being able to get what I want, so I can't afford to lose this opportunity.

What people don't tell you is that you can't show any weakness to shrinks. They'll jump on any excuse in these places. Before you know it, you're restrained and sedated while they wheel you down the corridor to solitary confinement. Loneliness is a foreign concept until you've experienced that intimidating slice of hell.

After a quick jog across the empty quad, I'm back at Oakridge and sprinting for the safety of my room. Hands shaking uncontrollably, I manage to get the door unlocked and slip inside before I slump against the wood.

"Uh, hey."

I nearly jump out of my skin, expecting some harrowing hallucination to be waiting for me. Looking up with fear, I'm shocked to find Kade sitting casually in my desk chair. A bright, megawatt smile is plastered on his face.

"Jesus fuck, what are you doing here?"

He simply shrugs. "Waiting for you."

"In my room? How did you even get in?"

He flourishes a spare key card. "Perks of the job."

Seriously? This guy has an answer for everything. I shrug off my leather jacket and sling it onto the bed. It's only then that I notice the paper bags waiting on the mattress. There are two of them, and they're jammed full of stuff.

"Care to explain?" I demand.

Kade clears his throat. "Don't get upset. We couldn't help but notice your lack of belongings, so we sorted some stuff to give you. It isn't much, but it'll make us feel better."

I stare, gaping. Frantically, I try to wrap my head around what he's saying.

"How... uh, what?" I stutter.

"Just some essentials. Nothing special, don't worry." He chuckles nervously, his hand rubbing the back of his neck. "Look, we want to help you out, okay? It's nothing shady. I promise."

This is unbelievable. Do they all pity me? Oh God, they came in here yesterday and saw the truth about how sad and empty my life truly is, utterly devoid of any meaning. They probably sat and laughed about me afterwards, trading jokes and insults.

Is this a trick? Some kind of sick game? Does he expect me to fall to my knees and blow him, like Paul did?

"Don't freak out, Brooklyn."

Kade stands, his hands now raised in surrender as he inches closer. I immediately step backwards, putting distance between us while my thoughts spiral.

"Why are you doing this?"

"We're trying to help, that's all," he tries to placate.

That can't be true. Nobody ever does anything out of the goodness of their heart. Not in this world, and especially not somewhere like this. Everything comes with a price—invisible strings attached that come back and bite you in the ass later on. He's trying to manipulate me into owing him a favour.

"Leave," I order.

"What? We're just looking out for you."

"I said go! Take your shit with you and leave me alone! All of you."

I point towards the door, my hand waving in the air. Every inch of my body feels hot, radiating indignation and fury. All remaining sense has left my mind. Kade stares at me for a long moment before nodding with resignation and gathering his navy pea coat.

"Keep pushing people away, and you'll end up alone. You'd do well to realise that."

"Spare me the fucking lecture, Kade. I never asked for this."

He pauses in the doorway, casting a sad look back at me. "Neither did I."

Slamming the door shut on his way out, I realise that he's clearly angry with me but unable to say another word without losing his temper. I'm left surrounded by their bagged gifts, feeling like the worst person in the entire world.

CHAPTER 12
KADE

DADDY - BADFLOWER

I STORM OUTSIDE into the falling rain, then freeze and turn straight back. Heading inside once more, I freeze again and turn back around. Once, twice, three times. I repeat this indecisive nonsense while fisting my hair and struggling to contain my emotions.

"Fuck!" I shout.

She's so infuriating. Her rejection stings as badly as before. Why do I even care? I get myself into these messes by always trying to save people's asses when they don't need or want it. Brooklyn does though, and that's the most infuriating thing.

God, she needs it. That girl is crying out to be helped and, ever the bleeding heart, I can't help but listen. One of these days, I'm going to be fucked over for the last time.

But not today.

Finally making a decision, I race back up the stairs for the final time, stomping all the way to the fourth floor. My jaw is set, and blood rushes in my ears. She doesn't get to push me away.

I'm already dealing with Hudson's need to self-destruct, and I can't take any others right now. I may not know a thing about her, but I've seen enough to know that she's worth saving. Beneath the ice-cold exterior and sharp tongue, there's more.

I hammer on the door, too blinded by anger to let myself in. Brooklyn doesn't answer. Soon, I'm smashing my fist against it even harder. Anger isn't usually my first response, but it's been a long week and this is the final straw.

"Jesus, will you keep it down?"

I glance to the side, following the familiar voice. Hudson's door swings open as he yells, stumbling out with his raven hair rumpled and inked chest bare. When he realises it's me in the corridor, he suddenly looks a lot more awake and scrubs at his eyes in confusion.

"Kade? The hell are you doing?"

"None of your business," I snap angrily.

I can't deal with that asshole right now as well. We still haven't spoken since the exchange over dinner. I have no desire to start a conversation with the dickhead until he bucks up and gets his head out of his ass for once.

"Seriously, what are you playing at?"

"Go back to your room, little brother. This doesn't concern you."

Another voice chimes in, this one female.

"Hud, baby. Come back to bed. Leave him to it."

I see Britt emerge in my periphery, peeking out with a standard-issue bedsheet wrapped around her stick-thin, naked body. When she sees the door I'm waiting by, a hateful look carves her features.

"Not that fucking whore. She broke Maya's nose. You know that, right?"

"That's hilarious," Hudson splutters, earning himself a punch in the shoulder.

"It's not! She's a psycho bitch. You best walk away, Kade."

I ignore them both, continuing to knock with persistence. Eventually, they slip back into the room, thankfully leaving me alone. You know what? They deserve each other. Britt is an ugly personality wrapped in a brittle shell. I hope she breaks Hudson's heart and leaves him.

That'll teach him.

Or, it would. If he had a heart to break.

I come to my senses enough to let myself in with my pocketed key card, preparing to lecture the hell out of Brooklyn until she bucks up and accepts my help. Instead, I'm left standing awkwardly, unsure of what I've walked into.

The setting sun blazes through the room, highlighting the picture of despair cowering in the corner. She's in a tight ball, knees to her chest and both hands clamped over her ears. I can see her shoulders shaking from here, bobbing up and down with heaving sobs. The sight is definitely not what I was expecting.

I creep over, unsure of how to approach this situation but knowing that I have to do something. Walking away isn't in the realm of possibility.

Sinking down to her level, I reach out and brush the top of her head. Her hair is like satin beneath my touch. She stirs, peeking out through the pale curtains covering her face.

"I told you to go," Brooklyn croaks.

"You know I can't do that."

Cupping her pixie face, my thumbs brush over her reddened cheeks to wipe the tears away. Her hands slowly begin to slacken, releasing the death grip she had on her head.

"I'm sorry for knocking so loud."

Shaking her head, her eyes drop. "It wasn't you."

I slide a digit under her chin, tilting her face back up. "Then what is it?"

Her lips press together. She shakes her head, refusing to answer like usual, using all of her strength to prevent the words from leaking out.

"Why are you doing this to me?" she eventually whispers.

"Because helping people is what I do, love."

Brooklyn pries my hands away from her face before gently pushing me back. She's rejecting me again, ever the stubborn bitch.

"Not me. I don't want to be helped."

"Why not?" I demand.

She presses herself further into the corner. "No."

My patience snaps. I hold her still, forcing her to listen to me. "Please let me in. Look at Eli. He was a mess when he got here six months ago."

I've caught her attention. She's listening to me.

"And Phoenix? First time I met him, he threw up on my shoes because he was coming down from a week-long bender and quivering like a leaf. You don't need to be ashamed."

A bitter laugh escapes her lips. "Don't I? You don't know me."

"You're right, I don't. But I want to. If you'd just let me."

I shuffle back and keep my distance, allowing her the space she clearly wants. I know the drill. At first, it's like approaching a wild animal. You've got to ease in and get them used to your presence.

Hell, it took Eli a month before he allowed me this close. The poor guy was so traumatised that he barely moved, let alone spoke. To this day, I've never heard his voice.

"I'll hurt you," Brooklyn whimpers.

"You won't," I assure her.

"It's what I do."

Ever so carefully, I stretch out a hand. Palm up in offering, I'm careful to leave distance between us. I have to give her the option to take it, rather than forcing it upon her.

"Come on, Brooke. Trust me. Just for a moment."

She daggers me with those steely eyes. Gunmetal grey and full of bleak defeat.

"And if I say no?" she murmurs.

"Then I'll leave."

The suspense threatens to cripple my confidence, but she blindly reaches out and grabs my hand. I tighten my grip, clinging to her now that she's on board. I refuse to let go for fear she'll run away from me.

We end up on the bed, paper bags tossed aside without another word. Brooklyn's body instinctively curls up, arms tucked close to her chest. I toss any reservations aside and stretch out opposite. Our heads are mere inches apart, and I make sure my legs don't touch hers. I don't want to scare her off now that we've gotten this far.

"Why are you here?" she asks.

My instinct is to lie, whether deliberately or by omission. That would be infinitely easier and less complicated for both of us. But the whole point of this isn't to do that. There's only a handful of people in this godforsaken place that know of my true purpose here.

"My brother," I reveal.

"Hudson?"

"You know him?"

"No, just heard his name around."

She's frowning to herself, like the name brings back bad memories or something, but quickly clears the expression away. "He's here?"

I breathe a sigh. "Yeah, he's here. It's complicated, but when he was arrested and charged, I was desperate to protect him. Having that power stripped away was tough. I was a student at the time, studying for my master's degree in mathematics."

"What happened?"

"To cut a long story short, I made a deal with our parents. My father is very active in local government and was able to cut a deal with the authorities in exchange for some fairly substantial donations to Blackwood's program."

"Seriously?"

"Yeah. I was given a free ride to this place, able to continue my studies online and also keep an eye on Hudson. I wanted to try and help him get better."

Her eyes are wide. "You did that for him?"

I look away, feeling a hot blush rising from my shirt collar. "He'd do it for me. It's not so bad, I help out with the admin and a couple classes, as you know. It's worth it to be there for him, even when he treats me like shit."

"That's why you're given free reign."

"Pretty much. But that stays between us, okay?"

Brooklyn nods her agreement, easing my nerves somewhat. "So, you're... uh, normal?"

"Well, I don't really care for that word, but sure. I'm here voluntarily."

She stares at me like I'm a puzzle she just can't fathom, her eyes searching with calculation that makes me nervous. "You don't take meds? Or go to therapy?"

"Ah, not so much."

I wait for her response, but none comes.

"What about you?" I ask gently.

"Me? Haven't you read my file?"

Fuck, she's got me down alright.

"I actually haven't."

"But you could have?"

I nod in confirmation. There's no point in lying about it. I did with the others, but something about her has held me back so far. Perhaps some faint hope that maybe she'd tell me herself, given time.

"I... I did something," Brooklyn utters. "Something unforgivable." An involuntary shudder seems to pass over her. "Please don't make me say it."

"You don't have to."

Taking a chance, I move to hold her hand. Our fingers automatically twine together in a way that feels almost natural.

"You're a good person. I'm not."

I shake my head resolutely. "I refuse to believe that. Look at the way you handled Eli on your first day. And standing up to Rio like that? It was a sight for sore eyes. He's been pushing everyone around for far too long and getting away with it."

"Those things don't redeem me of my sins."

That's far more than I can argue against. This is clearly ingrained into her, a belief as corrosive as it is false. She's internalised it so hard, I have no chance of digging the festering hatred out of her. But it's not like that's going to stop me from trying.

"Nobody is all good, Brooke. We're all somewhere on the spectrum of morality, dabbling in shades of grey. There's no such thing as good and bad. Not really."

Brooklyn listens intently, her eyes flicking over my face. Then she shifts her body closer, gradually closing the gap between us. I dare not move, especially now that I've gotten so far. Her knees brush mine, and I can feel her breath on my skin.

"Tell me then."

"Tell you what?" I murmur back.

"The worst thing you've ever done. I want to know." Her fingers squeeze mine. "I promise I can keep a secret. I'll take it to my grave."

It comes to me easily. Too easily. My most awful source of shame. She must see it on my face, and a dark smile pulls at her full lips almost with excitement. I want to tell her, on a primal level.

She's calling out to something inside of me, a layer of my personality that I've buried as deep as possible, hoping never to awaken it again. How did she find it within me?

"It was seven years ago," I admit. "Right before my sixteenth birthday."

The words burst free, refusing to be contained any longer. As I speak, Brooklyn's leg hooks over mine, tangling together to trap me in place. Her warmth pushes me to the edge, with more shameful secrets escaping my lips.

"There was this girl, Amy. She was a few months older than me. We were just kids, stealing kisses behind buildings and exchanging endless text messages. Within weeks, we were both besotted with each other."

She's hanging on to my every word, her attention almost too intense to handle. It's like she's greedily eating up my secrets, sneaking them away for her own use. This has stayed a secret for so long, but she's pulling the sordid shadows free. I'm powerless to stop.

"She got sick. Throwing up in school." I gulp hard, forcing moisture into my dry mouth. "I was terrified. When the test came back positive, confirming that she was pregnant, it was like the world was ending."

Brooklyn's eyes seem to soften.

"Looking back, I was so shallow." I scoff at myself. "It didn't matter, the world wasn't ending. But my father demands perfection from me. He always has. I knew that if he found out... that would be it for me. For my future."

"What did you do?"

I pause, Amy's face filling my vision. Sweet, rosy cheeks and brown curls, with a wide smile that charmed anyone and everyone. Top of her class, she was a wizard on the violin. Her talent was unrivalled. Even at sixteen, her bright future was secured.

"I threatened her, saying that no music school would ever take on a teen mum with a screaming baby. Her folks were obsessed with image and reputation."

Nodding along, Brooklyn hangs on to every word, even as I feel sick to my stomach for speaking this sordid truth out loud.

"I broke her down, scared her into thinking there was no other option but to get rid of it. She cried, begging for my help, telling me that we could make it... be a family. I said no. Never going to happen."

My eyes close briefly. The grief is overwhelming, even now. It's like I'm talking about a stranger, when realistically, the bastard in this story is me. My arrogant younger self. Like Brooklyn said, *unforgivable*. We've both earned that word, apparently.

"Where's Amy now?"

I prepare myself to admit the truth out loud for the first time. "She's dead. Has been for the last seven years. She never even made it to music school."

"How did she die, Kade?"

Brooklyn's voice is soft and mesmerising, coaxing me on. She's stealing my sins and swallowing them whole, greedy for more to hang on to.

"Complications from a back-street abortion. Dead within days of that damn test."

There's a loaded pause, both of us immersed in each other's gaze. The pain in my chest reaches its peak and ebbs away, along with the words that have just been vocalised. I can't take them back now, it's out there and beyond my control.

"I never stepped forward and claimed the child," I continue. "Everyone heard what happened and judged her, tossing about vicious rumours. Our fling was always a secret. We were both terrified of our families finding out. To this day... they still don't know it was me that knocked her up."

I'm ready for Brooklyn to pull away or toss me out of her room in utter disgust. She's within her right after hearing that story. I'd be repulsed too. Hell, I am every day when I look in the mirror and remember the past.

"You see, I guess I really do deserve to be here," I finish.

"No, you don't. Not one bit. You were an asshole, but who isn't?"

I can't help the broken laugh that comes out. "I was a fucking coward."

Her lips turn up in a tiny smile. "We're all cowards, Kade. Running scared from our pasts, avoiding the inevitable. It always finds its way back to us in the end."

Her head drops to the pillow, eyes sinking shut. She snuggles closer, almost like she's comforted by the skeletons in my closet that I've just revealed. When I was playing the good guy, she stubbornly pushed me away. But now that I've owned my mistakes and shared my darkness with her? She's cuddling up like a goddamn puppy, bathing in the grief.

This girl isn't right. Not one bit.

I couldn't save Amy, and I'll spend the rest of my life making up for that, saving all the other hopeless victims in her place. It doesn't matter how much it kills me inside every day. Hudson. Phoenix. Eli. And now? Brooklyn too.

We're family.

No one goes down on my watch.

CHAPTER 13
BROOKLYN

TEARS DON'T FALL - BULLET FOR MY VALENTINE

I'VE SURVIVED my first couple of weeks at Blackwood.

Adjusting to regular classes has been fine, especially with the boys keeping me company and helping with the workload. I have no intention of tackling the stacks of books on my desk. Group therapy doesn't begin until next week, so I don't have to endure that horror show yet.

I pace the room, evening light stretching through the small space. Kade is coming to get me for dinner soon. I'm just killing time. The paper bags of stuff he gave me before still sit under the desk where I threw them after he left.

How I managed to fall asleep in front of him that night, I'll never know. Sleeping is hard enough on my own, let alone in the presence of another. I'm starting to think that I judged him too quickly. With a defeated sigh, I empty the bags on the bed.

Did I even say thank you before I threw the gifts back in his face? I'm an asshole. No surprises there. They've given me an assortment of things, none of it new. This stuff clearly belongs to them and they've given it... to me?

The band t-shirts are definitely Eli's. He's the smallest, and I don't see any of the others sporting *Iron Maiden* merchandise. My fingers run over the soft hoodie buried underneath. It's a lighter shade of grey than his usual one. My heart somersaults, feeling the ramifications of this gesture. I raise it to my nose and take a sniff, relishing the familiar citrusy scent that I've come to associate with him.

Goddammit.

When did I start caring so much?

Phoenix's offerings consist of a cute beanie and an indigo blanket for the bed. I spread it out immediately, smiling at the cosy setup. There are also a couple of beers, which makes me laugh. Where did he get these? I can't even begin to imagine. I'm grateful though; I haven't had a drink in far too long.

Lastly, Kade. He gave me some fresh toiletries to replace my confiscated ones along with a basic backpack filled with stationary and new notebooks. I pause over them, that damned feeling in my chest ballooning.

Jeez, what are these guys doing to me? They're creeping in no matter how hard I try to block the feelings out. Nobody's ever done this for me before, not since my parents died and left me alone in the world. My eyes flick over to the bedside table.

The polaroids are buried in the drawer, hidden from sight. The temptation to look returns. My fingers near the handle, but I hold back, fearing the consequences. Last time I looked at their faces, I ended up needing three stitches.

In that case, maybe I should look so that I stop fucking around with counting pills and do things the old-fashioned way. But I know better than anyone that you have to do it properly to succeed.

That's why I've taken some extra time this past week to build my stockpile up even further. It's easy to pass out and only do half the job. Then I'll never get another chance.

I change into one of the new t-shirts, this one with *Red Hot Chili Peppers* scrawled across the front. Allowing myself a small smile, I slip on my pink Docs and grab my leather jacket, adding Phoenix's beanie on a whim.

I prefer to skip dinner usually since my stomach is too unsettled to deal with food. Turns out, stopping meds cold turkey ain't fun. But Kade has apparently taken it upon himself to fix that, hence why I'm being escorted to the cafeteria tonight.

Heading downstairs, I check for guards before lighting up a cigarette on the front lawn and leaning against some stupid decorative statue. Curious looks are tossed my way as patients pass by on their way out, but I ignore them all and keep smoking. My run-in during gym class last week has earned me a reputation.

"Hey, Brooklyn!"

Phoenix jogs over, his signature megawatt smile in place. He comes way too close and plucks the cigarette from between my fingers, backtracking as he takes a drag.

"You're actually joining us for once, what a treat. Nice hat."

"Don't get used to it. And thanks, some weirdo gave it to me."

"Huh, he clearly has good taste."

He gives me a flirty wink as the others join us. Eli shuffles up to my side, giving me a nod. His dark curls are fresh and bouncy. He must've just had a shower. Green eyes trailing over the shirt peeking out from beneath my jacket, he manages a smile that makes my toes curl.

Christ, I'm playing with fire here.

"You morons coming?" Kade calls.

My jaw nearly drops when I take in his casual outfit. The usual shirt and smart trousers are nowhere to be found, replaced by grey sweats and a tight, black t-shirt that reveals more toned lines of muscle than my brain can handle.

Holy smokes.

I'm literally screwed.

Phoenix links his arm through mine and drags me along, joining the hordes of people heading across the quad. I can feel Kade's eyes on me, but I don't react, deliberately keeping my distance. Things are still odd between us after the other night. He's more overbearing than ever, constantly studying me.

All I can think about is him laying across the bed from me, his thick lashes framing sad, hazel eyes. Or the feel of his leg on mine, and his face close enough for me to hear his breath as he confesses his sins. I can't move past that night. It's done something to me.

Don't get invested, I remind myself.

I can't afford to care about these guys.

Once in the busy cafeteria, we join the queue and load up our trays. I select a small salad that doesn't look too intimidating for my stomach, but Phoenix steals my plate, muttering as he dumps a giant serving of lasagna on it as well.

"Fucking eat it," he orders.

I kind of like this bossy version of him, all growly and harsh. We crowd around their usual table, with conversation flowing easily. There's something comforting about the ease with which they've inserted me into the group despite how badly I've behaved or my shitty attitude.

"Heads up, Kade. Hudson and Britt just walked in."

Phoenix's low whisper elicits a groan from his friend.

"That's just great."

"Hey, at least they've got clothes on this time."

"Makes a change," Kade grumbles.

I keep my head down and push the food around my plate. Fucking Hudson. That name is cursed. I'm not particularly looking forward to meeting someone who will only remind me of the past. Even if he's a decent person—which, from what I've heard, he isn't—I won't be able to get past that damn name.

"Kade! Didn't I say to cancel that fucking appointment?"

He must be close, marching up to the table with furious steps. That voice sends shivers right down my spine. It's earth-shatteringly familiar in its gruffness.

My blood chills as my stomach drops to the floor. Oh, fuck me gently. It can't be. The universe surely doesn't hate me this much?

With every ounce of willpower possible, I look up, taking in the man skidding to a halt beside his brother. Wearing dark, ripped jeans and a tight t-shirt, his outfit reveals chiselled abs that I know all too well.

I trailed my tongue over them many times, tasting the salty tang of his sweat after we fucked like rabbits in the dark. He's filled out and grown into his looks since the last time we spoke.

Five whole years ago.

It still hurts like it was yesterday.

All noise falls away. The bottle of water in Hudson's hand falls to the floor, his face slackening with absolute shock. His crystal-clear blue eyes go so wide that it's almost comical. A new eyebrow piercing disappears into his shock of pitch-black hair.

Locks I used to tangle my fingers in. Plump lips that used to worship me in the dead of night when they weren't whispering lies and manipulations to control me further. His corrupted soul took everything from me.

This can't be happening.

Ever so gently, I set my fork down. A strange sense of calm is quickly descending. I've waited for this day, dreaming about it night after night while nursing my shattered heart and plotting my revenge for if I ever saw his face again.

I stuffed the feelings so goddamn deep, they sank into the pits of my heart and poisoned everything around them. The memories haunted me for years to come in every guy that followed him. He ruined them all for me.

"W-Wha... Brooke?"

The table descends into heavy silence, with all eyes on me. Kade's glancing between the two of us with concern. Phoenix is poised to move closer. Even Eli is paying attention, his hood back and headphones out. They're watching the car crash unfold in slow motion, unable to stop the disaster barrelling straight ahead.

"Hello, Hudson."

My voice doesn't sound like my own. It's dark, angry and accusatory. Of course, he's here. It's where monsters belong. I shouldn't be surprised. He'll fit right in with the other treacherous bastards that frequent these halls.

He continues to stare at me, his hands quickly clenching into tight fists. "You're here."

"I'd think that was fucking obvious," I lash back.

He swallows hard. "How? Why?"

I slowly rise to my feet. Sliding my dinner knife up my sleeve, I maintain eye contact, never once allowing him a glimpse of the chaos beneath my steely exterior. I'm cold as ice and razor sharp, ready to give him a taste of his own medicine.

"Not sure it's any of your business why I'm here."

"This is... Jesus. I can't believe it's you," Hudson splutters.

"Bet you never planned to see me again."

Jaw clenching angrily, Hudson finally breaks and looks away. He casts his brother a pleading look, silently asking for assistance. Seems like cowardice runs in the fucking family.

"I never stopped hoping to see you. I tried to find you," he murmurs.

"Spare me the lies, Hud. Frankly, I'm glad you didn't find me."

A twisted memory comes back to me, filling my vision and solidifying my rage. My body straddled him as he wrapped a belt around my arm and filled a syringe.

He watched hungrily as I shot up, quickly relaxing and slumping onto the thin mattress. Warmth and adrenaline surged through me with the substance in my veins.

Fucking and getting high—that's all he was ever good for and inevitably, that's what set us on course for a cataclysmic ending.

"Brooklyn?"

Kade stands up, looking so confused and so lost. I almost pity him. He really has no idea about the kind of monster he's related to.

"I didn't realise that your brother is *this guy.*"

"How exactly do you two know each other?" Phoenix interjects.

A resentful laugh bubbles up. "You want to tell them or should I?"

Hudson's mouth clicks open and shut several times. He's pale, too pale. He looks sick to his stomach, and I fucking love it. I want to pound on his body until his bones break and his skin cracks, leaving nothing but a bloodied, crippled bag of dead organs behind.

Even then I won't forgive him.

"I... ah. Well..."

He's tumbling over his words like a scared child. Looking brokenly at me, the devastation on his face is so visceral that it makes my mouth water with need. That's exactly how I want him to look. Like that and worse. Much worse.

Ensuring the knife is securely hidden, I leave the table and get up in his annoyingly handsome, angular face, leaving scant inches between us. I'm close enough to bathe in his heady, masculine scent. So achingly familiar, I want to peel my skin off just to get it away from me.

"Say it, Hud. Fucking say it."

He shakes his head and attempts to grab my hand, failing utterly as I swing it out of reach. Silently pleading with me, he's begging me to relent. Let him off the hook. Whatever. No way in hell is that going to happen. Not after what he did to me back then.

"Brooke, blackbird. I'm so sor—"

Before he can finish, I strike him firmly across the face.

"How dare you! I'm not your fucking blackbird. Not anymore."

I follow the blow with another, hitting him over and over again until he falls to the floor. Scooting away from my savage attack, he tries to hold me back without physically hurting me, as if his gentleness now will make any difference.

The damage he inflicted long ago can't be undone. I almost want him to hurt me physically, to validate the wounds he created that can never be seen by anyone but me.

"Brooklyn! Stop!"

"Someone grab her!"

"Quick, security is coming!"

All I see is red. Not reality, nor the blossoming friendships around me or the care I've been shown. Just the pure, unadulterated need to hurt this bastard. To make him feel even a smidgen of what I went through. I may not deserve to live, but neither does he.

Make him pay. Make him hurt.

Cut him, the devil in my mind orders.

The knife slips down into my hand, and I go to town. Putting all my strength into the movements, I hope to cause maximum damage. My body is weak compared to his, but I still draw blood from each stab that I manage. It blooms through the thin material of his white t-shirt like a watercolour painting.

Fucking beautiful.

That's how it feels.

Hands grab my body and haul me up, dragging me away from Hudson. Kade steps between us, ever the peacekeeper. Fuck that. I'll hurt him to get to his brother if I have to.

Phoenix holds me to his body with arms like steel bands and tells me to calm down, but it's futile. Fury thrums through me, stronger than any drug ever injected. Fiery rage seals my determination.

I slam my head back, hearing Phoenix cry out in pain. Slipping his hold, I fling myself at Kade. I'm snarling and swearing like a rabid animal. This is what it feels like to lose control, and it's so damn satisfying.

In the end, it's the guards that break us up. Like invisible sentries appearing out of thin air, they remind us all that this isn't the real world. You don't just get away with stuff and simply walk away to lick your wounds. They're always watching, poised to intervene if necessary.

I'm sandwiched between the burly men, one yanking my arms back and crunching my fingers together until I release the weapon. Hot tears pour freely as my face is smashed against the floor. It's just like the good old days. The Clearview special, restrain and punish.

"Say goodbye, you psycho. They'll never let you out after this."

The guard is shouting, threatening me, but I don't care. Not one bit. In the seconds before I'm dragged away, I see Kade kneeling on the ground by his brother. Phoenix and Eli stand frozen, both watching me helplessly.

Then there's Hudson. His hand is pressed to his abdomen, but he doesn't even look phased by the bleeding injuries I inflicted. His attention is focused on me as I'm taken away, his expression caught somewhere between disbelief and pity.

I hate them. I hate them all.

I hope my death *kills* them.

CHAPTER 14
HUDSON

LET YOU GO - MACHINE GUN KELLY

I SCRUNCH the paper up in my hand, tossing it across the desk to join the others. Six attempts, and I still can't write a word. Kade watches silently from his seat opposite me before glancing back down at his laptop screen.

Taking a fresh piece of paper, my pen is poised. Right. Consumer marketing. *I know this, come on. It's fucking easy.* Pressing the nib down, I quickly lose focus and scribble angrily, so hard it tears a massive hole in the middle of the page and ink spills everywhere.

In my head, familiar storm-cloud eyes are peering up at me. Her pupils are blown wide and dilated while her lips are wrapped around my dick, taking it so fucking deep I can hardly contain myself for a second longer. She always knew exactly how I liked it and never disappointed.

My dirty little blackbird.

Another fantasy comes.

Her hands are secured to the bed frame with my belt, and her body is open and exposed. Perfect tits calling out to me, I tear my eyes away, focusing on the leg propped up on my shoulder. My fingers search for a vein to tap. Squirming and writhing, she begs for me to taste her sweet pussy as the drugs work their magic.

"Hudson?"

Kade's hand lands on my arm. I open my eyes, and the images melt away. He's looking at me with a frown creasing his eyebrows, his black-rimmed glasses sitting slightly crooked beneath his light-blonde hair. We're all stuck in an eternal state of anxiety at the moment.

She's been gone for a whole week.

People that go down into the basement, locked in solitary until they're stable enough to return… they come back different. More broken than how they went in.

The four walls closing in, time melting into insignificance; it's a recipe for insanity. I'm under no illusions. I've been there before. Two days was enough to scare me straight, relatively speaking.

"When are you going to talk to me?" Kade sighs.

Shaking my head, I gather my ruined papers and walk to the rubbish bin to shove them in with all my frustration. For good measure, I kick it too. Stupid fucking bin.

"I'm not. Ever."

He shrugs. "I'll only ask her about your history when she returns."

If she ever does.

"Don't you dare. Leave her out of it, Kade."

"How? Brooklyn's the reason you're in this state. She tried to fucking stab you! That's a big deal. What happened between you two? What did she do?"

"Nothing. It's not what *she* did, you idiot."

It's what I did. The unthinkable.

Kade slams his laptop shut before leaning back in the chair. His arms are crossed over his shirt as he evaluates me.

"Was this before or after you came to us?"

"Before."

"In foster care?" he clarifies.

The dark memories bombard me. St Anne's was a Catholic-run foster home where I first met my blackbird. Tucked away in a remote town in the countryside, it was far from the luxury of upper-class London suburbia where I eventually ended up.

Kade's family adopted me when I was sixteen. I left the misery of being in care behind. I left her behind, alone and utterly destroyed by everything I'd done. My blackbird was broken.

"Yeah, I knew her then."

That's all I can say. The rest is too awful.

"What happened?"

I slam my palm down on the desk. "Do you ever stop?"

"I'm just trying to help you, Hud. You need to talk about it."

"No, I don't. Because nothing is ever going to fix what I did."

Kade thankfully shuts up. I've dealt with him following me around like a fucking guard all week, and it's just too much. I get it. He wants to help, but it's entirely unwelcome. He should be in the warden's office convincing her to release Brooklyn.

I don't blame her for what happened in the cafeteria. I deserved it. But the way she came for me... she's not the timid, innocent, yet surprisingly fiery girl I once knew. This isn't where they send angels. We're all fucking devils here.

"You need to stay away when she gets back." Kade points a finger at me, his voice hard as nails. "I mean it."

"I can't," I mutter.

"You will. She doesn't need you and clearly doesn't like you."

The worst part is, I don't even care. Now that I've seen her, laid my eyes on her translucent skin with her billowing hair lighter than fresh snow, I'm enthralled all over again. Just like before, I fell hard and fast without coming up for air. I'll only hurt her by sticking around. So why can't I let go?

The door to the library opens. I glance up, my eyes searching for her.

Disappointment fills me as Phoenix and Eli appear instead. For fuck's sake, she's not coming.

Even if they let her out, I'm the last person she'll want to see. But she will have to face me soon enough. If she needs to scream and beat on me again, so be it. I'll take it. Whatever brings her back to me.

"Anything?" Kade asks desperately.

Phoenix shakes his head. "Nope. No sign of her."

All of their eyes are on me, matching expressions of anger twisting their features. Hands clenched, I turn my attention back to the textbook. I read the words without taking them in. My brain is caught in a state of complete numbness because I know this is all my fault.

Phoenix glares. "What do we do now?"

"No one will talk to me about her. I've been shut out," Kade states.

"You have to know something!"

"I'm just as frustrated as the rest of you. There's nothing we can do."

Shoulders slumping in defeat, Phoenix curses colourfully. "I hate this."

"Why the fuck do you guys even care?" I hiss at them.

Matching glowers are tossed my way, indicating that was entirely the wrong thing to say. Even my so-called friends hate me right now. It's not a great feeling, but I'm used to being the bad guy around here.

"While you've been busy screwing Britt and being the world's shittiest human being, we've been getting to know Brooklyn and helping her settle in," Kade rants. "So, lose the entitlement and wake up, Hud. You're not the only one who's pissed."

I almost want to pat him on the back for finally saying it how it is for once.

"We care as much as you do, if not more," Phoenix chimes in.

Even Eli nods, chewing on his lip anxiously. He's not looking great, even more washed out and jittery than usual as he furtively glances around. All three of them care. It's blindingly obvious. I can't help the jealousy the realisation brings.

"Fine, then help me fix this," I plead.

"How?"

"I don't know. Between the four of us, we have to think of something."

There's a chime, and Kade punches several buttons on his phone to quickly silence it. He needs to be more careful. We're technically allowed phones, but internet access is strictly monitored, along with all incoming calls.

"It's your appointment this afternoon with the lawyer."

He shoots me a loaded look. Just as I'm about to berate him for the millionth time, an idea hits me. Management will never listen to us; we're a group of fucking delinquents with records that shame most prisoners. They apparently won't even listen to Kade, who clearly has less sway around here than previously believed.

"That's it," I exclaim.

Kade is the first to catch on, of course. "Dammit. You're right!"

"Someone catch me up?" Phoenix whines.

"The lawyer. He's here to provide an update on my case, but we'll just use him to free Brooklyn instead. Say that they're holding her without cause or whatever. He'll know exactly what to do, and the punishment will never stick."

The words tumble free as my relief grows. This could work. If we leave her, they'll let her rot, regardless of the toll solitary will inevitably take on her mind. I can't just sit here while they slowly break her down, day by day.

Kade strides away. "I'll make the call."

"Then what?"

"Huh?" I turn to Phoenix.

"She hates your fucking guts, Hud. You've got to sort it."

I look away, feeling the hot, clinging embrace of shame. What's my plan here? Beg on my knees for forgiveness? I don't think I've ever apologised for a damn thing in my whole life. That's what drove her away in the first place—the inability to own my shit.

"I'll figure it out," I mutter.

"Promise?"

"Jesus, man. I promise, okay?"

Phoenix nods, clearly still unhappy but conceding for the time being. I don't bother looking at Eli, the deathly silent statue in the corner. I'm sure he's thinking the exact same thing, judging me with eyes that see far too much.

How do you rectify the worst thing you've ever done in your life?

"You've got to tell us what happened between you two." Phoenix sits back in his chair like he's an interrogator or some shit rather than my friend.

"Haven't we been over this, shithead? Not happening."

"We have a right to know."

I abruptly push my chair back and gather my stuff as he watches me closely. Rage slips beneath my skin and burns hot, scalding every nerve ending until I can't contain it anymore.

My empty chair breaks as I smash it against the wall. My roar of frustration startles nearby patients hiding from security in the stacks of books.

Phoenix jumps in shock. "Jesus, Hud. Chill the fuck out before security comes over! You need to cool it."

Standing amongst the splintered wood, my chest heaves and my cheeks burn. Even smashing the chair didn't release the heavy weight in my mind, the choking guilt. If only I could go back, punch my younger self in the face and tell him to do the right thing, no matter the consequences.

Instead, I ruined us both.

CHAPTER 15
BROOKLYN

MONSTER (UNDER MY BED) -
CALL ME KARIZMA

VIC GRUNTS, *his body flush against mine so our hips are glued together. Thrusting into me with tender strokes, he moans and kisses my neck. I feel sick to my stomach, but I can't pull away. He doesn't need to know what goes through my head when we make love.*

It'll break his heart.

"You're so fucking tight. God, I love you. I love you so much."

"I love you too," *I grind out.*

The words are killing me slowly, piece by piece.

It's not his fault. Vic... he's troubled. Kind and sweet when he wants to be, but scarily quick to anger. He's hateful of the distance growing between us. When we fight over the drink and drugs, he comes to me to apologise first before sweeping up broken glass or fixing shattered picture frames.

But he's also always the first to start swinging. Neither one of us is good for the other. The ghosts and shadows in my head are ripping us both apart.

Vic rolls off me, his breathing ragged as cold air hits my skin. The relief is acute, and is quickly followed by shame. This should be giving me pleasure, making me feel loved and wanted, not repelled, holding in my disgust as I fake the noises and an eventual orgasm.

"Did you try on the dress that I bought you?"

"Uh, it's not really me."

"Put the dress on. It's my sister's wedding, for fuck's sake," *he hisses.*

I'll be dressed up like a prized puppy. Fuck that. But if I refuse, I'm the bad guy.

"I... can't wear it, Vic."

He turns his eyes on me, wide and upset. The emotion quickly fades into anger that is never far beneath the surface. He's always mad at me for one thing or another.

"Why not? Did you do it again?"

Shaking my head, I'm ignored as he pins me down with his substantial weight and yanks my shirt sleeves up. He gasps and swears at the mess he finds, making me cringe back into the pillows to escape his inevitable wrath.

"Brooke! The hell are you doing to yourself? Fucking freak."

His fingers bite into my skin, aggravating the throbbing cuts like he wants to punish me. I try to pull my arm away, but his grip tightens.

He's furious, and the disappointment stings. Bile gathers in my throat, and I want to run and hide. These aren't his to look at. They're private. Personal.

"You promised."

"Screw promises. It's stupid," I mutter shamefully.

"How can we be together if all you do is lie? Does it mean nothing to you, the shit that spews from your mouth? You're fucking breaking my heart here."

No. It doesn't matter to me. I'm not even sure he has a heart to break, just a twisted, gaping hole where it should be. We're both assholes, but I'll lie, cheat and manipulate without blinking an eye.

That's the truth of it. This good-girl persona that he's constructed for me is not real. He's deluding himself and punishing me for failing to meet that standard.

"Leave me alone." I shrug him off, trying to escape.

"You don't get to do that, Brooke!"

He drags me back, refusing to let go. I struggle and fight, but it's no use. He's stronger than me, bigger than me. Determined to save me, or at least save the version of me that he believes exists.

What if I told him where I was last night?

What if he knew that less than twelve hours ago, I was fucking another man? Bent over a table in the closed diner, my uniform hitched up around my waist. I took it hard and rough from the chef in exchange for a baggie of coke. I didn't even ask him to use a condom, that's how little I care about myself.

Anything just to feel something.

No matter how much it destroys my soul.

The urge to throw the ugly truth in his face is overwhelming. But deep down, I'm fucking selfish. I don't want to be alone. Secretly, no matter how toxic this thing is between us, I want to be the person he thinks I am.

She's better than me, tenfold. No matter how long I stay in this hazardous waste of a relationship... the chances of me ever becoming her?

Zero. Nil.

I'm too far gone.

I shove Vic hard, breaking his hold. My head buzzes and my ears ring with panic. Screaming voices grow louder with every second, fuelled by my anger and always ready to taunt me some more. The accompanying shadows grow until they're chasing me from the bedroom, but I can't escape the dark suggestions that follow.

Kill him. Break his neck.

Slit his throat. Push him down the stairs.

I don't listen. I never listen. I've heard voices and seen the shadows for years, long predating my shitty relationship with Vic. I grew up with invisible friends that no one could see, until the friends became shadows that haunted my every waking moment.

The constant failure to live up to Vic's impossible expectations?

They don't like that. They want us to act, to punish him right back for idolising me when really I'm just a worthless bitch, coasting through life from one disaster to the next. It's his fault for making me feel bad for being my true, broken self.

Kill him. Kill him. Kill him.

Kill him. Kill him. Kill him.

I storm out of the room, locking myself in the bathroom. Searching frantically for the spare razor, I smash it on the sink to release the tantalising blades. Vic throws them out, and I buy more. It's a never-ending battle of wills.

Even when I promise to get better and we share a brief glimpse of a normal, happy relationship… it's all hot air. Fake words and easy lies to appease his own demons. Nothing can stop me.

Kill him. Kill him. Kill him.

Kill him. Kill him. Kill him.

"NO," I scream in response.

The shadows melt down the walls, bubbling and spitting with rage. They creep closer by the second, whispering their poisonous commands to me. No matter how loud I shout, they refuse to leave. Refuse to stop talking to me. Sometimes, I talk back just to appease them.

I can't kill him.

Please don't make me.

I can't do it.

I slice and slash my arms, fucking devastated by the ceaseless anger. The pain isn't even Vic's fault. I carried the scars inside for years before we met in a backstreet nightclub. Cutting myself viciously until the voices fade once more, I slump on the floor. I'm suddenly tired and drained of all hope. This is my routine. It always works.

But my biggest fear?

That one day, it won't be enough. Even this won't stop me.

And the shadows will win.

———

There's a metallic bang as the guard slides the food tray in. It rouses me from the nightmare of my past and sends me hurtling straight into the nightmare of my present. He slams the hatch shut again without uttering a word. Speaking isn't allowed.

Even if I had something to say, my body wouldn't cooperate. Nothing escapes my lips right now. They're numb, slippery with drool. Every inch of my body is empty. Immobile.

How long have I been here? A week? Month? Year?

Does it even matter?

I once spent a weekend in the hole back in Clearview. That was torture enough, and it felt shorter than this. But who knows? Time isn't real anyway, not anymore. Life ceased to exist for me a long time ago—when this sickness took root, invading my brain and corrupting my soul. It's all been illusionary since, dragging on without meaning.

Sleep returns as the black smog descends and envelops me. My food turns cold, and the sunlight fades. Flooding across the room through the high, barred window, it peeks into the basement level of the institute while setting. I can't escape through there.

Don't you think I've tried that?

Another day begins. Another tray of food. More sunlight, more rain, more numbness. Then another. Tray after tray. Day after day. I lay there, fading and withering. Tormented by ghosts and memories in my head. Voices and whispers of a time long past, yet still irrevocably tied to my present.

Truly, I envy people that can simply move on, like it's so fucking easy to do. Everyone should hurt as much as me. Everyone should suffer like I do. That's all I can think about. It's bitter and pointless, and I know I'm acting like an angry child. But inside, deep down, I still am that angry child.

The days blur into one another.

When my endless solitude is finally disturbed, I'm not even sure what's real and what's not anymore. The drugs have been forced in through an IV line, eroding all of the precious, painstakingly constructed boundaries in my mind. The medicine unhinges and destabilises me until I swear the padded room is watching me, laughing and sneering. Medication is meant to have the opposite effect, right?

Fucking psychiatrists.

It's all bullshit.

"Brooklyn? Can you hear me?"

I'm rolled over, and the thin, white sheets are pulled back as cold air hits my skin. Beady eyes peer down at me beneath a crop of white hair and wire-rimmed glasses. His skin is creased like old parchment and scented with expensive cologne.

"Time to get up now," he croons. "You're free to leave."

A guard is brought in to lift my flaccid body, forcing me to stand on legs that refuse to hold my weight. I'm removed from the cell and dragged out into a bleak corridor.

Shadowy and never ending, it holds more cells and barred doors that stretch onwards into the distance. I think I hear voices as we pass, but the whispers from behind the other doors are indecipherable.

My mind is groggy, unstable and short-circuiting. I can't process anything or even begin to question what's happening around me in the sinister darkness of this place. The scenery melts away into the background as we walk past.

"It's taken some time, but we're now happy for you to leave and rejoin the main population. The new drugs have you looking much more stable, hmmm?"

The odd-looking man is talking on and on in a regal voice. Signing release papers as he walks ahead of me, he tucks a fancy fountain pen back into his white coat once finished. The words float inside my head, all meaning lost in translation. One thing screams at me through the heavy fog.

This is not what better feels like.

What have they done to me?

Entering a nearby office in the basement, I'm deposited into an armchair. My head is propped up so I can see the doctor taking a seat at his desk, humming under his breath.

He's short and round, clearly well into his sixties. The striped bowtie and braces beneath his coat make him look like a fucking cartoon character. If I could feel my face, I'd laugh.

"Hmm, let's see. Well, well. Interesting stuff."

Continuing to mutter and ruminate, he hobbles over to a nearby mini fridge and rifles through the tiny, labelled bottles of drug cocktails like he's a fucking bartender and I'm a helpless punter.

When he sidles up to my chair with a hypodermic needle, I try to move, but fail. Nothing responds to me, not even my toes. All I can do is sit helplessly frozen as he finds a suitable vein and plunges it in.

"Very good. This should liven you up, dear. Such a good girl."

He retakes his seat and studies me intently. A loud grandfather clock ticks away in the corner of his resplendent, carpeted office. Thick persian rugs meet gold-framed paintings that depict countryside scenes in impeccable detail. It looks like a museum in here.

Gradually, feeling begins to return to my body. My fingers spasm painfully as pins and needles spread through my extremities. First, paralysing cold infects my cells, then burning heat. Looking down at my bare feet, ever so slowly, I manage to wiggle my toes.

Within half an hour, I can sit somewhat upright and form words again. I wipe drool from my mouth and lick my lips, my tongue feeling heavy and foreign in my sore mouth. Whatever he's given me, it seems to have kick-started my body. Was it adrenaline? Some experimental drug? I've lost count of the shit they've pumped into me. This isn't right. It isn't normal.

"H-How long?" I manage to say.

"Two weeks. Your lawyer has been giving us some trouble, missy."

"My l-lawyer?"

Don't fucking have one.

None of this makes sense.

I just want to go back to sleep.

"Yes, lawyer. A frightfully rude gentleman from the city. They love to swan in here making demands."

"W-Why?" I stammer.

"Well, we insisted on getting you into a healthy state before even considering a return to the general population. This is a mental health institution, after all. Treatment is our first priority, along with customer satisfaction."

His smile is wide, almost savage, and it makes me deeply uncomfortable. I need to argue back, to point out that drugging me to death isn't treatment. It's fucking sedation and abusing their power. Nothing about this is healthy. Not a damn thing.

"I w-want to go home."

The plea slips out unbidden. My voice is cracked and reveals more emotion than I want anyone to see. I hate the vulnerability, but I'm in no place to play games right now. Then it hits me, straight in the motherfucking heart.

I don't have a home.

The elderly man smiles, nodding with what should be kindness, but looks more like fascination. The restrained curiosity is so clear in his gaze, and it makes my skin crawl. Like I'm just another social experiment ready to sacrifice for the cause.

"You're clear to return back upstairs." He beams at me proudly. "I'll be taking over your treatment from now on. You'll return to me once a week for your shot and for therapy, not Mariam. She isn't equipped to deal with your... *specific challenges.* I have more suitable experience."

"Experience?" I repeat.

"Yes. We have lots to work on together. Exciting plans."

Ice travels through my veins, and I want to cry. Scream, refuse and flee from sight. Everything inside of me is saying that this guy is bad news.

But there's no proof or tangible evidence to suggest this isn't another one of my delusions. I try to wrack my brain, but the two weeks are all a blur. A twisted, amorphous cloud in my psyche.

Just get back to the room.

Get away from this man, this floor.

All of it.

He calls for the guard to return, giving him instructions to get me home safe. I can walk better now, but everything shakes and burns since every muscle is now unused to sudden movement after so long spent in a barred cell.

As we leave, I look back at the twisted little man for a final time, my heart hammering in my chest.

I can't hold the final question back.

"Who are you?"

He tips his head towards me, plastering a charming smile in place that would win over any jury.

"Professor Lazlo, my dear. Pleasure to meet you properly. I look forward to our appointment next Monday morning. Do rest up, we have plenty to crack on with. Plenty."

CHAPTER 16
PHOENIX

CATHEDRALS - ANIMAL FLAG

I KICK the ball to Hudson a little harder than necessary. It goes sailing past him and out of the pitch, causing a round of complaints. He flips me off and chases after it, giving me a burst of satisfaction. *Good*. Just the sight of his face right now is too much to handle.

I'm not a particularly violent person. Words are better weapons than anything else. You can cut someone far deeper with the truth than any blade. But what he did? I'm pissed off. Hell, I'm fucking furious. Everything was going fine until he showed up and it all went to shit.

Two weeks.

Brooklyn's been gone for two damn weeks. No matter what legal precedence is thrown at this place, she's under the custody of the shrinks. Her life has been signed away to them.

There's not much else to be done, and the attack on Hudson sealed her fate. With enough witnesses to verify what happened, even the fancy fucking lawyer from London couldn't get her out of solitary.

I'm going crazy. This girl, she's under my skin. I don't know how or why, but knowing she's in that basement, all alone.... it's doing things to me. Causing feelings that I didn't even think I was capable of.

Eli and I tried to break in the other night, but we nearly got tossed in there ourselves. Luckily, I'm squeaky clean and he's too fucking crazy to survive the hole, so we only got a warning.

Regardless, if she isn't back by the end of the weekend, we're going back down there. Consequences be damned to hell. I'd happily kiss my spotless record goodbye for the chance to see her again.

"If you're going to be a dick, we may as well stop," Hudson yells.

Well, that's pretty much guaranteed.

I march over, hating how angry I feel right now. This isn't me. I don't *feel* shit like this. He seems to think I'm coming to talk, but as soon as I'm close enough, I smash my fist into his stomach. Doubling over, he grunts in pain. I think I can appreciate the appeal of violence now.

"Think I've earned the right to be a dick," I shout back. "Fuck you, buddy."

Turning my back on him is a mistake. Next thing I know, my legs are swept out from underneath me and my head connects with the hard ground. Hudson looms over me, his face twisted in a mask of rage.

"Screw you, Nix. You think I don't feel the same way?"

"Yeah, well, I don't see you doing shit about it!"

Hudson grabs me by the scruff of my shirt, his face close enough for spit to hit my cheek. "You have no fucking idea. None at all. Don't talk about shit you don't understand or we're going to have a problem."

"Guys, come on." Kade sighs. "Let's not do this again."

"Piss off," we both reply at the same time.

A few punches and insults later, and we're walking away from each other and dusting ourselves off. There's no point dragging it out, we both just needed a release. Kade prefers to suffer in silence, pointlessly scrolling the internet for legal arguments and loopholes. It's a waste of time, if you ask me.

Eli is another breed altogether. For a generally unsociable guy, he's breaking records at the moment. Completely retreating into himself, his nose is always buried in a book. Yet, he never seems to finish it. In fact, I think he's been reading the same page for a while now.

"Let's go back to the room," I suggest. "We got some more beers off Rio."

"You really need to stop bargaining with him," Kade chastises.

"I'll pay him back, don't worry. He knows I'm good for it."

"I could use a drink," Hudson chimes in moodily.

We trail back to Oakridge in uncomfortable silence. Things between us have never been so tense. The repercussions of Brooklyn's attack on Hudson have been hard on all of us, but no one knows how to fix this mess. Not while we're wrapped in fear of what's happening to the little firecracker that barrelled into our lives.

I'm aware that I've become too attached, too quickly. It doesn't change a thing though. Every night, her stormy eyes invade my dreams. I see her lips on mine, and her body fitting against mine fucking perfectly while her sweet cunt is wrapped tight around my dick.

She was the best kiss of my life, and that's saying something. You can bet that when she's out, nothing's going to stop me from doing that again and more. Anything to bring some life to her. I need to see her reluctant smile, let it devastate my heart with a mere look.

"Hudson! Baby!"

Britt's shrill voice rings out across the quad. She's spotted our group and is chasing after us. *Stupid bitch.* Flinging herself at Hudson, he's forced to peel her off and take a big step back. His facial expression says it all.

"Where have you been? I've been looking everywhere. I miss you."

She's whining again, and Eli swiftly departs, literally striding away without a second glance. I know he can't stand her voice, but now Kade and I are stuck. We shift awkwardly as she gapes at Eli's retreating back, turning to meet Hudson's obvious rejection. Watching her get crushed into a million pathetic pieces is actually pretty entertaining.

Just me? Oh well.

Hudson runs a hand through his hair, lips pursed unhappily. "I thought I told you to leave me alone, Britt. We're done, for good. It's over."

"Baby, what are you talking about? Quit messing around already." Her voice becomes gradually more hysterical as she latches on to his arm. "Don't do this, Hud. You need me."

"Listen to me," Hudson barks. "We're through. That's it. No more."

Fat tears begin to roll down her cheeks, sparkling satisfyingly as her heartbreak takes root. It's fucking hilarious if you ask me.

"Don't say that. Please," she whimpers.

Hudson grits his teeth, forcing some patience. "That's the truth."

Bursting into loud, echoing sobs, Britt hangs off his body. She's clawing at his shirt like some kind of deranged kitten while mewling her pathetic pleas. Fucking hell, I should've run while I had the chance. She barely weighs a thing with her protruding bones, so Hudson swiftly places her back on the ground.

"Leave me alone. Move on," he orders.

Her pain swiftly morphs into anger as her face scrunches up and hands ball into tight fists. The slap comes as quickly as expected, leaving a big, red handprint on his cheek.

"Fuck you, Hudson Knight," she spits harshly. "You're a bastard."

He simply shrugs without showing any emotion whatsoever. Without even looking her in the eye, he acts like she's nothing more than shit on the bottom of his shoe. It's excruciating to watch, but morbidly fascinating at the same time.

After more shouting and cursing, Britt storms off in a cloud of rage, leaving Hudson to rub his sore cheek from where she hit him. He glares after her with exasperation.

"Man, she's hard work."

"We've been telling you that for months," Kade points out.

"Whatever, it's done now."

"Another victim," I comment.

He looks like he wants to kill me.

"What's that supposed to mean?"

I scoff bitterly. "You know exactly what it means."

"I'm sorry, how many guys did you fuck last week?" Hudson hits back. "Or last month, for that matter? Can you even remember?"

We argue all the way back to the dorms, trading brutal insults. In many ways, Hudson and I are far too alike. I lack his anger, but we both have a tendency to leave a trail of broken hearts behind us.

We fuck and chuck like there's no tomorrow. It's easier that way, and commitment is too risky. Getting attached never leads to anything good around here.

We reach the fourth floor of the building. and I'm in the lead, which gives me a clear view down the pristine corridor. My eyes are the first to fall on her. I have to blink to reassure myself that she's real, but I'm so shocked and relieved.

The guard gives her an aggressive shove and storms away without looking back. Brooklyn slumps against the door, her knees giving way.

"Holy shit," I breathe.

Taking off before the others can respond, I'm at her door in a flash, anticipation quickening my steps. It feels like forever has passed since I last saw her. Just seeing her again feels like a dream after the many nights spent imagining her platinum hair wrapped around my fingertips.

"Brooklyn," I holler.

Her head doesn't raise, and I pause, suddenly unsure.

"Brooke?"

She rests against the door, desperately failing to get inside. Her hand is shaking so violently that she can't scan the key card.

"I can't do it," Brooklyn whimpers.

Her hushed voice lethally stabs my heart. Leaning in, I tuck her hair aside and take a good look at the face hidden beneath. If she looked like a ghost before, she's nothing more than a corpse now.

Deathly pale and drawn, her eyes are swollen from crying. I can see the blue of her veins beneath her skin as she blinks hard, seeming to process exactly who I am.

"Hey, firecracker. It's me, Nix," I coax softly.

Tilting her head up, Brooklyn's silvery eyes finally meet mine. Faded and washed out, her pupils are blown impossibly wide. I can practically see the drugs swimming in her system. My thumb brushes over her sore bottom lip, so fucking gentle I surprise even myself.

"It's good to see your face," I whisper.

My words break the spell. She removes my fingers from her face, letting her expression harden. The display of vulnerability is stuffed down deep, and stubborn rage takes its place instead.

"Leave me alone," she grunts.

"What? No."

"All of you... just leave me alone."

We stare off as the other two finally catch up. Kade immediately comes to my side, slipping seamlessly into protector mode as he assesses and evaluates the situation with worried hazel eyes. He looks about as happy as I feel at the mess they've made of our girl. She can barely stand up, let alone open her door.

Hudson hangs way back, his face carved in thunderous lines. He's suddenly quiet now that she's here. I can practically taste the tension that explodes between them, but he's seemingly doing the right thing for once in his life by keeping his mouth shut.

"Brooklyn! We've been so worried," Kade rushes out.

I can see his hands clenching, itching to reach out and touch her. I know that feeling all too well. Brooklyn's head ducks down, ignoring our presence as she continues scrabbling with the door despite her hands still trembling violently.

Kade exchanges a look with me. "What's going on?"

I shrug, lost for words. All of that stress, two weeks of sleepless nights and guilt... and she doesn't even want to see us. What happened down there in the basement? She's changed. None of the spirit and fire is there, just this defeated shell trying to push us away.

"I don't want to see you guys," Brooklyn mutters.

"Give me the key card," I demand, trying to snag it from her shaking fingers. "Give it to me now!"

She tries to fight me off. "No! Fuck off, Nix."

"Give me the goddamn card, Brooke. This is ridiculous."

Stubborn as hell, she denies me again. Kade and I are suddenly shoved aside as Hudson's limited patience expires. He swiftly plucks the card from Brooklyn's grasp and unlocks the door, tucking it into the back pocket of his ripped, black jeans. Before she can finish getting an insult out, he scoops her small body up, crushing her to his broad chest.

"Put me down! Damn asshole," she yells.

"Shut up and do as you are fucking told," he bites back.

Storming into the bedroom, we follow hot on his heels. Kade seems slightly aghast at his brother's rough handling as he slams the door shut. Hudson deposits Brooklyn on her unmade bed, where she lands with a gasp. She continues to struggle against him as he tightly tucks her in.

"What part of don't ever touch me again do you not understand?"

Hudson shakes his head, clearly exasperated. "I never agreed to that bullshit, and you know it. Stop acting like a child."

"You're right, I shouldn't be surprised." Brooklyn's voice is dripping with acid. "Consent never meant much to you anyway."

Hudson flinches so hard, it looks like it hurts. He deliberately avoids looking at us. I can almost see the shame crawling over his suddenly blank face as he looks away from us all, hiding from judgement.

What the hell is she talking about?

What exactly did he do?

"Touch me again, and next time I'll aim for your heart," she promises darkly. "Final fucking warning, Hud."

"Give it a rest and go back to hating me tomorrow. Let us check if you're okay."

"Please," Kade adds emphatically.

Considering for a long, hate-filled second, Brooklyn eventually nods and sinks back into the pillows. "I'm fine. Just tired, okay?"

"No, not okay. We haven't seen you for two whole weeks. Going to need more than that," I grit out.

The need to shake her to make her understand what's happening here increases. We can't be pushed away like this.

"Just drop it."

Brooklyn's looking at me now, begging with her eyes. Nobody gets what they want with me; I take pleasure in rejection. But immediately, I want to relent just to make her happy. She looks like shit, but it's what lies beneath the surface that concerns me, something we'll have to carefully draw out of her.

"Maybe we should let her rest," I concede.

"No way," Hudson retorts.

She shoots him a fearsome glower that silences any further comments. Her cold stare makes me shiver. "You are the last person I want here. Learn when you're not wanted."

"I'm not walking away," Hudson insists.

Brooklyn glares at him. "Didn't stop you before."

"I never meant to hurt you, blackbird."

Tears begin to run down her face as she seems to grow even angrier. "You didn't, huh?" She shakes her head in disbelief, managing to sit up. "I don't want your excuses or apologies, Hud. I never did."

"I don't, fuck... I can't..." Hudson stumbles.

Jabbing a finger at her chest, Brooklyn's voice drips with contempt as she cuts him off. "You did this to me. You are the reason I'm here, why I'm screwed up beyond repair. Nothing, *absolutely fucking nothing,* will ever fix that. Walk away and never return."

She lays back down, dismissing us all. Hudson stares for a split second before turning and storming away, kicking the desk chair so hard on his way out that a dramatic crack splits the back. His departure leaves us both gaping and completely flummoxed.

"You guys too. I mean it, fuck off already," Brooklyn shouts.

I glance at Kade, who gestures towards the exit, apparently willing to give in. I'm tempted to stay behind and argue some more, but frankly, she's in no fit state. There's only so much I can do for someone so unwilling.

"You sure?" Kade asks gently.

Her hard, clipped response follows. "Are you still fucking here?"

His shoulders slump in defeat as he walks away. I make sure the bedsheets are pulled up tight to Brooklyn's chin and gently brush her tangled, platinum hair. I'm aching to do more, regardless of her feelings.

"You know where we are if you need us," I offer.

"I won't. Just leave and don't come back, alright?"

We reluctantly do as we're told, and it takes every ounce of respect for her privacy that I have. Whatever shadowy treatment the shrinks conduct in that basement, it's crippled her for good.

CHAPTER 17
BROOKLYN

TWISTED - MISSIO

FORCING my numb legs to move, I take the stairs two at a time. It's painful, but I push myself regardless, warming my body up in preparation for a gruelling run. I'll do anything to get the static out of my mind that refuses to lift, no matter how loud I scream into my pillow at night.

Nothing's been the same since I returned a few days ago.

Admittedly, I haven't really left my room in that time, only to visit the nurse's station for meds. They threatened to take me straight back to solitary if not. Lazlo has me on a strict new regime.

I now get a shot every week, along with my daily pills like before. There's no cheating. It's injected straight in, and rather than trusting me, I'm now watched like a fucking prisoner as I swallow each day. My mouth is inspected afterwards, ensuring there's no trickery and I'm actually swallowing them.

What a fucking joke.

As a result, all of the plans I laid are tattered and destroyed. I've been here for over a month, yet somehow, I'm still at square one. This was not how things were supposed to go when I agreed to the transfer from Clearview.

I can't recall a single thing that happened in the basement. It's all just a big, ugly blur in my mind, punctuated by awful memories of a time that I really don't want to remember. The endless days of solitude have brought all my demons back up to the surface, and now they refuse to be suppressed again.

I'm expected back in class today. Considering how far behind I am at this point, it barely seems worth it. I was supposed to be dead by now. If I hadn't attacked Hudson, I'd be free. Finally, after all this time, I was so close to getting what I wanted. I don't know who I'm angrier with: myself or him.

I take off into the early morning mist. Readjusting to taking meds again and the trauma of solitary have wrecked me, physically and emotionally. How I'll get through classes, I have no idea. I need a new plan to get the hell out of here. November is fast approaching.

During my time in the hole, an official search took place of all the dormitories. There's a huge contraband issue here, and everyone knows it. They tore apart the bedrooms in an attempt to hunt down the culprits.

I quickly found out that not only did they find and confiscate my stash of pills, but my blades as well, along with anything else that was deemed risky.

Looping around the perimeter twice, counting the guards and CCTV cameras as I go, I'm still not ready to head back. What used to work for me is no longer helpful. I can't seem to relieve the suffocating darkness in my mind.

Opting for a different route, I head behind the slightly smaller Pinehill dorms and cut through the rear gardens. Pristine greenery gradually melts away the further I run, growing unkempt and forgotten. Towering birch trees soon envelop me into the thick underbrush.

When I come to a towering security fence that marks the edge of the property, I search the perimeter in frustration, ready to admit defeat. I don't expect to find a tiny, passable hole hidden in the corner.

Squeezing myself through the barbed wire, I hold my breath and make it to the other side, breaking into a sprint just in case anyone is watching. The further I run, the more removed I feel. It's like I've entered into a different world, far from the nightmares of Blackwood.

Out here in the unknown, I can almost forget the trap I'm stuck in and the harrowing reality that I actually have to *live*. I've got four more weeks to make it out. Four weeks before the anniversary.

I jog into a clearing, finding an abandoned graveyard tucked into the Welsh wilderness. Black, wrought-iron gates encircle the space that's filled with crumbling gravestones and statues. There's a mausoleum at the back, which looks imposing in all its gothic beauty. Willow trees sway in the light breeze, and golden leaves coat the pathway leading me inside.

I trail my fingers over the faded names, overcome with pointless spite and jealousy. Why are they dead and not me? Why can't I be buried in this ground, cold and empty? It's only fair that we get to choose if we live or not. If someone wants to die, that's their decision. Not everyone wants to be saved.

Sinking to the frosty ground, I rest against one of the gravestones, savouring the peace and quiet that sinks beneath my skin. Except it isn't silent. Somewhere, there's a noise. It's tinny, almost like a muffled speaker.

I peer around, and my eyes land on a crouched form by the mausoleum doors, dressed in a familiar black hoodie and distressed jeans. Eli's headphones blare heavy rock music as he rustles in his backpack. His curly hair is messy and escaping from the scruffy cap he wears.

Pulling a tobacco tin out and searching inside, I'm unable to look away as he locates a small, razor-sharp penknife. He takes the time to methodically clean and disinfect it with a kind of ritualistic attention to detail. Then he slowly rolls up his sleeve, face pinched in concentration as he studies his arm.

I can't tear my eyes away.

My mouth waters as he presses the blade to his skin and draws it across, eliciting an immediate release. His shoulders slump and his face relaxes as the blood flows.

As I watch with fascination, he moves an inch down and repeats the process. It's like I'm watching an artist; the blade is his paintbrush and his arm is the canvas for him to create a beautiful, bloody scene of morbid proportions.

I'm so enraptured by the sight that my grip on the gravestone slips, causing a chunk to crash to the ground. His head shoots up, and our eyes immediately connect.

Fear and panic quickly melt into something else that I can't describe. He's looking straight at me with his lips quirked in a secret smile. It's like I'm some kind of voyeur to his most intimate moment, and he's getting off on the thrill of having an audience.

Screw it. He's clearly happy to see me.

I join him on the moss-covered steps, but neither of us speak. There's no awkward reunion or insistent questioning like with the others. Our attention is focused on the knife clutched tightly in his hand. Blood streams from his wrist to his elbow in crimson rivulets, and my fingers ache with the need to snatch it away.

But not to stop him.

Fuck no, I want it for myself.

I want to feel something, to elicit that sweet, euphoric release for just a second. Like a recovering alcoholic, I'm staring at him with raw need while eyeing the prize and wondering how to get some of it for my own pleasure.

As sick as it is, I'm not interested in stopping him from hurting himself. I understand the need to gamble with that delicate line, somewhere between life and death. Too deep, and that's it. Not deep enough, and you're left wanting more.

It's a vicious, addictive cycle.

I fucking love it.

Shining emerald orbs stare at me curiously as I run my finger over his palm, daring to move higher. Circling his wrist and the blue veins there, I follow the trail up to his weeping lacerations.

Spreading the trickles of blood beneath my touch, I'm creating a trail of crimson brushstrokes. Now we're both artists, imprisoned by this sick fascination together.

"I'm sorry," I murmur, trying to pull away.

His hand stops me, holding me in place as he shakes his head. That dark smile is lopsided and knowing. Fuck, he wants this as much as I do. How twisted is that?

But it doesn't matter. It doesn't stop me. This feeling between us, the tendrils of darkness and pure fucking sickness drawing us closer, it's irrevocable. Uncontrollable. Nothing exists outside of this moment.

Eli offers the knife to me, and my heart pounds faster than ever. I can't rip my gaze away from the glinting steel as he cleans and disinfects it. Before I know it, my fingers wrap around the handle. My hand is still shaking and pathetic, but he doesn't judge.

Not my Eli.

Rolling the sleeve of my sweater up, countless silvery scars and gnarled lumps of skin are revealed. His gaze burns like fire, and I actually enjoy it. Filled with this odd sense of pride, I want him to see my artwork and appreciate it for himself, one cutter to another.

It's like a rite of passage, this intimate sharing of our battle scars, inflicted by the ultimate enemy—ourselves. Everything about this is wrong. Unhealthy. Toxic. Messed up.

But at the same time, *oh so right.*

The serrated edge meets my sensitive flesh. A sigh escapes my lips at the familiar feeling, seconds before taking that tempting step. Then I'm moving the knife, trying to draw blood, but my quivering hand is preventing me from getting a good grip to press deep enough.

I huff, cursing the fucking medication I'm dosed to high heaven on. After a few more failed attempts, the frustrated tears are threatening to fall.

"Fucking hand," I growl.

Eli swallows hard, biting his lower lip. He gently eases the knife from my spasming hand. Giving me a long, hard look, he silently asks the question I know he can't say out loud.

My consent.

This complicated, broken man wants to help me in the only way he knows how. He even has the sweetness to ask before doing it. I'm nodding without thinking, trusting him intuitively with every fibre of my being. He lifts his eyebrows, seeking confirmation.

Rather than answer, I seal my lips on his. Just a whispered moment of affection, giving him a glimpse beneath the surface at the damaged girl tucked away behind layers of sarcasm and anger, who wants him to cut her when *she can't fucking do it herself.*

"Please," I whimper. "Make it better, Eli. Please."

As he draws it across my wrist, I wonder if he feels it—this unexplainable bond between us, like kindred souls reunited at last. We're two lone wolves circling one another, both intrigued and a little afraid. I wonder what that feeling tastes like to him.

My eyes sink shut as the release comes, hot and sharp with a bite of pain. I can't hold back the moan of satisfaction as he repeats this action four times. Methodically, precisely. Taking his time and care in doing so.

Once he's done, another sensation takes over. *Holy fuck.* It's his tongue, gliding across the skin of my wrist as he kisses his handiwork. He laps at the blood, his fingers digging painfully into my arm.

Send me to Hell, I don't care. I'm fucking wetter than I've ever been. My thighs clench with the flood of pure arousal.

"Eli," I whisper like a prayer.

Burying my fingers in his unruly curls, I yank hard until his bloodied lips are there for me to claim. Teeth clash with the violence of our kiss, and he's just as enthralled as I am. Grasping my face and exploring every inch of my mouth, his coppery tongue marks his territory.

Desire burns through me as I scramble into Eli's lap, wrapping my legs around his trim waist. Drawing our bodies together, I need to feel him everywhere. Now that I've had a taste, I can't get enough. I'm plummeting fast, and he's there to catch me before I drown.

Our hips grind together as his hand slips beneath my sweater, gliding over my stomach and ribs. His fingers undoubtedly feel the ridges and raised skin there too. He makes short work of getting inside my bra, teasing my stiff nipples. I rub myself against him even harder, the press of his rock-hard cock driving me wild.

"More," I gasp.

Eli looks at me, his eyes sparkling with mischief as he bites his lip. It's the most alive I've ever seen him, the most alert and present in reality. He's always hiding from the world, zoned out for his own self-preservation. But right now, Eli's here with me.

Swiftly undoing his jeans, I reach for the hard length trapped inside. His cock is ready for me, hot and pulsing. Eli yanks my shirt up, and I shift so he can remove the rest of my clothes.

Then his fingers glide over my skin, circling my thighs until he slips inside my dripping folds. Teasing the bundle of nerves there, I shudder a breath. He casts me another cheeky smile before he plunges inside my pussy with two digits, spreading me wide.

"Fuck yes," I moan.

Eli pauses, calculating for a devilish second before retreating and rubbing his fingers into my bleeding arm. Sizzling pain bites into my skin.

With the gathered blood, he returns to my pussy and slips his fingers back inside. Hot, sticky blood moistens my folds as I scream out. So fucking wrong, yet so right at the same time.

He quickens the pace, fucking me roughly with his fingers as I begin to work his velvet shaft. I can hear his rasping breath, and I'm enjoying the pleasure I know I'm giving him.

As the feeling builds and I'm wound tighter, I realise after years of suffering through shitty hook-ups that this is what I like. Depraved. Bloody. Twisted. But ultimately, fucking *incredible.*

Eli's lips work across my jawline and all the way down the slope of my neck, sucking and bruising along the way. I love it. He's owning me and I cannot get enough. Lowering myself on his lap fully, I spread my legs.

I'm straddling him perfectly as the tip of his dick presses against my red-stained opening. Eli hesitates, his hand wrapping around my neck to gain my attention.

Squeezing my throat until I'm gasping for air, the question in his eyes is clear. Even after all of this, he still wants my consent. That's a real fucking gentleman. The same gentleman that just sliced my skin and *liked it.*

"Please," I beg sheepishly.

He wastes no time, slamming his cock home deep enough for me to cry out. I'm so full, every nerve ending is on fire as his forehead meets mine. When I find my balance and begin to move, the euphoria only increases.

I ride him hard with my arms wrapped around his neck for support. He's still gripping my throat, squeezing tight enough to excite me further as breathing becomes even more difficult.

I'm chasing the high, insatiable and desperate for more of this feeling. Our bodies smash together as we both moan and gasp. Once I've screamed out my first release, Eli moves, assuming dominance and removing me from his lap.

I'm lowered onto the cold ground of the mausoleum steps. Hands grip my thighs as he hangs over me, and his tousled hair slips over his face, disturbing my view. I swipe it away.

The way he looks at me? It's fucking addictive. Like I'm the very oxygen he breathes.

Slipping back inside of me, Eli buries his face in my neck as I writhe and cry out. He fucks me hard and fast like his life depends on it. The open air only makes it hotter, kissing my bare skin.

There's something forbidden about screwing among the dead buried in this graveyard with blood leaking from both of our arms, evidencing our shared fascination for the art of self-destruction.

Twin flames destined for oblivion.

Neither of us can hold on for long. He's buried so deep inside of me, I feel like I'm going to explode. Climaxing again, I ride the waves of my release as Eli manages a few final pumps before finishing and slumping against my chest.

His hair tickles my cheek as he catches his breath, looking up at me with those damned knowing eyes. It's like he can hear my thoughts, despite the silence between us.

"Eli," I begin.

A loud voice interrupts, our heads snapping up in shock. I grab my clothes and Eli does the same, scrambling to cover himself as the voice nears.

Grabbing his hand, we jump down the steps and sneak around the side of the mausoleum just in time. A pair of sour-faced guards burst into the graveyard and urgently search around, reporting back into their radios.

"Nothing here. You sure she went this way?"

The radio crackles. "Yes, lieutenant. Use your eyes."

"It's empty. Check your computer again."

There's a crackling through the radio speaker, then some kind of scuffle before a new voice chimes in. "This is Augustus. Bring the asset back in range or pack your bags."

The two guards quickly resume searching, ducking behind gravestones and checking in the trees. Eli clings to my hand as one of them comes dangerously close, their heavy black boots stomping up the steps to the mausoleum. Both of us stop breathing.

There's a loud groan as the guard works the door open, yanking the ancient stone aside to peek into the darkness. We take the opportunity to move fast, fleeing around the back of the graveyard and sprinting all the way back to the security fence.

Eli doesn't release my hand until we're back in Oakridge.

Sweaty, bloodied, and satisfied.

CHAPTER 18
KADE

HURRICANE - HALSEY

CLOCKED in for my usual Monday shift, I'm tapping away on my laptop with anticipation. I check to make sure the warden is in her office before I pull up Brooklyn's institute records.

Moral considerations aside, I could easily lose my privileges here for doing this, but I honestly do not care. I need to know what happened in that basement. Brooklyn has become a ghost. Nobody has seen her all weekend, and I'm losing my mind.

I checked out Phoenix's and Eli's records after our very first interactions, knowing I had to do something to help them. Not everyone that comes here is a criminal, nor are they all court sanctioned to engage in treatment. Some are just plain crazy and of particular interest to the shrinks.

Technically, Phoenix was threatened with prison time for dealing drugs. From what I've heard, he was the ringleader for a notorious gang back in London.

If he didn't attend here and clean up his act, he would've ended up behind bars. Having a Bipolar diagnosis spared him that unpleasantness, along with the fact that he was an unstable mess at the time of his arrest.

Eli's the most innocent out of us all. It's not what he did, but what others did to him that led him to Blackwood. He has bounced around different facilities for over a decade, growing up institutionalised and medicated. His most recent transfer was from Clearview, the same place that Brooklyn ended up before here.

"Kade? You got that list for the Christmas market trip?"

Mike comes to a halt at my desk, leaning on his elbow. The deputy warden is a bit overbearing, but he's decent enough. A damn sight more approachable than the warden herself, Elizabeth White.

She oversees day-to-day business and spends most of her time in board meetings, but she's the real authority around here. The shrinks are just her lap dogs.

"Sure, I'll get it for you now. The one in early December?"

"Yep. We need to start making arrangements. Elizabeth is on my case again about rewarding those with good behaviour." He rolls his eyes dramatically. "You coming? I put your name down, and I could use the help."

Shrugging, I bring up the lengthy file and glance over the details. It's a small list of approvals. Very few have spotless records and no disciplinaries. Phoenix's name is on there, much to my relief. He's kept his nose clean ever since getting off the drugs.

"Why not?" I decide. "My online exams should all be done by then anyway."

Mike beams at me. "Gets you out of this place at least."

I sneak a glance out of the corner of my eye as Mike fiddles with his phone. His head is partially turned, so I have a chance to glance over the other names listed. It's an alright group, no one too difficult or dangerous. Naturally, Hudson and Eli are nowhere to be seen.

"You get the names from the shrinks?" I ask casually.

"Yeah, we had to get security clearance. Liz approved them already, but she barely looked at it," he complains with a frown. "The bloody woman is more interested in her emails than actually doing something meaningful around here."

I hum a response, pretending that I'm getting it ready to print. A tempting thought forms in my mind when I hear that it's already gone through the warden. Heart hammering, I type another name at the bottom, changing the automatic status from red to green to indicate that she's low risk.

What could possibly go wrong?

Brooklyn will be with us both, away from the suffocating surveillance at Blackwood. I'm fucking ecstatic just thinking about it, hungry for any opportunity to get her alone, even if she won't talk to us right now. We're not all like Hudson. I have to earn a second chance from her.

"Here you go." I give him a polite smile.

"Thanks, Kade. You're a good lad."

Mike collects the paperwork and wanders off back to his office, leaving me to return to my sleuthing. It was easy enough to get into Brooklyn's records—perks of the job and all.

Not being a genuine patient has its benefits, even if I did sign away my freedom for the privilege. Nobody can understand why I volunteer to help out, but there's a reason for it. I like to know what I'm getting myself into.

Control is power in this world.

My asshole father taught me that much.

Brooklyn's photo on record is a scary sight. Limp, unwashed hair and hollow cheeks frame her dead eyes. She looks even worse than when she came back from solitary.

It's backdated by ten months, from her first admission to Clearview. I scroll down, trying to glean as much information as possible while stifling my guilt for invading her privacy.

Brooklyn West, 21, Female.

Presented in an acute phase of psychosis. Pre-existing diagnosis of schizophrenia. Assessment needed immediately, case assigned to R Zimmerman for triage.

I read on further, curiosity burning inside of me as I scan through the brief notes from the psychiatric team that assessed her before she even got to Clearview.

Upon arrest at St Pancras Train Station, the patient was detained by police after a 48-hour chase. She has been put in custody to await psych evaluation. Presents with delusional thoughts, visual and auditory hallucinations, violent tendencies and an unstable personality.

See attached incident report for more details.

The cursor hovers over the attached file, but when I click it, a box appears to request a security code. Looks like it's locked for confidentiality and only the warden can give permission to access it.

I quickly close the screen and take an unsteady breath, glancing at her door. This is why I should mind my own business. Using my carefully cultivated computer skills, I quickly erase my presence from the system and catch all the hidden records.

This isn't my first rodeo, and whatever is in that file, it's nothing good. While I scramble to cover my tracks, a question blazes in my mind. What exactly did she do?

Despite that, the chances of it affecting this odd possessiveness I feel about her is low. I can't explain the way I get attached to people. It's like my heart claims them long before my brain has a chance to catch up. No matter who they are or what they've done, once I'm invested, there's no turning back.

A sharp bang on the desk bell has me jumping in my seat. Panicked, my heart leaps into my mouth. I glance up to find Hudson grinning at me in amusement, his black hair mussed up and sweaty from exercise. He must've been in the gym again.

"Hey, bro. Got some post for me?"

"Was that really necessary?" I demand.

"Yep, it was. Fucking scaredy cat. What've you got to hide?"

I shrug, relieved that I've already cleared my laptop. Reaching inside my satchel that's tucked beneath the desk, I pull the expensive, cream-coloured envelope out and slide it over.

"I was going to bring it to you after work."

"Don't bother," Hudson mutters.

I watch him rip into the letter, his blue eyes scanning over my mother's elegant writing. She uses personalised stationery emblazoned with my father's political campaign branding.

Our parents are rather image obsessed, but fuck if Mum doesn't love Hudson like he's her own child. No matter how insistent he is on pushing us all away.

"Any good?" I ask hopefully.

"Same shit. Misses me and wants to visit."

I force myself to keep a reasonable tone, biting back my frustration. "She's been asking for the last eighteen months. You could give the poor woman a break, Hud. One visit won't kill you. She's earned that at least."

He balls up the letter and tosses it towards the bin, landing a perfect shot. "I told her to forget about me. If I let her see me now, she'll never let me go."

I gape at him in disbelief, astounded by the sheer lack of human emotion. "She's your mother, for Christ's sake."

"No. She's yours," Hudson argues, his expression turning bleak. "I'm just the trash that got brought in and put her to shame."

His hands ball into fists as he stares at me. He's completely clueless to the trail of broken bodies he leaves in his wake. She couldn't care less about what he did, and Mum still loves him like any good parent would, adoptive or not. He's too blinded by the past to see that, trapped in his own head.

"She isn't ashamed of you. Not one bit," I bite out. "She cares, something you should learn to accept. Keep going and one day, nobody will anymore."

Before I know it, Hudson grabs hold of my spotless blue shirt and hauls me up. His angry face is right in front of mine, and his furious aquamarine eyes glare at me.

"I didn't ask for you to follow me here, brother," he hisses at me. "Nor do I want it. I did the crime, now I'm doing the time."

"Hud—"

"No. Don't talk to me about acceptance while you're here, wasting your goddamn life away when you could be out there actually living. It's enough that I've ruined my life, but you've got to add yours to my conscience too?"

I give Hudson a hard shove, causing him to stumble back and release me. I refuse to give him the satisfaction of intimidating me.

"I'm only trying to help you. There's no ulterior motive. You know what my first thought was when I heard what you did?"

Hudson looks away, his jaw clenched as he shrugs.

"I didn't worry about the other guy. I was worried about you. What this meant for your life, your future. And more importantly? What the hell I was going to do without my little brother, someone who came into my life when I was already an adult, but still managed to become family."

"Just leave it, Kade."

I take a deep breath, trying to manage my temper. "No. You'd do well to remember your family when you're going around beating on people, or fucking and boozing yourself into oblivion. There are people that care about you, even if you don't."

He reluctantly listens as I rant, beyond done with his bullshit. When I'm finished, he simply turns on his heel and stalks away. It's as if I don't even exist and my words mean nothing.

I gave up the best years of my life to be here. To support him and ensure that he isn't alone in this world. And what do I get for my loyalty? Nothing. Fucking nothing.

Glancing back down at my laptop screen, I bring up the ID photo that I took for Brooklyn. She actually smiled as I tucked the hair behind her ear, if only for a brief second.

Her wide eyes flickered with something other than pain before shutting down again, but I saw it. Something's there, buried beneath the surface. I'll find it again, no matter what it takes.

Hudson doesn't want my help? *Fine.* Let's see how he likes it when I steal his girl. Then he'll know how it feels to be disregarded.

CHAPTER 19
BROOKLYN

HIGHER - SLEEP TOKEN

I WALK into the classroom and avoid the dozens of eyes that immediately lock on to me. For the past handful of days, everyone has been all up in my business. As I've gradually returned to class, it seems I'm now somewhat of a celebrity. Everyone looks at me with fear and fascination.

I barely survived my first day of English class, sitting alone at the back as others whispered and gossiped around me. Yesterday, I stomped around in a cloud of rage, refusing to speak to anyone to avoid exploding spectacularly. Even the guys seem determined to get inside of my head.

They'll give up eventually and leave me alone. I can't afford distractions, not now that Lazlo has me on tight lockdown. Getting the hell out of here before next month is all I can think about.

I've listed all the potential methods in my journal, its ink-stained pages filled with hatred and regret. My options are limited at best.

When I ran back to the security fence to investigate further, hoping that would provide some opportunity, I found it had been repaired and electrified. Nobody is getting out for a casual stroll now.

Entering the packed classroom, I walk past tables filled with interested onlookers. Some patients seem awake and coherent while others are clearly heavily medicated as they drool on themselves. This place is fucking depressing.

Someone coughs. "Crazy bitch."

I have to stifle the urge to smile. *You got that right.* If anyone deserves to be stabbed with a blunt dinner knife, it's Hudson. My only regret is that I didn't have anything sharper on hand to remove his organs with.

I pass the assholes with my head held high. Phoenix and Eli are sitting in our usual place, waiting for me. I can't tear my eyes away from Eli's messy ringlets and blushing cheeks as he avoids looking at me. Does the memory of fucking me keep him awake at night as well? The way he looked at me as the knife dragged across my skin was pure fucking magic.

Schooling my blank expression back into place, I take my seat at the end of the table. Eli is wearing his usual worn hoodie and a pair of ripped jeans that show off the honed muscles in his legs.

Next to him, Phoenix's dramatic blue hair contrasts his black t-shirt and grey flannel, while bringing out the deep, chocolate depths of his irises. They both look delicious.

"Hi, guys."

Phoenix does a double take. "Well, look who decided to join us."

I can feel his attention acutely as I slip the gifted beanie off my head, revealing my still slightly damp hair. There's a smile tugging at his full lips, and it's driving me insane.

"You're looking better," he compliments, shamelessly checking me out. "Finally decided to walk among us living folks again?"

"Whatever."

This winds him up further, just as I intended.

"When are you going to actually talk to us? Come on, Brooke. I'm so over this stupid silent-treatment thing you've got going on. Whatever happened between you and Hudson, it's got nothing to do with me."

I can't help but melt a little at the sight of Phoenix's plump bottom lip jutted out for dramatic effect. Damn, I'd like to bite that lip, knowing exactly how it feels against mine.

"Look, I couldn't care less. He's your friend and that's enough reason for me to stay away," I explain simply. "As soon as I can request a seat change, I'm getting away from all of you. I don't need any more hassle in my life than I already have."

I relish the flash of pain in Phoenix's eyes. It feels good to be in control here. No matter what happens, I'm the one calling the shots. Letting others get close is an impossibility.

"You're being a stubborn bitch," Phoenix whines.

"Get over it and leave me alone."

We lapse into silence as the teacher walks in, immediately clapping his hands for everyone's attention. Crawley is tall, spindly and beyond creepy, but he's decent enough. After two weeks' absence, I'm clearly on his shit list.

As the others get on with their assignments, he dumps a load of work on my desk and demands that I catch up before the exams next week. Next fucking week. I don't bother trying to argue back, nodding and glaring daggers at his back instead as he turns to leave.

"Need a hand?" Phoenix offers.

I'm shaking my head before he even finishes.

"Nope, I'm good."

With a frustrated growl, his hand swipes through his spiky hair. "You know what? Screw you. Do what you fucking want. It's your choice."

"Damn right, it is."

Phoenix's caustic glare burns into the side of my head, but I don't bother to look as he lashes out. "Keep this up, and you'll end up alone for the next three years. That's all I'm saying."

"What makes you think that bothers me?"

"You really are a piece of work, aren't you?" He leans closer, deliberately trying to make me feel uncomfortable. "No wonder you have no fucking friends. Born alone, die alone, right? Good luck with that, crazy bitch."

He seems to think that I have a heart to hurt.

He's in for a fucking surprise.

I lick my lips and produce an amused smile. "I'd rather be alone than be friends with the likes of you lot. Do you have any clue who Hudson really is? What he's done? Check yourself before coming at me, dickhead. The grass ain't always greener."

"Hudson is a good guy... most of the time," Phoenix defends.

I laugh and snatch up some random papers, giving my hands a task rather than punching his pretty fucking face until he bleeds.

"Right. And you accuse me of being full of bullshit."

Apparently, this hits a little too close to home, as Phoenix turns his head and dismisses me by sticking headphones in. I grind my teeth, mentally chanting to myself that I'll be gone soon, no matter what it takes.

I've got to get away from these guys and their petty little feelings. The sight of Hudson at my bedroom door reminded me of the price you pay for letting people get close. No one's allowed inside my dead heart.

I won't survive it.

They won't survive it.

I get through the rest of the class by ignoring everyone, doodling little nooses on the corners of my textbook. The list of materials I should be reading to catch up is lengthy, but I toss it in my bag without a second look.

I don't give a damn about this class, the exam or the assholes in charge of this circus. They can kiss my ass before I write a fucking essay.

"What are you..." Phoenix trails off, his eyes on my book.

I quickly flip the pages and block the doodles from sight. He's really pushing his luck. Just as I'm about to get my shit and storm out to escape him, a loud alarm begins to ring. It screams through the air, and everyone starts moving to grab their bags.

Phoenix curses and begins jamming loose sheets of paper away, but my attention is focused on Eli. He's suddenly hunched over, his forehead pressed to the desk and hands clamped over his ears. I can see his body shaking from here, beneath his thick hoodie.

"Come on, it's a fire drill," Phoenix orders.

I ignore him completely, briefly debating with myself before walking to Eli's side. I can help him out without caring, right? Running my hand down his spine, he stiffens instantly, his face peeking to the side. Terror dances in his eyes as he stares, silently begging for help. Just like I did in that graveyard, where he obliged without question.

I offer him a tentative hand. "Let's get you out of here."

Eli pauses for a moment, utterly detached and controlled by his fear. I don't look away, waiting for him to gather some semblance of strength. When his trembling fingers link with mine, I offer him a small smile.

"Trust me," I say simply.

I wait an eternity for his eventual nod.

Together, we head out of the classroom and down the polished staircase, taking the steps two at a time. Out here, the alarm rings even louder. Eli clutches my hand painfully tight.

When the first hint of smoke whispers through the air, we move faster, practically running to escape. The air's getting thick, the acrid scent of burning growing stronger.

"Just a drill, huh?" I hiss at Phoenix.

"How was I supposed to know that it's real?"

Suddenly, Eli's hand is ripped from mine. I stumble, crashing into Phoenix's back. He steadies me before I topple down the stairs and we both turn to look back up the staircase.

Eli's crouched down, his head lowered and hidden from sight, and his arms are wrapped around his body as the trembling intensifies.

"Oh man…" Phoenix sighs.

"What is it?"

"He doesn't do fire. Fuck, okay."

Lowering to his level, Phoenix slides a finger under Eli's chin, tilting his head just enough so that their eyes can meet. Their lips are inches apart, while their faces are intimately close. If I didn't know better, I'd say they were lovers.

"I've got you, E. I'm not leaving you," he promises.

Eli stares without breathing, the ingrained mistrust clear.

"You're not alone, buddy," Phoenix adds. "Come on."

I stand transfixed, watching the exchange with bated breath. My eyes are beginning to water from the smoke, getting stronger and more noxious by the second. Eli watches Phoenix with empty eyes, his lips pressed together as he battles his demons.

It's almost like he doesn't believe a word his friend is saying, even though we'd never leave him. No person would when there's a fire raging nearby.

Phoenix repeats the same assurances, a little more forcefully. He's practically chanting it, begging Eli to trust him. It's heartbreaking to watch the terror that's holding Eli hostage, like he's trapped in his own mind and can't move a muscle, let alone speak.

An idea comes to me, and I ease down next to Phoenix, moving him out of the way. Eli can't listen when he's under the influence of his anxiety. That cruel motherfucker doesn't listen to rhyme or reason. I've got to break through, and I know just how he likes to do that.

"Eli? It's Brooke. We need to move, work with me here."

Snaking my fingers up the sleeve of his hoodie, I hold his eyes as I search for the ridges that I know I'll find. Four horizontal cuts, right where I watched him slice himself open a few days ago.

They're still raw and barely healed, so it's easy enough to dig my nails in to rip the fresh scabs away. I scratch at Eli's cuts until I can feel the blood flowing once more, warm against my fingertips. His eyes widen at the pain, teeth surrendering his abused lip.

That's it. Come back to me, little Eli.

I know just what you need.

A few seconds pass as he slowly comes crashing back down to earth. He latches on to the comfort of pain just like I knew he would. We're the same fucking person. When he gives a slight jerk of his head, I step back and allow Phoenix to haul him up, resuming our descent towards the smoke-filled foyer.

I can't help but stare at my red-stained fingertips as I follow the guys. I'm utterly fascinated by the sight of Eli's blood on my skin. Now we're even, both claimed in crimson by the other. I don't know what that means for us, but it leaves me feeling giddy.

We make it to the entrance of the building where patients are pouring outside to escape the thick, oppressive air. I cover my mouth with my sleeve before a coughing fit can take over, ducking lower to the ground and following the crowd.

Smoke pours from one of the classrooms, and I can make out the glow of flames attacking rows of textbooks and papers. Eli and Phoenix are lost in the crowd as my feet freeze. I'm rooted to the spot by the sight of the deadly fire. My mind is quickly consumed by an evil, penetrating voice.

Walk in. Give it all up and offer yourself to the flames.

This is your best chance. Do it. Give up.

It would be so easy. I'm standing in the middle of chaos, so there are no guards or teachers to stop me. CCTV cameras are obscured by smoke. There's a glimpse of freedom right there for the taking. I place one foot in front of another.

Each step takes me dangerously close to the blazing heat that I feel against my face. My hands curl into fists, nails biting deep into my palms. The voice intensifies, drowning out all other noise. I can practically taste it on my tongue, the sliver of hope in the form of inevitable death.

No more breathing.

No more suffering.

No more living.

For the first time since that fateful night nearly a year ago, when I completed my spiralling descent into Hell, I could be free again. Just as I'm about to reach out and grasp the door handle, tattooed, muscular arms wrap around my waist.

Fuck! No.

Not him.

Big, scarred hands hold me tight. I'm dragged backwards, further and further away from my salvation. I scream bloody murder, pleading for my captor to release me, but it's no use.

I know those hands.

I remember the fights that scarred those knuckles.

"What the hell are you doing? The room's on fucking fire."

Hudson's words send me falling back down the rabbit hole, into the sordid past. I can see the memories of him ripping the duvet off me in the foster home, or snatching pills from my hands, yelling and screaming vicious words.

One time, he burst into the bathroom at school, careless of the other girls that squealed at his entrance. He nearly smashed down the stall door just to get to me, snatching the scissors away from my bleeding wrist.

"Let me go!" I scream.

He's always touching me when he isn't wanted. Sticking his arrogant nose into my business, like he has any right to involve himself after what he did five years ago.

"It's a fire! You dumb bitch. We're leaving."

Hudson drags me all the way outside. We stumble into the fresh, midday air and collapse on the ground in a fit of coughing. Other patients huddle all around, gasping for air.

Hudson releases me, and I immediately move away like he burned me, not the fire. I'm shaking like a leaf, adrenaline and anger compounded into a toxic chemical in my blood.

"How dare you touch me," I yell accusingly.

Bright, chilling blue eyes stare back at me with the same barely restrained rage that poisoned our every moment together.

"You were seconds away from walking into that fucking classroom," Hudson shouts back. "Don't bother denying it. You always were unhinged. I just saved your damn life."

"What makes you think that I want to be saved?"

He looks at me like I'm mad, full of judgement and something resembling... pity? Oh, hell no. Hatred sits heavily in my gut as I stand and slap him firmly across the face for a second time.

"If you don't leave me alone, I'll report you and have you thrown into solitary," I threaten. "How would you like that? I can assure you, it ain't fun down there."

Hudson rubs his stubbly cheek, frowning in confusion. "You're kidding me, right? Are you that stubborn? Give it up, blackbird. I'm done fighting you."

"I'm not stupid, you brain-dead dickwipe. You seem to have forgotten why we're no longer together." I glare daggers at him, wishing I had a knife to slip into his gut again. "You can't just come strolling in after all these years and start acting like you give a shit. Not happening. It's too fucking late for that."

I turn my back before he can answer, pushing past gasping patients and frantic guards shouting their instructions. Phoenix tries to grab me as I pass him, but I quickly storm off, unable to bear any of them for a second longer. I feel Hudson's eyes on me all the way across the quad.

Of course, though, he doesn't have the guts to follow me. If only he cared this much before, we wouldn't be in this position.

CHAPTER 20
PHOENIX

TOXIC LOVERS - MASS OF MAN & MASETTI

I WRAP the duct tape tight around Scott's wrists, leaving him no room to wiggle as I attach them to my bed frame. Giving my handiwork a tug to check, he doesn't budge. He's firmly restrained and unable to move an inch without my permission.

Staring into his light-brown eyes, his lashes frame innocence and anticipation. Scott's far too meek and breakable to handle this, but I don't care. I'm not one for exercising my conscience often.

"N-Nix? It's a bit tight," he whines, biting his bottom lip.

I stare blankly at him. "Do I look like I care?"

I bet Brooklyn wouldn't complain if she were the one tied to my bed. Hell, I'd bet my life that she'd love it. But the narrow-minded, stubborn bitch herself is still avoiding us, and I'm fucking done with being ignored.

Scott sighs, batting his thick lashes at me. "I came to have some fun, but you're being a dick. Lighten up, will you?"

Pulling my hand back, I slap him firmly across the face. I relish the tears that spring in his eyes and the glorious red mark that appears.

"Shut the hell up, man. You came because you're bored. We're under curfew because of the fire. Behave or I won't lay a fucking finger on you or your cock tonight. Got that?"

He nods obediently. The little freak loves being roughed up, and I'm more than happy to do all the punishing. I hurt him because he reacts, and it's oh so sweet. At least I can get that out of someone, even if it isn't the person I truly want to surrender to me.

"Don't say another word," I warn.

Scott keeps smiling and nods, drawing in a sharp breath. I pull my dick free and palm it in my hand, watching his eyes travel down. He licks his lips as I rub myself, enjoying the feel of his eyes on my skin, but he's powerless to move. I've got him all trussed up with nowhere to go. That's the good thing about a metal bedframe.

"Please, Nix... Please..."

"What did I say? Keep your goddamn mouth shut."

To further illustrate my point, I silence him by shoving my dick deep into his welcoming throat. He gags and moans, a few teardrops leaking down his face as I choke him with my hard cock. I can tell that despite my roughness, he's actually enjoying it.

That's the sick truth.

People love to cry victim and play the innocent card when really, we're all equally fucked up in our own way. The only difference is that some of us wear it on our sleeves while others live a lie, denying themselves the pleasure of taking exactly what they want, when they want it. What a sad existence.

As my dick hits the back of his throat, I moan at the shockwaves of pleasure. I savour the pleasure, even if this feels wrong, like I'm betraying my own feelings somehow by screwing him.

"Fuck, yeah…" I mumble.

Scott means nothing to me, just like the rest of them don't. He's a means to an end. I'll take whatever I can get to escape this world. It used to be drugs, back when I lived in London. But in my sobriety, I have to rely on sex instead.

Dammit, some nights… I'd kill for a hit.

Just one more time.

Loosening the restraints enough to roughly flip him over, I push Scott's face into my pillow. He grunts, shivering all over as I run my finger over the ring of muscle ready and waiting for me. All the while, Brooklyn's grey eyes are stuck in my head. She won't leave me alone.

Am I sick for wanting to march over to her room and throw the past right in her pretty face? Spank her until she bleeds and tell her that she's a filthy fucking sinner? That would get a reaction.

I want her to acknowledge my existence. I'm desperate for a fix, and nothing else will cut it. She lured me in with her sad smiles and blood thirst, then pushed me away like nothing happened in that classroom on her first day.

I discard people when I'm done with them.

Not the other way around.

After grabbing some lube and prepping him, Scott grunts while I roughly fuck him from behind. My nails drag down his back, leaving angry red marks.

I have to shut my eyes to block him out and pretend instead that it's Brooklyn writhing beneath me, moaning and sweating as I give her something that she won't be able to ignore.

That thought is enough to finish me off, and I spill my load. Shoving Scott aside when I'm done, I leave him gasping for breath as I unwrap the tape holding him prone. I avoid his searching eyes afterwards. I don't do feelings. It's nothing personal.

"Want me to come back tomorrow?" he asks hopefully.

I collapse into my desk chair and grab a beer from the stash hidden in the fake bottom without bothering to offer him one.

"Nope. One time's enough. I'll find someone else for then."

He swallows hard and stands up, pulling his sweats back on as he readies to escape. "Fine. You know where to find me if you change your mind."

With a final lingering look, Scott heads for the door. He slips down the darkened corridor, running fast to avoid being caught by the guards patrolling every hour while we're under curfew. I don't bother to say another word. My thoughts are consumed by another.

I feel fucking guilty, which only infuriates me further. Why should I be sorry? It's her fault. I haven't done anything wrong, but I'm still getting the silent treatment from Brooklyn. We've all been lumped into the naughty corner together.

I need answers.

Quickly showering before I redress in comfy clothes, I feel trapped in my own skin. Even the quickie with Scott hasn't calmed me. If anything, I feel more rattled and agitated than before.

I get like this sometimes, my moods ebbing and flowing faster than the fucking ocean. Slipping into the corridor, I wait for the patrolling guard to turn his back and march in the other direction.

We're on full lockdown for the night, but it doesn't deter me from my mission for answers. I can easily blend into the shadows and move without being seen. It's second nature to me—becoming one with the darkness that eagerly welcomes me home.

I glance at Brooklyn's room as I pass, and I notice light spills out from beneath the door. She's still awake, then. The temptation to walk in reaches fever pitch, but I refrain, forcing myself to go to Hudson's door instead.

Eli answers the door when I knock, offering me a secret smile that makes my toes curl. Inside, the other two are playing cards and watching some football on Hudson's big TV. Having rich adoptive parents pays, I guess. It's twice the size of mine.

"Hey," I greet.

Their heads turn as I snag a bag of crisps from the desk, plonking myself down on the bed next to Eli. Kade and Hudson quickly resume their game of poker.

Shuffling to make space for me on the mattress, Eli settles back in his spot. He's captivated by a book and even quieter than usual after the morning's drama.

"Thought you had company?" Kade asks pointedly.

"Got bored. Thought I'd come and annoy you lot instead."

Hudson throws down his cards, grinning smugly at his brother. "Royal flush, motherfucker. You lose. Again."

Kade frowns. "You're a cheat."

"Nope, just better than you. You're overthinking it, and that's the problem. Aren't you mathematicians supposed to be clever and shit?"

"Don't start with me again. I'm not in the mood."

"Not my fault you're a sore fucking loser."

Kade gets up with an angry huff. He heads over to the packed bookshelf next to the bed, shuffling a couple textbooks out of the way to grab one of the cans of coke hidden behind. We had to restock after the big sweep the other night.

Every now and then, the guards get uptight and try to exert their power over us. Management riles them up and sets them loose on us. Most of the time, they don't give a shit. Then we're raided and they pretend to be responsible by stealing all of our stuff.

Hudson shuffles the cards. "You want in?"

I consider him for a moment. "What are the stakes?"

"Kade's doing my essays for a week. What have you got to offer?"

"I know what I want, but you ain't gonna like it."

"Try me," he counters.

"I want to know what happened between you and Brooklyn."

Hudson halts, chews his lip for a moment. His icy-blue eyes are focused on the cards in his hands. I can tell that I've hit a sore spot, but I don't care. I need to know what happened. It's been driving me crazy for weeks and I can't wait a second longer.

"Nope. Not my story to tell," he answers eventually.

"Mate, it kinda is. You're the one she attacked."

"If she knew that I'd told you, we'd never see her again."

I let out a laugh. "We don't see her anyway, thanks to you."

"Seriously, Nix, don't push it. Choose something else."

With a sigh, I accept my stack of cards. "Fine, start."

Hudson offers Kade a hand to play, but he politely refuses, content to watch. It's just the two of us facing off, and I'm determined to walk away with at least some idea of what we're dealing with.

"I want to know why you call her blackbird."

Hudson looks surprised, but that quickly turns to exasperation. "Bloody hell. You won't drop this, will you?"

"Nope. Time to fess up."

I can tell the others are interested too. Their heads perk up as we begin to play. Even Eli's paying attention, peering over his book when he thinks nobody is watching. I've got a pretty decent hand.

Despite Hudson's confidence, his face reveals too much. He always runs hot, full of emotion and anger. Where I'm cool and unfeeling, he's all fire and brimstone. I can use that against him.

"Fine," he concedes moodily. "But if I win, you have to convince Brooklyn to talk to me in private."

I snort at his demand. "You really think she'll go for that?"

"I didn't say to tell her the truth. Get her there by any means necessary. Lie if you must."

Huh, it looks like Hudson is ready to play dirty. I don't have any qualms with that. We play in complete silence, both spurred on by the prospect of our respective prizes. When I eventually win, he tosses the cards down with a disappointed sigh.

"You lose," I boast smugly.

"Yeah, whatever. We got anything to drink?"

Kade jimmies a loose floorboard up, revealing a hidden compartment full of contraband. He hands a beer to Hudson before slotting the wood back into place over our secret stash.

"We need to pay off our tab with Rio before he breaks the door down and kills us all." Kade chews his lip, looking apprehensive. "You know what he's like about late payment."

Taking a long draw, Hudson nods. "I'll handle it tomorrow."

We all settle back in for story time. Kade's face is stormy, tense. He knows we're in for a hell of a tale and, knowing Hudson, it won't be a good one. Eli refocuses on his book, but the tilt of his head indicates he's listening intently.

Rolling the beer in his hands, Hudson picks his words carefully. "You guys know that Kade's folks adopted me five years ago, when I was sixteen. Before then, I lived in foster care. I bounced around for a while, eventually ending up at a place called St Anne's."

"What about your mum?" I ask him.

"Too high or drunk to fight for continued custody of me. St Anne's was the alternative. It was a Catholic-run, abusive hellhole. Nothing about that place was holy."

Hudson drains his beer in a few desperate gulps. With a characteristic sigh, Kade fetches him another and passes it over.

"Here. Keep going."

"I was only there for a few months before I was adopted," Hudson continues, accepting the drink. "That was lucky compared to others who were swallowed by the system and forgotten. We all went to the same school a few miles away. On the first day, some assholes got hold of me. I ended up in the nurse's office with a black eye."

Sounds about right. He's always been a hothead and never one to run from a fight. Hudson laughs coldly, like the memory is funny somehow.

"Brooklyn was there too, sprawled out across the chairs with a bloody nose and a big, fat lip. When I sat down with the ice pack, she looked me in the eye and said *I hope the other guy looks worse than you.*"

Kade snorts, shaking his head with amusement. I spare a glance at Eli next to me. His furtive eyes are still hiding behind the book as he hangs on to every word. We're all in far too deep with this girl for our own good.

Hudson takes another sip. "I'd seen her around at the foster home we shared, but we never spoke before then. After that first encounter, I couldn't let her out of my sight. We were inseparable."

"So soon?" Kade frowns.

"Things moved fast. She was so damn tenacious. Fragile, innocent... but fiery when she needed to be. If she ever saw a kid getting bullied or one of the foster carers beating someone, she was the first person to throw herself into the fray. Even if it got her in trouble. Hell, she got off on the thrill of it."

"Sounds about right," Kade mutters.

Hudson's voice dries up. "Pretty much."

"What else?" I demand, running out of patience.

"The truth is, I... admired her. Everything about her. I'd sneak into her room at night whenever I heard her crying out and crawl into the tiny bunk bed just to hold her close. Man, she was so tempting and fucking beautiful."

I know the feeling. That girl is sin personified.

Hudson smiles at the memory. "She would spread her legs for me, and it was like nothing else mattered beyond the two of us. I couldn't get enough of her."

"How did she end up there?" I ask wearily.

"The others said she was one of the original kids at St Anne's. She'd been there since she was ten years old. Nobody knew why, and she refused to talk about her family."

I drum my fingers on my leg, growing more aggravated by the second. Why does Brooklyn's shitty childhood bother me so much? Or is it the idea of Hudson taking advantage of a damaged girl that was so clearly desperate for love? It sets my teeth on edge. I try to shove the feelings aside, but her grumpy face refuses to leave my mind.

"What about the nickname?" I prod again.

Hudson runs a hand through his raven hair. "I came home from school one day and found Mrs Dane, the head carer, beating the shit out of her. She was curled up on the kitchen floor, bloody and bruised."

We all lean closer, readying for the truth.

"I later found out that they'd caught her stealing food and sneaking off with it. When I asked Brooklyn about it that night, she made me swear that I could keep a secret."

Here we go.

Hudson swallows hard. "The answer was in the drawer by her bed. Inside, I found a tiny, injured blackbird. It was tucked away in a matchbox that she stole from Mr Dane. Brooklyn was feeding it crumbs that she stole and got beaten to pay for."

If possible, the room grows even quieter. Eli abandons his book entirely, giving Hudson his full attention. Kade nervously plays with his shirt sleeves, developing an anxious twitch.

I have a feeling that something awful is coming because I know Hudson too fucking well. The person he's describing isn't the real him.

Shuddering a breath, he picks the stack of cards back up to give his hands something to do. "Its wings were broken, and she used matchsticks to try and fix them. I told her that she was wasting her time, and it was just a stupid bird... but she wouldn't listen. She refused to give up on the little creature."

I watch Hudson's expression twist with raw, ugly rage.

"Why did it matter? The bird?" Kade asks, clueless.

"This girl had become my entire reason for existing in a matter of weeks, and she was ignoring me to watch this bird," Hudson spits. "It became an obsession. She was clinging to this thing like it was the centre of her whole universe. All of her attention was stolen by it. I was so fucking angry."

"What did you do?" I whisper.

"What do you think I did? I took the matchbox and killed the thing that took her from me," he reveals. "I told her that hope was a pointless emotion as I snapped its neck right in front of her and tossed the carcass aside."

Kade's jaw drops in shock and disgust. The real Hudson is emerging now, and bitterness invades his shadowy face.

"She was my fucking girl, and no one was allowed to steal her from me. Not even a stupid bird. After that... I called her blackbird every day. Just to remind her of who exactly she belonged to, and that nothing else was allowed to matter to her. Only me."

We all stare at him, speechless. The other two look equally as horrified by the truth. I'm guessing we're all on the same page now. I'm a depraved fucker, there's no two ways about it. But that story was a whole new level entirely. What can you possibly say to something like that?

Kade nails it as always.

"Well, she certainly earned the right to stab you."

CHAPTER 21
BROOKLYN

EVERYBODY GETS HIGH - MISSIO

"I COULDN'T BELIEVE it when Todd asked me." Teegan chatters away, not caring whether I'm paying attention. "I've definitely messed it up already. One look, and I ran in the other direction. I mean, it's just a date. Not a big deal. But in this place?"

I roll a pen in my hands, pretending to listen while lost in my own head. Her words wash over me, though none of them resonate.

"Movie night as well! Loads of people will be there, practically the entire block. Does he really expect it to be romantic?"

"Sure," I hum distractedly.

"I can't sit in a seat without a panic attack. There is no organisational system either, no matter how early you arrive. It's all beanbags and shit. Maybe I should cancel. Are you listening to me?"

A sharp elbow in the ribs rouses me.

"Sorry, rough night. I'm listening, I promise."

She looks unconvinced. "What's going on with you?"

"Nothing. I just haven't been sleeping well. The whole fire and lockdown thing has been a bit much this week. Did you hear all that screaming last night too?"

Or was it just in my head?

Teegan straightens her notebook so it sits at a perfect right angle to the library desk. "Tell me about it. We heard it even from the first floor. Apparently, they figured out who set the fire and dragged them to solitary. I heard it was Owen, the pyromaniac from the top floor."

"Seriously?"

"I mean, he's been caught playing with matches and burning people before. It's kinda his thing."

The mere mention of someone being taken to solitary has sweat breaking out on my palms. I can't even begin to unpack the new information about a crazed pyromaniac attacking people. Just another day in paradise, right? This place is a circus.

"How's that even possible?"

Teegan chuckles. "People find a way to do shit, especially in this place. Take someone's freedom away and they just find new ways to do what they want, each one more creative than the last."

"Has something like this happened before?"

She pauses, frowning to herself. "I remember when I first arrived, a little over six months ago, there was this girl, Tiffany. She'd taken so much acid over the years, her mouth was like a gaping hole. No fuckin' teeth."

I crinkle my nose. "That's gross."

"Anyway, she went cold turkey like the rest of the addicts do when they come in. As it turns out, reality was a little too much for her. They found her dead by the end of the month."

"How'd she do it?" I ask casually.

Not like I'm looking for ideas or anything.

"She died in the swimming pool. Somehow, she got hold of some crank. You can get most things here if you know the right people and have payment. Tiffany went for a swim and drowned her stoned ass."

Teegan takes a slurp from her water bottle, as if we aren't discussing the brutal death of a fellow inmate. Sorry, *patient.* Everyone is so desensitised here.

That's what mental illness does to you. It gets in your head and makes the line between life and death seem so small, you're no longer afraid to cross it.

Catcalls and heckling break our conversation as we both snap out of it. The noise is coming from the far end of the library, where Rio and his buddies are waving for my attention.

They grind against the air in a pathetic demonstration that I suppose they think is appealing. Do girls seriously find that attractive? Yuck.

"Ignore them. The stupid twats won't pass their exams anyway," Teegan mutters. "Not like I'm going to do much better. I'm so screwed."

She begins to anxiously scratch her hands, where I can see the skin is already mottled with burst blood vessels. Nervousness practically leaks from her and, to my own surprise, I want to hug her. She marched to my door earlier and dragged me over here to study, refusing to take no for an answer. Beneath the worry and fear that defines her life is a little ball of sass.

"You'll do fine," I offer.

"Yeah right. Ever since I transferred to a different subject, I've been lost. The teachers fly through the content, and I'm sitting there trying to count how many roof tiles there are just to keep calm. I miss science."

"So, transfer back. What's stopping you?" I point out.

"My parents are the ones who paid for me to be here. They pressured me into doing something *constructive* with my time. I felt like I couldn't refuse. Money and all that… it comes with strings, you know? Obligations and stuff."

I look at Teegan for a moment, taking in her shoulder-length, glossy red hair and various facial piercings. She's probably the mellowest, most friendly goth I've ever met— a complete softie at heart, beneath the anxious candy coating. I want to throw her parents' money back in their faces on her behalf. No one should live for someone else.

"If you want to do something else, then fucking do it. Screw your parents and their money. What kind of cruel assholes send you to a place like this anyway?"

"It was here or the psychiatric unit back in Birmingham. Apparently, you're not considered stable if you break into your neighbour's house to rearrange their furniture at three o'clock in the morning."

I choke on a mouthful of water, lowering my bottle as she stares at me, fighting back a smile. "Woah, hold up. You broke into their house?"

"Um, kinda. I couldn't sleep after glancing inside at the summer barbecue the week before. If I didn't straighten things out, I think I would've imploded from anxiety. Crazy, right? You can say so. I know I am."

Making sure she meets my eyes, I answer steadily, "Nope. Not one bit. Just a little quirky is all. Don't worry, all the best people are. Being normal is overrated, Tee."

She beams at me, a genuine smile that has me grinning back. Dammit, this girl is burrowing further beneath my defences with each passing second. When did I suddenly start giving a shit? I knew when I saw her getting bullied while having a panic attack that she is worth defending.

"Anyway, the exams. You haven't been given a free pass?" she guesses, changing the subject as we both look away, unused to the feeling of friendship.

"Nope. Not that it matters," I answer without thinking.

"Why are you so relaxed? They're right around the corner. It's a mandatory part of the treatment plan, you know. They think learning is therapeutic or some crap."

I scramble for an excuse, cursing my stupidity. I can't exactly say that I plan to fucking kill myself by any means possible, and some pointless exams mean nothing to me. They can shove their theories and treatment plans where the sun doesn't shine.

"I've been catching up, so it's chill," I lie easily.

"Well, you've got brains. You'll ace it. But me? Nah, I'm nothing but air up here." Teegan gestures to her head. "I've got about as much hope as fuckface over there with his idiotic mates."

We both turn to look at Rio. He's telling dirty jokes as loud as possible while his friends laugh and jeer. My stomach turns listening to the way he talks about his hook-ups with zero fucking respect or sensitivity. He's a purebred, entitled asshole if I ever did see one.

"I don't get it. How is he so popular?"

Teegan shuffles closer so that she can whisper without being overheard, her eyes darting about. "You know what I said about Tiffany getting gear in here? Well, if you want contraband, he's your guy. Anything you want. He runs shit."

"How does he get it past security?"

She wrinkles her nose in distaste, as if talking about Rio and his illegal endeavours offends her. "Beats me. One thing I do know? Money talks. I heard on the down low that his parents are investors. They own stately homes and titles or some shit."

"What the hell is he doing here then?"

"Clearly, money doesn't buy sanity." Teegan snorts. "They don't give a toss what their unstable, delinquent son does with his nest egg, as long as he keeps it quiet and doesn't fuck with their holiday plans."

I nod absently, filing the information away for later use. Bingo, I've got my source. It sounds like I'll have to put my morals aside and approach the jackass. It's fucking degrading, but I'm desperate. It's not like I'll be around for much longer to regret it.

"So, movie night. What do you think? Should I go with Todd?"

"Yeah, why not. He seems cute." I wink at her. "Go for it."

"You're right, I'm going to do it. What's the worst that could happen? Who in the dorms are you going with? The emo guy?"

"Like I said, that was a one-time thing," I defend quickly.

There's more wolf whistling directed my way, gaining the attention of the rest of the library. Lifeless eyes fall on us, and I glare back at them, hoping to scare the nosy patients off. Whispers and gossip circulate around us, much to my annoyance. I'll break their damn legs if I have to.

"Ignore them. They'll get bored eventually," Teegan mutters.

She returns to her studying, leaving me to daydream while staring out of the window. A long and torturous hour later, we're packing up for the day.

I've got a free period this afternoon. I already saw Lazlo for my weekly shot, and he postponed my therapy session to deal with some urgent, patient-related issue. It's fine by me.

I'm in no rush to spend time with him again. The mere thought of sitting in the same room as Lazlo for any amount of time is almost too much for me to handle. I have to take a deep, calming breath.

You're running out of time.

The anniversary is coming.

You better die before it gets here.

I conceal the shake in my hands by fiddling with my coat zipper, attempting to ignore the whispered voice. It isn't real. The ghosts in my head are watching my mental clock, ticking down every last second. The pressure is increasing with each passing moment.

Teegan slowly packs up her stuff, turning each item over in her hands four times before neatly slotting it into her backpack. I linger behind, moving deliberately slow as my eyes stray to Rio.

"I'll see you tomorrow for the movie," she says hopefully.

"Maybe." I cringe at the thought of movie night. "I'll see. I'm not sure if it's really my thing. But have fun with Todd."

She blushes beet red. "It's not like that, honestly."

"Sure, whatever. Have fun, and don't do anything I wouldn't do."

Teegan grabs her backpack and walks off, turning to laugh at my words. "That doesn't exactly leave much, Brooke!"

I look away as she leaves the library, feeling a weird warmth in my chest again. It's been a long time since I've had anything even remotely resembling friendship in my life. Part of me finds the idea of having someone close enough to care terrifying.

When I die... she'll only suffer.

And make no mistake, I will die.

Living is fucking overrated.

Slinging my backpack over my shoulder, I survey the room and slowly head over to the far corner. It's go time. Meeting Rio's eyes, I jerk my head towards the towering bookshelves that create a great hiding place. He casts a quick look around before following me with a wide, sleazy smile on his face.

"Well, ain't you a sight for sore eyes."

"Cut it out. I want to make a deal, not listen to your pathetic flirting."

"No beating around the bush, I see. You know most girls in this place would kill for a look in with me, right?" He flexes his biceps as he speaks, and I almost gag.

Rio is tall and blonde, with tightly packed muscles from working out on a daily basis like the other anger management patients. Beyond that, he's a slimy fucking creep.

I would rather break his nose than bargain with him. But this is the price you pay for shit in this world. Clearview taught me real quick that if you're willing to pay, then anything is possible.

"Most girls are fucking stupid," I point out. "Look, I hear you're the resident hook-up around here. I've got a list. What's it gonna cost me?"

I pull the scrunched-up note from my pocket. Subtly slipping it into his beefy hand, I glance around to ensure we're still hidden from sight. Rio shakes his head, enjoying this way too much. He takes a quick read of my list and whistles under his breath.

"Want me to bring you a fucking unicorn too?"

I take a step closer into his personal space, maintaining unbroken eye contact. His muscular chest is almost pressing against mine. The trick is confidence. You have to show them you're serious and not to be messed with. Reputations are earned, not given.

"I'm willing to pay a high price. Don't fuck around. I'm not some dewy-eyed bitch asking for nail polish. Fix me up, and I'll make it worth your time. Or should I take my business elsewhere?" I pout exaggeratedly. "Thought you were the boss in this place."

That makes him smile. My words hit their target perfectly. Rio inches even closer, his strong deodorant making my chest burn. I stand still, forcing my breathing to even out as he grabs a strand of my hair, twirling it around his finger.

"I hear you, but I don't take empty promises."

"What do you take?" I force my clenched hands to release.

Rio grins. "Proof of payment. Right now."

Goddamn arrogant bastard.

I have to force the descending red haze back and remind myself that I want the stuff on that list. Desperately. It's nothing I haven't done before. I let men fuck me over the bar at my old work without even getting their names. Back then, it was just to feel something for one damn second. If I do this, I'll be ready and equipped to check out for good.

"Do you have the means to fulfil my order?" I nod towards the paper now tucked in his pocket. I'm not fucking stupid.

"I'm a man of my word, believe it or not. I can fix you up fine. Trust me, my supply lines are good."

He's deadly serious; all signs of humour have been wiped aside. Gone is the laddish asshole that prances around like he owns the place, and he's replaced by a slick businessman capitalising on a gap in the market.

It's pretty scary, but every prison needs a supplier. Contraband is hot shit when you have little to lose and much to gain from disregarding the rules.

Casting another suspicious look around, I make sure the coast is clear. Rio's goons are guarding the perimeter, keeping watch on the few patients still in the library.

It's like they're his fucking bodyguards or something. How didn't I see it before? The power dynamic beneath all the bravado? It's plain as day that he runs the shop around here.

"Haven't got all day," he goads.

Here goes nothing.

Falling to my knees, I undo his belt and lick my lips. I can see his rock-hard shaft straining against his black boxers. I'm just about to wrap my lips around his cock when a scuffle breaks out. Swearing and bickering has me freezing, his dick still in my hand.

We both turn to look as a towering shadow rounds the corner of the bookshelf. Thick, black hair, dazzling, oceanic eyes and a shining eyebrow piercing frame an apocalyptically angry face.

"The fuck, man? Get out of here," Rio barks.

Bad move.

Hudson's eyes take in my position, from my knees resting on the floor to my hands in a very suspicious place. My mouth is scant inches away from Rio's erection. There's no mistaking this scene. He should know well enough what I'm up to—I spent plenty of time on my knees before him once, both publicly and privately.

With a smug smile, I lean in and press a gentle kiss to Rio's cock. I taunt Hudson with my eyes as he watches the show, his face turning purple with rage. *Doesn't feel so good, does it, motherfucker?* He watched before, in a situation not so different. Only then, he got something out of it, the selfish son of a bitch.

This is me taking back control.

One blowjob at a time.

"Is something the matter?" I ask innocently.

Hudson doesn't say a goddamn word. There's no need. I see the attack coming from a mile off as his fist sails towards Rio's face. The blow sends him flying back into a bookshelf.

Without stopping for a breath, Hudson advances and delivers brutal punch after punch. Bones crack and blood sprays as the pair beat on each other like cage fighters.

All I can hear is their grunting and the sound of fists meeting flesh. It takes all three of Rio's guys to pull the two men apart, both sporting injuries and future black eyes.

"You're fucking unhinged!" Rio yells.

Hudson laughs shortly, spitting blood on the floor and wiping his split lip. "Your point, asshole? Stay the hell away from her. You hear me? I'll fucking kill you next time. That's a promise."

Crystal-clear blue eyes turn to me, tinged with anger and disappointment. How dare he judge me? When Hudson tries to seize my arm, I dodge out of the way, storming off instead. He soon catches up and yanks my arm again, slamming the exit door open.

"Get off me, you son of a bitch!"

Hudson's fingers tighten on my arm as he drags me along. He's grabbing me so hard, I know I'll have a bruise tomorrow. It's not the first time his touch has stained my skin.

"Zip it, Brooke. I swear to God, if you say one more word, there'll be hell to pay."

Sparing one last glance over my shoulder as we flee the library, I catch the look that Rio sends me. His boys are running off to alert the nearby guards. Fucking tattletale, like he's the innocent one in this situation.

The look he sends me is downright cold, vastly different after Hudson's little performance. He pulls my note from his pocket. I watch him rip it to pieces—slowly, deliberately, with the threat abundantly clear.

CHAPTER 22
HUDSON

11 MINUTES - YUNGBLUD, HALSEY & TRAVIS BARKER

FUCKING WHORE.

Filthy bitch.

I'm losing my shit right now and spiralling fast, but hell if I care about staying calm. That shitshow merited violence, regardless of the consequences.

I'd do it all over again, no matter what they do to me. Rio will rat to his bankrolled, corrupted guards just to spite me. Screw him.

What happened to my blackbird?

This isn't the girl I remember from St Anne's. If I didn't recognise her, I'd say she's an entirely different person. Where's the troubled orphan that wore secondhand pyjamas and fell asleep while clutching old photos of her parents? Or the girl that crept into my room at night with stolen bandages to clean up after the older kids beat the shit out of me?

My precious girl wouldn't be on her knees with her mouth wrapped around another man's cock, trading favours like a desperate slut. Jesus, who am I kidding? I know what happened to her. It's all my fault. I fucking ruined her.

Shoving Brooklyn out the door, I watch as she trips and stumbles to her knees. Good, it serves her right. What would have happened if I didn't walk in at that exact second? Would she have let Rio fuck her against the wall? I feel physically sick just thinking about it. I roughly pull her back onto her feet. She struggles against my grip, tossing every insult under the sun in my face.

"Shut the fuck up," I growl, fisting her hair.

I hope it hurts. She deserves it. I ought to bend her over my knee right now for that shitshow back there. She won't be able to sit down for a week by the time I'm done with her.

"Let me go or I'll fucking report you," Brooklyn shouts.

Ignoring her threats, I keep walking back across the quad towards the dormitories. I refuse to release her, no matter how hard she fights me.

I've had enough of watching her flounce around here, acting like she doesn't even know me. I'll break her all over again if I have to, one stupid bird at a time. Whatever it takes to bring her back to me.

"What was he getting for you? Booze? Cigarettes?"

"None of your business."

I grind to a halt, slamming her body into a nearby brick wall. She cries out in shock as I pin her against it, invading her space until we're nose to nose. Her grey eyes are shining with unshed tears, the rage and fear mixing into a tempting maelstrom.

"Talk to me like that again, and you'll regret it," I warn darkly. "I asked you a fucking question."

She breathes rapidly. "And I said fuck off."

Her defiance isn't new to me, but she's even more stubborn now than she used to be. Fuck if I don't find it hot. The schoolgirl I once knew doesn't exist anymore. My blackbird grew up.

"I said, what was he getting for you?" I roughly grab her chin. "You will answer me, Brooke. I want to know what was so important that his cock was in your mouth instead of mine."

She stares up at me, her eyes burning. "Get your hands off me right now. Final warning."

After checking that we're still alone, I let out a frustrated growl. Yanking her arms above her head, I easily pin them there so she can't move or struggle. I'm holding her prisoner now.

"Want me to let go, huh? That's what you want?"

Leaning in, I steal her frantic breaths and inhale her scent. I want to bathe in her pure fucking essence. It's painfully familiar and reminiscent of the broken home we shared. She isn't allowed to breathe if it's not for me.

"Let go," Brooklyn repeats.

"So you can run back to that asshole and beg on your knees?" I taunt.

"If that's what I want to do, then you're the last person to complain," Brooklyn hits back angrily. "You have a shitty memory, Hud. All that time we spent together... who exactly taught me to beg on my fucking knees, huh?"

She moves so fast that I can't dodge the headbutt that comes my way. Her forehead connects with my nose, which bursts instantly. Hot blood streams into my mouth. She watches closely, waiting for my reaction. I know she's desperate to see my pain.

I don't give her the fucking satisfaction.

Licking my lips, I maintain eye contact, letting her see the chaotic tangle of emotions brewing beneath the surface. There's nothing left to hide from her. She's seen the absolute worst in me and hates my guts for it. It can't get any worse than that.

"I'm not letting you go until you talk to me," I state plainly. "You took one look and came at me with a knife. I'm not blaming you, I earned that. But it took two of us to ruin our relationship, blackbird. Own your shit already."

Brooklyn thrashes in my arms, trying to break free as her eyes sparkle with tears. "Own my shit? You're kidding, right? You should be in prison for what you let them do to me. I was sixteen years old! Goddamn you. *God-fucking-damn you.*"

Her words sting like acid as the buried memories roll through my mind. Brooklyn trussed up and restrained while I snorted coke off her bare breasts. Her knees knocking together as we shot up together for the first time before I fucked her good and rough from behind. Pulling on her pearly-white braids hard enough to rip her hair free.

That was just the way she liked it back then. Our late night hook-ups were more punishment than pleasure for both of us. Treading that fine while we both clung to a single moment where living wasn't a burden.

"Hate me all you want. But you can't ignore me forever."

She bares her teeth. "You walked away, not me."

"I didn't walk away. I was adopted."

"So, what, a half-assed apology and you're off the hook? You really thought that was enough? Five years you've been gone!"

"Brooke—"

"No! Five fucking years, and you want to argue that you're the victim here," she screams at me. "You left me alone in that hell and went swanning off into the sunset with your perfect new family. Do you have any idea of the damage you left behind?"

Anger sneaks back inside my mind like a silent assassin. It's my ever-present companion. I can't keep a cool head any longer for this conversation. She needs to be taught a lesson and reminded of who exactly owns her ass.

I wrap a hand around her delicate throat. Brushing her pulse point, I find her unsteady heartbeat. Just as her lips part on a sharp intake of breath, I squeeze hard, easily crushing her windpipe.

"I left when the girl I loved became a stranger," I whisper harshly. "You were like a ghost. Staying wasn't an option after what happened. So, yes, I fucking ran."

She tries to respond and fails, choking instead.

"Blame me all you want, Brooke. But you're the one that cut me off when you turned your back on me and said that you didn't love me anymore. I died that day, right then and there. It felt like this."

With all my strength, I choke her even harder, relishing her teary eyes and seizing chest. She's desperately trying to suck in a breath that's being stolen away.

I could kill her with my bare hands without batting an eye. I release my grip just enough to let her gasp before tightening it again, stealing back the privilege of breathing as she fails to fight me off.

"Does it hurt, baby? Your chest burning? Eyesight swimming? Good. I want you to fucking hurt, you little whore," I lash out. "When you turned your back on me and walked away like nothing between us ever mattered, I felt like you'd taken a knife to my goddamn stomach and gutted me."

I force a hand up Brooklyn's t-shirt as I speak, even though she flinches away from my touch. Finding them through nothing but memory, I stroke the soft scars that litter her hips, showing her just how well I know her dark secrets.

"You cut me deeper than you ever cut yourself," I murmur, teasing her soft skin. "That's why I never looked back. You took my heart and ground it into pathetic little pieces. Happy now?"

When I let go of her throat this time, she violently coughs and splutters. Tears are streaming freely down her cheeks as she sucks in deep, rattling breaths that sound agonising.

"Am I happy now? I fucking hate you," she sobs. "I'm glad you left. The only thing you were ever good for was ruining my life. From the day you walked into that nurse's office, I was doomed. Walk away, Hud. That's all you're good at. Leave me alone."

I stumble as she manages to break my hold. Rubbing her rapidly bruising throat, her eyes tear through my skin and penetrate my dead fucking soul.

Call me sick, but I can't help smiling at her. The yelling and hatred show that she still cares. Somewhere, deep down, there are feelings. I can work with that.

"What are you grinning about, you fucking psycho?"

I shrug nonchalantly. "It takes one to know one. You want to tell me what you're doing at Blackwood? Or are you gonna run off again like a scared little kid?"

"Shut your mouth. What I'm doing here is none of your business. You lost that privilege a very long time ago and, based on what I've heard from your *brother,* you continue to disappoint. This place is where you belong, asshole."

My heartbeat roars in my ears as she speaks. Her ruined voice isn't a single octave above a whisper, but it's as if she's shouting into my head, sneering at me and throwing Kade in my face like it's common knowledge that we're adoptive brothers.

The fucking cheek of this bitch. I know that I'm a disappointment, but I don't need reminding of that fact. Especially not from her. She was the beginning of the end for me.

"You always were fucked in the head," I insult, turning it back around. "If I belong here, then so do you."

I watch as Brooklyn's face falls. *It's not nice having the past thrown in your face, is it?* As she's about to reply, our standoff is interrupted. The door we fled through bangs open.

Two guards emerge, searching around until they spot us. I recognise them instantly as Rio's men. Everyone knows that they're slipped a tidy salary to make his life here a luxury. The bastard himself points in our direction, a smug grin on his face.

Brooklyn readies to flee. "I'm not going back to the hole."

"No reason we should both end up there. I got this, you go."

Jerking my head towards the dorms in the distance, I indicate for her to run away. She stares at me in complete confusion, like I didn't just offer to save her damn hide. This girl is infuriating.

"You'd do that for me? Why?"

"I'm the one that hit him." I shrug. "Don't get all soft on me. I don't want to see you go into that basement again and never come out. Go find Kade. He's in his room, and he'll stop them from dragging you off."

"But—"

"No buts. Do as you're told for once in your life."

I give her a gentle push to get her moving, fighting to keep my voice firm. No doubt, I'll be dragged down to solitary after the fiasco in the library, especially if Rio has tattled on me already.

The clinicians all know I'm a hothead. They look for any excuse to toss me back in a solitary cell.

"This doesn't make us even," Brooklyn responds, her eyes narrowed. "Not by a long shot."

"Yeah, I didn't expect it to. You're a stubborn bitch, you know that?"

"Learned from the best," she snarks.

Casting her a look, I focus on her soft, pink lips that are curled in a slight smile. Fuck, I'd give anything to kiss her one more time. Even if she did punch me after, it'd be worth it. Deciding to take a risk, I ignore the incoming trouble.

Yanking her thin body closer so it's trapped against mine, my hand grips her sharp jawline. Brooklyn freezes in my inked arms, her body rigid but unwilling to move. There's a magnetic force drawing us together, stronger than either of us can resist.

"For old time's sake." I press my lips to hers.

She's still pissed at me, but she doesn't object as her lips part like they're trained to react to me after the thousands of times we've done exactly this. Her tongue darts out to tangle with mine, and the taste of tobacco on her breath drives me wild.

I kiss her with every ounce of regret that lingers between us, trying to communicate the apology that feels hollow when said aloud. Words don't cut it. I need to physically show her how I feel. Her teeth clash with mine, giving as good as she gets and sending a message of hatred right back.

"Screw you, Hud. You can't kiss me like nothing's changed," she murmurs against my lips. "I still fucking hate you."

"And I still want to spank your ass for the shit you pulled back there. You best hide when I get out, because I'm coming for you. This time, you ain't running away again. I'm done chasing you."

Brooklyn stares, but I swear her mouth twitches in an almost smile. Much too soon, the guards catch up and drag me away. They snatch at thin air as she runs full speed without looking back.

Good girl. They're less interested in her, wrestling with me instead. I'm led away to the doom that I know awaits. It's a small price to pay to taste my broken blackbird.

Just like when we were kids, I'm fucking addicted all over again. All it took was one hit of her toxic poison to enthral me. One tiny taste, and I'm on my knees just where she left me, broken and begging for another chance.

But this time, I won't be walking away from her. She's been mine since the day I laid my eyes on her five years ago. When I get back, I'm gonna make sure she fucking knows it.

CHAPTER 23
BROOKLYN

HEROIN - BADFLOWER

LAYING ON MY BACK, I'm sprawled across the bed and staring up at the blank ceiling. Light from the rapidly fading sunset paints the surface, but I don't turn to watch it, even as my mum's words nudge the back of my mind. I hear her every night.

If she hadn't gone and gotten herself killed, then she could watch the fucking sunset herself. I wouldn't have to watch it for her, enacting the ritual like some kind of twisted dedication to her memory. The good memories, anyway. There are plenty of bad ones that I'd like to erase forever.

The truth is, everyone dies eventually.

One disappointment after another.

I roll onto my stomach and wrap Phoenix's navy blanket tighter around my body, half-heartedly picking up my copy of *The Handmaid's Tale*. I'm supposed to be reading it for class, but I only picked it up to tear pages out and see if I could cut myself with the edges.

It didn't fucking work, of course, but the words caught my eye. I kept reading and fell into a deep rabbit hole. My fingers trace over the sentence that I circled so heavily, my pen tore through the page.

It's those other escapes, the ones you can open in yourself, given a cutting edge.

What I wouldn't give to cut my way out of this life. I want to tear a hole big enough to squeeze through and disappear from reality. That's the thing about dying.

Those who battle hardest against it are the ones afraid of what they'll leave behind. But when you have nothing—nobody to grieve you or notice the chasm you leave behind in the world—there's nothing terrifying about death.

In the end, it's more appealing than living.

I hear Phoenix's loud voice before the knock comes.

"Brooklyn! You in?" he hollers.

Sighing, I get up and open the door. "Yeah?"

Phoenix and Eli both wait on the other side, dressed casually for the evening. My mouth goes dry as I study the acid-wash sweats and tight graphic shirt that Phoenix is wearing, showcasing refined muscles and broad shoulders. His blue hair is starting to fade, but it's still garish under the bright lights of the corridor.

Eli looks just as delicious in his tight, ripped jeans and signature hoodie with the word *Metallica* emblazoned across the chest. His dark curls are bouncy and freshly washed again, smelling faintly of citrus fruits. They stick out from beneath the green beanie he wears.

Fuck me, it should be illegal to look this good.

"We're here to bust you out," Phoenix declares proudly.

I stare, refusing them entry. "Bust me out?"

"Saturday is movie night in the block. You can't sit in here alone. I bribed Kade to arrange something decent. We normally get lumped with some vanilla PG shit, but I bargained for something better."

"Is that so?"

He quirks an eyebrow at me, leaning against the doorframe to close the distance between us. "Come on, you know you want to."

I don't budge, folding my arms and offering him a mean smile. "What makes you think I actually want to go with the likes of you two?"

Phoenix dramatically lays a hand over his heart, letting out a sigh. "You wound me! Put it this way—come downstairs, and we'll make it worth your while. We can be very gentlemanly when the mood strikes, firecracker."

He winks at me, and the sexual tension is electric. His flirting is relentless, moving beyond mere banter and into something more. I bite my lip, feeling heat rush through my body.

Eli stares, his intelligent green eyes layered with even darker intentions. He doesn't have to say a word for me to feel the lightning crackling between us. My hands are itching to reach out and touch his body again. But with Phoenix in the mix too? These two will be the death of me. How convenient.

"Fine. I'm bored anyway." I sigh dramatically. "But I expect to be thoroughly entertained."

"You got it. Let's go."

We head downstairs as a trio. Phoenix keeps close to my side. His hand rests playfully on my lower back, but I don't bother to move it. I've made my feelings clear, so if he wants to play a dangerous game, that's on him. I can't be blamed for whatever comes next.

"Is Kade joining us?"

"Nope. He got leave for the weekend to see his folks. Some family birthday shit," Phoenix replies with a shrug. "Being Blackwood's bitch has its perks, I guess. You don't see the rest of us making it home for birthdays."

"Bitter much?" I laugh.

Deep down, guilt settles in my gut. Is Hudson missing seeing his family because of me? No, don't fucking go there. He chose to start that fight with Rio. I didn't ask him to get involved.

Phoenix clears his throat, apparently uncomfortable with my question. "Haven't got any folks to miss. So, no, not bitter. But my sister turns fourteen in a few weeks, and I won't be there. My record is spotless too."

"You have a sister?"

"Yeah. My nana raised us both when Mum ran off with her latest exploit. I haven't seen that bitch in nearly eight years. Charlie doesn't even remember her."

"That sucks. Good riddance to shitty parents."

He immediately chuckles. "Agreed."

We head down through the foyer and past the guard station, deliberately avoiding the meatheads sitting inside, studying everyone that passes.

I don't have anything else constructive to offer Phoenix. Shit happens. Parents only disappoint, and us kids are always left to pick up the pieces.

We reach the movie room, where a bustle of patients are slowly filing inside in pairs. Joining the back of the queue, we filter through into a large, relatively modern space. This end of the building seems to be an extension added to the rest of the ancient institute.

Big, comfy sofas and beanbags are strewn about in the low-lit room, with brightly coloured blankets and cushions thrown in. A projector hangs from the ceiling, beaming directly onto a black wall at the front. It's warm and spacious, perfect for hosting a small group.

I take in the impressive arrangement. "This is fancy."

"None of that public hospital shit here," Phoenix says, grabbing my hand. "We're in the big leagues, baby."

I'm directed towards the back of the room, passing Teegan on the way. She gives me a wink from her spot next to her date. Eli trails close behind us, and we take the uppermost corner, where two beanbags sit unoccupied. Everyone seems to be spreading out automatically into what must be their usual places.

"Gotta bribe us to behave somehow, right? It's all an act," Phoenix informs me. "You only get compliance if you keep the masses happy with treats. Don't be fooled by it."

He takes one of the beanbags and sprawls out, offering me a hand. His fingers curl inwards to beckon me closer. I stare at him with an eyebrow raised in challenge. He's in top form tonight.

"I don't bite." Phoenix bares his teeth in a way that has my thighs clenching together. "Not much, anyway. Come play with us."

I end up sandwiched between the pair of them with my ass occupying both beanbags simultaneously. Phoenix slings his arm around my shoulders straight away as I shiver. Why is he making it so damned hard to stay uninvolved?

"You okay?" I whisper to Eli.

His eyes slide over to me, followed by a tiny nod of his head. I want to ask more, but a smartly dressed, middle-aged woman strolls in, flanked by two guards that look deadly serious. Their hands rest on batons that are strapped to their belts.

Phoenix's lips touch my ear. "That's the warden, Miss White. You don't see her around much even though she's in charge. She gets others to do her dirty work."

Miss White looks like a fucking sadist. Dressed in a neatly pressed pantsuit, her perfect, blonde hair is scraped back in a severe bun that highlights her beautifully cruel face. She strides to the front of the room, arms folded and heeled foot tapping impatiently.

"This is a reminder that only orderly conduct is permitted in this room. Don't try any funny business," she says crisply. "After recent events, my patience is wearing thin."

Phoenix laughs quietly. "I bet it is."

"Any illicit activities will be swiftly punished," Miss White continues her lecture. "No more verbal warnings. Am I making myself clear?"

I swear her eyes stray over to us, clocking our position at the back of the room. Eli tenses beside me, his leg jiggling to expel his constant flow of nervous energy. I lay a hand on his denim-clad thigh, silently urging him to take a breath.

"Taggert and Jackson will be staying behind to keep an eye on things." Miss White gestures to the two unfriendly guards. "Abuse this privilege, and it will be taken away. Enjoy the film."

She turns on her designer heels and stalks away, and the two guards shut the door behind her. They station themselves there with a perfect view of the room, studying us intently in what's clearly a shitty intimidation tactic.

Phoenix curses under his breath. "They'll be watching us in the bathroom soon too. What happened to human rights?"

I stifle the urge to laugh in his pretty face. "You're all too fucking spoiled around here. Back where I came from, a bathroom door was a rare commodity."

I swear I see the ghost of a smile on Eli's lips, like he knows exactly what I'm talking about, but my attention is stolen by Phoenix's hot breath against my skin.

"We're not all hardened badasses like you. Excuse me for wanting some privacy while I shit. It's my thinking time."

"Charming. Thanks for that image."

"You started it."

We continue to bicker as the credits roll. Some stupid sci-fi movie comes on the screen. Everyone seems pretty happy about it as they settle in, but I shoot Phoenix an incredulous look.

"Thought you got something decent put on?"

"Hey, it's usually childish shit. This is the best I could do."

We lapse into silence as the movie plays in the background. All I can feel is the suffocating warmth of their bodies around me. My hand still rests on Eli's leg and at some point, he adds his on top, drawing lazy circles against my skin.

Phoenix isn't much better, snuggling his body closer to mine until we're practically spooning. His muscular legs fit perfectly around mine, and something suspiciously firm is nudging my lower back.

"Problem?" Phoenix breathes.

His hand brushes my hip as he continues to toy with me. I exact my revenge by wiggling my ass, letting his erection grind into me as I hear him gasp.

"Nope, just getting comfortable. Thanks for asking."

"Quit moving then. You're killing me."

I'm killing him? I feel like I may actually melt into a puddle at any moment. It's been far too long since my steamy kiss with Phoenix or the graveyard tryst with the silent man on my left. I'm not ashamed to admit that I want them both. Who fucking cares? Life is short, and I intend to make it even shorter. I may as well enjoy it while I can.

Halfway through the movie, I'm ready to combust. The guards have long since gotten comfortable and are both focused entirely on the screen now. Being at the back of the room gives us the perfect privacy, and the two devils sandwiching me in are ready to play.

Phoenix takes the opportunity to snake a hand up my sweater, his fingertips gliding across my ribs. He gently rubs a thumb over my nipple, which is as hard as a pebble, even through the thin material of my bra. I bite my lip to hold a gasp in.

"Not ignoring me now, are you?" he says softly, his teeth nibbling my earlobe. "You've been a complete bitch, firecracker. Think that deserves a punishment, don't you?"

His tongue is hot on my neck, tracing down until it reaches my clavicle. Pressing open-mouthed kisses on my skin, his touch leaves a path of fire that ignites my core.

"I don't ignore you anyway," I moan.

"Give it up already. You've treated us like we have the fucking plague ever since Hudson came into the picture."

"Have not."

"Have to! But that's fine, I guess we need to show you what you're missing. Ain't that right, Eli?"

Suddenly, another mouth secures itself to my throat. Peppering kisses around the back of my ear, Eli shoots me a filthy look. His eyes are twinkling with mischief as he sucks on my sensitive skin. He barely has to do a thing and my cunt is soaked, begging to be filled by him again.

"I have done no such thing," I defend. "You're being a pussy."

Phoenix pulls the cup of my bra aside, his fingers painfully twisting my nipple. "Don't lie. You're punishing us all for Hudson's mistakes. I don't take shit like that lightly, baby. You best remember who was there for you on your first day."

Like soldiers executing a coordinated manoeuvre, they both attack my body. I writhe between them, imprisoned in desire. Eli tugs on my hair and battles with my jeans as Phoenix lavishes my breasts with his signature blend of borderline-painful pleasure. A hand clamps down over my mouth, swiftly silencing me.

"Not a word. Be a good girl and we'll let you come."

My pussy clenches tight at Phoenix's words, screaming out for relief. I groan under my breath, stifling the response that wants to escape. He laughs and bites my earlobe again.

"That's it, good girl. Quiet now."

Eli finally wiggles his way into my panties, and his fingers brush right over my swollen clit. Slow and gentle, driving me wild with need. He's toying with me, and I will combust if he doesn't do something soon.

"Show our girl why we're worth it," Phoenix orders him.

Eli slips two digits inside my slit without warning, the sneaky bastard. He invades my body while I bite down hard on my lip. Fucking me with his hand, he watches me closely for the torture he's inflicting on my nerves.

Phoenix decides to punish me even further. Capturing me in a searing kiss, his tongue sweeps through my mouth. I have no choice but to surrender to his lips, letting myself be devoured.

"You taste so damn sweet," he mumbles.

His tongue piercing is deliciously cold and oh so satisfying. I can hardly breathe between his expert lips and Eli driving me over the edge. Tension builds in my core, and I raise my hips, seeking more friction. Anything to relieve the ache building inside of me.

"Enough, Eli," Phoenix commands.

Then, Eli's hand is gone. He leaves me on the cusp of an orgasm, tearing his fingers from my cunt and cruelly preventing my final plunge into oblivion. I whimper against Phoenix's mouth while he chuckles like a fucking deviant.

"Doesn't feel good to be left hanging, does it?" he taunts.

Sucking on my bottom lip hard enough to hurt, he bites down with his teeth then soothes the sting with his tongue. He bites me repeatedly as his ministrations move down my jaw and neck. I'm being marked.

"Finish what you started here," I hiss at him.

I can see the enjoyment on his face. He's absolutely loving torturing me, exerting his power and control.

"Why should we? You're the one that's been a complete bitch to us. I thought you liked pain, huh?" Phoenix's fingers slide up my sleeve, digging into my fresh cuts. "Nice to know you hurt yourself as much as others."

"Screw you, that's none of your business," I groan.

Phoenix bites my throat, right above my skipping pulse, as his nails dig into my arm. I swear I die on the spot when he adds his teeth on top, sending searing pain throbbing through me.

"Am I not allowed to hurt you? Or is it just Hudson who has that honour?"

"Do what you want," I grunt. "Just don't bring him into it."

Phoenix snickers, pulling back to stare into my eyes. "That asshole doesn't speak for the group. If you want this, then you're going to put your drama with him aside. Quit ghosting us, and I'll hurt you, firecracker. I'll fuck you up as much as you want."

The two deviants share a loaded look as I prepare to relent. Because let's face it, I'm fucking done for. I was kidding myself if I thought I could keep my distance from them both.

"Fine," I growl.

"Is that a yes?"

"Fucking hell, Nix. It's a yes."

Eli grabs my chin with his free hand, refusing to let me look away. His emerald eyes speak a thousand words as he kisses me just as hard as Phoenix did.

His soft ringlets are tickling my face as his hand resumes driving me crazy. Just when I think it can't get any better, Phoenix shifts behind me. He tugs my jeans down lower, making sure I'm hidden by their bodies around me.

"Do you like that, firecracker? Eli fingering you like the dirty slut you are?"

"Yes." I shudder, lifting my hips higher.

"We're gonna do things to you that will push your boundaries. Don't expect sweet and sappy, because that ain't what we're about. You still want it?"

I nod frantically, watching Phoenix's pleased smirk. He planned this all along, and I've fallen into his nefarious trap. Bringing his fingers to my mouth, he slips them between my lips.

"Let's start here then. Suck," he demands.

I open my mouth without protesting, taking his slim digits in and moistening them with my tongue. Pressing further into my mouth, his fingers briefly slide down my throat and cause me to gag. Phoenix's smile broadens. He's seriously sadistic.

After a few seconds, he pulls them free and lowers his hand back into my jeans. I have to suppress a surprised squeak as he finds the ultra-sensitive nerve endings of my asshole. My entire body tenses in preparation. I was not expecting that.

"Say please." Phoenix circles the tight ring of muscle.

I swallow a scream as Eli adds another wet finger, stretching my pussy even wider. Phoenix continues to mercilessly toy with me, spreading my saliva around my back entrance.

Another climax spirals inside of me, ready to climb higher as they play me like an instrument, perfectly synchronised with each other.

"Please…" I moan, unable to resist.

Phoenix pushes the tip of his finger in. "Please what?"

I want to yell and tell him to go to hell, but every ounce of my self-control has left the building. I want them both to fuck me. Right here, right now.

Regardless of the room full of people, I'd bend over and take it without question if they wanted to.

Phoenix grabs my hair, yanking it to turn my head back towards him. My eyes water at the roughness, and a smug smile dances across his lips. He's thoroughly enjoying my pain.

"I asked, please what? Answer the question or Eli will leave you hanging again."

The fingers working in and out of my pussy pause as he speaks, and another whimper of pain threatens to escape my lips. Eli is his silent assistant, inflicting Phoenix's fucked-up will.

"Please fuck me," I mutter, blushing hard.

Goddammit, the son of a bitch is grinning at me.

"Not yet," Phoenix replies shortly. "But soon, Brooke. I can't wait to have you screaming my name while we both fuck you into oblivion. Is that what you want? We'll push every boundary you have and more. Final warning."

He bites my lip again, drawing blood and licking it clean off.

"Yes," I answer obediently.

"Now you're behaving," he praises. "Give me that attitude again, and I'll spank your ass raw."

Phoenix nods to Eli. My voice is stolen by his finger breaching my ass, gradually easing in as Eli returns his fingers to my slit. With them both inside of me now, I think I'm going to shatter into a million pieces.

I feel so full. It's been a long time since anyone touched me down there. As they play with me, I can't help but wonder what will happen when they both fuck me at the same time. Because that sure as hell is happening.

"This is mine, you hear me?" Phoenix states, fingering my ass. "A night with us and you won't walk straight for a fucking week. I can't wait to bruise your perfect skin."

Eli's mouth trails down my sweater until his lips capture my exposed nipple. Hell, the image of being trapped between them has me swallowing a cry as my release takes over. I bury my face in Eli's hair, breathing in his mouthwatering scent. I have to stifle my noises so nobody hears us.

When I manage to lift my head several breathless seconds later, I'm fucking wet again at the sight that awaits me. Goddamn sadistic bastards. Phoenix and Eli are kissing passionately, their mouths latched on to one another like hungry animals.

I'm entranced by the sight, and aftershocks from my orgasm still making my legs shake. Phoenix fists a handful of Eli's curls as his tongue dances across his lips.

He yanks hard, exposing Eli's throat, which he sinks his teeth into like a damn predator. Eli rubs the solid lump in his jeans, his breaths coming out as pained shudders. When they part, both men stare at me with hooded eyes.

"Damn," I comment breathlessly.

Eli's chest vibrates with a laugh that doesn't make it out for anyone else I hear. The son of a bitch looks mighty pleased with himself. Slowly raising his fingers to his mouth, he ensures that we're both watching before taking his time to suck every last drop of my come from them.

"Does our girl taste good?" Phoenix asks curiously.

They share a silent conversation in typical fashion, communicating without a single word being spoken. I glance around, the loud movie concealing our filthy conversation.

No one saw a thing; they're all entranced by the screen. Even the guards are none the wiser, fixated on the movie like the negligent twats they are.

Crossing my arms, I feign annoyance. "Are you two done already?"

Trapped between both of them, it's impossible to remain mad for long. Already, I'm wet and shivering, my body burning for more attention. When Phoenix winks at me, I'm like putty in his fucking hands.

"Nope. We're just getting started, baby."

CHAPTER 24
KADE

HOLY NIGHT - LANDON TEWERS

CROUCHED behind my father's vintage Porsche 911, I'm well hidden from sight as I spark up a cigarette. Taking a long drag, I blow the smoke out as my body begins to relax.

It burns my lungs, but I don't care. I need the relief it brings right now. I'm not much of a smoker, but when you're surrounded by stuck-up assholes commenting on shit that's none of their business, it's needed.

Why did I think coming home was a good idea?

"Kade! You out here?"

My head falls between my legs. I sigh, hoping that she'll give up searching for me. There's no such luck, though, as Cece peers around the car and her eyes land on me. She scoffs and sits down by my side, her hand held out to demand a drag on my cigarette.

"Come on, give it up. You know Mum won't let me."

"Fine," I grumble, passing it off to my baby sister.

Whereas Hudson is adopted, Cece is my sister by blood. She's several years younger than me, bearing the intelligence and quick wit of youth. Out of them all, she's basically the only one I can stand to be around because she's down to earth and level-headed in a way our parents aren't.

"Was it what Uncle Terrence said?" she guesses.

I manage a nod.

"Fuck him. He has no right to say shit about Hudson or his life choices. What happened to blood is thicker than water, huh? Stupid old bastard."

I snatch the cigarette back, giving her a shrug. "He'll wheel out the tolerance card when it suits him. We all know what he really thinks of Hudson, Dad too. It doesn't give them the right to talk smack about him in front of the entire family though."

"True. At least he isn't trying to act like he cares."

I guess that would be worse. We can rely on our father and his extended family to be cunts. My mum is the only decent one among them.

We sit in silence until the cigarette is gone, staring across the foggy grounds surrounding our family mansion. Seven acres of grass, trees and horses line the estate, with a giant circular driveway to fit Dad's extensive car collection.

The house itself is a million-pound monstrosity, full of antique crap that Mum proudly collects and displays, as if to suggest that her days as a housewife actually amount to anything.

I hate it here.

I hate everything about this life and the expectations that come with it. I'm aware how much of a privileged shit that makes me sound. The truth is, I'd rather be fucking poor and in control of my own destiny than in this prison of superficiality.

My whole life, I've been controlled by other people's plans and ideals. Dad knows exactly what he wants for us, whether we like it or not. I'm left trying to defend my rejected adoptive brother to relatives whose kids attended Oxbridge and boast several doctorates.

"How's boarding school?" I sling an arm around my sister.

"Crap, as usual. I hate it there so much. I can't wait to graduate, but now Dad won't let me apply for art school. Can you believe this shit?"

"Yeah," I answer drily.

He cares more about propriety than anything else. Why do you think he paid a fortune to hush up Hudson's arrest and pack him off to a place like Blackwood? Just so the embarrassment would fly undetected under the radar, without ruining his latest political campaign. To this day, our extended family thinks I'm studying abroad to explain my constant absence.

"How is he?" Cece asks.

She anxiously picks at her pale-pink dress. I can't tell her the truth—that Hudson's a wreck, barely scraping by, making zero progress and on track to be refused release. He's got a record longer than my arm and more incident reports than most prisoners. Right now, he's spending the rest of his weekend rotting in a solitary cell for getting into a fight.

"You know Hudson, he's never far away from trouble."

"But you're looking after him, right?" she prods, chewing her lip. "Just like you said you would?"

I clear my throat, forcing a smile on my face. "Of course. I promised, didn't I? I'll bring him home, Cece. We're halfway done."

"I can't wait until you're both back. These stupid family dinners aren't the same without you guys causing trouble."

I give her a squeeze, trying to convey the comfort that I can't manage to vocalise. There are so many empty promises that they threaten to drown me at every turn.

Will I ever come back here, to the life I so desperately want to escape? Even if I do, will Hudson be with me?

"Miss you too, kid. We'll be back before you know it," I lie.

"I'm not a kid anymore, Kade. Haven't been for a while."

I ruffle her hair, even as she curses under her breath. "You'll always be a kid to me," I reply with a smile.

Someone shouts our names from far off. We share a grim look before rising and walking back to the house. Mum stands in the door with her hands on her hips, looking suitably unimpressed. I get a whack around the head with a dish towel for my absence.

"What are you two doing out here?" she berates with a frown. "It's your father's birthday, the least you can do is join in. Is that smoke I smell? Bloody kids… if I find out—"

"Mum," I interrupt. "We were just catching up, okay? Calm down. Everything's going fine. You're worrying again."

Her smile is tight. "You know what your father is like about things being perfect when family comes over."

"Yeah, I know."

"Get back in there and spend some time with your cousins. I'll be serving dessert soon." She gestures for Cece to go, laying a hand on my arm to stop me before I can escape. "Not you. We need to have a chat."

Great. The universal words of guaranteed doom.

"Sure. Lead the way." I sigh.

She guides me through the grand reception area, past rows of priceless artwork and delicate vases. Raucous laughter and the clinking of glasses rings out from the formal dining area as we pass, but Mum keeps silent until we reach my father's study.

I hate this room. Flames are glowing in the open fireplace, and the huge mahogany desk is piled with neatly stacked paperwork. I sink into one of the high-backed armchairs and prepare for what I'm sure is bad news.

"How's Blackwood? Keeping up with your studies?"

Avoiding her eyes, I search for some enthusiasm. "Yeah, I guess. It's not exactly paradise, but we make do. You know how Hudson can be."

Her fingers dance across her throat as she sighs in relief. "Good, good."

"Mum?"

"Yes, dear?" she says absently.

"What is it? What's wrong?"

With a trembling hand, she wipes at her teary eyes. "I'm sorry to do this on your weekend at home, but I couldn't tell you over the phone. It's about Hudson."

"What about him?"

"There's been a new legal motion filed against him. They're pushing for a retrial in the new year to get a conviction this time."

A heavy weight settles in the pit of my stomach, and I swallow hard. "For… a conviction? I thought he was off the hook. It was self-defence. The judge agreed to three years at Blackwood, and he walks free. That's the deal we made."

Mum shakes her head, fingers worrying the hem of her dress. "That was the initial ruling to avoid him spending the next year rotting in a cell while he awaited trial."

"I know this. What's changed?"

"Now a witness has come forward with new evidence against him. They can't justify not proceeding with a prison sentence anymore. Things are a little complex, but we have a plan…"

Mum rambles on, throwing out names of fancy law firms and extravagant sums of money, but all I can hear is my heartbeat rushing in my ears.

It's like the ground has collapsed beneath me and I'm tumbling in a free fall. Eighteen months of my life, all sacrificed in the name of getting Hudson back on his feet and bringing him home.

Was it all for fucking nothing?

I can't lose him. Not like this.

"Who's the witness?" I interrupt her stream of words.

"Look, Kade. I don't think—"

"Tell me who it is!"

"I didn't mean to upset you…"

I grab her hand, squeezing it tight as tears fill my own eyes. We're both verging on a breakdown, faced with the prospect of Hudson's permanent removal from our lives. Say what you will about my shallow parents, but you can't fault Mum's dedication to my adoptive brother. She loves the bones of that asshole and has done so for the last five years since he joined our family.

Even when he broke her heart.

"Please. Who is it? I won't tell him," I reason.

She nods decisively. "Give me one."

"Huh?"

"Don't play dumb with me, boy. I'm your mother, for Christ's sake. I cleaned your bedroom as a teenager enough times to know what you were up to in there. Now, give me a cigarette before I lose my mind."

I reluctantly hand the pack over and light one for her. She leans back, breathing in a lungful and seeming to relax slightly.

"Your father would kill me if he saw this."

I shrug, watching her carefully. "I won't tell if you won't."

We sit in silence for a moment as she enjoys her cigarette. Meanwhile, I'm losing my mind, desperately trying to understand what could be gained from sending Hudson down for a crime that wasn't his fault.

The judge agreed that Blackwood was the best solution. Hudson wasn't in his right mind, and he still isn't. He doesn't need punishment, he needs help. Who could have possibly come forward after all this time?

"I need to know," I say, breaking Mum's little spell.

Her momentary relief soon fades as her face falls. "There was one person missing from the police interviews, Kade. One person that didn't talk and fill in the gaps."

"I don't understand… I thought there weren't any witnesses. Hudson was the only one there."

"That's… not exactly true." Mums hesitates, her cheeks colouring with embarrassment. "We went with that story to make things better for Hudson."

"You did *what*?" I exclaim.

"The lawyers figured out the whole thing. They made it sound like our only option if Hudson wanted to avoid life imprisonment. Who can prosecute when there's no one to testify as to what happened but a dead person?"

I pinch the bridge of my nose, battling with my temper. "So, someone was there that night? Someone saw what Hudson did... to him?"

"That's why he got off lightly." Mum nods in confirmation. "His voice was the only one that was heard. The witness acted like the whole thing was a bad dream, and we used that to our advantage."

Fuck. I feel sick.

"We pretended like she wasn't even there that night. The woman was drugged to high heaven, so it didn't take much convincing. But now... his account is being challenged."

The penny drops. It's an ugly realisation as I cast my mind back, recalling the weeks of anxiety as they analysed crime scene data and took accounts from Hudson, us, his friends and fellow college students.

They were piecing together the mind of a man broken by childhood circumstances, enough that he felt the need to sneak off from his ideal life with us back to a crackpot mother who abandoned him for drugs instead.

He wanted to save her, but he destroyed his life instead.

"It's his mother, Stephanie," I say distastefully.

Mum nods. "Yes."

Stephanie was there that night. All this time, I've been fed a big fat lie. They said that Hudson snuck home and she was gone, leaving her abuser behind, who didn't take too kindly to Hudson's return. It was self-defence, or so I thought. That was the story I was fed. Or more accurately... *the lie.*

"She saw the whole thing, Kade. He killed her boyfriend in front of her. She just refused to acknowledge it until now."

The image of Hudson's drug-addled mother swims in my mind. I've only ever seen pictures, the little snippets that I could glean from my traumatised brother who refused to acknowledge the childhood abuse that warped his mind.

"And now?" I press, knowing the worst is yet to come.

"Stephanie wants to testify against her own son. She's threatening to bring the entire thing down on us. What really happened that night... she's going to expose it all."

All I can do is stare into Mum's pain-filled eyes. The weight of responsibility is on my shoulders, slowly crushing me to the ground. All this time, I was fighting to protect Hudson from himself.

I couldn't see that the real threat was waiting in the wings, embroiled in lies and ready to strike at the opportune moment. Hudson killed for her, a truly pathetic excuse for a parent.

And now she's going to bury him for it.

CHAPTER 25
BROOKLYN

DARK SIGNS - SLEEP TOKEN

I STAND in the long queue outside the nurse's station, waiting to pick up my meds. All around me, countless zombie patients sway and stumble, lining up for their next dose of sedatives to get them through the day.

I'm just as bad. My hands are shaking, and my body is sweaty.

"Elijah Woods!" the nurse calls from her hatch.

I quickly look up, finding Eli in the crowd. He skulks forwards and accepts the little paper cup of pills, swiftly knocking them back before sticking his tongue out for inspection.

"Clear. Move along."

Eli tosses the cup away as he leaves, heading straight for the cafeteria. I watch every step he takes, his leg muscles pronounced through his tight jeans, strengthened from running.

The guys flash through my mind again—the way they played my body like a fine-tuned instrument as I was sandwiched between them over the weekend.

"Brooklyn West!"

Forcibly dragging myself out of the daydream, I retrieve my meds from the grey-faced nurse and swallow the numerous, brightly coloured pills. Choking them down without gagging is near impossible, but I've had a lot of practice over time.

"Tongue," she demands.

Her eyebrow is raised in challenge. Opening my mouth and sticking my tongue out as requested, I'm soon dismissed with a curt nod.

"Good. You're expected in Professor Lazlo's office at ten o'clock for your shot."

My stomach drops as dread fills me. Shuffling away from the queue, I fight to keep my breathing steady. Every inch of my body quakes involuntarily, despite my best efforts to remain calm. Why am I so afraid of him?

Voices blur around me as I stand stock-still, lost in my head. I tell myself that it's just the others talking, but fear creeps down my spine nonetheless.

No matter how many pills I swallow, the shadows and voices won't leave me alone. They refuse to return to that little box in my mind and instead sneak back in when I least expect it.

A hand latches around my wrist. I look up, finding Rio sneering at me. I step backwards, attempting to put distance between us that he swiftly ignores.

"Your boyfriend put on quite the show the other day. I do hope he's enjoying his stay in the hole. Send him my regards, won't you?"

"Screw you." I fight to escape his restraint.

"Not quite. He interrupted, remember? So rude and inconsiderate. Anyway, I don't deliver without full payment, Brooklyn. You owe me. We had a deal."

"I don't owe you shit. You tore up the list days ago. We're through."

Rio's hand seems to tighten, his nails digging deep into my flesh. "We're not through until I say so. Didn't I tell you how things work around here? I don't tolerate disrespect. Pay up or there'll be trouble."

"Pay for what exactly? You're a fucking lunatic. I don't see what I asked for."

I shove Rio's shoulder as he stumbles back, his eyes hardening.

"You need to learn your place already. Nobody fucking breathes in this place without my permission. You hear me, bitch? Piss me off and you won't live to see your precious Hudson again."

He glances around, giving a subtle nod to the nearby guard watching our exchange. I barely catch the knowing look shared between them before Rio shoves me against the wall.

Something cold and hard presses into my ribcage. The slice of pain tells me exactly what it is as Rio draws the shank across my skin.

"Like it?"

"Cute. Never took you for a prison thug," I hiss under my breath. "Just how many guards have you paid off with daddy's credit card? Or do you blow them in the store cupboard?"

He leans dangerously close. "Your smart mouth ain't doing you any favours. Here's the deal. I've got some blow for you, but my price has just gone up. Call it interest for messing around. Take it or leave it."

I'm so tempted to tell him to stick it up his ass, but my desperation is stronger. It soon dissolves any sense of self-worth that I have left.

"I'll take it. What about the rest?"

Please, I want to beg.

"This is it for now," Rio confirms, still grinning like a lunatic. "Make it worth my time, then I'll think about the rest."

His blade disappears, and the cocky asshole dances backwards like he owns the place, utterly unconcerned. No one says a damn word about the altercation.

His buddy on duty is literally looking in the other direction, acting like he's oblivious to what transpired.

"Meet me on the roof tonight at eight. Don't be late."

"The roof?" I repeat in confusion.

Rio winks, giving me a flash of the blade slipping into his pocket. I simply nod my agreement and turn away, swallowing the lump in my throat. I can't face the guys for breakfast now.

Not after agreeing to that.

It wouldn't be right.

Instead, I sneak back outside into the cold air, finding a bench to collapse on. My trembling hands reach into my coat pocket, quickly realising that I have no smokes left to occupy myself with.

I want to scream.

Pull my hair, slice my wrists and fucking shatter into a million pieces. Have you ever felt like a stranger in your own life? People talk to you, call your name... but none of it feels real. You're trapped behind glass watching your life simply pass by, one disaster at a time.

I sit there in the freezing autumn air until the bell rings and patients flood out from their first classes, indicating that it's nearly ten o'clock. Hell awaits me.

Managing to dodge through the crowds to make it back inside, I check in at the reception desk that marks the entrance to the treatment wing.

"Brooklyn, here for Lazlo." I flash my ID badge.

Bundled past the therapy rooms, I pass Mariam's door with a wistful sigh. Never thought I'd miss that over-enthusiastic bitch, but here we are.

The silent guard guides me through several locked doors until we reach a wide staircase leading downstairs. In my drug-addled state last time, I didn't notice the sign.

Level Two - Therapy rooms 20-35

Level One - Solitary confinement

Basement - Z Wing

Down the stairs to level one, I'm escorted past endless doors—a familiar sight from my last trip to the hole. Muffled crying and voices fill the air, whispering ghosts telling tales of insanity from behind locked doors. I struggle to repress the shiver wracking my body.

We pass an open door leading into one of the solitary rooms, and I sneak a glance that has my blood freezing in my veins. A pair of shrinks wrapped in their pristine white coats battle with a long-haired male patient.

One secures him in restraints while the other clinician brandishes a deadly looking needle. I hastily look away as they successfully get the screaming man sedated. The sight brings up far too many bad memories, both past and present.

Hurrying the rest of the way down the endless corridor, we descend into the basement. There's a final layer of security before we reach the Z Wing.

Lazlo's office awaits at the very end of the corridor. Stiflingly hot and cast in suffocating shadows, it beckons me back into the darkness as Lazlo opens his door on the guard's first knock.

"Good morning, Brooklyn. Come in, quickly now. We have lots to get on with."

I sit in the chair facing him, my arms wrapped around my jittery body. Lazlo takes a seat behind his cramped desk, studying me for a moment. It sets my teeth on edge.

When he goes to the mini fridge to retrieve my shot, I have to swallow the protests bubbling in my throat.

"Here we go, another dose. How are you adjusting?"

Let's see.

I can't fucking sleep. My mind feels alien. My skin itches, and I feel like a stranger in my own body. The trembles kill me, and delusions plague my every waking moment. Voices taunt me, shadows chase me and I'm losing my mind more and more each day.

I offer a simple nod. "Fine."

"Good. No more voices?"

Mutely shaking my head, I turn and study his bookshelves. I'll do anything to avoid his penetrative stare that threatens to uncover my darkest secrets. I can't give him any more ammo to use against me. I'll be tossed into a padded cell for the rest of my miserable existence.

"Well then, that's good news." Lazlo beams. "Now, just a little prick. It'll be over before you know it."

He slips the needle into my neck, and I flinch.

"What's this?" Lazlo runs a finger over my tender forehead, where I know a dark bruise is forming. "Have you been banging your head against the wall? Tut tut."

"No," I struggle out, swallowing hard.

Fucking idiot, Brooke. Too obvious.

"I've worked in psychiatry for forty years, Brooklyn. I know a self-harmer when I see one. Were you lying about the voices? Or is it the intrusive thoughts this time?"

I pick at my jeans, still avoiding his gaze. Fuck him. Fuck this room. Fuck Blackwood.

Lazlo chortles under his breath. "Okay, we can discuss this later. We hardly know each other, after all."

Relief rushes through me.

"Now that I'm your therapist, I've been familiarising myself with your case. We will be spending a lot of time together over the next three years."

He peers at me again, almost like he's expecting something. I remain silent, unprepared for his next words.

"Tell me about Victor Brunel."

"Hell no," I blurt automatically.

"Excuse me?"

I meet his curious eyes. "I said no."

Placing my thick file down, Lazlo sighs and folds his ugly spectacles. I can feel the lecture coming from a mile off as he plasters his best shit-talking-therapist smile on, ready to spew some patronising bullshit.

"Brooklyn, we both know why you're here. I've read your notes from Clearview and the various assessments conducted there. I am familiar with the details of your case."

"So what?"

"Schizophrenia is a weighty label in itself, let alone any others. Your destructive personality is something we can work on together."

I stand abruptly. "Can I leave?"

"No. Sit down."

Ignoring him completely, I begin to pace the darkened office. As I wring my hands, Lazlo watches intently and takes subtle notes that he thinks I can't see. I don't give a fuck if I look crazy. My spiralling thoughts take over everything and I need to *move*.

"Tell me what you are feeling right now," Lazlo suggests.

"Get out of my head."

"It's my job to be in your head," he replies curtly. "Come on, what's the worst that could happen?"

He could lock me up for the rest of my life, preventing me from ending my pathetic existence. He'll force me to live beyond the looming anniversary, and my mind simply won't cope.

It'll implode. The memories will be too much to handle, and I'm fucking terrified of what my mind does when it's had enough.

"I'm... pissed off," I admit reluctantly.

Lazlo crosses his legs, getting comfortable. "Why is that?"

"I don't like being analysed."

"Are you afraid of what I might find?"

Fucking smug wanker. Of course, I'm afraid of that.

"No," I lie easily, but it doesn't quite ring true.

Lazlo taps his pen. "It is our natural instinct to protect what we are ashamed of. But in this space, we are nothing more than therapist and patient. You don't need to be embarrassed."

I throw my arms up in annoyance. "I'm not fucking embarrassed!"

"Then tell me what's got you strung so tight right now."

I give up and sink to the carpeted floor, crossing my legs. I refuse to return to the stupid seat where he can study me like a damn specimen.

"The labels," I mutter.

Understanding dawns as Lazlo clicks his fountain pen, scribbling something else down. I resist the urge to march over there and snatch the notebook away or shove it so far up his ass he'll spit paper.

"Schizophrenia?"

A thick lump forms in my throat that is impossible to swallow. Ancient memories tickle my mind, and I don't have the strength to keep them at bay in the face of his scrutiny. It was a long time ago when the family sickness first reared its ugly head.

The car veers off to the side as my parents scream at each other. Mum battles an invisible enemy that none of us can see. She talks to it all the time.

We sail straight into a tree, twisted metal and smoke filling the space. Airbags burn my skin, and sizzling flames drown out Dad's dying cries. Broken ribs cut off all air as I battle against the seatbelt. Blood is slick beneath my fingers, my own and theirs mingling.

"Brooklyn? You with me?" Lazlo prompts.

I clear my throat, vision filled with smoke. "Yeah."

Blinking rapidly, I try to force the images away. Reality and imagination blur as their cries echo through my mind, mixing with the ever-present shadows that always appear to torture me further. I can almost feel them both watching me now.

Lazlo gives me a moment, watching my expression closely.

"I want to talk a little about your diagnoses. You've been aware of these issues for some time, I believe." He searches his papers again. "I can see that you had several psych evaluations growing up, and a stint in an inpatient unit then too."

Yeah, when the stupid foster carer stumbled in and cut me down from a noose. Interfering bitch.

"When did the voices start?" he asks conversationally, like he isn't prying into the deepest pits of my mind and shining a light where it isn't wanted.

"On and off for several years. Worse as I got older," I reply, hoping to appease him and prevent further questioning.

I deliberately don't mention the shadows that follow me around. Voices are crazy enough without adding horrifying hallucinations into the melting pot of madness.

"The drugs made your affliction worse, I presume?"

I shoot him a frustrated glare. "Don't bring the drugs into it."

Lazlo disregards my words, lacing his wrinkled hands together. "The relationship between drug use and psychosis is well documented. Narcotics are proven to increase paranoia, hallucinations and erratic emotions. In fact, I participated in a study which…"

"No," I interject firmly. "I said don't blame the drugs. We both know where it came from."

"Your illness?" he clarifies, catching on. "I see. Well, there is a genetic component to schizophrenia, a familial pattern that is also well established. Although a myriad of factors also impact…"

I abruptly stand again, my body coiled tight with tension. "I'm done talking about this."

"We still have an hour, Brooklyn."

"Please, not now," I beg, revealingly honest for once.

"I'm afraid it isn't up to you." Darkness invades his expression, twisting it into something terrifying. "I have a job to do. You will cooperate and tell me what I want to know."

"I'll tell you nothing. Bite me."

"It doesn't work like that, I'm afraid. Would you like to return to solitary confinement? Perhaps it will prove beneficial."

"You can't threaten me!"

"Can't I?" Lazlo deadpans.

With a chill running down my spine, I begin edging towards the door. Something inside me is screaming that this man isn't a normal doctor. My survival instincts are telling me to run from this reptile before he takes away the little freedom I have left.

"Brooklyn!" Lazlo shouts after me.

I ignore him completely and stride out of the office, passing a startled guard who's waiting outside. While he's exchanging furious whispers with Lazlo, I practically run from the building.

Every step mirrors the heavy beat of my heart. As I emerge into the reception area upstairs, I make a frantic dash for the exit. I can hear the guard following behind me, but I move too fast for him to catch up.

Breaking out into the fresh air, I stumble and end up falling to my knees in the quad. Hard gravel rips my black jeans and slices my leg. Hot pain races through my system from the deep scratch, but I don't react.

Sucking in air takes all of my attention. A full breakdown is threatening to take over. Lazlo's threats have left me shaken.

"Brooklyn?"

A warm hand lands on my shoulder, brushing my long hair aside. I note his familiar scent—fresh mint, cigarettes and coffee meeting my nose.

Kade is crouched down, peering at me with concerned hazel eyes behind his black glasses. "Hey there, love. What's up?"

I push his hand away, fighting to compose myself. "What do you want?"

"Woah, easy. Just making sure you're okay."

My head falls as I shove my emotions down, picturing the little box in my mind that all my monsters and demons barely fit into. It's bursting at the seams.

One day, it'll erupt spectacularly. I offer Kade a weak smile that doesn't feel particularly genuine.

"Sorry. Bad timing."

"Clearly. You alright? Need a hand up?"

He helps me to my feet, wrapping an arm around my shoulders. For a brief, glorious second, I relax into his slim body. I want to bury into the warmth and comfort that he offers without judgement, even if I've spent weeks running away from doing exactly that.

"Want to talk?" he murmurs.

I can feel his nose buried in my hair.

"Nope."

Pulling back, Kade stares down at me. In typical protective fashion, he's silently searching for my secrets. But for once, he doesn't pry or push me any further. Forcing a smile, he takes a step back, giving me some much-needed space.

"Okay. I'll leave you be. You know where I am."

"Thanks."

As I turn to race away from him, Kade calls my name again. "I almost forgot, I got you something. Don't tell the guys, though, because I didn't bring souvenirs from home for everyone."

After a quick glance around to check that the coast is clear, he subtly presses a brand-new pack of cigarettes into my hand.

"For me?" I ask with a frown.

Kade's cheeks flush pink. "Yeah. Come and find me later if you want some company. No pressure."

With that confusing offer extended, he quickly strides away. I'm left taken aback as the bitter clutch of despair around my heart loosens. Something else takes its place.

Warm, unfamiliar, fuzzy.

Something akin to gratitude.

CHAPTER 26
ELI

BEAUTIFUL WAY - YOU ME AT SIX

STANDING in the shade of a huge oak tree, I let the raindrops lash against my face. It's ice cold, the moisture burning my skin as the wind howls around me. The cigarette between my fingers fizzles out.

Without a care, I toss it aside. For once, there's a single taste in my mind. Untainted by the usual chaos. Rain tastes like regret. Bitter, acrid and sharp, like battery acid or the smoke from a raging house fire.

"I'm fucking cold. Coming in?" Phoenix shudders.

He only waits for a second when I fail to respond, taking my silence as agreement rather than actually communicating with me. It isn't his fault. I'd give up trying to talk to me too.

Phoenix tosses his cigarette aside and jogs back into the dorms, leaving me and the rain to continue our unspoken conversation.

After another futile speech-therapy session, I'm coiled tighter than a spring and ready to explode. It always brings up far too many memories that I fight every day to suppress.

Rio and his goons sprint past in a hurry, sparing me from their cruel taunts for once as they fight to escape the rain. I must look insane, drenched and staring up into the fathomless clouds.

It's not as though the opinions of inferior people matter to me anyway. I don't need them to understand. No one ever will.

Much later, I trail back inside, calmed by the ferocious storm that has me shivering. Violent thunder and lightning rattles priceless pieces of artwork trapped in golden picture frames. I skulk up the stairs, intent on a hot shower with my penknife. A quick glance at the clock tells me it's half past eight.

"Hey, Eli! Are you coming for a round of poker?"

Kade and Phoenix are walking down the staircase to meet me halfway. They're dressed casually in dark sweats and t-shirts, both settled in for a long, stormy evening. I shake my head, itching to escape and sort myself out.

"Are you sure, man?" Kade double-checks. "We'll be in the recreation room if you change your mind."

Leaving them to their game, I take the stairs two at a time. When I reach the fourth level, something catches my eye and halts my hurried steps. Brooklyn is descending from upstairs to her floor. With her face crumpled and tear-streaked cheeks, she looks devastated.

Who the hell upset her?

I'll kill them myself.

She freezes, and her eyes are shifty and filled with guilt. "Eli?"

I don't move. Seeing her looking so broken is almost too much for me to handle after an endlessly shitty day. I let her come closer to me, her chin tucked down and shaking hands wrapped around her midsection.

"What are you doing here?"

I dart my eyes up to the above floor where my room is.

"Oh. Well, I'll see you later."

Brooklyn tries to pass me, but I suddenly brace my hand on the bannister. As I block the way past, she visibly swallows, her gaze on her feet.

"Eli... please. I need to be alone right now."

She's absolutely soaked through, just like me. Was she up on the roof in the middle of a storm? How did she even get through the exterior door? The only person I've ever seen sneak up there is Rio and his thugs since they have the means to bypass security.

Risking a tentative step towards her, I let my fingers trail over the dripping sleeves of my hoodie. She's still wearing it then; I haven't seen her take it off yet. That thrills me a little too much.

"Please go," she whimpers.

I'm drawn in further. Her sad expression is calling out to me on a fundamental level. I cup her pale, tear-stained cheek and run my thumb over her bottom lip, slowly making my way up to the bruise across her forehead.

When I touch the tender spot, a hissed breath escapes her mouth. My beautiful, broken girl. We're far more alike than Brooklyn will ever know.

If only she remembered me, and if only I'd had the courage to approach her in Clearview. Tangling our fingers together, I decide to take action.

I can't stand the gaping hole in my chest that being in her presence creates. She leaves me feeling hollow, gutted by need and desire. I have to touch her. Taste her. Be seen by her, *heard* by her in any way possible. Even if I can't speak.

"Eli, don't."

I ignore her and run my fingers through her wet hair. Droplets of water cling to her dark lashes and trail over her translucent skin. It's like there's an invisible thread between us, tugging on my heart and silencing the demons in my mind.

All I can taste is my own desire. It's thick, heady and overwhelmingly concentrated. I tug her along, straight towards her door, and Brooklyn reluctantly surrenders her key card.

Soon, we're toppling inside. That's where my patience fails. I shove her against the wall, my knee spreading her legs apart as my mouth attacks hers, but she doesn't kiss me back at first.

"Eli, no. I can't. You don't know—"

I interrupt, letting my tongue tangle with hers and claiming her mouth. I can feel the clash of her teeth meeting mine. Her fingers bury in my soaked hair as I grind my body against her, struggling to hold a growl in.

Brooklyn suddenly shoves me backwards, sending me stumbling into her empty desk. Her silver-grey eyes blaze with indignation, and something else. Unintelligible. All consuming. Bleak.

It's regret, I think.

The rain has whispered to us both tonight.

"Why do you all insist on caring about me?" she snarls, barely above a whisper. "Can't you see that I'm worthless? I'm a fucking failure and a waste of air."

I try to advance, but she raises her hand in warning.

"No. I said no."

Words are clawing at my throat, so damn close but stuck behind an invisible barrier. Brooklyn shakes her head and disappears into the bathroom. She slams the door behind her, leaving me standing in her dark room.

Anger fills the silence and matches the brewing storm in my mind. I can hear the shower click on. I shouldn't go in there, because her refusal was clear.

The door to leave her room is right there. A better man would walk through it and never return, just like she wants. But fuck that. I never claimed to be a good person.

I slip into the steam-filled room against my better judgement. Brooklyn stands under the spray of hot water with her hands braced against the tiled wall as sobs wrack her body.

Standing there staring, I'm enraptured by her pain. She turns and looks at me through the glass, somehow unsurprised that I followed her.

"Fuck off, Eli," she croaks.

I shake my head.

"Leave me alone! I don't want you here."

I shake my head again.

"Why won't you talk to me? Just say it! Say that you're disgusted by me." Brooklyn sucks in a breath, her rage rapidly spiralling. "Say that you hate me. Don't stand there looking all pitying and shit."

I take a tentative stride closer to the shower. Softly sliding the door open, I step into the warm spray, still fully clothed. Her back hits the wall as I crowd the small space, her bare breasts brushing against my soaked t-shirt.

"You don't fucking give up, do you?"

This time, I answer her with a kiss. Brushing my lips against hers, it feels like with one wrong move, she'll break. I want her to break. Fall apart in my arms. Cling to me like a lifeboat.

Nobody has ever needed me before.

What would it feel like to be wanted?

Brooklyn grabs a handful of my dark hair, her lips firm against mine. Our tongues tangle as my hands roam her body, gliding across scarred skin to cup her butt.

She's kissing me like I'm the air she breathes, and I've never felt so fucking alive.

"Off," she orders.

All signs of resistance are gone as she tugs on my wet t-shirt. I freeze, my body flush with ice-cold dread. I can't let her see what's hidden underneath the fabric. She can never know how damaged I really am.

Backing away, I try to escape the shower as she pursues me, no longer running or afraid. I'm the prey, and she's here to devour me whole.

"I said *off.*"

My hand scrabbles with the handle, desperate to escape.

"I thought you wanted this?"

We've fucked before, but she's never seen the real me. Not fully. There's no turning back from that. All I can do is stare into her hooded eyes, hoping she can sense the fear in me.

Brooklyn's bruised forehead meets mine. Nose to nose, we inhale each other in a moment that feels infinite.

"You don't need to be afraid, Eli. Not from me. Please, trust me."

Hands grasping the hem of my t-shirt, she drags it up inch by inch. I'm on a precipice and about to plummet to my demise as she gently strips me.

Her gaze eats up my twisted flesh, which is more scar tissue than actual skin. I don't need to look to know it snakes all the way around my torso, across my shoulders and dips into the waistband of my jeans.

Understanding flickers across her face.

"Fire?" she murmurs.

I swallow. Try to breathe. Lick my lips. Nod my head.

You're a sinner, Elijah.

This is what sinners deserve.

Fire cleanses everything.

The smoke in my nose is too real, infecting my senses and blocking out reality. It isn't until she peels off my soaked jeans and frees my dick that I come back slightly.

Brooklyn spares me a knowing glance as she falls to her knees in the shower, her mouth secured to my hard length. She invades my mind with sensations that refuse to be ignored.

The mental fire recedes as I focus on the feel of her perfect mouth around my cock. I brace my arms against the wall when I hit the back of her throat. My breath hisses from between my teeth.

Fuck, it feels incredible.

When I'm on the verge of finishing down her pretty throat, I yank her up and pin her against the wall. On instinct, her legs easily wrap around my narrow waist.

Brooklyn's breathing hard, and her lips are shining. My fingers glide down her stomach, finding her throbbing clit. She's so fucking wet. Her cunt is a dripping furnace, begging to be touched.

"Eli…"

Silencing her mewling, I position myself and push inside her pussy in one slick move. I can't hold out any longer. Our hips slam together, ensconced in a bubble of frenetic need. Her walls are so tight as they clench around my cock. It's a snug fit. Goddammit, she's too perfect for me to express.

Beginning to move, I pound into her without any care for lasting long. I want to consume her. Devour her soul and keep it locked behind my ribcage where it can't escape.

Her nails bite into my back as she kisses me again. Roughly. Savagely. With her tongue invading my mouth, I pummel her cunt into oblivion.

When she breaks away for air, I duck my head to suck on her hardened left nipple. My teeth pull at her bud, biting and sucking her perfect tit hard enough to leave a bright-purple mark before gradually moving up to her neck.

I want to see my bruises all over her fucking body. I want to hurt her, see her pain and own her in the most twisted way possible.

Our movements grow more frenzied as we both chase an elusive high. We groan and cling to one another while the pressure keeps building until we're both ready to shatter into broken shards.

Brooklyn falls apart first, screaming out my name. Her pussy clenches around me, and I'm spilling into her seconds later.

"Fuck, Eli," she pants.

Even if I could speak, I doubt I could form words after that. Part of me wanted to savour this moment, but the minute I felt her tight walls hugging my cock, I was done for.

We breathe heavily as the scorching water continues to cascade around us. Grabbing a bottle of shower gel, I quickly wash up and rinse off before exiting the shower to escape her scrutiny.

My fucked-up body is still fully on display. Drying off, I hand her the towel next before panicking. My clothes are in a drenched heap on the floor.

Brooklyn grabs my hand. "Stay?"

With her chapped lip caught between her teeth, she looks impossibly young. Her platinum hair is wet and scraggly, and her eyes are lined with circles, holding more grief than anyone ever should.

I follow her into the bedroom like a dying man chasing a mirage. She climbs into the bed still completely naked, beckoning me to join her with a crooked finger.

"I'm not, ah…" Brooklyn gulps, running a hand over her face. "Not very good at this. The sticking-around-after thing. But with you"—her eyes flick back up to mine—"I want to be."

My feet carry me forwards and I climb into bed with her. Our bodies entwine, skin damp and breath mingling. My fingers bury in her wet blonde strands as her hand runs over my lower stomach, teasing the sensitive patches of burned scar tissue there.

I've never let anyone do that before.

Not even Phoenix.

"I wish you could talk to me," she blurts.

The sound of crashing thunder fills the room as light flashes behind the drawn curtains. Brooklyn clings to me even harder, her leg hanging over mine and scar-laden arms wrapping around my bare chest. I don't know where I end and she begins.

Brooklyn sighs. "Tell me something. Please."

Fucking Christ, I want to. More than ever before in my life, I wish I could say something. *Anything*. But I can't get a fucking word out, not even when her lips graze along my jaw.

"You really can't, can you? Not a word?"

My head hits the pillows in aggravation. Brooklyn stares for a second longer before disentangling herself from me. Leaving the bed to rustle in her coat pocket, she returns with a pack of cigarettes, popping the window open through the safety bars to light up.

Stupid fucking words.

I don't need them.

Not with her.

If she wants to know about my pain, I'll fucking hurt her myself, spilling her blood and claiming her heathen soul. Then she'll understand. Roughly grabbing her arm, I pull her back towards the bed before flipping her onto her back.

"What are you up to?" she breathes.

I'll tell you something, baby girl.

If that's what you want.

Brooklyn's luscious, trembling legs slide open. I settle between them, staring down at her with determination while cold air floods the room as the rainstorm rages.

I kiss my way down her soft thighs, my tongue flicking across her clit and causing her back to arch. She's already soaked for me again, betraying her anticipation.

"Fuck... Eli. Don't stop."

Tasting her sweet little pussy, I slide a finger in while rubbing her clit with my thumb. She's soaked again, her legs quivering at my mere touch.

Once she's mewling and ready to burst, my mouth leaves her cunt. I raise my head, slowly licking my wet lips. This girl. We're cut from the same fucking cloth.

I leave her shivering, searching for something to use to inflict my will. My eyes land on her battered Chucks next to the bed. I quickly steal the laces while she watches me intently. Back in bed, I grab Brooklyn's thin wrists, looping the laces around to tie her hands tightly together.

No escaping now.

Running away isn't allowed.

I snatch the still-lit cigarette from between her fingers and shift into position so that my cock nudges against her drenched folds. She groans as I tease her slick opening, taking the opportunity to lower the cigarette to her forearm.

"Oh fuck..."

She hisses as I burn her without mercy.

"Goddammit. Don't you dare fucking stop."

I slip fully inside of her, filling her tight pussy up as I burn her arm again. This time I do it for longer, watching her skin melt and form beautiful red welts.

Her walls clench around my dick and she moans, biting her lip again in a way that drives me crazy.

"P-Please... Eli. More."

Her legs wrap around my waist to pull me closer, causing my strokes to deepen. Her rounded tits bounce with each thrust, and I tug her wrists above her head, exposing more vulnerable skin for me to scar.

Burning her again, I'm enthralled by the bloody wounds that mark my path across her skin. Brooklyn hisses in pain and moves her hips, stealing more twisted pleasure from me.

I drop the cigarette into a plastic cup of water on her bedside table after I've inflicted several more burn wounds. Hurting her has only wound me up more. I want to do it again.

I want to cut her.

Make her bleed.

Make her cry.

We're both completely fucked up, and that's how I know she'd take it. Brooklyn grabs my hair with her restrained hands, manoeuvring my body into place.

She ends up on top, straddling my cock like the fucking queen she is. I grab her hips as she begins to move, riding me hard and pulling my curls tight enough to sting.

"You drive me insane," she groans.

We fuck frantically in the dark, our panting accompanied by the patter of heavy rain and the odd flash of lightning. As I'm ready to spill my load for a second time, I grab her by the throat.

I own her right now. Her breath. Her mind. Her pussy. It's all mine. My fucking property. Mine to destroy as I please.

Pulling her gorgeous face closer, my grip tightens, and her eyes grow wide. I squeeze tightly, my thumb teasing her skittering pulse point while she struggles for breath. The seconds crawl by as she slams her body down on mine.

I don't let her take another breath until everything explodes into spectacular pieces. Brooklyn slumps on top of me, sucking in deeply while our sweat mingles. Warmth seeps across my crotch when she eventually climbs off my lap.

"Don't worry, I've got an implant. We're good."

I hate the rapidly forming distance between us. I want to invade Brooklyn's every cell and possess her, until her whole world revolves around me alone.

Thoughts of restraining her fully and playing with my knife tickle my mind. Perhaps, I could fuck her senseless in a blood-slick mess while she screams my name. It makes my dick twitch already in excitement.

"Still got nothing to say to me?" Brooklyn smirks.

Pulling her back towards me, I wrap my arms around her sticky body. I can hear her roaring heartbeat as she burrows into my side, fitting perfectly against me, like we were made for each other in the deepest pits of hell.

"Maybe we don't need to talk," she adds, her leg rubbing mine. "That was good enough for me."

Settling into a comfortable position, she lets out a satisfied sigh. I don't intend to stay. The nights are the worst—when the dreams of being beaten with a Bible and of fire consuming my body sneak back in.

That's when I can't keep quiet any longer. The screams break free whether I like it or not. I don't want her to witness that.

As Brooklyn's breathing evens out and her hair tickles my chest, my eyes grow heavy. For the first time since I got my scars, I'm not afraid of someone seeing them.

CHAPTER 27
BROOKLYN

BLASPHEMY - BRING ME THE
HORIZON

I STARE at the selection of dreary breakfast foods. Fruit, cereal and toast. None of which looks remotely appealing. Even the coffee is fucking decaf, like caffeine is going to make us any crazier. A plate of eggs drops on to my tray, startling me.

"Stare all you want," Phoenix smarts, smiling broadly. "It ain't gonna get any better in the meantime."

He adds some more food to my plate. Grabbing my hand, I'm hauled onwards down the line. I let him pull me along with no energy to protest. The first couple of days after my shot are the worst. I feel so fucking numb, even his aggressive need to feed me doesn't matter.

Scanning both of our IDs to log the meal, he steers me through the busy cafeteria. I savour the feeling of his warm hand wrapped around my bicep. We take our seats at the usual table, which is deserted apart from Kade. Dressed in his usual crisp white shirt and trousers, his nose is buried in a scarily thick textbook.

Phoenix shuffles closer to me, pressing his lips to my ear. "Nice hickey you've got there, firecracker. Are there any more beneath that cute sweater of yours?"

I flush with embarrassment. "Is it any of your business?"

"It could be," he murmurs, his gaze full of heat. "I think I've earned myself some time alone with you, don't ya think?"

Snorting, I push the food around my plate. "Since when?"

Phoenix leans back, rolling his eyes at me. "That's how you want to play, huh?" His hand lands on my leg beneath the table, giving it a tight squeeze. "I know what you were up to last night with Eli. Must say that I'm a little disappointed at my lack of invite. Come find me tonight."

"Is that an order or an invitation?" I hum cheekily.

His hand skates higher, brushing between my thighs. "An order."

Kade drops his textbook with a curse, breaking the moment. Mopping up the spilled orange juice spreading across the table, he quickly realises that we've joined him and blushes.

"You been here long?"

Phoenix leans back, putting space between us again. "Nope, brainiac. What's so interesting in that book of yours?"

Kade shrugs, tossing the textbook aside. "Got an online exam tomorrow that I'm cramming for, that's all." His eyes flicker to me, his warm smile making me tingle inside. "How are you, Brooke?"

"Same old. Good luck with your exam."

"Thanks. I can't wait until it's over so I can relax again. Are you guys coming to the party this weekend? I've been planning it for months."

My eyebrow lifts. "A... party? Here?"

Kade shrugs, tucking his book away in his bag. "Halloween. It's this Saturday. When I say party, I mean crazy institute-friendly edition. Not exactly a wild rave, but it's the closest thing we get to fun around here."

I shudder at his mention of Halloween. It's yet another reminder that the clock is ticking down, and impending doom is growing closer with each day. Rio fucked me over with the order. I can't do anything with a single bag of blow. No blades, no pills. I'm getting desperate now.

Phoenix chuckles around a mouthful of toast, breaking my morbid thoughts. "Last year was zombie themed. Everyone fit in perfectly in this place." He gestures to the patients around us, and the varying degrees of alertness. "Especially the nutters."

"Hey," I interject with a frown. "You calling me a nutter?"

"Obviously. You're the queen of nutters, girl. Own it."

He waggles his eyebrows at me, his boyish face lit with humour beneath his mop of blue hair. I deliver a kick under the table that has him choking on a mouthful of breakfast. Kade laughs into his plastic cup while I grin smugly, surprising myself. My swinging emotions give me whiplash sometimes.

"Anyone seen Eli?" Kade asks once he's composed himself.

"He went back to his room to change," I blurt, before realising what I've said. All eyes firmly on me, I struggle to reign in my embarrassment. "I... think. I saw him going that way."

"Is that so?" Phoenix scoffs.

I shoot him a glare. "I don't know. Ask him yourself."

His eyes trail back down to my bruised neck, his lip curling up at the corner. "Oh, don't worry. I intend to."

We lapse into silence while eating until another tray hits the table. Whispers around us put me on high alert as I look up. My heart immediately leaps into my mouth. Hudson lowers himself down, giving his brother a small, terse nod of greeting.

Then his oceanic eyes are on me.

"Shit man, you're back!" Phoenix exclaims.

They exchange fist bumps as I stare into Hudson's weary eyes. The flawless blue colour is faded beneath the weight of exhaustion. His eyebrow piercing is crooked, and his rumpled black hair is impossibly messy, sticking up in all angles.

I struggle to swallow my anger. "Hi."

Taking a half-hearted bite of an apple, he nods. "Hey."

Kade's hazel eyes bounce between us as he watches the awkward encounter, before clearing his throat expectantly.

"It's good to have you back, bro."

Hudson doesn't respond, munching lifelessly on his apple. He's washed out, drained and extremely pale. Just like I was after a trip to the hole. Something about that place drains the fucking life out of you. There's nothing worse than being trapped with your own mind.

Kade forces a smile. "So, Halloween. We're all in?"

I toss my napkin down, giving him an unenthusiastic shrug. "I guess. Although I can't exactly get a costume together in this place."

"We'll sort it," Kade answers swiftly, holding a hand up when I begin to protest. "Seriously, don't worry. I've got you covered, love."

That warm feeling in my chest returns. I mentally berate myself for enjoying the thrill. *He's got me covered.* Why does that feel so damn good? How do I turn this feeling off?

Phoenix and Kade chatter away as I stare at my plate, entirely uncomfortable with the dark presence at our table. Hudson's gaze sears across my skin like Eli with his cigarette, but I continue to chew my lip and avoid his eyes. He went to the hole because of me. *Willingly.* Where does that leave us?

I can't forgive him.

I'll take my resentment to the grave.

Wrapped up in my thoughts, I don't hear the footsteps running up behind me until it's too late. Scolding hot liquid hits the back of my neck first, burning and running down my back. There's no suppressing the cry of shock and pain that slips out. I jump and trip over, landing flat on my ass.

A smirking, gaunt face grins down at me. "Oh gosh, I'm so sorry. Slipped on my shoelace," Britt exclaims, her hands flapping about dramatically as the room falls silent.

All three guys curse and jump into action. Britt stares down at me triumphantly, an empty plastic cup in hand and piping hot tea scolding my skin. The cafeteria's guards appear in an instant, swiftly yanking Britt far away from me.

"I'm sorry, it was an accident, I swear!"

They shove her against the wall, tightly restraining her arms. Phoenix sinks to his knees by my side as Britt makes exaggerated crying sounds, acting all fucking innocent but it's so obviously fake.

"It was an accident, I swear," she protests. "These floors can get so slippery! I would never hurt my friend here on purpose." Her bottom lip juts out and she bats her lashes.

Phoenix mutters a scathing insult and wraps an arm around my shoulders, gently lifting me up. His hand tracks over my soaked sweater and I hiss, angrily shoving him away from me.

"I'm fine, leave it."

"She attacked you, that is not fine." He turns to the two exasperated guards. "We all saw it, that was deliberate!"

"No! Me and Brooklyn are great friends," Britt defends. "It was just a little accident."

Her widened eyes turn to the deliberately silent asshole across the table. He's watching the incident with an empty expression.

"Hudson, tell them! Back me up!"

He stares at her blankly. "Why?"

Britt gapes at him, her eyes filling with tears. "What do you mean why? Because it's me!" Her voice turns shrill. "I slipped, okay? Accidents happen all the time!"

The minute she flashes me a look of hatred, I know just how false that sentiment is. I don't give a fuck what's going on between her and Hudson, it ain't got shit to do with me.

Rising to my feet and pushing Phoenix's hands away, I face the bemused guards. "It's fine, it was an accident." I shoot Britt a cold smile. "No problem, *friend*. I'm all good."

"What? Brooklyn, you can't be serious," Phoenix splutters.

I take my seat again. I'm utterly calm as the guards release Britt, moaning about incident reports and reluctantly backing off. As soon as their backs are turned, I spin in my seat and face her.

"Do you practise that wail all night? Your acting is shit."

"I'm sure I don't know what you mean," Britt replies sweetly.

As she turns to waltz away, my hand darts out and snatches her wrist. I glance at the retreating backs of the guards before roughly yanking her closer, getting up close and personal to ensure she hears my every word.

"I don't know what your game is but if you try that again, I'll make you regret the day your skinny ass landed in this hellhole. Got that, whore? Or should I demonstrate?"

Her lips part as she frowns at me, eyes lifting to look at Hudson again. "Stop slutting around with my boyfriend and you'll never have to look at me again. If anyone's a whore here… honey, it's you."

My fingers tighten around her bony wrist. I dig my ragged nails in, making her flinch. Satisfying droplets of blood begin to well up.

"That's what this is about? You are so far off the mark, you stupid cunt." I jerk my head at Hudson, who's watching the exchange with a frown. "He's all yours. Word of advice though?"

Britt swallows hard.

Meeting Hudson's eyes, I ensure he hears my next words. "Keep your eyes open, because he'll stab you in the back at the first chance he gets." I offer Britt a fake smile, loving the uncertain look on her face. "He'll break your fucking heart without batting an eye. Good luck."

I release her and pick up my tray, ignoring everyone's stunned silence as I stride away. Kade calls my name, but I ignore him. With my tray deposited, I'm out of the room. Daring to breathe again, my fists clench as I fight my rage.

That fucking idiotic bastard.

I march out into the freezing air of the quad. Turning and punching a wall with a shout, the skin across my knuckles breaks. It throbs in time to the fresh burns across my back.

I savour the pain. Public revenge isn't my style. I'll let Britt go running back to that asshole, and when the inevitable heartbreak comes, I'll dance on her fucking grave. That's what I call real revenge.

"Brooklyn?"

His broken voice calls out, rooting me to the spot. Indignation floods my body as I spin around, facing the man that stole my heart before crushing it into pathetic pieces. Hudson hangs in the doorway, a hand shakily running through his unruly hair.

"What?" I bark.

"Britt... she's just pissed off."

"Because you won't fuck her or because you stopped?"

Hudson looks away. "Stopped."

What a truly disgusting mental image that is.

"Tell your little hook-up that she has no need to be jealous and she can keep the tea to herself in future. I have zero fucking interest in you." I step closer, offering him a derisive sneer. "Frankly, if you died tomorrow, I would have a party in celebration."

Chilly wind whips between us. Hudson looks at me, his expression hardening. I knew the contrite act wouldn't last long.

"When did you become such a cold-hearted bitch?"

"Why don't you ask yourself that question?" I throw my hands up in exasperation. "I'm sure you'll find a suitable answer if you cast your mind back. What was it you said to me then?"

Hudson shakes his head, refusing to answer.

Coward.

I walk right up to him, gently cupping his cheek. He sucks in a startled breath. His eyes close slightly when I tenderly caress the stubble on his face with my thumb, like he's savouring my touch. With my lips scant inches from his, tricking him into thinking I'm here for a kiss, I fire my parting shot.

"You said to trust you because you love me and will never hurt me. Look where that got me. Don't lecture me on being cold-hearted, you piece of utter, utter scum."

I swing my leg back and kick Hudson right in the balls, hard enough to elicit an agonised cry. He goes rigid, eyes bugging out before crumpling to his knees. Just for good luck, I punch him in the face too.

"That's for ruining my motherfucking life!"

As I draw back, the other two guys break outside. They screech to a halt when they see our altercation. Hudson slumps on his side, spitting blood and cupping his undoubtedly sore crown jewels. That was so goddamn satisfying. I could watch him cower all day long.

"What the fuck?" Kade shouts.

He looks at me like I've lost my mind. Phoenix is staring too, although he looks somewhat more understanding. I gesture down at their groaning, pitiful friend.

"Why don't you ask your brother how he paid off his addiction before you swept him off into the sunset? I assume he hasn't told you that part."

Kade remains silent, confirming my suspicions. They don't have a damn clue, just like I thought. Hudson will never admit to the truth. He's too fucking ashamed to own his shit.

"I didn't think so," I summarise. "Word of advice? Don't believe a word this lying son of a bitch says. When you've heard the full story, then you can think about judging me."

"Brooke—"

I relish the dawning look of dread on Kade's face as he glances down at his groaning brother. "No, I won't hear it. Until then, mind your own business."

Stalking away with my head held high, I leave Hudson to pick up the pieces. All three men watch me go in stunned silence. I have to walk away before I end up killing every last one of them for my own satisfaction.

Prison sentence be fucking damned.

CHAPTER 28
BROOKLYN
HURRICANE - I PREVAIL

I BOUNCE ON MY FEET, glancing at the door to the group therapy room for a third time. Still shut. Conversation buzzes all around us, with patients standing in huddles and gossiping while they wait.

Teegan places a hand on my shoulder to still my movements. "Hey, chill. Thursday's group is a decent bunch. You don't even have to speak if you don't want to."

"Yeah, right. It was a rather unpleasant experience in Clearview though." Shuddering, I hug my stomach tighter. "It usually ended up getting messy, one way or another. Although the facilitator was one of the good ones."

After getting away with not attending so far due to a couple of rescheduled sessions and my lengthy stint in the hole, the doom that is group therapy has finally arrived.

The doors to the room swing open, causing the line of bedraggled patients to move. Anxiety curdles in the pit of my stomach. With a sympathetic smile, Teegan squeezes my arm.

"Try not to worry. It's forty minutes and then you're done. Besides, it's not too taxing. Just your standard shared pain fest and some meditation crap."

Delightful.

We slip into the large, well-lit room, heading towards the back. A collection of chairs have been lined up in a rough circle. I can practically see the tension leaking from Teegan as she chooses a spot, her hands gliding over the arms and legs precisely four times before she sits down.

"Here's good," she confirms.

"Sure?"

Teegan smiles. "Yeah."

Chatter continues around us as I take in my surroundings. The expensively carpeted floor and wallpaper is lit by chandeliers that cast warm light. Some of the group are dressed in sweats or pyjamas, while others wear jeans and actual clothing.

The ones that are dressed down seem to be more out of it, their eyes glassy or mouths slack. Then there's the walking skeletons, with their bones protruding as they eye up other people's weight. When Britt strolls in and shoots me a glare, I fight the urge to get up and leave.

"Ignore her," Teegan whispers. "When her hair falls out and she's got a feeding tube shoved up her nose, she'll be the one on the receiving end of hate for once."

I shake my head, despite the smile twisting my lips. "You're evil."

"Just realistic. Did I hear that you two had a fight?"

"Hardly a fight." I shrug, playing it off. "A few days ago, she threw her drink at me out of pointless jealousy. I doubt she'll be doing it again, or I'll break her gangly fucking legs to prove a point."

More people trickle in, gradually filling up the room. It's a real selection from across the two dorms, including some new patients that I don't recognise. Teegan leans closer.

"No way! That bitch. Aren't her and Hudson a thing anyway? Plus, I thought you're with Eli?"

I shush her before anyone can hear. "No! How many times do I have to tell you, it's nothing serious. She is with Hudson, sort of. But we have… history."

"Oh man, now this I've got to hear. How come you're pulling all of the cute ones?"

"He isn't cute. Hudson's fucking insane."

"Insanely hot, sure."

I deliberately look at Todd, seated by the door and cleaning his glasses on his loose t-shirt. "I thought you two were… you know." I waggle my eyebrows at Teegan, who blushes beet red. "Didn't you go to movie night together?"

"Yes," she admits with a nervous chuckle. "But it turns out, stealing a quickie when you're more worried about the lack of coordination in his bedroom is near impossible."

"Girl, your brain is exhausting."

"I know. Hilarious." Todd smiles at her across the room and Teegan looks away, cursing under her breath as her hands shake. "Maybe you've got a point."

The room falls quiet as our group facilitator arrives late. A short, curvaceous woman with strawberry pink hair walks in. Her bright shirt and loose linen trousers are instantly recognisable to me. When she turns, I almost laugh in surprise. She hasn't changed one bit in the months since I last saw her.

"Morning campers! How're we all doing today?" Sadie chirps, grabbing a chair and sitting down. "Great to see y'all again. Let's get started, shall we?"

Everyone seems to relax, their eyes automatically closing as they take deep breaths. Sadie finally spots me. Her mouth drops open, perfectly plucked eyebrows raising in utter shock. I offer her an awkward wave and a smile. *Later*, she mouths, giving me a grin.

"Great, let's begin with our mindfulness exercise."

A lot of pointless breathing and gratitude shit later, we're given Post-it notes and kiddie pencils. Sadie makes sure everyone has one before clapping her hands together.

"For the sake of our new members, let's do a bit of an intro. My name's Sadie. I'm a trainee psychologist here at Blackwood. In these group sessions we are working on our coping skills using teamwork and collaboration. Any questions?"

Awkward silence ensues, but nothing fazes Sadie. She's a perpetual fountain of enthusiasm, and she always has been.

"Good! Perhaps our newcomers would like to introduce themselves." Her eyes land on me. "Would you like to start?"

I glare daggers straight at her. She knows how I feel about being put on the spot. Back when she led the group sessions in Clearview, I seem to remember telling her to go to hell when she asked me to recite a poem. No fucking thanks.

"Sure," I grit out. "I'm Brooklyn. I've been here for a while."

"Got an interesting fact for us, Brooklyn?" she presses.

"Yeah, she's a fucking whore." Someone coughs.

I immediately meet Britt's malicious gaze. Sniggers sound throughout the room as all eyes land on me. I have to physically restrain myself from getting up and smashing that bitch's head into the wall.

"Sure," I state acidly. "Despite popular belief, I'm *not* a fucking whore. Anyone that thinks so is welcome to tell me to my face. I'll make the hole look like a holiday."

I give her a wan smile and cross my arms. Everyone's attention on me suddenly ceases, with many dropping their gazes in fear. Sadie coughs to smother her laughter.

"Well, thanks for that. Just a gentle reminder, this is a non-violent space. We're here to heal and grow. Who's next?"

Heal and grow.

I haven't missed those words being recited to me.

A couple of girls introduce themselves. Kate and Lana have both newly transferred from juvie prison. They can't be older than sixteen but wear their aggression like a coat of armour.

Lana has her mousy brown hair cut into a short pixie cut, with a thin scar bisecting her eyebrow. She spares me a chin jerk of respect. Apparently, my threat has earned me some street cred or something.

Sadie thanks the group and leads us through another stupid exercise. Once the torture is over, she lets out a relieved sigh.

"Isn't that better?"

Nobody answers.

We all seem equally unimpressed.

"Okay, today we are going to be working on fear. It's a powerful emotion, one that can lead us astray in so many ways. What we're going to do is this."

"Here we go," someone comments.

Sadie ignores them. "Each person will write something on their Post-it note that they're afraid of. These will all go in a hat and we'll each go around and pick one. That person must offer some constructive suggestion for tackling the fear."

After a collective groan from the group, Sadie tuts disapprovingly. "Come on now, let's give it a go. Remember, be honest. This is all anonymous, so really challenge yourself. Choose something that is important to your recovery."

We're all given five minutes to think. I spend at least four and a half minutes staring at my pencil. Not a single part of me wants to do this bullshit. Teegan seems stuck too, the paper crumpled between her clenched hands. Without having to say a word, I get the issue.

We're all ruled by fear. It's a dark, amorphous cloud that touches every life one way or another. Narrowing it down to any single thing is an insurmountable task.

"Thirty seconds," Sadie calls.

Lie. Make something up. Leave it blank.

The choices run through my head, but in the last five seconds of time left, I take a leap of faith. Scribbling hard enough to break through the paper, I angrily toss my answer into the hat.

"Okay then! Let's see what we've got." Sadie takes the hat and gives it a stir, walking around the circle and handing each person a piece of paper.

"Leon. Why don't you start us off?"

The blonde-haired, blue-eyed guy across the circle gives her a charming smile. He's one of Rio's goons, strapping and toned from spending his days in the gym. I've come to realise that's Rio's territory. This twat turns my stomach with a mere look.

"Sure, Sadie. I'm afraid that if I don't get laid pretty fucking soon, my dick's gonna fall off. You want to help me out?"

Raucous laughter erupts. Sadie gives him a scowl of disapproval, but even I'm struggling to hold the giggles in.

"Firstly, remember the group rules or you'll be put in front of the warden for a little chat. Secondly, you should be reading what's on the paper, not what you wrote."

He shrugs, fighting a grin. "Sorry, my bad."

"Okay, let's move on. Teegan?"

Taking a deep breath to steady herself, Teegan unfolds her bit of paper and clears her throat. "Um, this person is afraid of failure."

"Good. Now what would you suggest to that person to help them with their fear?"

Teegan sits impossibly still, riddled with anxiety as the entire group looks at her. "Ah, I guess I'd say that as long as you keep trying, it doesn't matter if you fail. The effort is what counts."

Sadie beams at her. "Very nice, I think that's good advice. We're all afraid of getting things wrong and letting people down. But as Teegan suggests, sometimes that is inevitable." Her eyes stray to mine momentarily. "Sometimes it's the showing up and getting your hands dirty that counts."

Subtlety was never really her strong suit.

A few more take their turns, their fears ranging from the profound to more sleazy jokes from the clearly sexually frustrated assholes in the group. When Lana picks up her note and reads it, she pauses for a moment, silently pondering before clearing her throat.

"This person said… I'm afraid of becoming the monster the world thinks I am."

A hush takes over the room. I school my expression, ensuring nothing slips out. Tension sits heavily in the air and Sadie casts a glance around, forcing an encouraging smile.

"We're all here for a reason, folks. Some more serious than others, but we share a common goal. We *all* want to do better than we've done before. To amount to more than what our mistakes make us. Lana, what would you like to say to that person?"

Lana gives a slow, cold smile while crossing her legs. "I'd say that when some cunt came at me in prison, I shanked her so fucking hard she's shitting in a bag now. So, fuck everyone's opinions. Nothin' wrong with a little blood and that ain't what makes you a monster."

Sadie's mouth falls open, slightly horrified.

Raising an eyebrow, Lana shoots me a wink. "You see, it's all subjective."

I can't help but return her dark smile from across the room, while others whisper to each other and giggle. Sadie's mouth is still hanging open as she struggles to find an adequate response.

"Well, ah. Thanks for that, Lana..."

"No problem," she replies casually.

The other's answers pale in comparison after that. I mostly tune out, happy to daydream rather than play Sadie's stupid little game. When the session's up, I make my excuses to Teegan and hang back as the room empties. Sadie shoves her stuff away and immediately comes to me, wrapping me in a tight hug.

"Dammit Brooke, it's good to see your face."

"You too. Never thought I'd have to suffer through more of your *Hakuna Matata* therapy shit, but here we are." I shrug, noting the strangely nervous look on her face.

"I transferred from Manchester to here shortly after leaving Clearview," she explains, keeping her voice light.

I have this instinctive feeling that she's lying.

"What are you doing here? Were you transferred?"

"Zimmerman gave up on me." I pick the loose threads in my jeans. "He sent me here for the three-year program."

"They gonna let you out when you finish?"

I have zero intentions of finishing this pointless shit.

"Apparently, although it depends on my behaviour and stuff. I don't know how they intend to cure the crazy in my head."

Sadie lays her hand on top of mine, giving it a squeeze. "You may not see it now, but the last time I saw you, there was drool coming out your mouth. You couldn't string together a sentence because they had you so drugged up."

I roll my eyes. "Thanks for reminding me."

"My point is that recovery is possible. Look at yourself and how far you've come. I'm so proud of you."

My gut twists in anger, no matter how irrational it is. Rule number one; never tell a crazy person they look better. We don't want to hear that shit. Nine times out of ten, you'll push them to self-destruct even more just to prove you wrong. Trust me.

Swiftly changing the topic, Sadie grows serious once more, casting an anxious glance around the deserted room. I swear she checks the CCTV cameras, confusing me further.

"Brooklyn, just promise me one thing."

I nod slowly. "What is it?"

"Just be careful. Blackwood has a good reputation, but that doesn't mean bad things don't happen here. Watch your back, okay?"

Fear slithers down my spine at her ominous words. She looks at me imploringly, all signs of her usual optimism brushed aside.

"What do you mean?" I ask with a frown. "What's wrong with Blackwood?"

Sadie plasters her usual bright smile back into place. "I've got another group to facilitate, I must go. If you need anything, you know where to find me." She holds my gaze for a moment, an unspoken message in her eyes. "*Anything* at all."

I force a smile when all I want is to scream in her face and demand to know what the hell she's going on about. But it's clear she doesn't intend to elaborate on her vague words, rushing to escape our conversation.

"It's good to see you," I force out. "See you around."

As I get up and open the door to leave, Sadie urgently calls after me.

"Brooke!

I look over my shoulder. "Yeah?"

"You aren't a monster. No matter what the world thinks, or what the newspapers print. You're a good kid that made some bad choices. Remember that."

She returns to quickly packing her stuff away, glancing at me one last time. My heart seizes, all of my suspicions melting away at her words. More than anything, I regret writing my biggest fear down. Now it's out there and I can't take it back. The truth is, it doesn't matter what everyone else thinks.

I already hate myself enough for what I did.

CHAPTER 29
HUDSON

IF YOU WANT LOVE - NF

SLAMMING MY DOOR SHUT, I toss the handfuls of papers on the bed. Fisting my hair, I fight the urge to scream aloud. Piping hot rage fills my every thought. Blinding, blurring, leaving no space for rationality or calm.

My fist meets the plaster wall, my skin splitting and blood smearing across the paintwork. I yell my frustration and keep punching, regardless of the pain in my busted knuckles.

Mariam says that I have to work through my anger if I'm going to have any chance of leaving this place. You know what? Screw Mariam. I'm never escaping this godforsaken cage because it's where I fucking belong.

Brooklyn hasn't spoken to me since our bust up. She passes me in corridors like I don't even exist, like that kiss outside of the library never fucking happened. I know she felt it, the instant electricity behind us. That spark paved our way for ruin five years ago, and we were always destined to burn together.

Meanwhile, our group is splintering apart. We sit in silence at mealtimes, the air thick with resentment. I get it, the guys blame me for screwing things up. That empty chair at the table is painfully obvious.

Kade silently plots, determined to win back his latest project. Phoenix is acting like a complete bellend, deflecting his pain by any means necessary while fighting off a manic episode. Don't even get me started on Eli. He's worse than ever and hellbent on destruction.

I can't believe I didn't see it sooner.

We're all caught in her orbit.

Every damn one of us.

I slump on the floor, my back against the bloodied wall. My head falls to my hands as I fight the overwhelming need to smash Brooklyn's door down and sort this toxic mess out once and for all.

I want to break her, scream at her, tell her that I can't stop thinking about her. Anything to fix this mess. I can't remain trapped in limbo, caught between loving and hating that bitch. The knock at my door comes before it swings open. Kade strides in. He takes one look at me on the floor and frowns, freezing on the spot.

"Hud? What's going on?"

I shake my head and flee to the bathroom, unable to express the intensity of my anger. Kade refuses to look away while I rinse my hands under the tap. Red swirls of blood trail down the drain along with chunks of broken plaster.

"Nothing. I'm good," I grit out.

He hesitates, seeming to choose his words carefully. "I thought you were working through this stuff, not giving in to it. What's gotten into you recently? Don't you want to go home?"

I wrap the towel around my sore hand, sparing him a withering glance. "Who are you, my fucking therapist?"

"Well, no."

Brushing past him, I take a seat on the bed. "Just mind your own business. It's got nothing to do with you."

Kade heaves a frustrated sigh. "It has everything to do with me."

I pinch the bridge of my nose. *Seriously? This again?*

"When will you learn to fuck off when you're not wanted? You think I wanted you to give up university to follow me here? Or that I wanted anyone to lie—"

I pause, teetering on the edge of revealing too much. Keeping up with the lies is exhausting. Kade takes three long strides and sinks to his knees in front of me, his hand landing on my leg.

"I know, brother. I know."

My eyes slide up to meet his. They're wide and certain, without a single crack of doubt.

"You... know?" I repeat slowly.

My heartbeat pounds in my ears as he nods. The entire fucking world ends with that admission. It has never mattered what everyone else thinks of my crimes, or the half-baked lie that we spun with cash and influence to conceal what really happened that night. All I've ever cared about is one thing. *Kade.*

He's my better half.

Everything I should be and more.

"You don't know," I mutter.

"Mum told me everything. The whole ugly truth." He grinds his teeth, struggling to remain calm and level-headed. "You should have told me. I deserved to know."

My gaze instantly drops to the floor, my cheeks burning and heart thumping erratically. I can still see the blood that poured from that asshole's battered body as I beat him to death. It streaked up the walls, peppered with fragments of skull.

"Tell you what? That what happened wasn't self-defence?"

Kade gulps, silently fighting his own conscience. "Yes."

The air feels impossibly thick as we watch one another, awful reality crushing us both.

"I didn't want you to know," I manage to say.

"Why? I don't get it, Hud. None of it."

"Because I didn't want you to think bad of me! That's why!"

I stride over to the barred window, staring out at the dark night. We used to spend every Friday night like this together before Blackwood. Before I became this person. Clubbing or drinking, we'd take a train into London to find some cute girls to chat up.

"You shouldn't be here," I mutter regretfully. "You're wasting your life in this place. They're never going to let me out, in three years or thirty. Not after what I did."

I glance back at Kade, noting the look of absolute devastation across his face. He chews his lip, carefully choosing his next words.

"Hud... there's something you need to know."

I wait for him to finish, knowing that whatever is coming, it must be bad. Enough to affect the unshakeable Kade. Enough to drive him to my room when he can barely stand to be around me as I slowly ruin my life even further.

"Just tell me," I command. "Tell me and go."

Kade joins me by the window, his hands clenched in balls. He can't even look at me, resolutely staring ahead.

"Mum says there's been a development in the case."

"Right... And?"

"Fuck, Hud," he curses, anxiously loosening his shirt collar. "Your Ma, she's come forward and wants to testify against you."

My stomach bottoms out. Ice floods my body and sickness muddles my mind. I can hear Kade saying my name, his hand on my shoulder, but it doesn't resonate. Nothing about this feels real, like I'm imprisoned in a twisted nightmare designed to fuck me up.

"She wants... to testify. Against me," I state emotionlessly.

"Yeah. You realise what this means, right?"

Stumbling to the bed, I sit down and put my head in my hands. "Of course, I fucking do. She's going to expose the lie. Your parents will be implicated. We're all going to prison."

I recite the prospects tonelessly, too overwhelmed to fully comprehend the almighty shit storm heading our way. Kade joins me on the bed, looking equally tense.

"*Your* parents too. They made this mess to protect you, dammit. Now they'll go down with you." He gulps loudly. "We need a plan. There's got to be a way out of this."

"It's perjury, Kade. We all lied."

I smash my clenched hand against my forehead, willing the truth to go away. How could I have been so stupid to go along with this? Fucking hell, I deserve that prison sentence. I can't let Kade's mum go down for my mistakes too. His father probably deserves to be in a prison already, but I sure as hell ain't putting him there.

"How do we protect them?" I ask through gritted teeth. "I'll march up to the judge and confess if I have to. They can do whatever the fuck they like to me. I can't let—"

My voice chokes up as I swallow hard.

"I can't let this happen. Your family saved my life."

Of all the responses, Kade laughs.

"What the hell are you laughing at?"

"Nothing." He chuckles weakly. "It's just... I think that's the nicest thing you've ever said."

I shoot him an incredulous look. "You kidding, right? That's what you're thinking right now?"

Sobering, Kade stands and looks down at me. "We're a family, whether you like it or not. We will fix this *as a family.* Nobody is going to prison. You are coming home. I made promises and I intend to keep them."

"What exactly is your plan?" I call after him.

"We're figuring it out," he answers evasively. "Mum is coming in a few of weeks to see us both. She's requested visitation. Hopefully, we'll have an update then."

"Sit tight? That's your plan?" I gape at him.

"Yes. In the meantime, keep your mouth shut. The lawyers are tying the investigation up in red tape to delay things. Sit tight and don't lose your shit, brother. We fixed this mess once..." He looks me right in the eye. "We'll fix it again."

I stare at the door long after it closes behind him. My vision is tainted by the memory of blood. It happened in a split second, a decision that changed everything for me. I drove down to see my mother in a daze, intending to finally confront her about the years of abuse that put me into the foster system.

Hudson, what are you doing here?

You can't be here.

Please go. If Ron sees you...

I should've listened to Ma. In fact, I should've never gone back to that hellhole, filled with pointless ideas about closure and finally healing from the past. I had it all laid out for me. This perfect life that Kade's folks provided. College. Friends. Good grades. A future. I tossed it all away to go back for that crackpot whore.

There's only one person that can possibly understand. My feet move automatically as I flee the room and march across the corridor. Fist banging on Brooklyn's door, my chest seizes and sweat coats my forehead. Everything is spinning and falling apart at the seams. She's the only person that has ever come close to understanding me.

No answer.

I rattle the handle, but it's locked. Darkness closes over my vision as I rest my forehead on the wood. This can't be happening. Kade and his family can't go down for my mistakes and stupidity. This is all my fucking fault.

"Hudson?"

I look up, desperately hoping it's my girl there. Disappointment coats my tongue as Britt stares at me, her eyebrows furrowed.

"Are you okay? What's wrong?"

I lose all sense of right and wrong. Marching over to her and grabbing her face, my lips are straight on hers. I don't want to kiss Britt. I fucking hate her guts. But if I concentrate hard enough, I can pretend that she's my blackbird. That her dry hair is long and luscious. That her thin body is soft against mine and lined with every scar that I've memorised.

"I knew you'd come to your senses," she pants.

"Shut the fuck up."

When she speaks, I remember who she really is.

Dragging her to my room, I shove Britt up against the door and grab her body, craving the release I know screwing her until she screams will bring. Just as she mewls and begins to get my door open, there's a gasp from nearby. A noise that's a razor-sharp dagger to my heart.

Brooklyn stands by her door, frozen in place. Her eyes are trained on us with a look of horror. Face splintering with pain, she swiftly wipes it away as soon as I look up. My hands fall away from Britt's body, like I've been shocked with electricity.

"Brooke, wait!" I shout frantically.

She turns and flees into her room. I run to follow her and smash straight into the door as the lock quickly turns. Kicking it and yelling for her to come back out does nothing. She's gone, leaving me locked in the corridor with nothing but my regret and self-loathing.

"What the fuck is wrong with you?" Britt marches up to me and slaps me hard enough to sting. "What does she have that I don't? You can't keep using me, I will not be disrespected for a second longer!"

"Go then," I reply cruelly. "Get the fuck out of my face and don't come back."

Eyes filled with tears, Britt sniffs and nods solemnly. "Fine, I will. That's it, we're done. Don't you ever come back to me when you need someone to pick up the pieces."

Running away while sobbing, she leaves me alone and surrounded by nothing but the remains of my petty selfishness. All I do is hurt people. I'm no good for anything else. Brooklyn always managed to see the good in me, even when I broke her in the worst possible way.

Now, there's nothing good left to see.

CHAPTER 30
BROOKLYN

WHATEVER LETS YOU COPE -
BLACK FOXXES

TEEGAN HANDS me a tube of black eyeliner, chewing on her lip as she inspects me. "Try this. You'll look even hotter."

"I'm not trying to look hot when I don't even want to go to this stupid fake party." I roll the eyeliner between my fingers, glowering at her. "Why can't I just stay behind?"

"You've moped around all week long and I'm sick of watching it. Where's the badass that punched Rio on her first day or broke those girls' noses?"

"Leave it be, Tee."

She raises a pierced eyebrow at me. "No! The only way to teach those guys is to go to the party looking drop dead gorgeous, might I add, and hook up with someone even hotter than them."

I flop back on her neatly made bed, crumpling the stupid Halloween costume beneath me. "First off, I'm not moping. Second, I don't give a fuck about what they think and never have."

Teegan snorts. "Yeah right. You're so full of shit."

With a frustrated growl, I stand and snatch up the bloodied nurse's outfit. "Fine! I'll go to the idiotic Halloween party with you if it'll shut you up."

I turn away from her smug, victorious face and go to the bathroom, slamming the door behind me. This is the problem with having friends. They don't know when to butt the hell out and leave you alone. I don't want to fucking celebrate Halloween, because that means it's two weeks until the anniversary emotionally assaults me. Two weeks to get my ass out of here, with zero leads and limited opportunities to do just that.

I'm screwed.

Trapped and powerless.

Maybe I'll go to the party and get absolutely fucked up to forget. I still have the gear I scrounged off Rio. If I'm lucky, my body will simply give in to my broken mind's demands. I unwrap the tacky costume and shake it out, staring down at the short, skin-tight dress.

The fact that Kade picked this out makes my palms sticky. Despite me ignoring them all, he still left it outside my door last night. All week I've been set on avoiding this shitty party and the confusing men that will undoubtedly be attending it. Just seeing Hudson with that slut wrapped around him has me in a tailspin.

"Do I seriously have to wear this?" I yell through the door.

"Yes! Stop fucking whining and get dressed already."

Cursing under my breath, I strip off my usual jeans and t-shirt. My body is pale and slim in the mirror. On my right arm, the almost-healed slashes are peppered with angry cigarette burns. I haven't seen Eli since the night of the storm. He's retreated into himself and disappeared off the face of the earth recently.

I can't keep doing this, letting them close enough to hurt me. If I never met them, would I be dead by now? I've allowed these men to distract me.

"Hurry up before I come in there and dress you myself!" Teegan bellows.

Taking one look at the cheap white tights that came with the costume, I toss them aside. The dress isn't much better as I pull it up my bare legs, fastening the poppers and scowling at my reflection. I look like a slutty nurse that would certainly get fired for this get-up.

My boobs barely fit inside and way too much cleavage spills out. My long legs are also entirely on show. Teegan's eyes light up when I step out to show her.

"Holy fucking damn. Kade chose that strategically, right?"

"I cannot wear this in public," I grit out.

"Dude, you've got to. Besides, it's only Oakridge dorms attending. Pinehill is celebrating tomorrow. Too many people to manage all at once."

"That isn't comforting."

Teegan frowns, her eyes on my legs. "Although you should probably avoid the warden. One look at you and she'll give you a disciplinary."

Handing me the eyeliner along with a tube of contraband red lipstick, she shoves me back in the bathroom. "Sort your face out and let's split. I told Todd we'd meet him outside at seven o'clock."

"Who are you to lecture me about guys when you've got that poor fucker right in the friend zone?" I ask snarkily.

Teegan slams the door in my face.

"You get over your relationship drama and I'll get over mine!"

"Not a relationship," I mutter back.

Brushing through my pearly hair and adding some winged eyeliner, I consider the lipstick. I'm going to be attracting all the wrong kinds of attention like this. With a grin, I swipe it across my lips, a devious plan forming.

After tonight, maybe those persistent guys will finally take the hint and leave me alone to my plans. Even Eli. I'm done hurting and being vulnerable around him. It's time to finish what I started.

As Teegan grabs our coats and key cards, I prise the lid from the toilet. Reaching into the tank, I search for the waterproof bag I stashed inside. This is the only way

I'm getting through the night. Running it under the tap, I tip a line of snowy powder on to the edge of the sink and squeeze my eyes shut.

Snorting it up, I devour the whole line, then another for luck. Bitterness hits the back of my throat as I flinch back, rubbing my nostrils. I can't feel it yet, but this shit will be worth the price I paid. I don't want to feel a single fucking thing tonight.

The door handle rattles. Teegan sticks her head in, her eyes widening with surprise when she sees me wiping the excess away and stashing the bag in my bra.

"Jesus, what are you doing?"

"None of your damn business. Let's go."

I brush past her and grab my leather jacket from her hands, before slipping my bright pink Docs on. We head out, descending the staircase in silence. It's freezing cold outside. Jogging through the drizzly rain to reach the cafeteria, we find Todd standing at the entrance, waiting for us to arrive.

"Hey, Teegan! It's so good to..." His eyes land on me and his jaw drops. "Oh, um. Hi Brooklyn." He offers a limp wave.

Choosing to ignore him, I light up a cigarette and bounce on my toes, shivering in the cold. Thankfully, there are no guards around to catch me smoking. Teegan stands awkwardly between us, and I give her a subtle nudge.

"Doesn't she look hot?" I waggle my brows at Todd.

"Y-Yeah, of course. Tee, you look... really, um, cute."

They're both as bad at this as each other. With the blood rushing through my head and the coke dissolving my manners, I grab Teegan's face and press my lips to hers.

Kissing her good and proper before I pull away, I turn back to Todd. He's watching the exchange excitedly. Men are so easy to manipulate. I grab his hand and place it in Teegan's.

"Have fun, kids."

Strutting inside, I chance a look back and find them making out against the wall, their hands all over each other like horny teenagers. That shit works every time. I'm happy for her.

The corridors seem to bend and move as I march towards the cafeteria, stumbling straight into the wall at one point. An overfriendly arm snakes around my waist. I right myself, looking up into an unpleasant set of eyes.

"Hey good lookin', did you miss me?" Rio sneers.

"Like hell I did," I slur.

"Fuck me. You're high as a kite. How is it? Good shit, right?"

Grabbing a hold of his generous bicep, I offer him a grin. "Almost worth the price I paid."

He laughs and links his arm with mine, guiding me down the corridor. We pass several guards that stare at me suspiciously, but Rio gives them a subtle nod, holding me close. No one says a word as they let us go on our merry way. Not suspicious at all.

"Babe, I've got plenty more where that came from."

Rio's lips brush against my neck, his breath hot and sticky. I shudder, suddenly cold despite the narcotic fire burning beneath my skin. Gently disentangling our arms, I meet his eyes with certainty.

"You know what I want. Shame you tore up the list."

He swears under his breath, a hand reaching out to grab my wrist. "I'm all ears. Tell me again."

With my breasts brushing against his chest, I smirk as his eyes widen in surprise. My lips ghost along his jaw before I reach his ear to whisper quietly.

"I want your key to the roof."

Rio laughs. "You never cease to entertain. That's gonna cost you a damn sight more than a blowjob, sugar. Are you fucking insane?"

I tilt my chin up in defiance. "I want that key."

"What for? I ain't taking blame when you throw your pretty little ass off that roof."

"You've got enough strings to pull to conceal your involvement. Unless you're objecting for some other reason?"

I raise my eyebrows in challenge without denying the insinuation. It's not like he's gonna stop me from doing it, the asshole doesn't care about anyone but his shady business.

Rio looks into my eyes for a second before shaking his head in disbelief. "Bloody hell, you really are crazy. I'm outta here."

He turns and strides away, muttering to himself about lunatics wasting his time. Fucking coward. I'll get that damn key, and it'll be the last thing I do.

Walking on wobbly legs, I enter the cafeteria and toss aside my jacket. The lights are low and coloured strobes are dappled across the floor from the stereo set up in the corner.

There are several tables full of food, the paper bowls overflowing with approved snacks that have been dolled up to look interesting. Despite the mass of patients dancing and enjoying themselves, there's still an undercurrent of reality.

The drinks are all non-alcoholic.

Guards line the perimeter in their dozens.

Cameras capture everything.

Drugged up patients stare and drool.

I skip past a pumpkin carving station, equipped with kiddie plastic tools and fake candles. The party is busy, more popular than I thought it would be. Various costumes ranging from vampires to zombies are showcased, although most look homemade and pretty shit if I'm honest.

I snag a lemonade from the drinks stand, smiling cheekily at the sour-faced guard who frowns at me. He's one of Rio's pals. I recognise him from the library incident.

"Ain't you cold, girl? Seen more clothes on a stripper." He leers at me, checking me out a little too obviously to be appropriate. "Anything I can help you with?"

"Nope." I give him a wink as I pass.

Joining the dance floor, I wiggle between various bodies and join in, swaying my hips like no one is watching. For a brief second, this almost feels like real life. I could be out in a club, dancing the night away just like everyone else my age is doing.

My back suddenly connects with a firm, muscled chest. I peer over my shoulder, finding tousled blue hair, amused, chocolate brown eyes and a painted skeleton face staring back at me.

"Fancy seeing you here," Phoenix taunts.

He wears all black, including a t-shirt that's been printed with white bones. When his arm wraps around my waist, he pulls me close to his body, and his other hand lands firmly on my hip. He squeezes hard.

"What are you wearing, firecracker?"

"An outfit. Ask Kade." I smirk.

Hand skating even lower, Phoenix's fingers stroke the skin of my inner thigh. He's brushing dangerously close to my throbbing pussy. I grind my ass against him, enjoying the feel of his lips at my ear. I hear him gasp as his dick grows hard.

"What's gotten into you?"

Tugging my dress up a little higher, I glance around to ensure no one is watching us. All of my inhibitions have vanished under the influence of drugs. All I can think about is him bending me over and fucking me right here, right now. Regardless of those watching.

"Nothing. Just having some fun. Got a problem with that?"

"Hell no," he answers quickly.

Concealed from sight by the packed bodies on the dance floor, Phoenix's hand meets my wet pussy. He traces the damp cotton of my panties in a gentle tease. His teeth nibble my earlobe as I moan, shifting my ass against his crotch even harder.

"Jeez, have you been body snatched or something?"

I spin to face him, finally meeting his eyes through my thick lashes. He studies me, his full lips parted. He's seconds away from kissing me when the penny finally drops. His expression hardens in an instant, all of the playfulness dissipating.

"Christ… are you fucking high?" Phoenix hisses.

Running my hand over his hard pecs, I roll my eyes rather than replying. The urge to laugh hysterically bubbles up. I can't help but giggle, which only infuriates him further. I'm in trouble now.

"I knew it. Your eyes look like flying saucers. Dammit, Brooke!"

With his hand latching around my wrist, Phoenix forcibly drags me through the packed bodies, no matter how loudly I protest. I'm still laughing, hilarious tears fighting to break free.

"Niiiix, don't be a bore. Let's dance and then fuck, hmm?" Yanking my hand free and planting my feet, he's almost yanked off balance. "You know you want to."

His hand tightens on my chin, jerking my head up. "You're a fucking mess. I don't do drugs anymore. You should damn well know that. Come on, let's get you some water."

I'm guided over to the back corner where the kitchens are open. Kade's dressed as the Grim Reaper and talking to some clueless staff members, soaking up the appreciation for his party planning. As soon as we approach, his white-painted face drops. Phoenix jerks his head towards the kitchen.

"Ah, excuse me. Just need to check on dessert," Kade lies easily.

He jogs over to us and grabs my other arm, effortlessly smiling to direct any suspicion away. Between the two of them, I'm muscled through the doorway and straight out back into the kitchen.

Another familiar face awaits. Eli's head shoots up from where his nose is buried in a book. He looks rough, even in my blurry vision. Far gaunter and paler compared to the last time I saw him, like Caspar the ghost, minus any costume.

"What on earth is going on?" Kade demands.

Phoenix deposits me in a chair, letting out a huff. "What's going on is Brooklyn is fucking stoned. I had to get her out of there. Look at the state of her!"

"Not stoned," I correct, raising my brow at him. "I don't do weed."

Eli stares at me wordlessly, quickly tossing his book aside. His emerald eyes scan my face, and he frowns, as if trying to bury beneath the surface to find the truth. Kade yanks at his hair in exasperation, unable to even look at me, and Phoenix curses colourfully.

"Why are you all being such grumpy assholes?" I pout at them. "Isn't this meant to be a party?"

Wobbling to my feet, I tug my skimpy dress back down to cover my bare thighs. Kade finally looks at me, his eyes bouncing over my bare skin with a visible gulp.

"Thanks for the dress."

I invade his space, giving him a wonky smile. His hands run over my shoulders and down my mottled arms. I don't miss the way he catalogues the devastation across my skin, both new and old. His eyes flick over my shoulder to where Eli sits, before he turns his stern expression back on me.

"What have you taken?"

"None of your business," I hit back.

"I'm being serious, Brooklyn. You can't just do what you want around here. There are consequences."

"Says who? Nobody gives a damn either way."

Kade pushes me into a chair. "Says me, alright?"

I shove his attentive hands away. "News flash. I can do whatever the fuck I like, when I like, and there's nothing you guys can do about it." I flick my eyes over Phoenix and Eli, including them in the sentiment. "Stop trying to pull me into your fucked up little family dynamic here. I'm done."

I stagger to my feet and head for the door, breezing straight past Phoenix's grabbing hands. My good mood has evaporated as I start to come down from my high. I need another hit to perk me up again. Too many feelings are threatening to take over. As I near my escape, Kade's cold voice makes me freeze on the spot.

"What did my brother do to you to screw you up so badly?

My heartbeat roars in my ears. Heat flushes my tingling skin, and the amusement drains from my body like blood down a plughole. Digging my nails into my palms, I spin to face Kade. Fuck Hudson. I'm done keeping his filthy secret.

"Did you ever ask him how he paid off his drug debts before coming to you?"

The resultant silence is thick with confusion.

"I didn't think so." I scoff, turning to Phoenix. "You were a dealer before, right? Okay, so tell me what happens when someone doesn't pay up. Enlighten us."

He keeps quiet.

I laugh again. "Don't be shy now. What happens?"

It feels like forever before he finally answers. "You threaten them," Phoenix mutters, rubbing the back of his neck in shame.

"Precisely. And if that doesn't work?"

He tries to move towards me, but I lift a shaking hand to halt his steps. "Answer the goddamn question." I face him, refusing to back down. "Tell Kade exactly what his brother did to me. Why I'm like this. Why I'm stuck *here*, forced to justify my fucking high to you lowlifes."

"Brooklyn, please," Kade pleads, his handsome face marred with pain. "We just want to help you."

I shake my head in distaste. They still don't get it.

"I don't want your help. I don't want anyone's help!"

Eli shoots to his feet, almost as unsteady as me. His angular face is troubled, and his steps are hurried. We're both breaking apart at the seams but that doesn't mean I want his help. I backtrack further, unwilling to let him even remotely close to me.

"Will someone answer my question?" I shout at them. "Or are you all too scared to face the truth?"

"You pay with whatever you have," Phoenix admits.

Bingo. You pay with whatever the fuck you can offer, regardless of the consequences. All four of us face off, locked in a deadly battle of wills while music pulses through the room. No one will meet my eyes. The truth weighs thick and suffocating between us, along with the notable absence of the man in question.

"You wanted the truth. There you have it," I sneer at Kade. "You want to know why I'm so screwed up? The answer is simple. Your brother paid his debts with the only thing he had."

He flinches, remaining silent.

I turn to Phoenix, hating the pity on his face. "Me. He paid with me."

"Brooke..." Kade begins, trailing off in horror.

He looks at me with unimaginable pain in his eyes. Wiping my stray tears away, I'm sure my eyes reflect the same emotion. Even five years down the line, the wound is festering and deep, forever raw from the lack of resolution with the man that ruined me.

"The fucking blackbird is not the only thing he killed," I spit, my emotions spiralling out of control. "That's your truth."

Marching out while searching for the baggie in my bra, I'm determined to eliminate the agony ripping both my mind and body apart. The twisted feelings of hatred and anger that have somehow escaped their prison to torment me further.

Nobody follows me.

CHAPTER 31
BROOKLYN
GUEST ROOM - ECHOS

NUMB. Sweet, meaningless, irrefutable numbness.

All the anger, indignation, gut punching rage… it's gone.

Finishing my second line and wiping my nose, I clamber to my feet. The toilet lid is dusty and spotted with white flecks. I don't bother to clean up after myself. Snorting cocaine in the bathroom on my knees is a new low, but luckily, I don't care anymore.

"Leave me alone!"

A door slams, followed by muffled crying and the sound of a lock sliding across the neighbouring stall. I brush myself off and sneak out to splash my face. Eyeliner streaming down my cheeks and red lipstick smeared, I look like a deranged clown. I stare into my own eyes, watching my drugged-up smile fade.

I am my own destroyer.

Every single solitary moment of my life, I've been fucked over, abandoned, forgotten and used. By everyone and everything. And somehow, it all comes back to me. There's no one else to blame but myself. I'm a failure, a goddamn failure.

"I hate you," I shout at myself, a deep frown marring my brows. The pressure in my chest still doesn't relent so I shout even louder. "I fucking hate you!"

My fist sails into the glass. It cracks right down the middle, my blood smearing beautifully. With all the coke swimming in my veins, I don't feel the pain from my busted hand. Crimson rivulets spill down my skin and I stare, enraptured by the sight.

I deserve this. People like me shouldn't live. I'm a waste of air and if I died right now, I'd be doing the world a favour. No one would even notice.

"What are you doing?"

Britt emerges from the stall, trailing mascara and pink cheeks staining her face. She looks from the smashed mirror to me in disbelief, unwilling to move even a step closer, like she's physically afraid of me.

"Seriously, Brooklyn? Hello?" She waves a hand in the air as if to attract my attention.

"I...I..." I stumble, blinking rapidly.

What am I doing? Why am I here? Nothing makes sense anymore. Shadows creep into the edges of my vision and begin to mutter, tipping reality on its head. The voices won't be far behind. All I can feel is my heartbeat threatening to break my ribcage open.

"You look fucking insane right now." Britt slowly crosses the bathroom, hopping up on the counter next to me. "But who am I to judge, right?"

"Right," I croak, splashing my face for a second time.

I try to force the crescendo of invisible voices from my mind, to seem somewhat in control as Britt watches me with critical eyes that see far too much. She clicks her tongue, a knowing smile blossoming as I contemplate breaking her jaw.

"Where'd you get it?"

"Why should I tell you?" I counter.

She hops down from the counter and gets in my face, her lips pressed together. "Don't be a dick. Just tell me. You got more?" Her eyes trail over my skimpy outfit. "Although I can't imagine where you'd be storing it in this slutty get up."

The insult snaps my remaining self-control. I shove her back, watching in delight as she stumbles and falls on her ass. Something that looks a lot like fear flashes through her eyes. I prowl closer, looming over her, my fists clenched tight.

"Who exactly are you calling a whore? Tell me, Britt," I spit her name hatefully. "How many times did you spread your little legs for Hudson, hmm? Bet you took every scrap of attention he threw at you, like the desperate whore you are."

"You don't know what you're talking about."

I shoot her a grin. "How does it feel now he's gone?"

"Fuck off! If it wasn't for you, he would still be with me."

I bat my lashes innocently to screw with her further. "Nothing to do with me, sweetheart. Guess he just got bored of breaking you over and over again. It loses its thrill after a while. Trust me." I meet her eyes without shame. "I know."

The shadows have nearly taken over my entire line of sight. They won't stop until I do something far worse to her. Turning to leave before I kill the bitch, her choked voice stops me dead.

"You know what? You and Hudson deserve each other. You're both screwed up, selfish, unlovable psychopaths." Her voice drops low as she glares daggers at me. "I hope you kill each other. Better yet, hurry up and kill yourself. God knows you won't be missed."

Britt looks away to face herself in the mirror. My stomach bottoms out when I see the reflection looking back at me in the cracked glass. A ghost is waiting for me.

He's standing next to her, soaked in spilled blood. Clothes torn and saturated with crimson, his body is slashed beyond recognition. Looking so real, I'm convinced that if I reach out, I'll be able to touch his broken form.

Vic. He's here.

I'm terrified that he'll escape the glass and kill me himself. Watching the slow smile spread across his blue lips, I break into a run, desperately fleeing the bathroom and the demons inside.

The party still rages in the cafeteria. I can hear the pumpkin competition being called over the microphone. I can't go back in or face the men that see the good in me that I can't. They are safer far away from me.

With my body trembling from the hit rushing through my system, I run back down the deserted corridor. Britt's words echo on a loop in my head. All I can think about is opening a vein wide enough to end this shit for good. I can practically see the puddle of blood in my mind's eye, forming a dark halo of death around my still corpse.

Vic's voice whispers through my mind.

Hurry up and fucking kill yourself.

I shake my head, but he refuses to be silent.

You know you want to. Come join me.

"Brooklyn!" Teegan calls as I pass her, without even sparing her and Todd a glance. They watch me go with concern, repeatedly shouting my name while I grapple with reality.

I don't stop running until I'm back in the dorms. Taking the stairs two at a time, I trip and stumble multiple times, burning my hands against the carpet. I don't stop until I finally reach the fourth floor, skidding to a halt.

There's a shadow slumped against the mahogany door. Black hair wild and untamed, his head is hanging low between his legs. My feet backtrack as his head raises, two brilliant blue eyes spotting me. They dissolve everything around me until nothing remains but the distance between us.

"Blackbird," Hudson whispers reverently.

I should run. Turn around and flee. Hide. Shout. Anything to escape the devil at my door. But my feet move of their own accord, guiding me forwards with the magnetic pull of Hudson's defeated eyes. I stop in front of him, my lip curled in derision.

"Get out of my way."

Hudson clambers to his feet, his generous height towering over me. Jaw set and expression hard, his sorrow melts into something darker, more primal.

"The guys sent me to look for you. I've been waiting."

The stench of alcohol comes off him in waves. Clearly, I'm not the only one funding Rio's little contraband operation.

"You're drunk, Hud. Go home."

"I'm drunk. You're high. What better time to have this conversation?"

With that, Hudson bends down and picks me up. A shocked scream escapes my lips as he lifts me in one smooth move, before tossing me over his broad shoulder.

"Put me down! Put me down this instance!"

"Shut the fuck up before you wake everyone," Hudson growls, spanking my ass as he stalks to his room.

Scanning his key card with one hand, he kicks the door open and marches into the darkness. There's a distinct click as the lock slides shut. I'm roughly tossed on to his messy bed.

"I'm done running circles around you." Hudson discards his phone and key card, turning his unfathomable expression on me. "You continue to forget the lesson I taught you when we were kids."

Standing at the end of his bed, his luminous eyes prowl over my splayed out, vulnerable body. He offers me a bleak smile.

"You're fucking mine, blackbird. You've always been fucking mine."

"You're mistaken." I shake my head, desperately scrabbling backwards to escape him. "I was never yours to begin with. You stole everything from me. My sanity, sobriety, education. Everything." Reaching out to grab a nearby lampshade, I toss it straight at him as hard as possible. "Fucking everything!"

The light narrowly misses his head, smashing against the wall instead. Hudson doesn't even flinch at the pointed shards cascading down around us. He just huffs and pulls the duvet towards him, dragging me closer while I battle to escape.

"You're a monster," I shout.

His hands grab my ankles and pull until I'm hopelessly caught beneath him at the end of the bed. He traps my body between his powerful legs, pinning my wrists above my head. Simmering blue eyes burn a path straight down to my damned soul.

"You think I don't know that?" Hudson hisses at me. "Every single day for the last five years, I've had to live with the knowledge of what they did to you." His Adam's apple bobs, betraying his emotions. "Of what I *let them* do to you."

His hand releases me to cup my cheek. Glossy black hair falls across his eyes. Rather than tenderly brushing it aside like the old me would have done, I take the opportunity to swing my fist, punching him straight in the face.

"Fuck you!"

Hudson stumbles back, wiping his split lip. My chest seizes as he glares at me, his very limited patience crumbling into ruins.

"Why do you continue to fight me?" he asks.

When he tries to come close again, I kick my leg out, so it connects with his jaw. He reels back and I leap up to advance, pushing him into the bookshelf. It groans and wobbles precariously for a second before toppling over. Books, picture frames and debris fly everywhere, showering down and bruising us both.

"Because you took away my ability to fight," I yell back.

We continue to battle each other, and both end up on the floor. We're gasping for breath, surrounded by destruction. Before I can launch another assault, Hudson scrambles across the floor and pounces on me. As his heavy weight presses into me, I writhe and scream.

"Come back to me," he demands.

The minute his lips land on mine, something inside of me gives. It snaps and fucking dissolves as my lips part, automatically reacting to his familiar mouth against mine. His kiss is desperate, unapologetic, riddled with grief.

For a second, I allow myself to feel something, and then it all comes crashing back in. Every reason why this is a terrible idea that will only hurt both of us all over again. As I come to my senses, I bite down on his lip until he yelps and releases me.

"You fucking bit me." Hudson frowns.

"You fucking kissed me," I counter furiously.

Then his lips are devouring mine again, smearing the fresh blood between us as copper dances across my tongue. Hudson grasps the cheap poppers of my costume and rips them open in one swift move. My bra soon disappears, exposing my bare breasts. He groans, his mouth blazing down my neck and along my collar bone, skating ever closer to my hard nipples.

"Don't you dare," I protest.

He takes a rosy bud in his mouth, teeth teasing the soft skin. My breath catches as my hips buck, unable to suppress the reaction.

"Stop. Please stop."

"No," Hudson answers simply, kissing his way down my flat, scarred belly. "I won't fucking stop."

Undoing the remaining poppers, he exposes my cotton-covered pussy. His eyes close briefly, like he's memorising this moment, unable to believe that it's actually real. With one hand pinning my arm, he tugs the material lower, his fingers brushing against my pulsating clit.

"I said stop…" I plead again.

Hudson's lips brush against my cunt, his tongue slipping between my folds as hot pleasure zips straight up my spine. He pleasures me with his mouth, licking and sucking as I fight for every breath. Protests are lodged in my throat. When his teeth pull at my sensitive nub, I scream against the back of my hand.

"Stop?" he asks innocently, his devilish eyes meeting mine.

"Yes," I squeeze out.

I'm unsure if I'm arguing or agreeing anymore. Ignoring me, Hudson's eyes stray to my discarded dress and land on the baggie that I had tucked away inside.

"What's this?" He studies the remaining powder.

I attempt to snatch it away. "That doesn't belong to you!"

The look Hudson shoots me would scare even a grown man. I am so fucking dead. He's going to bury me alive.

"I thought I interrupted that little session you had going on in the library. How'd you pay for it, Brooke?"

I desperately try to escape, but Hudson sits on my legs and traps me beneath his crushing weight. He dangles the bag in front of me like it's a fucking murder weapon and I'm on trial.

"I said, how did you pay for it?" His fingers trail down and meet my dripping folds, toying with my slit. "With your tight little pussy, or that sweet mouth of yours? Fucking whore."

"None of your goddamn business!"

The anger on his face is so familiar, I feel like I've fallen back in time. With a livid shake of his head, he shoves his fingers deep inside of me. I gasp, reacting to his expert stroking. His other hand carefully tips a line of coke out on my stomach, trailing down to meet my belly button.

"You're acting like a slut," he comments cruelly.

My fingers fist in his coarse hair. He greedily devours the line, his nose teasing my hot skin, moaning in pleasure as the drugs hit.

"Learned from the best, you arrogant asshole."

Eyes filled with hatred scan my face. "You do remember."

I gape at Hudson as he kisses over my scarred hips, his lips meeting my wet heat again. I'm shocked to silence as he proceeds to dump the remaining coke straight on my clit, smirking to himself.

"Yet you seem to have forgotten who owns your ass though."

My back arches, my whole body alight with stimulation from the drugs mingling with my juices. I yank his hair hard, and he snorts the powder straight from my pussy, licking away the rest with his perfect tongue. Desire twists in my core, traitorous fucking desire that he doesn't deserve.

"Just like the good old days, huh, blackbird?"

"I hate you," I moan.

My knees tremble as the pleasure builds. The sound of his belt being removed has my half-lidded eyes flinging open. My gaze lands on his straining boxers. Fuck, he's still so big.

Hudson grabs his t-shirt and yanks it over his head, exposing deliciously chiselled muscles and endless inches of black ink across his skin. The tattoos are new, but I don't have time to study them as he prepares to tie me up.

"You're not allowed to finish yet," he informs me tersely. "Not until you answer my question."

My foot connects with his bare chest. I kick him away from me, snatching my dress up to put back on.

"I don't want anything from you. Not anymore."

As I get to my feet, readying to escape, a hand tangles in my long hair. With zero apologies, Hudson yanks me back. He tears strands of my hair out just like he used to, the scheming bastard.

"Tough shit. You don't get to walk away." Hudson pulls at my scalp, his hand tightening around my throat. "I will not lose you again."

"You... walked... away," I choke out.

Walking me backwards until my legs hit the bed, we sink into the mattress. His hard cock rocks against me through his boxers, brushing against my soaked slit. It feels too fucking good.

Hudson takes the opportunity to slip his leather belt around my wrists. He moves fast, quickly securing me to his bed frame, far too smoothly for this to be the first time he's done that.

"Perfect. You always looked best when at my mercy."

I yank on the leather restraint, trying to slip my wrists free. It's no use. He's got me utterly trapped. When his cock presses against my inner thigh, my hips buck involuntarily to seek out more friction. No matter how loud my head is telling me to scream, my body is betraying me.

"You left me no choice but to walk away," he murmurs.

His mouth glides over my torso until he's stationed above me, in a position of complete control. Hudson's hand grabs my throat again, squeezing impossibly tight, offering me slivers of air.

"You're fucking mine," he states possessively.

"You don't own me. You never did."

"That's a lie and you know it. Let me remind you."

His cock strokes my pussy lips without entering, teasing the slick opening and driving me insane. His hand tightening further, my lungs burn from the lack of oxygen. I writhe beneath him, still fighting to escape. Anything to end the sick, familiar torture.

"Something to say, Brooke?"

Hudson's teeth graze my ear, the burst of pain lancing through me as he bites down. Heat pools in my core, despite my inner protests and raging anger. When he releases my throat just enough for me to respond, I desperately suck in precious air.

"Only... c-cowards... r-run," I stutter.

Hudson pulls back to look at me. I headbutt him so hard, my teeth knock together. Finally, my hands work free from the belt. I shove his tattooed body off me, relishing his yelp of pain. Fleeing the bed, I intend to take the coward's way out and run away myself.

"You're fucking unhinged," I snap at him.

Giving Hudson a final glance, the sight of him sends my plan up in smoke. He's given up, slumped against his pillows and wearing the most guilty, ashamed look. Hudson simply nods and rubs his sore head.

"I was a coward. For what it's worth, I never should have left. No matter how hard you pushed me away. Walking away was the biggest mistake of my life."

His oceanic orbs flash open, piercing my skull with the intensity of his gaze. He looks so broken, utterly devastated.

"Blackbird... *I'm sorry.*"

The drug haze dissipates as we study each other like foreign specimens, caught in a bubble of malicious, festering regret. There's so much mutual suffering and hatred pulsating between us, but there's also a thread of something else. I can't quite name it. Not fucking forgiveness, I'm not that stupid. But something else.

"You're sorry?"

Hudson gulps. Nods. Silently begs me with his eyes. He's a fucking monster... just like me. I can't resist his darkness. Within seconds, the roles are reversed. I'm climbing on top of him, straddling his generously inked body with confidence.

He grunts in shock but offers no complaint as I land my lips on his. I'm being driven by wordless need. Pure, frantic need to simply be *owned* by someone again. The empty void in my chest is demanding relief.

"I don't fucking forgive you," I snarl, lining his dick up with my entrance.

"Wouldn't expect you to."

Hudson's eyes roll back as I sink down on him. He fills my pussy so deep, I have to bite my lip to hold the groan in. I start to move, riding him at a fast pace that has me ready to fall apart within minutes. There's nothing gentle or tender about it. His hands are tight on my hips, guiding our momentum.

We're like two broken shards of glass, smashed and scattered beyond repair. As the pieces mingle together, you can't tell which bit came from where. It doesn't even matter anymore. You just have a worthless mess, but it's still irreplaceable.

Hudson is too broken for anyone else. I am too broken for anyone else. I fucking hate him, but there's a hellish part of my brain that is still addicted. We need each other, there's no denying that ugly truth. Like a heroin addict needs his next fix.

"Come for me baby," he orders.

My release crests, flushing my body with heat and sensation. Hudson takes the brief reprieve to gain the upper hand, flipping me over and pressing my face into the pillow. He yanks my ass high and plunges his cock back in. I hiss, relishing the sting of his palm cracking across my butt cheek.

"That's it, take your punishment like the filthy bitch you are," he goads. "Next time you decide to go off the handle and get jacked up, I expect to be invited along for the ride."

Hudson fucks me rough and hard from behind, his nails digging painfully into my back. A long, slender finger reaches around and trails teasingly over my clit, moistening it before he finds my asshole. The digit slips inside, and I scream into the pillow, relishing the intrusion.

Hudson spanks me another time, jolting the finger buried deep in my ass. "You always liked it dirty. Your pussy is mine, no matter what you say. Don't fucking forget that fact ever again or there will be hell to pay."

His speed increases, every frenzied movement growing wild. Heat twists inside of me like a freight train, barrelling straight for destruction. When his hand returns to my throat, he cuts off my cries. It's all too much. I soon fall apart, overstimulated while Hudson steals the orgasm from me.

"Say my fucking name," he commands. "Say it."

"Hudson," I moan, unable to stop myself.

He gruffly bellows and hot release spreads through me. We collapse at the same time, our sweaty bodies slumping and legs entangling. I gasp for breath, lacking the energy to push him away.

After several silent minutes of catching our breath, Hudson tucks hair behind my ear and traces my chapped lips. He's being far too gentle for my sanity to take.

"Stop looking at me like that," I whisper.

He brushes his lips across mine ever so softly. "I can't."

When I try to move and dislodge his body, he lets out a huff, pressing me back into the sheets. "Don't go. Please blackbird, don't leave me."

Featherlight fingers brush down my arm, teasing the solid ridges and scars. He circles the blindingly obvious cigarette burns for a second, pausing to take them in, before his fingers intertwine with mine. Despite everything, I don't have the strength to pull away.

"I have to." I sigh, sounding reluctant in a way that is completely alien.

Hudson grabs the duvet and yanks it back up to cover our bare, tangled bodies. His heavily inked arms wrap around and pull me close, until my cheek rests against his firm chest.

"For once… just forget. For one night, stay with me."

There's nothing left inside of me to fight him. Millions of reasons why I should leave cross my mind, but not a single one of them matters. The feel of his skin and his achingly familiar scent erodes my control, until I sling my leg over his and curl up close.

"One night. That's all you're getting," I grumble.

"I'll take it."

CHAPTER 32
KADE

THE KILL - THIRTY SECONDS TO MARS

I TAP my foot impatiently as Phoenix grabs his denim jacket, attempting to smooth his electric blue hair in the mirror. Eli stands next to me, equally unimpressed but maintaining his constant silence.

"Dude, come on. We're going to miss breakfast otherwise."

"Coming, for fuck's sake. I'm tired," he complains. "It's Sunday. No one should be awake this early."

"You were the one that offered to stay and help clear up after the party last night," I point out.

He slings on the jacket. "Didn't think it through."

We pile out into the corridor, all rubbing our eyes and yawning. I doubt anyone slept well after the altercation with Brooklyn. She disappeared and never came back. Traipsing down to Hudson's door, I bang on the solid wood.

"Hud. Get your ass out of bed. We've got to talk."

There's no answer. I know he's awake, I can hear the tell-tale scuffling and rustle of clothes from inside the room. He needs to be involved in this conversation, so I knock again, readying to let myself in when he finally flings the door open.

"What?" he grunts, pulling sweats up with one hand.

Phoenix slumps tiredly against the door frame. "Food. Dictator Kade here is dragging us down for a family meeting."

He shoots me an exasperated, worn out glare.

"We need to talk about Brooklyn," I state simply.

Hudson runs a hand through his wild bed head, his eyes lowering shiftily. He steps further into the corridor and tugs the door shut behind him, dropping his voice.

"Look, now is not a good time. Frankly, there's nothing else to talk about. She's a big girl."

"Did you find her last night? Talk some sense into her?"

Phoenix snorts. "Yeah right. She won't listen to anyone, least of all him."

The sound of someone throwing their guts up and a toilet flushing echoes from inside his room. All of our eyes widen. Phoenix smirks, looking far too amused.

"I knew you wouldn't stay away from Britt for long," he taunts. "Looks like we're interrupting Hudson's morning delight."

I peer suspiciously around him, but Hudson blocks my view. I knew telling him about the impending court case was a mistake, but I didn't think it would send him running back to that bitch. I'm about to lecture him when the door swings open. I think all of our jaws drop in unison.

"Oh shit," Brooklyn exclaims.

She's standing there in Hudson's t-shirt and nothing else. I can see the curve of her breasts through the material, hanging low enough to cover her ass while leaving her luscious legs on display.

Hudson stares at me, clearly trying to communicate something important. The three of us remain silent, utterly bemused by the sight of Brooklyn, looking significantly worse for wear, inside of Hudson's bedroom.

Eli's the first to react. He simply turns and strides away without a single word, his steps heavy with annoyance. Brooklyn watches him go, the pain shuttering her eyes. I feel Phoenix shift next to me, straightening and folding his strong arms across his chest.

"I see. Well, this is cosy," he comments snidely.

Brooklyn narrows her eyes at him. "Talk some sense into me? That's why you sent him after me? Fucking mature. Didn't we discuss this issue last night?"

I force a controlled smile, attempting to level with her stubborn ass. "We were worried about you, that's all. Will you come to breakfast so we can all talk?"

Laughing under her breath, Brooklyn grabs her belongings and slips straight past all three of us. She heads back towards her bedroom. I cast Hudson an unimpressed glare and follow hot on her tail.

"Wait, hear me out. We only want to help," I call.

"Leave me alone. Like I said, I don't want or need your help."

"But you'll happily fuck our friend?" Phoenix retorts.

Brooklyn swivels, casting him a furious glower. I'm just about to try and de-escalate the situation when Phoenix grabs her wrist and pulls her close, his fingers tilting her chin up.

"You're playing a dangerous game here, firecracker. Don't start something you're not going to finish. Hudson's not the only one that's involved here."

She smacks his hand away, scoffing incredulously. "Since when is it any of your business who I fuck?" Her lips spread into a slow, twisted smile. "Are you jealous?"

Phoenix meets her challenge, shrugging nonchalantly. "You asked for it. All bets are off."

What exactly does that mean? She's tearing our group apart at the seams and loving every second of it. I've got to intervene and stop this before it's too late and the damage is irreversible. We can't be undone by a screwed-up chick with zero morals.

Grabbing Phoenix's arm, I muscle him away. "Leave it. We're going."

Brooklyn watches us as we head back down the corridor, leaving a half-naked

Hudson to return to his bedroom. Her door slams when we reach the stairs, and I finally release Phoenix.

"What the hell, man?"

"I was doing you a favour." I shrug.

"Don't get involved. She's slept with both Eli and Hudson, and you're just okay with that? Seriously?" He throws his hands up angrily. "I can't ignore my feelings."

Phoenix storms away, abandoning me and returning to our room. I'm left alone on the stairs, entirely frustrated and unsure of how we even got to this point. We're fighting like children over a fucking *girl*, some nobody that strolled in here like she owns the place and doesn't give a shit about hurting us.

I can't lose them.

None of us will survive this place alone.

Since day one, I have been in charge of keeping us together, so that's what I'm going to do. She's not the only one that can play dirty. My next moves will make or break us, but I don't see any other options. Someone's got to wade in and sort this mess.

I march back down the corridor and storm into Brooklyn's room without knocking. I kept the spare key card for exactly this reason. She's braced against the wall, her head lowered and breathing heavy. Just as she looks up and begins to protest, I grab her by the shoulders. Spinning her around, I pin her body against the wall.

"You've got me and my best friends in a tailspin," I growl at her, surprised by the aggression in my voice. "My family means everything to me. I refuse to lose that because of you."

She squeaks in surprise, attempting to writhe from my grip. I shove her against the wall even harder, keeping her trapped.

"It's all or nothing, love. You don't get to turn us against each other."

I can't hold back, finally doing what I've been dreaming about for the last two months. Securing my lips to hers, I cup her cheek and pillage her mouth. Brooklyn tastes so fucking sweet, her soft lips melting against mine like they belong.

I twine my fingers in her tangled hair and lose myself to the kiss. Our tongues stroke, breath mingling, bodies grinding against one another. All of my instincts are telling me to keep this car crash of a person as far away from my family as possible.

She's going to be the death of us all, but as I press my painfully hard dick into her body and hear that breathy little moan, I stop caring. Brooklyn breaks the frenzied kiss first.

"Kade, I can't..."

"Stop screwing with us. You're playing with fire. I don't want to see anyone get burned." Stepping away from her needy, shivering body, I raise an eyebrow. "You're in or you're out. It's that simple. Choose us or walk away and don't look back."

"Choose you?" she repeats.

"No, all of us. Since the day I welcomed you to this place, I've tried to bring you into the fold. You've fought me at every turn, fucking with my friends behind my back."

Her gaze drops in something that looks like shame, but I tilt her head back up. She can't hide now. It's too late to run.

"We aren't a family by blood, but necessity. You don't get to pick favourites or turn us against one another. We all care about you."

"I don't understand," she mutters.

"Let me make it simple for you then. I'm a nice guy, but when someone threatens those I care about, I can be your worst nightmare. Either pull your shit together and join the group or get away from us all. No more playing childish games."

It's the only thing I can think to do. She can't choose only one of us. It will kill us all with jealousy. Anyway, the truth is, I don't want her to choose. We all need her, in different ways. She's the missing piece of the puzzle.

Brooklyn's steely grey eyes pierce mine, with all the bullshit stripped away, leaving her open and vulnerable. She licks her lips, carefully selecting her next words.

"What if I don't deserve you guys? What if you'd all be better off without me here?"

"Bullshit," I call her out. "Every single one of us has issues in some way. Why the hell do you think we're here?"

My knee slides between her legs, spreading them wide. I trail my lips over her soft skin, my heart skittering.

"Phoenix is a dealer turned addict who sold his soul to the devil to provide for his family. You haven't seen him in a manic episode yet but trust me it ain't pretty."

Brooklyn gulps hard.

"There's Hudson," I continue. "The hot-headed asshole who can't go a day without beating on someone or fucking to deal with his guilt. Then you've got Eli, the silent, tortured soul, so traumatised by his past that he can't look at a match without breaking down and cutting himself. He hasn't spoken since he was a kid."

I brush my lips over hers, gentler this time, coaxing her compliance. I've ensnared her in, slowly but surely. This is my final chance now.

"You know how far back my demons reach, Brooke. I'm a control freak who can't help but pick up lost causes to try and fix, no matter how pathetic and desperate for love that makes me."

"You're not pathetic," she whispers.

I press my forehead to hers, my chest tight with emotion. "Aren't I? None of us are perfect, but you don't have to be to take up space in the world. None of us are getting out if we don't have each other's backs. I'm offering you the chance to *belong*."

I step back, letting Brooklyn's body sag against the wall. Her cheeks are wet as she glances up at me, her face broken and troubled in a way I can never truly fix. But I'll damn well try my best because she's like me. Frantically treading water in the hope that someone will rock up and pull her out of hell.

I'll save this stubborn bitch even if it's the last thing I do. I wait. Watch. Hope and pray. When she raises her chin with determination, hope blossoms in my chest. Brooklyn nods once. It's tight and forced, but it's a fucking nod in agreement.

"Get dressed," I order immediately, without betraying my relief. "Get your ass down to breakfast, then we're going to the library to study. You're passing that exam next week. Come on, move it. You've got five minutes."

I leave her bedroom, slamming the door behind me as I make my way back to find the others. I'm going to drag their sorry asses downstairs too. I will keep this family together, one way or another. If Brooklyn wants to screw with my guys, then there isn't going to be any special treatment.

We're a fucking family, and families *share*.

CHAPTER 33
BROOKLYN
THE HILLS - THE WEEKND

"TIME'S UP! Papers at the end of your desk."

I finish scribbling my final words and stack the papers, sliding them over to Phoenix. He grins at me and places them at the edge of our table. Crawley promptly collects them. Eli's already long finished, his arms crossed as he stares blankly out of the window, clearly lost in thought.

"How'd it go?" Phoenix asks.

"Alright. Kade's tutoring this past week has helped, I think."

"I'm sure you nailed it." He bumps my shoulder with a wink, playfully ruffling my blonde hair. "Come on, let's get out of here. It's celebrating time."

We gather our bags and prepare to leave, with the two guys sandwiching me between them. Phoenix casually slings his arm around my shoulders and Eli grabs my hand, neither saying a word about touching me in public. My cheeks burn hot as we pass several staring patients. I stuff my embarrassment down.

I have no idea what they're both playing at, but I'm not going to complain. Kade apparently had a little chat with them last week, after the humiliating incident with Hudson. Since then, things have been different.

"Where are we meeting the other two?"

Phoenix and Eli share a look as we head downstairs, inching through the crowd of patients leaving their afternoon classes.

"They've got a meeting or something. It's just us for now. I think they'll join us after."

I shrug, adjusting the heavy bag on my shoulder. "Sure, whatever. I know how I want to celebrate." Smiling sweetly at Phoenix, I give him a heated wink. "You've been promising me a go on that game of yours all week. Time to pay up."

He snorts, clearly expecting me to say something else entirely. "I see. Fine, video games it is. But don't cry when I beat your ass."

We head back to the dorms to escape the cold, making a beeline for Phoenix's and Kade's shared room. Once inside, I ditch my heavy bag, laden with books, and flop on the neatly made bed.

Kade's scent immediately invades my nose, the smell of peppermint and expensive aftershave clinging to his soft bed sheets. Phoenix ditches his denim jacket and scuffed Chucks, smiling as his eyes travel over me sprawled out on the bed like I own the place.

"I'll get the game loaded. Eli, sort snacks."

While the two boys prepare for our evening's entertainment, I subtly press my nose into the pillow and breathe deeply. My eyes fall shut. Kade's gruff words come back to me from last week, having plagued me ever since.

I'm offering you a chance to belong.

This is wrong. I'm pretending like I fit in here, that I accept his offer, when really my desperate need to self-destruct is growing by the day. I should push them all away and break their hearts, at least that would offer them some protection from inevitable pain.

"Yo Brooke. Shift your ass and get over here."

I will walk away, but not yet.

Let me pretend just a little longer.

Shoving the darkness to the back of my mind, I turn to Phoenix. He's set up two beanbags in front of their large, flat screen television. He pats the spot next to him and I shake my head to clear the haze, trying not to think too deeply.

Taking my place next to him, he passes me a controller and begins to load the game. I can hear Eli shuffling about in their secret stash. He returns with snacks, spreading bags of crisps, pretzels and sweets around.

"What are we, twelve years old?" I gesture towards the binge foods.

Eli offers me a shrug while silently nudging me to move closer to Phoenix. He's been even more isolated than usual for a while now. I long to ask what's going on in his messy little head. Unfortunately, it's a slippery slope. I need to keep my own cards close to my chest. He can keep his secrets for now.

Trapped between them both, my breath hitches as the scheming assholes sandwich me in impossibly tight. I'm not sure what the plan is here, but I'm certain there is one.

"Want to make this interesting?" Phoenix smirks.

"What are you thinking?"

"Best of three?"

I shrug, examining the buttons on the sleek controller. "Hardly seems fair. I've never played. Plus, you'll probably cheat."

He chuckles, his leg brushing against mine teasingly. "Scout's honour! Promise I won't cheat. Hell, Eli can even help you. I'm nothing if not a gentleman."

Yeah, right.

I lose the first game within minutes. My little pixelated head is blown to pieces as Phoenix whoops in victory. Eli ignores him completely and tugs on my sleeve, spreading his legs wider with a lifted eyebrow. As the next game loads, I hop into his lap and relax against his firm body.

"Behave," I admonish, feeling his lips against my ear.

Slim but muscular arms wrap around my torso. He moves to hold the controller over my own hands. With his help, I beat Phoenix easily at the next round. He's left pouting, muttering under his breath about cheating.

I grin at him. "It's best of three. You could still win."

"Game on."

Eli's lips trail down my neck, causing a shiver to run through my body as we prepare for the final game. I shift on his lap, my ass grinding against the rapidly hardening lump in his ripped jeans. When his teeth nip my skin, a sigh escapes my lips, causing Phoenix to shoot us a heated look.

"Stop distracting me," I complain.

Eli's spare hand gently brushes over my breasts. I jump a little, causing my character to promptly die on the screen. Phoenix cheers and waves the controller over his head. The satisfied smile he shoots me is so fucking smug, I almost want to flake out on our deal just to wind him up.

"Who's the cheater now?" I jab my finger at Eli, who's trailing his fingers up and down my arm in a teasing rhythm. "No fair using him. That's poor sportsmanship."

"It worked, didn't it?" Phoenix goads.

Clambering out of Eli's lap with a huff, I snag a bag of crisps and deposit myself back on Kade's bed. Both of the guys watch me like hawks, and the air is suddenly heavy with sexual tension. Despite the stalemate between us all week after my little slip-up with Hudson, their intentions are still far from honourable.

"So, the question is, what do you want as your prize?"

I pop a crisp in my mouth and watch as they silently confer, seemingly coming to a decision without uttering a single word. Do they read each other's minds or something? My pulse is racing, but I don't let my excitement show. They aren't the only ones that can play games.

"Play truth or dare with us." Phoenix relaxes into the beanbag.

I shake my head, crunching through a mouthful of salty goodness. "You really are big kids, aren't you? We're not fucking teenagers at a sleepover."

"Technically, I'm still nineteen, so there's that. You really don't have much of a choice, winners pick." Phoenix eyes me up with a smirk, looking entirely too pleased with himself.

I flop on my back, waving my hand for him to start. "Fine. I pick truth."

"Let's start simple. Favourite booze?"

"Tequila."

"Food?"

"Sushi."

Phoenix laughs. "Seriously? That fishy shit?"

"What? It's good. There was a sushi bar across from the diner where I used to work." I shrug, tossing the half empty crisp bag aside. "Anyway, that's two. My turn."

He waits as I wrack my brain, my curiosity burning. There are too many questions to count, so I settle for the most pressing one.

"What did Kade say to you last week?"

I almost don't expect him to answer, but Phoenix doesn't disappoint. "That you can sleep with whomever you please and it's none of our business."

"And what did you say?"

Phoenix waggles his finger at me. "Nope, that's your lot."

"Ugh, fine. Eli?" I pause, wondering how exactly to do this, given his inability to say a damn thing. "Dare?"

He nods simply. I can't help the smile that creeps on my face. Rolling onto my side and propping my head up, I have the perfect viewpoint to observe them both from. I'm dying to see this.

"I dare you to kiss Phoenix. No half measures either, I want to be thoroughly entertained."

Neither of them hesitates. They're magnetised to the other within seconds. This cannot be their first time fooling around. The chemistry between them is electric as Eli grabs a handful of Phoenix's midnight blue hair, yanking his face closer and positioning his body.

"Like this?"

Phoenix simpers as Eli's lips tease his jawline, working up to his plump, vulnerable lips. I watch the simple kiss with bated breath, my thighs automatically clenching together. The sight of them touching each other has me so fucking wet.

"Too nice," I respond drily. "Come on, Eli. I know you can give much better than that. Kiss him like you fucking mean it and I'll make sure your efforts aren't in vain."

Brilliant green eyes flick over to me, his eyebrow raising in challenge. Before I can tease him further, he's straddling Phoenix and kissing him hard enough to have my pussy quivering. Phoenix holds Eli's narrow hips and kisses him back. Their tongues tangle as their hands explore each other. By the time they break apart, I can't sit still for a moment longer.

"More to your liking, ma'am?" Phoenix jokes.

They both turn to look at me, their gazes loaded with pent-up desire and frustration. I clear my throat and nod once, not trusting myself to speak. They both settle into the beanbag together without separating. My eyes track Phoenix's hand as it lands on Eli's thigh, dangerously close to the bulge between his legs.

"Firecracker, truth or dare?"

"Dare." I smirk.

Phoenix contemplates me for a second before wiggling his finger for me to come closer. "Eli's been feeling a bit down of late. Why don't you come and cheer him up?"

I roll my eyes, my heartbeat suddenly picking up. Crawling across the bed to join them on the floor, I consider the beanbag for a moment and deposit myself on top of them both. They're both trapped beneath my weight.

"Room for one more?"

"Always." Phoenix grins.

He disentangles himself from Eli, allowing me to slip in the middle of them. I stare hungrily at the dark haired ghost before me, his chest seizing, and his lips parted. My fingers trail up his leg and undo his jeans, brushing teasingly across the skin of his scarred abs.

"Like this?" I ask innocently.

My hand slips into Eli's boxers and wraps around his straining dick inside.

Fuck, his hot length is pulsing with need. I feel Phoenix move behind me, pushing me onto my knees as he braces my body between them.

"You got it, baby," he praises.

Freeing Eli's cock, I glance up at him through my lashes for consent just like he did for me. His jerking nod is all I need to wrap my lips around the tip of his shaft, my tongue skating over his velvet skin. I bob my head for a moment, getting acquainted before greedily taking the rest of his length. Fingers dive into my hair and hold me tight as his dick hits the back of my throat.

"Fucking beautiful," Phoenix groans.

Sucking Eli off, I'm powerless to respond as Phoenix grabs hold of my waistband and slowly works my own jeans down. My ass rises in the air, and he shifts behind me, dragging my panties down too. Throbbing need fills my body all at once.

"Keep going, firecracker. You're not allowed to stop."

I twist my head and keep working Eli's cock between my lips, one hand splayed across his lower stomach and the other reaching down to cup his balls. For a second, I swear I hear Eli moan out loud, an actual noise escaping his mouth.

Then Phoenix's mouth is between my legs, his expert tongue spearing my slit. I gasp around Eli, my watering eyes squeezing shut. His tongue piercing is cold against my sensitive nerves, enhancing every sensation pounding through me. When he kisses around to my back entrance, his tongue tickling the tight muscle there, I swear I see stars.

"Have you ever…?" Phoenix enquires.

I wiggle my ass in response, hoping he can sense my enthusiasm. It's not my first rodeo. Phoenix pauses for a moment and delivers a punishing smack to my butt, his wet thumb pressing against my asshole. I can't help but groan, gagging for a second on Eli's generous length as he continues to ride my mouth.

Phoenix wraps his hand around my loose ponytail, wrenching my head back and leaving Eli bereft. He pins me to his body from behind, while his hands swiftly remove my t-shirt. I watch the fabric go flying, with Phoenix's deft fingers stealing my bra next.

"Kiss those perfect tits," he orders Eli, his hand still wrenching my hair. "I wanna see."

Teeth and tongue meet my breasts, nibbling across the solid peaks. I bite my lip, eyes rolling back in pleasure as Phoenix removes the rest of his clothes. His hand lands on my lower back, pushing me back down into the perfect doggy position.

"Eli's lonely, finish the job," he orders.

I take the Eli's cock back into my mouth, blowing him with everything I've got. Phoenix starts to play with my clit from behind me. The minute his hard cock brushes my inner thighs, my pussy spasms in anticipation, ready to finally have him inside of me. His length teases my opening for a second, the excitement building.

"Please," I whimper.

It's all the encouragement he needs.

"Dammit," Phoenix groans as he slams home.

If I could scream around Eli's dick in my throat, I would. I move my body in time to Phoenix's powerful thrusts. Each one sends shockwaves through my core. Eli tenses beneath me, bucking his hips and chasing his own release.

Hot seed spills into my mouth, pouring down my throat. I obediently swallow every last drop. The minute Eli finishes in my mouth, he collapses. Phoenix pulls out of me in a punishing move.

"Argh," I hiss, angered by the sudden withdrawal. "Don't fucking tease me."

"Shut the hell up or I'll gag you."

Eli wraps a hand around my throat, cutting off my snarky response. I glare at him, licking my lips as his eyes widen at the insinuation. He starts kissing me, invading my mouth and rewarding me for my efforts, despite the fact I was swallowing his come mere seconds ago. He must be able to taste himself on my tongue. That's so hot.

"Dammit, you two," Phoenix hisses.

His nails dig into my butt cheeks as he shifts again. His cock finds my back entrance. I forget how to breathe for a second, even with Eli still choking me, and internally high-five myself.

This is how I should be spending my last week alive.

Phoenix rubs my wet cunt again, gathering moisture on his fingertips. He transfers it to my ass, sliding a finger in to spread me wider in preparation. I suppress a growl as he adds another finger, loosening up the muscle.

"So tight," he comments.

I can hear him spitting and lubricating his length next. Sliding his fingers from my asshole, he gently presses his cock against the tight muscle. It takes time, but he gradually enters me inch by inch. Eli swallows my screams with his invasive tongue, allowing me a sliver of air.

"You're fucking ours."

Phoenix hisses as he starts to move faster, pounding into me. I can feel him spiralling, his movements growing wild as he repeats the declaration like a prayer.

"You're all fucking ours, Brooke."

Eli releases my throat and skates his nails down my arm. His fingers press against the healing cigarette burns that he inflicted. My climax slams through me with the burst of pain, pushing me straight over the edge. I swear I hear him whisper something, sounding a lot like *ours*.

Phoenix bruises my hips with his grip, still slamming into me with desperation. When he comes undone, he spills into me with a roar. His body slumps on top of me, and I fall forwards, straight into Eli's open arms. We all collapse into a tangled, gasping dog pile, barely fitting on one beanbag together.

"Next time, I'm gonna tie you up and we'll both fuck your sweet little pussy," Phoenix whispers in my ear, nibbling on the lobe. "How'd you like that? Both of us inside of you?"

If I'm still alive then.

"Sure," I reply instead. "Although next time I might pick truth though, you never know."

He snorts, managing to get to his feet and offering me a hand. We traipse to the bathroom and rinse off separately, removing all traces of the sordid affair that just occurred. I steal a shirt from Phoenix's wardrobe and slip it over my naked body, foregoing any panties or bra. The bed is calling me. Eli has already burrowed beneath the covers, his arms open and waiting for me.

The three of us cosy up together, stretching the mattress to maximum occupancy. Phoenix flicks a movie on and throws an arm around us both, his fingers absently teasing Eli's curls. It's seconds before the silent member of our group falls asleep, succumbing to his exhaustion.

"Phoenix?"

"Yeah, baby?"

I glance down at the peaceful look on Eli's sleeping face, where he usually looks so tortured by the world.

"What's going on with him?"

Phoenix gets comfy and draws the blanket tighter over us, his strong legs entangling with mine. "You can't say anything, but I heard his papa is sick. Terminal cancer."

"Shit, that's awful."

Eyebrows raised, Phoenix slowly shakes his head. "No, it's not. Who do you think gave him those burns? The man is a child abuser and religious nutcase. He's dying in prison as we speak. They reckon he has days at best."

I softly stroke Eli's shoulder, reassuring myself with the soft rise and fall of his chest. "His father did it to him?"

"When he was eight years old. Locked him in the sin closet and set the damn thing on fire. Apparently, he thought Eli was possessed by a demon. He used to beat him whenever he spoke. Eventually he stopped talking and he hasn't said a word since."

Bile rises in my throat. My fingers twitch with the need to hit something, I'm so furious. He literally beat the voice out of Eli. It's fucking sick. I'm disgusted, utterly heartbroken on Eli's behalf. He was just a kid, and they stole his tongue, before trying to steal the rest of him too.

"He was convicted?"

"Yeah. Child abuse, false imprisonment and attempted murder. Eli survived, obviously. Spent years in and out of burn wards before he was eventually sectioned. Kade says there were at least five attempts on his file, possibly more. He hasn't been free since."

I hug Eli's body even tighter, furious tears filling my eyes. There's no point denying how I feel about him. The thought of everything he's been through devastates me. No wonder he doesn't speak or function normally, dependent on self-harm.

He burned me… just like he was burned.

We lapse into silence with the movie playing to itself. I doubt either of us are watching it. I'm drowning in guilt because this time next week, I have no intention of being here. One way or another, I'll be leaving these beautifully broken souls behind. That's the deal I made with the devil in my head. A bargain with the darkness that whispers endlessly to me.

You're not allowed to live. Even if it kills them.

Even if they want to follow you to hell.

CHAPTER 34
HUDSON
WAITING GAME - BANKS

I SCRAPE my thick hair away from my forehead, staring at my tired blue eyes in the mirror. They're lined with bags and more burdens than I care to admit. My gaze flickers back to the bed, sheets rumpled and messy. It looked a hell of a lot better with Brooklyn in it.

Goddammit, the way she came apart beneath my touch. The memory has been seared into my mind ever since. Every stolen kiss and late-night fuck when we were kids pales in comparison. She acted like she didn't want it, but the minute I touched her dripping pussy, I knew the truth.

She's as hung up on the past as I am. Neither of us has moved on in the last five years. I can't stop thinking about her. Every day that she ignores me is fucking torture. I hate her and hate how powerless she makes me feel.

I'm nothing more than a puppy trailing after her, begging for any crumb of attention. Yet every night since she was in my bed, I jerk off to the memory and imagine ways to lure her back. Excuses to talk to her. Ways to get into her room. Conversation starters and scenarios in which we could actually be good for each other.

Yet every time, I come up empty handed.

Attempting to tame my hair, I startle when Kade breezes into the room without knocking.

"Hey, are you ready to go? It's nearly four."

"Since when don't you knock?" I groan.

"Since you stopped answering when I knocked. Come on, we're going to be late."

I straighten my shirt collar, tugging at the uncomfortable material that threatens to choke me. Kade looks me up and down, giving me an approving smile.

"You look good. Mum will be pleased."

"I can't believe you're making me do this."

"She hasn't seen you in over a year. With the legal shitstorm heading our way, the least you can do is act like you care," he criticises, causing guilt to bloom in my chest.

I follow him outside, leaving my phone but grabbing my ID badge. There's not much of a defence I can offer, I've behaved like a fucking asshole. To my adoptive mum and to many others. We walk over to the reception in tense silence, neither of us bothering to make small talk.

Once inside, we head through several brightly lit corridors, the walls lined with art that probably costs more than my entire tattoo sleeves. Everything's clean and tidy the closer we get to the visitation area, with even more finery than the other buildings. Like the wealth of this place isn't clear enough, they've got to rub it in just that little bit more.

At another reception surrounded by equal grandeur, we check in and get our IDs scanned. A burly guard sizes us both up. He frisks us and checks for concealed contraband, anything we could be trying to get out or trade with the visitor.

"Out," he demands, placing his hand under my chin.

I spit the gum out. "You done? We've got somewhere to be."

Several more seconds of aggressive patting down later, we're finally permitted to enter the room. It's kind of like a restaurant, with tables and chairs spread out. Refreshments are available from the hatch and elevator music plays in the background. The only difference is the barred windows, heavy security presence and multiple cameras dotted about.

"Smile," Kade orders as we take a seat.

"I'm an adult, I know how to fucking behave."

"Do you? That's news to me."

My leg jiggles under the table, betraying my anxiety while we wait for our visitor to show up.

"No need to be a dick. I know you're jealous."

Kade scoffs incredulously. "Of what, exactly?"

"I'm the only one that's had her in my bed." I smirk at him, "And that's driving you crazy. Don't worry, bro. I'll take good care of Brooklyn."

The laugh he lets out hurts my confidence a little, it's so full of humour and disbelief. "You really are delusional. You think you're the only one?" Kade turns in his chair, giving me his full attention. "She agreed to stick around, that doesn't mean she's all yours. The other two are with her right now doing God knows what."

I swallow the lump in my throat, refusing to entertain the possibilities of what could be happening at this exact moment with my goddamn girl.

"So, what, are we sharing her now? Like she's some piece of meat to pass between us?"

Kade settles back in his chair, shaking his head. "Look... I don't know. We're looking out for each other, that's it. You know that we all care about her, that's why we've brought her into the fold." He hesitates, fidgeting nervously. "The rest of it is up to her."

"I don't share," I growl automatically. *Hell no.*

"She's sleeping with Eli already, Hud. Probably Phoenix too. You gonna say no if she comes to you?" Kade asks simply. "All I care about is getting everyone out of here alive, then starting fresh. Nothing else matters. We stick together."

I hesitate, feeling a brief blossom of hope that's quickly crushed. I don't want to lose the guys, and I can't begin to contemplate losing Brooklyn now that I've found her again. But *sharing* her? How the hell would that even work? It's insane to say the least.

"You're happy to fuck someone that's also screwing your best friends?" I snort.

"Would you rather lose it all?" Kade snaps back. "Open your eyes. Nothing about our lives is normal or reasonable. I'm simply proposing an alternative route forward."

Just as I'm going to hit him with another snide comment, the entrance door buzzes and opens. We both stand as Janet walks in, her expensive kitten heels clicking against the floor. She hasn't changed in the past year since I last saw her, crying in the courtroom when I was escorted away in cuffs.

Her coiffed blonde hair is dabbled with grey, framing kind eyes and perfectly applied makeup. She still wears the silver locket around her neck that Kade bought for her fiftieth birthday, with pictures of all three of us enclosed in it.

"Oh Hudson... my boy," she cries out.

I adjust my shirt as Janet approaches, silvery tears already tracking down her cheeks. She rushes at me and pulls me into a fierce hug, her tiny body holding me tight despite the fact that I tower over her by at least a foot.

"Hi Janet," I manage to reply.

"Let me get a look at you," she gripes, fussing over me. Her hands run over my shoulders and hair, fingers pinching my cheeks. "You look too skinny. Aren't they feeding you?"

"I'm fine..." I offer, prising her hands away.

"Don't give me that. I haven't seen you for over a year, young man!"

I cringe at the anger in her voice, sinking into my seat. She pulls Kade in for a quick hug, this time not lingering too long as the guards will only come and break them up. Once we're all seated, her attention is back on me, studying and analysing just like her son does.

Kade breaks the heavy silence. "How was the drive?"

"Fine. I had to drop your sister back in Warwick. She says hello. Your father is away on business, else he would have come." Janet offers me a small smile. "He sends his love."

I nod tightly. Somehow, I very much doubt that's what he said. Leroy Knight isn't a good person. Janet was the one that truly brought me into their family. Putting up with all my shit, paying for tattoos to win me over, and basically doing whatever necessary to make me feel welcome.

"Your studies? They're going well?" she asks me.

"Yeah, it's fine." I shrug nonchalantly, trying not to feel her palpable disappointment. What more does she expect? This place isn't some summer camp. I'm not here by choice.

"How are the other boys? Phoenix and Eli?"

Kade links his hand with hers, casting me an impatient look as I struggle to find any words to offer.

"Everyone's good, Mum. We're all keeping busy."

"Good, good. Listen, we don't have much time." Her eyes flick to me, full of sadness and regret. "I know your brother has informed you of the... *little problem* we have."

"Yeah, he told me." I lower my voice, forcing the words out despite my choking guilt. "I think I should just come clean. Tell them the truth."

"No!" Janet exclaims, a hand flicking to her throat. "You will not put yourself at risk like that. Why do you think we're in this predicament?" Her eyes dart around, checking that no one is listening. "I couldn't see you go down for something that wasn't your fault."

I take her other wrinkled hand when she offers it, so the three of us are connected. More tears leak down her aged face as I bite my lip, fighting to keep my own emotions in check. It was my fault, but she still doesn't see it that way.

"What now?" Kade says gruffly.

"We're throwing legal challenges left, right and centre, trying to discredit Stephanie. Claiming she's unhinged, or that she doesn't know what she's saying." Janet nods to herself in reassurance. "It buys us some time. For now, keep both of your noses clean and heads down. We'll sort something."

Her eyes connect with Kade's. He nods, but I'm too lost in my mind to question the look shared between them. The mention of Ma's name has me spiralling into the past, down the black pit of memories that I've tried to purge from my soul with little success.

"She isn't right in the head, Hudson. Accusing her own son... it's sickening. She won't get away with this, I will not allow it," Janet declares, squeezing my hand tight.

"It's the truth though, isn't it?" I reply tonelessly. "I did it. I killed—"

"Stop," she interrupts swiftly. "We're not going through this again. I refuse to sit here and let you torture yourself." Her hand releases mine and grabs my chin, forcing my eyes up to meet hers. "You're my boy, not that witch's. Keep your head together and I will fix this mess."

I stare back at her, pain wrapping around my heart. Despite everything, all the shit I've put her through... Janet still has my back. I don't fucking deserve it. All I can think to do is hand myself in, get it over and done with. No one else should suffer for my mistakes.

"I'll keep my mouth shut," I agree reluctantly, before quickly shutting down her relief. "*For now*. The minute you or anyone else comes under threat, that's it. I'm telling the truth. I don't care what they do to me, where they send me."

"We'll be fine," she argues.

I nod to myself. "I want to protect my family, whatever it takes. You can't stop me from doing that."

"It won't come to that."

We all cling to each other for a second, savouring the contact until the timer at the front of the room buzzes. Janet presses a quick kiss to both of our heads, her eyes shining with tears as she plasters a strong smile back in place.

"I'll be back with more soon. Kade, look after your brother and keep in touch."

"Yeah, always. Bye Mum," he replies.

She turns to me, her eyes softening. "You're a good man, Hudson. Don't forget that. I love you so much."

As she leaves, we both watch in silence, taking a second to gather ourselves. Her words stick in my mind, however distasteful they seem to me. *Good man.* I'm nowhere near the person she thinks I am. Not even on a good day. But I'll damn well try to be just for the chance of making her proud.

"Come on." Kade clears his throat. "Let's find the others."

He takes charge, checking us out of the visitation room and leading the way. I walk numbly. Each step feels like it's sealing my fate, the agreement we just made is weighing me down. I should have refused, demanded they both give up on me.

"Stop it," Kade orders.

"Huh?"

"Stop fretting. You know how she gets. There's no way you were going to win that argument."

I scan my ID badge and let us into the dorms, holding the door open for Kade enter behind me.

"Yeah, I know. Just wish she'd admit defeat once in a while."

"She cares about you." He shrugs, as if the explanation is simple. "We all do, even when you act like an arrogant, self-obsessed prick."

"Probably the nicest thing you've ever said," I laugh darkly, throwing his own words back at him. "Fucking love you too, brother."

We walk back to his bedroom, letting ourselves inside. The sound of a movie playing comes from the corner, where the darkness is lit by the screen. It takes me a moment to find the shape of sleeping bodies crammed into Phoenix's bed.

"Looks like we missed the fun," Kade comments.

He flicks on a bedside lamp, chasing away the shadows. My eyes immediately land on Brooklyn. She's snoring lightly and curled around Eli like a spider monkey.

"Nice of you to join us," Phoenix mutters from beneath the covers.

"What did you do to them?" Kade laughs, sitting down on the bed opposite to pull his shoes off. "They're bloody sparked out."

"Nothing, just comfy." He smirks at me.

Kade looks at the two snoring cuddle buddies. "So I see."

Phoenix reaches over, pulling the covers tighter around Brooklyn and gently brushing Eli's hair away from his face. "It's good to see her getting some decent rest."

I linger in the doorway, my hands tightening into fists. Just seeing him touch her has piping hot anger racing through my veins, along with raw possession and the need to pummel his smug face. She's *my* fucking girl. I should be the one looking after her.

"You gonna stand there all night?" Kade asks wearily.

"What exactly do you suggest?" I remark. "You all look pretty fucking cosy to me."

Phoenix rolls his eyes, keeping his voice low so as not to wake them. "Give it up, Hud. You've been a pain in the ass all week. You think she doesn't see it?" He glances at the sleeping beauty inches away. "If you're not careful, you'll drive her away completely."

Kade nods, standing to grab his sweats and change. "There's beer hidden in the loose roof tile. Just chill and watch the movie before you have a brain aneurysm."

He disappears inside the bathroom, leaving me to retrieve the goods and settle on the floor. My back rests against the bed. I resolutely ignore the clothes strewn over the floor, refusing to contemplate what went on while we were in visitation.

She agreed to stick around, that doesn't mean she's yours.

Fuck Kade if that's what he thinks.

I know the truth.

I'm close enough to hear my blackbird breathing. I cling on to the sound just like Mariam taught me, using it to centre myself. Brooklyn's always been my anchor, even in the years since we've been apart. It always came back to her, the memory of her soft skin and sharp eyes. The horrifying night that eventually tore us apart.

Phoenix begins munching on snacks, snuggling up to her and making sure I'm watching as he does so. The asshole clearly has a death wish. I'll hospitalise him if he keeps playing up.

"Touch her again and I won't be accountable for what happens," I warn.

"She isn't your fucking property. Besides, she wasn't complaining earlier. You're not the only one that cares about Brooklyn. Time to face the facts."

The movie continues playing. My body begins to relax with the beer, every sip soothing my ceaseless rage. I manage to avoid breaking the blue-haired wanker's legs, even when he falls asleep and joins the snoring dog pile in the bed.

I'm counting that as a win.

She's still fucking mine though.

CHAPTER 35
BROOKLYN

CRAZY - LOWBORN

DO you ever stop to think about how the past defines you? Most people don't. They just shake it off and move on. I've never been like that.

I can remember every single event that led me right here. Blow by blow, slowly chipping away at my sanity, gradually adding to the expanding mosaic of my fragile mind. Every memory, twisted secret and filthy sin.

As the clock strikes eight o'clock, the final week of my life begins. I stare up at the ceiling in contemplation. This is it. The end that I've been waiting for all this time.

Why does the thought of dying hurt so bad?

I dress methodically, my movements stiff like a robot. Two outfits lay on my bed. One for each remaining day before it's show time. The final ensemble is my favourite t-shirt and jeans that I intend to wear tomorrow for the big day. I have a plan.

Phoenix's belt lies stolen beneath my mattress. That's the back-up option if I can't steal one of Eli's blades. I know exactly where he keeps them. I should be ashamed, stealing from them to end my own life. It will only twist the knife further when I'm gone, but I've never proclaimed to be a good person. Not once.

I slip my Docs on and manage a smile as I contemplate the bright pink material. It's a shame they can't come with me. I'll be sure to dispose of all my secrets beforehand. My journal, the photos and any other personal effects. I can't have the vultures picking at my corpse after.

Leaving the dorms and heading across the quad, I peer about to ensure none of the guys are around. Dinner last night was weird. Nobody knew quite what to say after Friday night's antics, and me sneaking out long past midnight to hide from them after sleeping with both Phoenix and Eli.

My silent sinner is even more broken than I thought. I can't fucking stand the thought that I'll only make that hurt worse, but the pain of living is far heavier. There are no easy choices anymore, just shitty options and a tonne of guilt.

Checking in at reception, I wait to be escorted down to Lazlo's office for my weekly shot. The corridors seem even gloomier today, with whispered moans and cries escaping from behind the numerous doors. A dinner lady I recognise from the cafeteria takes the trolley from door to door, accompanied by a guard to unlock the solitary cells and slide a tray in.

My eyes land on a skeletal, ghostly white body strapped to a cot inside. An IV line is attached and feeding the necessary fluids to suspend life. His hair is long and unkempt, like he's been locked away from society for a very long time. Our eyes lock through the door. I quickly look away, suddenly afraid.

That'll be me if I don't get the fuck out of here.

"Brooklyn! Good morning," Lazlo greets once we get to his office, bustling me inside as he checks his watch. "9.50. You're early, I'm impressed. Just can't wait, eh?"

"What are you doing to the people here?" I bark at him.

"In solitary?"

I nod tightly, sitting stiff in my usual armchair. Gooseflesh breaks out across my skin as he retrieves my usual dose from the mini fridge. Crystal clear fluid drips into the syringe. Lazlo eyes it intently, tapping the glass to remove any air bubbles.

"They are here for many reasons, Brooklyn. Poor behaviour, violence, suicide attempts, just to name a few. You spent two weeks here yourself, or did you forget?"

I shudder, fighting back the dark cloud of dread. "I didn't forget. But it's all... a bit blurred."

Lazlo leans on his desk, his short legs crossed and smile sadistically wide. I contemplate his thick grey hair and glasses, framing the mind of a man that thinks punishment is acceptable for the mentally unwell. Fucking shrinks. I'll never get over my disdain for them.

"You were acutely unwell. That's why it's blurred," he answers simply.

That's a lie, my mind whispers to me.

He's lying out of his ass.

I flinch back into my chair, my eyes squeezing shut to push the voice aside. That damned needle is coming for me and I'm irrationally fearful, even more than before. What's changed? I'm not going to be here for next week's shot. It doesn't matter what he puts in me.

"What medication am I on?"

The needle slips beneath my skin, icy fluid rapidly spreading as Lazlo watches my reaction. "Experimental anti-psychotics, dear. Blackwood is a pioneering institution in the psychiatric community. You're all forwarding the progression of science. Isn't that good?"

Lazlo retakes his seat behind the desk, shuffling back through my heavy file. If only I could get down here and burn it to shreds before I depart. A final farewell to the bastards that have plagued the last twelve months of my life. *And the rest.*

"Last time, we were discussing your diagnoses and you mentioned your family. Mind if we discuss that a little further?" He peeks at his notes quickly. "Your mother, specifically."

"I told you there's nothing to discuss," I snap.

"It's important to acknowledge the past. These things don't stay quiet in their tidy little boxes. What have you been carrying around with you, Brooklyn?"

Bereavement.

Drugs.

Assault.

Murder.

"Nothing," I state coldly.

"How old were you when they died? Ten?"

I squeeze my eyes shut, pressing my fingers into my eyelids until I see stars. Anything to avoid the familiar faces that swim to the surface, despite being buried deep and rotten to the core. My original wound is ancient yet still tragically present.

"Your mother was a paranoid schizophrenic," he presses.

"She was sick and loved her imaginary children more than me," I blurt out, my hands fisting in Eli's soft hoodie to hide the tremble. "She lost her fucking mind and died, that's it."

"What makes you think that she loved her hallucinations?"

I cross my legs and swallow hard.

"You acknowledge that she was sick," Lazlo points out, tapping his pen.

"But she didn't fight it. She just gave up and was consumed by her insanity. That's what took them from me," I choke up, my voice wavering. "She didn't want to live but couldn't leave us behind."

We're going for a drive, Brooke.

You, me and Daddy.

A nice long drive together.

"Are you 'fighting it', Brooklyn? Unlike her?"

Lazlo looks at me, calm as anything, while I feel like a tornado is ripping me apart. What gives this dickhead the right to ask me that? I've spent every day since that car wreck *fighting it*. Since my mother lost her battle and tried to kill us all, just to appease the monsters in her mind.

"Yes," I mutter, my cheeks flaming.

It's a fucking lie.

I'm done fighting.

Utterly, inarguably done.

"What would happen if you were to just give in?" Lazlo muses, his chin resting on folded hands. He cocks his head, beady eyes far too big behind his thick glasses.

"What... what do you mean?" I gulp.

"You tell me. What's the worst thing that could happen?"

He holds his pen poised, ready for my answer.

"Nothing. I will just... disappear. Like ashes in the wind."

"Hmm. It's almost too easy, isn't it?" Lazlo smiles at me.

Fear washes through me; not irrational, pointless fear, but visceral terror. The feeling when you know that something is wrong, without any evidence or support to explain why. I glance up at the camera blinking away in the corner, capturing our exchange.

"What are you doing?" I ask in a small, timid voice.

I sound entirely unlike myself. He's getting beneath my skin, unhinging me.

"Just exploring your thought processes. Tell me, how would you do it?"

The camera blinks. Lazlo stares. Distant shouts and cries echo through the room. My skin begins to itch, and I pull my knees to my chest, seeking the intrinsic comfort as a threatened child would.

"I don't want to talk about this."

"Are you afraid of the way it makes you feel?"

I shake my head as if to force him out. "No, I just... No."

"Don't you want to see your parents again?"

"No," I whimper, my teeth breaking skin as I gnaw my lip. "I don't..."

"Don't what?"

"I don't want to die!" I scream, feeling my tears spill over. "I'm fucking afraid. I don't want to die! But I have no choice, I have to do what they tell me to. That was always the plan."

Lazlo's fingers drum on the table, entrancing my gaze. His face looks completely different to me now. Gone is the fragile old man, replaced by a wolf in human skin. I blink, trying to disperse the image, shadows creeping up from the corner of the room.

"Who? The voices?" he guesses.

I swallow the bitter lump in my throat. "I... I'm not sure. Why are we talking about this?"

"Because it's November 13th today."

The room seems to freeze around me, detaching from reality and existing in an entirely dark world of its own. Lazlo flips through the papers, humming under his breath. When he selects a glossy photograph and slides it across the desk, my world implodes.

Vic's face stares back at me.

Bright, happy and *alive*.

"Does he look how you remember him?"

"Why are you doing this?" I whimper.

The photo seems to stare at me, his pixelated eyes wide and terrifying. When I manage to look away, someone stands behind Lazlo. Escaped from his mirror and grinning at me, his slick blood pools across the cream carpet. Pearly white teeth reflect the sparkling light, his fingers reaching out to point towards me.

You will join me, Brooklyn.

I've waited a year and your time is up.

I can't help it. I scream bloody murder, leaping up and tripping over the coffee table. Splayed across the floor, I scramble on my hands and knees, frantically putting distance between myself and the shadowy ghost my mind has created.

"He's here for you, Brooklyn." Lazlo smiles at me encouragingly. "All debts must be paid in the end. Time to face the devil and take your punishment."

"Please help me," I beg. "Don't let him hurt me. P-Please."

"I can't help you. People like you cannot be cured."

The world is closing in around me, the blinking camera seeming to pierce my head along with Lazlo's intent gaze.

"Run along now. The clock's ticking," he adds.

I fight the urge to throw up. Confusion and fear are reigning supreme inside of me. Gathering enough sense to find my feet and flee the room, Vic's bloodstained footsteps follow me along the way.

I sprint down twisting corridors, passing guards that pretend like I don't exist. I'm just a ghost passing through these sordid halls, hidden from sight and protected by my insanity. Am I alive? Is this even real? Sobs wrack my chest. I fight to remain present, so close to disassociating completely to escape the impending hell.

The gruesome hallucination of my demon follows me all the way back upstairs, until I'm bursting out in the reception area and skidding to a halt. I have to take a moment, a stitch burning my torso. Breathing is completely impossible. Checking several times to ensure nobody followed me up, I brace my hands on my knees and break down.

There's something wrong with this place.

Sadie was right.

Bad things happen here.

"Brooklyn? Are you okay?"

Someone crouches in front of me. I flinch back, my fists clenched protectively. Kade backs off, raising his hands as if to steady me. His warm hazel eyes are calming, but I'm in too deep. Spiralling beyond salvation into whatever cataclysm of death awaits.

"What's wrong? Did something happen?"

"Lazlo," I pant, fighting for every gasp.

"Yes... your session stars in half an hour. You're early."

My brain threatens to implode, pain lancing behind my eyes and sweat coating my palms. I feel weak at the knees, ready to collapse, throw up or both. Kade just stares unwittingly, analysing my every move but coming up empty.

"Are you worried about the session? Is that what this is?"

"But I just..." I spin, finding myself on the wrong side of the room, as if I entered through the door in preparation for my session. "What time is it?"

His eyes widen even further, anxiety seeming to enter his expression. Kade attempts to step closer, forcing me to take a shaky step back. He's tracking me down like an injured animal ready to be euthanized.

"It's 9.30, Brooklyn."

He doesn't have a chance to grab me as I run away. Each step takes me further and further away from this twisted nightmare. I lose my battle with my stomach and violently throw up once outside, pausing to wipe my mouth before sprinting back to the dorms.

I need to get a locked door between me and the world *right now*, so I can figure out if I'm losing my fucking mind, or if I'm dead already, and this is just my punishment in hell.

CHAPTER 36
ELI

SNUFF - SLIPKNOT

"THE PRISON WILL TAKE care of the funeral arrangements," Miss White informs me, barely sparing me a glance. "There isn't much in the way of an estate, but I assume a solicitor will be in touch given time. Any questions?"

I stare at the carpet, refusing to answer her. For once, there are no words niggling to escape. I have nothing to say, not a single thought or flavour in response to the sudden news. It isn't long before the cold-hearted bitch dismisses me, ready to get on with more pressing matters than some sick old bastard's inevitable death.

Leaving the warden's office as fast as possible, I carefully fold the letter passed along to me, taking time to make sure the edges are straight before slipping it into my pocket. His last words will stay with me forever.

The envelope gets scrunched in my fist, paper on purple flesh, bruises marring my knuckles from punching the wall. Gently, with more self-control than I feel, I take careful steps back to reception. Kade waits for me, already studying my face.

"Is it...?" He trails off.

I nod once. It's over. He's dead.

I've outlived the devil, once again.

"I'm so sorry, Eli. I can't imagine how you must feel."

His words sit heavily in my mind, tasting utterly unpleasant and futile. Like washed out dishwater swirling down a plug hole, debris and remains littered in a vortex of waste.

"You've got Mariam now, right? Maybe she'll help?" Kade tries hopefully.

I don't respond. Not even a look. There's no way to describe how I feel about my father's death.

"Look, we're here for you. Okay?"

My hands brace on the desk. I manage to meet his eyes. Kade fucking flinches, as if he's afraid I'm going to attack him or something. I look away, hot shame flooding every nerve. It isn't his fault, he just picked all the lost causes and has no hope of fixing us.

"Did you see Brooklyn on your way over by any chance? Running?"

Shaking my head, I roll my shoulders until they crack. The mention of Brooklyn doesn't even scratch the surface. I'm too ensconced in my confusing grief to clock his words. Kade sighs, clicking on his computer as the guard comes to escort me to Mariam.

I don't look at Kade again. I can't bear the disappointment and lack of hope I'll find there.

Back in Mariam's office, she begins with some lacklustre condolences, offering me the space to talk about him. I decline, my pursed lips and hard eyes portraying my refusal. Even if I could talk, there's nothing to say. Nothing can make this better.

Mariam continues to talk endlessly without paying any attention to me. The words simply pass over my head as they always do. I've spent months enduring this pointless therapy designed to cure my mutism. What a joke. Some people simply aren't curable, that's a fact. We're too fucked to be cured.

"The sky is blue. Yes or no?"

Mariam watches me expectantly, her smile a poor attempt at comfort. The flavour of vile, acidic spoiled milk sits heavy on my tongue, denoting the fear pulling at my skin. It mingles with my volatile emotions. *How dare he fucking die and escape his punishment early.* I'm still trapped, the real prisoner in this screwed up situation.

"Use your cards, Eli. Come on, we can do this."

I reluctantly study the two slips of paper, the words *yes* and *no* printed across in big letters. My entire body judders as pins and needles spread, anxiety pulsating through every nerve. It takes me nearly a full minute to find the courage to lift the *yes* card.

"Excellent. Well done."

I cringe internally at her pointless reinforcement, the fake enthusiasm only adding to the storm brewing beneath the surface of my mind. He used to be enthusiastic too, that pathetic excuse of a parent. Beating on me and starving me with pleasure, all in the name of purging a devil that didn't exist.

"Next statement...Tomorrow is Tuesday."

I study the wall behind her, watching flames in my mind that don't exist.

"Give it a go. There's a commissary credit up for grabs."

My hand shakes as I nudge the *no* card, forcing myself to appease her. The sooner she gives up, the sooner I can escape. I need to find a quiet corner to cut myself in, alone this time. I don't want any witnesses to this impending breakdown. Especially not *her*.

"How about telling me yourself? Can you do that?"

Fucking persistent bitch. She still doesn't get it, even after all this time. Mariam thinks I can be treated, and that I will speak again with enough therapy. She doesn't fucking understand. It's not that I can't speak. I choose not to.

Words only bring punishment. Pain. Fists and blood. Fire and ash. That's what he taught me. Keep quiet or else you'll pay the price. I will hold my tongue for the rest of my life before I subject myself to that particular form of evil again. I have the scars to prove it.

My collar bone clicks as I tilt my head, remembering the break that sealed my lips for good. The baseball bat connected with my little body as I swallowed the screams, his sermon of pain torturing me endlessly. Any sound would have only resulted in further punishment. I knew that well enough even as a kid.

"Try this one... My name is Elijah. Yes or no?"

I shudder, the name cracking like a whip on my skin. Mariam tries another smile, forever playing the doting mother that I never had. Staring at the thick carpet and resolutely ignoring her, more flavours invade my overwhelmed mind.

Expectation and hope tastes like ripe fruit. Sweet, but underscored with something rotten. Ultimately disappointing when I refuse to give in. I'm trapped in a vicious fucking cycle. The silence breeds my Synaesthesia, my senses strung tight from all the words trapped inside. Yet the more overwhelmed my mind becomes, the less I'm able to communicate.

I can't escape the perpetual hell.

Not like he did. He's free now.

"Look, Eli. You know that I want to help you. I'm just struggling to see any route that leads to progress. You won't be allowed back into the community until you show signs of improvement. Don't you want to go home?"

I don't have a home.

Not since it burned to the ground.

"Tell me what you think." Mariam sighs, trying to find some hope in this situation. "Give me something to work with."

Feeling increasingly angry, I flip the *no* card at her. She stares at me, her hands laced together and lips pursed. We're both frustrated, drained of patience.

"Well, I've asked a colleague to consult on your case. Perhaps some trauma-based therapy will prove beneficial. It's clear that this isn't working. How does that sound?"

I study the crystal chandelier hanging from the ceiling. Imagining it crashing down and crushing me, the glass slices my jugular as blood pours free. Metal punctures my chest and pierces my heart. Anything to end the season of despair that is my life.

"I'll be in touch with the details. Please think about what I've said. You need to start engaging, or I fear that Blackwood may be deemed inappropriate for you. You'll be sent back to Clearview with no opportunity to leave. This is your last chance."

Ice wraps around my heart, cold fingers of death and misery. Not that place, I won't survive it again. Especially without her there. My troubled girl with her dark, haunted eyes. I take Mariam's dismissal and flee, eyeing the blinking camera above the door on my way out.

Blackwood, Clearview.

It's all the same thing.

People like me, we're born to die. Failures bred from our very first breath. I would never survive on the outside. I've been in and out of institutions since I got my scars, so much that I've forgotten what it feels like to have free will. To experience normality. To breathe without being watched. To have aspirations, dreams, *hope.*

I begin to head to class but draw to a halt in the drizzly quad instead. I can't face them. Phoenix. Brooklyn. The people that actually care about me and see beneath the walls I've constructed. The walls *he* forced me to create.

I need to expel the dark energy swirling in my chest. I need to be fucking punished because I shouldn't be alive. What kind of cruel joke is it when I'm stuck here, and my goddamn abuser is at peace in death?

I see Brooklyn in my mind's eye. Curled up between us, her face slack and relaxed. *Trusting.* Letting her impossibly high guard down just long enough for me to sneak in. I'll never be able to tell her how I feel. Not now, not ever. The others will make her laugh, tell them they love her, poke fun at her grumpy morning face and sassy comebacks.

I'll always be the odd one out. The runt in the pack. The worthless piece of shit that my nutjob father made me. When all is said and done, I'll be the one left behind in this place. Hudson and Kade will go first. Then Phoenix, Brooklyn, and every other fucker that plays their cards right.

I'll be alone. Always alone.

I should have died in that fire.

You were born broken, Elijah. Shut your unholy mouth or I won't put food in it for another week.

His voice is loud and awful in my ears, along with the crackling of flames. It's too far ingrained for me to remove, no matter how hard I try. He's always there. Stumbling through the afternoon rain blindly, my feet guide me to the football pitch.

I'm not thinking straight, my only thought is to punish myself just like I've been taught to do. He's not here to do it, but I know the drill. Bad Eli deserves to be punished for his sins. Rio's guys are kicking a ball and messing around on the wet grass, just like I knew they would be.

"Get off the pitch, freak!"

"Fuck off before we make you."

"Come to get your ass kicked?"

"Look lads, it's the resident sociopath."

The insults fly, cutting my skin as much as any razor blade. I don't know what I'm doing. Nor do I care. After all these months, I'm buried beneath the mountain of my failure. Letting Brooklyn get close enough to care has only wounded me further. It's a constant reminder of what I lack, a future stolen from me before I even knew what it meant.

My fist connects with a jaw, I don't know whose. The provocation doesn't go unchallenged, as I planned. The assholes circle, boxing me in. Taking advantage of the CCTV blind spot, the sneers and laughs escalate the adrenaline flooding my body.

Fucking hurt me, I want to scream in their faces.

"You've got a death wish, you psycho!"

I allow myself a sick smile as the many punches land, my skin breaking and bones crunching. Pain explodes in all directions. I slump to the ground, gladly taking the beating. I could laugh, it feels so good. Beautiful, bittersweet agony. Blood runs down my throat. I cough, spitting crimson globules out.

"Come on lads, let's leave him."

They start to retreat, but it's not enough. My mind still buzzes with frenetic, destructive energy. I've got to release it, this desperate need is corroding me from the inside out. Hand searching around, my fingers latch on to a rock. I throw it with my remaining strength and watch as it sails into the back of someone's head.

"Ow! Dammit, this asshole's tripping. You stupid fuck."

Surrounded again, I blink through blood as they pull my leg at an odd angle, yanking it just right. Something snaps, the bone splintering and sending a wave of nausea through me. But still, I don't make a sound. Even as they break my fucking leg, and any remaining air escapes my lungs.

Father trained me well.

Quiet is good. Holy. *Pure.*

"Stay down or we'll break the other one too."

Forcing my eyes open, I catch sight of Rio standing behind his thugs, watching the show with amusement. Forever the ringleader, he's protected by his privilege. He epitomises the evil at Blackwood's centre.

Taking a final boot to my ribs, I curl inwards like a child, finally sated as the tsunami of pain overwhelms my bloodied body. At last, relief comes. Like a trained lab rat, I'm addicted to the pain. My attackers laugh at me and walk away without a second glance.

I'm ashamed to call you my son, Elijah.

You got the devil inside.

But don't worry, I'll get it out.

Let's call it a baptism of fire, eh kid?

I stare up at the angry sky as my consciousness fades, along with the constant whisper of nightmares in my head. No one's looking for me or even cares about me. Not really. I'm fucking thankful because all I want is to lay here, broken and beaten, until my sorry ass is finally permitted to leave this world behind.

Some people leave empty spaces where they used to be. I'm already empty. I don't exist.

The rain pours, heavy clouds thundering down on my broken body; the falling droplets slowly turning red around me. A halo of death encircles my desecrated remains.

CHAPTER 37
PHOENIX
BLOOD SPORT - SLEEP TOKEN

THE SOUND of buzzing and voices rouses me. Uncomfortable pain immediately rises to the surface. I stretch out, my limbs stiff from spending the night curled up in the medical wing's shitty waiting area. The others look equally exhausted. Kade is resting in an armchair as Hudson's towering frame stretches out across several chairs.

I'm so fucking angry, I could kill with my bare hands.

Whoever attacked Eli yesterday... they left him there to die. Alone, beaten within an inch of his life, his fucking leg broken. It wasn't until the afternoon gym class came out that he was discovered. Thinking about him lying there, completely abandoned by the world, makes me long to strike a match and burn this entire institute to the ground.

I'll find out who did it.

Then I'll fucking kill them for it. *Slowly.*

"Shit..." Kade curses, stretching his arms. "Anything?"

I shake my head, staring down the corridor where the treatment rooms lie beyond. "Nothing. What's taking so long? Why won't they let us in?"

"Standard procedure," Kade growls, rushing to his feet. "I'm his emergency contact, but they still wouldn't let me in yesterday. It's fucking ridiculous."

He swiftly kicks a chair with uncharacteristic anger. The loud bang wakes Hudson up, who blinks rapidly and rubs his face.

"You're his emergency contact?" I frown.

Kade collapses back into the chair and shrugs, staring up at the white ceiling. "He doesn't have anyone else. We're it. I put my name down the day we took him in."

If there's one thing about Kade that I admire most, it's his determination to fix the entire goddamn world. I'll tell you another thing—it's going to be the death of him one day.

"Calm down, they'll let us in eventually," Hudson states groggily.

Kade glares at him. "Don't tell me to calm down. I'm done being the calm one in this stupid fucking family."

Things are definitely fucked if Hudson is going to be the new voice of reason. We each fall silent, sitting in this damned empty hallway that smells of bleach and cleaning products. Kade's head falls in his hands. Hudson slowly wakes up, groaning about his aches and pains.

We refused to leave last night. Nobody wanted to go without seeing Eli first. We're a family, and we shoulder mutual blame for his relapse. Even if it was bound to happen again sooner or later. He's never far from another implosion, each one worse than the last. This time, he could have died.

The thought makes me want to scream.

"Has anyone spoken to Brooklyn?"

Kade and Hudson both shake their heads. Everything happened so fast, we'd completely forgotten the devil walking in scarred skin who has us wrapped around her fucking finger without even realising it.

"She should be here," I mutter.

"It will only upset her. Leave it until we know more."

"She probably already heard," Hudson reasons. "The entire institute likely knows by now."

We lapse back into silence, neither one of us speaking again until the entrance door swings open. Doctor Andrew strides in, shaking rain from his umbrella. He takes one look at us, rumpled and grumpy after twelve hours in this godforsaken waiting area, and he rolls his eyes.

"Are you lot still here?"

Kade stands, brushing down his creased shirt and wild blonde hair. "We told you that we're not leaving until we see him."

Doctor Andrew deposits his damp coat and grumbles under his breath, attaching various items of medical paraphernalia from his bag. "This isn't a bloody hotel. You shouldn't be here."

"Let us in and then we'll go," I counter.

He turns to me, still glowering, before acknowledging Hudson with a slight nod. Doctor Andrew has patched up Hudson on many an occasion, and this isn't the first night we've spent stubbornly waiting for an update. We all stand as he finally walks over, sighing in frustration.

"One visitor only. You've got ten minutes, keep it brief."

"You're kidding?" I glance down the white corridor. "We all need to see him."

"Well, you all just have to wait," he chastises. "Eli is concussed. We've got to take him for more X-rays at eight o'clock for his leg. Take your pick and the rest of you go home."

He points towards the exit. Hudson immediately puts his arm around my shoulders, dropping his voice low.

"Come on man, let's leave Kade to it. We'll come back later."

"But I'm his—"

"Emergency contact?" Kade snarks.

Best friend, asshole.

I'm his best fucking friend.

"You're seriously gonna be like that?" I ask him furiously.

Kade stares back in response like I'm the one being unreasonable.

"Fine." I swallow my anger, trying to focus instead on Eli. "Just make sure he's being looked after."

Hudson and I begrudgingly leave, heading for the cafeteria. We're both in a seriously shitty mood. I want to go back there and punch Kade's fucking lights out for being a smug git, but apparently, it's rude to punch your so-called friends. Who the hell knew?

"Quit grinding your teeth," Hudson snaps at me.

"Tell your brother to get his head out of his ass and I will."

"Like he'd ever listen to me."

We grab some breakfast and walk over to our usual table, resolutely ignoring the looks cast our way. News of what happened has clearly been circulating and the tension is brewing big time. When one of Rio's goons smugly asks how Eli is, I have to physically drag Hudson away before he gets us both thrown into solitary.

"They did it," he protests as I sit him down.

"I heard," I grind out, battling my own need for violence. "But be smart about this. We can't help anyone if we get ourselves locked up. Now isn't the time or place for this."

His hands ball into fists beneath the table. He's barely controlling his rage. We watch the huddled group of assholes whispering and trading jokes. Every laugh serves to escalate the thick tension between us. Worst of all, that slimy bastard Rio stares at us, ensuring we know *exactly* who orchestrated Eli's beating.

"I'll break all of their fucking legs," Hudson snarls.

"You can't take them all."

"Wanna bet? I'll tear their goddamn heads off one by one for what they've done."

"And land your ass back in solitary?" I bite into an apple.

"Who cares? It'd be worth it for the satisfaction."

I cast a glance at the looming security presence at every door. The guards are always watching with their dark, beady eyes. Cataloguing every move and word uttered without alerting anyone.

"One day they'll stop letting you out of that place," I mutter.

"They ain't letting me out of here, period. Get over it."

We finish up quick and dump our trays, making sure to walk straight past the boasting dickheads with our heads held high. I walk Hudson to class and check my phone, finding nothing from Kade. That wanker better at least update us after the shit he pulled back there.

When I get to the history classroom, I'm too late to slip in unnoticed. I glance through the door instead, finding our usual table deserted. No sign of Brooklyn. Anxiety immediately attacks me as I stare at the empty set, my stomach turning.

Where is she?

I try to remember the last time I saw Brooklyn, realising with horror that it was Sunday night in the cafeteria. A whole two days ago. Kade briefly saw her yesterday. He mentioned that something seemed off, but we were quickly swept up in the drama. Everything moved so fast. Fucking idiots. In our fear for Eli's health, we've left her all alone.

What if she was looking for us?

We've screwed up big time.

I break into a jog to get back to the dorms. Once inside, I take the stairs two at a time to reach Brooklyn's door. Rattling the locked handle, I press my ear to the wood, straining to hear but there's nothing coming from inside. The bad feeling in my gut spirals. It seems completely irrational, but something is wrong. I just know it.

"What the hell are you doing?"

I spin, desperate hope blooming inside of me, but it's quickly replaced with disappointment at what I find. Britt stands there, frowning, her hands on her narrow hips like she owns the place.

"Looking for your psycho girlfriend?"

"Is it any of your business?" I snap.

"Where's Hudson?" She tilts her chin up, eyes straying to his nearby door. "I've been waiting for him."

"Leave Hudson alone. He doesn't want to see you."

Britt stalks closer, sneering in my face. "What exactly do you all see in her? She must have the tightest snatch in England to have all four of you losing your minds."

My brewing anger flares hot. I grab her by the throat, shoving her against Brooklyn's door. Her eyes bug out and I snicker, leaning close enough to see her yellow-tinged eyes.

"She ain't a bag of skin and bones, for starters. I wonder how long it'll be before your heart just gives up." I scan over her with disgust, my fingers toying with her brittle hair. "You're fucking nothing. You got that? *Nothing.*"

Glorious tears brew in her eyes. I lean even closer, my nose brushing against her vulnerable throat. I can almost smell her fear.

"Keep starving yourself and you'll crumble to ash, where you fucking belong," I whisper into her ear.

"You weren't saying that when you fucked me last month," she spits, yanking her hair out of my clutch. "I thought you boys were all family and shit. Wonder what Hudson will think about you screwing his girl. Or better yet"—a devious grin lights her face as she winks at me—"*your precious Brooklyn.*"

No one threatens my firecracker and gets away with it. Britt tries to escape as I tighten my grip, flexing proudly while she struggles to breathe. I've got her completely trapped against the door, unable to run from my menacing smile.

"You dare tell them. I will *ruin* you. Got that?"

"Don't worry, Nix. Our little secret, right?" she chokes out. "That's what you said."

I dig my nails into her skin, baring my teeth as she flinches. "That's right, honey. I'm the fucking monster under the bed. Your literal worst nightmare if you start playing games with me."

I finally release her, watching as she turns and flees, her broken sobs echoing down the corridor. I can't believe I was ever stupid enough to sleep with that bitch.

Worst mistake of my life. Now, she's trying to pull some twisted shit and screw with us. That's not gonna happen. Kade isn't the only one that would do anything for his family.

I consider Brooklyn's door for a moment, ready to resume knocking when a thought crosses my mind. My feet hurry to the next floor. I reach Eli's bedroom and test the handle, finding it unlocked. Just like I thought. They probably searched the place top to bottom after he was hospitalised. Safety and all, they can't have a dead kid on their hands.

That would be bad for business, right?

Slipping inside, I find the room pitch black with the curtains drawn across the autumnal day. As I move to flick the bedside lamp on, a soft whimper freezes me on the spot. Tension radiates down my spine. I flinch at the barely audible noise, laced with so much fucking pain.

"Firecracker?" I whisper into the dark.

It's got to be her.

Where else would she go?

Tripping over books and dirty t-shirts, I stumble to the bed. A cowering shadow betrays her presence. She's tucked into the corner, hugging Eli's pillow tight, buried in dark sheets that don't immediately reveal their secrets. Relief floods my body.

She's here. She's okay.

"Hey," I say softly.

Her cries are the only response.

My relief is very short-lived. Heartbeat roaring in my ears as I inch closer, I finally notice the dark stains on the fabric. Icy tendrils invade my body as copper fills my nose. Everything stops. Nothing exists beyond the sheer terror that infects my mind at the sight of Brooklyn.

Blood.

Everywhere.

An impassable crimson ocean separating us.

"Brooke? What...." I trail off, my fingers touching wet sheets. "Oh, holy fuck..."

"Go away, Nix," she mumbles drunkenly.

What have you done, baby?

I crawl across the bed, quickly spooning Brooklyn in my arms. Her sticky blonde hair is stained red, splayed out across the pillows. As soon as I touch her, she jumps, struggling to break free from my embrace. She's still trying to run from me, like I'd ever let her go willingly.

I hold her to my chest. "Don't move."

"Why are you here?" She grabs a handful of my shirt, her weak voice trapped on a sob. "Leave me the fuck alone. All of you. I want to be alone."

"So you can die? Is that what this is? Goddammit," I curse furiously. My fingers slip on blood-slick skin, searching for the source. "What the fuck did you to do yourself?"

I lay her down on the bed, flicking on the bedside lamp. Horrifying destruction is revealed on her skin. My mouth goes dry at the deep, uneven slashes, blade parting flesh without mercy. There are too many slices to count, weeping red from both of her arms. She can't have cut herself that long ago if she's still conscious, but it's pouring out of her too fast.

So much blood.

I'm losing her.

"I made it stop." She sniffles.

I gulp hard. "Made what stop, baby?"

Shrugging my jacket off, I wrap Brooklyn up and lift her into my arms again. Panic rules my every thought. All I can think to do is fix her, no matter what it takes. Her head lands on my chest, her nose burrowing into my neck as she shudders a pained breath.

"Everything. The world. Voices. Guilt."

"You have nothing to be guilty for!"

Vicious newspaper articles and dark allegations threaten to contradict me, but I forcibly kick the thoughts out of my mind. None of us are bloody innocent here. She may be a monster, but she's *my fucking monster*. I decide whether she's guilty or not.

"You're not allowed to die," I declare, my decision sealed.

I can't take her to the institute's medics. They'll lock her away for good. I've got to fix this myself. Striding from the room and kicking the door open, I glance around to check the coast is clear. Tightening the fabric around her body, it conceals the almighty mess inside.

"Keep quiet," I say tersely.

Jogging down the stairs, I move fast. Once we're safely back in mine and Kade's room, I take her straight to the bathroom. Brooklyn's legs immediately collapse beneath her. I growl in frustration, depositing her in the tub.

Jesus Christ.

She looks even worse underneath the harsh bathroom light. Her already pale skin is waxy and smeared with bright red blood. Eyes barely open. Mouth slack. Cheeks stained with tears.

You're not allowed to fucking die on me.

Not today.

I turn the tap on, letting cold water spray across her fully clothed body. Brooklyn gasps, her back arching.

"What the… Phoenix?"

"Wake the hell up. No sleeping," I order.

Rooting around under the sink for the stashed emergency kit, I find it under the false bottom, along with my cigarettes, spare cash and a couple of back-up mobile phones. We put it together after Eli's last bad incident. He needed stitches then, too.

The noise that slips past Brooklyn's lips pierces my damn heart. Caught between a cry and a scream, her rage flows freely.

"You should have left me," she yells at me weakly.

"Not happening. You hear me?!"

I lose patience and roughly shake her, hysteria buzzing in my ears. "No one checks out early. Do your fucking time and walk away free. Your sins don't have to define you."

Brooklyn's head rolls to the side and her eyes slide shut, causing panic to seize hold of my lungs. I shout her name, but she remains limp and barely responsive. In my desperation, I take the kit and climb into the tub with her.

Both underneath the icy spray of water, I prise her eyes open and force her to look at me. She's hanging on.

"How'd you do it? Eli's room was cleaned out by security."

Her semi-conscious grin makes my skin crawl. "E-Eli's good at h-hiding stuff. I'm g-good at finding it."

Trying to be gentle, I take her in my arms and slip my hand around the back of her neck. "Hold your breath, this is gonna hurt."

One, two… three.

Dumping the bottle of antiseptic on her shredded skin, my teeth clench at her swift and immediate scream.

"It's okay, breathe…" I coax, holding her head to my chest. My own hands are trembling violently as she fists my wet shirt.

The bathwater turns a shocking shade of red as it leaks down the drain, the pungent antiseptic scent hanging thick in the air. Brooklyn goes limp, but I can hear the rattled breaths coming from her chest. She's still with me. Battling against the clock, I prop her up and grab the kit, expertly threading the needle in seconds.

"Here." I offer my jacket cuff to her, slipping it in her slack mouth. "Bite down and try to keep quiet. We don't need company right now."

It takes me an hour to get the deepest cuts stitched, cleaned and bandaged. She missed the major arteries but still managed to screw herself up good and proper, enough to threaten her life. She needs blood. I'm so mad, I can barely think straight, keeping myself strictly disciplined to focus on one problem at a time.

Then I'll punish her for trying to leave me.

"I'd offer you something for the pain, but that's kinda the point, right?" I bark at her.

"Fuck you. I didn't ask you to help me."

I gently extricate her ghostly white body from the tub, ignoring the bloody mess left behind. Carrying her to my bed, I set her down. Wide, unnerving eyes glare up at me. My fingers tighten on her chin, and I fight the urge to bend her over my knee right here, right now, like she fucking deserves. Verging on death or not.

"You're selfish and you give no regard for anyone else's feelings," I accuse, staring down at her.

She collapses against the pillows, eyeing the thick bandages encasing her arms. "Are you real?" Brooklyn asks me.

My stomach bottoms out. "Of course, I'm real."

I cup her cheek so that she can feel me, and she automatically leans into my touch. I'm beyond terrified, more than I've ever felt in my life as I stare at her numb, confused gaze. What happened to her? First Eli, now my firecracker. The world feels like it's ending.

"It's the anniversary," Brooklyn murmurs.

"Of what, baby?"

She tries to hold it in, but the words tumble free, followed by near hysterical tears. "One year ago, I became a monster. I'm not going to drag you all down to hell with me. You deserve better than that. Let me walk away now and it'll be simpler for everyone."

I collapse next to Brooklyn, pulling the sticky, stained t-shirt over my head. I can't fucking think straight while covered in her blood. It's unhinging my sanity, reminding me of how close we just came to losing her.

"That's today? Fuck, baby…"

Brooklyn stares up at the ceiling, muttering a weak *yes*. I can see her eyelids fluttering, sleep beckoning her under. There's enough blood in Eli's room and the bathtub to warrant her unconsciousness. I watch her until she finally gives in, burrowing down despite still being dressed in her soaked, ruined clothes.

This girl will destroy me, and everything I've worked for. Already I can feel the impending mania niggling in my head, burning behind my eyes as it battles to the surface. It's all too much, I can't keep doing this. Picking up everyone's fucking broken pieces over and over. I've got enough of my own to contend with.

I strip off Brooklyn's jeans and t-shirt, being as gentle as possible. She barely stirs, her body limp beneath my touch. I slip one of my shirts over her head and tuck her in. Re-checking the bandages to make sure they're done tight, I retreat to Kade's bed to study her.

We need blood.

Medication.

Sedatives.

A fucking psychiatrist.

Real medical attention, other than just me. But if I hand her over, that'll be it. They'll most likely send her back to Clearview, with no hope of ever leaving. That or she'll end up in solitary, where nothing good ever happens.

There's no right answer here. I'm being forced to choose between losing my firecracker and saving her damn life. When my phone vibrates in my pocket, I startle, noting Hudson's name before answering.

"Where are you? I'm sat alone at lunch like a fucking freak."

Pinching the bridge of my nose, I sigh. "Long story. Come to my room."

There's a long, loaded pause before he replies. "I have a meeting with Mariam. You good for an hour?"

"No. Fucking hurry up."

I hang up and continue my silent vigil, my hands clenched tight as I wrestle with my emotions. Brooklyn can't escape her past while it continues to torment her. I'll never be able to fix that, no matter how many times I stitch her up or make her smile. Some scars simply run too deep.

I raid my stash of pills and break two of the capsules open, carefully tipping it into a glass of water. Rousing Brooklyn long enough to get it down her is easy, and the hefty dose soon takes effect. She passes the fuck out. Safe… for now.

I can't lose my firecracker to the demons in her head.

None of us will be able to live with ourselves.

CHAPTER 38
BROOKLYN

LITTLE MONSTER - ROYAL BLOOD

One Year Ago

"THANKS FOR THE RIDE."

Grant watches me grab my handbag, a hand slipping into his pocket. My mouth waters at the bag of white powder he pulls free and slides over to me.

"Least I can do. This should hold you for a while. Hit me up when you want more though."

I squeeze my legs together, trying not to wince at the burn. Sex with him is never gentle, but at least I get something from it. Even if I have to do it all over again next week in order to get some more drugs to tide me over.

"Sure thing. See you at work tomorrow?"

"Later, B."

I climb out and watch him go, itching to get inside and tuck into my next dose. Vic's home from visiting his parents, so I'll have to be fucking high to deal with his possessive shit all night. My nails dig into my palms as I take the crappy elevator all the way up to our apartment, my dread and anxiety spiralling.

Slit his throat and run away, the devil whispers in my head.

"Nope," I mutter under my breath, digging my keys out. "I'm not listening to you."

They whisper to me non-stop now, the shadows. Forever my dark and sinister companions. Tuning them out becomes harder with every passing day, but the alternative is even more terrifying. I know what happened to my mother when she stopped fighting. It's not pretty.

Once I get inside the apartment, Vic surges to his feet and meets me in the kitchen. His dress shirt is unbuttoned, revealing tanned muscles that hold no appeal for me anymore.

"Where were you?" he demands.

I drop my keys on the counter, shrugging off my leather jacket. Cold air chills my bare legs and crotch beneath my shitty uniform. I couldn't wear those panties home, not after letting Grant fuck me once we closed up the diner.

"Late shift, customers," I lie, shrugging. "I needed the overtime."

"That's fucking bullshit! You're lying to me again."

Vic wrings his hands, and his face is bright with fury. He grabs my arm and shoves me into the wall, ignoring my squeak of shock.

"Stop fucking lying through your teeth!"

He shouts and raves, yelling in my face like he thinks I'm listening. He's drastically changed in recent months, growing angry and violent the more I push him away. The truth is no longer a hidden secret between us.

Every day, I fuck and shoot up, and he suffocates me with his demands that I stop slowly killing myself. I'm used to the regular screaming matches now. All I can do is stare blankly at him when he's like this because the voices in my head are far louder. Growing stronger with each second, outweighing his pathetic moaning.

Kill him, Brooklyn.

He's worthless. Kill him.

You know you want to.

I clutch my head and squeeze my eyes shut. Vic grabs my wrists and wrenches them away, yelling right in my face. I see red, overwhelmed by the pressure in my mind. My fist connects with his jaw and as he reels back, his eyes blown wide with fury.

"Don't touch me," I yell at him.

"What has gotten into you? I don't even recognise you anymore."

It would be so easy to slip a knife into his gut and feel the hot, satisfying blood pour. So damn easy. I bite my lip, refusing to answer his question. Acid burning in my throat steals my voice.

The shadows creep up the walls, infecting my sight. They twist and weave through the air to reach me, bigger than I've ever seen before. They're like towering angels of death, determined to claim what remains of my black soul.

"No! Stop it! Go away!" I attempt to flee the visions.

"Don't run away from me, Brooklyn!" Vic yells, mistaking my reaction. "I'm talking to you!"

He storms after me and grabs me by the hair, slamming my body into the kitchen table. My eyes burn from the pain across my scalp as he tightens his grip on my throat.

"Who is it, hmmm? Who are you screwing?"

His furious eyes sear my skin and dissolve any remaining control I have left. I can't keep this act up any longer, playing at domestic bliss. Realistically, everything is twisted and poisonous between us. This isn't living. I give up the pretence, letting my hatred flow.

"Anyone. I'll fuck anyone as long as they aren't you!"

The brief sense of victory is snuffed out by the cruel blow he delivers to my face. Stars burst behind my eyes as blood pours from my nose.

"I knew it! You're a psycho bitch, you know that? All these months I've watched you drink and drug yourself into oblivion." Vic shakes his head, a despicable sneer twisting his lips. "I should have let you die. You clearly want to. Go join your parents."

"Why don't you let me die then? Walk away."

"Because I love you! All I ever wanted was to share my life with you, but it's like the girl I loved has been fucking body-snatched by the devil. She's still in there though, I know it."

"She doesn't fucking exist!" I screech, slapping him hard.

Big mistake.

You don't poke the beast and get away with it.

Vic blinks, his pitiful mask slipping to reveal the hidden demon inside. A disturbed mind disguised by a pretty face and charming words. I'm not the only one making this relationship toxic. He hits me again, this time smashing my face into the table. I'm bent over and exposed, my naked legs trembling from the sudden wave of fear.

"Don't you love me anymore? You'd rather fuck someone else?"

I scream and fight back uselessly. "Get off me. I don't love you!"

"Too bad! You don't get to say that."

He spreads my legs with his knee, causing sickness to swirl in my gut. I continue to struggle against his weight, attempting to break free. He's so much bigger than me, strengthened by his rage. I'm his prey, trapped and vulnerable.

"Please don't," I beg, giving into my terror.

"All I've ever done is love you," Vic responds in my ear, his breath hot and sticky. "This is all your fault, Brooke. You're making me do this."

"It's over! Just stop! Stop it now!"

"No! It's not over. You'll learn your fucking lesson and give me Brooklyn back," he demands. "Not this screwed up whore that's taken over recently. Love me back!"

I can't protest anymore, tears flowing down my cheeks as his jeans rustle, the belt clicking open. Every second feels like its own individual death, repeated on an endless, hellish loop. Paralysis has taken over, imprisoning me in this nightmare. I bite my tongue and hold back the sob of pain when he roughly shoves his dick inside me. Agony rips through my insides.

"That's it, remember who loves you," Vic goads, his fingers digging deep into my hips.

Kill him. Kill him. Kill him.

An angry mob of voices fills my head, combining all the different monsters until they blur into a tsunami of murderous rage. I open my teary eyes to watch the shadows leaking down the walls like black tar. Crawling ever closer, they promise temptation and sin along the way.

Kill him. Kill him. Kill him.

Vic grunts his release and pushes me aside. I collapse bonelessly on the floor, curling inwards for protection and hugging my knees. Warmth seeps between my legs, blood mixing with his semen. I'm suddenly overcome with memories of the past and the last man that assaulted me, four long years ago. All while the person I loved most in the world watched.

Hudson. My first love.

He wasn't an abuser like Vic. That flawed, blue-eyed fool was trapped against the wall by the drug lord's thug, forced to watch as the tears streamed down his face. What happened broke him as much as it did me.

I haven't loved anyone since, the hurt ran too deep. It opened a chasm in my chest that paved the way for every moment of agony since. It's all come down to this very moment, every sin and secret creating a monster of its own.

Me. I'm the product of evil.

I'm ready to inflict some pain of my own.

Vic goes to the kitchen, grabbing himself a beer. "We're moving. I don't care where, any place. Pack up your shit and hand your notice in. That's a fucking order, Brooklyn."

Kill him. Kill him. Kill him.

"No," I croak.

The word is nothing more than a whisper. It doesn't matter. The voices will protect me. They know what's best. I've just got to do as I'm told. Getting my legs beneath me is an impossible task, but I force my broken body to move. Vic spares me a disgusted look and heads to the sofa, putting on the football like nothing just happened between us.

Don't let him get away with it.

Punish him. Bathe in his blood.

"I'm not going anywhere," I say, this time a little more forcefully. I reach for the knife block in the kitchen and grab the cleaver. It's heavy in my hand but feels terrifyingly good.

"You're talking nonsense again. Go start packing."

His eyes are on the TV. He's completely distracted while he simply orders me around. My entire body trembles as I walk over, the weapon clutched behind my back. Lucifer himself rests on my shoulder and beckons me onwards with his unholy demands.

Go for the neck first.

It's soft, tender, vulnerable.

Then finish the job.

"Shower as well while you're there. I can't stand the smell of that diner on you." Vic snorts, downing the rest of his drink. "Scrub your filthy cunt too, get whatever asshole has been screwing you erased. We'll never discuss it again."

I pause directly behind him, close enough to smell the earthy beer. One move and this will all end. *Just do as the voices say,* I remind myself. The rest will take care of itself. My heart is pounding, chest thumping as sweat runs down my face. The seconds crawl by. I raise the blade, a triumphant smile escaping.

That's it, good girl.

Give him what he deserves for hurting you.

I slash and stab, screaming like an animal. Vic fights back at first, his eyes blown wide with delicious fear. I have the element of surprise. The wickedly sharp blade parts flesh and he slumps to the floor, the beer bottle shattering. Blood gurgles from his mouth, spurting and pouring from exposed arteries in his neck. Vic slowly chokes, clutching at the air for help that will never come.

I smile sweetly. "I'm sorry, babe. I do love you really."

The blade slips into his torso and pierces his organs as I viciously attack, leaving no part of him untouched. By the time I'm done and my thirst for revenge is sated, his eyes are empty. Nothing but a butchered carcass remains, soaking my cream carpet with a crimson river.

Well done. Didn't that feel good? The power?

You can hurt whoever you want.

Take their lives and dance in their blood.

You know you want to.

I stroll to the bedroom, smashing endless framed photographs along the way. Then I stare at my horrifying reflection in the mirror. A new version of myself exists now—someone beyond redemption and irrevocably lost to the world. Shadows wrap around my ankles, voices whispering their applause in my mind.

Blood coats my uniform and skin. I rub circles in the sticky liquid with fascination. So beautiful. Vic had to die. Just like me. I raise the blade to my arm and hold it in position, ready to rip a hole in my artery.

No, Brooklyn.

You have to run, not die. Sort the body.

There are plenty more people out there who deserve to die.

Find them.

Shaking my head, I argue with the voices and defend my case. Death is the only option. I'm too far gone to continue. But ultimately, the shadows control me. I leave bloody footprints all the way back to Vic's cooling corpse. He's too large and heavy for me to move. I'll have to get creative. I can't disappoint, I've been given a task. It must be completed.

I've got to finish the job.

A handsaw ought to do the trick.

CHAPTER 39
HUDSON

THE JESTER - BADFLOWER

"YOU'RE GOING to tell me exactly what happened here, or I will slowly and painfully break every single fucking bone in your body."

Phoenix shushes me and drags me to the corner of the room, further away from the fitfully sleeping girl in his bed.

"Keep it down, will you? The longer she's out, the better."

He runs an anxious hand through his hair, eyes straying back over to her. I follow his gaze, pain blooming in my chest at the devastating sight. Brooklyn's tightly wrapped in sheets, moaning in her sleep. Bright white bandages peek out, revealing the extent of our current predicament.

"I crushed a load of my sedatives into her water," Phoenix informs me. "A double dose. She needed it."

"You spiked her drink with your medication? Dude, what the fuck? She isn't manic."

He glares at me indignantly. "Would you rather she tries it again? If I hadn't walked in and stitched her up earlier, she would have died. Bled out and fucking *died.*"

My mouth turns to ash, the bitter taste on my tongue refusing to be swallowed. It feels like a snake has wrapped itself around my insides and is squeezing tight, removing all available air. *Died.* She would have left me again, this time for good. The thought fucking destroys me.

"We can't turn her in. They'll throw her in the hole for her own protection."

"Or ship her back to where she came from," I say grimly. "If they deem her too unstable for Blackwood's program."

"Goddammit!" Phoenix curses. "What the hell do we do then?"

"We deal with this ourselves! We have no choice!"

"We can't. She needs medical attention."

He stares at me, shaking his head like I'm the one that's unstable. I fight the urge to yell at him some more. He walks over to the bed and sits down, his hand ghosting over Brooklyn's exposed shoulder.

"Tell me honestly, right now, how you feel about her."

"Huh?" I frown at him.

"Just answer the fucking question. All cards on the table."

I sink to the floor, my legs stretched out as I struggle through the mess of thoughts in my mind. There are too many to count. Love. Hate. Lust. Shame. It all mixes into one giant shitshow that has my head spinning. But one thought burns too bright to ignore.

"I can't lose her. Not now I've found her again," I admit. "She's different now, not the person she was before. But it doesn't matter, my feelings haven't changed."

Phoenix nods solemnly, his serious attitude so unlike him. But when faced with a crisis, we all have our redeeming qualities. He's cleaned Eli up many times in similar circumstances without a single complaint.

"You should know that I'm falling in love with her," he adds.

I wish I could say that I'm surprised, but I've seen the way they look at her. You'd have to be a fool to miss it. The guys are all fucking enraptured, just like me. Inexplicably drawn to the beautiful, chaotic disaster that is Brooklyn West and her crazy goddamn head.

"We all care about her, so we've got to find a solution here." I look back at my girl, comforting myself with the rise and fall of her chest. "I'll get Kade, he'll know what to do."

Phoenix snorts. "Yeah, right. He's busy fixing the other idiot hellbent on self-destruction."

"What exactly do you suggest then?"

He continues to stroke Brooklyn's skin, gnawing his lip. "She'll be out for a few hours. We need to get everyone together to talk some sense into her."

"Talk to her? That's your solution?" I repeat.

Is he for real?

"We've got to convince her to stick around."

Fighting my initial reaction, I consider his idea for a second, shoving the tendrils of jealousy aside. Will it work? Between us all, maybe we have a slim chance of success. Very fucking slim.

"I'll find Kade and fill him in," I concede.

"Good," Phoenix mumbles, nodding to himself. "We need to pull ourselves together for when she wakes up. It's now or never. All of us need to be there."

Huffing a breath, I walk to the bed and stare down at my sleeping blackbird. She clutches at the sheets, tormented even now. Surrounded by us, temporarily safe from her own mind. Fuck, there's no way this will work. We can't give her what she needs. How can you convince someone to live when they don't want to?

"It'll work," Phoenix reassures, reading my mind.

"How can you be so sure?"

"Because there's no other option. It's this or let her implode. The shrinks aren't getting a look in here. They'll bury her so deep, she'll never come out again. We're her last chance."

"Yeah, I know."

He glances up at me, offering me a bleak smile. "Get it done, Hud. For her."

"Keep her safe until we get back later? I'll bring the others. Just… watch over her." Gulping, I let some of my desperation leak out. "We can't afford to fuck this up."

"Yeah, got it," he mutters.

I press a kiss to Brooklyn's forehead and leave them behind, forcing myself to focus. I'll need the exact right words to offer her, to make her see that she has a reason to live. Phoenix is right, it'll take all of us. And if we fail, I can't even begin to contemplate the repercussions. Losing my blackbird is unimaginable.

I burst into the reception area after sprinting over like a madman, struggling for breath. Kade's on duty and his head snaps up as I enter at full speed.

"Hud? What's wrong?"

I jerk my head towards the back. He has a quick glance around, checking the coast is clear. We slip into the rear office for privacy, and I slam the door shut.

"I need to tell you something."

"Um, okay. Anything wrong?" he worries.

"Just… don't freak. It's Brooklyn."

Kade stills, the colour draining from his face. "What happened?"

I'm so fucking angry and scared, I can barely see straight. It takes all of my self-control to keep calm and rational. The thought of Brooklyn bleeding alone in Eli's bed is a nightmare playing on repeat in my mind. We don't have time to waste right now.

"She tried to kill herself," I blurt.

Kade's mouth drops open as he goes white. "What?"

"Phoenix found her bleeding out." I pause, shoving the chilling image from my imagination. "She's alive, out of it currently. We need to be there when she wakes up. And she needs medical attention. Phoenix has done what he can."

Kade fists his hair, panic gripping him. "Are you fucking insane? We should take her to Doctor Andrew right now before she tries it again. Jesus Christ, where is she?"

I shake my head frantically "No! Don't you see? They'll take her away for good this time. If we turn her in, we lose her. Permanently. Don't be a fool."

Kade's face falls. His eyes move without seeing, as if searching for options and coming up blank. "But we can't do nothing! Isn't it better that she's alive, even if it takes her away from us? She's a loose cannon and you know it."

I can't help myself, I punch the blithering idiot.

"Ow! Dammit Hud, what was that for?"

"To knock some sense into your thick skull. She will *rot* if they take her away. You know that Blackwood is the only way out of the system. We're talking about her life here."

"And I'm trying to save it," Kade spits.

Turning my back, I walk away to prevent myself hurting him further. Sometimes, he sees the world far too plainly in black and white.

"What exactly was your idea then? Screwing her to make it better?" he adds.

He's got a fucking death wish.

"Don't push me right now, I will break your fucking legs. Of course, that's not what this is about!" I collapse into a desk chair, gathering myself. "I don't know what else to do."

Kade kneels in front of me, his expression an open wound of shame. "What is happening to us? First Eli, now Brooklyn." His eyes fall shut, hard lines carving his forehead. "I've failed you all. We're falling apart at the seams."

I place my hand on my brother's shoulder, summoning some reassurance that I really don't believe myself. "We'll fix it. That's what family does, right? You said so yourself."

He manages a half-hearted smile, sparing me an appraising look. "Careful, brother. You're starting to sound a little too optimistic for your own liking."

"Well, don't get used to it," I mumble.

We both stand and clasp hands, nodding in acknowledgement. It's probably the first time we've agreed on something in the eighteen months we've spent here. Brooklyn's brought us together against the odds. Now, we've both got to work to save her. Kade holds my hand for a second too long, overcome with a moment of clarity.

"Good to have you on my side," he offers.

"Don't get all weepy on me, we've got shit to do."

We leave the office, heading back to the reception. My attention is drawn by the guard leading someone up the stairs from the basement level. My eyes clap on his proud smirk first as he sees us standing there, watching in dismay.

"Gentlemen," Rio taunts. "How's Eli's leg doing? Bit sore?"

I try to move, determined to pummel him into the ground and release the anger slowly choking me. Kade grabs my arm, muttering under his breath.

"He's not worth it. I reported him to the warden for the attack. He'll be punished the correct way."

Rio struts past us, heading for Miss White's nearby office. My fingers twitch with the urge to punish him myself, but I focus on the task at hand, keeping Brooklyn front and centre in my mind.

"I hope they bury you in solitary," Kade snaps.

Before Rio can respond with some inflammatory response, a stern voice barks at us. "What exactly is going on here?"

We all turn to see the warden herself appear from her office, her hands on her hips and face unimpressed. She's wearing another impeccable pantsuit, matched with loose, blowdried blonde hair.

"Kade, if you wish to keep your job, I suggest you get back to work. You and your friends are already on *very* thin ice. My patience is limited."

Her cold eyes stray over to me, bitter resentment taking over her face. "You best pray that Rio here doesn't wish to press charges against Elijah for starting the fight. This could get very messy."

"What the fuck?" I gasp in shock. "You can't be serious. You're taking his side?"

Kade and I gape incredulously at her words, utter disbelief taking over. This is fucking unbelievable. Rio and his group of untouchable lowlifes literally beat the living shit out of Eli, even broke his fucking leg. Why are they defending this asshole?

"Eli's the one in hospital, beaten within an inch of his life," Kade points out acidly.

Rio holds his hands up innocently. "He attacked my friends. It was self-defence."

"There isn't a single fucking scratch on any of you!"

Miss White's patience expires, and she turns to the silent guard. "Please escort Rio inside my office. I will deal with this and join you momentarily."

We both fall silent and watch Rio pass us, slipping into her office. He shoots me a hateful look before disappearing, promising retribution. My mouth waters at the thought. Fucking bring it. I'll rip the cocky shit apart, piece by piece.

"Kade, your privileges here can be removed as quickly as they were given. Don't forget that," Miss White says, her face pinched with displeasure. "There are protocols for a reason around here. Elijah attacked a fellow patient, therefore he is the one at fault."

"That's bullshit!" I interrupt.

She glares at me threateningly. "Silence! Or you'll spend the rest of the bloody year in solitary. I've had it with you, Hudson Knight!"

We both stand still, angry beyond words as the warden gives us meaningful looks, ensuring her authority is clear.

"Leave Rio alone and worry about yourselves."

She turns and marches away, slamming her office door hard enough to rattle priceless artworks up and down the hallway. We stare at each other, completely bemused by her blatant favouritism. What the hell has Rio got on her? Has he paid off everyone in this corrupt institute?

Kade rubs his forehead with a pained frown, clearly unhappy. "Rio will get what he deserves one day. There's something wrong with this place. I refuse to tolerate it for a second longer. Nothing about Blackwood makes sense, least of all that asshole's power."

"What are you suggesting?"

"Right now? Nothing. We need to sort our current mess and keep Eli out of their reach. One problem at a time, Hud. Come on, we need to convince Doctor Andrew to release Eli and see about stealing some supplies to treat Brooklyn."

We leave for the medical wing together, both struggling with the injustice. Nothing about this unholy place is right, it never has been. In an enclosed world with its own rules and social norms, of course things will be a little strange.

But that doesn't explain the growing list of worrying incidents that don't stack up. I have a feeling that we've only glimpsed the horrors that happen behind closed doors.

Even if we save Brooklyn and Eli...

Blackwood Institute will swallow them whole.

CHAPTER 40
BROOKLYN

BORN TO DIE - LANA DEL REY

I LAY STILL, my body numb and tingling. The sound of the shower running fills my ears, providing the only sense of reality in the pitch-black room. My mind is heavy, weighed down by an eternal burden that refuses to shift.

I shouldn't be awake right now, judging by the metallic taste of chemicals on my tongue. Phoenix saved me. Stitched me. Drugged me. If it wasn't for him, I would certainly be dead by now. Little did he know, I didn't want to be saved.

I'm beyond redemption.

I test my limbs, gradually moving from the stiff position. His little cocktail of drugs kept me out for a while, but after twelve months of incarceration, I've built up a tolerance. He miscalculated. It takes more than a handful of sedatives to keep me down these days.

This is my final chance.

No drawn-out goodbyes.

No pain or heartbreak.

I'll just disappear, and they can all go back to their lives like I never even existed. From the very first day I set foot inside of Blackwood Institute, I never intended to stay. This was just a brief stopping point, a layaway on my inevitable road to promising oblivion. I allowed the guys to distract me from my true purpose in being here, however briefly.

Fucking foolish.

I'll never be like them.

My sins are too great.

I walk barefoot and swaying, the room buzzing all around me in a kaleidoscope of confusion. It takes great effort not to fall over, but I've got just enough sense left to keep moving, past the bloody, ruined clothes that Phoenix stripped off on his way to freshen up.

I bided my time.

Calculated my moves.

Waited for his guard to fall.

This is my final move. Check mate. No failures this time. Slitting my wrists is too risky, we've proven the odds are unfavourable. These relentless men will just keep patching me back together with their hopes and desperation. Forever seeing something in me that simply isn't there.

Vic saw it too. In his own twisted, possessive way. He refused to let me die and paid the price for his stupidity. I killed him; intimately, brutally, *happily*. The shadows were my guide back then. They mark my steps now.

I leave Phoenix and this warped reality behind, softly clicking the door shut. My feet ghost across the thick carpet, bare and bloody. There's one more thing I need, my back-up plan. It'll have to do, I'm out of options. I'll hang myself and choke to death if that's what it takes to escape, no matter how messy it will be.

I get back to my room and lift the loose ceiling tile, my hand searching in the cobwebs until it meets paper. The package of accusations and hatred has taunted me for the last two months, ever since Mariam handed it over. I didn't break once in all that time, saving them all for this exact moment.

It's only fair that I read the letters now. At the end of this chaotic journey, it's a fitting memorial for this inevitable day. I've lived a whole year longer than Vic got to. Time to right that wrong. I stuff the bundle in my leather jacket and slip it on, too out of it to contemplate putting proper clothes or shoes on. My mind is numb and broken beyond repair.

My eyes stray to the phantom girl in the mirror. She looks haunted. Gaunt, tired, and inarguably *done*. The longer I look, I see him staring back at me. The golden boy hiding his evil, who hurt me in the worst possible way and died choking on his own blood. I watch myself smile. It's twisted and sick. Shadows curl around my limbs and begin to whisper, growing stronger.

He deserved it. You do too.

Come on, Brooklyn. Time's up.

Taking one final glance around my room, I swallow the rising emotion that threatens to distract me. It's messy in here, scattered with books and clothes. I note the reminders of the past two months, snippets of normality and belonging that prolonged my inevitable end.

Phoenix's beanie.

Eli's hoodie.

Kade's backpack.

Hudson's t-shirt.

Life is fucking temporary, fleeting in its brutality. It ends and begins, trapped on an endless loop that most are powerless to escape. I'm taking off early, unable to stomach any more of this rollercoaster. The guys will soon forget and move on.

Whatever feelings that I have for them… it's irrelevant now. I've got to finish the job I started one year ago and pay back the outstanding debt on my life. I'll end it and free all four pieces of my heart from this toxic *thing* between us.

There's a knock on my door before it swings wide open. I prepare to fight whoever is trying to save me this time. I'll hurt them if I have to. They can't stop me again.

"Hey, Brooklyn."

Dread seizes me. I force myself to look up, finding Rio in my doorway. He grins at me, his eyes slowly travelling over my body, noting the bandages on my arms and skittish look on my face. Smiling slow and sinister, he easily excavates the truth from my soul.

"Still want that key?"

I try to speak, my mouth impossibly dry. Nothing comes out.

"Some people have forgotten their place around here and need to be taught a lesson."

All I can do is stare.

"We don't tolerate disrespect here at Blackwood. They need reminding." Rio gestures behind to the corridor, where Kade and Phoenix's room is located. "You want to help me out with this? Free of charge. Call it a parting gift."

I nod, but not a sound passes my lips. Morbid hope balloons in my chest.

"Follow me," he orders.

Leaving my room behind, we climb the stairs together to the top floor. Passing several guards along the way, they simply nod at Rio, deferring to his authority. It's almost like he's the one in charge, not them, which makes zero sense. I wait outside his bedroom door, trembling all over while he gets the key. The sound of a floorboard slotting back into place reverberates through my mind. I'm close, I can almost taste the freedom.

Lazlo's question flashes through my mind.

Don't you want to see your parents again?

There's a strange feeling in my chest, desperately battling to break free.

"Ready?" Rio offers a slim key card to me.

I clutch it tight, managing another nod despite my body trying to defy me. It feels like I'm being pulled in two directions, ripping my entire psyche apart straight down the middle. I stare at him, wracked with uncertainty and a heavy dose of panic.

"Don't worry about a thing, it's planned out for you," Rio informs me, his words going straight over my head despite the immediate alarm bells. "I'll have a guard testify and say that you stole the card from him. Might even rough him up a bit, make it believable. Schizos can be so unstable, you know. I'll take care of everything."

Why?

Who are you?

Why are you doing this?

Questions rise to the surface like demons refusing to drown. I shove them aside, ignoring the terror of reality. This is my chance. I won't waste it. No matter what pieces on the chess board are carefully manipulating me, a clueless pawn.

We take the steps to the roof with solemn proclamation. Like the Grim Reaper guiding his victim, Rio hides from sight and gestures to the CCTV camera. Counting down the seconds, he gives me an encouraging nod as the red light blinks out.

"It's time." Rio gives me a long, hard look, as if savouring his victory. "Got anything you want to say?"

I stare at him, unfathomable pressure threatening to break my mind apart. Confusion and panic rise like an erupting volcano, but it remains locked out by the numb cloud coating everything. I should say something. Anything. Yet I can't think of a single word.

"You played the game well," he offers with a conciliatory smile. "I didn't think you'd last this long."

Game?

Rio laughs, plucking the key card from my shaking hands and scanning it to unlock the exterior door. His hand strokes over my tangled hair, and his lips twist with satisfied amusement.

"Nothing about this place is real, Brooklyn. Don't you see that yet? It's all just..." He pauses, grinning and searching for the right word. "An illusion."

Freezing cold air rushes through the gap, entangled with voices that beckon me up.

"Off you go. I can't wait to tell the others about this, I'll be given a fucking promotion. You've proven mighty interesting. I'm glad Augustus decided to bring you into the program."

"Augustus?" I choke out, barely above a whisper.

Something is screaming at me from deep inside, protesting against the slow realisation. This isn't right, his words mean something. I should be fucking running, not taking an offer that is simply too good to be true. But everything is so loud in my mind, I'm too exhausted and defeated to fight back.

"Oh, yes. Shame you'll never meet him," Rio goads.

Say it, Brooklyn.

You know the truth. Say it.

"Y-You're not a real patient. Are you?"

Rio strokes my cheek with something akin to pride, happy to boast his true status. "You've been fun, but it's time. Goodbye, Brooklyn."

My feet move of their own accord, giving me no choice but to comply. I take the steps up, leaving the devil behind. Voices scream in my mind to keep going. We're so close and nothing stands in our way anymore. Even though on a subconscious level, rationality is itching to escape.

This is too easy.

Wind whips my hair as I emerge on the roof. The sky is marked in shades of indigo and purple, an angry sunset just disappearing on the horizon. I think of my mother putting herself in the way of beauty. She's here with me now, her arms open and ready to welcome me home.

I make it to the edge of the building, my feet nudging brick that melts into thin air. I'm glad it's ending this way. With day fading into night, life morphing into death. Thing is, I've never lived in darkness. The darkness lives in me.

I take the bundle from my pocket and carefully undo the knot, letting endless letters fall all around me. Allison's penmanship screams at me from the ink-stained pages, the words taking life in my mind as sharp voices whisper her hatred. I open the first letter.

You took my brother from me.

I hope you rot in hell, where you belong.

It falls from my hands. The next one is marked with a date from the following week.

We had to bury him in pieces.

That's how you left him.

Unrecognisable.

I scrunch it up and toss it over the edge, watching the paper fall through the air, marking the path that I shall soon follow. They continue in order; week on week, for nearly ten months. Each letter spews hatred that I most definitely deserve. Countless notes telling me to die and remove my evil stain from this earth for good.

I'm more than happy to oblige.

Stepping up on the edge, my body wobbles in the suddenly thin air. Mere inches to go and I'm free. The final letter is clasped in my hands, bending under the weight of my anticipated grip.

I don't think that everyone is evil. Some deserve forgiveness, but that's just not you. What you did to my brother... that's not sickness. That's depravity. You're a monster, not a victim.

My eyes slip shut. Breathing halts. The voices quieten. Everything waits for the eventual fall. As I ready to throw myself into the comforting arms of the unknown, faces flick through my mind. Bright hazel eyes and perfect blonde hair. A silent, secretive smile and soft brown curls. Playful blue waves and an optimistic grin. Inky black strands and overwhelming regret.

I teeter on the edge and reply to the images in my head.

Goodbye. I'm sorry.

In the split second before throwing myself from the roof, a blood-curdling scream pierces the air. Followed by shouting. Yelling. My name. Multiple voices. Desperation. My head turns and I see them, this time for real. Running towards me with their hands waving frantically.

"Don't come any closer!" I shout.

My pursuers freeze, gripped with terror as I dangerously sway on the edge. Bricks crumble and topple off from the roof, barely supporting my weight. Kade steps forward and raises his hands placatingly, his entire body fraught with tension.

"Brooklyn, listen to me carefully—"

"No!" I scream back.

Kade flinches, his face collapsing with fear. He searches for help. Phoenix tentatively steps forward next, leaving Hudson behind as he holds a wriggling Rio in a headlock.

"Firecracker... it's me," Phoenix offers.

He approaches me like a startled animal. There's blood smeared on his face from a recent fight. His knuckles are cracked and bleeding. I can see that Rio's nose is pouring while Hudson continues to choke him.

"Don't move. There's nothing left to say," I say in a robotic voice.

"There's everything left to say. You don't have to do this. Please let us help you."

I shift my right foot. More bricks crumble and my body sways again. "One more step and I go," I interrupt him. "Stop fighting this. All of you."

"Blackbird, stop!"

"Brooklyn, don't!"

"Firecracker, please!"

They all shout and plead as I inch my left foot back, so fucking close to falling. The wind picks up and a squeak escapes my lips as I teeter, struggling to maintain my balance. All of them shift closer, ignoring my raised hand holding them back.

"No! This is my decision and mine alone!" I cry out, tilting my face up to feel the falling rain. "I must be punished for what I've done. I'm sorry, this is the only way."

Beginning to turn away from them, I face the towering drop. I lift my right foot to fling myself into the air, my heart bruising my ribs as it threatens to break free, but a different voice stops me.

Harsh. Grating. Raw. Disused.

"D-Don't... go."

I tremble on one foot as the sound of crutches against concrete approaches. Tears stream down my cheeks and freeze in the gradually increasing wind. In that moment, the final scrap of light disappears from the sunset. Ceaseless darkness invades everything.

"S-Stay."

Stuttered. Broken. Pained. Unpractised.

I look over my shoulder through the thick curtain of tears. He stands mere metres away, his leg wrapped in a cast and face marked in unnatural shades of colour. Brown curls matted and unwashed. Lips parted on words spoken only to me, breaking years of silence.

Eli drops one of his crutches and raises his hand. His fingers are outstretched to beckon me closer. I stare into his wide green eyes, full of horrors of both past and present, understanding in a way only kindred spirits can be. My foot lowers of its own accord as we face off in the gathering storm.

"I can't... don't make me," I manage to reply.

Those perfect lips turn up in a smile just for me. Thick eyelashes frame dazzling emerald eyes, begging me to step down. Eli wiggles his fingers; coaxing, encouraging, imploring me to return to him.

"L-Live," he struggles out. "W-We... live."

He hops closer to close the distance between us.

"Please stay away." I sob brokenly. "I don't... want to live."

Eli stops mere inches away from me, but he doesn't move any closer. His hand hovers in the air, encouraging me to close that final gap. I reach out automatically. I can't help myself, our fingers entwine. His palm is warm and dry. Steady. Reassuring. *Alive.*

"Neither do I."

His voice is raw but flows like honey through my veins. My feet move back from the edge without thinking. Only slightly, but enough for him to see. His devastating gaze burrows beneath my skin and attacks the tendrils of hatred around my heart. I take a shuddering breath. More tears fall. My body shakes. The wind howls. Eli's hand clutches mine painfully tight.

"Live... f-for me. For us."

His words ghost over my skin, caressing my fractured soul. Invading my mind in a way that no one else ever will. All because Elijah Woods is me. Broken pieces held together by bitter resentment and determination to take up less goddamn space in the world.

There's a sudden, brutal gust of wind just as I resolve to step down. I teeter in the air for a terrifying second before finally losing my balance.

EPILOGUE

ELI

"IF ANYONE HAS any further information about the tragic events that transpired last night, I urge you to come forward. You won't be in trouble. We need witnesses to shed some light on what happened. And remember... suicide is never the answer."

Miss White casts a serious look around the cafeteria, her dominance and authority stifling. There are more guards than you can possibly count in this room, a clear show of force after the chaos of the last twenty-four hours.

Phoenix grips my hand so hard it turns white. I touch his frantically jiggling leg, trying to communicate my silent support. We've got to keep it together in front of everyone.

"I understand that you're all shaken by what happened yesterday. A full investigation will take place," she adds meaningfully. "I can assure you that we will get to the bottom of this."

"Fucking lies," Phoenix hisses under his breath. "All of it."

His acrid rage dances across my tongue. I swallow, forcing the bitter flavour aside. *Hold it together, just for a few more seconds. Got to keep a brave face, don't let them see the truth.* This is torturous, sitting here like nothing is wrong, but it's necessary.

Miss White sighs and shuffles her papers, her brows furrowed. "That's it for now. Classes are cancelled for the rest of the week."

There's a scraping of chairs as a handful of therapists rise, including Mariam and Sadie. They all watch us carefully, their faces schooled into heartfelt sadness. Like any of them actually care.

Miss White clears her throat, forcing a horrid smile that really doesn't suit her. "This institute will mourn the loss of one of its own. Rest assured, if anyone was involved... there will be punishment. You're all dismissed."

The room bursts into a flurry of movement, with patients rushing to escape. We allow the crowd to dissipate, then Phoenix hauls me to my feet and offers me an arm. I get my crutches into position and resolutely ignore the pain wracking my body.

"You good?" Phoenix asks.

I nod curtly, keeping my expression neutral. We slowly stumble past the warden, who turns away from the conversation she's having to watch us suspiciously. We avoid all eye contact.

"Think they know?" Phoenix whispers once we escape outside.

I shake my head. *Who fucking knows at this point?*

It takes an age for us to get back to the dorms at my snail's space, but as we tackle the stairs, I notice the dorms are eerily quiet. Everyone is trying to avoid returning to where last night's tragedy took place. The entire institute is shaken to the very core.

Back at his room, Phoenix roots in his jeans pocket for the key card. He scans it shakily, letting us both in. Kade shoots up as soon as we enter the bedroom.

"How was it? What happened?"

I release Phoenix, letting him collapse and sink to the carpeted floor. He immediately buries his face in his hands, taking an uneven breath.

"They're scrambling, searching for information."

"But nobody gave any?"

I shake my head. Kade's body visibly sags with relief. He runs a hand through his messy hair, his face pale and exhausted. None of us slept a wink last night. We were too traumatised to sleep. We're running on empty, clutching at straws as we scramble to cover our asses.

"We need to get our stories straight in case they question us," Phoenix mutters. "The warden is ordering a full investigation."

"Way ahead of you." Kade sighs. "I'll brief everyone later."

I ignore them both, I shrug off my jacket and round the corner to bring Phoenix's bed into view. Two bodies are safely tucked inside where we left them. Hudson is sound asleep on his back, an arm tightly wrapped around Brooklyn's shoulders as she naps on his chest. He hasn't left her side since the roof, possessively clinging to her out of fear.

"They've been out of it for a while," Kade explains, contemplating the occupied bed. "Sadie gave her more sedatives when she came to finish the transfusion. We're out of the woods for the time being."

I nod again, grateful that the trainee agreed to help us.

"Good shout involving her, she's on our side here," Kade praises me.

She's the only person here that I even remotely trust. Sadie cared about Brooklyn in Clearview, so I knew we could approach her. It's not like the others know that. Thankfully, she kept her mouth shut about the past.

Phoenix pulls himself together and joins me by the bed, wrapping an arm around my waist for comfort. Kade comes next, completing our group, his attention on the unconscious girl that narrowly cheated death mere hours ago. Our entire world rests in that bed.

We're her family now.

Come hell or high water.

"What next?" Phoenix asks fearfully.

I don't answer, deferring to our leader. He's the one in charge of this car crash, though I expect he's making it up as he goes along. Kade lets out another sigh and meets both of our eyes. His hazel depths are wracked with overwhelming uncertainty.

"We figure out how to keep her alive, no matter what it takes."

"What about Blackwood?"

Kade gulps hard, more afraid than I've ever seen him.

"Something's wrong with this place. We need to find out what is really happening, and somehow conceal the fact that it was us who threw Rio off that fucking roof."

BONUS SCENE

BROOKLYN

Five Years Ago

"Pull her hair! Kill the bitch!"

Trapped between a gaggle of screaming girls, I throw frantic punches and kicks at random. There are five of them in the cheaper, rougher equivalent of a clique here at the academy.

We don't really have high-society, designer-clothes-wearing popular girls here; everyone is dirt poor and desperate. Popularity comes down to one thing—how well you survive.

Grabbing Candice's greasy plait, I use it to swing her around and straight into a brick wall. She wails like a banshee as thick rivulets of blood spurt from her nose.

"My fucking nose!" she screams. "You broke it!"

"Consider it an improvement, whore."

In retaliation, Gretchen's clenched fist slams into my stomach. I double over, trying not to empty my guts on their shoes. Food is rare enough in foster care. I can't afford to puke it up now.

"You slut!" Gretchen yells.

"Bet you didn't call your sleazy boyfriend the same thing," I wheeze back. "What's with the double standard, huh? He offered me the weed in exchange for a blowie."

"Liar! He wouldn't do that."

If I weren't doubled over in pain, I'd roll my eyes at her blatant self-deception. Her so-called boyfriend is the scummiest piece of shit around. She can't be that blind.

"Ask him, bitch. He could hardly wait to finish when I sucked him off."

"Liar!" she screams again.

Another fist connects with my face. I feel my nose crunch as pain overwhelms me and a river of hot blood courses into my open mouth. The injury only spurs me on.

Pain is supposed to scare you. It's a survival instinct that's screaming at you to run for your life and never look back. But it has the opposite effect on me.

I want to hurt. Break. Bleed. I like the sharp burn of suffering when I drag my razor blade over my veins, over and over again. Without pain, I'm dead already.

Taking another blow to the ribs, I lose my balance and hit the hard gravel. Instinct takes over, and I curl inwards for protection. The kicks keep coming, one after another. Left, right and centre.

Pain explodes through every part of me. Hot. Throbbing. Blinding. It feels fucking incredible. Suddenly, the blows cease as someone blows a loud whistle, calling for our fighting match to a halt.

"Enough! Break it up!"

"But, Mrs—"

"Don't make me ask again, Gretchen! Back up!"

I spit out blood and saliva, wiping my mouth with the back of my tatty blazer. I've worn the same uniform for three years now. Mrs Dane doesn't spend the money the government gives her on us. We're cash cows to her.

"Brooklyn? Can you hear me?"

Mrs Lyons, a fearsome sixty-year-old who's been hardened by years of service to the school, stares down at me. She's a sour-faced cunt, but I like that about her. I know where I stand with assholes.

"Fine," I grind out. "Just a misunderstanding."

Straightening, she faces the gaggle of my attackers next. "You girls wanna tell me what this is all about?"

Ignoring her offered hand, I find my own feet. My smashed nose is gushing blood, but it doesn't stop me from glaring at the five bitches that decided to gang up on me.

None of us would dare rat on the other—that'll get you stabbed in a place like this. I'd be knifed in the gut in a quiet corner where no one is watching and left to bleed out.

"Well?" Mrs Lyons demands.

"Nothing," Candice mumbles.

She looks unimpressed. "Look, ladies. I couldn't care less who slept with whose boyfriend this week. But the moment you cause trouble on my lunch shift, it becomes my problem."

Giving us all a meaningful look, we mutter half-hearted apologies. She plays a good game, but Mrs Lyons doesn't give a fuck. Nobody here does.

They aren't teaching us or growing miniature humans into world-changing adults. This is a zoo, plain and simple, built on an empire of poverty and crime.

"Brooklyn?" she prompts.

"Like she said." I wince while touching my bruised ribs. "Nothing."

"Well, go to the nurse. You too, Candice."

"I'm fine, Miss. I'll be late for class."

"Fine. Get outta here then. Any more trouble this week, and I'll have all of your skins. You hear me?"

Everyone recites a dull, monotone *yes* before we're set free. Exchanging scathing glowers with Candice and Gretchen, I watch them lead their posse away. They don't look much better than me, bruised and limping.

Clothed in threadbare uniforms, unable to afford lunch after spending their meagre money on cigarettes or weed, we're cut from the same impoverished cloth. That's exactly why we fight amongst ourselves.

"Go on," Mrs Lyons barks. "Off with you."

I traipse towards the maths building. It's a grey, ugly cinder-block construction, housing student services beneath the land of numbers and doom.

Passing the headteacher's office and reception, I limp towards the back of the building while gingerly poking my sore nose. I know the nurse's room well.

"Sandra?" I moan, pushing open the creaking door. "It's me again. I don't wanna hear it, I know I promised I wouldn't be back so soon."

The blare of a radio precedes the office door slamming open. Standing at just over five feet with huge, glossy-black hair, Sandra peers at me through her spectacles. Her ebony skin is smooth and unblemished, and is complemented by the gold hoops in her ears.

"Brooke! What the heck have you done now, girlie?"

I try for a wry smile. "Walked into a wall."

"For the second time this week?"

"Well, it's a very persistent wall."

Collapsing onto the scratchy material of one of the chairs in the waiting room, I kick my legs up onto the coffee table. Sandra grumbles and fetches tissues for my nose, then several ice packs.

Before long, she's got me kitted out. I pinch my nose and incline my head without being told. It's permanently crooked after being struck and broken far too many times. The stuffiness and blinding pain is routine for me.

"You're gonna sit there for half an hour," she orders.

"Go back to your crossword puzzle. I'm fine."

"You're a stubborn little shit, aren't ya?"

"Geez, what a compliment."

"Hardly."

She disappears back behind the sliding glass partition that grants her some reprieve. I stare up at the stained ceiling, marked by water damage. That entire fight was so fucking stupid.

I've seen Candice and Gretchen on their knees for a gram of weed countless times, and the dicks in their mouths never belong to their boyfriends.

Candice's hookup of the week, Neil Waters, is a piece of shit. But he's also well connected. I'd touch his slimy dick if it gets me a joint or two. I couldn't care less what other bitches have staked their claim on him.

"Nurse? Am I in the right place?" a deep voice booms.

Peering through the wedge of blood-soaked tissues against my nose, I catch sight of a newcomer. Standing at Sandra's window is a tall, broad-shouldered boy. My throat immediately tightens.

He's well built, like the assholes that play sports and drink beer up the top of the field. Stocky. Heavyset. Carved from muscle and bad decisions. Cheekbones that are sharp enough to slice my wrists wide open sculpt the features of his scowling face.

Boasting a thick crop of unruly, jet-black hair, his uniform is similarly ratty and faded. When he glances over his shoulder and two frost-bitten blue eyes clash with mine, I realise that I recognise him.

We regularly get new arrivals at the foster home where I live. Kids come and go, either adopted or forgotten. Cutie here is one of Mrs Dane's newest charges. I caught a quick glimpse of him last night when he arrived.

"What in Christ's name happened to you?" Sandra exclaims.

"Nothing," he drawls.

"Don't tell me you ran into a wall like this troublemaker. I wasn't born yesterday."

"Seems like there are some pretty violent walls in this place."

Cursing his smart mouth, Sandra hands him an ice pack and banishes him to the waiting area. I heave myself up so he can take the seat opposite, curling my legs beneath me instead.

My split lip is throbbing, but my nose has finally dried up. I toss the tissues into the bin beside me, replacing them with an ice pack to reduce the swelling. I'll have two matching black eyes before long.

The low groan of pain that escapes my lips gains the attention of the newcomer as he collapses into a chair, grunting in pain himself. Hell. He's gorgeous. I can't help but make a shitty joke.

"I hope the other guy looks worse than you."

Pressing the ice pack to his split lip, he doesn't respond. Fine. I can do awkward silences. I kick back, studying him subtly from the corner of my eye. The hard set of his jawline tells me all I need to know.

"The other kid started it," he eventually rumbles.

"Yeah, I hear that a lot."

Slumping in the chair, the air whooshes out from his lungs. He looks old enough to be in my school year. I'm nearly seventeen. If I pass my stupid exams in a few months, I'll be free from this hellhole.

My eighteenth birthday is the only thing keeping me in this crappy town. When I age out of the system, I can finally escape the torture that is foster care and forge my own path, far from angry fists and vicious insults.

"You got a name?"

Hottie is staring at me with one aquamarine eye, the other now covered by his ice pack as he moves it around his face.

"Me?" I blink at him.

His unyielding gaze scrapes over me. "Mrs Dane didn't bother with introductions last night. She told me to keep my distance from the other kids. You live there too, right?"

"Right."

"So, what's the old bag's deal then?"

"She's worried we'll form a super group and overpower her." I shrug humourlessly. "Like the X-Men, but with more malnutrition and bad attitudes."

"You got a sign-up form or something?"

Beneath his sharp stare, the smile on his lips is cocky, self-assured. I grin back. I can't help it. He's prickly and rugged, but there's something fiery in his eyes—a familiar anger that I can see reflected in myself.

"It's Brooklyn. Well, Brooke."

He offers me a hand that's painted in dried blood. "Hudson Knight. But if we're doing nicknames, then it's Hud."

"I'd say that it's nice to meet you, Hud, but this place is a shithole. Welcome to Hell."

"Thanks. You been at St Anne's long?"

I drop his gaze. "Since it opened."

"Jesus. That's a long time."

"Long enough."

We fall back into awkward silence. I sit there until my ice pack turns to slush, and then ditch it in the nearby bin. Sandra barely spares me a glance, waving her permission for me to leave. She's engrossed in a dog-eared copy of the newspaper.

"What class are you in?"

I freeze halfway to the door, turning on my heel. Hudson's staring at me as he tosses his own ice pack in the bin to reveal the dark, violent bruising around his eye socket. Someone went to town on him.

"You're talking to me?"

He lazily inspects the room. "Do you see anyone else in here?"

"Uh, chemistry. Dr Udale likes to torture us for the last hour of the day."

"You know where the humanities building is? I have some philosophy bullshit."

"Sure."

"You gonna show me there or what?"

Blinking, Hudson waits for me to lead the way like I haven't got anything better to do. I seriously hate presumptuous assholes. There's enough of them in this school as it is.

"You're not from around here, are you?" I ask with a huff.

"Nah. Just moved here."

Leaving the nurse's office, I feel him following hot on my heels. The rest of the maths building is quiet since classes have resumed after the lunch break. Adjusting my blood-stained uniform, I shuffle my feet.

"Let me guess. New town, same rules. You came in, threw your weight around and the dicks who think they're in charge soon put you in your place. That's a hell of a black eye you've got there."

Hudson's frown deepens. "What is your problem?"

"Show yourself around. I'm not a fucking chauffeur. I bet they all fell over their feet to kiss your ass back home."

"You don't know me," he splutters.

"I know enough. Mr and Mrs Dane don't give a fuck about the kids they take in. Some stay, others leave. We see more people coming and going than an airport. You've got charm. You'll be adopted before long."

The corner of his mouth hooks up. "You think I'm charming?"

Ignoring the steady throb of my injuries, I wave towards him. "Look at you. If it weren't for that uniform, I'd say you're in the wrong school."

"Wow. I don't know whether to be offended or flattered."

"It wasn't a damn compliment."

"Kinda sounded like it was." His stare is full of challenging fire. "So, is that a no then? Shame."

He is infuriating. I wish I could tell my skittering heartbeat that. His gorgeous, rugged looks and smart-ass tongue aren't enough to sway my decision. Favours are not a common currency in this school.

Leaving him speechless, I march back down the corridor despite the agony the fast movement causes. My hand grasps the door handle before fingers wrap around my thin, scarred wrist.

Wrenching back around, I'm slammed against the door by a solid weight. Hudson looms over me, leaving me trapped against the door. His short, clean nails slice into my skin.

"I came from a place far worse than this," he sneers in my face. "Kids fought with knives in the lunchroom to steal a fucking sandwich. You don't know my story."

"Take your hands off me right now."

"I ain't here to make friends, but I won't have you being disrespectful to my face."

"I said let *go*!"

His grip tightens. "You better watch yourself. We sleep under the same roof now."

He's really hurting me. The bite of his fingertips around my wrist feels like sharp needles slipping beneath my flesh to deliver their payload of sweet, numbing ecstasy.

"So, how about that tour?" he purrs, his eyes dark and deadly. "As fun as this is, I doubt either of us should be seen like this."

"Worried about your reputation?" I snort back.

"You think I give a fuck about that?" Hudson shakes his head. "You've got a lot to learn about me, Brooke."

As a last resort, I bring my knee to his crotch. Hudson grunts, releasing my wrist as he cups his dick.

"I'll pass," I whisper hoarsely. "Stay away from me, and I'll grant you the same courtesy. Good luck finding the humanities building."

Despite gasping in pain, the asshole actually grins up at me. Fuck, he is seriously unhinged. I can see the gleam of amusement in his eyes. It's hard to suppress my own grin as the tension crackles between us.

"See you around," he offers.

Shoving the door open to slip past him, I pause to glance back over my shoulder. "Doubtful."

PLAYLIST

LISTEN HERE:
BIT.LY/TWISTEDHEATHENS

Had Enough - Mouth Culture
    Phobia - Nothing But Thieves
    Jaws - Sleep Token
    I Want Out - Lowborn
    Sail - AWOLNATION
    I Fall Apart - Post Malone
    Kiss - Lil Peep
    Gasoline - Halsey
    Serotonin - Call Me Karizma
    Let Me Be Sad - I Prevail
    Follow You - Bring Me The Horizon
    I'm Not Well - Black Foxxes
    Daddy - Badflower
    Tears Don't Fall - Bullet For My Valentine
    Let You Go - Machine Gun Kelly
    Monster (Under My Bed) - Call Me Karizma
    Cathedrals - Animal Flag
    Twisted - MISSIO
    Hurricane - Halsey
    Higher - Sleep Token
    Toxic Lovers - Mass of Man & Masetti
    Everybody Gets High - MISSIO
    11 Minutes - YUNGBLUD, Halsey & Travis Barker
    Heroin - Badflower
    Holy Night - Landon Tewers
    Dark Signs - Sleep Token
    Beautiful Way - You Me At Six
    Blasphemy - Bring Me The Horizon

Hurricane - I Prevail
If You Want - NF
Whatever Lets You Cope - Black Foxxes
Guest Room - Echos
The Kill - Thirty Seconds To Mars
The Hills - The Weeknd
Waiting Game - BANKS
Crazy - LOWBORN
Snuff - Slipknot
Blood Sport - Sleep Token
Little Monster - Royal Blood
The Jester - Badflower
Born To Die - Lana Del Rey
The Funeral - Bands of Horses
Stop Trying, Be Nothing - Boston Manor

SACRIFICIAL SINNERS

BLACKWOOD INSTITUTE #2

TRIGGER WARNING

Sacrificial Sinners is a why choose, reverse harem romance, so the main character will have multiple love interests that she will not have to choose between.

This book is very dark and contains scenes that may be triggering for some readers. This includes self-harm, suicide, graphic violence, sexual assault, psychological torture, and strong mental health themes including psychosis.

There is also explicit language used throughout and sexual scenes involving blood play, breath play, knife play, and mutual self-harming.

If you are triggered by any of this content, please do not read this book. This is a dark romance, and therefore not for the faint of heart. Additionally, this book is written for entertainment and not intended to accurately represent the treatment of mental health issues.

PROLOGUE

LAZLO - 1984

"WHO CAN TELL me what Zimbardo's aim was for the Stanford Prison Experiment?"

Staring out at the bright, hungry students latching on to my every word, I wave the book in the air like a preacher with his Bible, waiting for someone to answer my question.

"Anyone? What does this augmented reality mean?"

The anticipated silence stretches on. I take the time to meet each pair of eyes in the packed auditorium. All desperate for knowledge, minds open and ready to be filled with whatever I please.

"Come on, folks," I cajole. "What do you get when you lock a group of volatile individuals up in a confined space? Give them assigned roles, make them feel like they're in control... that they have power, however fickle it may be."

A cute blonde sticks her hand up. "He wanted to investigate the origins of evil. Figure out if brutality is a result of the environment or something deeper. Hidden darkness buried inside our minds."

I nod, pleased with her answer. "Correct. Zimbardo constructed a fake prison inside his university to make the volunteers believe that it was real."

"How?" someone asks.

"Simple. The experiment conjured a whole new reality that was so convincing, they all inevitably fell victim to their own inner depravity. One by one, each participant was broken."

Another hand shoots up as I take a swig of coffee.

"Um, Professor? I was just wondering... how can environmental factors make someone turn bad? Deep down, aren't they just plain evil?"

Hopping down from the lectern, I take a seat on the stage. My captive audience leans a little closer, all succumbing to the sway and authority that any decent teacher deftly wields. Removing my glasses to polish the lenses, I offer the student a smile.

"We are all made up of an intricate tapestry—infinite combinations of traits and experiences that create the human mind. Every moment matters on a fundamental level. Evil isn't simply born; it's created by the world around us."

I pause, flicking through the pages of a dog-eared book that features in every lecture, *The Lucifer Effect*.

"As Zimbardo himself said, if you put good apples into a bad situation, you'll get bad apples. The power, ladies and gentlemen, lies in manipulating the human mind."

"Why?" another student asks.

"Because the man who holds the secret to manipulating the morality of others is truly indestructible," I answer.

As the bell rings and they all file out, I glance down at the pages clasped in my hand. Highlights and notes reigning chaos through my desperation to soak up knowledge during my many years of study. Even now, a decade later, as a world-renowned psychiatrist, I haven't forgotten the topic that stole my heart.

"Professor Lazlo?"

I meet the eager eyes of the blonde girl from before.

"Jenny, right? Good answer earlier. You're clearly keeping up with the course. It's a difficult topic at times."

"It's fascinating," she admits, gnawing her lip. "I was wondering if I could run an application past you? Since you know what you're doing and all."

Straightening my bow tie, I swipe a hand through my hair and offer Jenny a charming smile. "Of course. I'll check my schedule and pencil you in."

She thanks me before she flees the room. I turn to pack up my things, feeling rather smug. These college girls are easy prey, begging for attention. I bet she'll let me nail her over my desk just for a few pointers.

"Ahem, Lazlo, is it? Professor of Psychiatry?"

The door to the lecture theatre slams shut as a man enters. I frown, taking in his pristine black suit, polished briefcase, and nondescript features. My skin crawls immediately. This isn't the first time I've had other universities trying to poach me.

"I'm not interested, I already turned Oxford and Cambridge down. Don't bother."

The man smirks, helping himself to my papers and scanning the scrawled notes. I try not to feel violated, despite the obvious intrusion.

"I represent an organisation that is interested in recruiting you. My name is Pollark."

"That's not a real name," I point out.

"That's the only name you're getting."

Shaking my head, I gesture towards the door. "Get out of my lecture hall."

Pollark snaps open his briefcase, sliding a slim file free. He offers it to me, gesturing to the thick, expensive paper attached. My gaze falls on a cheque boasting more zeros than I'll likely ever see in my life.

"Is this some kind of joke?"

"Not at all. My employer is keen to recruit you. I can assure you this project has deeper pockets than you'll ever know. There's plenty more where that came from."

Gesturing for him to take a seat, I quickly scan through the papers, my eyes widening in disbelief. The attached proposal immediately captures my interest, however ambitious it may be. Not to mention immoral, against every oath I took as a clinician.

"This is ludicrous." I laugh.

He refuses to budge, raising an eyebrow in challenge.

"You will never get funding or clinical approval for this kind of venture. Are you writing a movie or something? Is that it?" I guess, waiting for the penny to drop. "Because my time is far too precious to waste with this kind of nonsense."

Pollark opens his suit jacket, carefully appraising me. When he flashes me the concealed gun inside, I realise this isn't a joke. There's a real-life shark in front of me, prowling and waiting to strike. He wants me to take a job that will amount to career suicide.

"I can assure you this is very real," he informs me. "We have a location and funding secured from the private sector. All we need are clinicians that share our… goals, shall we say, and who want to be involved in cutting-edge psychiatric research."

I gape at him for a few seconds, looking back down at the intricate proposal. Despite everything, my mind buzzes with excitement. He's caught my interest. It's almost too good to be true, but two tantalising words refuse to be ignored. *Free reign.*

"Is the salary negotiable?" I ask, playing down my eagerness.

"Put it this way, professor. You'll want for nothing for the rest of your days if you agree to join our organisation. My employer is nothing if not accommodating. Your efforts in this endeavour will not go unrewarded, should you choose to accept."

I look back at the battered book peeking out from my bag. Pages telling tales of experiments that wouldn't be allowed these days, a mere ten years later. Science is now beholden to the rules and regulations of civilised society, preventing any research with actual promise from taking place.

"Might I ask what the regulatory bodies think of your proposal?"

Pollark leans closer, flashing a cold, emotionless smile. "The organisation I represent has approval from the highest level in the land. Our investors are quite persuasive, not to mention well connected." He raises his thick eyebrows at me. "Are you in or not? I need your answer before I can tell you anything else. You'll need to sign an NDA, of course."

My fingers skate over the intricate crest in the upper-right corner of the page, an initial mock-up of what looks like an official emblem.

"The name?"

Pollark's smile widens.

"Blackwood Institute."

CHAPTER 1
BROOKLYN

NIGHTMARE - THE VEER UNION

MY FINGERS GRAZE THE MIRROR, smooth beneath my touch. The harrowing truth stares back at me, undeniable in the cold light of day. Sallow eyes. Dark circles. Gaunt skin. I look like a corpse reanimated back to life.

I'm dead.

This isn't real.

I fucking died.

I turn the tap on with shaking hands and splash water on my face. Fear coats my tongue, poisoning my every thought. Memories continue to assault me, but they're all blurred and foggy. The words are lost like ashes to the breeze.

"How long has she been in there?"

"Take a breath, Hud. We're not patrol officers. Lay off."

Their concerned voices float through from the bedroom.

"Two days ago, she was inches from falling to her death. How can you trust her right now?"

"Because it wasn't her. Don't you see that yet? He took her up there. Open your eyes to what's going on around you."

My forehead presses against the glass, seeking any sensation to ground myself with. I feel like I'm drowning, set adrift with nothing to hold on to. A fist hammers on the door and I nearly jump out my skin as my heart threatens to rip free from my chest.

"Brooklyn! Open the fucking door; I said five minutes. Don't push me."

"She just woke up, seriously you need to back off. Are you trying to scare her?"

"I'm trying to keep her safe!"

The voices continue to filter through, still sounding detached and faraway. I must be imagining them—I fell from that roof, and this is just a dream. I'm not alive, I can't be. This isn't real.

"That's it, I've had it."

With a violent smash, the door crashes open. Splintered wood flies like lethal daggers through the air. My knees give out and I cower in the corner, squeezing beneath the sink to hide from whatever monster has found me.

"Brooklyn?"

Clasping my hands over my ears, I curl up as small as possible. Smaller and tighter, like an imploding star that collapses from within.

"Look what you've done now."

"Shut the hell up, I've got this."

I jumped. I died. This isn't fucking real, I mentally chant. Warm skin meets mine, fingers rough and insistent, attempting to pull me back no matter how hard I fight against it. A very life-like hand cups my jaw and tries to gain my attention, but I burrow deeper into myself.

"Blackbird? It's me. Don't be scared."

I manage a tiny shake of my head.

"Come on, baby. I'm right here."

His fingers press my face, like he's trying to probe the broken mind within. I fight instinct as long as I can, eventually succumbing as my clenched eyes open. Two brilliant jewels stare back at me, turquoise flecks swimming in the crushing depths of the ocean.

"There you are."

"Hudson?" I murmur, my mouth impossibly dry.

"Yeah, it's me. I'm here."

Brows furrowed and face carved in concerned lines, he looks more like a demon than an angel. I must be in hell—after all, I was always destined to end up here.

"Where are we?"

Hudson frowns at me, real fear entering his crystalline eyes. "We're in Kade and Phoenix's bathroom. You just woke up a little while ago."

"No," I shake my head at him, "I said *where* are we?"

Something moves behind him, causing me to flinch back further. Another figure appears, although this one definitely looks like an angel. All shining blonde hair and tangible hope, not a scrap of doubt in sight. He attempts a comforting smile.

"Brooklyn? It's Kade. You're in Blackwood."

I shake my head again, this time more aggressively.

What am I missing? Why are they here?

"I escaped Blackwood," I tell them, glancing down at my tightly bandaged arms, the steady ebb and flow of pain confusing me. "I... died. This isn't real."

Hudson curses, taking a step back to gather himself. I watch him go with wide eyes, the rejection stabbing my chest. Kade quickly takes his place, falling to his knees.

"It's okay. You're going to be fine, love. I promise."

His voice brings it all back. Screaming at the top of his lungs, telling me not to jump, the others slowly inching closer. I wince at the sudden realisation in all its alarming detail. Someone was there to catch me in the violence of the storm. *Eli.* My silent saviour.

"Kade," I whimper.

"Shhh. I've got you, you're okay."

He grabs my body and gently draws me out from under the sink. Strong arms wrap around me as I'm pulled into his lap, enveloping me in reassuring warmth. Burying my face in Kade's shirt, I inhale the familiar scent while Hudson silently watches.

"This is real?"

"It's real. You're real," Kade confirms.

Hot tears sting my cheeks. The truth runs away from me as the room blurs, hidden behind a curtain of despair.

"What happened on the roof?"

Kade doesn't answer at first, continuing to stroke my hair. I try to grapple with the fog clouding my mind, but it slips through my fingertips. All I remember is Rio leading me up the stairs to my death. Every step I took towards that moment... he wanted me to. He baited me in my lowest moment.

"We caught Rio after he led you up there, sneaking back down," Kade explains. "He was on the phone, gloating about his success to someone. It was sick. He was supposed to—"

"Don't," Hudson interjects.

I blow out a shaky breath. "Tell me."

"She needs to know," Kade reasons. "She's the one that nearly died because of him. We all need to be on the same page here."

Hudson finally loses it, his fist smashing into the bathroom door. He lets out a furious roar before storming away. I remain in Kade's lap, watching the retreating tornado of emotion.

"Ignore him. We're all just..." Kade heaves a sigh. "We're strung a bit tight after what happened to you, that's all."

"Where is he?"

"Who? The others?"

Swallowing my fear, I look up into his hazel eyes.

"No. R-Rio."

Darkness seems to invade Kade all at once, a shadow passing over him. "He took you up there, love. We heard him recanting the entire thing to his mate on the phone."

"I don't understand."

"Honestly, I was hoping you'd be able to shed some light on it."

My eyes flicker shut as I trawl through the whole mess in my mind. "Hudson had him in a headlock while Eli..." I trail off, shame burning hot in my veins.

"Talked you down," Kade adds.

Guilt threatens to choke me, wrapping around my windpipe. This wasn't part of the plan. You never give a thought to the aftermath because who the hell intends to survive something like this? We console ourselves with the knowledge that we won't have to deal with the mess left behind. That's a job for the living.

"Where is he now? Rio?"

"Let's go to the bedroom before Hudson goes crazy."

Kade climbs to his feet, holding me close to his chest. I cling to his t-shirt, ignoring the mirror as we exit the bathroom. I don't need to see how bad I look again.

Back in the other room, Hudson sits on the bed, head hanging low between his parted legs. The sight breaks my heart as we sink on to the bed opposite. They both look exhausted. Kade wraps a blanket around my shoulders before pinning me to his side, unable to keep his hands to himself.

"We took care of Rio," he blurts.

"What do you mean?"

Hudson's head lifts, revealing an expression fractured with pain. "He was clearly involved in some messed-up shit. I don't know why he took you up there, whether for his own amusement or whatever. But we heard what his buddy wanted, and that ain't normal."

My voice is tiny, barely audible. "What did they want?"

"A picture."

Kade studies me as his brother speaks. He looks desperate, but I don't have any answers to give. It's all just an awful, traumatic blur. I have the vague sense of a conversation, but for the life of me, I can't recall a single word.

"When we overheard, Phoenix went crazy." Kade sighs. "They started to beat the shit out of each other. Hudson had to restrain him while we went after you."

Battling a tsunami wave of sickness, my head falls into my hands. More tears escape as I'm unable to hold myself together for a moment longer.

"Why did you run? Before your session with Lazlo?"

"I can't do this," I sob in response.

There's a shuffle and next thing I know, Hudson is kneeling in front of me. He pulls my hands away, forcing me to look at him. Fiery determination burns in his irises.

"You're safe with us," he whispers.

Fervent lips meeting mine, he kisses me for dear life. Every stroke of his tongue grounds me in the present and with Kade holding me close, I come back down to reality.

Melting into the kiss, I tangle one hand in his wild black hair, the other clasped in Kade's tight grip. Hudson brushes his nose against mine, using his thumbs to wipe my tears away.

"Nothing will take you away from us. Not Rio, not Blackwood. Not even yourself. You're not alone anymore and we will face this together."

Kade plants a gentle kiss on my temple. "No matter what."

I'm forced to lay back down, trapped between two solid lumps of muscle. Hudson wraps an arm around my waist from behind, and Kade lays a possessive hand on my leg. Neither seems able to leave or let me go, needing their own reassurance of the truth.

I'm still alive.

CHAPTER 2
PHOENIX

FACE ME - THE PLOT IN YOU

MY FOOT TAPS impatiently against the floor while dozens of nurses and patients walk past. Friday is always busy with the latest arrivals experiencing their first taste of misery. I have to look away when they bring one in with bruised arms, boasting obvious track lines. His entire body shakes, accompanying the nonsensical rambling.

That was me once.

Unstable and broken.

I've painstakingly rebuilt my life since I set foot in Blackwood. The guys have always supported me, but some things you have to do for yourself. Choosing to get clean and sort your shit out can only come from within.

I've been terrified since finding Brooklyn bloody and half dead. We may have saved her life, but convincing her to live is an entirely different challenge. I don't know if we'll succeed when we can't even look after our own.

Right on cue, the recent failure in question comes hobbling out of the examination room with his leg cast in thick plaster. I rush to Eli's side, giving Doctor Andrew a forced smile.

"Physio first thing Monday morning," he orders.

Eli rolls his eyes at me like this entire mess is funny. I'm not laughing, and neither is he. I can see the pain that he's trying to hide. He repositions his crutches, failing to keep me from the truth.

"He'll be there," I reply on Eli's behalf.

Doctor Andrew looks like he wants to say more, giving us both a final once-over before moving on to the next patient. We take off down the thickly carpeted corridor, and Eli shrugs my hand away. His plaster-cast leg makes his steps slow and awkward, but he's a stubborn son of a bitch.

"Should've accepted the wheelchair," I mutter.

The furious look he shoots me matches my own pent-up anger.

"Fine, do what you want. What do I know?"

Eli suddenly stops, glaring like it will make me get off his case or something. I grab a handful of his faded t-shirt and wrestle with my desire to beat the shit out of him, even if he was left half-dead after getting his ass kicked on the football pitch.

"Don't look at me like this isn't a big deal!"

Uncertainty and fear flash in his emerald eyes.

"You and Brooklyn have a lot to answer for, alright?"

Unable to stop myself, my lips land on his, teeth sinking into his plush bottom lip. The kiss is fast and intense, a taste of punishment for daring to leave me alone in this world. Eli quickly comes to his senses and shoves me away, his gaze accusatory.

"This isn't over," I growl at him.

He hobbles onwards, putting distance between us. I don't try to help him again, trailing behind as we make our way to the cafeteria. Once seated with our food, we both shove it around our plates and study the room.

Morale is at an all-time low after recent events. Rio's asshole friends stew in silence, while the guards stare and wait for the next drama to kick off. Nobody knows what to think. The truth is a dirty secret that we'll take to our graves.

"The hell you looking at? Fuck off," I bark.

The patients at the next table that were staring at Eli's leg quickly look away. *Nosy bastards.* I'll kick their asses if that's what it takes. They should be minding their own fucking business. Eli nudges me, silently commanding me to calm down.

"Whatever. Let them stare then."

Stabbing at the food on my plate, I tune the world out. Agitation pulls at my skin and my body is wound so tight, I feel like I'll shatter into a million pieces at any moment. Ever since we got Brooklyn safely sedated, I've been unable to escape the image of her teetering on the edge before she fell back on to the safety of the roof.

"Evening, gentlemen."

Two dinner trays hit the table. Hudson places one tray in the empty seat next to Eli, keeping the other meal for himself. He looks about as good as I feel, which is pretty fucking awful.

"What are you doing here? Who's watching Brooklyn?"

"She's awake," he answers.

Head snapping to the side so quickly it hurts, my eyes search the line for my firecracker. I spot her immediately. She's dressed in too-loose sweats and one of my old band t-shirts, her signature neon pink Doc Martens in place. I'm suddenly nervous, my hands balling into fists.

"How long?"

"A few hours. She's confused, so we thought getting her out would help."

Hudson's jaw ticks as he watches Kade guide our girl forwards. We all watch as Teegan runs from her table, wrapping Brooklyn in a bone-crunching hug. Kade sticks close by to supervise, ever the control freak.

"Confused?" I repeat.

"Yeah. About what happened and shit."

"What did you tell her?"

Hudson sighs. "It's complicated."

I seethe at his words. We're all falling apart and it's her fault. Losing our damn minds but sticking around regardless, that's the power Brooklyn has over us. Whether she knows it or not, that bitch has brought us to our knees.

"What does that mean?" I urge.

"We haven't told her anything, just that we sorted it."

"And she actually bought that?"

"She's a mess, Nix. Hardly in a state to question anything."

Eli continues to poke at his meal, acting like he isn't listening, but I can tell he's hanging on to every word, his expression splintered with guilt. I reach out and grab his hand, gaining his attention.

"We've got to keep it together for her. Got that?"

He gulps hard, quickly shutting down and pushing the emotion aside. When he nods, I release my grip and try to relax my own body, rolling my stiff shoulders.

"Relax. She's freaked out enough."

I glower at Hudson. "That's helpful. Thanks."

He shrugs, rising to his feet as Brooklyn and Kade join us. Our girl is shaking like a damn leaf, despite the supportive arms around her. Kade helps her slide into the space next to Eli, where her food awaits.

"Here we are."

Great idea, fuckface. Put the two most unstable members of our group together. She's an empty shell of her former self, not even bothering to look at any of us. Her fingers reach out and run across the table, as if verifying that it's real.

"Blackbird?"

Hudson waves a hand in front of her, causing her head to rise. I'm so angry at her, full of betrayal and resentment. But in this moment, not a single ounce of it comes to mind. Everything I prepared in my head vanishes as my desperate need for her attention takes centre-stage.

"Firecracker?"

The corner of her mouth tilts up.

"Hey, Nix."

I hold her gaze, internally screaming at myself to walk away. She's a vicious hurricane intent on our mutual destruction, but despite all the heartache and pain, I'd still do anything to put the life back in her soul.

When Brooklyn turns to Eli, they both seem to freeze, locked in a silent conversation that I can't translate. She reaches out with a trembling hand and cups his cheek. Eli's eyes sink shut, and he automatically leans into her touch.

"Good catch," she whispers.

Eli takes her hand and laces their fingers together. I think the entire table takes a collective breath as we all relax, relieved to see the pair of them here in one piece. Hudson orders Brooklyn to eat and Kade sits down, casting a surveying glance around the room.

"What did the doc say?" Kade asks.

"Physiotherapy and six weeks in a cast," I answer for Eli.

He nods and we lapse back into silence, no one knowing quite what to say next. Brooklyn munches lifelessly on a piece of bread and studies her tray, still clinging tightly to Eli's hand. Everything feels almost normal, until someone starts shouting from the other side of the room. The argument quickly escalates into a fight.

"Have some fucking respect!"

"Get out of my face, dickhead."

"Your friend is dead. Act like it already!"

"Rio killed himself! Not my damn problem."

The ever-present guards swarm in, dragging the two arguing guys apart. I instantly recognise Rio's closest friends and all-round assholes, Leon and Jack. Fists fly as they turn their rage on the guards instead and manage to land a few decent hits, chaos quickly descending.

"Fucking idiots," Hudson mutters.

Kade watches closely. "They're angry, it's understandable."

"Whose side are you on here?"

"I'm just stating facts."

We all watch as they're removed from the room, screaming curse words at the top of their lungs. Another guard demands that everyone stay calm and rests a threatening hand on the baton strapped to his hip. It isn't until the cafeteria quietens down that I look back at Brooklyn, who has turned an alarming shade of snow white. Her eyes are blown wide with awful realisation as the truth sinks in.

"Holy shit. R-Rio..." Her breathing speeds up as panic visibly takes hold, and she starts to heave. "I'm going to be sick."

"Shit. Hang on," Hudson orders.

He extricates her from the bench, and they make a beeline for the nearby bathroom as all three of us watch. With her gone, the fury comes rushing back. I'm shaking all over, angry not only at her for this entire fucking mess, but at myself for letting her get away with it. I can't just forgive and forget. She deserves to be punished.

"That went well," I snark.

"We couldn't protect her from the truth indefinitely," Kade replies.

I glance around to check that nobody is paying attention. "You mean the fact that Hudson threw Rio off the roof, and we've covered it all up? Allowed everyone to think he killed himself?"

"Keep it together, Nix. We're on the same side here."

"The truth will come out one way or another," I argue. "We're protecting her when she didn't give a second thought to killing herself, despite what it would do to us. We all know the institute won't let Rio's death pass unexplained. She's ruined us all."

Kade doesn't reply, but he does flinch at my words. Every single one of us has been hurt by her choices, whether they admit it or not. To make matters worse, Eli's suddenly fascinated by his shoes and won't even look at me. I'm the only one acting like there's something not quite right about this entire mess.

"I'm out of here."

I don't look back as I storm out. The guys are acting like strangers rather than my family. Brooklyn is a selfish bitch who abandoned everyone that loves her when she took the blade to her veins.

I'm at my absolute limit and the thought of shooting up has never seemed so damn appealing. Where can I get some gear? *Oh yeah,* we tossed the resident dealer off the motherfucking roof. Perfect.

CHAPTER 3
BROOKLYN

WHY YOU GOTTA KICK ME WHEN I'M DOWN? - BRING ME THE HORIZON

WITH MY EYES tightly squeezed shut, I latch on to the pain of fresh bandages being woven around my arms. Sadie tries her best to be gentle, muttering assurances under her breath. Let's face it, I've made a mess of things. I deserve the pain.

Once finished, she pats my hand and returns to her medical kit, packing away the supplies.

"The stitches can come out next week. Here, take these."

Fear fills me at the sight of more unknown drugs.

"It's pain meds and your usual prescription. I'm not trying to trick you," she reassures.

"Then what are you doing here?"

Sadie drops the handful of pills on the desk. I can't help but feel ashamed, a toxic emotion that I'm all too familiar with. She takes a seat beside me, sitting close enough for her shoulder to brush against mine.

"I'm not the enemy. Who do you think patched you up? Gave you the transfusion? The boys trusted me to look after you. Doesn't that tell you enough?"

My head falls into my hands, and I grit my teeth, trying to hold my shit together. She wraps an arm around my shoulders, offering comfort while I breathe through the panic. It's like my mind has become an alien entity, completely beyond my control.

"I don't know what to believe anymore."

"I need to know what happened up there, Brooke," she implores, forcing me to focus. "What did Rio say to you? Why did he unlock the door? Help me understand what I'm dealing with here."

Her eyes trail over the bandages hiding my shredded arms. She saw what I did to myself—well, what I tried to do but failed to finish. Feeling exposed, I turn away and hide from her gaze.

"Just go. Leave me alone."

"You can trust me," she repeats.

"Why should I?"

"Because Rio must have taken you up there for a reason."

I flinch at his name, acid rising up my throat. The wrong person fell to their death in that storm. The memories lurk below the surface, clear as muddied water. My traumatised brain has locked it all out, rather than face something truly awful.

"Kade mentioned that you had a therapy session the day before."

Sadie watches for my reaction. I shudder, the twisted memory barrelling into me. That incident I remember all too clearly. It pushed me over the edge. By any means necessary, I was determined to end it.

"What happened? Did you see Professor Lazlo?"

I can't tell her the truth—that I must have hallucinated the whole thing. There's no other explanation. Like a fever dream, it comes back to me in graphic detail.

The thick, black shadows dripping from Lazlo's walls. His harrowing taunts, and the sight of Vic, bloodied and deranged, intent on exacting his revenge.

Don't you want to see your parents again?

How would you do it?

My chest seizes and I begin to hyperventilate.

"It's okay, I'm here. Don't worry," Sadie recites.

"No, I didn't see him," I stutter.

"Are you sure? You can tell me what happened."

Clutching at my t-shirt, I dissolve into a gasping fit. Dream and reality blur inside of me, crumbling what remains of my sanity. There's no coming back from this, I'm truly broken now. It takes nearly an hour for Sadie to calm me down enough to breathe again and she makes the wise decision not to push any further.

"You're going to be okay."

I swallow my hysteria. "Nothing about this is okay."

"But it will be. I promise."

Her eyes bore into me, steady and certain. *Is she real? Am I alive right now?* Paranoia eats away at me, and I find myself glancing around the room, searching for shadows. Sheer terror forces me to choke down the handful of pills and I note the familiar red sedatives. It's been a long time since I've needed these.

"Just lay down, come on." Sadie helps me settle in bed, tucking the covers up to my chin. "Rest and you'll feel better when you wake up. I'll come back and check on you later."

After finishing packing up the last of her equipment, she prepares to leave. Part of me wants to tell her, to spill the whole ugly truth that's eating away at me. But she still works for Blackwood, regardless of helping me. I'll spend the rest of my days locked in solitary if I'm not careful.

"Are you sure there's nothing else?" she prods.

"I'm sure," I answer, forcing an even tone.

"This is just a minor setback, okay? Everyone's allowed to slip and fall. It's what you do next that counts, not the past. You're going to get through this and come out even stronger."

She doesn't believe you. You're fucking crazy.

Who hallucinates something like that?

Kill her before she tells everyone how insane you are.

I bite my lip, ignoring the voice screaming inside my head. She's my friend, not the enemy. I don't want to hurt her if I don't have to. I've just got to stick to the lie.

Once she's gone, I fall apart. My ragged nails dig into my palms, and I try to remember, forcing myself to head back down into that basement, the memories resurfacing. There's no one I can trust with this, not even the guys. They will wash their hands of me without a second glance if they realise just how broken I am.

The truth is, this could all simply be a fucked-up dream. I'll wake up in Clearview, locked in solitary for the rest of my days. With the floodgates open, my hallucination comes back to life in terrifying detail.

Vic's bloody corpse chasing me, screaming for his revenge. Lazlo's smile, full of evil promise. The sharp scratch of another needle, more drugs slipping into my veins. Time bending and twisting, erasing everything that happened.

It was a nightmare of my own making.

I scream into my pillow to release the pressure threatening to bust me open. It isn't enough, I need to hurt. Choking on more endless sobs, I punch the wall hard enough to break skin and bright red blood smears across the plaster. How do I know that I didn't really die? After all, this is purgatory, a prison for the insane.

Maybe I hallucinated the whole thing.

Maybe they want me to think that.

Maybe I'm still locked in solitary.

Maybe I never left Clearview.

As the sedatives begin to take effect, I curl inwards like a child. Vulnerable and beaten, the only comfort I can find is in the four men that kept me alive for this long. In my final moments, swaying in the violent wind, their faces came back to me.

Real or not, I clung to their presence when faced with death. My thoughts were of blue hair, hazel eyes, a stolen tongue, and dark tattoos.

I don't deserve them.

They are better off without me.

CHAPTER 4
KADE

LONELY - PALAYE ROYALE

SITTING BEHIND THE RECEPTION DESK, I remove my glasses and rub my aching temples. The stress of the past week has caught up to me; keeping Brooklyn safe on top of monitoring Eli is a lot of work for one person.

Phoenix and Hudson are both hanging by a thread themselves after what happened. It's down to me to keep us all together—a responsibility that I don't take lightly.

Pulling myself together, I gulp my lukewarm coffee, caffeinated, thanks to Mike's secret machine. But before my headache can abate, Sadie draws to a halt at the desk.

"How come you're working on a Sunday?" she asks.

"Mike asked me to cover. The weekend receptionist is sick."

"We need to talk." Her voice lowers. "*Privately.*"

Glancing around the foyer, I clock the usual guards. They're all sipping hot drinks and preparing for the day, not paying any attention to me. I'm trusted and therefore invisible. Giving Sadie the all clear, we slip into the back office. As soon as I shut the door, she rounds on me.

"I need to clarify some things with you."

"Great. Sounds like fun," I groan.

"Cut the attitude, Kade. You owe me after this weekend."

"Owe you?"

She shrugs, refusing to retract the statement.

"I thought Brooklyn was your friend."

"She's my patient," Sadie argues.

"So why haven't you turned her in? Told the warden and shipped her off to solitary for her own protection? Don't bullshit me, I'm running very low on patience today."

Of all the reactions, I don't expect Sadie to laugh in my face. Before she can slide into one of Mike's armchairs, I grab her arm. There's a camera tucked into the corner that covers his desk, capturing everything he does. Being invisible pays off —the warden has no clue that I know about it.

Making sure she stays hidden, I skate along the wall. It's located in the top right corner of the packed bookcase, the perfect angle to capture his desk. Sadie watches in disbelief as I fumble with the wires, carefully detaching the correct one so the red recording light winks out.

"There. Go ahead."

"What the hell?" she exclaims.

"Miss White isn't the trusting type, that's all I know. She installed it last year when Mike first came into the post. As far as I'm aware, he doesn't know it's there."

Sadie collapses into one of the chairs, deflating all at once. I'm clearly not the only one running on empty. Keeping stubborn-ass people alive is a full-time occupation.

"How is she?" I ask.

"She was drowsy last night, the increased dosage is doing her some good. I was on my way over to check on her when I thought I'd catch you. I want to talk about Rio. What do you know about him?"

Taking the chair opposite, I consider her question. Rio's involvement in this entire mess is baffling, none of us saw it coming. He was the resident hook-up and a general asshole, but nobody expected that from him.

"He was privileged, cocky. Paid off half the guards in here to smuggle contraband in. Whatever you wanted, he could get it. Drugs, booze, razor blades. His influence always shocked me."

"How is that possible?" Sadie frowns.

"Never stopped to question it before."

"Did you manage to get into his phone?"

Pulling it from my pocket, I hand the phone over to her. It's long since run out of charge, and we had no luck getting inside. Whoever was on the phone to Rio, demanding proof of Brooklyn's body, we're none the wiser. It was most likely a mate getting his rocks off. Some people are into twisted shit. I vocalise my theory, and Sadie shakes her head, unconvinced.

"There are too many coincidences. Come on, Kade. Patients don't just rule these places, not unless management wants them to. We know Rio wasn't working alone. So, who was helping him?"

An awful feeling bubbles in my gut, like swallowing a lead weight. I was furious when the warden let Rio off for beating Eli. It was obvious what happened, but she stood by him regardless.

"I'm not sure what you're insinuating, but it's insane," I point out.

"Is it? You're a smart lad. Think about it."

"You think the warden wanted Brooklyn dead? Why?"

Sadie shrugs. "It's a working theory."

My phone vibrates in my pocket, interrupting our exchange. Hudson's name flashes on the screen and I answer with a sigh, ready to tell him to fuck off. I'm unprepared for the sound of distant screaming down the line.

"Hudson?! What's happening?"

He doesn't answer at first, growling instructions at someone else. I think I can hear Phoenix's voice too, beneath the frenzied screams that set my teeth on edge.

"Hudson?"

"I'm here. We need back up, right now."

"Where are you?"

"Back fence where the exit to the old graveyard used to be."

He hangs up, leaving me gaping at the phone. Sadie caught the whole conversation and leaps to her feet. I quickly reattach the wire to the camera, and we escape into the reception, leaving one at a time to avoid arousing suspicion.

"You can't come with me."

"What? We're wasting time, come on," Sadie whisper-shouts.

"You really want to get caught helping us? They will kick you out of this place in an instant, qualifications be damned. Go to your office and leave this to me. I'll call if we need your help."

She deflates, but eventually nods. Leaving her to sulk, I race across the quad, bypassing the morning flow of traffic to breakfast.

I've only been to the old graveyard once when Eli went missing a few months ago. Phoenix had to give him four stitches after that particular incident. According to patient gossip, it was sealed up after recently being breached again.

No prizes for guessing who did that.

I follow the security fence to my destination, my heart plummeting when I find the unfolding situation. Hudson and Phoenix remain at a distance, trying not to crowd a frantic, sobbing Brooklyn. She's covered head to toe in dirt and blood that's leaking from deep slices inflicted by the barbed wire fence.

"What the fuck is going on here?" I demand.

"I went to try and convince her to come to breakfast," Hudson rushes to explain. "She flipped out, ran from me. We spent an hour hunting her down. She's been talking to herself since we got here."

I've never seen my brother look so afraid before, she brings out the emotion in him like nothing else. Brooklyn pays no attention, clawing at the ground like a deranged animal. She's completely out of her mind, slicing her hands in her mindless desperation.

"Where the hell is Sadie?" Phoenix hisses.

"Sadie can't help us, we have an image to maintain. If management catches her, we lose our inside help and then there's nothing we can do for Brooklyn."

"Fuck the image. We need her!"

"Let's hand Brooklyn over then, let them drag her down to the hole!" I yell, losing patience. "We can end this right now, but we will never see her again. Is that what you want?"

They both remain silent.

"That's what I thought. Get out of the damn way."

Once they've inched back to give me some space, I slowly approach. Brooklyn is now curled up in a tight ball, rocking herself. Falling to my knees, I bring myself down to her level.

"Love? It's Kade. What're you doing down there?"

"I've got to get out. This place is all wrong. Out, out, out!"

Her chanting splinters my heart. I glance over my shoulder, finding Phoenix struggling to remain calm. Hudson has already turned his back, needing a second to gather himself. It's excruciating to see her so vulnerable, victimised by her own mind.

"You're safe. Come on, let's get you cleaned up."

I offer her a hand, which she eyes mistrustfully.

"It isn't safe here, Kade. Nowhere is safe."

"We'll look after you. I promised, didn't I? Rio is gone, he can't hurt you anymore. You don't have to go anywhere you don't want to, but you can't stay here. If the guards catch us, we're all in trouble."

Some awareness inches back into her expression, but the storm clouds of her irises are still muddied with confusion. Like the rest of us, she's hanging by a fucking thread. We should have seen it coming; this breakdown was inevitable.

"Don't leave me," she whimpers.

"I'm going nowhere. Take my hand."

Brooklyn finally slumps, allowing me to scoop her up. Her body shakes in my arms, drained of all fight. She can't leave us again, we won't survive it.

When she spent two weeks in the hole what feels like a lifetime ago, we were out of our minds with worry. And that was before... everything. Feelings. Complications. Emotional baggage.

"Get her back to the room. Phoenix, have you got more of your meds stashed?"

He nods, but refuses to look at the state Brooklyn is in. They've got some serious shit to resolve, but I know beneath the bullshit, Phoenix still cares.

"Give her another dose. We've got to keep a low profile. She can't hide forever, classes start back tomorrow. We have to pull it together and get through this."

Hudson takes Brooklyn from me, clutching her close to his chest like a vulnerable child. He disappears with Phoenix, and I'm left behind, staring at their backs.

We've got our work cut out for us.

I'm not ready to lose Brooklyn—she's the missing member of our family and I know the guys agree. Ever since she stepped foot in this hellhole, we've been caught in her orbit. She challenges us, pushes us to be better, to do better. We will get through this. There's no other option.

Making my way back to reception, I retake my seat behind the desk. Bringing up Blackwood's record system, I type in Rio's name and impatiently wait for the results. Some basic information pops up but just like with Brooklyn's file, I'm halted by a firewall.

There's no bypassing it, his file is locked by the warden. I need clearance to get in. Quickly erasing my tracks, I slump back in my chair as Sadie's hair-brained theory comes back to me.

Why would the warden lock both of their files?

What exactly is she trying to hide?

And from who?

CHAPTER 5
BROOKLYN

CAREFUL WHAT YOU WISH FOR -
BAD OMENS

LAZLO'S SMILE IS WIDE, *eyes sparkling with malice. He's the devil in disguise, evil wrapped in wealth and authority. The dream blurs and I'm running down darkened halls, every footstep painting blood across the floor with the trail leading back to hell.*

Crimson drips from the walls along with terrifying shadows, while bones crunch against the knife clutched in my hand. I slash and stab, desperate for an escape. Vic refuses to die, pinning me down to hurt me all over again.

Then everything changes and the scene fades away, a new horror show beginning. This recurring dream only makes an appearance once in a blue moon, when my traumatised mind is too tired to keep it at bay any longer.

A dark, familiar staircase stretches before me while screaming echoes upwards and plays on a sickening loop. No matter how tightly I hug my small, vulnerable body, there's no relief from the terror. I cry for daddy to come save me, to ship her far away from here where she can't hurt us anymore.

Mummy is the monster now.

———

"Come on, there you are. Time to wake up."

Shooting upright in bed, my heart threatens to break out of my rib cage and run for the hills. Sweaty sheets are tangled around me, clothes sticking to my damp skin.

As I fight to breathe, I meet Hudson's gaze in the shadowy room. His hands are outstretched and ready to shake me again if needed.

"Are you okay?"

I force some moisture into my mouth. "Fine."

"Bullshit. You were screaming in your sleep again."

"Stop watching me sleep and it won't be an issue then, will it?"

His black hair is typically messy and well overdue for a trim. It hangs across his forehead, begging to be touched. I hold back, retreating to the corner of the bed as far away from him as possible. He's dangerously adept at getting under my skin.

"Do you remember what happened earlier?"

Searching my mind, I come up empty. The sun is setting outside the window, but the rest of the day is a blur. I can't remember anything after waking up from another tortured night's sleep.

"Should I be remembering something?"

Hudson glares at me and I study my hands in shame, finding them covered in dozens of painful cuts. Someone has washed the blood away and applied antiseptic cream, but the odd fleck of mud remains.

"Did I hurt someone?" I ask in a tiny voice.

His long pause sends a burst of fear right down my spine.

"No. You didn't."

I try to hide my relief, but Hudson knows me better than I know myself. He can spot the truth on my face, no matter how hard I try to lock him out.

"You were hysterical, trying to escape and wrestling with barbed wire like it was a fluffy fucking kitten. What the hell were you thinking? Do you want to get thrown in the hole?"

"Clearly, I wasn't thinking," I mumble.

"You need to get your shit together. If the warden finds out what happened on that roof, we're all going down. Rio is dead. Do you understand that?"

By the end of his rant, my throat is thick with emotion. I wipe my cheeks, taking a shuddering breath.

"I never asked for this. You guys don't have to look after me. You don't have to care. Just let them punish me and go back to your lives, forget any of this ever happened."

"Walk away? Just like that?"

"Yes. For your own sakes."

I'm terrified he'll do it.

But he doesn't leave.

He doesn't walk away.

I forgot that this is Hudson Knight. Untameable, uncontrollable, fucking irrevocable. His eyes darken with rage, all softness and fleeting affection dissipating. He cracks his knuckles, as if trying to scare me.

"You're a selfish bitch," he accuses darkly.

"I'm not denying that."

"The others may be fooled by this act, but not me. I know the truth, blackbird." He sneers, looking me up and down with disgust. "You gave up without a second thought for the people that care about you. Rio may have helped you, but you were on that roof because you wanted to jump. You wanted to die and take the easy road. You're a fucking coward."

I scramble out of bed to escape his wrath. It's too much, this onslaught of truth. The need to scream bubbles up within me. If I do it loud enough, I'm convinced that I'll wake up and find myself back in solitary, maybe even Clearview. Not stuck here, being lectured by Hudson of all people about being selfish.

Oh, how the tables have turned.

"Tell me I'm wrong," he demands.

I wordlessly shake my head.

"You can't because I'm right."

"Please stop."

"Make me," he challenges.

I want to tell him everything. The entire fucked-up truth that led me out into that storm. He needs to see the sickest parts of me before he walks away for good, even if I'm terrified to be alone.

Hudson marches over to me and I'm shoved into the nearby desk, sharp pain blooming in my back. I don't struggle, not this time. Our collision is inevitable.

"You don't get to walk away from me."

"You did," I point out.

"Doesn't mean you get to. I own you."

"Like hell. Leave me alone, Hud."

"No fucking chance."

Grabbing me by the hair, his lips meet mine in a bruising explosion of aggression and rage. Our tongues tangle and he yanks on the limp blonde strands, coaxing my whimpers of pain free. He's got me pinned, locked in place while he takes what he needs.

I might be the bad guy right now, but the feeling is mutual. I fucking hate him and everything he represents. But *goddammit*, if I don't want to crawl inside his body and die there just so we will never be parted.

Lifting me on to the desk, Hudson slides between my parted legs without stopping for a single breath. I'm consumed by the passionate kiss, completely at his mercy. He strips my shirt off and kisses along my jawline before sinking his teeth deep into my neck.

"You're hurting me," I whisper.

Hudson bites me again; deeper, rougher, a growl rumbling in his chest. "Good. You hurt me. You hurt all of us."

Manhandling me back to the bed, I'm roughly sprawled across the mattress as he tugs his own shirt off to reveal inches of inked skin. I bite my lip, holding back my protests. His lips twist in a dark, knowing smile like he can read the indecision on my face.

"It's high time I remind you who you belong to."

"I belong to myself," I insist.

"That isn't true, and you know it."

Grabbing me by the ankles, I'm yanked back down the bed as he strips off my sweats, exposing my cotton-clad pussy that's begging for relief. His mouth trails up my left leg, ankle to thigh, breath hot against my skin.

As he bites my inner thigh, my hips buck to increase the friction. The roughness of his scruff of facial hair is killing me, burning my over-sensitised flesh.

"You can yell, scream, tell me to stop. Fight back all you want. Tell me you hate me. Act like a spoiled, selfish brat." Hudson kisses my cunt through my panties before removing them. "It doesn't change the fact that I've owned your goddamn soul since the day we met. I'll fuck you while you beg for mercy if that's what it takes to prove it to you."

Ensuring I'm watching, he brings the damp material to his nose and inhales deeply. Then his mouth is back between my legs, tongue gliding through my wet folds. I cry out as Hudson strokes my clit, shoving a finger deep inside of me.

"You like it when I play with your tight pussy?"

"Fuck you, Hudson."

He adds another finger until I groan.

"Soon, baby," he croons.

Leaving me soaked and shaking, he stands to remove his jeans. My mouth goes dry at his tented boxers, which he pulls down to reveal his thick cock.

I'm caught between running for my life, and taking his length in my mouth. Every last punishing inch of it, just like he taught me to all those years ago. He knows it too, smirking at me with such damn confidence.

"Stop looking at me like that."

"Like what?" he says innocently.

"You know what. I'm not playing this game."

I scramble back, needing space to think before I make another mistake, but Hudson isn't a man to be messed with. He quickly covers my body, pinning my arms above my head before I can escape. Stretching my cotton panties around my wrists in one deft move, he ties me to the bed frame.

"That's better. No more running." He smirks.

"Let me go, you asshole!"

"Not happening, blackbird."

He's loving every second of this. Thriving on my inner conflict, exerting his power over me. My eyes sink shut as he kisses my breasts, tugging on my stiff nipples until I gasp aloud. His erection presses into me, but rather than giving me what I want, Hudson leans back and delivers a hard slap to my pussy.

"Scream, bitch. I want to hear it."

I relent, hissing in pain as his fingertips coast over my hips, caressing endless scars and gnarly lumps of flesh. It's too exposing, too intimate. I feel like he's excavating the darkest corners of my mind and examining them for his own amusement.

"I remember this one," he murmurs, his expression carefully blank. "It was a bitch to stitch up. You nearly passed out."

"Your needle work was shitty."

"I was sixteen and terrified. You were covered in blood, barely responsive. That was the day I realised how alike we are. Both so angry and lost. I was glad that I got to stitch it and leave my mark on you, however small."

I glare at him, rage burning through my veins. "I'm not a piece of property for you to own. You never understood that."

Empty eyes meeting mine, he's devoid of emotion. Reverting back to the safety of blessed numbness. It scares me, this version of the boy I used to know. He's not a boy anymore. He's not even a man. Hudson Knight is a monster—*my monster*.

Lining himself up, he doesn't wait for permission before slamming into me without remorse. I cry out, biting my lip hard enough to draw blood that Hudson quickly licks clean. He sets a frantic pace, like the world is ending around us and this moment is all we have.

I'm filled to the brim, barely holding on to lucidity as he thrusts into me with wild brutality, his grip on my hips bruising. Heat soon barrels through me, but Hudson doesn't stop or give me room to breathe, continuing to fuck me senseless while I catch alight.

"Tell me you love me," he commands.

Forcing my eyes open, I look at his devastatingly handsome face. Still closed off and unreachable, needing to dominate me to find some sense of control. I won't give it to him. He doesn't deserve to be in control. I want him to free fall with me, sink to the deepest depths of the ocean and drown alive.

"Go to hell."

"Say it, Brooke."

"No."

"I said say it, fucking whore."

His grip moves to my throat, nails digging into my flesh. Squeezing hard enough for tears to leak down my cheeks, he cuts off my air supply without apology. I fight against the restraints holding me prone, desperate for the air that's being choked out of me. With enough fighting, the cotton panties snap.

I manage to slip free, but rather than run for my life as I should, I slam my lips against his. Kissing Hudson is easier than breathing, and in this moment, I'd happily suffocate. I don't want to exist if it isn't for him, no matter how fucking angry that makes me.

We battle for dominance, both fighting the other, as we always have and always will. There's no relief until we're both falling apart. The world begins to blur from lack of air as heat unfurls inside of me, spiralling into a blistering explosion of pleasure.

Hudson chases his own release, and his final, brutal strokes feel like he's battering the truth into me, proving every hateful word. This cold-hearted bastard owns me—mind, body, and soul. Even when I wouldn't admit it to myself.

I'm crushed beneath his weight before he rolls off. His grip on my throat finally loosens, and I suck in a deep breath. My lungs protest against the pain, but I revel in the glorious rush of adrenaline and pure ecstasy the relief brings.

"I still hate you," I whisper hoarsely.

"And I still hate myself. We're even."

Turning over to face the man that demolished my heart, I give in and brush his tangled hair aside. All I can see is his younger face as old memories take over. His cheeks stained with bruises and tears, not a single word escaping. Both of us trapped in mutual horror, bound by trauma and regret.

"You used to tell me that you loved me," Hudson grumbles, his brilliant blue eyes meeting mine. "Every day and every night for nearly a year."

"That was before."

"Before you became a bitch?"

"No, you narcissistic dickhead. Before you let your dealer rape me to pay your drug debts."

Everything grinds to a halt. Pain rolls through us both, obliterating everything in its path. Hudson shudders, reliving the horror just as I am. For the first time ever,

I regret my cruelty. I'm still running from the truth, punishing us both for all the pain that tore our lives apart.

Hudson may have opened the door for them and struck the deal. He kept quiet, rather than shout and scream. Silently crying as they held a knife to his throat to ensure he didn't change his mind. But deep down, I'm certain that for every agonising thrust I endured, he felt it too.

"You think I let them?"

"You didn't stop them, Hud."

"That's not an answer. Do you think I let them do it?"

I snap, unable to look at him. "I don't fucking know any more!"

The chasm in my chest expands until it feels like I'm falling, spiralling into darkness. Hudson grabs his clothes and attempts to run away, unable to even look at me. As tears obscure my vision, a wave of desperation forces me to do something.

We're drowning in the vast expanse of the past, but it changes nothing. The years haven't cured my weakness for this monstrous man. I can't forgive him. I still love him. I still hate him. But fuck, the son of a bitch is right. I can't live without him.

"Please... fuck, don't go."

Hudson freezes at my broken plea, his tattooed back facing me. Unable to stop myself, I trail a gentle hand over his ink, hoping to coax him back. Pain strangles me while he suffers in silence.

"Hudson?"

"Just stop. You're right to hate me," he blurts. "On the roof, all I could think about was protecting you. Keeping you safe where I failed in the past. I savoured the sound of Rio's skull splitting open as he hit the concrete. The sight of his blood spreading made my mouth water. It was for you, blackbird. To punish him for trying to hurt you."

"But you were right," I admit softly.

"No. I wasn't."

"Just listen, dammit. I wanted to jump. I chose to follow him."

Grasping his clenched hand, I force him to turn around and come back to bed. We're both stark naked and vulnerable, but he doesn't fight me. Not anymore. I rest my head right above his heartbeat that betrays the conflict we both feel.

Our relationship has never been normal or healthy, and certainly never pure. We're just clinging to whatever scraps of light we can find.

"We're not good for each other." Hudson sighs.

"You're right, we're fucking toxic."

Studying his ink up close for the first time, I discover a tattooed blackbird just below his heart. The sight sends me reeling once more, processing the ramifications. He never forgot about me.

Tracing the dark feathers with the tip of my finger, Hudson's chest rumbles with a pleasured noise. We've both been marked by the other, claimed by scars and permanent ink.

"We should stop before someone gets hurt."

Hudson huffs. "You already got fucking hurt."

Neither of us moves.

CHAPTER 6
ELI

I THINK I'M OKAY - MACHINE GUN KELLY, YUNGBLUD & TRAVIS BARKER

SCANNING over the news article on my phone, I swallow the taste of death that lingers on my tongue. It's a pathetic piece, bullshit more than anything. Half the details aren't even correct.

While it's been a long time since the house fire, my father's case is still notorious. News of his death has finally leaked to the press, dragging up the past all over again.

Most of them speculate that I'm dead as I've been a ghost for the last ten years. A scarred, unlovable monster—who the hell would want to live like that? In their minds, the only rational conclusion is that I killed myself. Not for lack of trying, yet here I am.

Breathing.

Living.

Suffering.

Phoenix stretches out beside me in bed. The alarm went off half an hour ago, but we were up late. I was surprised to find him at my door after night-time checks, silent as the grave, but so clearly in need of a friend.

"Eli?"

His hand glides over my bare chest, lingering on the hard muscles of my abdominals. I wonder if he's going to take it any further, but the hand disappears. He climbs out of bed and starts to dress, smoothing his mussed-up hair.

"We're going to be late, come on."

I try not to let my disappointment show, the emotion bitter and heavy on my palate. This confusing, undefined thing going on between us is starting to fuck with my head. I grab my crutches and awkwardly tuck some clothes under my arm, before fleeing to the bathroom.

With the safety of the door between us, I breathe a little easier. All these emotions are so overwhelming, the conflicting flavours are screwing with my control.

Bitter ashes and hatred.

Sweet honey and desire.

Sour lemon and frustration.

Harsh chemicals and rage.

Hands balling into fists, I fight the urge to locate my penknife and release the tension in the only way I know how. I can't do that to Phoenix, not after recent events.

"Dude, hurry up. Class starts in twenty minutes."

My forehead collides with the door. *Fuck the class.*

"Elijah Woods, I can hear your attitude from here."

I smile to myself. He's a son of a bitch, but man am I glad to have him by my side. Complicated feelings or not. When I emerge from the bathroom, Phoenix is ready to go. He shoots me a shit-eating grin while throwing my bag over his shoulder.

"I've got you. Let's move."

It takes longer than usual to reach the classroom, but we eventually make it. Crawley immediately spots me and slides a memo across the table. It's a note from reception, signed off by Kade. Mariam is requesting my presence for an urgent meeting.

"What does she want?" Phoenix asks.

I shrug, scrunching the paper up in my hand. Probably to give me another pep talk. In our last session, she did her best to scare me straight.

Phoenix offers to come with me, but I wave the offer away, sliding my bag on to my shoulder and heading out of the classroom. Getting back across the quad without his support is tricky, but luckily, I bump into two familiar faces outside.

"What are you doing out here alone?" Hudson snaps.

He's walking Brooklyn to her usual session, his arm casually slung around her shoulders. Pointing at the main building to answer his question, I glance at Brooklyn. Her eyes dart about, studying her surroundings as if searching for an escape route.

If Rio wasn't already dead with his head caved in, I'd slice him into pretty pieces and dance in his blood for hurting her. Anger is my go-to emotion at the moment, but the flavour has changed. It now tastes like the dreams of mad, incarcerated children.

Our rage is all we have left.

They fall into step beside me, and we enter the reception, where all hell is breaking loose. There's a cluster of at least twenty black-clad guards studying us like specimens, and I don't recognise a single one of them.

Behind his desk, Kade widens his eyes at us, silently communicating—*stay out of this*. We've just walked into a battle ground.

"Why wasn't I informed?"

"With all due respect, I don't answer to you."

"I am the warden of this institution. You all answer to me."

Miss White comes storming out of her office mid-argument, her kitten heels clicking against polished wood. Her outfit is rumpled, matching her frazzled expression.

"We have a world-renowned security team, all highly trained in their expertise. I do not appreciate some meatheads storming in to seize control. This is completely unacceptable!"

Following behind her is a middle-aged man. He's stocky, built like a damn horse. The light from the chandeliers gleams off his bald head, and I don't miss the bulge of concealed weapons in his cargo pants.

Miss White stares as the other guards stand to attention, before the man nods, indicating for them to ease.

"I demand to speak to your superiors. Who are you?"

"The name's Jefferson, ma'am. You'll get your chance, Doctor Augustus is arriving shortly. In the meantime, we have orders to follow directly from the board. So, if you'll excuse us."

"Stop! You have no authority here."

Jefferson ignores her, nodding to another guard. "Halbert. You're with me, let's get this shit done before the boss arrives."

With an additional four guards flanking them, Jefferson and his cronies take off down the long corridor that precedes the treatment rooms. He stops to murmur something to Kade, who looks more than a little unnerved.

Miss White remains frozen on the spot, all colour drained from her face. Whoever this Augustus is, she looks none too pleased about his arrival. The name seems familiar somehow, but for the life of me, I can't place it.

"What the hell was that all about?" Hudson hisses.

I shake my head and Brooklyn doesn't speak either, her attention focused on Jefferson, who takes the staircase to the basement level. There's no ignoring the tremble in her hands as she tugs her braid, wincing and seeming to focus with the burst of pain. We approach Kade's desk, and he quickly pulls us to one side.

"You guys shouldn't be here."

"She's got her session," Hudson points out.

"That meathead just cancelled all of Lazlo's upcoming appointments. Take her away from here before they change their minds."

The life drains out of Brooklyn all at once, and she nearly collapses, leaning heavily on Hudson's arm. We're acutely aware of the many cameras and listening ears surrounding us, constantly monitoring.

"Yours is still going ahead, Eli," Kade informs me.

Brooklyn's hand suddenly shoots out, grabbing my sleeve. Her wide eyes meet mine, the grey depths twisted with exhaustion.

"No. Don't leave."

Propping one crutch against the desk, I cup her cheek. My thumb travels over her chapped lips and she lets out a breath, eyes fluttering shut. The way she unconsciously gives in to me is fucking addictive.

"Go," I murmur in her ear.

She shudders at my rough voice, still clinging to me tight. There are too many witnesses around, else I'd throw her against the wall and devour her lips, leaving no room for fear. But we have careful façades to maintain. Love is weakness, and I refuse to give anyone the ammunition to break us.

Leaving them behind, I hobble down to Mariam's office. She's lingering in the doorway, exchanging words with Sadie across the hall as they watch the situation unfold. Worry is etched on to their faces and Sadie abruptly slams her door shut.

"In you come, Eli," Mariam greets. "Quickly now."

I take my usual seat, awkwardly manoeuvring into it with my bad leg. Mariam takes the other chair, deliberately positioning it so the camera in the corner can't capture her face. Her odd behaviour immediately sets me on edge.

"I'm sorry for calling you here at such short notice. It couldn't wait, I'm afraid," she says in a low voice. "Every national paper in the country is carrying your story today. I'm sure the prison tried to suppress the news of your father's passing for this very reason, but it was bound to happen eventually."

It's just bullshit gossip, over-sensationalised media. It will soon blow over. What do I have to worry about? The world thinks I'm long dead.

"You need to take this seriously," she snaps, reading my expression. "The institute does not like publicity, and if your presence here were to get out, I fear there would be consequences for you. They will pay for your continued silence, one way or another. Do you understand what I'm saying to you?"

Her words don't scare me.

The look on her face does.

I nod once, slowly inching my chair away from her. Mariam seems to snap out of it, glancing around the room like the walls have eyes. This place is evil incarnate, the way it makes you doubt every fucking thing. Not even the therapists are immune.

"Eli... I need to ask you something. You have a choice to make, right now. It will define what happens to you next, so I need you to think carefully about your answer."

Grabbing my usual cards, she busies herself to make it look like we're doing speech therapy for the blinking red light recording our session. The paperwork is laid out and Mariam forces a cheerful smile, still keeping her voice barely above a whisper.

"I've protected you from this place. You and Hudson. They took Brooklyn from me and gave her to another therapist, but I tried my best. We're not all bad, I promise you. But with the changes coming, that name I just overheard... I don't know how much longer my protection will last."

Her fingers quake as she offers both cards to me.

"I can have you returned to Clearview before nightfall. Just say the word. It will be safer for you there, far from this place. You're a complex case, Eli. They love complex cases to get their teeth into. Let me help you."

Meeting her eyes, I'm astounded that she's being deadly serious. Mariam is genuinely offering to return me to that hellhole and describing it as better.

For a brief, shameful moment, I consider her offer. Fear is infectious, overwhelming me with the tart, stomach-churning flavour of acrid flames and battery acid.

I force it aside. There's no way in hell that I'm leaving my family, the girl who gets me out of bed in the morning and gives me a reason to keep going.

Reaching out, I flip the *no* card. Her smile drops, but she quickly recovers. It's a performance, choreographed to perfection. There's a thick undercurrent of worry in her next words.

"You will regret this. I'm offering you the chance to survive, to live in peace. Do you want to be a scientific curiosity? They won't let you out of here, they'll pick your mind apart piece by piece, document it, toy with it. Do you really want that?"

I don't have a choice.

Leaving is not an option.

"No," I whisper.

The word slips out and Mariam startles, mouth hanging open in shock. I don't want that, of course I fucking don't. But if I'm going down, it'll be protecting the people I care about. I can't do that from Clearview. We need each other to survive, no matter what comes next.

CHAPTER 7
BROOKLYN

MONTREAL - THE WHITE NOISE

TRUDGING TO THE CAFETERIA, the patient population is as silent as the grave. In the past few days, the game has changed. All the rules have been revised, and new players are on the board. We're just mindless pawns, clueless and vulnerable.

Rumours of an overhaul began last week while I was out of it. The warden cancelled classes after what happened, but no one expected to come back to this— dozens of new guards, so much additional surveillance it's impossible to breathe without someone knowing, and added discipline for breaking the rules.

I watched one of the new asshole guards knock a patient out with his baton yesterday for talking back; hardly a major offence. We're lower than scum to them. The perfect victims. Easy amusement for others to exploit.

"Blackbird?"

"Coming," I mumble.

Taking a long drag from the cigarette Hudson provided to calm my nerves, I use him as a shield to prevent anyone from noticing. We're close to the doors and the abyss lies beyond. A hastily called, mandatory assembly can't mean anything good.

The other guys are trailing behind us. Phoenix has barely spoken a single word to me all week. He won't even meet my eyes. Kade is his usual self, plastering on the reassurance thick to keep us all together. Hudson and Eli are both winning awards for their impenetrable silence, neither able to hide their own fears from me.

Filtering through into the cafeteria, the high ceilings and expensive wallpaper hide a multitude of sins. We're all frisked as we walk in, humiliated without so much as a second glance. Once the guards declare us clean, we take our usual table.

Hudson slides in next to me while Kade takes the other side, leaving Phoenix and Eli to find their own place. I try not to wince at the sight of their hands tangled together. I'm not jealous, even if I'd kill to be sandwiched between them.

Okay, so maybe I'm a little jealous.

But only because I thought I was in the equation somewhere. Now, I'm not so sure. They seem happy without me, with their intimate silences and lingering looks.

"Play it cool," Kade instructs the group.

Hudson's hand lands on my leg, squeezing hard.

"There are so many of them. What's that all about?" I ask.

Kade shakes his head. "I don't know."

Every single wall is lined with guards, new and old mixing together. The uniforms have all been upgraded, new batons and alarms added to their packed belts. I'm sure there are more weapons concealed, non-regulation items that have to be hidden to maintain appearances. They sure as fuck aren't here to look after us.

I meet Teegan's wide eyes from across the room. She walks in with Todd, the pair sticking together like glue. They weave through the crowd to join us, sitting down at the end of the table. Hudson glares, but I elbow him.

"Cut it out. She's my friend."

"You trust her? Because I don't," he snaps.

"You don't trust anyone. Get your head out of your ass."

"She's right, Teegan is harmless," Kade chimes in.

Hudson's grip on my leg tightens even more, hard enough to leave a bruise. He's a possessive fucker, and Todd averts his eyes at the obvious threat, but Teegan refuses to back down.

"You good, B?"

"Peachy."

"Good. Don't let these guys push you around."

I offer her a weak smile. "Never."

Kade rolls his eyes, while Hudson gives her the death look.

We lapse into silence as the doors to the cafeteria close, with all of the faculty present. At the front, the therapists and teachers sit in their own bubble, ranked by seniority. Mariam and Sadie sit close together, whispering to each other. To my relief, Lazlo is nowhere to be seen.

"Silence! Let's begin."

The wicked witch of the nuthouse steps forward. Miss White is dressed in a perfectly pressed pantsuit, hair slicked back and expression severe. Not an ounce of mercy or sympathy in sight. In fact, she looks thunderous. The whispers and chatter die out in an instant.

"In light of recent events, we have made some overdue changes," she announces. "Security has been increased for your own protection, and we have several new members of staff. The safety and wellbeing of you all is our number one priority here at Blackwood."

Hudson takes my hand, while Kade shifts closer so that our arms brush. It's like they can sense the threat and they're closing ranks around me. Nobody believes a single venomous word that leaves the warden's mouth.

"I'm sure that you're all understandably shaken by what's happened. I will be speaking to everyone in the coming days to offer my support and personal condolences. In the meantime, your regular therapists and support workers are available for added guidance," Miss White adds.

"More like ready to trick us into implicating ourselves," Phoenix mutters.

Kade kicks him under the table, levelling him with a glare that screams *shut the fuck up*. We all know what this is. Shifting the blame on to those incapable of defending themselves. She's looking for a scapegoat.

I tighten my grip on Hudson's hand, a red haze descending. If she comes for him, I'll gut her with a rusty fucking spoon before letting her take him away for what happened that night. Only I'm allowed to punish his stupid ass.

"You're all expected to comply with the upcoming changes and anything the security team may require. This is all for your own good and—"

The slamming of the cafeteria doors interrupts her rambling. All heads turn to study the latecomers. I instantly recognise the guards from the other morning, including Jefferson, flanked by his men.

He strides in with an air of satisfaction that turns my stomach, but the real concern is the person he is defending, protected on all sides. Everyone seems to take a collective breath as the power in the room shifts.

"Thank you for the invitation, Elizabeth. How considerate of you to hold this little meeting while I was on a conference call. We'll be discussing your disrespect for my authority later on."

His voice cracks like thunder, and the warden's eyes bug out as we all watch the show unfold. Jefferson and his men fall back, revealing the walking predator dressed in his finery; tall, slick, and formidable.

"Doctor Augustus. I apologise, we couldn't wait."

"Naturally."

Voice dripping with venom, Doctor Augustus marches to the front of the room. His glossy black hair is slicked back to highlight his angular face, paired with unmistakably intelligent eyes.

While he isn't overweight, his frame is corded by thick muscles that bulge against his designer charcoal suit. Miss White shrinks back, allowing him to take her place.

"I'll introduce myself then," he snarks.

She doesn't lift her gaze from the floor, fully submitting to him. I'm not gonna lie; seeing her stripped of all authority and control is fucking beautiful. The evil bitch deserves to have her throne toppled.

"My name is Doctor Warren Augustus," he declares grandly. "I am the head of Blackwood's board of directors. I'm here to replace Professor Lazlo as a part of the clinical team, and to oversee Blackwood's upcoming enhancements."

His pearly whites gleam with threatening confidence, the smile wide and savage. My lungs immediately constrict at the mention of Lazlo's name. I clutch my chest, trying to hide my reaction but it's no use. Sadie's eyes connect with mine across the room.

"I can assure you all, patients and staff alike, that the integrity and success of this institute is my highest priority," Augustus continues. "As the warden has said, your cooperation is required for the coming adjustments. Every single one of you is privileged by this unique opportunity. You're at the heart of a world-renowned treatment programme."

Pausing for effect, his cold eyes scour the room.

"Do not squander this chance with disobedience."

As he wraps up, the coiled tension in the room snaps. There's yelling from a nearby table where Rio's friends reside. Leon appears to have stood up, intending to disrupt Augustus's little speech. One of the new guards has launched at him, slamming him against the table to restrain his arms.

"Let go of me! I just want to ask a question."

"No questions," the guard growls.

"This is bullshit! Get off me, fuckface."

Rio's other friends, Jack included, remain silent as they watch the debacle with fear in their eyes.

"Halbert, let him speak." Augustus sighs.

The guard shoves Leon as he releases him. Everything about this is so wrong. They shouldn't have the authority to hurt us at will, like we're animals waiting for slaughter.

"My friend died last week. What are you going to do about it?" Leon shouts.

"As far as I am aware, he took his own life. A tragedy, no doubt."

I might be losing my shit, but I swear there's a gleam of amusement in Augustus's gaze. Rio's other bereaved friends all refuse to back Leon up, recognising the undeniable authority and control that should be sealing his lips right now.

"He did not commit suicide, he was killed," Leon insists. "I demand answers. This institute is a fucking joke, the world needs to know what happens behind these walls. You're all sick."

Bad move.

Rule one, never poke the beast.

At the silent command of his superior, Halbert whips Leon across the face with his baton in one smooth move. Blood hits the table as Leon falls, clutching his busted nose. His knees meet the floor, and Halbert strikes him again for added measure.

"We have a zero-tolerance policy for violence, inmate."

I shudder at the word *inmate.*

Halbert drags Leon to his feet and marches him from the room, his cries echoing in the stunned silence. The doors close behind them, like the gates of hell slamming shut.

"Anyone else have a question for me?" Augustus barks.

Silence.

Not a single word.

"Good. Everyone back to class."

Patients flee the room with renewed vigour, desperate to get away from the violence. I stare at the therapists, cataloguing their reactions in the aftermath.

Some, like Mariam and Sadie, seem utterly shocked and sickened by what they just witnessed. Others seem perfectly comfortable with the punishment. It's clear whose alliances lie where. We can't trust any of them.

"What in the living fuck was that?" Teegan whispers.

"Not here," Kade answers.

We leave together, sticking close to one another for protection. I don't miss the way the warden studies our group, and I hold on to Hudson's arm until we gather in the quad, where we're safe and out of earshot.

"Surely they can't do that?" Phoenix begins.

Teegan shakes her head. "That wasn't justified or necessary. It's abuse."

Eli slumps on the bench, taking the weight off his leg. I join him, uncaring about whether he's chosen Phoenix over me. I need to feel him, to know that he's still with me.

Our hands entwine and I snuggle into his side, seeking warmth. The brush of his lips against my temple is a small victory. Clearly, Phoenix isn't the only one he wants. *Hallelujah.*

"They can do whatever the hell they like," Kade says solemnly. "Just because they haven't so far, doesn't mean they won't. Who would believe us? We're nothing in the eyes of society."

"This Augustus dickhead is bad news," Hudson growls.

There's a chorus of agreements, and I look up to find Phoenix glaring at me. Like the mature person that I am, I bury my face in Eli's neck and clutch him tighter, my lips grazing his skin.

Two can play that fucking game.

"Look, we all need to get to class and act normal," Kade instructs. "Don't give him an excuse to bust you. Do whatever they ask, and this will all blow over."

Teegan and Todd mutter their agreement before leaving for class. Hudson has his session with Mariam and presses a kiss to my cheek before I can react and shove him away. Who the hell is this touchy-feely person he's become?

Kade gives me a meaningful look before following after his brother, leaving me with the happy fucking couple.

"We've got class too," Phoenix declares.

No time like the present.

"What's your problem? You haven't spoken to me in days."

"I haven't got time for this."

"Don't you want me anymore? Is that what this is?" I demand, my anger quickly rising. "You'd rather run off into the sunset with Eli, now that you've used me and realised it's him you truly want. I should have known you're too selfish to share."

My words are the final straw. With a glance around to ensure nobody is watching, Phoenix drags me from the bench and slams me into the nearby wall hard enough to send a hot burst of pain straight up my spine.

"You really want to do this here?"

"Be my fucking guest," I snarl.

"Fine. You're the one who walked out of that room and tried to jump. You left me behind, covered in your fucking blood, with no regard for the consequences. I saved your worthless, pitiful life… and you didn't even care."

His nails dig into my arms deep enough to leave grooves as he runs his nose up my throat, almost like he's marking his scent. Preparing for the kill before he intends to break my neck.

I don't move. Don't blink. Don't breathe. Every word burns me, and I revel in the torture. I deserve this and worse for everything I put him through.

"I never meant to hurt you."

Phoenix scoffs, his lips inches from mine.

"You betrayed our trust, put your faith in that scumbag Rio when you followed him up to the roof. I thought we were family."

"Please, Nix. I want to fix this."

"You can't fucking fix it."

Seizing his hand, I tug him around the corner, so we're tucked behind a towering oak tree and hidden from sight. Eli follows, his gaze nervous as Phoenix boxes me in. With my back against the tree, he invades my personal space without apology.

The hatred-filled silence between us crackles with tension, his knee parting my legs and hips pinning me in place. I can't move or run, submitting myself to Phoenix's will.

He can do what he likes to me; I don't care anymore. Choke me. Hit me. Bruise my skin. Reopen my stitches and let me bleed to death. Whatever it takes to ease the overwhelming shame that's crippling me.

"You think you can just spread your legs and all will be okay?" He sneers, the firm press of his erection up against my crotch.

"Of course not."

"So why is your pussy wet and begging to be touched?"

Without having to touch me, he already knows exactly the effect he has. I'm barely able to stand, my legs turned to jelly as Phoenix suckles my neck. I can practically feel the aggressive bruise left in his wake where everyone will see it.

Ignoring Eli behind us, Phoenix shoves his lips on to mine and I let him probe my mouth with his tongue, searching for answers I cannot provide. His cock rocks against me with each thrust of his hips, racketing my desire even higher.

"Please," I mewl.

"Please what?"

Reaching into his ripped black jeans, I stroke his length rather than answering, hoping to appease him. It seems to have the opposite effect as Phoenix grabs me by the hair, forcing me down to my knees.

"You want to make it up to me? Let me fuck your pretty little mouth like the slut you are, and perhaps we'll call it even."

Licking my lips, I strip his jeans down and greedily take his dick into my mouth, his length hitting the back of my throat. Phoenix growls, tugging on my hair again hard enough to hurt. I bob on his dick until the tears are running down my face, caught between hatred and desire.

Eli watches in silence, making the sensible decision not to intervene. This toxic exchange of rage and despair is necessary for our survival. It's how we communicate, beyond stupid words and excuses.

As Phoenix's thrusts quicken, fucking my mouth with his frantic strokes, the heat between my legs builds. I want them both. No matter the fact that I was the one to walk away from them.

Phoenix notes me rubbing my thighs together and smirks, using a handful of hair to wrench my mouth from his cock. I wipe my lips, daring to look up at him through bleary eyes.

"Are you wet, firecracker?"

I obediently nod, keeping silent.

"Bet you want me to fuck you right here, right now, where anyone can walk past and see. Ain't that right?"

Biting my lip, I nod again.

"And you think that if you let me, you'll be forgiven?"

He doesn't wait for my response, pulling me to my feet and checking we're still safely hidden from the rest of the quad. But if anyone ducks behind the tree, we'll be caught in an instant.

"You gonna keep your mouth shut?"

To answer his question, I turn and place my hands on the tree trunk, pushing my backside out in encouragement. I can hear Phoenix's sharp intake of breath and it fucking thrills me, the power I wield over him, even as I surrender my own.

He grips my waistband, teasing me without pulling it down. I quiver with need, on the verge of begging him like the desperate fool I am. But relief never comes.

"You're fresh out of luck, Brooke."

I look over my shoulder, finding Phoenix zipping his jeans back up and staring at me with raw lust as he slowly inches away. As if the distance between us will protect him somehow.

"What the hell?" I snap.

"Take care of yourself for once. I'm done here."

And with that final barked insult, Phoenix turns on his heel and strides away. Heat burns my cheeks and I stare at my feet, feeling like complete trash. To make matters worse, Eli seems torn as he glances between us both, his loyalties divided.

"Just go. He needs you more."

With a final lingering look of sadness, Eli nods and follows in Phoenix's wake. By the time they both disappear from sight, I've sunk down to my knees on the wet grass, empty and broken.

I would expect this kind of bullshit from Hudson, but not Phoenix. Not my blue-haired prankster. I'm a naïve idiot for believing that everything would be okay after what happened. These wounds can't be so easily fixed.

I've ruined the only good thing to ever happen to me. We're too broken to function as individuals, let alone manage a complicated, polygamous relationship. This thing between us is doomed, but it's also the only reason that I'm alive right now.

Without it, life doesn't seem worth living.

CHAPTER 8
BROOKLYN

NO ANSWERS - AMBER RUN

WAITING OUTSIDE SADIE'S OFFICE, I watch the streams of patients going about their business. Just another day in paradise, even if every day feels like a step in the wrong direction.

I spent so long clinging to a single date, planning my entire existence around my unshakeable need to be dead long before it came to pass. Caught between my desire to live and my need to die, I'm too scared to commit to either. The days and weeks are passing in a blur as I remain stuck in this living death.

Kade and Hudson have kept me company while Eli's doing his best to cling on no matter how far Phoenix pushes us all away. We're falling apart at the seams and there's nothing I can do about it.

The door to Sadie's office opens as she lets her morning patient out, catching sight of me propped against the wall. She gestures for me to enter, casting a look down the corridor.

"Expecting someone else?" I ask, helping myself to a seat.

"Afternoon to you too. To what do I owe the pleasure?"

"Quit playing around. We need to talk."

Sadie nods, flicking through paperwork as she walks over to the large bay window that looks out across the grounds of the institute. Rain is falling thick and fast, obscuring much of the scenery. I glance up at the CCTV camera, wondering not for the first time, who exactly is watching us.

"How have things been?" she asks.

"Fabulous," I retort. "Nothing like a near-death experience to sharpen your perspective. Maybe we should all try killing ourselves once in a while, give us all a new lease of life."

"Who's playing around now?"

Letting out a heavy breath, I brace my elbows on my knees and take a moment to rein myself in. She's the only one that seems to have the answers around here, I won't get anywhere by pissing her off.

"Look, I need to know what you know. It's been weeks, and no one is telling me shit. The guys treat me like I'm broken glass and I'm so over it. Tell me the truth."

She takes a seat behind her desk. "About what?"

Walking over, I snatch the paperwork straight from her hands and toss it into the overflowing bin on the floor. Sadie glares at me, pointedly looking at the camera above us.

"You trying to get yourself in more trouble?"

"I'm trying to make some goddamn sense of everything."

Sadie frowns. "And what makes you think I can help you with that?"

"You're a fucking therapist, aren't you?"

Sighing, she gestures for me to take a seat. "I can't make your friends forgive you, Brooklyn. That's something you will have to do on your own. All I can do is help you get through this in any way I can. So, talk to me."

Reluctantly accepting her offer, I collapse into a chair.

"I don't want to talk."

"Of course, you do. Why else would you be here?"

"I don't know why I'm here," I admit. "Here... *alive*. Any of it. Nothing makes sense anymore. I've ruined the only good thing in my life and to top it all off, we're being tormented like fucking animals waiting for slaughter."

I don't need to elaborate, she knows exactly what I'm talking about. Each day in the past few weeks has brought fresh horror. Guards playing sadistic games with patients and punishing them for the smallest infractions, each time more brutally. The entire institute lives in fear of Halbert and his merry band of bastards.

"Careful," Sadie lowers her voice to say.

"I don't give a fuck if they're listening."

"You should."

With a quick look up at the CCTV camera, she seems to come to a decision. Rooting in her desk drawer, Sadie pulls out a small remote and with the click of a button, the red recording light winks out.

"We have five minutes unmonitored. Make it count."

"What the hell?" I exclaim.

She shrugs. "We all have secrets, Brooke."

I bring my chair closer, panicked now that the race is on. "Look, I'm not stupid enough to think you helped us out of the goodness of your heart. You said to me that bad things happen here. Well, news flash. Bad things are fucking happening. I need answers."

Sadie bites her lip. "There are things you don't understand, and I can't tell you. I tried to warn you about Blackwood and that still stands. You aren't safe here, none of you are."

"You've got to give me something," I plead.

"How about the fact that all of Lazlo's notes, treatment plans, and years' worth of data have been wiped like he never existed. Hell, I can't even prove that he was treating you at all."

Reeling back, I have no response. She looks triumphant, like I've proven something by my silence. The mere thought of Lazlo makes me feel physically ill.

"Tell me what happened down there," she commands.

"Nothing. We just talked."

"About what?"

I glare at her. "It was therapy, Sadie. We talked about all kinds of shit. What do you want from me? Lazlo was a creepy old bastard, that's it. There's nothing more to say."

I hope she buys it. My entire body is locked down tight, practically trembling with exertion from keeping it all in.

Endless sessions poking around in my brain.

Needles and unknown drugs.

Hallucinations and clocks rewinding.

What else can I tell her? That I have no fucking clue what happened down there in the dark? She'll lock me away herself and throw away the key.

"You're hiding something," Sadie deadpans.

"You're a fine one to talk. Why did you help us? Why haven't you told anyone what really happened to Rio?"

"I have my reasons and I don't need to explain myself to you."

Hands curling into fists, I fight the urge to shout and rave. The double standard is pissing me the hell off. She's proven that we can't trust anyone in this place. Including her.

"For all I know, you're just one of Augustus's sadistic little minions. You're going to throw us all to the wolves and take the praise for catching Rio's killers," I lash out.

"You seriously believe that?"

"I don't know what else to believe, dammit!"

Sadie deliberates for a moment. I can see that I'm breaking her down, piece by piece. Truthfully, I don't think it's an act. She was the only shining light in the hellhole that was Clearview. You can't fake that. It's rare to find a therapist who cares about more than their paycheck at the end of the month.

"Look, I'll level with you," she concedes. "There are people here who don't have the patients' best interests at heart. This place isn't what you think it is."

"Then why are you here?"

Storm clouds roll across her usually sunny expression, wiping all traces of my happy-go-lucky friend away.

"You can trust me."

She shakes her head. "It's not a matter of trust."

"Then what is it?"

"Self-preservation. You're not the only one at risk here."

With defeat, she clicks on her laptop and turns the screen so I can see the full-sized photograph that she's pulled up. I stare at the young man, probably in his early twenties. A bright, energised smile and boyish brown hair frame kind, golden eyes. The same lovable energy that I see in Sadie.

"This is Jude," she whispers.

Judging by the pure agony splintering her face, I know this isn't going to be a happy story. I'm not sure those exist within these hallowed halls.

"What happened to him?"

Refusing to look at the laptop again, she slams it shut. "He accepted a job six years ago, after graduating and training to be a doctor. Jude wanted to dedicate his life to helping others, and what better place to do it than the prestigious Blackwood Institute?"

A lead weight settles in my stomach. "He worked... here?"

Sadie nods. "Moved all the way to Wales and pursued his lifelong ambition. It was love at first sight, he was so excited to finally be doing what he'd spent years planning. This place was a dream come true for him."

"What happened?"

Looking down at her folded hands, I'm shocked to see tears leaking down her rosy cheeks. All I want is to give her a hug, but I sense it wouldn't be welcome.

"Within six months, he was gone. Vanished without a trace."

I gape at her. "How is that possible?"

"The institute claimed he was offered an exciting position in Europe, training under some fancy shrink hoping to open a hospital out there. Even produced a letter from him, along with plane tickets and other evidence. The police weren't interested."

"That makes no sense."

Her hopeless shrug breaks my heart.

"Blackwood has connections in all the right places, Brooke. If they want someone to disappear, then that's exactly what they'll do. It's plausible that Jude is out there somewhere, living it large in a new country, but I don't believe it. He's dead."

Debating whether to voice my opinion, I throw caution to the wind. "It's also possible that he simply left and didn't have any family to inform, or a reason to stay here."

Expression hardening, Sadie looks uncharacteristically furious at my suggestion. I lean further away, still uncertain on where her loyalties lie.

"Bullshit. He wouldn't leave without saying goodbye."

"Why not?" I press.

"Because Jude is my brother, alright?" she shouts, more tears spilling over. "I was a teenager when he vanished. Our parents died when we were young, and no one would listen to a grieving kid. The investigation was shut down before it even began. Nobody remembers him now; only me."

Allowing her some privacy to gather herself, I reel over this new information. I knew there had to be more to it—this elusive air of inside knowledge that she's been strutting around with for months.

"That's why you're here," I guess, the puzzle pieces clicking into place. "You're trying to find out what happened to him, aren't you?"

Gulping, Sadie nods again. "I've spent years planning, retracing his steps, and applying to endless jobs. Clearview, Manchester. Now here. This is the end of the road. Whatever happened to my brother... it happened to him at Blackwood Institute."

The sound of voices and chatter outside in the quad reminds us that we're still here, beholden to rules and expectations. We can't pretend like none of this matters, getting to the truth isn't as simple as asking the right questions. Not here.

"What happened that night?" Sadie urges.

"I've told you everything."

"You haven't. Please be honest with me. I just want to find the truth and expose those responsible for all that goes on here. You can help me to do that."

Quickly standing, I begin to retreat.

"No, I can't."

"Why are you protecting him? Rio?"

"I'm not protecting anyone."

Sadie follows undeterred. "Then tell me the truth!"

Unable to keep it at bay, I fist my hair and bite down hard on my cheeks to prevent myself from spiralling out of control. The sense of implosion is so acute, triggered by the mere mention of the roof, like I physically cannot comprehend what happened up there.

"I can't tell you because I don't remember," I finally admit.

"You just need to try harder, take yourself back to that moment—"

"No! It's not that. I don't... it's like I don't want to remember. I've tried everything."

"Then try harder! We don't have time, I'm sorry." Sadie grabs me, her grip iron-tight. "You could be the missing piece of the puzzle. A living testimony to what happens in this place. I need you to do better than this."

"Let go of me..."

"Just think, dammit. What happened? I need to know! People are counting on me."

Her voice rises, adding to the pressure threatening to blow me open. I peel her fingers from my arms and run for the door, needing an escape route before I do something I'll regret. Her harsh, tear-logged voice has me freezing.

"Brooklyn! I'm here because Blackwood is sick, it's a twisted regime portrayed as a medical marvel. No one makes it out alive, it's all a lie. You're never leaving this place."

Glancing back over my shoulder, I meet her weary gaze. "The minute I stepped through that door, I was never leaving this place. Some of us don't deserve a second chance. I'm sorry, I can't help you."

Running like the coward I am, I leave her behind to her conspiracies and ghosts. The sound of her crying follows me, the guilt threatening to derail me further. I have no choice but to flee, ducking through crowds and ignoring the sound of someone calling my name.

Just before breaking outside, I catch sight of Augustus talking to Jefferson in the corner of the reception, both watching me through the crowd of patients.

I swear, I see him fucking smile.

Like somehow, this is all part of the plan.

Back in the safety of my room, I hide from the guys for the rest of the day. Filling endless pages of my stashed journal, battered by my frantic scrawl.

No matter how fiercely I write and dig around in my foggy brain, trying to coax memories free that will offer some scrap of hope—the truth still eludes me.

I have no idea what happened in that storm and why I can't remember it. Rio's involvement and the truth behind the undercurrent of criminality and contraband are the least of the unsolved mysteries lurking inside Blackwood's grounds.

Finding the truth is impossible.
The final clue disappeared along with Professor Lazlo.

CHAPTER 9
PHOENIX

ANIMAL IN ME - SOLENCE

FACING myself in the bathroom mirror, I add some more eye drops to my dry lids. It's become my usual routine in the past few weeks, covering up the previous night's activities with deception and lies.

I'm sure nobody believes this pathetic act I'm putting on, but ignorance is bliss, right?

After drugging myself to death with Jason last night, one of the junkies I've befriended, I wasn't ready to deal with almighty Kade and his lecturing bullshit. Thankfully, Eli let me sleep over, as I have done many times recently. I batted away his silent questions, even though it's obvious I've been using.

Splashing my face and running a hand over my messy blue hair, I leave Eli's bathroom to face the music. He's resting on the bed with his leg propped-up, frowning at his phone. I know for a fact that Kade and Hudson have been trying to pressure him into talking me around—*no pun intended.*

"Ready?"

His head snaps up, a guilty look crossing his face.

"You're the one who wanted to go watch the movie."

With his phone safely tucked away, he grabs his crutches and gestures towards the door. I deliberately avoid eye contact, hoping to conceal my post-high jitters. I've got enough to get me through the next few days; numbing out is the best option at the moment.

Making our way downstairs, we join the usual queue to lead into the Friday night movie, acutely aware of the many guards watching us like slavering dogs.

This Augustus asshole isn't fucking around, cracking down hard and fast. I'm so busy cataloguing their obvious weapons and new gear, I don't realise that a third member has joined our group.

Brooklyn.

Goddammit.

My firecracker looks... hell, she looks so fucking perfect. All heartbroken and sleep-deprived, barely standing on her shaking legs. Our gazes collide and I find so much sadness there, it makes my mouth water with need.

I can still feel her lips around my cock, and I dream about that day late at night when the drugs inevitably begin to wear off again. I want to steal some of her sadness for myself, lock it away for safekeeping and relish the power I hold over her rotten heart.

I'm glad she's hurting. Hell, I want to be the one to hurt her. Break her down and make her feel the pain I fucking feel.

"I don't remember inviting you."

"Free country." She shrugs.

"Well, I'm sure Teegan will have a spare seat for you."

Sighing, she shuffles on her feet. "Leave it out, Nix. I'm not here to fight with you again. I just want to watch the movie and get some sleep without Kade or Hudson up my ass."

Eli limps over to her, throwing an arm around her shoulders as his lips crush against hers. I see red, my hands curling into fists. It doesn't go amiss, and he shoots me a placating look.

My head is a fucking mess. I want to be the one to kiss her, but at the same time, I want to end her miserable life for good. What I wouldn't give to rewind a few weeks before shit got complicated, and I cared too much to let this bitch die in a pool of her own blood.

Taking the easy option, I storm off and find our usual spot at the back of the movie room. Eli tries to get Brooklyn to sit between us, but she takes his place instead, forcing him to slot into the middle. A peacemaker in the midst of our gruelling battleground.

I cut him a glare. "You're an asshole."

His lopsided smile would warrant a thorough spanking if we were alone, platonic bullshit be damned. Taking a cleansing breath, I focus on the movie and try to ignore the patrol of guards ensuring that for once, there's no funny business in the shadows.

An hour into the movie, I look over to the other two and find Brooklyn fast asleep with her head pooled on Eli's lap. She looks impossibly young, her arms curled close to her chest and seemingly at peace.

No matter how many times I blink and will the image away, all I can see is her long ash-white locks stained with blood, every inch of visible skin sliced by her own hand.

It haunts me at night, that damned image. Fuck, it haunts me when I look at our stupid bathtub. I'm running from the memories, but they still manage to follow me every step of the way, forever scarred on my psyche.

A loud, ringing alarm abruptly cuts the movie short and all the lights suddenly slam on. I instinctively reach for Eli and Brooklyn, prepared for some unknown threat.

One of the new guards strolls in, this one wielding a scary amount of power based on the way his peers shrink in his presence.

"Mandatory head count! Everyone outside," he booms.

"In the rain?" someone complains.

He reaches for his baton and twirls it like a damn circus performer, a ruthless smile in place. "Got a problem with that? Feel free to submit a formal complaint, I need something to wipe my ass with later."

There's a chorus of laughs from the other guards, like this is all some funny joke. One by one, we're herded out from the warmth of the movie room and tossed into the dark night.

I don't fight Brooklyn as she sandwiches Eli between us, ensuring the guards can't target him for walking slower. I have a feeling we'd both draw blood to keep *our* little Eli safe.

Heavy rain lashes the ground like machine gun fire, soaking us all to the bone. Forced to stand in humiliating lines, the sour-faced guards count each and every person three times.

More stream from the entrance as each floor of Oakridge is turfed out, some even in pyjamas. They don't give a shit that a torrential downpour is hammering us all.

Angry whispering draws my attention and I glance over to the other line, finding a couple of Rio's remaining friends that haven't been silenced. They've kept their distance after Leon was tossed into solitary, and Jack is now standing apart from them. We don't acknowledge each other, despite the fact I was buying coke from him mere hours ago.

"Little psycho couldn't even die right." Taylor laughs.

His mate agrees, stepping out of line to take a closer look at Eli. "Hey, fucking freak. What did you do to our goddamn friend, huh? Slice him up like you cut yourself? You're a sick bastard."

Eli grabs my sleeve, as if to hold me back.

"Let me have them." I hiss.

"You'll end up in a joint cell with Leon," Brooklyn warns.

"Screw you, firecracker. No one asked for your opinion."

She narrows her eyes at me before turning back to Taylor, straightening with such lethal confidence, I'm hard just watching her. *Goddammit*, this girl.

"Who are you calling a freak, dickhead? Last time I checked, your friend was dead. Clearly you're a shitty friend 'cos he killed himself. Case closed."

It's fucking hot how sadistic she is, rubbing Rio's death in their faces when we all know why the groundskeeper had to scrape his brains off the concrete.

"Rio didn't kill himself," Taylor defends.

"You deaf?"

"Nah, just immune to your bullshit, West. Quit protecting your sicko boyfriend. He should face me himself, like a real man."

Brooklyn squares her shoulders, ensuring Eli is safely behind her. "You really want to start something out here in front of these new assholes? I'll wipe the floor with you, good luck getting laid after that."

With the guards distracted by emptying the dorms and counting patients, Taylor takes a swing at Brooklyn, but he's far too slow. She weaves through the air like a fucking goddess and slams her fist into his stomach. Her attention turns to Dean, who can't quite believe that a girl took down his friend.

"Care to take a shot, fuckface?"

He raises his hands in surrender.

"I'm just minding my own business."

"That's what I thought." Brooklyn sneers.

She turns back to face us and it's a mistake. I see the hit coming long before she does. Taylor's face is red with rage, and he barrels towards her, easily capable of breaking her skull with his sheer size and weight.

I shove Eli back and intercept Taylor, using the momentum to carry us away from the line and into the darkness. We tumble through the soggy gardens until we're far away enough that the guards can no longer see us, concealed by towering trees.

Time moves like lightning as my fist sails into Taylor's face over and over again, not stopping even as his hot blood coats my knuckles. I'm not much of a fighter, never have been. But *fuck me*, there's something good about breaking an asshole's nose.

"Jesus... Phoenix, stop!"

I ignore the girl who demolished my heart. The screams from the dickhead beneath me, and the ache of my busted knuckles. This is what it feels like—beating the shit out of others rather than hurting them with words alone.

I see the appeal; Hudson's right. Just as Taylor begins to cough blood, someone else tackles me from behind and we roll through the thick mud again. When we come to a stop after smacking into a tree, I find Brooklyn shivering beneath me.

"What the fuck did you do that for?" I shout.

"You were killing him. I just saved your ass from prison."

"Look around you, this is a fucking prison!"

I grab handfuls of her soaked, muddy t-shirt, covering it in blood. Every breath feels like a mammoth effort. I want to scream and rave until the world makes sense and I don't have to drug myself just to feel in control again.

"Nix," she croaks.

"No. You don't get to do that."

"Do what?"

"Make this about anything but what it is," I answer angrily. "He insulted Eli, so I beat the worthless motherfucker. Don't look at me all dewy-eyed and shit, thinking I'll forgive you rather than kick your ass too."

"If that's what you need to do, then do it."

Our foreheads collide as the torrential rain continues to pour, drowning out the entire world but us. All I can feel is the beat of her cruel heart, and I study the tears clinging to her eyelashes, begging to be unleashed.

"Punish me. Hurt me. I don't care anymore," she implores.

An exasperated laugh slips out. "That's exactly the problem, firecracker. You didn't care enough to stay before, and despite everything, you still don't. Not enough to make a difference."

My words hit home, and her expression hardens back into familiar rage. I love seeing her control fray and disintegrate.

"When are you going to grow up, huh?"

"I watched you fucking die," I yell.

Brooklyn recoils, trying to run from me, but I have her pinned in the mud, the howling wind and rain sealing us in a destructive bubble. It all comes boiling to the surface; every last scrap of hatred and impossible love I have for this infuriating creature.

"You were bleeding out in my arms, and I stitched your lifeless body with my bare hands. Twenty stitches, to be precise. You can count them in the scars left on your body by my hand."

I release her soaked t-shirt and wrap my hands around her throat instead, needing to wield some control over her. She tries to prise my fingers from her windpipe as blood trails down her flesh from where my nails dig in, eliciting sweet pain that makes my heart pound. When she fails, Brooklyn's expression dissolves into malice.

"You want the truth? I hate you for saving my life."

Her choked words lash like acid, and I tighten my grip, squeezing the life out of her. No one can stop me. Not the guys. Not Blackwood. Not even the devil himself. If I wanted to kill her, right here, right now, I fucking well could.

"You should have just let me die," she struggles out.

I loosen my grip enough for her to speak unobstructed, seeking the sick punishment of her words. "Is that so?"

"Yeah, it is. I'd be far from this hellhole and every last piece of shit in it. You had no right to take that from me. No right. Now I'm alive and it's your fucking fault."

"Jesus Christ. You're a selfish cunt."

Burying her fingers in my wet hair, Brooklyn tugs sharply on the strands until I meet her dead-eyed gaze again, ensuring there's no mistaking her confession.

"Who could stop me from going back up to that roof and finishing what I started? Nothing and nobody but me can decide what happens next. Being alive is my choice."

Despite the toxic smog engulfing us both, our lips collide in a hungry, animalistic clash. She tastes like death and damnation, my ruin and my salvation all wrapped up in a ball of fiery hell.

I let her dominate, defeated by my traitorous need to feel close to her for the first time in weeks. Even if she makes me want to beat the shit out of her on a daily basis.

"Then why are you still here?" I break the kiss to say.

"I'm here because this bullshit life is the last thing I have left."

I laugh, biting down on her lip. "You didn't care about that when you were cutting open your veins or ready to throw yourself into that storm."

Pausing, she manages an inhuman smile.

"You wanna hear a secret?"

Ignoring the raised voices and shouting that marks our impending disruption, I stare deep into her eyes and nod once.

"It didn't hurt when I cut myself deep enough to disfigure my arms. The only pain I felt..." Brooklyn brings a hand to her chest, above her heart. "Was right here."

All at once, the fight drains out of me. I can't hide it anymore. This angry person isn't me, I hate who I'm becoming. I hate what *she's* made me. Releasing Brooklyn's rapidly bruising throat, I ball my fist and smash it into my forehead.

"I feel that pain. It hurts so fucking bad."

"Let me make it better," she begs.

I almost give in. *Almost.* The urge to cave, to sweep her off into the sunset and take this broken, twisted brand of love is so damn tempting. Whatever scraps of recognition and attention she will offer me. But with the last shred of self-respect I possess, I shake my head.

"You can't. Not now, not ever."

"Nix, please—"

"I said no."

Leaving Brooklyn sprawled across the blood-stained grass, I run like the coward I am at heart. Taylor is already gone, disappeared to lick his wounds in private without the entire institute knowing. Eli waits for me, but he's clearly expecting Brooklyn to follow, and frowns when she doesn't.

"Leave me alone. Both of you," I order.

With nothing more to keep me here, I walk away from them. Alone. Hurting. Dying for just one more hit to make the pain bearable again, even though it will never be enough.

CHAPTER 10
BROOKLYN

CARRY ON - FALLING IN REVERSE

SLEEPLESS NIGHTS and tormented days follow.

I reach an uncomfortable level of acceptance, pretending like the world isn't falling apart. Life is an excellent distraction even as it burns down around you.

After coming so close to death, everything feels… *more*. I see the world like I've never seen it before. It's fucking terrifying, but also strangely exhilarating.

Curled up on Teegan's bed, I study her gothic room. Bookshelves packed with records that fit her bright red player, a true vintage she assures me. The string lights shaped like little skulls, a homemade bedspread printed with her favourite albums, countless black outfits obsessively organised in her wardrobe.

"I've never seen your room before."

"You haven't?"

Shaking my head, I abandon the pretence of studying and roll on to my back, finding perfectly spaced glow in the dark stars stuck to her ceiling. "Seriously?"

"What? I'm afraid of the dark."

"You're kidding, right?"

A pencil bounces off my head as she nervously giggles, straightening the trinkets on her desk. "Just because I'm a goth, you think I can't be afraid of the dark?"

"I'm saying nothing."

With an eye roll, she returns to her exam paper. Part of me wonders what it must feel like to be fully alive. A larger part of me is afraid of the answer. Living doesn't always equate to better.

"What are your plans for Christmas? You know it's next week, right?"

Her question startles me, and I head for the packed bookshelves to inspect her record collection, needing the distraction.

"Like I give a shit when it is. I'll be here, obviously."

"You didn't apply for leave?" She frowns.

"Does it actually get granted?"

I watch as she realigns her notebook with the corner of the desk for a fourth time, before placing her pen at a perfect right angle. She stares at it for a few seconds before shaking her head, willing herself to move on.

"I've never had a problem. I suppose I'm deemed low risk. I'll be travelling back to Birmingham and spending three days with my parents before they drive me back."

Swallowing my bitterness, I force a smile.

"Nice."

"Did you apply for leave at all?"

"Even if I had someone who gave a shit, do you really think they'd grant me leave? Unstable, violent offender who was literally caught doing a runner from the crime scene?"

Teegan gulps and I realise that I've let on more than she knew. My past is a well-kept secret that not many have access to.

"At least you'll have company with your men." Teegan smirks.

"Stop fishing, I'm not telling you anything."

She waggles her eyebrows and strolls over to her record player. I nearly got a lady-boner when I first spotted it, all retro and glossy, surrounded by her endless stash of records.

Teegan takes my hand and drags me back to bed as the familiar sound of *Pink Floyd* plays through the speakers. In the low evening light, the glow in the dark stars light up in a regimented constellation of her madness.

"Where did you get your collection from?" I ask out of the blue.

"My dad owns a record shop. This is nothing compared to his. When I was a kid, we'd go hunting in thrift shops for hidden treasures. It's been years since we could do that together."

"How long have you got left?"

"Fourteen months." She sighs.

"Then that will be the first thing on your list."

She smiles at my words, but I'm distracted by the familiar song in the background. It reminds me of home, my dad grooving around his garage while fixing up the truck. It's a bittersweet memory that I would usually push down, but instead I let it wash over me.

I'm not prepared for what follows.

Sudden screaming pierces my skull with such volume, I'm convinced the awful sound is real. Struggling to breathe, I wrestle with the memories and visualise that bloodied box in my mind, stuffing the shadows back into the welcoming darkness.

"You good?" Teegan asks.

I clear my throat. "Yeah, fine. What were you saying?"

She stares at me a little too long, but once again proves why I love her crazy ass by not prying into my weird behaviour.

"Well, I need more info. Specifically on your little harem."

"My what?"

"You know, *harem*. All the guys are obsessed with you."

I choke on a laugh. "Hardly."

"Oh, give it up already. I've seen enough to know that you're obviously

involved with them all. I'm dying to hear which ones you've slept with already."
She snickers.

"We are not having this discussion."

"What? I'm curious, and a little horny. Spill the beans."

Her smile is wider than the Cheshire Cat's. I've never seen a happier goth, cloaked in black clothing and scarily dark makeup, yet giggling like a teenage girl eating ice cream with her gal pals. She's a fucking enigma.

"Only Kade," I concede.

"You've only slept with him?"

Coughing, I muffle my answer. "Only *not* slept with him."

Her excited scream can probably be heard in the darkest depths of the basement. I slam my hands over my ears, waiting for her to calm the fuck down. This whole girly friendship thing is still new to me, but she makes it easy to love her.

"Now I've got to know. When? Where? Who?"

I cover my face with a pillow. "You know who, dammit."

"Were they all separately? Or..." Her cheeks flush pink. "Together?"

Using the pillow to smack her around the head, she crawls away from me to change the record, giggling to herself.

We should really leave for dinner, we've hung out all weekend and left the guys to their own devices. They'll be getting worried soon and giving me all their possessive bullshit.

"Answer the question, Brooklyn West!"

"A bit of both," I admit.

Teegan fans herself dramatically. "Hot damn. What's the deal?"

"Fuck if I know."

"Do you have feelings for them all?"

I make myself get up again, grabbing Eli's hoodie and throwing it over the *Shinedown* shirt I stole from Phoenix a while back. It still faintly smells of him and I need the comfort of feeling close to him.

He's now avoiding me like the plague after our angry shouting match. I'm waiting for him to agree to a hate fuck to clear the atmosphere, but he's stubborn as hell.

"Brooklyn?"

With a sigh, I concede. "It's complicated. Until recently, I hated Hudson and couldn't stand to be in the same room as him. Now Phoenix hates my guts, I think Hudson wants to try again, who knows what the hell Eli is thinking, and Kade has barely touched me since we kissed weeks ago."

Teegan whistles. "Jesus. No wonder your head is a mess."

"Exactly. Come on, we should go down. Least we can do is show our faces," I say, needing to escape this conversation and all its messy complications. "Besides, Sunday night means roast potatoes."

"The holy grail."

"Move it, horny bitch."

We head over to the cafeteria in the dark, following the glow of lights that penetrate the thick smog. Winter has arrived right on time, and I'm hit with another memory, this one from last Christmas. The demons won't stay quiet at the moment, growing louder each day.

I spent it in solitary after attacking an orderly for trying to involve me in carol singing with the other patients. Safe to say, 'tis the season to be fucking miserable if I want to. Holy Spirit and Santa Claus be damned.

Dinner is in full swing, so we grab our food and sneak over to the table. Hudson is glowering at me without saying a word, despite the fact we've been texting ever since he presented me with a phone from their stash, demanding I check in regularly.

Possessive assholes, the lot of them.

"Nice of you to join us," Kade remarks.

I roll my eyes at him, sliding in opposite Eli who immediately looks up and smiles. He tips his head in a specific way and I nod my answer, confirming that I'm good. He jerks his chin and I pick up my cutlery, submitting to his demand to eat. I love our new secret language.

"Phoenix not with you?" Hudson asks.

"Why would Phoenix be with me?" I scoff. "We all know he's still giving me the cold shoulder. I've barely seen him all week."

The guys seem exasperated with Phoenix's behaviour, and I bury the guilt that rises, drowning it in potatoes and gravy. It hurts because I know his treatment is justified, and there's not a single thing I can do to fix it.

As we're wrapping up dinner, Halbert begins his usual routine of circling the cafeteria like a predator hunting its prey, seeking any excuse to lash out. All of the new guards seem to have a violent streak, treating us more like prisoners than patients here to rehabilitate. Of course, we're the silent masses, with zero rights or ability to speak up for ourselves.

A kleptomaniac from the first floor is his next victim. He catches her trying to sneak out food wrapped up in her pocket and she's restrained against the wall in no time. The following search turns my stomach, and she's silently crying by the end, running at full speed when he frees her.

"Fucking bastard." I hiss under my breath.

"He's unfit for service, the guy probably belongs here himself," Hudson agrees, lowering his voice. "He came into class the other day for a spot check, busted someone for carrying cigarettes. Even the teacher was scared when he got the poor sod in a chokehold and threatened him with indefinite solitary unless he revealed his source."

"Do we know the source?" Kade chimes in.

"Not Rio, that's for sure."

There's a wicked glint in Hudson's eye that sends delicious heat flooding between my legs. The sadistic bastard knows exactly which buttons to press. *Later,* I mouth with a wink, and he grins at me.

Halbert circles back around, twisting his baton in his hands. When his gaze lands on Teegan, sitting next to Eli and minding her own business, it's scarily triumphant. He stands over her, faking a reassuring smile.

"Hey there, enjoying your dinner?"

Teegan flinches. "S-sure. Thank you."

"Where'd you get the piercings, kiddo? Got some buddy that'll stick a needle in you for a quick blowie? That's contraband, inmate. No facial jewellery allowed."

I bite back my need to correct him.

We're not fucking inmates.

"It's never been a problem before," she stutters.

Her eyes slide over to Hudson with his obvious eyebrow piercing, but Halbert has already chosen his victim. He's like a dog with a bone and refuses to look away from her.

"Well, that was before. We're here now. Take them out."

I'm weirdly proud as she faces him straight-on, concealing her fear. My girl has a backbone. But this asshole doesn't like to be defied and smashes his baton against the table with a resounding *crack.*

"Final warning," he utters.

If he makes another move, I'll be the one on my way to solitary for assaulting a guard. No one messes with my friends, uniform or no fucking uniform.

"Piercings are allowed. Ask Miss White," Teegan argues, her voice squeaky with nerves. "Better get your facts straight next time."

"Miss White is no longer in charge of this institute."

We all exchange shocked looks at the news. Even Kade seems taken aback and he usually knows all the gossip. Taking advantage of our surprise, Halbert's arm raises to strike Teegan.

Moving on instinct, I launch myself across the table. Teegan topples back and I take her place, the baton connecting with my jaw. I have enough sense to grab Halbert's wrist before he retreats, twisting until his bones crunch. He shouts for backup like I'm some out-of-control lunatic, not just defending my friend.

The backhand takes me by surprise, and everything goes blurry as I crumple to the floor. Next thing I know, Hudson has leapt on Halbert, delivering a swift punch to the face. Eli rushes to help me while Kade goes after his brother, trying to de-escalate the situation.

"What on earth is going on here?!"

The deep boom of authority freezes everyone. Augustus himself storms into the cafeteria, his coat flapping behind him, revealing the deep red silk inside that matches his black shirt and diamond cufflinks. The minute he sees us, his mouth turns down with displeasure.

Eli wraps an arm around me, and I cling to his t-shirt, swallowing the blood in my mouth. My face aches from the blow, but I refuse to let it show.

"Just dealing with a situation, sir. We'll get it cleared up," Halbert rushes to explain, shoving Hudson into a table and pinning his arms.

"Get off him, we did nothing wrong," I shout.

Augustus's attention turns to me, cataloguing my position on the floor. With Eli's help, I struggle to my feet. They don't deserve the satisfaction. I was defending my friend from a dangerous predator, regardless of his position.

"Insolence will not be tolerated," Augustus declares.

Without dropping eye contact, I lift my chin in defiance. The slightest smile tugs at his lips, like he's enjoying the show I'm putting on.

"Your attack dog tried to hurt my friend for no reason." I gesture to where

Teegan sits paralysed with fear. "We have the right to defend ourselves. Maybe you should train your staff in ethics and basic decency."

Augustus shifts from amused to enraged in seconds. He slithers over to me, the weight of his gaze suffocating, like he can see into the darkest corners of my mind with a single look.

"That's some attitude you have, Miss West."

Something is screaming at me, standing in front of this snake dressed in the skin of a man. Like I'm missing something important. I can feel the answer hanging on the edges of my mind, just out of reach.

"Well, let's see if a night in solitary will inspire a change of heart. There is no room for defiance in Blackwood. We're rehabilitating you to re-join society, not wreak havoc on innocent employees simply doing their job."

"Innocent?" I repeat.

Augustus's perfectly shaped eyebrows raise in challenge. I'd be dumb to keep this up, he'll lock me away and toss the fucking key. Instead, I ease myself out of Eli's embrace and surrender to Halbert. He abandons Hudson and restrains me instead.

"Little bitch." He sneers.

"Thought I was an inmate."

His grip tightens until I wince, causing Hudson to let out a string of colourful curses. Kade has to lay a hand on his shoulder to prevent another fight breaking out.

Turning on his heel, Augustus barks at the silent audience of patients to continue with their dinner. No one will look at me as I'm escorted away, like the pathetic sheep they are.

I'll happily spend the night in a cell if that's what it takes to protect the guys and Teegan. Nobody fucks with what's mine.

"Quite the show you put on back there," Augustus chuckles.

Escorted behind him, I'm taken to my worst nightmare, the awful corridor heading down to where the basement awaits.

I don't dignify him with a response, even when Halbert twists my wrists at a sharp angle and pain burns beneath my skin. I can play this game all fucking day long.

"Some time to reflect then perhaps, before we begin our work."

That breaks my resolve, fear inching in.

"Our work?"

Augustus tosses me a grin. "You're my patient now, Miss West. I have been preparing to continue with Professor Lazlo's work and help you on your journey towards recovery."

The mere thought of having this monster dig around in my mind is far more terrifying than the darkness of the basement. I'll happily be chased by hallucinations and ghosts long before I surrender my sanity to Augustus.

"Bring it on," I challenge.

"I do like a willing candidate. We'll see how long that lasts."

CHAPTER 11
PHOENIX

HOSPITAL FOR SOULS - BRING ME THE HORIZON

LINGERING OUTSIDE THE GYM, I bounce on the balls of my feet to keep warm. At least Rio was punctual. Jack is a poor replacement, but there aren't many drug dealers in a secure mental institution.

Only the well-connected ones.

My phone vibrates and I curse at the name flashing on the screen. Kade's been chasing me all day, trying to lure me into a family meeting. Brooklyn has been kept in solitary for an extra night, so he's demanding action. Once again, she's the source of further drama. *We're shocked.*

"Hey. Sorry, I'm late."

Jack offers me a fist to bump, gesturing towards the shadows around the back of the gym. He picked up where Rio left off, exploiting the demand for contraband, and tapping into his old supply lines. I've kept this secret to myself; the others would kill me if they found out.

"Here," he offers, palming me a bag of coke.

"Thanks, man."

I stuff it in my pocket and offer a wad of notes which Jack eagerly accepts. It feels pretty shitty to be stealing money from Kade, but I've reached the point where I no longer care.

"You want something stronger? I can get whatever you want."

I clear my throat. "Nah, I'm good."

"You sure? No judgement here, bro."

Snorting cocaine is one thing, but I sure as hell ain't touching the other stuff. Going sober damn near killed me and I'm in no rush to repeat the experience. I'd rather die.

"Hit me up when you want more." Jack shrugs.

"Yeah, see you around."

I head into the gym and find a vacant bathroom to cut a line, snorting it up and sighing as the bitterness hits. When I started again last month, I promised myself only once. Just one more hit and that would be it.

I'm a clueless motherfucker if I thought I could only ever have just a taste of the world I left behind. But the way I see it, if Brooklyn can attempt to launch herself off a building and still get puppy dog eyes from the others, then I can have a harmless hit.

Back outside, I have to dodge a cluster of guards hooting and patrolling the grounds, an unsuspecting patient trapped between them. I don't recognise the poor bastard, so decide not to intervene. They will play their sick little games regardless of anything we do—we're not human to them.

"Phoenix!"

Ignoring the voice, I race up the stairs to Oakridge without stopping, but of course it isn't enough to deter his majesty, Kade the dictator.

"Phoenix! Jesus Christ. Wait up."

"Leave me alone, Kade."

He catches up just as I reach the fourth floor, escorting me back to our room. After swiping his key card and shoving me inside, I slump on my bed while Kade rages.

"Why haven't you answered your fucking phone? Family meeting. We need to get Brooklyn out of the hole, they can't keep her in there for days on end."

"Sure, they can," I mutter, tapping on my phone.

Kade snatches it from my hand. "What the hell is going on with you? I've got enough going on with Hudson behaving like a reckless idiot. I don't need you losing your shit too."

"I'm sorry, are my feelings inconvenient to you?"

He deflates, shaking his head. "Of course not, but the only way we get through this is together. You've kept this up for well over a month now, it's time to get over it."

Scoffing, I ignore Kade and stare up at the ceiling. Above all else, he has to be in control. Unfortunately, there isn't a whole lot of that going around at the moment.

"Go deal with your murderous brother and girlfriend." I roll over, giving him my back. "Go on, fuck off."

Just as I think he's going to give in and go back to being everyone's fucking saviour, there's a long exhale.

"We're your family, Nix. This whole childish feud has to stop, we can't be fighting each other when we've got enemies closing in all around us."

"Enemies?" I laugh.

"Hudson's mum is getting louder by the day and trying to bury us all. Eli's getting dragged through the shit in the nation's media, and my goddamn friends are intent on killing each other before the rest of the world takes a shot."

Turning back over to glare at Kade, I find him uncharacteristically losing his shit. He ceases pacing and grabs his coat, ready to storm back out into the dark.

"Give it up, she'll be back tomorrow," I concede.

"You really want her to spend another night in the hole?"

"Maybe that's where she belongs, man."

His glare is caustic. "You don't mean that."

"Don't I?"

Rather than explode at me, he slams the door shut loud enough to wake Satan himself. I stare for a few seconds before dropping to the floor, beginning an aggressive round of pushups.

I've got too much energy slamming through me to focus. Abandoning that, I contemplate the neat room around me. Kade keeps it obsessively tidy, always picking up after me.

Fuck that.

Fuck him.

Fuck everyone.

I left everything behind when I came to Blackwood. Family, friends. I haven't seen my sister, Charlie, since I arrived, and Nan isn't getting any younger. I sacrificed it all when I took the fall and was arrested, electing to come here in my desperation to avoid a prison sentence.

Family was how I consoled myself. The family I found, not the one I left behind. Without them, I have nothing. I'm just another failed junkie.

I break down, shoving the nearby bookshelf with all my strength until it crashes down with an almighty bang. Books, papers, and hidden contraband go flying, but I don't stop there. Everything must go.

Eli finds me an hour later, curled in the corner amongst destruction and carnage, bruised and sweating. Nothing remains of the room. I smashed each piece of furniture, tore papers and books, shattered light bulbs and picture frames.

"Get the hell out," I shout, my voice wrecked.

Abandoning his crutches, Eli tentatively picks through the debris to make his way to me. His annoyance melts away, leaving awful pity behind. I fucking hate it and want nothing more than to wipe that goddamn look from his face.

"Are you bloody deaf?"

Eli shrugs, managing to sink down next to me.

"I'm not in the mood to do this with you right now."

He raises a single eyebrow.

"This emotional shit. Whatever you want to call it."

We stare at the bomb site around us, lapsing into comfortable silence. I've always been at ease around Eli, there's no pressure to speak or fill the quiet with stupid, meaningless words. Especially when talking fixes nothing.

Eli's head lands on my shoulder, surprising me. His dark curls tickle my cheek and our hands somehow find each other, fingers interlinking. It feels more natural than breathing, but part of me is still afraid.

"I don't think I can do this, Eli."

Stroking his jean-clad leg without thinking, I don't realise that his muscles are tensing beneath my touch.

"You shouldn't be here. I'm not safe to be around."

"Don't c-care…" he stutters.

The rasped words surprise the shit out of me, and I gently lift his chin with my index finger, needing to see his green eyes. They're full of dark understanding that I should never take for granted.

I want him to see it all, the twisted part of me that wants nothing more than to break him, make him feel the pain that's choking me to death. It's the only way.

Eli moves before I can, his lips landing on mine. Kissing me like it's the last thing he'll do, all teeth and tongue, he communicates with far more than pitiful words. Each hungry clash is its own claiming, an irreversible brand across my heart.

Automatically, my hand slips around his throat and I squeeze, deepening the kiss. The room seems to shrink, pushing us closer together. In a moment of madness, I drag him into my lap so he's straddling me, keeping my hands splayed across his back.

It's an awkward manoeuvre with his plaster-cast leg, but I'm done being gentle. The hard press of his erection has me groaning against his mouth, needing a hell of a lot less clothing between us.

It feels wrong to touch him without Brooklyn present. Like we're cheating somehow, breaking an unspoken rule. The thought only makes me more ravenous. I want to rip apart the rule book and take him over my knee, punish him for the shit he pulled on the football pitch.

Eli pulls back, gasping for breath. His irises are blown wide with pleasure, and he licks his swollen lips, contemplating me for a moment. When he reaches for my waistband, reality comes crashing back in.

"We should stop," I whisper.

He shakes his head.

"I can't be your fucking friend, Eli. Not anymore." Panic lances across his face and I rush to explain. "Not like this. I need more."

Running my thumb over his bottom lip, I wrestle with myself. He wants it too. We both do. To blow this whole friendship charade to hell and begin anew.

"I want to hurt you the way you hurt yourself," I admit softly.

Eli nods his consent. The flutter of his dark lashes is my kryptonite. Taking control, his hand winds into my jeans and palms my hard cock, making his intentions crystal clear. I don't have the will to push him away.

Raising my hips, I let him take my erection in hand as air hisses out between my clenched teeth. He strokes me with confidence, never once taking his eyes from mine. I bury my fingers in his hair and guide him down, needing to feel his silent mouth around my dick.

He takes me deep, hollowing his cheeks and driving me to the edge of desperation. We work in perfect synchronicity until I'm unravelling, spilling my load straight down his pretty throat.

Eli swallows with such obedience, sparing me a knowing look, I'm seconds away from bending him over and fucking his tight ass until he finally speaks.

"Leave now or I won't be responsible for my actions," I warn.

He doesn't budge. Not like every other guy that ran for the hills by the time I was done with them. We'll see. There's still time.

Pulling my clothes back into place, I clear my bed with a sweep of my arm, sending rubble flying everywhere. Eli watches, allowing me to pull him up and dump him on the mattress, careful of his bad leg.

My fingers spasm with need as I undo his fly, no longer afraid of crossing the line between harmless flirting and something more. I'm done denying myself.

He's fucking *mine*.

Flipping him over, I expose his perfect ass and admire the view. Untarnished, framed by thick scar tissue that peeks out from beneath his t-shirt. With a single finger, I trace the glimpse that's exposed at his waistline and watch as Eli shivers, fighting the urge to run. I've seen glimpses of his scars before, but I want to see it all now.

"Don't hide from me, Elijah," I chastise.

He stops fighting, surrendering to the pleasure as I reach around and grab a handful of his thick cock. With a few strokes, he's putty in my hands.

I want nothing more than to finally fuck him, but not yet. Despite everything, I can't quite contemplate the thought of doing that without her to watch. My evil goddamn firecracker.

"Why did you get yourself beaten up?" I whisper into his ear. He doesn't answer, writhing against the sheets as I work his length. "You and Brooklyn have royally fucked things up. I think that warrants a punishment, don't you?"

Eli nods.

"Let me hear that voice."

I lean in and gently bite his earlobe, letting my tongue trail down the vulnerable slope of his exposed neck. Shuddering, Eli lets out a barely-there whisper of agreement.

"Good little Eli. I want to see you. All of you."

I can see how much strength it takes him not to push me away and run for his life. Instead, Eli grabs the edge of his acid wash t-shirt and slowly drags it up, tossing the fabric aside.

I sit back, studying his back and gently guiding him over so I can see the front too. His entire torso is warped by horrific burn scars, rigid lumps, and lines from his precious blade.

"So beautiful," I murmur.

His glare speaks a thousand words.

"You don't need to be ashamed, Eli. Not in front of me. You're fucking perfect the way you are, goddammit. I wish you would believe me."

Eli studies me for a second, mulling my words over before coming to a decision. He flips back over, laying his head down and raising his ass, encouraging me to spank him. I try to decipher the silent message he's sending me.

"This isn't what friends do."

This time, he speaks. "N-No."

"If we're not friends, then what are we?"

He doesn't bother to answer.

I don't think either of us knows.

Retrieving my hidden belt from beneath a loose floorboard, recovered from Brooklyn's room after she failed to kill herself, I swallow hard. Running my fingertips over Eli's scars, I caress the masterpiece of agony that fascinates my messed-up imagination.

Cracking the belt against my palm in warning, he doesn't flinch or run. The next strike hits the sensitive flesh of his left butt cheek, bright red blossoming against creamy white. I'm hard again already, despite finishing in his mouth minutes ago.

"Final chance to run, Eli."

He poises himself, indicating his consent.

Ten strikes.

Each one counted out in time.

When I'm done, panting and thoroughly sated, Eli collapses on the bed. His skin is mottled with new marks of my own, but I feel no remorse. Maybe I should. But for every bit of grief and pain they've put me through—him and Brooklyn—I've taken it back. Doled out my revenge. I'm in control.

"N-Nix."

Eli turns over, tugging his jeans back up.

"Now you want to talk?" I laugh bitterly.

His gaze is steady as he cups my cheek. My first thought is to run. Kick him out, retreat to my safe corner, far from any complications. But I can't run from him. Eli knows my fucking soul and won't allow anything but the truth.

Instead, we curl up together amongst the destruction with his head on my chest, right above my skittering heartbeat.

"Better?"

His whisper is like music to my heathen soul.

"For now. I'm losing control and it scares me."

Eli shifts until we're nose to nose. He peels back my layers with a mere look, exposing every last secret. Carefully tracing the bags under my eyes with his fingertip, there's no hiding my dilated pupils from the hit I devoured in the gym.

"I know I've let you down."

Eli shakes his head.

"I have, don't deny it. I'm sorry."

His lips meet mine in the briefest of kisses, accepting my apology. Something bubbles between us; a powerful, terrifying emotion. I try to pull away, needing to escape like the coward I am. This time, he's the one doling out the orders.

"Stay," he demands.

His voice, all breathy and harsh, is better than any drug. I know the truth now. Eli is my lifeboat, preventing me from sinking into the bleak, lifeless depths of the unknown.

"Don't tell the others about the drugs. It won't happen again."

We seal the agreement with another kiss.

It's our little secret.

CHAPTER 12
BROOKLYN

THOUSAND EYES - OF MONSTERS AND MEN

AFTER SLAMMING my body into the solid metal door for the fifth time, I collapse on the stained concrete floor in defeat.

The first night in solitary, they brought food and I ignored it. The next tray got thrown at the wall, forcing a cell swap while the mess was cleaned. Hitting the guard in the face with a bowl of lukewarm soup was the final straw. I was sedated and awarded another night for my antics.

Augustus made a brief appearance to turn his nose up at me, studying me like a specimen beneath his microscope. It's like he's waiting for my defiance to fizzle out. He jammed a familiar needle right into my neck and left, but his skin-crawling words haven't left me since.

"You will submit. They all do in the end."

The darkness of night in the basement brings fresh horror. Whispered threats and taunts ride the air with invisible evil. I've never heard so many screams in one place, over and over.

Tossing and turning on the hard cot, I begin to tremble uncontrollably. There's no warmth to cling to in this subterranean paradise of death. I cover my ears and attempt to block out the noises, but it's no use.

I'm going to die here, I know it.

It's just a matter of how long it will take.

After days of nothing but pain and suffering, the cell door opens again with a bang. I don't have the strength to turn over, staring at the cracked wall and trying not to contemplate what the dark patches are.

"Leave me alone," I mutter.

"You've held up well. I'm impressed."

With a huff, I roll over. The awaiting sight shocks me. One of Augustus's new guards is propped against the wall. I take in his pearly blonde hair, tied back in a loose knot, with strong features and a knowing smile that promises trouble.

I feel exposed as he studies the bruises covering my body, the swell of my right cheek from that dickhead Halbert's blow.

"Who the fuck are you?"

Silence.

"Tell Augustus to come do his own dirty work."

Crouching down to my level, he watches me like I'm a naughty child waiting to be scolded. I fight to move my aching body up against the wall, putting maximum distance between us.

"There's nothing brave about your defiance," he offers.

"My defiance is all I have left, asshole. Get out of my cell."

Maybe he'll beat me bloody until I promise to behave. Or touch me in all the wrong places, defile my splintered soul a little more. There are no rules in Blackwood, I know that now. It's all a façade.

Instead, the guard stands and smooths his cargo trousers. I stick to my guns, ready to defend myself. I hate the way he's looking at me, like he knows all my darkest secrets despite being a complete stranger.

"Who are you?" I repeat shakily.

Without answering my question, he turns and leaves. Augustus is clearly grasping at straws, sending in random guards to threaten me with the silent treatment. It'll take a hell of a lot more than that to break me.

Tucking myself back into the freezing corner, I hug my knees to my chest and will the night away.

When the sun rises, I'll be free.

This nightmare will end.

———

"Bring her. I'm done with this nonsense."

Strong arms clamp around me as I startle awake, still trapped in another harrowing dream where Vic chases me through darkened woods, leaving bloody footprints in his wake.

Snapping my eyes open, I realise what's happening and scream at the top of my lungs. Someone slams a hand over my mouth as I'm dragged from my dark cell, still cloaked in night-time shadows.

Fighting is futile.

Instead, I go limp and let them sling me around like a piece of meat. The two unknown guards have to tug my boneless body past countless locked cells, each more terrifying than the last.

Screams and shouts echo all around me, seeping through locked steel. I recognise the corridor of the Z Wing. This isn't a place of healing, we're descending the seven circles of hell.

"In there," Augustus commands.

He gestures towards the door that features in my nightmares, watching me with sheer hunger on his face. Despite every fibre of my being screaming at me to fight, I'm forced to return to the scene of the crime—Lazlo's old office.

The interior has drastically changed with its new occupant. Gone are the dusty tomes and dreary artwork that reminded me of Dracula's lair. The new curtains are made of thick, blood red velvet. New shelving has been installed, packed with countless books. Old photographs hang on the walls, depicting Blackwood's history in black and white ink.

The two guards shove me into a stiff, high-backed chair, before nodding to Augustus and retreating. I face a perfectly organised desk without a speck of dust or single item out of place.

"You can't do this. I have rights," I declare, my voice slurred.

Cool and collected, Augustus gives nothing away. He slams the door shut, making me flinch as he slides into the seat opposite. Even with inches of mahogany desk between us, I feel unsafe. His mere presence is a threat to my sanity.

"Attitude is not tolerated here, Miss West."

I blink, certain I misheard him.

"I watched your man attempt to beat my friend for no reason. You want to talk about my attitude? This is unbelievable."

"Where do you think you are?"

I don't answer him, it's a trap and I'm no fool. His tactics are transparent to me. Half of psychology is manipulating others to say exactly what you want to hear.

"This isn't some fairground for you to prance around on, Miss West. There are rules for a reason. Or have you forgotten that you are court sanctioned to be here? Three years is a long time to spend locked in a cold, dark cell."

Don't give him anything.

Fear is for the weak.

You aren't weak. You're a cold-blooded killer.

Concealing my shiver, I ignore the voices screaming through my mind. They've picked up in my time spent down here and I'm too exhausted to stop the shadows that begin to infect my vision, clinging to the walls like sinister angels of death. Like he can see every turning cog in my mind, Augustus watches me closely.

In another life, I'd consider him handsome. He's well on his way to middle age but carries it well. No doubt filthy rich, well-groomed, and put together in his designer garb. *Pretentious twat.*

Licking my lips, I summon some bravery.

"Where is Professor Lazlo?"

"Early retirement."

He's lying.

Cut his fucking tongue out.

"I don't believe you," I say instead.

"What reason do I have to lie? The dear old professor had an impressive tenure, but this role requires the utmost commitment. I'm here to continue his good work. That includes taking you on as my patient, Miss West. So, if I were you, I'd start cooperating. Sooner rather than later."

A hot burst of panic hits me hard enough to blur my vision. The thought of endless hours spent in this claustrophobic office, with this... *reptile.* No fucking way.

"Give me one reason why I shouldn't toss you back in a cell."

His dark smile is edged with amusement as he waits for my answer. I bite back my sarcasm, forcing myself to be rational.

"I want to speak to the warden."

Augustus laughs. "Miss White has moved on to other pastures. I'm in charge now, and I asked you a question. You best answer it."

Scrambling for another escape, I settle on a bold-faced lie. "My friends have connections. Lawyers that won't hesitate to sue."

Augustus fucking *shrugs*.

Like it doesn't mean a damn thing.

"They could bring lots of unwanted attention to your institute."

"Good for business," he drawls.

Scrambling for some crumb to offer him, I'm startled when his hands slam on the desk, disturbing loose paperwork. He rises from his seat, towering over me to assert his dominance.

"There is no threat you could level that will buy your freedom. So, here's how it's going to go."

Augustus grabs a file from his drawer, ready to pass it over to me. I dread the content, more haunting photographs to throw in my face or painful reminders of the past.

Just as he opens his mouth to speak, chaos descends. An ear-shattering alarm goes off, making us both freeze. The sound of heavy boots mirrors the unsteady beat of my heart, and by the time the door opens, Augustus is already marching out into the corridor.

I should run, take this chance, and flee. But idiotic me can't stifle my curiosity and I soon follow him, tentatively peering out into the mayhem.

One of the cell doors is wide open. The sounds floating out turn my stomach in the worst possible way. A meaty thud of flesh hitting flesh, bones crunching, hysterical screaming.

Is this what it sounds like from the outside? Death? I've never been the witness and not the perpetrator.

"It's Patient Seven, sir. He's lost it."

"Restrain him! Call in back-up," Augustus orders.

Security floods in to restore order, turning the basement into a warzone. My nails dig into the doorframe as I watch a tangle of stick-thin limbs being wrenched from the cell.

Dragged by his ragged hair, the patient attacks like a rabid animal, his gaunt face consumed by murderous rage. A red trail marks his escape on the wipe-clean floor.

Blood... *fuck*, it's pouring from his mouth.

It's everywhere.

My horror intensifies when they pull a nurse from the cell, her body limp and unresponsive. More blood spreads into a growing puddle, gushing from a wound on her neck that's lined with deep, clear teeth marks.

He's torn her goddamn throat out.

With his bare teeth.

I take one last look at the monster, Patient Seven. He's fighting off various needles, but it's no use. The sheer volume of armed guards overwhelms him. Taking my cue to leave, I begin to run and smack straight into another unwelcome figure.

"Gotcha." Jefferson laughs.

"Get her out of here," Augustus barks.

Clamping down on my arms, I'm hauled back upstairs without another word. He dumps me into the darkened reception, still locked up and deserted at this early hour.

Just as Jefferson looks ready to speak again, a howling noise echoes from the basement. I startle when the radio attached to his hip crackles.

"Leave her. We need backup down here."

"Copy that," he responds. Replacing the device, Jefferson sneers at me. "Back to the dorms, inmate. I'll be seeing you soon."

I waste no time running for my damn life, out into the frigid air. With every step, the adrenaline abandons me, and terror sinks in.

All I can think about are the thick trails of blood coating Patient Seven's pearly whites. It hits a little too close to home. I have to rub my hands together to convince myself they aren't covered in blood anymore.

You can't wash the blood away. Not really.

You deserve to be locked up down there too.

"Leave me alone," I shout at thin air.

There's nothing there. I'm haunted by something far worse, an invisible monster that no one can fight for me. Attempting to outrun my own mind, I race back to Oakridge.

I'm close to safety when a towering shadow steps out, blocking the dorm's entrance. I have to fight the urge to scream in terror.

"What the hell do you want?" I shout.

The basement asshole tucks a loose strand of hair behind his ear, considering me. "Just making sure you got back safe. The dark can be disconcerting sometimes."

"You're following me?"

He folds his arms across his chest and refuses to move. I decide to hell with it and try to bypass him, completely unprepared as he slams me into the side of the building. Grunting in pain, I compose myself enough to hide the flash of weakness.

"Stay away from me. I'm not scared of you!"

"You need to watch your back. There's no place for heroes here. I don't want to see you get hurt," he implores.

Staring into his unfathomable eyes, I'm surprised that I don't feel threatened by his words. It feels more like a warning, a flash of something more beneath the calculated mask.

"I'm not trying to be a fucking hero. I just want to survive."

"No one survives, Brooke. You're never leaving this place."

Managing to shove him away, I race for the entrance and slide my ID from my bra, where I stashed it the other morning. You can never be too careful. With a final glance back, I feel sick to my stomach when I find that he's gone. Skulked back to serve his master.

Refusing to slow down until I reach my room, I slump once the door is locked behind me and let myself into the bathroom, intent on scrubbing the scent of death from my skin.

I nearly die of fright instead. Staring back at me, dripping gelatinous blood across the tiles, is a ghost who looks far too real.

You thought you could run?

I slam my hands over my ears. "You're not fucking real."

Somehow, I can still hear Vic as he moves closer, skin sloughing off like a shedding snake to reveal white bone and muscle beneath.

I'm as real as anything.

"Leave me alone," I whimper.

His smile is deranged, flashing rotting teeth and decay.

You broke the deal, babygirl. Now you're living on borrowed time. Don't think I'll let you get away with this. You owe me. A life for a life.

Unable to hold myself up for a moment longer, I fall to my knees and hug my midsection, keening like a mourning animal. My brain begins to shut down into self-preservation mode. When I dare to peek an eye open, a new monster awaits.

Time for your shot, Brooklyn. There's a good girl.

I skid backwards, running from Lazlo and his sharp needle. My back collides with the bedroom wall, and I can't suppress my scream, unable to run any further. His wide, ravenous smile resembles a shark preparing to devour its prey.

"Brooklyn!"

"No," I moan, squeezing my eyes shut.

"Come on, blackbird. Come back to me."

"No... please, don't hurt me."

"Shhhh, it's okay. I've got you. Open your eyes."

Fingertips press against my face as I continue to writhe, tormented by images and memories on an endless loop.

Screaming.

Crying.

Begging.

Dark staircases and bloodied tiles. Ghosts digging their way from shallow graves, intent on revealing the long-buried truth.

"Grab her, Kade. Over to the bed."

A hand clamps down over my mouth, silencing my moans. I'm sandwiched between two solid blocks of heat and slowly, the world comes crashing back down. Someone is stroking my hair, whispering words of comfort.

"That's it, love. Come back."

"K-Kade?" I gasp.

"I'm right here. Hudson too."

When I summon the courage to look, the blood and gore is gone. Lazlo has returned to his locked box, along with my other tormentors.

I'm crammed into the middle of my bed with a well-muscled brother on either side, Kade cupping my cheek and Hudson holding me tight.

"How did you f-find me?"

"We were trying to break into the basement," Hudson admits.

"What the fuck?"

"To get you out." Kade watches me with concern.

Hudson squeezes me from behind and I cling on to him, using the feeling of safety to ground myself. The hallucinations are gone. They can't hurt me.

"That asshole Halbert tossed us out. We were having a smoke when you came running past like a bat out of hell," Hudson explains. "What the hell happened?"

"I d-don't... I'm not sure. Something in the basement, some... *guy*." Burrowing into their embrace, I let my eyes slide shut. "Please... just make it all go away. I can't do this."

Kade presses a kiss to my temple, gathering me in his arms. Their scents intermingle, tobacco and fresh cotton, a wicked blend of comfort and possession. Two pieces of my broken heart click back into place and before Kade can pull away, I draw his lips to mine.

Driven by pure instinct, he grunts in surprise but soon reciprocates, submitting to the swipe of my tongue seeking entrance. Hudson's grip on my hips tightens, and I can feel something hard brushing up against my backside.

Even though I'm kissing his brother, he's loving it.

Kade breaks the kiss with reluctance, forcing me to relax into the mattress. Without his lips devouring mine, the adrenaline rushes out of my body all at once, leaving me feeling impossibly heavy.

"You're safe," Hudson murmurs.

"Rest now, talk later," Kade adds.

Little do they know, none of us are safe.

Not here.

CHAPTER 13
BROOKLYN

DESIGNER DRUGS - FNKHOUSER

"FOR THE HUNDREDTH TIME, you're not going."

"Are we still discussing this?" I sigh.

"This isn't a discussion."

Hudson stares at me possessively, blocking the bedroom door. Kade watches our standoff with amusement, choosing to stay well out of our current disagreement.

"I'm going. Kade signed me up for this trip months ago!"

"You just got your ass out of solitary, now you want to sneak off on some stupid Christmas trip you don't have clearance for?"

"I covered our tracks, she'll be fine," Kade interjects.

I cut him a glare. "She can speak for herself."

Smirking, he grabs his navy peacoat and leaves me to deal with our resident moron, who would like nothing better than to chain me to his bed like a caveman.

"I need some fresh air, this place is driving me crazy," I coax, closing the distance between us.

Hudson remains hard-faced and immovable, even as I wind my arms around his neck and press my body against his.

"I need this, Hud. We'll be fine, Kade is going to be there."

"Phoenix too," Kade supplies.

"Like that asshole is any help these days." Hudson scoffs.

Rolling my eyes, I brush my lips against his one last time before releasing him to grab my leather jacket and battered Chucks. Even if I have to kick his ass to get out this room, I will. I swapped one cell for another, and I refuse to live in fear of Augustus.

Kade brushes straight past Hudson, holding the door open for me. "We'll be back tonight. Keep an eye on Eli, we've got babysitting Phoenix duty. Call if there's any issues."

"Lucky fucking us." I snort.

Hudson crosses his arms over his bare chest, looking like he wants to snap Kade's legs for siding against him. "Stick together and come back in one piece. I'll kill you both myself otherwise."

I drag my gaze from the lines of hard muscle on display that make my mouth go dry. "Yes, sir. No killing today, thanks."

"I mean it, blackbird. I'm running low on patience as of late. If I find you've gotten yourself in more shit, I'll burn down this institute to get you out. Got that?"

Ignoring the grumpy dickhead, I slip into my jacket and cover the stolen *Machine Gun Kelly* shirt that still smells of Eli. Sadie removed my bandages yesterday, also giving me a similar lecture about keeping my nose clean. I'm grateful for the long sleeves to hide my arms, which are more scar tissue than skin now.

"I could tie you to the bed," Hudson muses.

"Sounds like fun. I'm game."

"To make you stay, dammit."

"Then I'll punch you for being a controlling wanker."

"You're a goddamn pain in my ass," he snaps. "I never agreed to be all soft and shit with you, so quit appealing to my humanity because we both know I don't have any."

Glancing at my sickly reflection, I call it quits and try to brush past Hudson, but he's still having none of it. He grabs me by the throat, and we wrestle as he pins me against the wall, his erection pressing into my lower belly.

"We both know that's not true," I counter.

His smile is dark, all raw possession. "You're looking for something that isn't there. I'm not a good man."

"You think I don't fucking know that?"

"I think you forget it, far too often."

"Let go of me, Hud. I'm done with your shit."

His grip loosens enough for me to break free, and I glower at him, warning him to back off.

"Just come back to me," he growls.

I manage a tight nod. "I always do."

Following Kade out into the corridor, the door slams shut on Hudson's annoyed expression. We take off downstairs before he kills us both, and head across the quad while sharing a cigarette.

"Just act normal," Kade advises.

"Not sure I know how to do that."

He snorts. "Figure it out. Copy everyone else."

"Everyone here is insane. You're not helping."

"Let's just get the hell out of here."

We join the chaos that rules inside the packed reception, patients queuing up to be frisked by guards before being ticked off on a spreadsheet. Mike runs through a quick headcount as he directs people outside. I let Kade go first so he can help out, leaving me alone to deal with these assholes.

"Dump your shit and arms up, inmate."

I find Halbert waiting for me, a sick leer on his lips. Lifting my arms up, his hands linger far too long on my chest and rear, despite the fact I'm clearly not hiding anything.

"How did you swing this, huh?" he demands.

"I have no idea what you mean. I'm a model patient. Can't you see my halo?" I gesture above my head with a smirk.

"Bullshit. Do us all a favour and keep your tight little ass in line." Reconsidering, he shakes his head. "No, scrap that. If you fuck up properly this time, I can lock you in a cell for the rest of your life. See how long it takes until you're cracking your own skull to escape."

"Gee, you're a real charmer."

"Halbert! Keep it moving," someone yells.

Reluctantly declaring me clear, Halbert moves on to terrorise the next patient waiting behind me. I grab my stuff and follow the flow of traffic, unnerved by the sense that I'm being watched.

Augustus is nowhere to be seen, but the beady eyes of CCTV cameras catch everything. If he's watching, why isn't he stopping me from leaving? Does he even care? Is this a test?

Glancing around, my gaze catches on familiar grey eyes—tucked away in the corner, hidden from sight. The guard's long hair is loose and messy, unlike his previous ponytail. Augustus's guard dog isn't bothering to hide the fact that he's staring right at me. He lifts a single eyebrow, so I run and don't look back.

To my surprise, he doesn't follow.

Escaping on to the safety of the coach, I make a beeline for my assigned seat. My stomach plummets at the person sitting next to me. Phoenix doesn't even acknowledge my existence, headphones in place and gaze fixed out of the window.

Great. More silent treatment.

"Attention all!"

Mike stands at the front with his clipboard in hand, while Kade takes the seat reserved for staff as he's officially here as an assistant today.

"We've got a few group rules to go through. The new warden, Doctor Augustus, has been kind enough to allow this trip to continue. Don't abuse this privilege, alright?"

New warden.

I try not to shudder and fail.

"Stay in your assigned pairs, no wandering off," Mike recites. "Best behaviour and normal policy applies too, so if there's any funny business, we'll be driving back before you know it."

There's a series of muttered agreements from all twenty patients attending. How I got clearance for this trip, I'll never know. Kade is fucking sneaky, and here I was thinking he's all straight-laced and shit.

With the boring safety procedures done, we set off. Phoenix's eyes are screwed tightly shut so he doesn't notice me leaning over him to study the scenery.

Man, I forgot what the world actually looks like. I'm convinced that if I blink, it'll disappear. There's something magical about the mundane after so long locked inside a wannabe prison.

"What the fuck are you doing?"

Tilting my head, I find Phoenix frowning at me after removing his headphones. His blue hair is fading badly, but it's the dark circles under his eyes that trouble me.

We haven't spoken since that movie night. I'm desperate to touch him, to feel him somehow. This forced distance is killing me. I just want my happy-go-lucky friend back, even if it's more than I deserve.

"I forgot what it looks like." I sigh.

"Huh?"

"The real world."

"Since when did you give a shit what the real world looks like?" Phoenix replies in a hard voice. "Thought it wasn't enough for you to stick around anyway."

Sinking back into my seat, I try not to let his words get to me. I've got his attention now, but all I want is to jump off this moving coach and run as far away from dealing with my problems as possible.

"You're talking to me now then?" I snark instead.

Great move, Brooklyn. Piss him off even more.

"You were the one practically sprawled across me."

I frown, watching the fine trembles that wrack his body. He looks wired, coursing with an invisible electrical current. His knee bounces uncontrollably and he hits his forehead a few times, as if trying to knock sense back into himself.

"Are you okay, Nix?"

"Leave me the fuck alone."

His eyes close again and he turns as far away from me as possible, cutting off all conversation. *Well, that was a disaster.*

I should just give up, it's not worth the hassle. But the weeks of constant upheaval have worn my patience thin, and I don't have it in me to fight him anymore. Resting a hand on top of his knee, I bring my lips to his ear.

"Please talk to me."

He turns to stare at me. "Why should I?"

"Because I'm tired of fighting you."

"Well, I'm far from done, so suck it up."

Darkness swirls in his eyes, offsetting the obvious gleam of hysteria. I hold my breath as Phoenix glances around to ensure nobody is watching, before aggressively shoving his lips on to mine. I'm so shocked, I surrender to the searing kiss.

His tongue immediately invades my mouth, shoving out all thoughts of running. Heat unfurls in my belly, and I grab hold of his t-shirt, dragging him closer to hide from the rest of the coach.

I groan against his lips when he skates a palm over my breasts, teasing my stiffened nipples through the thin material. Working his way down, Phoenix's nails finally scrape against the seam of my jeans, right above my throbbing clit.

"Want me to touch you, firecracker?"

"Yes, Nix."

"Say please, goddammit."

Biting down on his bottom lip, I sigh. "Please, *sir*."

Phoenix grins, but there's no sign of the man I used to know, cracking jokes, and giving up his favourite beanie for me to wear. This is a different Phoenix; all dark, animal possession and heartbreak, driven by his need to break me down into controllable pieces.

Casting another look around, he deftly reaches inside my now-unzipped jeans and shimmies into my damp panties, finding my clit. I grit my teeth to hold the moan of pleasure in, relishing the feel of his expert hand sliding between my folds.

"So wet. You really are a whore," he murmurs.

"You're the one touching me," I point out.

Thrusting a slick digit inside my slit, Phoenix snickers. "You're fucking begging for it. Spreading your legs like a goddamn bitch in heat for all of my friends but me. How is that fair?"

"You haven't spoken to me in weeks, let alone found your way into my bed. How is that fair?"

Using his fingers to work me into a puddle of gasping need, Phoenix secures his lips to my throat and sucks my skin between his teeth, marking me for the entire world to see. It gives me the faintest glimmer of hope that somewhere deep down, he still wants me. I can fix this shit.

Surrounded by unsuspecting patients as he fucks me with his hand, it doesn't take long for the wave to crest. This is hotter than I'd care to admit. I've always had a kink for public places.

Just as I'm about to bite down on my coat sleeve to keep from crying out, Phoenix laughs. A cold, broken sound. Then he rips his hand from between my legs, leaving me right on the edge of a blistering orgasm. I fight the urge to scream in frustration.

"Doesn't feel good, does it?" he utters, furious gaze searching my face for the pain he desires. "Being promised one thing and getting another. You're not allowed to come on my hand, firecracker. Never again. Want to know why?"

I whimper, pathetically writhing in the seat.

"Because you're a soulless bitch."

With a final loathing look, Phoenix turns and faces the window, completely dismissing me. I stare at the back of his head, tears prickling my eyes. *How fucking dare he?* I feel humiliated.

Uncomfortable and painfully turned on, I spend the entire journey thinking of ways to break his skull. Phoenix replaces his headphones, blasting enraged music while he twitches and jiggles like a damn live wire.

I see it now.

The sickness thrumming through his veins.

He could be high, but this could also be something else. The others warned me that Phoenix can become... unstable. Manic. Cruel and hateful. The thought manages to scare me, despite his hurtful words.

When the coach eventually parks up in a reserved space, Mike orders everyone off. We're all lined up, paired off with guards on either side. I watch Phoenix stumble and fall from the coach steps, striding straight past me without a second glance.

"Kade?"

Joining me, he follows my line of sight. "He upset you?"

I shrug. "No more than usual. Something's wrong."

Kade's smile doesn't quite reach his eyes. "Nearly losing you was devastating for all of us, that's why he's lashing out. He'll come back eventually."

"This is something else... he's not well."

"I'm sure everything is fine. Come on, let's go."

Flanked by beady-eyed guards, we head into town. I try to forget about Phoenix being a stubborn asshole, focusing instead on drinking in my surroundings and committing it to memory.

Colourful shop fronts, the hum of people milling about, endless cars streaming past and blaring festive music. It's easy to forget that Blackwood exists out here, the shadows chased away by something far more dangerous—*hope*.

The market is still quiet, allowing the guards enough space to carefully watch us. Phoenix disappears with a couple of other patients to find food, while I trail behind Kade to a nearby stall. He hands me a towering hot chocolate and I can't help but grin at him. Fuck, this feels too good to be true.

We find seats underneath a huge, decorated tree, content to watch the crowd in silence. Kade polishes off his drink and slings an arm around my shoulders, the casual move making my heart skip a beat. *He's so fucking cute.*

"Thanks for the drink."

"You're welcome." He smiles.

"This feels totally weird. What are we doing here?"

"Being alive, Brooke. Enjoy it."

Lapsing into silence, I savour the thick, chocolatey goodness and ignore Kade's smirking as I moan my enjoyment. By the time I'm done, his smile has fallen away, leaving worry behind.

"Look, I need to tell you something."

There goes my good mood.

"What is it?"

"I'm only telling you this because I trust you. I've never seen Hudson so... stable. You've changed him. He's been coasting along for so long, but you changed everything."

My feelings are too complicated to express when it comes to that insufferable son of a bitch, so I shrug in response.

"He's in trouble, Brooke." Kade sighs.

Fire immediately races through my veins, and I take a deep breath, ready to slice and stab my way out of whatever mess we're in now.

"What is it?"

"He'd kill me if he finds out I've told you."

"Just spit it out. I can keep a damn secret."

Kade's voice drops an octave, filled with icy hatred. "His mother has come forward with new evidence to help prosecute him. I'm going to convince her to retract her statement and clear his name."

I reel for a second at the bombshell. That's fucked-up, though I'm hardly one to talk when it comes to happy families. I never met his mother, that was way before my time.

"What's the evidence?"

"That he killed her lover in cold blood rather than self-defence."

"Holy shit. Is it true?"

Kade nods, his jaw clenched tight. Am I sick for finding some thrill in the fact that I'm not the only one with blood on my hands? Hudson's always had a glorious dark side; you only have to look at Rio's messy end to know that. It used to scare me when we were younger, before I realised how alike we actually are.

"I'm assuming you have a plan," I guess.

"One he knows nothing about, yeah. We've kept him in the dark, me and my family. You know what Hudson's like, he'd want to go in all guns blazing."

I shake my head. "Stab first and ask questions later, right?"

"Exactly. We need to tread more carefully than that."

"And if it doesn't work?"

Kade shoots me an intense, searching look. "Then it goes to trial. We'll be dragged across the coals, my entire family. They will want to call every witness possible to defend Hudson. *Everyone.*"

An awful feeling pools in my belly as I realise what he's saying.

"Fuck, you mean me?"

"It's a possibility. Something to think about."

"Jesus Christ, Kade. Seriously? I hardly think I'm the right person to defend Hudson."

"You're a witness, someone who's known him for a long time and can attest to his character—what he was like before we even met him. We need to discredit his Ma, prove that she's talking complete bullshit."

"All I can prove is that I gave my heart to a monster, and he left me to die." I make myself look away, hiding my emotion from Kade. "It was a slow death. Waking every day, looking in the mirror and seeing... what he made me."

"You have a chance to do better than him," he points out.

Tossing my empty cup, I no longer feel carefree and at ease. This entire trip was just an excuse for Kade to get me alone, to convince me to do something I can't even think about. Imagine standing in front of a jury and recanting the worst moment of your life? *No fucking thanks.*

"Nice try," I hiss, climbing to my feet. "You bring me out here, tell me to relax and enjoy the break. All you want is for me to cover Hudson's lying, waste of space hide. Right?"

"He's saved your skin enough times," Kade responds hotly.

"And he's fucked me over just as many."

Kade follows, determined to win this argument. Little does he know, I can be just as stubborn. No way in hell am I going to tell a room full of strangers what happened all those years ago.

As I'm about to demand he fucks off already, there's a high-pitched scream that comes from the market. Sharing worried looks, we race back towards the crowd we left behind.

A large group has gathered around the Ferris wheel, draped in Christmas lights and festive decor. At first, nothing appears to be amiss. Kids cling to their parents and grating music continues to play, all jingle bells and happy fucking shit.

Then I follow the path of pointed fingers and gasp, covering my mouth in shock.

"Oh, fuck," Kade curses.

"Is that... *Phoenix?* Oh my God."

Climbing his way up the moving wheel, the blur of faded blue and familiar ripped jeans is most definitely him. Along with one of his mates, he's scaling the unstable structure by hand, his feet slipping against the slick metal.

I scream his name, shoving my way through the panicked crowd. This can't be happening. He's going to fall and break his stupid neck.

"Halt the wheel!" Mike orders.

Guards swarm all around us, pushing through civilians as they encircle the fairground ride. The operator hits the emergency stop and the carriage grinds to a halt, trembling in the winter wind. The sudden movement causes both Phoenix and the other guy to shudder mid-air, fighting to cling on.

"Phoenix! Jason! Don't move!"

I wait for their screams and calls for help. Unbelievably, laughter and excited hoots follow instead. The pair of idiots holler, waving down at us while Mike rearranges the guards to cover all bases.

"We're fucking flyin' free," Phoenix yells.

Kade grabs my hand, staring up in fear. "He's going to fall."

"No, he won't move. They'll get him down."

"He's either high or in the middle of an episode. Goddammit."

"I fucking told you something was wrong!"

The awful Christmas music abruptly stops, leaving nothing but whistling wind and the halted breaths of both the patients and public. A couple of guards are attempting to follow in their footsteps, scaling the metal beams of the Ferris wheel in their desperation to prevent this from turning ugly.

"I'm king of the goddamn world," Phoenix bellows.

"Is he for real right now?" I gape in disbelief.

Kade shrugs, glancing over to where Mike has tracked down two burly police officers. "When he's... in this state, he often says shit like that. Thinks he's someone else."

"What's happening? He's manic?"

"It's been coming for a while," he mutters.

One of the police officers flourishes a megaphone from his patrol car. He aims the speaker up at Phoenix, who now hangs perilously from one leg hooked over a metal bar, freeing up his hands to fist pump the air.

"For your own safety, do not move!"

I watch in horror as Phoenix flips off the police officer, laughing and beginning to climb even higher. His Chucks briefly slip before he regains purchase. To make matters worse, his friend Jason follows, spindly legs barely supporting his weight.

"Fuck you all!" Phoenix hoots.

"We're never going back!"

"Death to Blackwood!"

"We want to be fucking freeeeee!"

Another two police vehicles come screaming into the market square, the blaring siren distracting us all. Life always happens in these brief, distracted moments.

Tragedy strikes and nine times out of ten, there's nothing you can do to stop it. A split second is all it takes for the world to end.

Kade lets out a panicked yell, clutching my hand tight enough to grind bones. I clutch him back with equal desperation, sick to my stomach at the unfolding nightmare.

A blur of unidentifiable, dark clothing abruptly falls from the Ferris wheel, colliding with a metal bar and falling, falling, falling.

Nobody breathes.

Nobody blinks.

Nobody fucking exists.

All I see is the human-shaped blur sailing closer and closer to the cold, hard ground.

Then... impact.

CHAPTER 14
KADE

IMPERSONA - WHAT HAUNTS YOU

QUICKLY LACING MY RUNNING SHOES, I take off into the morning mist. It cloaks the institute in mystery, that skin-crawling sense of danger that never quite abates. The snow has been falling non-stop in thick swathes that obscures the gothic beast beneath it.

It doesn't take me long to catch up to her. Brooklyn has been running every morning without fail, as if she can outrun the problems threatening to drown us all. I know the feeling.

Her feet slip and slide through icy puddles, but it doesn't deter her. She runs like the world is burning to the ground behind her, and the merest hint of hesitation could result in guaranteed death.

"You can't run forever," I call out.

Her feet don't miss a beat. "Leave me alone, Kade."

Managing to draw alongside her, I chance a look at her hollow eyes. Cheeks sallow and gaunt, haunted by regret. I know she isn't sleeping again, not until her body physically passes out from exhaustion.

"How long are we going to do this for?" I ask.

"I have no idea what you're talking about."

Grabbing her arm, I force her to stop running.

"Phoenix is alive. A fucking idiot, but alive. Jason chose to follow him up there and he paid the price. You can stop punishing yourself, there's enough of that going around."

She braces her hands on her knees, drawing in shallow breaths. "That's not what this is about. You lot can play happy families and exchange presents, I'm not about that."

"This has to stop. We can't keep fighting each other!"

"There is no *we*," she deadpans.

Staring down at her, I laugh coldly.

"That's low, even for you."

She heads back in the direction of the dorms. Another figure waits on the snow-covered steps. Eli's plaster-cast has been removed, leaving a leg brace behind, but he still can't run for several more weeks. Brooklyn takes one look at him and walks straight past, now ignoring us both.

"Merry Christmas to you too," I yell after her.

The slam of the door answers me.

"Charming."

Turning to Eli, we share a silent conversation. He's as frustrated as I am, worried about Phoenix and the ramifications of what happened. No one has seen him since the trip. When I enquired, Mike refused to give me any answers. I can only assume he's in solitary, which never leads to anything good.

"Can you keep Hudson occupied? I've got to do something."

Eli nods, taking my offered hand up. We wind back upstairs, accompanied by the excited shouts of patients looking forward to their one day of relative normality.

Some are lucky enough to get leave for the holidays, while others will have family visiting. I postponed my usual festive visit beyond Blackwood's walls and opted for something else instead.

It's time to take back control of our lives.

Today is the beginning.

After stopping to change into a smart outfit fitting for such an occasion, I let myself into Brooklyn's room with the universal pass I stole from Mike's stash after her attempt. Her safety is more important than boundaries.

Settling on her bed, I wait for Brooklyn to finish in the shower. When she emerges, wrapped in a threadbare towel that barely covers her luscious legs, I duck my gaze.

"Are you familiar with the concept of privacy?" she snaps.

"Feel free to use my shower and walk around half naked anytime."

"Hilarious."

"I can assure you, I'm not joking."

While she bangs about in her wardrobe, I check my phone. It's nearly time and this is an appointment we can't miss. I'm only half hoping Stephanie, Hudson's estranged and troublesome Ma, will turn up to visitation. The promise of money should be impossible to refuse—especially for a drug-addled junkie.

"What do you want, Kade?"

Glancing up, I find Brooklyn tugging a *Royal Blood* t-shirt over her head, covering countless inches of scarred skin. I clear my throat, trying not to focus on the beckoning curve of her hips.

"We have a visitor. You're coming with me."

"Huh?"

"On the trip, I informed you about our little… *problem.*"

Crossing her arms, she levels me with an unimpressed look. "I told you, I'm not going to testify. No way. Tell your lawyer to stick that stupid idea up his well-paid ass."

"Our lawyer is female," I retort.

"Stop being fucking pedantic."

Smirking, I slowly inch towards her, causing her to back up against the door. I've kept my distance, bided my time. Allowed my brothers to have their way with the one thing that could keep this broken family together for good. I'm done. No more subtlety, it's time to fight fire with fire.

"You will come with me," I command.

"Says who?"

"Says me."

Lifting her chin, she faces me with defiance. "And if I refuse?"

Brushing my knuckles against her cheek, along her jawline and up into her pearlescent tresses, she visibly shivers. Her lips part while her body involuntarily leans towards me, silently begging for more.

"Why haven't you kissed me?" she suddenly asks.

My hand freezes. "I wasn't sure if it was welcome."

"I kissed you the other night."

Brooklyn takes a decisive step forward, turning the tables to invade my space this time. Her fingertips drag down my striped navy tie, curling the fabric around her fist.

"My feelings haven't changed."

I can't help but grin. "I'm intrigued to learn more about these feelings of yours."

"I'll tell you all about them… for a price."

"And what would that be?"

"You," she answers simply.

Settling my hand on her hip, I slip one finger beneath her chin to expose her plump lips, mere inches separating us. It's been so long since I kissed her, not the other way around, but I can't do with just a taste.

I want it all. Her obedience. Her control. The assurance that she'll fall to her knees at my command and help me save my asshole brother's life before giving herself to me.

"Come with me and you can have whatever you want."

"I told you, I'm not meeting any lawyers," she says.

"You're in luck then." I inhale the scent of her body wash which smells suspiciously like Phoenix's. "I've invited Hudson's mother to discuss the terms of her testimony withdrawal."

Brooklyn's eyes widen as she stares at me in shock, not running or arguing back as I expected. Something burns deep within her irises; a fierce, protective need that could work in my favour.

"Help me convince her and I'll reward you, love."

"How will you reward me?" she breathes.

My hand trails down lower, over her hip and along her inner thigh. Without breaking eye contact, I brush my fingers over the seam of her jeans, where her sweet pussy lies below. Even through the thick material, I can feel her warmth. She's fucking begging to be touched, owned, and controlled. I can do all three.

"Trust me, I'll make it worth your time," I add.

Cursing under her breath when my hand withdraws, she offers me a decisive nod.

"I'll hold you to that, Kade."

"I would expect nothing less."

Entangling our hands, I pull her from the room before she changes her mind. Eli can only keep Hudson busy for so long, and I really don't need him catching wind of this.

The plan is simple—offer the heartless bitch that calls herself his Ma enough money to make this mess go away. Mum has it all planned out and ready, but I insisted on doing the honour.

Giving Stephanie a glimpse inside Blackwood gives me an advantage. She'll be shaken, vulnerable. It won't take much to exploit that fear and make her realise who holds the true power here.

Inside the visitation area, we suffer through the usual security checks and squeals of near-delirious patients dying for a glimpse of their families. The room is packed as we trail in, taking a seat in the furthermost corner.

Brooklyn holds on to my hand for dear life, glancing around like she's studying an alien planet.

"I hate this," she mutters.

"You've never been here before?"

"I don't get many visitors. Well, none."

I tuck our hands under the table to prevent a guard from noticing and blowing a gasket. She's trembling all over, fighting to keep a straight face. Every inch of the room is covered in garish decorations, throwing the festive fucking spirit in your face.

"I'm sorry to put you through this."

"It's fine, I don't give a shit. Who needs to celebrate anyway?"

"I went home last year, left Hudson to his own devices." I frown at the scarred table, recalling the drunken mess I returned to. "It wasn't pretty."

"Is that why you're staying this year?"

I nod, not trusting myself to speak. She doesn't need to know how messy my home life is. The prettiest façades often hide the darkest truths. Money and luxury are no substitute for a real family—one I've found in this hellhole, not in the empty, echoing halls of the mansion I once called home.

I've lost count of the times I've been awoken by the distant sound of my father beating Mum when he thinks Cece and I are asleep. Punishing her for threatening his political career with something as trivial as children, or for drawing the wrong kind of attention to his campaign. His standards often prove fatal.

"Do your parents know that she's coming today?" she asks.

"Only Mum," I answer reluctantly. "We're trying to deal with this discreetly. She cleared it all, got Stephanie on the approved list under a false name. The quieter we keep this, the better."

"And palming people off with cash is discreet?"

"This world isn't a fairy-tale, love. There's no such thing as decency, we have to live in reality. It runs on money and favours, two things my father has in abundance. He won't miss a small withdrawal that will silence the threat hanging over us all."

Her voice is uncertain. "I hope you're right."

We wait for Stephanie to arrive and cling to each other for strength, blocking everything else out. The doors eventually open and families flood in, carrying their approved gifts that have been unwrapped and thoroughly checked for contraband.

At the very back of the line, I finally catch sight of her. Entirely awkward and out of place amongst the rest of the visitors, watching the room with furtive, clearly dilated eyes.

"She's here," I mumble.

Brooklyn straightens in her seat. "Show time."

Stephanie recognises me immediately. I have no doubt she's done her research. Her short black hair is limp and unwashed, collarbones sharp enough to cut steel, cloaked in worn clothing in need of a good wash.

But the biggest head fuck is that she has the same bright blue eyes as Hudson. Sometimes, I forget he isn't my brother by birth.

"Kade Knight." She sneers, sliding into the seat.

"Thank you for coming."

"Like I had a choice."

Turning her attention to Brooklyn, Stephanie frowns. She can't place her, which was exactly what I wanted. Throw her off the scent. This is a show of force, proving to this worthless bitch just how much backing Hudson has.

"Who are you then?" Stephanie snaps.

"She's with me," I answer.

She hits me with a sour look. "I ain't playing no games with you people."

Reaching into the pocket of my crisp white shirt, I discreetly retrieve the cheque that Mum signed off in advance. Sliding it across the table, hidden under my palm, I offer Stephanie a glimpse.

"Take a look."

She gulps hard, studying in the generous sum.

Lowering my voice, I check to ensure the nearby guards are out of earshot. "Let's cut to the chase. We're willing to offer you a substantial amount to officially retract your statement and fuck off as far away as possible. You're going to tell the authorities that you made a mistake, the drugs muddled your mind."

Stephanie eyes me with disgust. "Why should I listen to you? You're locked up in here too."

"My family has enough resources to make your life a living hell," I say simply. "If they can get me in here to look after the son you abandoned, they can rain down shit and misery on your head too."

Her eyes bug out a little at the revealed information. She almost looks like she's considering the offer before darkness seeps back into her eyes and she bares her teeth.

"Hudson killed Ron. He ripped him apart like a goddamn animal. My son is evil, he's unstable and you should get as far away from him as possible."

"Do you like Blackwood?" Brooklyn asks out of the blue.

"Huh?"

Leaning forward on her elbows, Brooklyn faces Stephanie without an ounce of fear.

"You think Kade just enjoys the shit food and occasional beat downs? Perhaps. Maybe we should tell his connections to lock you away too, see how you like it. You can have the room opposite Hudson, repeat your spiteful venom to his face. Trust me, there's no one to hear you scream in this place."

Her words have the desired effect, even better than I could have done myself. Stephanie looks around the room with terror, taking in the armed guards, countless CCTV cameras, and dead-eyed stares. She gulps, like at any moment a pair of handcuffs will be snapped around her skinny wrists.

"Alternatively," Brooklyn singsongs, "I could remove the shank from my jeans and show you what evil really looks like. It won't take long to bleed you out, even with these assholes watching. I have nothing to lose. Real monsters walk these halls, and you're threatening the worst of the worst."

"You wouldn't," Stephanie keens.

My dick stirs in my slacks as Brooklyn cracks her knuckles, offering Stephanie a lethal smile. She doesn't have a weapon, I know that. But the act is so fucking convincing. Even I'm a little afraid of her, though it wouldn't stop me from bending her over this table and fucking her tight pussy until she begs for relief.

"Final offer." I indicate to the hidden cheque.

Studying us both with fear, I wait for Stephanie to crack. She won't hold out for long, the walls are closing in as the seed of doubt grows. One more push and she's ours. I can play along, wear the skin of my violent brother if that's what it takes to win this game.

"Perhaps just cut her throat, it's cleaner," I whisper to Brooklyn.

She laughs coldly. "You think I care about cleanliness? I'll tear her to shreds and bathe in her blood if I want to."

Stephanie chokes a little, watching our exchange.

Regardless of our audience, Brooklyn shoots me a heated look. "Might even let you fuck me in it. How would you like that?"

My mouth goes completely dry, and I forget about Stephanie staring at us like we're from another planet, slowly inching her chair further away. The darkness in Brooklyn's eyes has never looked so damn appealing.

"Maybe I like it." I grin at her.

"Trust me, you would."

"Care to demonstrate?"

"Don't tempt me."

In perfect synchronicity, we both turn back to Stephanie, leaving our entwined hands on show this time. Hudson's evil witch of a parent is now only half-seated, ready to bolt at a moment's notice. None of the guards are close to us, she has no back-up for several precious seconds if we wanted to hurt her.

"What will it be then?" Brooklyn drones in a bored voice.

Stephanie gulps. "I want double. Then I'm gone."

Before I can add more zeros to the amount and deal with this quietly, the ticking time bomb beside me decides to explode in spectacular fashion. Grabbing a handful of Stephanie's greasy hair, Brooklyn smashes her face into the table in one brutal move.

Stephanie screams, blood gushing from her nose. Before the guards can make it across the room to intervene, Brooklyn yanks her across the table and punches her in the throat.

Her lips meet Stephanie's ear, who's choking on her own blood. "Take it and fuck off, else you'll meet a worse fate than your junkie boyfriend. Got that?"

"Please... let me go."

"Come for Hudson again and I'll skin you alive. That's not a threat, it's a fucking promise. Go."

Two of the nearest guards vault over several tables and finally restrain Brooklyn while the entire room watches in open-mouthed shock. Clutching her throat, I catch Stephanie palming the abandoned cheque and tucking it into her bra before she runs.

Brooklyn is tossed across the room, fighting back against the two guards determined to pin her down. I try to follow, intending to defend her, but a third guard slams me into the wall.

"Stand down," he orders.

"Let her go!" I shout.

Unable to escape his restraint, I'm forced to watch as they crack Brooklyn's skull against a table, causing several horrified visitors to scream. Now limp and compliant, she's weighed down like an animal for slaughter.

"Get the hell off me! I have fucking rights," she slurs.

"Silence, inmate."

The guard brushes himself off, already murmuring into his radio for back-up. When he realises that he has an audience, he cracks his baton on the table, regardless of how bad this looks.

"Visiting hours are over. Everyone out!"

There's a groan from the surrounding patients, while their visitors look disturbed at the sheer violence of what they just witnessed. It's easy to forget this isn't the normal world in here, we're so attuned to the madness and violence.

The room empties in a heartbeat as parents and crying children flee, the rest of the patients being herded in the opposite direction. I curse when a smug face glides into the now empty space, his usual silk shirt stained deep red to match the Christmas decor.

"Miss West. Causing more trouble, I see." Augustus sighs.

Brooklyn writhes on the floor, attempting to escape the knee being pressed into her back and cutting off her air supply.

"Just living up to my reputation," she chokes out.

"Escort her down to my office. It's time for a little chat."

The rest of the guards form a wall of muscle to prevent me from chasing after her. I catch Brooklyn's gaze just before she's escorted from the room, and she spares me a dark grin, utterly unafraid of whatever punishment is heading her way.

Dammit.

I've screwed up badly.

"Get this shit cleaned up," Augustus bellows. "I want a full debrief, contain the situation, and make sure no one talks. We don't need this getting out."

"Yes, sir," another guard responds.

Augustus spares me a warning look that speaks a thousand words. He sweeps from the room after Brooklyn, his expression thunderous. Something bad is coming her way. I'm guided through the mess of overturned chairs and discarded presents, shoved back out into the waiting area.

Fisting my hair as I stride out into the snowy quad, I wonder how the fuck I'm going to explain this to Hudson without him breaking my legs.

CHAPTER 15
BROOKLYN

SMELLS LIKE TEEN SPIRIT - MALIA J

DRAGGED by my hair all the way down to the basement, I find myself laughing hysterically at the entire situation. Stephanie's warm blood still coats my skin, and my mouth waters at the memory of it trailing from her broken nose, mixing with snot and tears. Hurting her felt so fucking good.

Standing on patrol at the entrance to the Z Wing, I find Jefferson waiting with a pair of handcuffs hanging from his finger. He waggles them at me, far too pleased with himself.

"Back so soon?"

"What can I say, I missed this place."

He snaps the cuffs around my wrists, taking me from the other two guards that are swiftly ordered away. Forced down the low-lit corridor, I battle against his hold despite the fuzziness in my head from being cracked against the table.

"Where's your buddy, Halbert? Off killing bunny rabbits or plotting his next sadistic game to play? Nice guy, real sane."

Jefferson glowers. "Silence, inmate. We're not here to chat."

"Could've fooled me. You're just so damn friendly."

With an aggressive shove, I'm deposited inside Augustus's stiflingly hot office. I briefly consider running, but I won't get far. The heat from the roaring fire leaves no oxygen to breathe and I stumble into several pieces of furniture before falling to my ass.

"Graceful, Brooke."

Glancing up, I find the long-haired asshole at his post in the corner, studying me with his perceptive eyes. I manage to climb to my feet and collapse into the empty armchair opposite Augustus's desk, my head throbbing steadily.

"Didn't take you long to get back into trouble." He sighs.

I cut him a glare. "You got a name, fuckface? I could keep calling you that in my head or come up with something more creative if you'd prefer. Besides, what kind of low life has nothing better to do than work here on Christmas Day?"

He rolls his eyes at me. "It's Logan. What kind of low life breaks their visitor's nose on Christmas Day?"

"Me."

"And I'm here. Deal with it."

Cutting off our exchange, the door to the office crashes open as Augustus strides in, tossing his expensive coat aside. He levels me with a searing look of hatred.

"I see you've forgotten our chat about attitude, Miss West."

"Just keeping you on your toes, doc."

He leans against his desk. "I was prepared to be patient, gentle even. Perhaps I was mistaken—clearly that approach proved futile for the esteemed Professor Lazlo too."

Despite the oppressive heat in the room, I can't help but shiver. Augustus nods to himself, heading over to the mini fridge that I know holds countless vials of unknown liquid.

"Enough of this. Time for a push," he declares.

"Wait..."

I trail off as he loads a syringe, tapping the air bubbles out. Attempting to escape, I leave the armchair and press myself into the corner, my hands still cuffed behind my back. Augustus is in no mood to play and places the needle down, retrieving his laptop instead.

Setting it down facing me, he taps a few buttons to bring up a screen split into three, showing several CCTV feeds that I recognise from across the institute.

"What is this?" I ask fearfully.

"Consider it a warning."

Studying me like a caged animal, there's no questioning his intentions. I can see it in his eyes. The hunger for power that only comes from owning another person. Logan shifts in the corner, crossing his legs so casually, it makes me fucking mad. I'll show these wankers.

"I'm not playing this game, whatever it is."

Augustus taps his laptop again, changing the feeds. This time, the outside of Oakridge is pulled up. Two figures stand in the snow, half-hidden behind a towering willow tree, smoking cigarettes where they think nobody can see them.

Eli and Hudson.

In the next moment, Kade is racing across the quad to them, clearly panicked. I know the minute he recants what just happened, because Hudson stiffens and attacks his brother, pinning him up against the tree.

"Now that I have proven this is a live feed..."

Augustus changes the cameras again. The screen is plunged into darkness, a single spotlight illuminating a familiar concrete solitary cell, holding one figure.

Covering my mouth in horror, I watch as a near-hysterical Phoenix hammers his fists against the door, screams silenced by the muted laptop. He paces across the cell, pausing to punch the wall regardless of the dried blood staining every surface.

He's a mess; wild-eyed and frantic, hands swollen and bruised. It feels like an eternity has passed since the trip. He looks like he hasn't slept in years.

"Mr Kent has been in solitary confinement for nearly six days," Augustus recites, lacing his fingers. "I have no doubt that if left to his own devices, he will experience a full loss of lucidity. He's already deep into a manic episode."

"You're breaking him," I whimper.

"Correction—he is breaking himself."

I have to look away as Phoenix pulls sharply on his hair, falling to his knees and slamming his forehead against the floor once, twice, three times. Eventually, he loses consciousness. Slumping in a helpless, battered ball.

"I've also encouraged his deterioration," Augustus adds.

"You're supposed to be a doctor!"

"That I am. You see, Miss West, I have a very specific responsibility when it comes to Blackwood's program. Where the other clinicians rehabilitate, I serve a greater purpose."

Unable to look away from Phoenix's limp body for long, I console myself by the steady rise and fall of his chest, desperate to reach into the screen and throw my arms around him.

Augustus takes the opportunity to retrieve his discarded needle and sneak up on me, jamming it deep into my neck. I let out a scream but it's no use, the icy liquid flows straight into my veins.

"That wasn't so hard now, was it?"

I slump, falling from the armchair. My body hits the carpeted floor, but the feeling doesn't connect. I'm completely numb from my fingers to my toes, paralysed by whatever Augustus has shot me full of. Far worse than anything Lazlo ever used.

Augustus smirks. "Feel free to take a moment."

I garble a response, struggling to form words. The minutes tick by while the room spins, my body uncooperative and alien. When I finally rouse, everything feels wrong. Like there's something inside me, a parasite in my mind.

"Take a seat, Miss West."

Remarkably, I do exactly as he says. My feet move of their own volition and there's not a damn thing I can do about it. Augustus's smile is full of sickening satisfaction.

"Here's how this is going to work. I will release Mr Kent in good time, but only in exchange for your cooperation."

"Cooperation?" I manage to say.

Augustus chuckles. "You know, there isn't a single thing that happens here without me knowing."

Flustered by his smug grin, I begin to spiral and panic. We've all got secrets that can never see the light of day, some more recent than others.

"Why was Mr Knight's mother visiting you?" Augustus asks.

It takes great effort to conceal my relief; I half expected him to drag in Rio's rotting corpse just to prove a point. Nothing is beyond this man, I'm realising that now.

"She was threatening them."

"I see."

Augustus refocuses on his laptop, switching the feed back to the others. Eli is standing alone in the snow, watching as Kade chases after a furious Hudson.

"You've become attached to Elijah Woods too, and Kade Knight."

Instinct is screaming at me to lie, do whatever I can to offer some flimsy protection to all four pieces of my dead heart. If Augustus can torment a manic patient like Phoenix with no repercussions, I dread to think what he can do to the others.

"I don't… I'm not attached," I splutter.

"We both know that's not quite true, don't we?"

With the tap of a button, the video of Eli is brought into full focus. He's ducked behind the tree, rooting around his pocket. I blanch at the familiar penknife he pulls free, rolling up his hoodie sleeve in a moment of pure desperation.

"Elijah is a fascinating case, I must say," Augustus muses.

"Leave Eli alone!"

His smile is far too confident. "The traumatised mind has always intrigued me. In Elijah's case, he does not function without the safety and security of others to ensure his well-being. When you remove that, rip apart his support structure at the seams…"

We both watch as Eli takes a deep breath, violently slashing his arm three times, without his usual control. He doesn't even bother to clean the blade or find a hiding spot as is his ritual. The cuts are uneven and jagged, his head falling between his knees with relief.

I can see him trembling from here, overwhelmed by all the fighting and shouting. Without Phoenix or Kade there to intervene, he falls back on the only coping mechanism he knows.

"Does his destructive nature entertain you?"

"Nothing about this is entertaining," I seethe.

Clocking me with perceptive eyes, Augustus's lips turn up in a pleased smile. He retrieves his phone from his pocket, holding it to his ear without looking away from me.

"You know what to do. The mute first."

My heart leaps straight into my throat. On the screen, Eli is rolling down his sleeve to hide the bleeding cuts and breathing hard, vulnerable on his own with no one to protect him.

To my horror, Halbert and another guard walk around the corner, dragging him out from the tree by the scruff of his hoodie.

"What should we do to him?" Augustus wonders.

Internally, I'm freaking the hell out. Not Eli. Augustus can do whatever he wants to me, but Eli isn't strong enough to withstand it. I chance a look at Logan, hoping for back up. But of course, he doesn't help me. Just stands there; an emotionless, empty shell in front of his superior.

"Leave Eli alone, I mean it," I say with more conviction.

Augustus smiles, straightening his tie like his men aren't physically assaulting a patient at his command. The fear on Eli's face is soul-destroying as he's restrained by the two guards, one on each side, both laughing and yelling. Halbert reaches into Eli's pocket and retrieves the stashed blade, waving it like a toy.

"One move, that's all it would take to end his life. Nobody is looking for Elijah Woods." Augustus stands, striding towards me. "He's nothing. Actually, he's a liability with all these newspaper articles and speculation. What if I told Halbert to slit his throat? What could you possibly do to stop that from happening?"

"No... Please..."

Tears spring free from my eyes without my permission, stinging my cheeks. I can't wipe them away, handcuffed and barely in control of my own body. Complete and utter powerlessness is the worst feeling in the entire world.

Vomit rises up my throat as I watch Halbert spot Eli's braced leg. He kicks him right where it hurts and Eli collapses, unable to hold himself up. I can feel his pained cry, trapped behind his pursed lips. It reaches inside me and sets alight the spark of defiance.

I struggle to my feet, drunkenly throwing myself at Augustus. He tosses me aside like trash and I smack into his desk, winding myself before ending up back on the floor.

Kneeling beside me in complete and utter control, Augustus strokes a slender finger along my jaw, caressing me like I'm a precious treasure that will make him rich.

"I will hurt every single person that you have ever cared about, Miss West. Inside Blackwood, my word is law. Don't think I won't do it. Accidents happen in these places, it would be a simple enough task."

"What do you want from me?"

Augustus looks satisfied with my broken question. "Everything. No more games. You will be my willing participant for important psychiatric research. Sign yourself over to me and I'll leave your little boy toys alone—the Knight boys, Elijah, even troublesome Phoenix. You have my guarantee."

Despite everything, a single image comes back to me. Patient Seven, inhuman and screaming, his teeth stained with innocent blood. The people down here aren't human beings anymore, picked apart piece by piece until nothing remains. If I give myself to Augustus, there will be no going back.

Swallowing acid, I manage to ask, "If I say no?"

"Then you will watch as I slowly unravel the minds of your friends and turn them into empty shells of the people they used to be. Elijah first—with fire, I think. Phoenix and his beloved drugs. Hudson, Kade. Even the Teegan girl, I know she's your latest pet. Madness is contagious, Miss West."

Rising from the depths of their mental prison, the room fills with writhing, spitting shadows. Angrier and more demanding than ever before. Their screams fill my head, but I can't block them out. It's no use. There is no running.

I'll tear myself apart if it keeps them safe.

Feed myself to the fucking wolves.

Sell my soul to the devil himself.

Whatever it takes.

Augustus doesn't need me to answer, he already knows that he's won. Hefting me back into the armchair, he hums under his breath and returns to the cupboard beside the mini fridge. Wheeling out a familiar looking machine, terror wraps around my lungs and claws its way up my windpipe.

"Now, sit nice and still for me."

I don't fight as he sets up the EEG machine, weighing me down with electrodes stuck to my body. It's not the first time; I've been tested before when I was younger. They thought the hallucinations were merely a brain injury after the car accident, not the family sickness rearing its head.

Once fully set up and ready to go, Augustus slides in behind his desk and opens a drawer, retrieving the same file from last time. A grainy photograph is placed right in front of me.

No.

This can't be happening.

I stare at myself, little more than five years old, sporting a huge black eye and split lip. I forced a smile for the school photographer and accidentally broke the scab, the camera snapping a shot of blood running down my chin.

"Such a pretty girl," Augustus croons.

Somehow, I manage not to puke.

"Where did you get this?"

"I have many resources, Miss West."

Without tearing myself away from the reminder of my childhood, the voices reach a crescendo in my mind. All from the same demon. I can still hear her screaming at me from all those years ago, more dark memories entwined and locked away by my psyche.

Who are you, devil child?

Answer the question.

I'll make you bleed if I have to.

She only ever saw one of her invisible monsters, not a frightened child who just wanted her mummy back. The first blow hurt, but after a while, I stopped reacting. She was enjoying it too much.

Dad would come home and lock my sick mother in the bathroom, ordering her to cool off. He always protected her, even as she beat us black and blue, too enamoured to protest.

With the machine beginning to pick up a reading of my distress, Augustus settles back with a fresh notepad and pen, his evil smile dripping with anticipation. The realisation hits me like a tidal wave, and I can't help but choke out the truth.

"Lazlo... that final session. It was real, wasn't it? I didn't imagine the things he said. He wanted me to lose control."

"Professor Lazlo worked for me," Augustus confirms my worst fears. "I will continue where he failed. We have work to do, Miss West. Blackwood has a reputation to uphold as the cutting edge of modern research."

Pen poised, he looks to the beeping machine then back at me.

"Now... your story. Start from the beginning."

CHAPTER 16
ELI

HIGH WATER - SLEEP TOKEN

THE MOVIE PLAYS in the background on Kade's laptop, but nobody is watching it. We're all too wired, anxiously awaiting Phoenix's return. The institute has dragged it out for as long as possible, but whatever deal Brooklyn struck, it's time for the bastards to pay up.

Stretched out beside me, her legs are curled around mine as she shifts impatiently. After the fourth time, I pin her against my chest. My hand sneaks under her shirt and I feel her breathing halt as I traverse over her scarred stomach and ribs, until my hand rests right above her heart.

Alive. Alive. Alive.

Each thump a promise of more.

Shallow comfort, but I'll take anything.

Burying my face in her long hair, I indulge in a deep inhale. The scents, both real and imagined, intermingle inside of me. Fresh waffles and syrup. Fire and burned, cooking flesh. Blooming wildflowers and falling leaves. Slick blood and the bitter tinge of pills. Everything I think home should smell like and the dark reality of the world we actually call home.

"He should be here by now." She sighs.

My lips brush over the shell of her ear, tracing down to her soft, vulnerable neck. There are no words to offer, even if I had the strength to try. Augustus agreed to release Phoenix. He just didn't say when.

"He'll come home," Kade offers.

Him and Hudson sit on opposite sides of the room, maintaining their stubborn silence. It's been going on for days, this pointless feud. At least they have stopped beating on each other now.

As far as I can make out, Kade saved his skin, but endangered Brooklyn in the process. We should count our blessings that Kade is still alive after pulling that shit. If Hudson had his way, I doubt he would be. Brooklyn arrived back, seemingly unharmed, but she refuses to discuss Christmas any further.

"Did we get it all?" Hudson chimes in.

We all take a collective glance around the semi-reconstructed room. With typical attention to detail, Kade had the furniture all replaced in the blink of an eye.

Phoenix didn't stop to think that by destroying everything, he revealed all his secret hiding spots. We've spent days flushing drugs and pills down the toilet while keeping watch for nosy guards.

"It's all gone," Brooklyn confirms.

Kade seems uncertain. "He could always get more."

"Then we track down the source and ensure they don't sell him anymore," she snaps. "Blackwood is a small place, it will be easy enough to find out who took over from Rio."

"Leon never made it back from solitary. He would be the first logical choice," Kade muses.

"True, but he had other friends that would be in the know," Brooklyn adds.

Hudson cracks his knuckles. "Leave it to me."

Before we can discuss it any further, the beep of a key card being scanned ends our painful wait. The bedroom door opens, and I catch a glimpse of a guard tucking his pass away, stepping back to let Phoenix enter. Everyone takes a final, anticipated breath.

Limping and nearly dead on his feet, our final family member crosses the threshold. My heart fucking squeezes as I scan down his body, dressed in borrowed sweats and an oversized shirt.

He's clearly lost weight after so long in solitary, but that isn't what worries me. Something is missing. There's an emptiness in his gaze as he looks between us all, hesitating for the first time ever.

"Phoenix?" Brooklyn whispers.

His eyes snap to hers. "Firecracker."

I release her and watch as she crosses the room, approaching him as you would a scared child. An anxious part of me is preparing for Phoenix to run as far from us as possible, continuing on his destructive cycle. He slumps in defeat instead.

Brooklyn catches him, until his entire body weight rests on her. She takes his shaking hand and gently pulls, guiding him back to where we've pushed the two beds together to form a kind of nest.

Phoenix finally sees me, those bright eyes dulled by exhaustion.

"Eli."

I smile, beckoning him over.

An invisible cord seems to tie our two separate halves together, and he's magnetised back to me, crawling between the sheets. I fold him into my arms and kiss his lips, regardless of everyone watching. His head falls to my shoulder, too heavy to hold up alone.

"I'm sorry," he mumbles.

I wrap my hand around the back of his neck and squeeze, needing him to know. None of us are perfect. None of us are sane. All we have in this world lies in this very room—and that, above all else, is worth suffering for.

After a round of greetings, Kade slapping Phoenix on the back and Hudson giving him his usual furious stink eye, I tuck him into the tightest corner of the bed where he can't escape.

Brooklyn watches us both, something holding her back from climbing into bed. I realise that she saw us kiss. She knows that we're… *more*. Undefined but still more than we were.

I beckon her with one finger.

She shakes her head. "You don't need me."

Before I can grab her, a tired voice answers.

"We do."

Phoenix can barely keep his eyes open, crashing hard from his manic episode, but he has enough strength left to hold out his hand. An olive branch, and perhaps, a chance to escape the perpetual hell of the past few months.

I'm terrified she'll take it, and terrified she'll leave. This chaotic web tying us all together is toxic and unnatural, but without it, none of us will make it out alive.

"I've hurt you," she states.

Phoenix doesn't budge. "And I've hurt you."

"Perhaps we can all agree it's time to stop fighting each other, and start fighting everyone else," Kade suggests, his gaze bouncing between us all.

Brooklyn's feet begin to inch closer, carrying her to salvation. A few more steps and I can pull her over the edge myself, just like I did in that storm. She needs a lifeboat and I need an anchor. We can't let this go, not yet. I'm ready to fight for the chance of something more.

"I'm sorry," Brooklyn whispers.

She looks between us all, exposed and emotional, her impenetrable defences stripped away after months of fighting it.

"I put you all through hell, but you're still here. I took you for granted and couldn't see beyond… myself."

"Nobody blames you, blackbird." Hudson sighs.

She shakes her head, biting her lip.

"I did," Phoenix admits.

Hudson shoots him a murderous look, but Phoenix doesn't take it back. He stares at Brooklyn, his face an open wound of hatred and desire mixed into a hurricane of emotion.

"I thought… it would be easier if you had died."

Kade dropkicks Hudson before he can launch across the room and break Phoenix's skull, while Brooklyn stands gutted and alone. I don't move, whatever point Phoenix is trying to make, it needs to be said. This is the only way we can move on.

"You saved my life," she says in a choked voice.

Phoenix nods. "I did what I had to do. But that didn't make it any easier, stitching you back together cut by fucking cut. Your life was in my hands. It was the single most terrifying experience of my life. Then you walked out and made it worse."

Tears spill over and leak down her cheeks. Seeing her cry so openly, not hiding her feelings from us all, it's something else. I want to take her in my arms and drink every last salty drop.

"I don't know what to say."

"Don't say anything," Phoenix concedes. "I thought that if you had died... it would be easier to forgive you. To rebuild and forget. Forgiving a ghost is easier than forgiving a living, breathing person."

"You don't have to forgive me. I don't," she answers sadly.

Running a hand over his face and washed-out hair, Phoenix seems to shake himself. Willing himself to go on, rather than run.

"I want to. It'll take time, but I want to try."

The faintest glimmer of hope burns in Brooklyn's eyes, an ember amongst the ashes. "I really am sorry, Nix."

"Yeah," he mutters shamefully. "Me too."

"I'm going to get some air. Rest."

Turning on her heel, Brooklyn flees the room. I reposition Phoenix and follow before Hudson can; he's too angry and volatile right now. It needs to be me.

Chasing after her, I follow the flash of ash-blonde hair fleeing up the stairs as fast as she can. By the time I get to the top floor, my braced leg is throbbing with pain.

She's still ahead of me and I spot her ducking inside Rio's old room, making dread bloom in my chest. The door remains unlocked, no one has moved in since its inhabitant fell to his grisly end.

I find her standing in the middle of the empty space, staring out through a barred window at the fading sunset. She doesn't react as the door clicks shut, like she knew I would follow. I'll chase her to the end of the goddamn earth if that's what it takes.

"He's alive."

Wrapping my arms around her from behind, I nuzzle her hair.

"Maybe that's as good as we can ask for."

"Yes," I whisper, kissing her neck.

This isn't her fault. Phoenix is always a stone's throw from implosion at any given time. Fuck, who isn't? His breakdown was always going to happen, regardless of her involvement.

"I need you to promise me something, Eli."

She turns in my arms, hands pressed against my chest. Up close, I can see the veins beneath the surface of her parchment skin. I long to trace them with my tongue, press the blade to her flesh and watch the crimson river flow. It's sick how turned on that makes me, my need to hurt this fascinating creature.

"Eli, if something happens to me, promise me that you'll keep them safe."

I grab her face, searching for whatever it is that has her looking so afraid. I'll gut anyone who dares to hurt her again. Brooklyn covers my hand with her own, letting her eyes slide shut.

"Promise me, Eli."

My lips fasten on hers, endless words clogged in my throat and cutting off my air supply. I need to know everything. Her pain. Her fear. What the future holds and how we will survive it.

She kisses me back with fervour, swallowing my emotions whole like pebbles of death. I'd cut out my heart and hand it over if that's what she needed.

Her fingers snake around my wrist, inching their way up my sleeve. I abruptly pull away, realising exactly where she's headed. The shame and guilt it will reveal. Brooklyn doesn't let me run as she finds the fresh cuts; her touch a gentle, reverent caress.

"You don't need to hide from me. Not now, not ever."

Holding her eyes, I seize the shred of courage her words inspire, and grab hold of my shirt, tugging it over my head. I remember the time I was too afraid to show her anything. Now, every ugly mark and twisted inch of flesh on display, I feel no fear.

She is mine and I am hers.

My scars are her scars.

Brooklyn bites her lip, reaching for her own shirt and removing it. Stripping off her sweats, she stands bare in only a pair of cotton panties. I take my time drinking her in; every last stroke of a blade, the healed cigarette burns and fresh bruises, a true history of violence.

"I need to hurt, Eli. Help me."

Who am I to refuse?

Trailing my fingers over the curve of her hip, I grasp her slender arm. The evidence of her recent attempt is hard to look at, even for me. She tries to pull away as I take my time studying each bright pink slash, the new skin pulled taut.

I don't let her go, even when she tugs her arm again. My lips brush over the pulsing vein at her wrist, travelling upwards to kiss each scar in turn, one by one.

"I did this," she sobs.

Tears course down her cheeks, and I brush my index finger along her skin, catching the moisture. Brooklyn watches as I lick the tears from my finger, savouring the salty taste of despair. Her sadness keeps me alive. It reminds me that I'm not alone.

"Please hurt me. Make me pay for what I've done."

Dropping to her knees, head lowered in submission, she offers herself to me. I reach into my pocket, seeking the penknife that Halbert and his asshole friend tossed back, telling me to kill myself if I wanted to. Like it would please them somehow.

I retrieve it now, flicking the sharpened blade out. The noise has Brooklyn's lips parting as she peers through her thick lashes.

I summon another scrap of courage. "B-Beg."

Her gorgeous breasts heave as her breath catches, teeth sinking back into her lip. Falling to my knees, I join her on the floor of Rio's room—the man we killed to keep her safe. Now, we stain his grave with hallowed heathen blood.

"Please, Eli."

She offers me her slim wrist, pale and begging to be bloodied. I shake my head, indicating for her to lie down instead. Brooklyn gulps but obeys nonetheless, her back hitting the bare carpet and legs parting for me to slide between.

Tightening my grip, I bring the edge of the blade to her clavicle, pressing it deep enough to bring a drop of blood to the surface. Slowly, I drag the blade down over her sternum, between her breasts, leaving a deep slice to mark my path. I then move it to her pert right nipple, dragging the lethal, sharp tip over her flesh. Brooklyn moans, her back arching.

I place my finger over her lips. *Silence.*

Moving the knife to her rib cage, this time I press even harder. The cut is deep enough to make her gasp as blood runs down her flat stomach, pooling at her belly button.

With a smirk, I run my tongue along her inner thigh before lapping at the coppery puddle, drinking her mortality from the source.

"Fuck... more, Eli. I need more."

This time, to remind her to be quiet, I slap her left breast hard enough to leave a bright mark. Her mouth parts in a silent 'O' and I can smell her arousal through the thin fabric keeping us apart.

She watches through lowered lids as I take the knife to her cotton panties, efficiently slicing them down the middle to reveal her perfect, dripping cunt.

Mine.

All. Fucking. Mine.

Flipping the knife so I'm carefully holding it by the blade instead, I offer it to her. Brooklyn soon catches on, taking the slim handle into her mouth and sucking. Fucking perfect.

Once it's coated in her saliva, I bring the handle to her pussy and gently slide it between her folds. She writhes and lifts her hips, seeking more. I push her legs open even wider and drag the handle all the way over her sensitive clit, until I reach her tight hole.

More courage. "B-Beg."

She obliges immediately, mewling for my touch. I slide the knife inside her wet slit, holding the sharp blade at a safe distance, and begin to fuck her with it. Close enough to kiss the danger without cutting her on it, each stroke makes my hard cock scream for relief.

It doesn't take long to steal an orgasm from her lips. I bite down on her leg, over and over, leaving a violent trail of bruises. With my teeth dragging across her clit, she shatters into a million pieces and I set the blade aside, using my tongue instead to make her come for a second time with two fingers buried deep in her pussy.

When I'm done, with her spent and exhausted, I take my dick in hand and touch the fresh cuts on her body, using her blood to spread over my shaft. Brooklyn watches as I pleasure myself while studying her. The cuts and bruises inflicted by my hand. The tang of blood still coating my lips. Her frantic, unsteady breathing.

She drops her hand between her legs and begins to play with herself, already wet again. Somehow, this feels more intimate than sex. Sharing the moment with no space left between us.

"I want you to come on me, Eli."

My lips twist into a grin. *Hell yeah.*

"Show me how much you want me."

Watching as she satisfies her pussy with practised strokes, I work my shaft almost aggressively, chasing the elusive high. We don't break eye contact, staring deep into each other's souls.

I want to own her. Break her into perfect little pieces and stick them all together again. Tie her shattered psyche in ribbons of my blood, until I'm swimming in her veins, never to be parted.

"Now," she commands.

Positioning myself, I let out a grunt while coming all over her flat stomach, blood and seed mixing in an abstract collision of pain. She's coated in me, our substances mingling, becoming one. Branding us far more permanently than words ever could.

"Fuck," Brooklyn curses.

I smirk at her. *Precisely.*

Struck by a dirty thought, I drag a finger over her hip to gather a sample of the mess before tasting myself. It should be disgusting, but the heat in her gaze strips away any shame I might feel. We have nothing to hide from one another.

"Eli?"

Brooklyn tangles her fingers with mine, pulling me close enough to whisper directly into my ear. The volume of life's most intimate moments.

"I'm in love with you."

I stop breathing, certain I misheard.

"I fucking love you, Elijah. Quit looking at me like that."

I can't believe it.

Love. For the first time, I'm actually loved.

Licking my lips, I beg the universe on my knees for a voice. Just for a moment. A second. More than a broken stutter that's more pain than relief. A real voice, worthy of her love. Worthy of surviving the fire and everything that followed.

Fucking Christ, just give me a voice for once in my shitty life.

"You don't have to say it. I know."

Curling up in my lap, Brooklyn clings to me like a second skin. No space between us, we share the same blood and bone. Two people. One body. One twisted, sick mind.

And in this moment, I finally realise what it means to be loved by someone. Another monumental realisation guts me—that despite my stolen tongue, I love her too. More than anything in my entire fucking life. Even more than my blade.

I'm the sick boy she fell in love with.

She's the sick girl I'm obsessed with.

Perhaps, we're each other's antidotes.

CHAPTER 17
BROOKLYN
MADNESS - RUELLE

"STATE YOUR NAME FOR THE RECORD."

Staring into the dead, blinking eye of the camera, fear threatens to overwhelm me. Augustus sits in his usual position of power, hands laced, his attention fixed on me.

I see it so clearly now; the truth I was ready to deny. Lazlo, Augustus. They're all the same. Monsters profiting on the weakness of others. It was all a lie. Blackwood was never real.

"Brooklyn West."

"Good. Let's begin."

After a whole month of these sessions, I'm familiar with the procedure. Twice a week, I'm escorted down to the freezing basement, where I take my usual seat. Augustus injects my shot and retrieves his fancy machine.

I always sit rigid as he attaches the electrodes, preparing myself to delve back into the toxic waste of the past. He questions me while taking measurements and writing meticulous notes. The cycle repeats, on and on.

It's like he's preparing for something. Performing background research before the real work begins. If this is just prep work, I'd rather fucking die than be here for the main event. But my life is the only thing standing between Augustus and the people I care about.

My pain… is their protection.

That's a price I'm willing to pay.

"Let's return to where we left off last time," Augustus prompts.

Right on cue, I'm unable to escape his suggestion. My eyes fall shut as an explosion of colours bursts behind my lids. At this point, I can no longer tell where the past ends and the present begins. We're swimming in the muddied expanse of the unknown.

"Where are we, Miss West?"

Looking far too real for my liking, I sit in a darkened room, painted in my favourite shade of yellow. Shelves filled with picture books and teddy bears line the walls, fairy lights casting a faint glow that reveals Augustus beside me.

He invades my hallucination, inspecting a battered bunny rabbit with the ears chewed and fabric worn from my anxious habits. When Mum screamed the house down, punching invisible enemies and begging for help, Dad had to restrain her. I would get so scared, but bunny was always there to soak up my salty tears.

"Home," I say in a small voice.

"Interesting."

Augustus places the stuffed rabbit down and studies my childhood bedroom, hands clasped behind his back. For weeks now, we've been working backwards to unwind the complex tapestry of my mind. Each session reveals more horror, countless buried memories. I think he's searching for something.

"What's that sound?"

Tuning into the distant wails that have haunted me for the last fifteen years of my life, I curl up into a tight ball just as child-me would have done. Anything to escape the inevitable. They're fighting again, but this time... fuck, this time the monsters will win.

"She saw bad things. Dad couldn't kill them for her."

"When did the hallucinations begin?" he questions.

Searching for the answer, I hit a brick wall. The truth is there, locked behind glass. No matter how hard I batter my fists, I cannot knock down the mental barrier that seeks to protect me. I suppose I should be grateful for small mercies.

All I can remember is her sickness. I loved her so much, but in every happy memory, the darkness pervaded. Finding the courage to leave the tiny bed, I creep out of the bedroom and linger before a hauntingly familiar staircase.

The blood-curdling screams are louder out here, a perfect representation of the past, presented like priceless art. Their voices are clearer now, revealing the truth.

"Please stop! It's not real! Let me help you."

"Get away from me, demon!" she yells furiously. "I'll cut you! Get the fuck away."

"No... p-please... Brooklyn is upstairs!"

The crash of smashing glass makes me jump, and I hug my aching midsection, longing to escape this nightmare. I'm trapped in my own past, shackled by forces beyond my control.

Augustus sinks down on the top step, beckoning for me to join him. Together, we listen to the soundtrack of death below us.

"When did you first realise she was unwell?"

"She always picked me up after school," I whisper, voice quaking with terror. "One day she was late, and I started to walk home alone. I didn't want to miss the start of my favourite show. I stumbled across her in the alleyway. The neighbour's cat was dead at her feet."

Augustus writes that down. Even in this twisted dreamscape of my imagination, he's still taking his fucking notes. I know this isn't real, but I still want to shove the paper so far down his throat, he chokes to death.

"What is she doing down there?"

"Can't you tell?" I hiss.

"This is your mind, Miss West. All of this is controlled by you."

"Does that mean I can kill you?"

His smile is dark, proud even. "If that would please you, yes."

I can't suppress the tears rolling down my cheeks like acid rain. Every drop burns me to the bone, and I cry as more awful screams echo up the staircase.

Mum isn't the one screaming. The sound is deeper, more masculine. I cover my ears and battle the memories rising to the surface, cloaked in dripping shadows.

Someone touches my shoulder and I leap away, expecting some horrifying hallucination to be waiting for me. Lazlo and his smile, or perhaps Vic and his disgusting touch.

Someone else waits by my side where Augustus previously sat, a figment of my imagination that looks so real, my heart disintegrates into irreparable pieces.

"Hey, baby, it's okay," he murmurs.

"Daddy?"

"Come here, Brooke. I've got you."

Smile radiating pure love, he beckons me into his arms. The perspective of the nightmare suddenly changes and now I'm standing beside Augustus, watching as child-me throws herself into her dad's arms.

I can practically smell his achingly familiar scent, inches away but trapped in the past where I can't reach him. I watch the hallucinatory scene with a longing so strong, the memories threaten to rip me apart atom by atom, until nothing but soulless dust remains.

"I c-can't do this anymore."

"We're not finished," Augustus chastises.

"Fuck your questions. I'm done."

Spinning around the room, I search for an escape. I'm locked in here, there are no doors to run from my past. I can't escape the constant screaming and the gentle murmur of Dad's voice that makes me want to peel my fucking skin off.

"If he's upstairs with you... who is downstairs?"

Augustus's question is one too many. The mental doors slam shut, and I'm filled with sudden pain, my mind bursting at the seams. It's all too much. There's a reason I locked this stuff out.

With my eyes squeezed shut, I crash back down into reality and find myself in Augustus's gloomy office, surrounded by books instead of death. He's still watching me from behind the desk, unmoved this entire time, his pen poised.

"Fascinating." He beams.

I start yanking his stupid wires off my face.

"I'm done."

"Not until I say so."

His words inflame the raw wounds tearing me apart, and I walk right up to the camera still recording our session, punching it with all of my strength. The lens cracks against the hardwood floor and I follow, smashing it to pieces without realising that I'm screaming too, cursing the entire universe.

I turn to Augustus, snarling in response.

"We're done when I say we're done, not you. This is my head, my memories, my goddamn life that erupted in a fucking mega-tonne explosion. Count yourself lucky that I'm letting you in at all, even if it's only to protect my friends."

The lunatic with far too much power simply smiles, like he's proud of me for finally snapping and this is all part of his master plan. Slowly breaking me down, layer by layer, unpeeling secrets and information that I've made myself forget.

He closes his notebook, pages heavy with pain I never want to be reminded of. "Are you scared of the truth, Miss West?"

"I'm not scared of the truth." I clutch my bleeding fists, picking out embedded glass. "I'm terrified of reality when men like you can manipulate it into whatever they want."

"Fight all you want. This is your truth." He smirks.

"Like hell it is."

Augustus notes something down, still smiling. "Miss West, your past made you who you are today. It made you stronger."

Slamming my hands down on his desk, he actually startles a little and shifts back, the briefest flash of fear in his eyes. I long to reach over and cave his head in, too furious to think straight.

"I was a fucking child," I seethe, voice low and dangerous. "I didn't need to be stronger; *I needed to be safe.*"

Without caring whatsoever for the consequences, I storm from the room before I kill him and score myself another life sentence. Every step loosens the weight on my chest, further from the monster in the basement and his clever games.

I don't stop running flat out until I reach the perimeter of the institute, with the towering security fence sealing my fate. Gasping for breath that escapes me, I fall to the hard earth and bury my face in my hands.

A month of this torture is more than I can take, and we still haven't hit the worst bits. I'm so fucking scared of just how far he'll go to get his precious answers.

A tall shadow falls across me, the crunch of leaves revealing his presence. I look up to find Logan standing at a safe distance, hands raised in surrender.

He's always there, every week. A constant witness and shadow, invisible in his corner. Occasionally, he offers a joke or talks to me while we wait for Augustus. Trying to lessen the pain somehow, in his own way.

"Tell Augustus to suck my dick. I'm done," I snarl.

Rather than return to his sadistic boss, he offers me a hand. I eye it like he's a poisonous snake ready to sink his venom into me. Rolling his eyes, Logan joins me on the ground, the snow thawing as winter crawls by.

"Running from him won't help you," he says.

"Nobody else is going to help me. Not even you."

"You're the only one capable of stopping this now, kiddo."

"Stop fucking calling me that."

The nickname started early on, in those brief moments before Augustus arrived or was delayed finishing up a phone call. Logan isn't my friend. I don't know what we are. But still, we're in this together, trapped by circumstance.

"What does Augustus want with me?"

"Do you really need to ask me that? I thought you were smart."

"And I thought you were Blackwood's bitch, but now I'm not so sure. Who the hell are you?"

I take a second to consider his steely grey eyes staring back at me with a desperate kind of protectiveness. We should be natural enemies. He's in league with Jefferson and his cronies. Somehow, Logan doesn't feel like my enemy—but he also isn't my ally.

"Are you real?" I blurt.

His smile is crooked, amused even.

"What do you think?"

Considering, I find a logical explanation. "I think you're another one of Augustus's mind games. He sent you to get close to me, get my guard down for whatever comes next. I think you're a ticking time bomb and I'm an idiot for sitting here with you."

"Imaginative, I'll give you that." He snorts.

"You're a fucking asshole."

"And you're an uncooperative bitch."

A sudden, sharp scream has me jumping out of my skin. I spin on the spot, searching the trees around me that line the perimeter. We're alone in the gloomy daylight, whipped by icy air. My demons can't follow me out here into the real world, their territory lies beneath the ground in Augustus's basement of horrors.

"How long do you think you can postpone?" Logan asks.

"Postpone what?"

"Augustus achieving his goal."

"I don't know what his fucking goal is," I snap, throwing my hands up. "I'm just trying to survive, okay? That's it."

"No one survives, Brooke. Not in this place."

I watch in horror as Logan's face... changes. Consumed by dark shadows, engulfing his body and beginning to grow, melting flesh and bone. I still have one foot in the past and the screams intensify, until I'm covering my ears and sobbing uncontrollably.

"Please... h-help me, make it stop," I weep.

But Logan is gone, consumed by the evil inhabitants of my darkest hallucinations. In his place, striding from the tree line with assured steps, Vic's ghoul-like presence finds me broken and alone.

I can follow you anywhere, babygirl.

Remember that.

"Get the hell away from me. Get away!"

He reaches out, skeletal fingers inches from my face.

You can't outrun what lives within you.

I'll always be here, no matter what.

Slamming my hands over my ears, I dig deep and let all the fear out in a roar of desperate, all-consuming terror. A plea to anyone out there, someone with the power to unshackle whatever control Augustus has infected me with.

"Brooklyn! Wake up!"

A distant voice creeps in, high and panicked.

"Teegan?"

"Fucking hell, breathe. Open your eyes."

Sudden pain stings across my cheek and I fling my eyes open, finding myself… slumped in a bathroom stall.

What the fuck just happened?

The perimeter fence and thick, gloomy woods are gone, leaving behind polished tiles and gold fittings. I'm curled up in a tight ball on the floor, tucked into the furthest corner. Teegan stares at me, on her knees.

"Holy crap, that was scary," she mutters.

"How did I get here?"

"You just went rigid in the library and started talking complete nonsense. I followed you in here before someone called security, said that I'd make sure you're okay."

She's visibly trembling all over, her eyes wide and forehead slick with anxious sweat. The door is locked behind us, trapping us in the relative safety of the stall.

"I was… I thought…" I stutter.

"We should call the guys, I don't know what to do," she frets.

"No! Don't call them. They can't know."

"That you're sick? Come on, girl."

Forcing my exhausted body to uncurl, I get my back against the wall and hug my knees to my chest for protection. "No, that I'm losing my shit. Please, Tee. Don't tell them."

Shaking her head at me, her eyes bounce around the tight space, clearly searching for something to straighten and control. With no distraction available, Teegan curses under her breath and pulls a pack of cigarettes from her pocket. I think my eyebrows disappear into my hairline, I'm so shocked.

"Shut it. You scared the shit out of me."

"You don't smoke." I laugh weakly.

"They're Todd's, but I do now."

Lighting up with shaking hands, Teegan passes me a smoke first before taking her own. I can't help but giggle as she coughs and chokes on the first drag, frowning at the little stick of death like it's dynamite about to explode.

"That is so disgusting."

I exhale, letting my eyes close. "You get used to it."

She flaps her hand in the air to disperse the smoke, remembering that we're still in the public bathroom. I'm pretty sure smoking will be frowned upon by the guards, but there's little more they could do to me at this point. I'm already beyond saving.

"Brooklyn… talk to me."

"I can't. I'm sorry."

"We're friends, aren't we? I was so alone before I met you. You were the first person to look at me as more than a freak." She smiles, taking another awkward drag. "I know something bad is happening here. Everyone does, but no one talks about it. I guess we're all just fooling ourselves."

"Sometimes the world we pretend exists is better than real life."

"But dreams don't last forever, you always have to wake up," she says gently.

Finishing my cigarette in silence, I drop it into the toilet bowl and manage to climb to my feet. Offering Teegan a hand up, I then wrap her into the tightest hug imaginable, bone-crunching and so fucking perfect.

"Thank you for being my friend, Tee. I know I don't always show it, but I was alone too. You're the one doing me a favour by being here."

Her eyes sparkle with tears. "Dammit, B."

"Not a word to the guys, got it?"

She reluctantly nods. Letting her go first, I linger and take a look at myself in the bathroom mirror. Bright lights illuminate my zombie-like state, eyes sagging with exhaustion and raw from crying. Hair brittle and dry from my lack of eating, no matter how many times Hudson threatens me over the dinner table.

I'm losing control.

I feel like each day brings me closer to death, but this time, it's not on my terms. I've actually decided to live, for the first time in my life, and the world has said no. Not this time.

Living is reserved for good people, not monsters like me. Logan is right, there's no escape. I'm going to fucking die here.

Augustus wants me for one thing—my mind, and the scientific value it holds. I have no doubt he won't stop until he owns every inch of me.

CHAPTER 18
HUDSON

VIOLENT PICTURES - DREAM ON DREAMER

"GIVE IT UP ALREADY. You're wasting my time."

Sinking my fist into Tyler's gut again, I grin sadistically as he doubles over, gasping for air. Another blow to his head and he lands on the ground, smacking into a nearby tree in the process.

I watch the blood pour from a cut in his forehead, weeping down his slack face. The sight has my mouth watering with anticipation.

"I d-don't know…" he sobs.

"I saw you snorting it, dickhead. Who is your source?"

"Please… it w-wasn't me…"

Booting him in the ribs, he cries out and lands on his back, now hugging his broken midsection. I wipe my hands on my jeans, the ripped black denim soaking up the blood. I could do this all day. It feels good to be doing something, albeit more violently than Kade instructed.

"Don't think that just because you used to fuck Phoenix, I won't kill you," I warn, crouching down beside the pathetic creature. "I'm running very low on patience, Tyler."

"Ask… Phoenix… he gave it to me!"

Staring at him, my temper flares and I have to stop myself from actually strangling him. Kade and I questioned Phoenix weeks ago when he returned from solitary.

He turned over his source—some lowlife from Pinehill dorms. The asshole was dragged away on an anonymous tip-off the next day, thanks to us. Then we found another wrapper of coke in Phoenix's discarded jeans last night. This isn't over.

"Stop lying through your teeth, before I break them," I warn.

Tyler tries to drag himself up, but I press my foot into the middle of his chest and keep him pinned to the ground. He's crying freely now, it won't take much longer to break him.

"You're fucking that addict now, aren't you?" I increase the pressure on his chest. "Zade, is it? Maybe I should pay him a visit too, he might be more obliging."

"Leave him out of it," Tyler splutters.

"Give me what I want then."

Wiping away snot and tears, Tyler finally breaks. "It's Jack."

I curse my stupidity. Of course, it's him. The rumours were that Leon was Rio's right-hand man, before he was dragged to solitary and never returned. They say he's been transferred to another unit, unable to remain here after losing his friend.

Fucking hilarious. I should have killed him myself for what he did to Eli, they could have shared a goddamn grave.

"Breathe a word of this to anyone and I'll pay you a visit in your sleep. No one will ever find your body, not even here. You understand me?" I threaten.

Tyler looks like he's going to shit himself, wiping blood from his eyes. I remove my foot, leaving him to pick his sorry ass up and go back to drugging himself to death. If Phoenix is buying again, then he needs an intervention. We're not having a repeat of Christmas.

"Yeah?" Kade answers as I dial his number.

"I got the source. I'll deal with it."

"Tyler?"

I shove back hair from my eyes. "He won't be a problem."

"Jesus, Hud. Did you really have to hurt him?"

"You don't get answers playing fucking nice."

Hanging up the call, I tuck my phone away and stomp back through the trees, ducking to avoid patrolling guards. Not like they give a shit anymore.

Even if they found me with my hands wrapped around Tyler's throat, they would probably laugh and grab some popcorn. Our insanity entertains them. Augustus is taking us all kicking and screaming into a very dark chapter of Blackwood's reign.

It doesn't take long to track Jack down. I know exactly where to look, following footsteps that I haven't entertained in several months. This walk of shame used to be my daily routine, now it's a distant memory of how desperately alone I was before my blackbird returned to me.

The door to the art room is shut, but I can still hear the over-exaggerated moans that set my teeth on edge. Bursting in, I inwardly cringe at the sight of Britt splayed across a table being piledriven while Jack's pasty ass faces me. She doesn't spot me at first, but her eyes bug out when she does.

"Hudson! What the fuck?"

Jack doesn't stop, sparing me a brief glance but continuing to slam into her relentlessly. "Be right with you, mate. Gimme a sec."

"Take your time." I sigh.

Propping myself against the store cupboard, I stare out of the window. It's almost too familiar to handle. Back then, I was doing whatever necessary to survive. Hour by hour, day by day. Drowning myself in misery and vices, preparing for a lifetime of this shit.

Now... things are different. I spend my nights stroking Brooklyn's bare back and dreaming of a life beyond these walls, far from Blackwood. Fantasising about what kind of future we could possibly have together when all is said and done.

After grunting his release, Jack yanks his jeans back up and shoves Britt aside. She hops down from the table, scooping her panties from the floor while glaring daggers at me.

"Jealous?" she asks hopefully.

"Not much to be jealous of, Britt."

"Of course, you are. Jack's a real man, he treats me with respect. Far more than you ever did."

Glancing around the room, I sneer at Britt.

"This is respect?"

Her cheeks flame bright red, and she straightens her clothes before snatching her bag from the floor.

"I hope you and Brooklyn fucking die. I'm outta here."

"Wait up," Jack calls, sliding a clear baggie across to her.

Britt takes the pills and stuffs them deep in her pocket, sparing me a final longing look before fleeing. I feel sick watching her lope from the room, a reminder of my lowest point in the two years I've been here. Sometimes, it takes a shift in perspective to make you appreciate just how far you've come.

"What will it be? I've got the best shit," Jack asks.

"I'm not here to buy."

"Got a special request or something?"

Cracking my blood-stained knuckles, I slide a hungry smile into place. I'd love nothing more than to break this asshole's legs and leave him to rot. He must have been there that day, beating on Eli for entertainment.

"Yeah. Stop selling to Phoenix Kent."

Jack barks a laugh. "You're not his damn keeper."

"I bloody well am. Leave him alone, got it?"

Uncrossing his arms, all signs of humour dissipate. Jack reaches into his pocket and flourishes a deadly, sharpened shank. Rather than having its desired effect, I laugh in his expectant face.

"You really think that scares me, big man?"

"I am the new big man around here, asshole. Best fall in line."

"You're nothing." I scoff.

"Is that so?"

Facing him, I don't notice that the door has opened, and two others have snuck into the room. A sharp kick to my legs has me stumbling and falling into a table covered in canvases, unprepared for the next blow to the side of my head.

"Evenin' boys." Halbert chuckles.

Shoved into a stack of wet paintings, I'm boxed in by the two guards. Expecting them to bust Jack, I watch in disbelief as he sidles between them, perfectly at home. Jack peers down at me with an annoying-as-hell smile, holding his contraband shank in full sight.

"You really ought to pay more attention, Hudson. Throwing your weight around doesn't mean shit anymore. You're in my debt, after all. Some wouldn't mind throwing you to the wolves, but I think you're fun to keep around. Keeps things entertaining, eh?"

"What the fuck are you going on about?" I snarl.

Halbert reacts first, dragging me up before pinning my arms behind my back. He's surprisingly strong, getting nice and close as his hot breath meets my ear.

"Fall in line, son. Before things get messy."

"Why are you protecting him?"

"We're just keeping you safe, that's our job." His snort is full of confidence as he takes the shank from Jack, pressing it into my side. "Fancy a nice trip to the medical wing? Because that's what will happen if you keep causing trouble."

"He's the one selling drugs and contraband to the entire institute. You've been tearing the place apart for months looking for this son of a bitch. But I'm the one pinned to a goddamn table?"

"If you weren't protected, you'd be dead already." Halbert laughs.

"Protected by who?" I shout.

The press of the blade vanishes, and they skulk backwards, amused by my obvious confusion. Jack accepts his shank back and slips it away, still eyeing me. The trio of shits are fucking working together, whatever the hell that means for the rest of us.

"We'll see how long that protection lasts," Jack adds.

"I have no clue what you're all talking about, dammit."

"Perhaps you should check the news. See you around, Hudson."

Leaving me alone in the art room, I stare at their retreating backs. Halbert and Jack joke like old friends, with the other guard bringing up the rear to ensure that I don't follow.

I'm so fucking confused, I spin around the room and look for anyone else, certain I imagined the entire thing. I'm alone. No witnesses to back up the headfuck that just happened. Seconds later, the CCTV cameras flash back on, beginning to record again.

What the actual fuck?

Fishing my phone out, I find multiple missed calls from Kade. His text messages grow more frantic, demanding that I call him back. I ignore them all. He's still an asshole for the crap he pulled last month.

Protection.

Dead already.

News.

Overwhelmed by panic, I hit the red button on another call from Kade and bring up the national news station, scrolling through countless mundane headlines. Just as I'm about to release the breath I'm holding, the blow lands.

I'm staring at a picture of my fucking face, bruised and pale, at the top of an article. The mugshot from the police station two years ago when I was arrested on suspicion of murder. It's the same thing on every website I check, my face blazoned for the world to see—right next to a campaign photo of Kade's father.

Politician's Family Accused Of Perjury.

Corruption & Scandal Rocks Local Government.

Witness Steps Forward, Claims Blackmail & Conspiracy.

The phone crunches in my grip as I take in the dozens of stories, each more vicious than the last. Kade's father is a national hero and well-loved local politician, among his other business ventures.

Blackwood silenced my fate two years ago when he threw enough money at it, ensuring the conviction didn't impact his precious reputation or re-election. But clearly, money wasn't enough to cut out my bitch mother's tongue.

"Stop fucking calling," I answer my phone.

"Screw you, Hudson. You seen it?"

"Yeah, I've bloody seen it."

Kade's sigh rattles down the line. "We're screwed."

"It'll blow over, Ma's full of shit. The money must've run out so she's trying her luck again."

Leaving the art room, I look out for Halbert or Jack waiting to jump me again but find the corridor thankfully deserted.

"Don't panic, brother. We'll figure this out."

"He's called me home, Hud."

My feet halt and I curse. "When?"

"Immediately."

My stomach flips with the rush of anxiety. The thing about perfect families is that it's all a careful mirage, like the illusive lake of water in a bone-dry desert that disappears when you get close enough.

Janet Knight is a saint—there's no denying that. But she had the misfortune of marrying a man who cloaks himself in lies and money to hide something far darker.

"Don't go. Just stay here."

"I've got to. Mum called too, I can't leave her to deal with this."

"What can he do? It's all clickbait, the press will back off eventually."

"Stephanie won't stop running her goddamn mouth." There's a long pause before Kade speaks again, his voice lowered into fearful tones. "Not until he makes her."

Despite everything, all the shit and misery she's put me through, I can't help but feel sick at the thought of something happening to my shitty, only remaining parent.

That's what dragged me back to that hell two years ago, leaving my perfect life behind—some misguided, unshakeable sense that I owed her the chance of a better life too. And look where it fucking got me.

"We need you here," I argue.

"I won't be gone long. Just enough to mediate and make sure this doesn't get out of hand. Brooklyn has you, Phoenix has Eli. You'll all be fine."

"And you have us. We do shit together, not apart."

"Not this time. I have to do this alone."

He ends the call and I curse up a storm, searching for some way of keeping him here. It's not that I don't trust Kade to handle himself, more like I'm afraid of what his father is capable of when threatened and pissed off.

I still remember one of my first nights in that house, the black eye he came back to our room with for daring to stand up for his mother. Leroy never wanted children, let alone an adopted bastard with a chip on his shoulder. The benefit to his public image was the deciding factor.

If Kade has to go, then I'll be the one to step up.

I can keep our family together in his absence.

And kill his asshole dad if needed after.

CHAPTER 19
BROOKLYN
SAVE ME - OMRI

SHOOTING upright in Hudson's bed, I clutch my hammering chest. The air refuses to reach my lungs which burn steadily, almost like I'm being choked by invisible hands.

All I can see is the dark, harrowing staircase leading downstairs, punctuated by screams and the warmth of my dad stroking my hair, telling me to stay in my room where it's safe.

I should have listened to him. I should have run from that house and all its inhabitants when I had the chance. *Foolish Brooke.* Now look at me.

"That's the third nightmare tonight."

The soft voice startles me, and I find Kade smoking a cigarette out of Hudson's window. The tip glows in the dark of the room, illuminating his drawn face. Grunting in his sleep, Hudson tightens his arms around me, attempting to pull me back into the warm sheets.

"I'm fine," I whisper, wiping tears from my face.

"You're not."

"Get off my back, Kade."

"When are you going to tell me what's going on?"

I manage to peel Hudson's arms away and stand, joining Kade in the window. He offers me the last of his cigarette and I take it, sucking in the smoke while he watches.

"Why are you leaving?" I counter.

"You know why."

"You don't have to leave, let your folks deal with Stephanie. Stay here with us. I can't look after all these assholes alone, you know."

Kade tries not to laugh. "You'll do just fine."

"That's not true."

Laying my hand over his, our fingers curl together and he meets my eyes. There's something buried in his gaze, a fear I've never seen from him before.

Kade is our immovable mountain. Without him, I'm terrified of how we'll stay afloat.

"We don't work without you," I plead.

His thumb skates over my knuckles, a gentle touch that leaves me wanting more. Kade studies my hands, too distracted to notice the intensity of my desire to throw him against the wall and tear the grey sweats from his swimmer's body.

"I need you to trust me, Brooke. I'll come back."

"I've never not trusted you."

His lips turn up in a dry smile. "I don't know about that. You fought pretty damn hard for months to stay as far away from us as possible. You were running so fast, you didn't stop to realise that it was never needed."

Closing the remaining distance between us, I step between Kade's legs and rest my forehead against his bare chest, my lips skating over his warm skin. Sleeping between him and Hudson is still a relatively new thing, an unspoken arrangement as we glided together naturally over time.

"Kade?"

"Hmm?"

I lean in to brush my lips against his. "You owe me that reward still. Don't think I've forgotten. Take me somewhere."

His hand sneaks up to cradle my head, holding me in place as his lips caress mine, his tongue seeking access. I rest a hand over his heart, letting him take control and devour me, despite Hudson sleeping mere inches away.

The jealous bastard would probably push Kade out of the window if he caught us. Sleeping in a bed together is one thing; this is another entirely. I can't help but fantasise about what it would be like to be with them both… at the same time. *Fuck.*

"Where?" Kade breathes.

"Anywhere but here. I… I want you."

His eyes darken with need, the mood shifting. "Now?"

"Now, Kade. Before you leave me alone in this hell."

When he kisses me again, the element of control has been obliterated. His teeth nip along my jaw before he kisses me with fervent need, fingertips gripping my arms impossibly tight.

Kade climbs down from the window and walks me back to the bed, pulling me into his lap. Once I'm straddling him, I can feel every inch of his hard cock pressing right up against me through his sweatpants.

"Fuck, love. I want you too."

"So, take me."

I grind on him, loving the feeling of power. His hands slip beneath my t-shirt and glide over my hips, finding my bare breasts. Taking one in each hand, he squeezes hard and tugs on my nipples until I gasp aloud. The sound stirs Hudson, who mutters my name in his sleep before rolling over.

"Come on, I have an idea," Kade whispers.

Placing me back on my feet, he throws a shirt on before taking my hand. I follow on bare feet, too excited to think about anything else. Months of sexual tension has my knees weak and heart ready to explode.

We sneak upstairs in the dead of night, the dorms relatively silent, given the late hour. Guards patrol each level, but Kade is stealthy, waiting for them to switch over before racing up the stairs. We manage to get up to the top floor unnoticed, but I freeze when I see where he's taking me.

"No way," I whisper-shout.

"Thought you trusted me?"

Glancing between him and the final stairs that lead to the roof, I wrestle with the fear making me tremble all over. I haven't been up there since the night of the storm.

The guys kept Rio's key card; I found it when we were searching for Phoenix's stash and promised myself that I wouldn't go back again. Not so soon.

"I'll always keep you safe, love," Kade offers.

"It's not you I'm worried about."

Backing me up against the wall, Kade slides a knee between my legs until I'm utterly trapped, forced to look at him. His index finger drags over my bottom lip, as if committing every inch of me to memory to be recalled at a later date.

"This is where we lost you," he states, softly kissing the corner of my mouth. "I want to fuck you for the first time up there and prove that nothing will ever part us again."

His words have me near-disintegrating in a puddle of need. I frantically nod, wrapping my arms around his neck. Kade picks me up and cradles me to his chest, carrying me up the few short steps to the roof.

With a quick scan, the door clicks open and freezing cold air meets us. I look back at the CCTV camera recording everything and imagine Augustus watching, taking his notes. He said that nothing happens here without him knowing. I flip my middle finger up and smile.

You can't control me, asshole.

The roof is so dark, I can't see a thing. Only the faint glow of the stars and crescent moon offer any relief from the suffocating weight of night. Kade holds me tight, tugging my hair to expose my throat for him to work his way down.

He presses me up against a brick wall, the cold leaching into my bones, but it does nothing to stifle the heat gathering between my slick legs.

I mess his perfect blonde hair up as my legs wrap around his waist to remain upright. Between him and the wall, I'm at his mercy. It's fucking perfect.

"I don't want slow or gentle, Kade."

"Next time perhaps," he muses.

I bite down hard on his ear lobe until he grinds into me, his dick pressing against my sleep shorts. "Maybe. Right now, I want you to show me everything you've been thinking about for months."

Kade palms my ass, still holding me up. "Yes, ma'am."

He deftly pulls my sleep shorts down, holding me with one arm while he slips them from my body. I'm not wearing any panties beneath, just an oversized t-shirt I stole from Hudson to sleep in.

Kade's tongue explores my mouth as his hand slips between us, easily finding my wet pussy. I grind against his hand as he coats his fingers in my juices.

Then he surprises the hell out of me by pushing one inside of my slit, and slowly breaching my asshole with the other.

"Fuck," I moan, loving the sense of fullness.

"You're so fucking dirty, love."

Finger-fucking me in both holes, I'm weak and ready to explode within minutes. But Kade isn't so willing, ripping his hand away and dropping me back on my feet.

His confident smirk doesn't falter as he grabs my hips and spins me around, taking a handful of my loose hair to hold like reins. I place my hands on the brick wall, ready and waiting.

From behind, he whispers in my ear, "I've wanted to do this since the day we met."

"Then do it."

Instead, he shocks me again by spanking my ass hard enough to have me groaning. He soothes the pain with a soft caress, before hitting me again and tugging on my hair still wrapped around his fist. I'd expect this from Hudson, but not my gentle Kade.

"Bend over, little slut."

Holy smokes. Kade dirty talking is next level hot. I arch my back so that I'm at the perfect angle and wait for the relief to come. Sweet, charming Kade won't make me work for it. He won't make me wait and beg as the others do... *surely?*

"Tell me how much you want my cock."

Peering over my shoulder, I meet his gaze. Seemingly, people can always surprise you. My shining knight watches me with raw possession, so far from the innocent man I know.

I want this intense person even more, tinged with blood and death, dipping his toes into the darkness we all know so well.

"Please, Kade."

"I love it when you say my name like that."

Dragging his fingers through my folds, I gasp as his wet thumb meets my asshole this time, pressing inside. Kade smiles at me like a predator finally capturing its long-awaited prey.

With another sharp tug of my hair, I hiss in pain, and he secures his lips to my throat. I don't realise that his sweatpants are pushed down until his erection brushes against my pussy, so close to where I want it. Without making me wait a moment longer, Kade surges into me in one smooth thrust and I swear I see stars.

"Jesus. You're so damn tight."

Sucking on my neck, I know there'll be a hell of a mark tomorrow. I couldn't care less, panting hard as Kade fucks me against the wall. The open air and cameras only make it hotter.

Anyone could walk up and catch us, maybe Augustus will send his men to watch and laugh. They wouldn't get the chance. I'd slit their goddamn throats and let Kade screw me in their blood.

After I've climaxed once, Kade pulls out and encourages my legs to return to his waist. He pushes back inside me at an even deeper angle, my back meeting the wall again.

"Hold on, baby."

Clinging to his broad shoulders, I bury my face in his neck while he worships my body. Pumping into me with ragged breaths, hand buried in my hair and strong legs holding me up. The coiled spring in my lower belly draws tight again, ready to unfurl in another almighty explosion.

"Are you close?" he murmurs.

"Yes, don't stop."

"Couldn't if I fucking tried."

Pulling back to look at him, I slide the glasses from his face and rest our foreheads together. The sight of Kade losing every ounce of his precious control will stay with me forever. Surrendering his power, perhaps for the first time.

"Come for me, Brooke," he orders.

I silence him with a violent kiss, sucking on his bottom lip. Kade hammers into me with renewed speed, like he's chasing his demons by possessing every inch of me. I find myself wondering who exactly this person is. My back will be black and blue by the end of this, but I wouldn't change it for the world.

We end up collapsed on the roof, with me straddling Kade as I ride his dick like it's my day job. He kisses every inch of me, chasing his own release. I coax the pleasure from him, taking his sheath at a deep angle until I'm ready to fall apart too.

When we both come, it isn't quiet or tame. There's no holding it in, after months of dancing around one another. I want the whole institute to hear me claiming him as my own. Kade slumps, battling for breath as I ride out the aftershocks of my own orgasm.

"That was…"

"Long overdue," I finish, replacing his glasses.

His chuckle is like warm honey on frayed nerves. We breathe in tandem, the intimacy stifling, but I don't want to run. He's beneath my skin and wrapped around my bones like a parasite. Kade and his fucked-up family of outcasts own me. I belong to the four of them, for better or for worse.

Releasing me to locate his clothes, I tug my sleep shorts on and spare a glance around the roof. Memories of that night slink towards me like smoke on the breeze, licking at my skin. In my vulnerable, post-sex haze, I'm unable to block them out.

I think Kade is saying my name, but the sound is drowned out as I peer into the darkness, my heart rate picking up. Footsteps fill my ears, inching closer. They've come to punish us.

No.

Something worse comes.

"Leave me alone," I whimper.

Dragging his desiccated skeleton, Vic smirks at me through the blood dripping from his demolished face. He stops mere metres away, eyes trailing over my bare legs as I tug my shirt down, hating the way he looks at me, even in my imagination.

You fucking whore.

No one touches you but me.

You're still mine, little Brooke.

"This isn't real," I chant, staring at him.

Of course, it is.

I live inside your head.

I own you, babygirl.

"No. You're dead. You're fucking dead!"

Vic comes even closer, working off the belt still wrapped around his waist. I know what's coming. The pain. The blood. Losing all sensation and control. Leaving me broken in shards of smashed glass and the remnants of his rape.

Distantly, I can feel someone else shaking me, begging me to come back, but I can't tear my eyes from Vic's. He's inevitable.

I will never leave you alone.

Not until you kill yourself.

Come back to me.

"I can't come back. Please... fuck, this can't be happening."

If I'm dead, then you must be too.

Just like Rio wanted.

You should have finished the job.

Everything falls into insignificance as his whispered words tug at the unravelling thread in my mind. I crash to my knees, pain splitting me open. Memories hit me like a tonne of bricks, and I scream at the shadows, desperately pushing them away. I don't want to acknowledge what happened up here. I don't want to feel it.

"Stop! Just stop!"

Come on, babygirl.

You'll have to break eventually.

The pressure builds to a breaking point and I think I pass out from not breathing for too long. Next thing I know, I'm being cradled in someone's warm lap, shielded from the wind whipping the roof. Vic's gone, slinked back to his shallow grave.

"Blackbird?"

"Love?"

Clutching my throbbing head, I whimper in pain. Two familiar scents register, and I latch on to them, forcing aside the image of Rio tormenting me, his grin wide with satisfaction. I watch his lips move with words, but nothing comes out.

No.

I refuse to remember. Not yet.

I manage to wrestle my eyes open, meeting two blue jewels of anxiety and fear. Hudson's fingers clutch my chin painfully tight, refusing to let me look away as the tears roll down my cheeks.

I've got to get this monster back where it belongs, but there are too many. Vic. Rio. Lazlo. Mum. Even Augustus. I'm being strangled to death by fucking ghosts.

"C-can't b-breathe," I stutter.

"Copy me," Hudson orders.

He mimes slowly breathing in and out, forcing me to follow his lead. Kade stands behind him, letting his brother take control. When that fails, I'm unprepared for the sharp sting of Hudson's palm across my cheek, the strike snapping me out of it. I suck in a deep breath of sweet, glorious air.

"The hell did you do to her?" Hudson growls.

Kade looks so guilty, keeping his distance from me.

"Nothing. We were just... and she... *fuck.* This was a bad idea."

"You think? Up here? Jesus Christ, Kade."

"I wasn't thinking, alright?"

They bicker until I find my voice, small and weak.

"Please… s-stop fighting."

Hudson flexes his arms around me, lifting me up like I'm little more than a child. In my fragile state, I snuggle closer to him and for once, allow myself to be comforted. Even by him.

"What happened, Brooke?" Hudson asks gently.

"Exactly what they want to happen," I whisper.

"Who? What are you talking about?"

Unable to keep my eyes open any longer or explain myself, I succumb to the darkness once more. It's a welcome relief.

CHAPTER 20
KADE

SAINTS - ECHOS

PACKING the last few items into my overnight bag, I reluctantly ditch it by the door. Phoenix is still asleep in his bed, wrapped around Eli with his bare chest on display.

We're alone in here, Hudson took Brooklyn back to his room after she passed the fuck out. He was far too angry to trust me with her after what happened on the roof.

"You've got to watch them," I implore.

Eli blinks, raising a single eyebrow.

"I don't fucking know, figure it out. Just go to class and act normal, don't let Brooklyn out of your damn sight until we know what's going on with her. I'll be back tomorrow."

He gestures towards Phoenix, still sleeping.

"Him too. Jack's been warned, but I don't trust him."

I'm asking a lot. Eli has his own shit to deal with, but we're running dangerously low on good options. It feels like all of our chickens have come home to roost at the same time. I've got to level the field and get back in control of this situation.

"We'll be fine," Phoenix groans sleepily.

I roll my eyes. "Well, excuse me for not trusting you right now."

"Get over it already, Kade. I've got my shit together."

"Have you? Really?"

Phoenix throws the covers off, his blue hair sticking up in a million directions. Beside him, Eli still chews his lip and looks between us both, fearing another argument.

Shielding him from harm is becoming difficult, and the impact of him being constantly triggered is on the long list of worries that keep me up at night.

"Just go, we got this," Phoenix repeats.

Dressed only in his boxers, he disappears into the bathroom. I fight the urge to flip him off, meeting Eli's eyes again. He nods, indicating for me to leave.

I feel like a fucking asshole but there's no refusing my father's request—I have no doubt he has the power to drag me out of Blackwood by force if necessary. Whatever Dad wants, he gets.

Leaving the pair of them to it, I stop by Hudson's room but can't bring myself to knock. The best night of my life turned into a nightmare and it's all my fault. I never should have taken her up there. Without saying goodbye, I flee the dorms and sign out at reception.

Jogging down the winding paved road that welcomes you to paradise, I leave the looming institute behind. Every step between me and the others adds to the weight pooling in my gut.

Shaking it off, I make a beeline for the bright red sports car parked on the curb. I had expected Mum, or perhaps a driver.

"Look what the cat dragged in," Cece calls out.

Sliding into her stupidly expensive car, I pull my sister into a tight hug. "You finally passed your test then. Fourth time's the charm. Nice ride."

"It gets me around." She laughs.

I barely have my seatbelt in place before she peels back on to the road, driving like a maniac on speed. Blackwood disappears in the rear-view mirror, and I swallow hard, forcing myself to focus on the task at hand. I need to have my game face ready, with no distractions.

"So, how come you're home?"

Cece shrugs. "Dad called me back too."

"What? Why?"

She bites her lip, not wanting to answer.

"Just tell me, Cece."

"It's just… things at school got a bit messy. Everyone's seen the news, I was getting some shit from the other girls about Hudson. They called him a psychopath, Kade. How fucked up is that? They don't even know him like we do."

"I'm not entirely sure he isn't a psychopath." I sigh, flipping the mirror down to inspect my appearance for any imperfections. "But he's family. That comes first."

"Not sure Dad will see it the same way."

"Then we make him see it that way. For Hudson's sake."

Nodding, Cece presses down on the accelerator, and we lapse into tense silence, the miles ticking away. Neither of us is happy to be returning home, it's hardly a cause for celebration.

By the time we pull up to the state-of-the-art security gate that grants access to the sprawling mansion in the distance, I feel like my shirt collar is strangling me to death. My phone vibrates with a text message and I welcome the distraction.

Brooklyn: Thanks for saying goodbye.

Kade: I'm sorry, love. Be safe.

Brooklyn: And you be careful, asshole.

Kade: I will. Don't have too much fun without me.

Brooklyn: Hardly. Come home soon.

Cece swings her car in next to Dad's gleaming Porsche 911, letting out a heavy sigh. She eyes the mansion with the same dread that I do. Reaching over the console, I take her hand in mine.

"Leave this to me, okay?"

"I'm not making you face him alone," she mutters.

"I'll be fine. Keep Mum occupied and away from this."

"She's stronger than you think."

I climb out of the car, smoothing my shirt. "So am I."

Once inside the entrance hall, Cece gives me a brief squeeze before carrying her bag up the grand double staircase, keeping her footsteps deliberately light.

I glance at my reflection in the nearby gilded mirror one more time. With no more excuses to stall, I wave off the housekeeper that comes to greet me and head to the study, knocking once.

"Enter."

Inside, the curtains are drawn against the drizzly day, and a roaring fire burns in the corner. The huge mahogany desk piled with neat stacks of paperwork lies empty, while two high-backed leather armchairs before the fire are occupied.

I linger awkwardly in the doorway as whiskey glasses are clinked and knocked back. Dad takes his time to down the measure before waving for me to come forward.

"Well, well. The prodigal son returns," he declares.

Leroy Knight is an imposing man—always impeccably dressed in a three-piece suit and cufflinks that cost more than most houses, his bald head polished to utter perfection.

I have his eyes, though the hazel in his is offset with more green flecks and shines with calculated intelligence. Taking his time to look over me, Dad stubs out his cigar.

"Your tie is crooked, son. Fix it."

Looking down, I see no fault but straighten it regardless.

"Sorry, sir."

"What took you so long getting here?"

"I had classes to finish yesterday. I apologise."

"When I call, I expect you to respond."

Gulping, I look at the other armchair. If possible, my unease heightens even more, and I take a careful step backwards. Dressed in a charcoal shirt and slacks, fake smile firmly plastered in place, Tony raises his glass to me before finishing his mouthful.

"Nice to see you again, Kade."

Dad has many business partners, more than I can keep track of. None turn my stomach more than Tony does. He deals in the somewhat *shadier* aspects of running a political campaign and multiple successful business ventures.

While Dad's hands remain spotlessly clean, his subordinates' bear enough blood to warrant an admission to Blackwood. Success isn't possible without paying a heavy price in this world.

"We will join you shortly," Dad snaps, gesturing for Tony to leave. "Come sit, son. We have much to discuss."

Smirking at me, Tony smooths his trousers and leaves the room. Once alone, I settle into the leather armchair beside Dad and stare deep into the pits of the fire.

"Where's Mum?"

"Resting. She has a migraine."

Dad pours himself another measure, without offering me one. I could use the liquor to steel my nerves, already fraying at the edges. I wasn't expecting to see Tony here, nor for Dad to be so lethally quiet. That's never a good sign.

"Tell me, which one of you came up with the idea of asking Stephanie to attend Blackwood for a private meeting? You or your stupid mother?" Dad barks.

I flinch. "Me."

"Naturally. I thought I paid for your fancy education for a reason. Perhaps you're not as clever as you'd have us all think. Has that street rat made you soft, Kade?"

"Hudson isn't a street rat," I whisper.

I don't see the punch coming. I'm a fool. The force of it has me falling from the armchair, splayed on my back before the crackling fire. Dad's face is purple with rage as he towers over me, his expertly polished shoe crunching my wrist until I'm screaming.

"That fucking boy has been nothing but trouble. I put clothes on his back, accepted him into our home. Put him through college and school. What thanks do I get?"

The crystal whiskey glass sails into the chimney above the fireplace, shattering into pieces that rain down on me. I cover my eyes with one hand, still pinned by Dad's foot pressing into me.

"Not only did you go behind my back and disregard the risk involved in negotiating with this worthless skank, but you brought her to the very place we arranged for Hudson to attend for its privacy," Dad seethes, staring down at me with utter contempt. "You've brought shame on this family, Kade."

Moving his foot so it rests on my neck, crushing my windpipe, I make myself go limp and submit. Fighting back will only make this worse.

"I was only trying to help," I choke out.

"You disobeyed me. You and your mother."

"Mum w-wasn't involved, it was all me."

"Her goddamn name is on the paperwork. But this isn't about her, she's already learned her lesson." My heart leaps into my mouth at his words, but Dad isn't done. "Now, it's time you earned your place in this family. We will deal with this matter once and for all. My way."

Dad hauls me up, his grip on my neck threatening to break bone as he escorts me into the depths of the mansion. Down through the ancient servants' quarters that are no longer used, a passageway leads to a subterranean level from the prohibition era.

These days, this private part of the house is used for his late-night poker games and business meetings. I still remember sneaking down as a curious child and being beaten within an inch of my life for disobeying the rules.

Tony awaits at the bottom of the staircase, smoking a roll up, with one hand casually in his pocket. I clock the bulge of a holster beneath his suit jacket. He's packing as always.

Dad roughly shoves me into the waiting room and they both block the exit, leaving me to face the dark level lit by flickering candlelight.

"No need for introductions," Dad tuts.

Backtracking until I collide with the damp wall, I stare into the terrified eyes of Hudson's Ma. Stephanie looks even worse than last time we met, nothing more than skin and bone now.

Her lip is split, and entire face swollen with bruises, but more stomach-turning is the way her hands are cuffed above her head, connected to a water pipe.

"What is this?" I gasp.

"A lesson, son."

Removing his designer suit jacket, Dad pockets his cufflinks and begins to roll up his shirt sleeves. Tony follows suit, unveiling a gun tucked into his leather holster. I look over to the exit, finding the door locked and bolted. No escape.

"Twenty grand didn't get you far then, huh?" Dad chuckles.

"Please... I'll s-stop, I won't say a w-word," Stephanie sobs.

"No doubt you snorted your way through that in no time. So, you figured you'd kick up a fuss, milk me dry for all my goddamn money? People like you make me sick."

Following his words with a swift and brutal punch to the face, Stephanie lets out a scream as her head slumps. Blood drips on the stone floor, joining an already dried puddle.

"You threatened the integrity of this family," Dad snarls.

"What integrity?" Stephanie shouts.

He delivers another punch, this time to her stomach. I look away as she retches, more blood than vomit. Tony watches from the corner with sick pleasure, laughing under his breath.

"My entire career is built upon this foundation." Dad turns back to me, wiping his knuckles off on a handkerchief. "Isn't that right, son?"

I don't answer. I can't speak. It's a crumbling foundation, laced with fear and resentment, corroding from within. We're a perpetuated façade of domestic bliss, hiding a far darker reality.

"Please... I'll retract my statement, tell the press I made everything up," Stephanie begs, all of her weight on the cuffs as her knees give out. "You'll never see me again. I s-swear."

Ignoring her begging, Dad turns to me. I blanch when I see that he's now holding Tony's gun, hand outstretched to offer it to me.

"Take it, Kade."

"I can't," I mutter shamefully.

Boxing me in, Dad grabs hold of my tie to bring us nose to nose. I can smell the liquor and cigar smoke on his breath, and it turns my stomach.

Suddenly, the gun presses to my temple with terrifying weight. What scares me even more is the flash of desperation inside me that wishes he would just pull the trigger and get it over with.

"Take the gun or you will never see Hudson again."

I stare deep into Dad's eyes, realising I have no choice. No control. Nothing. I've been fooling myself for years. Amy and our baby died to protect my so-called precious image—the person Dad wanted me to be, when all along, the path ends here. In this unthinkable moment.

Like the coward I am, I take the gun.

Gripping my shoulder tight, Dad guides me forwards until I'm standing metres from Stephanie. She begs me with her eyes, still coughing great globules of blood.

"Such a waste. Suicide really is a tragedy." Dad sighs.

Tony sniggers. "Couldn't live with herself and the lies, clearly."

"You won't get away with this," she weeps, helpless and alone. "The world will know what happened here. I won't be silenced."

"We control the narrative," Dad intervenes. "You should have taken the money and ran, you fool. Now, we will discredit every last toxic word you printed. Every lie. You came to my home and threatened me and my wife. High on drugs, no doubt."

Stephanie screams her frustration and I feel my own desperate tears spill over, the gun trembling violently in my hands. Dad doesn't loosen his grip, keeping me pinned in place.

"You admitted to deceiving the entire world just to get one last fix before putting a bullet in your own skull," Dad finishes. "My brilliant son, visiting home after studying hard for his degree, witnessed the whole ordeal. Thankfully, he was here to protect his old man."

Delivering me a wink, Dad steps back. I'm left centre stage and it becomes clear exactly who will be putting the bullet in Stephanie's skull. What he expects of me, to protect those I care about. This is the final test of my vow to keep my family safe —Hudson and all the others.

"Do it, Kade."

My finger dances over the trigger. Internally, I see my ten-year-old self, shaking and afraid as Dad took me hunting for the first time. Forced me to learn every step, until I shot my first deer and watched the life drain from its beautiful chocolate eyes. Only this isn't a deer. This is a real life, breathing person.

"Please, Kade… help me," Stephanie keens.

I don't see her.

Not anymore.

All I see is Hudson, handcuffed and vulnerable in her place, begging for his life. Then Brooklyn. Eli. Phoenix. Cece. Mum. Everyone I care about, pinned and at Dad's sick mercy. No one is safe from him. I have to play the game, no matter the cost.

A guttural scream slips past my lips as I finally squeeze the trigger. In an instant, Stephanie's skull shatters. Hot copper splashes against my lips and I stand frozen, drenched in her blood.

"That wasn't so hard, was it?" Dad heckles.

Unable to look at her broken body for a moment longer; I stumble to the corner of the room and throw up repeatedly until nothing remains in my stomach.

"Remember what happened here, Kade," Dad warns. "I won't tell you again."

His threat is the final straw and I run. They both laugh at me, shouting their praise. I don't look back. Fleeing on numb legs, I leave them to dispose of Hudson's Ma, another eliminated threat to this empire of corruption.

I have no doubt that Stephanie and our little problem will vanish with enough money. Her story dies with her. Just like them all. The people who threaten Dad's throne or defy him in any way.

Bursting out into the entrance hall once more, I catch sight of myself in the mirror. The person that walked into this mansion is gone.

Staring at my reflection, dripping red with the odd fragment of bone too, I'm numb. If there were anything left inside of me, I'd throw up again.

"Kade?"

Arms wrapped around her trembling knees, Cece watches me from the top of the staircase. I wipe blood and tears from my eyes, trying to pull my broken pieces back together for her. It doesn't work. I fall to my knees instead, until she's flying down the stairs and holding me.

"What did he do to you?" she whimpers.

"We're leaving."

"What about Mum?"

Cece helps me to my feet, deathly pale as she looks over my once-white shirt now blooming with deep crimson swirls. I gently push her away, towards the front door.

"Get in the car. I'll follow."

"No, wait—"

"Do it, Cece!"

Leaving her to flee, I make myself take the stairs up. Each step feels like the last thing I'll do, an unbearable weight pressing me down. I stop by my old room and rip the bloodied clothes from my body, fighting nausea the whole time. I have to get them off.

By the time I've quickly changed and arrived at Mum's room, I feel like I'm dead already. This is my penance, the price I must pay for all I've done to assist the monster smoking his cigar.

I was sent to Blackwood for a reason.

After all, investments need monitoring.

My father has sunk a small fortune into the institute over the years, one of the elusive private donors. After paying off the authorities to ensure Hudson's admittance and making my life comfortable as hell, I soon realised I was expected to... *watch over* certain things.

Dad isn't a sentimental man, the truth is far more heartless.

I'm his fucking mole.

Months of lying to everyone, digging into information that's none of my business, watching the politics of clinicians and the patients they pick apart... I've reported it all back. Seemingly innocent information, but in the wrong hands, a lethal weapon if needed.

"Mum? You awake?" I whisper.

Peering into her dark room, fear swallows me whole. There's a lump beneath the bedsheets, human-shaped and silent as the grave. She's always kept a stash of sleeping pills around, allowing her to escape this hell when needed.

Slowly, I peel back the sheets and brace myself for inevitable impact. Every inch of mottled skin confirms my worst fears.

She's black and blue.

Beaten within an inch of her life.

"K-Kade?"

Her voice is a broken whisper that stabs me in the heart. I try to soothe her, my own eyes burning with angry tears, but she brushes my searching hands aside.

"Go h-home. It's not safe f-for you here."

"I'm not leaving you!"

Turning over to reveal her bruised face with an eye swollen shut, Mum offers me a helpless smile. "He c-can hurt me, but not you. I'll be okay as long as I know you're safe."

"No... We can go somewhere far from here. Anywhere."

"Someone has to stay behind." She cups my cheeks, brushing my hair aside. "I know y-you don't believe me, but you've always made me proud. Your b-brother and sister are lucky to have you. Keep them safe, Kade. Please."

Her words cut so fucking deep, I fear I'll never recover. Not after what I just did. There's never been anyone less worthy than me. Mum pushes me away with her remaining strength, trying her best to manage a smile, revealing a chipped tooth.

It takes everything in me to leave her behind. I make myself think of the other people depending on me, at risk without me there to keep them safe. Dad's power reaches everywhere, including Blackwood. I have to get home. Whatever comes next, it won't be pretty.

"What are you doing?" I bark at Cece.

She still stands in the house, not safely ensconced in the car. Crying uncontrollably, she looks up to where Mum's door lies. I drag her out, regardless of what she wants.

"Where exactly do you two think you're going?"

His voice crashes like thunder, setting dread deep in my bones. The front door stands open and rain lashes against the ground outside, but greater evil lies within. Cece clutches my hand tight as we both turn and face our father together.

"We're leaving, Dad."

"I hardly think so. There's still much to discuss."

Clearing the thick emotion from my throat, I summon every ounce of courage to straighten and face him without fear.

"Cece is going back to school and I'm returning to Blackwood, to Hudson and my friends. We won't be back here."

"You're a fool if you think I'll let you walk away from this family," Dad warns, casually lighting another cigar. "Back upstairs, Cece. Let the adults speak in private."

Before I can stop her, Cece drops my hand. She walks right up to Dad and his smile oozes confidence as she falls in line.

"Good girl," he praises.

Cece preens beneath his touch, her eyes screwed tightly shut. I feel sick to my stomach watching the power he holds over her. As I prepare myself to do whatever necessary to save her stupid life, even if I have to drag her out by her hair, Cece surprises me.

"I am ashamed to be your daughter."

Striking our father across the face hard enough to elicit a sharp crack, Cece strides away without a backwards glance. Dad looks genuinely shocked, touching his red cheek, before it turns to rage.

"You'll pay for this, Kade."

I stare him down. "I already have."

Wasting no time, I chase after Cece, throwing myself in the car as she floors it. We take off in a spray of gravel, racing back up the long driveway.

Glancing at Dad in the rear-view mirror, he stands on the threshold, staring after us with fury. This isn't over yet.

Far, far from it.

"You shouldn't have done that," I shout.

Cece blasts well past the speed limit to escape the mansion's grounds, tears pouring from her eyes.

"I know."

Looking away from the road, she gives me a watery grin.

"But it was fucking worth it."

CHAPTER 21
BROOKLYN

15 MISSED CALLS - MOUTH CULTURE

"SETTLE DOWN! REMEMBER THE GROUP RULES!"

Sadie lectures the room as she scrawls across the whiteboard. We're supposed to be compiling a list of so-called positive coping mechanisms, but it's dissolved into a pissing contest as the assholes in the room compare exploits.

Britt is doing everything within her power to piss me the hell off, and after spending all night being questioned by Hudson about what the fuck happened up on the roof, I'm struggling not to react.

Kade isn't here to stop me from killing the skinny bitch and burying her fucking body where no one will find it. Therefore, I'm not responsible for what happens if she doesn't shut the hell up.

"This is a waste of time," Teegan mutters.

"How much longer?"

"Another fifteen minutes."

"You've got to be kidding me?" I groan.

Sadie shoots me an unimpressed look from across the room, still trying to reign in the rest of the group. I smile sweetly, drawing a little halo above my head with my index finger. Her eye roll tells me how much she appreciates that.

"You hear from Kade yet?"

"Nope. He's supposed to be back today."

Teegan bumps her shoulder with mine. "Stop worrying, he's a big boy. How about we blow off lunch, go back to my room. Dad sent some new records, you'll freak out when you see them."

"Which ones?"

Her grin is full of mischief. "Nirvana, limited edition."

"You're speaking my language. I'm in."

Casting an impatient look around, I make the mistake of meeting Jack's eyes on the opposite side of the circle. He slid right into Leon's vacant spot in the group, almost like he never existed.

No one seems bothered by the fact that Leon disappeared after asking too many questions and causing a scene. These clueless sheep are fucking stupid.

"Sometimes things happen in life that we can't control," Sadie drones on, her handwriting filling the board. "All we can control is our reaction to these events, and whether we let our emotions define our actions."

"But we're all different," someone argues.

Sadie nods, capping her pen. "Of course. But that doesn't mean we can't learn from each other. What works for one person might also work for the next. This group is an opportunity to share ideas and grow your own skill set."

Britt sticks her hand up and Sadie nods, casting me a placating look.

"We're not all equal though, are we?" Britt says, her voice shrill and infuriating. "I mean, we've got literal murderers in the group. I have never killed a man and sawed him into easily disposable pieces."

A lethal silence descends. I clench my hands into fists, taking a breath to maintain some semblance of calm. Teegan casts me a nervous look, filling in the blanks that I haven't wanted to discuss. *Fucking Britt.* I won't rise to it, she's just pissed because Hudson hasn't acknowledged her in months.

"We're not here to discuss private information," Sadie chastises.

"It's hardly private, the internet is filled with news reports and all the gory details. Who else feels comfortable sharing a room with the notorious boyfriend killer? She's a fucking psychopath."

The short, barked laugh of our resident hard-ass, Lana, soon wipes the smile from Britt's face. She's been in my corner since our very first session together and never shies away from the cold, hard truth. My kinda gal.

"News flash, princess. We're all psychopaths," Lana drawls. "I've killed more people than anyone else here. First time, my stepdaddy snuck into my room to touch my baby sister the same way he touched me. Wanna know what I did?"

Britt blanches, resting on the edge of her seat like she wants to run as far from Lana as possible. I don't get involved, enjoying the show far too much.

"Maybe now is not the best time to...." Sadie begins.

"I cut his goddamn dick off and made him eat it like an ice lolly," Lana interrupts.

The entire group stares at her with varying expressions of shock, disbelief and... *amusement?* Perhaps they aren't all prudes here as I'd previously thought.

"Run along now." Lana laughs darkly. "I'm sure Daddy will lick your wounds when he comes to deliver more laxatives shoved up his asshole. Does he make you blow him for it? Or do you just bend straight over like a good little princess?"

Britt flushes an ugly shade of red, looking like she wants the ground to swallow her up. This is fucking priceless. I expect her to run from the room like the coward she is, but there's a sudden blur of movement as she launches herself across the circle and tackles Lana to the floor.

"You fucking whore! How dare you?"

Hands wrapped around Lana's throat, Britt lets out a furious wail. I'm almost impressed. Sadie is useless, shouting for them to stop. While Lana could handle herself easily, I decide to intervene and grab Britt by the hair. She screams as I toss her across the room, a handful remaining clenched in my fist.

"You crazy bitch," she wails.

"Leave Lana alone, slut. You're outnumbered here."

Britt attempts to retaliate and grabs my ankle, flailing about like an idiot. Taking full advantage of Sadie's hesitation, I slam my foot down on Britt's fingers and wait for the satisfying crunch of broken bones. Fuck my resolve, I'll take the punishment if needed.

"Keep your mouth shut in the future or it'll be your legs next," I warn.

Dropping the loose strands of hair at her feet, I leave Britt to sob and offer Lana a hand up, sharing a smirk. She's right about one thing; Britt doesn't belong here. Not anymore. The queen's throne has long been toppled, let the reign of crazies begin.

"That's it! Group dismissed, everyone out immediately," Sadie shouts, hands on her hips. "Brooklyn, stay behind," she adds.

Limping out while clutching her head, boasting an impressive new bald patch, Britt doesn't look at me again. Teegan mimes for me to call her and follows the others, leaving me alone in the empty circle of chairs.

The minute the door slams shut, Sadie rounds on me.

"What the hell do you think you're playing at?"

"She fucking started it," I snap.

"You cannot do stuff like that, Brooke. It's unacceptable."

"Are you saying this as my friend? Or a clinician?"

"How about as a human being?"

I snatch up my bag and march over to her, getting real close. All of the anger and exhaustion boils into red hot rage and Sadie paces backwards, seemingly afraid of me.

"Stop kidding yourself that you're doing any good here." I sneer, wanting to hurt her. "You're following a dead trail that leads back to a ghost, while the rest of us suffer and endure the hell that Augustus is raining down. Investigate that, you fucking coward. Otherwise, get the hell out of my face."

Fresh out of fucks to give, I storm from the group therapy room before I do something worse like deck her. Sadie doesn't shout after me for once and when I glance back, I find her hunched over, hands covering her face.

I should feel guilty, but I don't have the luxury of caring about anyone else's feelings anymore. She's earned that dress down.

"That wasn't very nice, you know."

I walk straight past Logan waiting in the corridor, and he rolls his eyes, soon chasing after me.

"Ignoring me now. Mature."

I spare him a withering look and keep walking. I'm in no mood to play along with his little games today. "Leave me alone."

"No can do," he replies, falling into step beside me. "Keep drawing attention to yourself, see what happens. These people aren't your friends. They won't protect you from this place."

"Apparently, neither will you."

"I'm on your side here."

"That's bullshit. Decent pay, is it?" I shake my head. "Augustus is a fucking piece of work, I don't know how you sleep at night."

"And how do you sleep, huh?"

He stares at me with interest, waiting for my answer.

"I don't sleep. Not anymore."

Leaving him in the corridor, I burst out into the quad and light a cigarette, my hands still shaking. Augustus can fuck himself, Logan too. If he's going to pick around in my brain for a living, I'm having a damn smoke.

Unable to even consider facing Teegan after Britt dropped that bombshell on those who didn't already know, I hide out in the library through lunch, needing some alone time to decompress.

It's probably the quietest place in the entire institute, removed from the constant state of alertness and fear. Towering mahogany shelves packed tightly with books offer protection from the outside world, and for a moment I can almost convince myself that I'm far from here, living an ordinary life. It doesn't last long.

"Mind if I join you?"

Glancing up from the page I'm half-pretending to read, I find Jack leaning against a stack of books, observing me.

"Free country," I mutter.

He drops his bag and takes a seat opposite me, picking up a book at random to prop open on his lap. Like he needs the cover, we all know who he is now. Blackwood's newest bitch.

"What do you want?"

His smile is crooked. "Just to talk. That's all."

"I have absolutely nothing to say to you."

"Your boyfriend had plenty to say the other day."

I cut him a glare. "Hudson is not my boyfriend."

"Isn't he?"

The amusement on his face has me twitching with anger. This is the man who kept Phoenix supplied for weeks, helped to beat the shit out of Eli, and protected Rio from punishment for all his transgressions. If anyone deserves a beatdown, it's him.

"You should walk away before I do something I'll regret," I warn.

"I have no doubt that you wouldn't regret it." Jack laughs. "But, in the interests of moving forward, I'm here to propose a truce. I've been told to keep my distance from your group of boy toys, and as much as I'd like to see Hudson rot in hell, I'm a man of my word."

Staring at Jack, I realise he's being serious.

"Who told you to keep your distance?"

He frowns, then lets out a laugh. "You don't know? Oh, man. This is going to be so fucking good."

"Answer the question before I make you."

Jack draws to his feet, smothering more laughter. He tosses the book aside and grabs his bag, pausing to spare me a final amused look.

"And here I was thinking you're smart. Almighty Brooklyn, Augustus's favourite whore. Watch your back, bitch. He can't keep you safe forever."

Scrambling to my feet, I follow him out of the library just in time to catch Halbert waiting by the entrance. Together, they leave and head back into the quad. To the unassuming bystander, it would look like Halbert is escorting him.

I can see the truth. The guards look at Jack the same way they looked at Rio—with deference and fucking respect.

Still can't remember, huh, babe?

I squeeze my eyes shut, shaking my head to clear the voice.

You'll soon catch up.

Time's running out, Brooke.

Even in my hallucinations, the smell of cigarette smoke is unmistakable. Clasped between his stiff, dead fingers, Rio takes a leisurely drag while watching me from a few metres away.

"Not real. Not real," I chant.

He strolls right up to me, close enough for me to smell his rotting flesh. I look around at the handful of patients nearby, but no one makes a sound. I'm the only one who can see Rio, or rather, his decomposing corpse.

I'm as real as everyone else.

Rio taps a finger against my temple, the brush of bone making my stomach revolt.

Reality can be whatever you want.

It's all up here.

My phone vibrates in my bag, and I'm startled by the reminder that I'm actually awake. This isn't some twisted nightmare. By the time I've pulled it out, Rio's disappeared from sight. Only the faintest curl of shadows lies in his place.

"Hello?"

"Blackbird. Where are you?"

I let out a relieved sigh. "Hudson."

"You okay? What's wrong?"

"Nothing, I'm fine. Just needed to get some reading done."

He makes a low grumble, not sounding convinced. When have I ever been bothered about keeping up with Blackwood's curriculum? I flee the library, getting out into the safety of fresh air where I can attempt to breathe a little easier.

"We're back in the room. Kade's here."

"Fuck, I'm coming."

"Stay where you are. I'll come and get you," he demands.

"Jesus, Hud. I'm perfectly capable of walking alone."

I hang up the call, pocketing my phone before he can say another word. My relationship with Hudson is still akin to walking through a deadly minefield, certain that at any moment, one will go off. It's not a matter of if, but when.

By the time I get back to Kade and Phoenix's room, our designated hangout, I almost have my shit together. *Almost.* Smoothing what I hope is a normal expression into place, I let myself in and find everyone waiting in tense silence.

Eli's eyes connect with mine first as he drinks me in, searching hard for all the secrets I'm struggling to hide.

"You missed class," Phoenix smarts.

He sits propped against the wall, ignoring the stacks of work surrounding him that Eli is gradually working through. I flip him off, ditching my bag and coat before heading for Kade's empty bed.

Hudson sits at the desk, feet propped up with his usual glare in place. "I thought we agreed that nobody goes out alone."

"We agreed that you're a controlling asshole and that was never going to happen," I respond, pulling my legs up to my chest. "Sometimes I need space."

"Cut the bullshit. We all heard about what happened in group."

I drop my forehead to my knees. "Fucking Teegan."

"She's worried about you," Hudson reasons.

"I said that I'm fine. Britt had it coming, she's been gunning for me ever since you stopped screwing like rabbits. I took care of the problem. That's it."

Phoenix snorts, earning himself a clip around the head from Eli of all people. The pair share a silent conversation and I look away, searching the room for Kade. The hum of the shower running answers my question.

"You know, eventually the *I'm fine* excuse will run out."

I find Phoenix staring at me, ignoring the warning look that Eli gives him.

"You're a fine one to talk. How's sobriety going?" I ask.

He searches for another word. "Good."

"Good? Really?"

"Fucking *amazing*. It's the best."

I roll my eyes. "No need to be sarcastic, Nix."

"You're both full of shit." Hudson shakes his head.

"Fuck off, Hud," we both say in tandem.

Phoenix can't help but grin at me, for the first time in so fucking long. My stomach flips and I smile back. Our bickering is halted as the bathroom door opens, a rush of steam billowing out.

Kade emerges with a towel tucked around his hips, scraping wet blonde locks from his face. My excitement is quickly extinguished by the deep purple bruise on his neck, shaped almost like the tip of someone's shoe. Another swells his left cheek, framed by heavy eye bags beneath his glasses. He clearly hasn't slept.

"Kade?"

I watch his Adam's apple bob as he finds us waiting, a look of fear cemented in his tired gaze. Kade isn't afraid of anything in this world. It's all just another puzzle to be understood and solved to him. This person... doesn't look like my Kade.

"Let me put some clothes on," he mutters.

I exchange worried looks with Hudson while Kade dresses, bypassing his usual smart stuff to throw a pair of faded sweats on, leaving his chiselled chest bare.

Rather than join me on the bed, he folds himself into the corner, far away from us all. Opening the window, he lights a cigarette.

"What happened?" Hudson demands.

Fucking subtle. Kade smokes in silence, staring out at the falling rain. Once the cigarette is done, he's unable to avoid us any longer. The nerve in his jaw works overtime as he wrings his hands, now staring at the thick carpet.

"I went home. Cece too."

Hudson blanches. "Is she okay?"

"Cece's fine. I made sure she got back to school. I stayed the night there, then took a cab back to Blackwood this morning." Kade looks up, his eyes briefly meeting mine before returning to Hudson. "I can't... fuck. I don't know what to tell you."

I feel physically sick as I watch him deliberate, certain his next words will change everything.

"Dad invested in Blackwood a decade ago, and multiple times since. He has eyes and ears everywhere. For the past two years, I've been feeding information back to him. Weekly reports about the goings on, staff and patient alike. Anything he can use if needed."

"Use for what?" Phoenix asks.

Kade shrugs. "Leverage. Dad's on the board of directors."

"Wait, what?" I blurt.

"Has been for years now. I didn't tell you guys because I figured the less you know, the better. He doesn't like loose ends. I was trying to keep you all safe."

Hudson stands, hands on his hips. I move to the edge of the bed, ready to jump in if needed. I don't like where this conversation is going. Kade keeping secrets for all this time isn't going to go down well at all.

"What about Ma?"

Kade's shoulders slump. "I'm sorry, Hud."

Hudson's hands clench into fists and I lay a gentle hand on his shoulder, trying to ground him.

"Where is she? What did he do to her?"

"I never meant for any of this to happen..."

Pushing me aside, Hudson marches up to his adoptive brother. Phoenix and Eli watch fearfully, equally engrossed by the impending car crash. All we can do is brace for impact now.

"Where is she?" Hudson repeats.

Kade seems to crumble, collapsing inwards with visible grief. He felt nothing but disdain for Stephanie, so he isn't mourning her loss. This is something else. Something worse.

"I'm supposed to be the good guy," Kade whispers, removing his glasses to scrub his reddened eyes. "I'm so fucking sorry, Hud. I had no choice. He threatened you all, Mum too. This was the only way."

The bond between parent and child is an odd thing. They have the power to tear us down inch by excruciating inch; abuse us, break us, traumatise us until nothing but broken pieces remain.

I know that all too well. Hell, we all do. But somehow, our inner child will always love the monsters that brought us into the world. It's ingrained too deep to dig out.

"No," Hudson pleads.

Kade breaks down fully. I've never seen him cry or look anything but strong and dependable. He sinks to his knees before Hudson, offering his life as recompense, begging for execution.

"I k-killed her. I killed your Ma."

CHAPTER 22
ELI

HIGHER - SLEEP TOKEN

PILING INTO THE CLASSROOM, I hold on tight to Phoenix's hand and let him drag me over to our usual seats. Brooklyn clings to my side, sandwiching me in between them.

The three of us are sticking together like glue; safety in numbers and all. I wish I could say that were the case for the rest of our group, but life loves to fuck us all over one way or another.

When I picked Phoenix up from his room, Kade was already gone—locking himself away with stuff to do now that Mike's managing the ex-warden's workload for Augustus.

It's obvious bullshit. He's been avoiding us all, not even turning up to eat dinner. Hudson neither. The pair of them have fallen in at the deep end and show no sign of emerging anytime soon.

Phoenix pulls my chair out for me, and I slide into it, dropping Brooklyn's bag from my shoulder. She does this girlish little smile when I carry it for her, almost like we're a normal couple. Not this complicated triangle with an even more complicated web on top.

Maybe it's best we don't label it. Me and Brooklyn. Me and Phoenix. The others too. What we are together, and what we are apart, there aren't words to describe it. Maybe there doesn't need to be. I don't want to make us fit into one of society's tight little boxes, because it will only lessen what we have.

"You heard from Hudson?" Phoenix asks.

Brooklyn drops her notepad and pen on the table, running a hand over her loose braid. "He had therapy with Mariam this morning. Obviously, he couldn't talk about what happened, but I'm hoping it helped. He's shut me out, won't even let me in the room."

"He'll come around."

"Seems like I'm always waiting for someone to come around."

Pressing his lips together, Phoenix fiddles with his phone for a distraction rather than replying. Their temporary truce has offered some respite, but we're far from out of the woods.

After I had an anxiety attack when they started to argue again, they agreed to keep things amicable around me. At least for the time being, while the rest of our group is splintered apart.

Once the room is full, Crawley begins the lecture and at least half the patients fall asleep in the first ten minutes. The guards have taken to performing random spot checks, chucking people out in the dead of night to ransack their rooms.

"Guys?" Brooklyn nods towards the door. "Look."

Two guards have slipped into the room, coasting around the perimeter. Her hand lands on my leg and squeezes, urging me to remain calm. I've become a regular victim of their bullying, a figure of ridicule.

"Over my dead body," Phoenix grumbles.

Brooklyn studies them both. "Agreed."

"You two stay out of this. Let me handle it."

"Like hell! They'll kick your ass, pretty boy."

Phoenix glares at her. "Who are you calling pretty boy?"

"We both know I throw a better punch than you."

"Wanna bet, firecracker?"

"I'd bet my damn life," she boasts.

"You're on."

Brooklyn shuffles her chair closer, so our bodies are touching at all available points. Her warmth offers me some calm, and I let her scent wash over me.

Home. Safety. Security.

I take his Phoenix's hand under the table, trying to keep him under control. I used to wonder why people were so afraid of being sectioned. These places exist in a realm beyond the norms of society. Nothing happens amongst the dead and disturbed, trapped in stasis.

But in this new, enhanced version of Blackwood... it's the real horror show. I finally understand what fear of the system means.

"Is there a problem?" Crawley exclaims.

The two guards remain silent, waiting for the door to bang open and bounce off the wall. Brooklyn curses under her breath as Halbert strides in, kitted out in pressed uniform and more non-regulation items than I can count.

"Nobody move," he orders.

Phoenix rests his arm on the back of Brooklyn's chair, glancing at me. He's determined to keep us both safe, but I'm more worried about what punishment the guards will dole out if he causes a scene.

"What the hell is this?" Crawley demands.

"Move aside."

"This is unacceptable. I'm trying to run a class here."

Halbert offers him a dangerous smile. "If you have a problem, feel free to take it up with Doctor Augustus. He's always open to... *feedback.*"

Crawley backs down, the spineless shit.

We'll have to protect ourselves.

Halbert props himself against our table, casual as anything. I'd love to wipe the smug look from his face and break his nose. Phoenix catches my eye and I know we're in total agreement.

"Ahh, Miss West. A pleasure as always."

"I don't have a session today." Brooklyn sighs.

"You go where I say so, inmate."

"Fuck off, Halbert."

"You assholes have no right to terrorise us," Phoenix adds.

Halbert glares at him, hand resting on his baton. "We're just doing our jobs. Back off, kid. I don't like your tone."

"That's doing your job?" Brooklyn points towards one of the more fragile patients, who's sobbing while straightening her clothes after a pat down.

"You lost your right to privacy the minute you stepped foot in here," Halbert answers, taking advantage of the distraction to get Phoenix in a headlock. "Insolence will be met with force."

Both of us backing into the corner, I attempt to shield Brooklyn with my body. They can do whatever the hell they want to me, but not her. Crawley looks away, no help at all. Not even a mere protest at the fact his class is being hounded like animals.

Halbert tries to grab Brooklyn next but ends up tackling me instead. I'm shoved down on to the hard floor, a knee pressing into my back until I can't breathe. The guards restrain the others under the pretence of searching them, but we all know it's a charade.

"We're clean! Get your hands off me," Brooklyn shouts.

Once thoroughly searched and released, we all huddle together and watch as the rest of the patients in the classroom are subjected to the same humiliation. One person is escorted out when the guards pull a sharpened piece of plastic from his pocket. Who walks around with a homemade shank? *Amateur.*

"Woods. You're coming with me," Halbert calls.

Phoenix immediately bars his arm across my chest, refusing to let me go. "Not a chance. You didn't find anything on us."

"He has a visitor, you nosy shit. Back up or I'll throw you in solitary," Halbert threatens.

They both look at me with matching confusion and my heart plummets. There's only one person who would visit me here, I've been expecting it for a while now. I shake my head, indicating it's fine, before grabbing my backpack and following the guards out.

Halbert clamps his iron-grip around my bicep and drags me along for added measure. The slamming of the door behind us silences Phoenix's protests and I'm towed outside, across the quad in front of everyone milling about.

"He's the mute I was telling you about." Halbert sniggers.

All of the surrounding guards stare at me like I'm a damn exhibit, laughing at my expense. Halbert refuses to loosen his grip, despite my entire arm radiating pain.

"You fuckin' slow, kid?"

"Daddy fucked him up good and proper, I bet."

"Look at the little freak, he's shaking."

"I heard he ain't been outside in ten years."

Smothering the urge to bash all of their brains in, I stare straight ahead. The sadistic guards want a reaction and I'll die before giving it to them. I'm used to the hatred and disgust.

We finally arrive at the reception, and I'm deposited in the waiting area, roughly shoved into a seat. Mike stands frowning at Kade's empty desk, but soon wanders over when he spots me waiting.

"Hey, Eli. Sorry about all this."

I clutch my backpack, my anxiety catching up to me. I've been dreading this moment, but there's no postponing the inevitable. Best to just get it over and done with.

Smoothing my *Blind Channel* shirt, I follow Mike into the back office. He's given up his desk for the lawyer, Mr Freeman. I recognise him from the various court hearings. He waits for me in his fancy fucking suit, with a discarded briefcase on the table. Whatever the contents, it's for me.

"Elijah, pleasure to see you again."

Nodding, I hug my shivering body tight. I couldn't give a fuck what my father did with his will, the man doesn't deserve to be remembered.

I'd rather erase every last sickening memory, but no matter how deep I slice my skin, how much blood I shed in payment, his ghost refuses to budge.

"I'm here to discuss Mr Kenneth Woods's estate."

The urge to explode is pulling at my skin and I look down at my folded hands, waiting for the torture to finish.

"I'm afraid there isn't much in terms of monetary offerings, the majority of his assets were expunged in the... *incident*. The rest were spent on legal bills or during his prison sentence."

Part of me wants to laugh at his choice of words, but I focus on breathing through the awful taste of hatred instead.

Bitter ashes.

Acid.

Blood.

Flames.

I'm losing my fucking mind and want nothing more than to run at full speed, far away from this place and the memories it brings to the surface of a time I'd much rather forget.

"It's my legal obligation to execute the will of my client, therefore I have an item to give to you today as instructed. Given your personal circumstances, it seems inappropriate, but unfortunately a will is legally binding. You understand?" Mr Freeman's expression is sympathetic.

Reaching for his briefcase, he snaps it open and pulls out some paperwork. I quickly sign while he prepares whatever else is inside, hidden from sight. It takes great effort to make myself put the fountain pen down, the razor-sharp nib taunting me.

"Excellent." Mr Freeman nods. "Well, here you are then."

My surroundings dissolve into darkness as I stare down at Mike's messy desk, the entire world revolving around that fucking briefcase. Nestled amongst the paperwork is a plastic evidence bag. Mr Freeman reluctantly places it in front of me, nervously glancing at Mike in the corner.

Do you know why we pray, Elijah?

For repentance. For God to forgive our sins.

Get on your knees and kiss the bible, son.

Blackened and fire-damaged, the book inches from my fingertips has haunted my dreams since I got my scars. Through every hospital, transfers, and repeated sections, it followed me. I squeeze my eyes shut, assaulted by too many memories to separate from reality.

Endless nights spent shivering and hungry in the sin closet. Being dragged out by my hair come morning, forced to kneel, and seek forgiveness. My lips grazing the Bible for a moment, before my father raised it high and used it to beat me bloody.

A cold, detached haze descends over me, and I accept the item, sliding it into my backpack. Mike looks astounded, like he expected me to disintegrate into a blubbering wreck.

I'm far too focused for that. With the lawyer satisfied, the meeting ends and I'm free to go. I run out without hearing anything else, preoccupied by the heavy weight in my bag. With a quick text sent to Phoenix, I relay where to find me.

There's only one place to do this. Somewhere hidden, out of reach to the rest of Blackwood. We discovered it last year while searching for somewhere to hang out altogether. I cut through the thick forest behind the main building, dodging guards and the usual CCTV cameras that I know off by heart.

At the back perimeter fence, if you follow it far enough into the darkest corner of the institute, there's a section just loose enough to slide under. It pries away from the ground, allowing me to slip into the world beyond.

Blackwood has many secrets.

I discovered one by accident.

Nestled amongst the gloomy woods that surrounds the property, lies an abandoned chapel. Crumbling into ruins, the stained glass has long since cracked and disintegrated, with the spiked metal fence half-collapsed in places.

Heaving the rotten door aside, I slip inside the ancient space and wait, crouched by the last remaining piece of furniture—ironically enough, an altar.

It doesn't take them long to find me, Phoenix knows the way by heart too. The door heaves open, admitting them into the ruin.

"What the hell is this place?" Brooklyn exclaims.

Shutting the door against the cold, Phoenix follows her down the aisle. "It was abandoned before the institute even opened. This is protected land so they couldn't demolish it."

Both racing to join me, they seem equally relieved to see me in one piece. Phoenix pulls me into a tight embrace while Brooklyn watches.

"What happened? Are you okay?" she demands.

I shrug, dropping my backpack to search inside.

"What are we doing here, Eli?"

Pulling the evidence bag out, I have to physically stop myself from throwing it far away from me. I grasp the fragile Bible inside, careful not to damage the blackened pages while placing it in the centre of the altar.

"Holy shit," Brooklyn breathes.

"Is that…"

I nod, taking Phoenix's offered hand. Brooklyn joins us, and with their strength on both sides, I'm able to look at the last remaining piece of my childhood. It looks so unassuming, but the fire-damaged pages tell tales that no one will ever hear.

"Your Papa's will came through then," Phoenix guesses.

Brooklyn eyes me. "What are you going to do with it?"

Fierce need bubbles within me, a sheer desperation that blocks out all fear and anxiety. I fucking hate the person that my father made me. He's weak. Damaged. Irreparable. This book represents everything that's wrong with me; it doesn't deserve to exist.

Retrieving my stashed cigarettes, we each take one and light up, savouring the smoke in silence. It takes several minutes for me to gather my flimsy courage; what little I have left.

"No m-more," I stutter.

Stepping forward, I leave the safety of their embrace behind to stand on my own two feet. My entire life has been defined by that night. The sick man who saw evil, where there was nothing but a hungry child who begged for mercy.

I haven't seen the real world, outside of inpatient units, in… *fuck*. It's been so long, I don't know anymore. Over half of my life. I'm terrified of it.

"You can do this, Eli," Brooklyn encourages.

Drinking in the reassurance of her voice, the explosion of comforting flavours that her mere presence brings, I grind my cigarette on the dry, flammable pages and wait.

It doesn't take long for the embers to spread like a sickness. We watch the Bible burn to a crisp, the charred husk collapsing into beautiful nothingness.

When nothing but ash remains, I let my eyes slide shut. All my life, this weight has held me down. Infected every possibility of happiness and kept me trapped in the past.

Every reminder of my father has now been wiped from this plane of existence, leaving nothing but memories behind. His death felt like a sick taunt, but this… I think I can live with. He's gone, and I'm still here. Unbeaten. Unbroken. I fucking won.

"We should celebrate," Phoenix declares.

Brooklyn grins. "What did you have in mind?"

"Oh, I can think of a few things."

His heat-laden gaze bouncing between the two of us, Phoenix drags Brooklyn into the middle. I let my hands fall to her hips, her ass brushing right against my crotch. Phoenix stares at me over her shoulder.

"Eli… hell, I'm fucking proud of you."

His words wrap around my heart like a shoestring, and I reach over Brooklyn to cup his cheek. Keeping her tightly sandwiched, our lips meet. Phoenix kisses me in a violent clash of teeth and tongue, towing that fine line between pain and pleasure.

I wouldn't be here without them both.

Something binds us together; an unbreakable bond.

Brooklyn melts between us, grinding against me and desperate for attention. It feels so fucking right, having them here to witness this moment. I'm complete with them by my side.

"Problem, firecracker?" Phoenix smirks.

"Nope."

"You jealous?"

Biting her lip, she doesn't deny it. I let my lips trail over the shell of her ear, down to her neck. Sinking my teeth in, she lets out a moan as I bruise her pale skin.

"You want us to touch you?"

"You know I do," she moans.

"Then you gotta work for it, baby. Show us how much you want us to fuck you, and maybe we will."

With an annoyed growl, Brooklyn spins around to face me. Phoenix grabs a handful of my shirt and pulls me closer, encouraging her to kiss me.

When her lips meet mine, he lets out a low hum of approval. She tastes so good, like a heaven-sent miracle tempered by sickness and despair.

"On your knees, firecracker."

Her tongue brushes along my lower lip before we break apart, searing need written across her face. Brooklyn obediently falls to her knees before me, peering up at me through her eyelashes.

"What do you want me to do to him?"

Phoenix glances at me. "Use your mouth."

Reaching for my waistband, her hand slips inside my boxers, palming my rock-hard cock. Phoenix licks his lips, watching with excitement as Brooklyn takes me deep in her throat, hollowing out her cheeks. I grab fistfuls of her hair, guiding her bobbing mouth on my erection. She's a fucking pro.

Phoenix grabs me and kisses me again, his tongue claiming every inch of my mouth while Brooklyn drives me to the edge of desperation. Before I can finish down her pretty throat, Phoenix grabs her by the hair and slows her movements, taking back control. She stares at me with hunger.

"Let me finish the job."

"Not yet," Phoenix snaps.

Hauling her up, he glances around the ruined chapel, as if searching for the perfect place. When his gaze lands back on the altar, still coated in smouldering ashes, he nods.

"Perfect. Move it, both of you."

Brooklyn takes my offered hand up and we converge around the altar. The idea of fucking our girl together, on top of the burning remains of my father's legacy... *goddammit*. I'm nearly blowing my load just thinking about it.

"On you get."

She gapes at Phoenix. "For real?"

"Do I look like I'm fucking kidding?"

Suitably chastised, Brooklyn hops up on the altar, narrowly dodging the smoking remains of the Bible. Phoenix grabs her by the ankles, yanking her into position until she's spread-eagled across the surface.

"Lie down," he commands.

"I'll burn myself."

"And?"

Grinning darkly, Brooklyn shoots me a loaded look before easing back on the altar, surrendering herself to the smoking embers of my shitty childhood. She hisses, burning her back in the process, but still does as instructed. I'm impressed.

Phoenix tosses her shoes aside, stripping off her jeans until she's shivering. Running his tongue from her ankle to pubic bone, I watch as he places a gentle kiss to her cotton-clad pussy.

"You should be grateful," he mutters.

"How so?"

Beckoning me forwards, we stand side by side as Brooklyn writhes. Her panties are slowly dragged down her legs, exposing her glistening, pink cunt to the chapel's air.

"I've wanted to fuck little Eli here for a long, long time. But because we're gentlemen, we didn't do it without you here to watch. Ain't that sweet, firecracker?"

I fight the urge to roll my eyes. Gentlemanly is an overstatement, more like we both wanted our girl here to watch when we cross that final tempting line. Phoenix's words have their desired effect and Brooklyn raises her hips, begging to be touched.

"I want you both," she begs.

"Shut it, slut. We're in charge here."

Grasping her t-shirt, Phoenix pulls it over her eyes and secures it there, effectively blindfolding her. Brooklyn's entire body quakes with need, and we both revel in the thrill of her being trapped and at our mercy.

"You want to go first?"

I shrug, gesturing for him to go ahead.

Spreading her legs wide open, he drags his tongue between her dripping folds while freeing his own erection. I watch with fascination as Phoenix plays with her clit, getting her nice and wet before pressing his head against her slick opening.

"Say the word, firecracker."

"Please," she responds immediately.

Phoenix smirks at me before surging inside, eliciting a breathy moan from Brooklyn as she writhes on the altar. Finding his rhythm, he holds her hips while slamming into her, before glancing back at me.

"Her mouth looks empty, Eli."

Taking my cue, I step up to the altar while stroking myself. With Brooklyn's head tilted to the side, I shove my cock into her welcoming mouth, below the makeshift blindfold.

"Good boy," he praises.

Brooklyn takes us both without complaint, Phoenix piledriving into her as she chokes on my length, still managing to drive me insane. It feels so right, sharing her like this, claiming her sinner's soul together.

Before he can finish, Phoenix pulls out and jerks his head, indicating for me to take his place. We quickly swap over and he helps Brooklyn on to her hands and knees, so her perfect ass is raised high in the air for the world to see.

Beautiful red welts cover her back with burns from the remains of my father's Bible, and my mouth fucking waters at the sight. Seeing her scarred and bloody, mirroring my own twisted flesh, soothes something deep within me.

I crack my palm against her butt cheek, relishing her sigh of pleasure, then glide a single finger through her soaked cunt and up to her asshole.

"Goddammit," she curses.

Easing a slick digit inside, I play with her tight hole, stretching her wider with another finger. Lining myself up to her pussy, I give in to the urge to fuck her senseless. There's no way for her to know who is inside of her, and she willingly takes Phoenix's dick into her mouth at the same time I enter her.

"You like it when we fuck you?" Phoenix chuckles.

She mumbles unintelligibly around his dick, but the heat between her legs answers well enough. With one hand holding her hip, I thrust into her while studying the fresh welts scarring her back, the sight spurring me on until Phoenix pauses.

"I reckon she can take us both, Eli."

I stare at him, intrigued by the thought.

"Come on, don't be shy now."

Both pulling out, Phoenix continues to work his shaft as he removes Brooklyn's blindfold, guiding her down from the altar. She stands on trembling legs as he indicates for me to take a seat on the stone steps.

Helping her climb in my lap, I slip back inside her tight pussy, relishing the deeper angle. It's like she was fucking made for me. Phoenix watches the show, face lit with anticipation.

"You ever had two cocks inside you?" he asks.

Brooklyn bites her lip. "No."

"First time for everything."

Wrapping my hand around her throat, I fasten my lips to hers and bite down, needing to taste her sweet, coppery blood. Brooklyn whimpers, feeling Phoenix's heat at her back. Sinking his teeth into her shoulder, he breaks our kiss to press his fingertips to her lips.

"Suck, baby."

Brooklyn moistens his two digits, still riding me hard while following orders. I watch her eyes blow wide with surprise as Phoenix brings his fingers to her asshole, slipping one inside. She groans, her pussy clenching around my length.

"So tight," Phoenix murmurs. "Let me add another."

I watch with fascination as he stretches her further, making Brooklyn shudder with desire. "More, Nix."

"Don't be impatient."

"You're both mine, aren't you?"

We glance at each other and Phoenix grins. "Damn fucking straight, we're yours. Just like you're ours to share."

Pausing to drop saliva on to his cock, he works the lubricant across his length, before transferring more moisture to Brooklyn's back entrance. She's practically trembling, submitting to his preparations while I continue to pump into her.

"Phoenix," she breathes, uncertain.

"Shut it, Brooke. If I want to fuck your asshole, then I damn well will. Now, kiss Eli like a good little patient and maybe we'll let you come, okay?"

Still holding her by the throat, I drag Brooklyn's lips to mine. She gasps into my mouth, and I know the moment Phoenix begins to nudge inside her back entrance. Jesus, this should be illegal.

"Good?" I murmur.

Brooklyn growls. "Yes."

"No complaints here," Phoenix quips.

Pausing on my lap while she adjusts to the gradual intrusion, Brooklyn shifts until she finds the right position. Phoenix is taking it slow, letting her squirm as he inches deeper inside, until we're fucking our beautiful girl together.

I must've died.

This is fucking heaven.

Overwhelmed by endless waves of blistering pleasure, I have to fight to keep going. I can feel Phoenix inside of her, rubbing right up against my length still buried deep in her cunt. We exchange grins, both relishing the feeling.

Working together as the perfect team, we service our girl until she's begging for mercy, pausing for the occasional kiss over her writhing body. Phoenix is gentle at first, guiding her into it before he begins to increase the pace.

Between us, we have Brooklyn's screams echoing through the chapel as she surrenders control. It's a glorious sight; watching her shatter into a million pieces. Finding my own release, I stare deep into Phoenix's mischievous gaze. I want to watch him lose control too.

With his lips bruising mine, his thrusts grow more ragged until he grunts, finding his own climax. We awkwardly collapse in a tangle of limbs, laughing as Phoenix trips down the steps and flashes his bare ass. He ends up spread-eagled across the floor, cursing up a storm.

"Graceful." Brooklyn snorts.

"Shut up, firecracker."

"Look, it's a butt-naked ballerina!"

"Hey, I'm a damn good dancer. You'll see."

"Promises, promises."

Stifling a laugh, I hold her to my chest as Phoenix collapses next to us, grinning ear to ear. When Brooklyn looks at me, her smile melts away.

"I don't want to go back."

Phoenix swipes hair from her forehead, before pressing a surprisingly gentle kiss to my temple. With us both in his arms, he looks whole. Complete. Happy for the first time in months.

"Me neither," he admits.

"Can we stay here for a while?"

I nod, tightening my arms around her. Cuddling together for warmth, we rest in peaceful silence, ignoring the sun setting outside. I want to stay like this forever. I don't give a fuck where we go, or what the future holds, as long as they're both in it.

"We should get back." Phoenix sighs.

Brooklyn spares me a glance. "You ready?"

Nodding, I release her to search for discarded clothing, taking a moment to gather myself. Something feels different inside of me. Lighter, somehow. Breathing in deep, I find the answer.

No flavours.

No anxiety.

Nothing.

My father's voice has gone.

For the first time, I can taste the real world.

Elijah Woods is dead. Only Eli remains.

I'm fucking free.

CHAPTER 23
BROOKLYN
IF I SAY - MUMFORD & SONS

"PLEASE, KADE. LET ME IN."

Smacking the door again, I'm awarded with no response. Kade has shut himself away, refusing to leave the room for classes or even work now too. He's become a ghost.

None of us have seen him in over a week. Phoenix has been staying with Eli to give him some privacy, even though I said it was a bad idea to leave him alone.

We've allowed this to go on for too long, indulging his need to self-destruct. There's no one more qualified than me to understand exactly what he's going through, so I banished Phoenix and Eli to class, staying behind to deal with this shit once and for all.

"Kade! I'm not leaving until you talk to me."

Silence.

Fuck this.

"Don't make me break the door down!"

Hand sore from beating on his door, I slump with my back to the wood. He's in there; alone and hurting. I get it. My life changed forever as Vic took his final breath; now Kade must bear the same burden. But he doesn't have to do it alone.

"It isn't your fault, Kade."

There's a shuffle from inside, like he's slumping against the door to be close to me, then more silence. I can almost feel him through the wood.

"Please talk to me."

I must sit there for hours, waiting for an answer that never comes. Patients walk past me, sparing me the odd look but keeping their opinions to themselves. I have a reputation now and nobody wants their fingers breaking or worse.

"This isn't over. I'll be back."

Standing on numb legs, I reluctantly leave Kade to his silent treatment and make my way down the corridor, despising the opulence and wealth around me that once took my breath away.

It makes me sick now, the gleaming exterior hiding a system designed to break its inhabitants. I'm losing the people I love and there's not a damn thing I can do to stop it.

Hammering on Hudson's door like a woman possessed, I'm ready to break my fucking hands if necessary. Someone will talk to me. I refuse to take this for a second longer. As the door clicks open, I nearly fall inwards but manage to catch myself.

"Hudson?"

"Go away, Brooke."

Slowly inching inside, I catch him disappearing back into bed, the early spring sunshine casting light into the bomb site of his room. Clothes, books, and torn paper litter the carpet, the odd beer bottle foolishly on display.

When I find several empty baggies, peppered with the remains of white powder, I lose my shit. He was supposed to stop Phoenix's supply, not keep the confiscated drugs for himself.

"What do you want, blackbird?"

I linger at the end of the bed. "To talk."

"Then you should go, because that's not happening."

Burying the need to rage and scream, I hold back instead. When I woke up after the storm, Hudson was there. It's always him. The boy who hurt me in the worst possible way has done his damnedest to fix his mistakes, to do better.

I can be more for him.

I fucking *have to be.*

Toeing off my Doc Martens, I pull Phoenix's *Deftones* shirt over my head and lose my ripped jeans. Dressed in just bra and panties, I pad over to the bed and slide between the covers, finding Hudson stretched out in the corner. Throwing one leg over his waist, I burrow into his body heat.

"I'm not fucking leaving."

"You should," he murmurs.

"Not this time. I'm right here."

It doesn't take long for him to cave, burying his face in the crook of my neck. I'm engulfed in his broad, inked arms, pressing me tight against his bare chest. We lay there in heavy silence, breathing each other in just like we did as kids.

"Have you seen him?" Hudson whispers.

"No one has. He needs you."

"I can't look at him, blackbird. I love him, but every time I close my eyes, every goddamn night…" His hot breath ghosts along my skin in an agonised sigh. "All I see is Ma's face. Bruised and beaten, right before I killed that boyfriend of hers and landed myself in here. For a second, she was relieved. She was still Ma, beneath it all."

"I'm sorry, Hud."

Lifting his head, his bloodshot eyes meet mine. "I'll never see her again. She was a bitch, but she was family."

Cupping his stubble-strewn cheek, I brush my thumb over his cheekbones, committing every inch to memory. He still looks like the person I knew—a little rougher around the edges, hardened by time and circumstance. But my broken, twisted boy is in there, beneath the bravado and rage.

"She made her choice. That isn't Kade's fault."

"He took her choice from her."

"His father took it," I remind him.

Peeling my hand from his cheek, he places a gentle kiss in the centre of my palm. "You've never been the forgiving type. How can you defend him so easily, after everything?"

"Because I know how it feels to be responsible for the worst thing you've ever done, and to live with the knowledge of what you took without permission," I admit shamefully. "It's the most intimate form of hell to be alone with your guilt."

The tiniest, near-invisible tear rolls down Hudson's cheek before he can stop it; a flicker of humanity when so often he buries it deep, until nothing but his monstrous side remains.

Men cry too, even when stupid society tells them they shouldn't. *Fuck that bullshit.* I'll catch all the tears he needs to shed.

"You know what it feels like to hate yourself."

"Fuck, Brooke. You know I do."

"And you know how destructive guilt can be."

"Well, obviously. What's your point?"

"Then please, just listen to me. Kade is your brother, he's your family now." I wipe the tear aside, placing a kiss at the corner of his mouth. "For his sake, it's up to you to fix this. You have the chance to save him before it's too late. Neither of us had that luxury."

Hudson sighs, with the tiniest hint of a smile. "Christ. I told you before about appealing to my humanity."

"And I told you that we both know… you're more human than you'd care to admit. That's not a bad thing."

Trapping me beneath his muscled body, Hudson's nose brushes mine. "Stop being all mature and shit, it's freaking me out."

"What can I say, it's personal growth."

"You've changed, Brooke."

"No, I'm just done running."

Crushing my lips against his, I feel no need to hide the truth him. Our days of fighting this are over. He's as irrevocable as the night swallowing the sun each day, casting us all in the comforting warmth of shadows.

"Blackbird?"

I stare into his aquamarine eyes. "Yeah?"

"I want you to know, dammit. I need you to know—"

Hudson's forehead meets mine, our breath intermingling.

"Truth is, I've loved you since I was sixteen years old, and you gave me shit for getting beat up," he whispers. "I loved you when I walked away because I couldn't look at you without seeing what I'd done. And I loved you when you took one look at me and stabbed me in the cafeteria. Hell if it didn't turn me on a bit."

I can't help but laugh, and his smile is devastating.

"I still fucking love you. I never stopped."

"Hudson—"

He shakes his head, placing a finger over my lips. "I know you hate me. I don't expect you to say it back; not now… fuck, not ever. What I did was unforgivable, and I will never forgive myself, let alone expect you to. This place fucking sucks, but I'm glad one thing has come out of it all. Blackwood brought you back to me."

With every last barrier stripped away, I see him clearly now. The raven-haired monster I fell in love with so many years ago.

Jaded and miserable, with a smile that only shone for me. Possessive enough to kill an injured bird to make me love him. Broken enough to walk away when I needed him most. Good enough to hold me in my lowest moment and tell me that it's going to be okay.

Layer upon layer of imperfect human being, much like us all. Somehow, he's still it for me. The beginning and the end.

"I hate you, Hudson Knight."

His smile doesn't falter, hanging on to my every word.

"But the truth is, I loved you the moment I laid eyes on you in that goddamned school. And right now, even though we're doomed to end badly, I'm still yours. I have been all along."

"You don't have to say it," he interjects.

"Let me fucking finish, asshole."

Grinning, he bites his lip and waits.

"Hudson, I love you."

"You said it." He beams.

"Don't get soft on me now."

"I'm afraid I just might. Don't tell anyone."

We collide like twin flames destined for destruction, teeth and tongue and sheer desperation to become one. Hudson presses me into the bed and covers me with his tattooed body, every inch of skin telling the stories of his past that we used to exchange in the darkness of our foster home.

I give myself to him, surrender to the inevitability of us falling together as we always have, and always will.

"Wait," I break apart to say.

"No taking it back now, baby."

Rolling my eyes, I place a hand on his chest to push him away. "We can't do this right now. Kade's locked in his room and won't answer to anyone. Go to him."

"Right now? Seriously?"

"Seriously. Fix things, I'll still be here."

Groaning into a pillow, Hudson drags himself from bed, giving me a flash of his strong thighs and chest. I watch in appreciation, heat flooding between my legs.

"Stop looking at me like I'm a tree you want to climb."

"No can do." I grin.

He throws his usual ripped jeans back on and a discarded shirt, staring at me with longing. "I'll get back in that bed and make you scream if you carry on."

Flicking the covers back, I make him watch as I trail my fingers over my belly, before sliding into my panties. I'm soaked already, even more so with him watching. Dipping a finger inside my pussy, I spread my legs so he can watch me play with myself.

"Blackbird," he growls.

Bringing my wet finger to my lips, I taste myself and moan, making a show of sucking on the digit before winking at him.

"Go. Hurry back."

"You're evil."

"But you love me."

Hudson smirks. "Damn fucking straight I do."

As he storms out, I slump back on to the bed. There's this weird, light feeling in my chest. I have no idea what it is, but perhaps... this is what it feels like. I won't say that word, it's a curse. But one day, I hope we can find it. The elusive thing that all humans are seeking.

The slam of the door has me sitting back up, frowning.

"Back so soon?"

I don't expect to see Jefferson's dark, hungry smile lighting up the room. He rounds the corner, one hand on his baton, the other clutching a familiar pair of handcuffs that have my lungs seizing.

"Get the hell out of here," I shout, backing into the corner.

"Nice to see you too. Get your ass up, you missed your session."

"I'm busy. Tell Augustus to fuck himself."

"You don't choose when to attend," he warns, inching dangerously close. "If you don't put your clothes on and come with me, I'll drag your pasty ass outside myself. The whole institute can see you for what you really are, a little fucking freak."

I cross my arms, covering the scarred skin on show.

"Alternatively, I can go and grab Elijah instead," Jefferson suggests. "I've seen him outside, smoking away with that blue-haired bastard where they think we can't see them. Maybe he can cover for you instead, hmm? That'll keep Augustus busy."

My heart leaps into my throat but I don't let it show, snarling at Jefferson instead.

"Turn around so I can dress, pervert. I'm coming."

CHAPTER 24
BROOKLYN

MY BODY IS A CAGE -
ARCADE FIRE

SHOVED INTO AUGUSTUS'S OFFICE, I catch myself before I fall flat on my ass and stumble into the bookshelves instead. Jefferson snorts, offering me a wave before slamming the door shut.

He wouldn't even let me leave a note for Hudson, so I'm gonna get my ass kicked later on for the whole vanishing act. *Great.*

"Your shirt is on backwards."

Whirling around, I find Logan in his corner. "Your buddy gave me ten seconds to get dressed before he threatened the cuffs, so excuse me if my outfit isn't perfect."

"Why were you naked in front of Jefferson?"

Glaring at him, I quickly shove my arms back through the t-shirt and right myself, muttering obscenities under my breath.

"He doesn't understand the meaning of a locked door."

Logan chuckles, averting his eyes to give me some semblance of privacy while I adjust myself. When I'm done, I glance around Augustus's office and find it more dishevelled than usual.

The mahogany desk is stacked with several newspapers and piles of unorganised notes, cluttering the polished surface. With a quick glance at the door, I sneak over and grab the first paper, scanning over the headlines.

Local Politician Vindicated After False Accusations.

Conspiracy Accuser & Addict Commits Suicide.

Philanthropist Thanks Institute For Treating Troubled Son.

Unbelievable.

They have tied the whole story up in neat little bows. Stephanie, unstable and high, made up a story to target one of the most powerful families in the country. With her plan quickly unravelling, she took her own life in a drug-fuelled rage.

According to the papers, the esteemed Knight family emerged unharmed and stronger than ever, vowing to stand by their innocent little lamb and adoptive son.

Fucking hell.

I think I'm going to puke.

"There's not even a mention of what Hudson did in here," I hiss, rereading the article. "Kade's father has twisted the whole narrative to fit him and benefit his career. Hell, this probably just won him the next election. Goddammit."

"Money weaves many a web of lies, kiddo."

"I thought we discussed the nickname, motherfucker."

He smirks. "What? I like it."

"And I'd like you to fuck off."

Tossing the newspaper aside, I take my usual seat. Augustus will be over the moon, this entire fiasco is one giant advertisement for Blackwood. He'll have new patients pouring out of his gold-plated asshole, begging for a plea deal to reduce their sentence.

Logan watches over me from the corner as we wait for Augustus, his familiar presence offering a crumb of comfort. When the evil bastard himself arrives, the door crashing shut with fury, I can't help but flinch.

Augustus removes his luxurious wool coat and scarf, running a hand over his slicked back hair. He spots me and glares.

"You missed our session, Miss West."

"Yeah... something came up."

"Rolling around in bed with your convict boyfriend is not an adequate excuse to skip our time together. Or have you forgotten the deal? I'm happy to refresh your memory if needed, bring one of them down here for a live demonstration."

I keep my gaze averted. "That won't be necessary."

"Good. Don't let it happen again."

There's a shuffle behind me, and I'm startled by an additional presence in the room, hovering by the open fireplace. Standing at well over six feet, the ghost-like creature awaits further instruction. Beneath shaggy brown hair long overdue for a cut, two haunting, caramel eyes spare me a glance.

It's him.

The monster from the basement.

I fight the urge to run for my fucking life. I almost didn't recognise him without blood dripping from his chin, snarling like a rabid animal whose meal was interrupted.

"You remember Patient Seven. He will be joining us today."

Gulping, I offer him a nod. "Hi."

There's no response beyond his vacant, unnerving stare. Almost like there's nothing beneath his skin but blood and bone, an empty void where a person used to be. He defers back to Augustus like a trained dog, chin dipped in submission.

"Patient Seven has been working with me for several years now in another facility," Augustus boasts, proud of his creation. "The mind is a funny thing, so malleable and resourceful. It can be moulded like clay, transformed into something new."

Walking around to the other side of the desk, Augustus leans on the slab of mahogany and faces his patient.

"But you can't make an omelette without breaking a few eggs."

My skin crawls at the sense of power dripping from the demon clothed in authority and accolades. While the newspapers print the bullshit they're paid to roll out to the world, the truth lies buried in our living graves.

"Why don't we show our guest how much progress you've made?"

Augustus tucks a strand of hair behind Seven's ear, leaning in to whisper his command.

"Let's see how long it takes for you to put your head through that wall."

I swallow the burning acid rising up my throat as Seven nods, taking measured steps towards the wall. He faces the concrete, pausing for a tense moment.

This has to be some kind of game or sick joke, a scare tactic. Augustus casts me a look, ensuring I'm watching the show.

"Come on now, you have your orders."

The crunch of bone makes me shudder, reverberating throughout the room. Smashing his forehead into the wall, Seven doesn't stop. Even as his skull fractures and skin splits, leaving crimson trails on the wallpaper.

"Again," Augustus commands.

Once, twice, three times.

Each blow sprays more blood and my stomach twists painfully, threatening to revolt at any moment.

"Please... stop," I beg.

"More, Seven."

Augustus watches without a single flicker of remorse as his patient slowly caves his own head in. When Seven stumbles, on the verge of losing consciousness, the doctor finally orders him to stop. I've never been so horrified and relieved in all my life.

"Well done. You may take a seat now."

Falling into his seat beside me, Seven struggles to keep his eyes open. I stare at the endless river of blood gushing from the self-inflicted wounds in his head.

"How much do you know about Blackwood's history, Miss West?"

The question catches me completely off guard and I drag my eyes away from the creature beside me.

"I... I don't understand. Nothing."

Augustus retakes his seat, fiddling with his diamond cufflinks. "You see, the field of psychology was booming in the sixties and seventies. So many promising experiments and fields of enquiry, pushing the boundaries of scientific knowledge. Exciting times. Blackwood was purchased in the early eighties and repurposed for use, with the intention of providing cutting-edge care."

"Purchased by who?"

Smirking at my question, Augustus glosses straight over it and gestures to a framed photograph on the wall. I've never noticed it before, too distracted when I'm in this room.

I walk over to study it closer, noting the familiar building lined with staff dressed in old-style nurses' outfits and white coats.

"Blackwood Institute." I trace the label. "1984."

"This soon became a haven for the dangerous and disturbed. An alternative route, beyond the confines of criminal justice and punishment," Augustus explains as I retake my seat. "Do you know what the best thing about criminals are, Miss West? People who have no choice but to accept their fate here?"

I wring my sweaty hands. "They have nothing to lose."

"Correct. But also… they are expendable. Replaceable. Outcast from society and ultimately, forgotten about. When you leave this place, there will be no one waiting for you. No one to miss you or welcome you home. You're alone in the world and that is… *advantageous*."

Augustus flicks his eyes back over to Patient Seven, issuing another silent command. Before I can run, his skeletal body wraps around me like a coiled snake.

I don't have time to scream or fight back, clawing at his hands crushing my windpipe. There's wildfire in his soulless eyes, a burning inferno that will devour me whole.

With me subdued, Augustus loads a sharp needle with a shot, the liquid a darker colour than the usual concoction. I attempt to throw Seven off, but the room is blurring from lack of air.

All I can feel is the pain in my lungs, then a sharp scratch as Augustus dispenses the shot directly into the vein in my neck.

"I don't treat patients, Miss West. I carefully, meticulously… *break them*."

The world slips away, and I float on a lake of unconsciousness, falling back into the depths of my mind. Programmed by endless, agonising sessions, it follows orders perfectly.

I drag myself back to that imagined staircase without being told, every painstakingly constructed wall collapsing. Screaming echoes around me; begging and pleading.

The awful soundtrack crackles back to life, overwhelming every remaining sense. I savour the warmth of my dad's arms around me, his breath whispering against my hair.

"I'm sorry, Brooke. It's going to be okay."

Begging.

Sobbing.

Crying.

Nothing compares to the desperate plea of the dying. I thought I learned it from Vic in his final moments, bargaining for his life. It made the kill oh-so sweet, watching the light drain from his body as I sunk my knife deeper into his abdomen.

"She's hurting him, Daddy."

"Shhhh, it's okay. Go back to your room."

Leaving that scared girl and her desperate father behind in the depths of my memory, my nightmare changes, exploding outwards like spilled ink.

This time, I'm heading up to the roof, filled with horror but unable to stop myself. Rio grins at me, waiting for the CCTV camera's light to wink out on command. His lips move and this time, I can hear the words.

Nothing about this place is real.

It's all just… an illusion.

Sucking in an excruciating breath, my eyes fling open again. The room spins around me, ticking and buzzing. I'm staring up at the ceiling of Augustus's office and he's back behind his desk like nothing happened, scanning over some paperwork.

Patient Seven is nowhere to be found. The wall… it's pristine. Not a single speck of blood, a mere smudge or dent to suggest anything happened at all.

"Welcome back. You passed out, Miss West," Augustus informs me. "The shot can be unpleasant, please take your time. We're in no rush to begin our session."

Dizzy and disorientated, I lay broken on his carpet, finding no comfort in his satisfied smile. It takes an eternity for me to drag my uncooperative body back into my seat, where Augustus is setting up the machine as usual. Rio's voice refuses to leave me.

I'm glad Augustus decided to bring you into the program.

I'll be given a fucking promotion.

I can't run or scream as the truth reveals itself. There's no escaping it now—the program. I fed myself the illusion at will, but months of denial have prevented nothing. I still ended up here, staring at a clean wall, my sanity splintering apart.

Rio won.

Augustus won.

Blackwood fucking won.

"I want to focus on a specific memory," Augustus begins.

I gulp, too terrified to even move.

"I think this memory will benefit from some further inspection. Trauma can do extraordinary things to our minds. Bending, blurring time… removing reality. The truth can become quite unrecognisable. We will find it together."

Augustus opens his notebook, pages thick and filled with notes. The EEG machine explodes with noise, dozens of wires tracking the tornado ripping through me. I frantically look around the room, searching for something.

There's no Patient Seven.

No Logan. Nothing.

I'm alone, dancing with the devil and *losing it*.

"Tell me about the cat, Miss West."

"Cat?" I mumble, my voice alien.

Flicking to a page in his notes, Augustus chuckles.

"Poor little Brooklyn, alone in the world and begging for love she will never receive. Desperate to get back for her favourite show, she stumbles across something that terrifies her. Her mother laughing and delirious, a strangled cat clasped in her hands."

His words paint a picture and instantly, I'm that little girl again, trembling like a leaf and running as fast as my legs will carry me. Mum follows, screaming and shouting, drawing the attention of the entire neighbourhood. Dad would have to apologise to them later, and explain that she's overwhelmed by motherhood.

"What happened next?"

Licking my dry lips, I find my voice. "She g-got worse. Terrified of her own shadow. Talking to things that w-weren't there, s-singing to invisible children late at night."

"And this is when the beatings began?"

I nod, feeling the tears soak my cheeks. "Dad called the doctor, begged him to help. He said she was sick, that she had to go away for a while to get better. It t-took months, but she did come home. She was never the s-same again. Cold… e-empty."

Augustus leaves his designated place behind the desk, taking the empty chair next to me instead. Front row seats to watch as I fall apart. The memories won't relent now they've been set free. Deep down, I'm still that scared little girl, running from her own mother.

"What next?" Augustus prompts.

"So m-much screaming. On and on and on…"

"Who was screaming?"

Agony erases all rational thought and I clutch my forehead, begging for it to stop. I don't want to remember. I beg for the memories to leave me alone, ignorant and at peace.

But no matter how hard I lock down those tightly packed boxes, the time has come. I no longer possess the strength to keep it all at bay. The truth is coming for me.

"Go down the stairs. Take me with you," he instructs.

Augustus's voice takes me back into the nightmare. My small, child-sized feet sink into the carpet as I sneak downstairs. Dad went moments before, making me promise to stay in my room. But the screaming has stopped, so it must be safe now.

There's nothing to be worried about.

Daddy will look after me.

Adults always mean what they say, right?

With Augustus hot on my heels in this twisted dreamscape, I inch through the darkened house until the kitchen lies ahead. There's a strangled, broken sob coming from inside, one that doesn't sound human. Like an injured blackbird being crushed to death in furious hands.

"My poor boy… What have you done, Melanie?"

"He was sent here to spy on me. I had to!"

Shuddering at the tone of Mum's voice, I halt in the doorway. My eyes track over polished tiles, white and clean… but there's something dark spreading across them.

Choking on a sob, I follow the expanding puddle to its source and find Dad on his knees, begging for the lord's forgiveness. There's something across his lap. No, *someone.*

"And here we are," Augustus celebrates.

Dad lets out an awful keening sound, cuddling the limp body to his chest. I can't see his face, but I know who it is now.

For the first time in over a decade, I remember who stood between Mum and me, time and time again, sparing me another beating. Who held me close at night and rocked me to sleep, promising of a life far from this place. Who gave his life to protect me from her insanity.

I have an older brother. *Had.*

"Daddy?" I whisper.

His head snaps up, wide eyes meeting mine. "Oh no, Brooklyn… don't look, sweetie." Voice dripping with devastation, tears leak down his pale face. "Go back to bed, I'll come read you a story. I just need to look after Mummy."

I'm a good girl, so I do as I'm told.

My fluffy bunny rabbit's ears take a battering as I chew my way through the fabric, listening to the shouting below. They argue about what to do, who to call. One word embeds itself in my brain, too traumatic to ever forget, sneaking down into the depths of my psyche.

Handsaw.

"I won't let them take you from me, darling…" Dad declares.

He was too pure for this world, weak and co-dependant. Addicted to her brand of love, blinded by the sickness determined to consume us all. Trapped in the nightmare, I scream myself to sleep as my mind breaks into pieces that will never be fixed.

Their actions were the beginning of the end. The voices and shadows soon followed in the months to come, after the fateful car crash that left me alone and orphaned.

Parentless. Brotherless. Broken.

"We have to move him. Bit by bit. Get the saw."

"No! He's my son, I want to bury him."

"Don't let them take me away, Ian. Please… I beg you…"

"Calm down, Mel. I'll fix this. I promise."

Cowering in the corner of Augustus's office, I leave the vision of child-me behind, the past melting away as I return to the real world. The final memory has been unlocked.

Furious sobs tear me apart, and I hug my knees to my chest, hoping that if I can make myself small enough, the demons will leave me alone. Even the one sat in the chair, studying me.

Not real.

Real.

Not real.

Real.

"I k-killed him," I scream into my hands.

"Who? Your brother?"

Shaking my head, I fight to get words out. "Vic. I killed h-him and… sawed him into pieces. Just l-like the voices told me to. Just like my f-father did. Just how I f-fucking learned to when he butchered my brother to protect the m-monster he loved instead of me."

Augustus beams at me, like this whole time, he was waiting for those exact words. The filthy, murderous pearl at the heart of this tragedy. Months of work and he has his answer.

He faces me with anticipation, the professional persona slipping away once more. Something sinister takes its place.

"You see, the truth is that Blackwood Institute was never intended to cure the insane," he reveals conversationally.

"What?" I whimper.

"Some are here to rehabilitate and return home, but nobody leaves this place without my approval. We treat those with families and build our good reputation, enough to fool the outside world, while I keep the most promising of the crop for my own purposes."

Placing a steady hand on top of my head, he gently strokes my hair. I try to shrink away and run from what I know is coming. There's no escaping him. No hiding or pleading, no chance of redemption.

My soul belongs to Blackwood.

It always has.

Augustus crouches down to my level, his finger tilting my chin up to meet his eyes.

"We're here to learn and pioneer beyond the constraints of civilised times. Like my predecessors, I study evil in all its forms. And you, Brooklyn West... are the perfect subject. Not only a victim, but a perpetrator. An untainted product of pure evil. You will be my greatest creation yet."

He kisses my forehead just like any father would.

"You will be... Patient Eight."

CHAPTER 25
PHOENIX

ADRENALINE - ZERO 9:36

THE SOUND of a dying animal wakes me up.

Begging, whimpering... like somehow, it's trying to speak to me. Desperate to be understood yet doomed to die alone.

I turn over in bed, clutching the empty sheets where Brooklyn is supposed to be sleeping, in safe distance and under our constant surveillance. Instead, she's fucking gone.

"Kade? Wake up, man."

He groans, tapping his phone to shine light into the dark room. I've been back in my own bed for a while now since he decided to re-join the world of the living.

We've been rotating Brooklyn between us all, taking turns to watch over her after things escalated. The other night, we found her slicing her leg deep enough for eight stitches, completely delirious and out of control.

I don't think any of us have slept right since.

"This better be good," Kade mutters.

I peer around the room, unease trickling down my spine.

"You hear that?"

We lapse into silence, listening to the sound.

"It's coming from the bathroom."

I leap out of bed, padding across the room on light feet. The optimistic side of me wants to believe that she went to pee, but I'm not an idiot. There's no room for hope here, that's the most dangerous of all emotions for the incarcerated and insane. We hid all the sharp objects for this exact reason.

Opening the bathroom door, I look inside.

My heart stops dead.

I'm terrified of finding her bleeding out like before, the residual trauma threatening to overwhelm me. I don't think I would survive it again.

Instead, there is no blood in sight. I think she's okay. Flicking the light on, I realise just how fucking naive I am. There's nothing remotely okay about this scene.

Brooklyn stands with her hands braced on the sink, staring at her own reflection in the mirror. Her gaze is empty, devoid of recognition. I don't even think she's awake. A thick curtain of tears stains her cheeks, pouring freely.

My firecracker looks irreparably broken.

"Baby? What is it?"

Pulling her into my arms, I rub circles into her back, noting the gooseflesh covering her entire body. She's still naked after we fucked earlier and shivering violently.

"She's k-killing him, Daddy. Save h-him."

I'm too terrified to even breathe. "What are you talking about?"

"You're supposed to s-save him. Stop her, she's killing him."

Giving her a rough shake, she doesn't look at me, her eyes still glued to the mirror. Waving a hand right in front of her blank face, there's still nothing. Brooklyn is nowhere to be found, imprisoned by her nightmares or something far worse. *Memories.*

Shouting for Kade, I hold her tight and wait for help because I'm freaking the hell out here. He takes one look at the chaos and assumes control, sweeping sweaty hair back from her face to peer into her unfocused eyes.

"Brooklyn? It's Kade, wake up, love."

He clicks his fingers, also finding no reaction.

"Come on, firecracker," I plead.

Kade glances between the mirror and Brooklyn's trembling bottom lip, disappearing into the room again. I know for a fact Sadie left a stash of meds for emergencies, but the others don't trust me to know where they are yet.

"Don't hurt h-him…" she moans, swaying on her feet.

"Shhhh, it's okay. You're safe with me."

Pressing a kiss to her tangled hair, Brooklyn lets out another agonised sound. I take a step back, hoping more space will calm her. Instead, her expression transforms into something else. She draws her fist back and before I can stop her, smashes it into the mirror with a furious shout.

"I don't belong to you, Vic. I never did!"

Shards of glass fly through the air, and I tackle her until we're sprawled out on the bathroom floor, littered by sharp fragments. She continues to writhe beneath me, tortured by an invisible enemy.

"Kade! Hurry the fuck up."

"Coming!"

Reappearing into the doorway, he takes Brooklyn from my arms and cradles her to his chest, making soothing sounds. I struggle to my feet, bleeding from several small cuts but the pain barely registers, I'm too focused on her mumblings.

After managing to dress her in sweats and a discarded t-shirt, we bundle her into Kade's bed, tucking the covers into tight folds that would make any military man swoon.

Brooklyn fights the restraint as sweat drips from her flushed face. Her lips are parted on a gasp laced with such pain, it breaks my heart into even more pieces.

"What do we do?" I ask in a panic.

"Hang on. Love, drink some water for me. Come on."

By some miracle, Kade manages to get a glass down her. I don't miss the unmistakable swirl of dissolved powder laced in the drink, a drugs cocktail that should buy us some time to figure out what to do next.

These episodes have been coming every day for a while now, worsening by the hour. We can't ask anyone for help, not until we know why she deteriorated so fast. Something pushed her over the edge. Or... *someone.*

Collapsing on top of the covers beside her, Kade holds our girl tight until she finally drops off. Her eyes continue to move behind her closed lids, but the awful gasping sounds are gone. He tightens his arms around her like a straitjacket.

"Any bright ideas?" I ask desperately.

"I got nothing. Things have gone to shit recently, it must have destabilised her."

"That's bullshit, Kade."

I know what this is.

Blackwood Institute.

Run by the insane, for the insane.

Kade shuts off the light, and I force myself back into bed, the grip of exhaustion taking over. We like to kid ourselves with the falsehood that any of us are safe here, in control of our own destinies.

The truth is a bitter pill to swallow—we're never safe. Not here, not anywhere. And especially not when the threat comes from within and can't be so easily beaten.

Dropping back to sleep, I focus on the soft sound of Brooklyn's breathing. Any hope of a peaceful night's sleep is rendered futile by an ear-piercing scream a mere hour later, just as dawn begins to peek through the window.

"Fuck! Where is she?"

Kade falls from the bed, clutching at empty sheets. We throw clothes on, racing out into the hallway. A handful of other patients have emerged from their rooms, searching for the source of the commotion.

Down the staircase, we locate the culprit. Zero shame, I'm fucking relieved to see someone other than Brooklyn sprawled at the bottom, bleeding and broken.

A familiar nurse is being tended to by one of the night-time guards, her leg twisted at an unnatural angle as the blood pours from her head. *What a glorious sight.*

"Did she fall?" I laugh.

She's the bitch who always sticks her finger down my goddamn throat, thwarting my efforts to stash pills. Hell, she deserves to be pushed down the stairs.

"Do you think..."

I don't finish that thought, Kade knows what I'm alluding to. He looks worried, glancing down at the nurse a final time before declaring that we should split up.

I race back upstairs to grab Hudson while he goes for Eli. We need to find our girl, and fast. It takes a few minutes for Hudson to answer, slamming his door open with a growl.

"Phoenix, man. Seriously... fuck off."

"We have a problem."

"Goddammit. Let me grab my shoes."

After tearing apart Brooklyn's empty room, we grow desperate. She's nowhere to be found, I even checked under the damn bed.

While Kade urges everyone to remain calm, Hudson loses his shit and smashes the bathroom door with his fists, and Eli watches the madness with barely suppressed terror.

"Any ideas before we have to involve security?" Kade sighs.

I begin to protest right as Hudson hisses his disagreement too. We bicker and toss ideas about, but Eli remains resolutely silent. It's only when he stiffens, sprinting from the room with an odd-sounding squeak, that we pay attention and chase after him.

Each step upwards echoes like a thunderclap, dread squeezing tight around my heart. He takes us right up to the top floor. It's quiet up here, cloaked in darkness broken by the rising sun.

Making a beeline for the exit, my mouth goes dry at the memory of the last time we ended up on the roof. It haunts me every night without fail. The exit door is slightly ajar, open just enough for no one to notice unless looking.

"You told me that you tossed the key after that night," Kade accuses.

Hudson flushes. "I meant to... fuck!"

We burst out on to the gloomy rooftop and find Eli frozen, staring into the distance. Deja vu slams into me with enough force to make me dizzy. There, sitting on the ledge with her feet dangling over, is Brooklyn.

"Stop!"

"Brooklyn!"

"Firecracker!"

Screeching to a halt behind her, she looks over her shoulder with a frown like we're the lunatics for making a racket.

"What are you shouting about?"

I take tentative steps to close the distance between us, hands outstretched in readiness to grab her at the first chance we get.

"Just come away from the edge," I coax.

She gives me a crooked smile. "I'm just sitting here."

Crowding around her, I exchange worried looks with the guys. Her voice is all wrong, light and unfamiliar, like someone else has invaded her body and stares back at me. She looks awake this time, swinging her legs back and forth over the edge.

"Doing what?" Kade asks uneasily.

"Talking."

"To... who?"

Glancing to her side, she frowns at thin air but soon plasters her smile back on. "Myself. I like it up here. It's quiet and loud at the same time, the wind drowns everything else out."

Kade studies her. "Did you push the nurse?"

She doesn't answer, smiling broadly. While Hudson snorts, Kade looks uncomfortable—like he can't reconcile this version of Brooklyn with the one that exists in his head.

"She didn't see me." Brooklyn giggles.

Cursing colourfully, Kade takes a step back and fists his hair. Taking advantage of the distraction, Eli manages to get close to Brooklyn without spooking her, sitting down by her side.

She reluctantly accepts his arm around her shoulders, and he whispers something in her ear, making her laugh before glaring back at Hudson.

"You broke my bathroom door?"

"You were missing," he snaps.

"I was thinking, not missing. I'm fine."

We all settle down at various points on the ledge. Kade has the most calming presence, but he can't bring himself to speak. I know he's thinking of the nurse and her broken leg, shoved down the stairs without remorse.

His conscience has taken an absolute beating as of late, but he still loves to tell himself that we're good people, not the monsters the rest of the world sees.

Brooklyn stares up at the sky, her expression fluctuating between contented and… grief-stricken. Like she can't decide how to feel or what the hell is happening inside her brain.

"You guys always find me, don't you?"

Hudson huffs. "Even when you run from us."

"But I didn't always have you there. I was alone for so long." Her voice trails off, eyes filling with tears. "Did you know that I had a brother? A long, long time ago."

While the three of us wait for her to expand, Hudson catches my gaze over her shoulder and there's real fear there.

"Blackbird… you never had a brother."

"You don't know everything about me, Hud."

Looking to him for confirmation, Hudson shakes his head again. We've had the rundown on her childhood, the waste of space parents who died in a mysterious car crash, leaving Brooklyn orphaned and alone like the rest of us.

"He was tall like my dad. Good and kind, but grumpy too. Protective of me. He'd always ask me these profound questions, like he was the little voice of conscience in my head. Trying to teach me to be more than our mother, I suppose. She didn't set the best example."

"What was his name, firecracker?" I prod.

Brooklyn stares out into the distance, her hands shaking in her lap. Hudson takes one and clutches her tight, clearly sensing that something is amiss here. Physically, she looks the same. But I can't shake the sense that we're not talking to our Brooklyn anymore.

"I… don't know. Can't remember."

No one knows quite how to respond to her obvious confusion. She's clearly talking nonsense and won't listen to us. So, we watch the sun slowly rise on the horizon, bathing us all in brilliant light.

The guards change over from the nightshift, exchanging greetings and incident reports. A medical team carries the nurse away, crying and confused about what happened. The kitchens start up for the day, preparing to feed the insane masses. The world continues to spin, even as reality crashes down around us.

"Let us help you," Kade finally says.

"You can't help."

"We want to try," I add.

Brooklyn casts me a look, something a lot like terror in her gaze. Whatever she needs, I'll do it. I'm done hating her. This place wants to tear us apart, the lone wolf is easier to break that way. Not on my watch.

"We should go in," Hudson grits out.

I help Eli to stand and offer Brooklyn a hand, before passing her off to Hudson before he loses his shit. Once she curls up in his arms, he takes a much-needed breath, briefly crushing her to his chest and then passing her over to me. We all need the reassurance after that debacle.

"You're freezing."

"I can't feel anything," she mumbles.

Her words terrify me. She's too thin, too breakable. I'm the only person allowed to hurt her. She's mine to bruise and scar, mine to love until death fucking parts us. And even then, I'll haunt her goddamn ass to the ends of the earth.

"Don't come up here alone. Just tell me or someone else," I beg.

"Sometimes I need to be alone."

My lips graze hers, seeking comfort. "You're not alone. You never need to be again. We're your family, Brooke. All of us."

She reciprocates the kiss, but still can't hide the torment in her eyes. Not from me. The others may believe her shit, but I know the truth.

I've kept enough secrets of my own to know what it looks like, the toll it brings to carry such a heavy weight around. Unable to share the burden or seek relief.

Brooklyn is lying to us.

She's lying through her fucking teeth.

And I'm going to find out why.

CHAPTER 26
BROOKLYN

DESTROYER - OF MONSTERS AND MEN

DOMINOES WAS my favourite game as a kid.

Easy entertainment when my parents were shouting the house down, on the verge of killing one another. My dad always said that the more we love, the harder we fight.

When I was younger, I never understood what he meant by that—how love could be something far more imperfect and toxic than the stories told by Disney movies.

Lining the tiny ivory slabs up into perfect circles, I'd long for the thrill of tapping just one solitary domino, and watching the entire thing spiral out of control. Like a butterfly that flaps its wings a thousand miles away, yet causes a tornado nonetheless.

Actions have consequences.

I understand that now.

I thought that by killing myself, I could atone. Foolish, right? Trapped here, there is no forgiveness. Only evil. Now I must learn how deep the darkness goes.

Without Logan playing bodyguard today, Augustus faces me from behind his desk, tapping ash from his cigarette into a silver tray. He's never smoked in front of me before, but we're beyond pretences now.

"How did it feel to watch her fall?" he asks.

I remember the excitement that built in my chest as I snuck up on the nurse. That was my homework—find someone worthy of punishment and make them hurt. I've watched her treat patients like dirt for months, using her authority to inflict misery. Seeing her broken and in pain clicked something into place inside of me.

"Good," I admit.

"I watched on the cameras. Impressive work."

"You watched?"

"Naturally."

Everything that happens in Blackwood is under his control. Even when we think we're free, it's all a lie. Augustus wants bad things to happen. He wants patients to take drugs and trade contraband, fight and fuck, hurt themselves and wreak havoc.

It's all invaluable data for his calculations, an untapped well of knowledge and power. Rio worked for Blackwood to feed the corruption, ensure the flow of information. Supply the madness and watch it all spiral out of control for the sake of experimentation.

"Let's talk about your brother," Augustus suggests.

"No."

"You're not in charge here, Miss West. Don't you think it's curious that you erased him from your memories? An entire person, simply gone." Augustus snaps his fingers. "The human mind never ceases to astound me."

"If you're done jerking off over my brain, I'd like to move on."

Glossing over my attitude, Augustus takes his pack of cigarettes and slides them across to me, eyebrows raised. I hesitate, certain it's a trap. He merely smiles, encouraging me to help myself.

"We still have much work left to do."

Breathing in the familiar comfort of nicotine, I repress my shudder at his words. Part of me still refuses to believe the horrifying truth that we unearthed. A decade's old secret lost in the darkest recesses of my mind.

"There's no more story to tell," I drone.

"I'm no longer interested in your story."

"Then what?"

"I've told you why Blackwood exists. Now you must see for yourself."

Opening his desk drawer, Augustus flourishes a glinting pair of handcuffs. My heart skips a beat as he advances. I should run as far from this godforsaken room as I possibly can. Take my chances in the wildness, beyond the barbed wire fence. Hypothermia would be better than another day spent being his lab rat, dancing upon command like a ballerina in her music box.

"I've told you about disobedience. Things can get a lot worse for you," he warns.

I have no choice but to let him cuff me, the metal digging into my flesh. We exit the office and find my favourite sadist in the hallway, his lecherous gaze scraping over me.

"Evening boss," Jefferson greets.

"Are the arrangements taken care of?"

"Yes, sir. We finished up with Patient Seven an hour ago."

I keep my mouth shut as I'm guided away, leaving the relative safety of the office behind. Never thought I'd see the day that I called this place familiar or comforting, but the damp-ridden darkness of the sprawling rooms beyond are another realm of hell entirely.

"The Zimbardo Wing was constructed shortly after opening, to keep the two purposes of Blackwood separated," Augustus explains, escorting me down another endless corridor.

Every step feels tantamount.

Like I'm towing the line between life and death.

"Zimbardo... *Z Wing*," I mutter.

"The last true pioneer in the psychological field of evil," Augustus confirms. "He longed to understand the depravities of the human mind, what caused certain individuals to take the path less-travelled from good to bad. Genetic predispositions or the influence of environmental factors."

We pass locked and bolted doors, no indication of what horror lies beyond. Supplies, empty holding cells... or something far worse that doesn't bear contemplating.

"In this day and age, research is bound by ethical constraints that prevent anything of true interest being investigated," Augustus continues, smoothing his silk shirt.

My feet slow to peer inside an open door, and I gape at a giant steel bathtub placed in the exact centre. Vomit rises up my throat, each fresh horror assaulting me.

Dark streaks across the floor.

Red swirls on rusted metal.

Cuffs built into the tub to restrain its occupant.

"Why am I here?" I dare to ask.

Augustus peers over my shoulder. "Ah, the bathtub. A little old-fashioned, I know. Sometimes the best tactics are the old ones, Miss West. Don't worry, I have something special planned for you."

Pure glee is printed across Augustus's face as we stop outside the final door. Assuming control from Jefferson, he removes my cuffs and steers me into the awaiting darkness. I feel around, grasping at thin air until a switch is flicked and brilliant light floods the space.

"Welcome to the isolation chamber."

I try to flee, but Jefferson draws back his fist and smashes it into my stomach. He follows it with a swift kick to the ribs, before retreating from the room.

"I thought you'd know better than to run by now." Augustus sighs.

"You... s-sick fuck," I cough.

He tuts, twirling the cuffs in his hands. "I'm a scientist, a researcher. One day, the entire world will know my name. It will be written in the history books for all that I've contributed to science simply by getting my hands a little dirty. No reward without hard work, right?"

"I'm not your fucking science project."

Groaning, I pull my body up and catch his amused smile.

"You will be whatever I want you to be. We've explored your past, the genetic predisposition to evil. Now, time for a little push. Those crucial environmental factors often prove effective."

Turning on his heel, I scream insults and curses as the door slams shut. Left alone in the chamber, I search for an escape. The walls are smooth concrete, leeching all of the heat from the room. No windows, no doors. No place to run. I have to kid myself that the stains on the floor are simply dampness.

I wonder how many people have died in here.

I wonder if I will die in here.

I wonder if... after everything, it'll be a relief.

With an odd crackling noise, the lights dim, all but a single beam that projects on to the nearby wall. Clouded by dust particles hanging in the air, I wrap my arms around myself as a grainy video is painted across the concrete.

"Smile for the camera, Brooke! Show us your big teeth."

No.

It can't be.

I watch the home video play out with Mum cuddling me from behind, ruffling my platinum pigtails. She places a sloppy kiss on my cheek before seizing the camera, turning it around to face Dad. Smile lines and warm eyes, staring back at her with so much fucking love, it turns my stomach.

"My beautiful wife." He sighs happily.

"Don't get all soppy on me now, Ian. Come on, let's take her to the sea."

Passing off the camera to someone else, I slam my hands over my mouth to hold the ugly sobs in. It must be him—my brother. His laughter is high and pre-pubescent, watching our parents walk me across the sandy beach. They swing me between them, like a real family.

"I'm sure by now you must be wondering where I got this tape."

Augustus's voice whispers through a loudspeaker, tucked in the corner. I fumble around for anything I can use to smash the fucking thing and remove his evil stain from this place. The video continues to play, shredding the remains of my control.

"There are a great many things you don't know, Miss West."

"I'm not playing this game with you!"

There's a long pause before my punishment arrives. I collapse to the floor, clamping down on my ears as an earth-shattering explosion of sound fills the room. The intense ringing bounces off the walls, reverberating around me until I feel like my head will explode.

I don't know how long it goes on for. But when I finally release my ears, still ringing despite the silence, my hands come away bloody.

"Next up on our little trip down memory lane," Augustus singsongs.

Peering through bleary eyes, I'm unprepared for the next assault. The new video is even older, blurry around the edges and dipped in greyscale. I spot the timestamp from the early nineties as the news reporter gestures up to the institute behind him.

"As you can see, Blackwood is the future of psychiatric care in England. Top of the line clinicians and facilities, it has become a haven for those too acutely unwell for the outside world. Look—here's one now!"

Like a zoo animal being masqueraded before a captive audience, I watch in horror as the white doors to a van are slammed open, two guards dragging a female out.

The minute the camera swings close enough, they capture her face. Cloaked behind a tangled blonde curtain, yet unmistakably familiar.

Holy motherfucking God.

She doesn't fight or scream, doesn't hurl hateful curses or threaten death. This woman is younger than my memories, untouched by the cruelty of sickness and irreversible damage. Hopeful. Unbroken. Alive.

Mum.

"Spot anyone you know?" Augustus taunts.

I stare into her timid eyes as the reporters follow her like vultures. The video is dated as several years before my birth, but it's undeniably her. The rush of shock soon dissolves into rage. He's beneath my skin, sinking his claws deep into my brain and scrambling it for entertainment.

"Melanie West, twenty-nine years old. Admitted for postpartum psychosis and declared a successful candidate after three years."

Listening to Augustus recite her information, I drag my nails against my scalp, as if I can peel the skin back and reorder everything becoming so twisted inside of me.

Postpartum.

I wasn't even an idea at that point, still years off my birth date. It's irrevocable proof that what we discovered is true. I did have a brother. A family. I lost it all.

Forcing myself to look back at the tape, I watch as the guards escort Mum to the gates of the institute. A small team awaits, gathered for the press to take photos and spread the word, attracting even more investors to expand the horror of Blackwood.

Realisation trickles down my spine as I drag myself closer to the images, close enough to make out the grainy faces. Sandwiched between two nurses, I recognise him immediately.

Youthful and less wrinkled, wearing the same damn glasses and sinister smile. My fist sails into the wall and I scream at the pain of my busted knuckles, hot blood slipping over my skin. No matter how hard I punch, I can't hurt the images being projected far beyond my reach.

"Professor Lazlo pioneered Blackwood's programme for nearly thirty years," Augustus muses.

"This can't be happening… it's not real."

Augustus zooms the video in, so Mum's face is undeniable.

"Stop lying to yourself, Brooklyn."

The video cuts and I curl back into a protective ball as sound is blasted into the room again. It feels like the world is ending, each seismic realisation underscored with the pain and confusion of sensory overload. They're trying to unhinge me.

I realise that it's working.

I realise that I can't fucking run from this.

Sobbing into my bony knees that are pressed to my stomach, it feels like an eternity before the sound stops. The pain exploding through every part of me fills my pores like a cancer, leaving no room for anything else. Not even myself. I can feel it slipping between my fingers; the scraps of lucidity that remain.

"Melanie proved to be one of our best patients," Augustus reveals. "She had such savagery within her, a glorious darkness that Lazlo pulled to the surface with a little encouragement. I'm intrigued to see if you will live up to her standards."

"Never," I gasp, wiping tears from my face. "She was my mum, not your pet psychopath. You did this. You're the ones who made her sick."

Augustus cackles away, enjoying my terror.

"Melanie was Lazlo's favourite experiment. In the three years she spent here, he achieved truly incredible things. I have a whole file on all the killings that took place by her hands. He created the perfect monster."

Sucking in a searing breath, I find the dreaded answer to my question. "Before releasing her into the wild."

"Like a trained tiger returning to its natural habitat," Augustus surmises. "What point is there in sculpting the human mind if it does not retain the new shape? Lazlo's work needed to be tested for efficacy. Naturally, when your father called the authorities on her years later, Melanie returned to Blackwood."

It was him. *Lazlo.*

He was her doctor all along.

Slamming my head into the wall, hoping for unconsciousness, my body falls back into the comfort of pain. My entire life was a lie. All these years spent blaming my cursed blood, the 'family sickness' that ruined my life—*wasted.*

I remember the day they took her away from us, I was so scared. But when she came back… any glimpse of my mother had been extinguished. It was a matter of weeks later when that fateful night happened.

"She murdered my brother," I sob.

"Melanie did as she was trained to do. The truth is, Miss West… Blackwood is your home. It courses through your veins, even as you fight us at every turn. You have always belonged to this institute. Your life was born to serve this program, just as your mother did. This is your destiny."

I retreat to the furthest corner of the room, huddling into a defenceless ball. The slam of the door raises my head, where Patient Seven's blank face waits for me.

"Let us play a game." Augustus chuckles. "Seven is my most successful project. Not quite your mother, but he's damn good. Add enough pressure to a piece of coal, and you will create a diamond. A glorious, crimson blood diamond."

Seven advances, his gaze firmly locked on me. There's nowhere else to run, I'm backed against the wall. He stops mere inches away from me, his nostrils flaring with each breath. I'm terrified to realise that I hope he breaks my skull against the wall.

I'd welcome the relief.

"Here is the deal. Prove yourself worthy of further investment and you will walk out of this chamber. Fail to impress me and I will bring Elijah down here into the darkness with you," Augustus explains. "See how well he fares during a trip down memory lane. Fortunately, there is plenty of footage surrounding his little fiery accident. It won't take much to break him."

"You promised to leave them alone," I whimper.

"Bargain with the devil and find yourself damned, Miss West."

Without further warning, Seven roughly grabs me and tosses me across the room. I hit the ground, pain shooting up my spine. He advances without emotion, kicking me in the face hard enough to break my nose.

As I choke on an endless river of blood, he straddles my body and wraps his big, strong hands around my throat. That's when the squeezing begins.

I silently plead for mercy.

Whether for death or salvation, I don't know.

The room narrows until it's just the two of us, both imprisoned in this mutual hell. Neither of us is free. He flexes his grip, teeth bared as he slowly crushes my windpipe. Just as I resign myself to my fate, preparing to let my eyes fall shut, something flashes in his gaze.

A brief sliver of recognition.

Perhaps, a human being inside the animal.

Leaning close enough for his lips to meet my ear, hearing his voice for the first time shocks me out of my stupor.

"Fight back or you will die. Hit me. Hurt me. Make me stop because I don't want to kill you."

Drawing back, he gives me the tiniest nod and loosens his grip just enough for me to get some much-needed air. Then I unshackle the beast inside of me and attack, drawing on every ounce of strength I have left.

His skull cracks against the floor as I pounce, my fists splitting and breaking against his pulverised face. Blood thirst takes over. Pure survival instinct.

If giving myself to Blackwood keeps Eli out of this basement, I'll sign my name in blood and willingly accept my fate. The crunch of shattered bone and wet, squelching flesh doesn't even register. I'm screaming as I relentlessly beat on Seven, a primal sound of indulgence.

When I'm done, Jefferson has to drag his body away. Limp, bleeding, and broken. No longer recognisable as a human being. I'm not even sure if he's alive, beneath the crimson waterfall.

My head hangs in exhaustion, my muscles screaming in protest. I don't realise that Augustus has entered the room until his hand brushes over my blood-stained hair; a caring, tender gesture.

"Well done, Patient Eight."

"Eli?" I whisper brokenly.

"He will remain free, as will the others. But their freedom comes at a cost."

CHAPTER 27
HUDSON

DEATHBEDS - BRING ME THE
HORIZON

TAKING a long drag from the joint, I hold the smoke in my lungs and bathe in the rush of calm. Blowing it out, I pass it off to Kade. We share in silence, studying the institute beneath us.

"You believe her?"

He shrugs, stubbing the joint out. "I checked the records, the other girl was admitted to solitary by the books. We have no reason to believe that she's lying."

After coming back a few days ago, black and blue, Brooklyn's refused to speak a word to any of us. She's been holed up in her room, and none of us know what happened, only that she claims to have gotten into a fight.

While the others may be gullible idiots, I know she's lying. My girl would never let anyone hand her ass to her like that.

"You got anything on Augustus yet?"

"He's squeaky clean." Kade sighs. "All of his qualifications and background history checks out, I was thorough. Looks like he was working at another place up north before relocating to Blackwood. There's nothing to suggest he's... I don't know. Involved somehow. We know Brooklyn's not well. Look where we are, for fuck's sake."

"I don't give a shit about that," I snap. "I know her better than she knows herself. This isn't her. I'm telling you, Augustus is bad news. We're missing something here."

I don't say that I only half believe my words. We all know what Brooklyn is capable of. Kade hesitates, but I gesture for him to spit it out already.

"With all due respect, she's here because she killed someone. Maybe we don't know her as well as we think we do. Brooklyn is unstable. She's mentally unwell and we're only encouraging her."

I flash him a warning look. "Careful, brother. Glass houses and all. Your hands aren't as clean as you seem to think. Need I remind you?"

He flinches, the colour draining from his face.

"That's what I thought."

"Give me a break, Hud. I'm just saying what we're all thinking."

"No one else is thinking that," I argue.

"She pushed that nurse down the stairs without a second thought. She broke Britt's fingers, stabbed you in the cafeteria, fucking killed a man without any remorse. I don't think I need to go on. We're protecting an animal."

"Our fucking animal!"

"I care about her too," Kade defends.

"Doesn't sound like it to me."

"Don't twist my words." Flicking the finished joint aside, Kade deflates. "All I'm saying is that we can only keep her safe for so long. If she continues to spiral, eventually the institute will step in. There will be little we can do to prevent that from happening."

"The institute is the one doing this!"

"Fucking with our heads and tormenting patients for fun? Yeah, sure. But you're talking about a full-blown conspiracy. Do you have any idea of the repercussions? It's bullshit."

His words set my ceaseless rage alight. I stand, pacing around the roof. I'm so sick of constantly being two steps behind everyone else. All the pieces are there, this broken jigsaw that seems to have a life of its own, yet it refuses to fit.

"You're the one who said something is wrong here," I point out.

"You're trying to pin this on the clinicians to escape the truth," he replies sadly. "We're all in love with an unstable, broken human being that can't control herself. She's here for a reason and we've blinded ourselves to that fact out of sentimentality."

Seizing Kade by his perfectly pressed shirt, I pin him against the brick wall. His eyes bug out and he claws at my wrists, trying to relieve the pressure.

If he wasn't my brother, he'd be dead already. As he so aptly put it, sentimentality is a fucking bitch, but it's the only thing keeping him safe right now.

"What happened to family is forever?"

"Running from reality won't help any of us," Kade wheezes.

"You want to talk about running from reality? Okay, let's do this then. You killed my fucking Ma. *You*. No one else."

"Hudson... Please..."

"No! Enough is enough. I don't give a shit what happened, it doesn't change the facts. She's dead because of you. I was ready to let you drown in your guilt, and Brooklyn was the one who convinced me to reach out and help you."

Pain overwhelms Kade's expression, and he silently pleads for me to stop. I'm not done. Far fucking from it.

"You're running from your demons and lecturing the rest of us for doing the exact same thing," I shout in his face.

"Get the hell off me, Hud."

Instead, I slam him into the wall hard enough to knock the air from his lungs. Kade gasps and tries to fight back, but I'm stronger than him. He can't run from the truth anymore, I won't allow it.

"Admit it. You killed her."

"She was trying to bury our family for helping you."

"She was still my goddamn mum! Now she's dead."

I've been mourning a ghost because no matter her faults, she was flesh and blood. Family. The woman I killed to protect, landing myself in hell on earth. Kids are broken because they can't help but love the monsters that breed them.

"I'm sorry," Kade begs.

"That means nothing to me."

"Please, Hud. I'm so fucking sorry."

"If you'd let me turn myself in, she would still be alive. Janet would be okay. Your father wouldn't own our goddamn asses. Cece wouldn't be hiding in her school out of fear, with no home to return to. You had to save me and sacrifice everyone else."

Tears race down Kade's cheeks. "Because you're my brother."

"I'm not. I never was. You just needed another victim to save, another lost cause to add to your repertoire of failure." I snort like the whole thing is funny. "You compensate for your own shortcomings by boosting your ego, acting like a saviour. None of us need saving by you, Kade. You need to fix yourself."

Shoving him aside, he scrambles away from me in fear. I've never seen him look so afraid before. But staring into my eyes, the undeniable truth thrown in his face for the world to see, he's scared. There's nothing more terrifying than facing your own flaws.

I fire my parting shot. "You call yourself a good person, but you're a selfish prick. We promised to protect Brooklyn from whatever came next, whether that be herself or someone else. You've given up on her. Truth is, you're full of shit. I'm fucking ashamed of you."

He collapses, crying freely.

The Kade we knew is gone.

With a scoff, I leave him on the roof to wallow. He can do whatever the hell he wants. I walked away from Brooklyn once before and it was the worst mistake of my entire life. I've failed her so many times and I refuse to add another to the long list.

Out of them all, no one expected me to be her protector, but I'm the only one strong enough to do it.

Stomping back down to her room, I let myself in with the pass I stole from Kade. I find Eli asleep in her bed, curled around her for protection while unconscious. Brooklyn's wide awake, staring up at the ceiling as she thinks.

"Blackbird?"

She startles, glancing up at me. The black smudges beneath her eyes hurt me on an atomic level. We've failed her and each other. Blackwood has broken us all.

"What are you doing here?" she whispers.

"I came for you."

"Why?"

"Because it's my fucking job, baby."

She gently removes Eli's arm from around her. He looks so young tucked up in her bed, innocent and vulnerable. I'm shocked to realise that he isn't wearing a shirt, revealing skin I've never seen for myself.

Thick scores of twisted flesh cover every inch, pulled taut and painful. Brooklyn catches me staring and pulls the blankets up to his chin, covering the scars from sight.

"You've never seen them before?"

"He's a private person," I reason.

"Wouldn't you be too if someone did that to you?"

She climbs from the bed and grabs her cigarettes, walking over to the window. Her hands shake as she lights up. At this point, the rules are redundant. None of us even pretend like we're afraid of punishment anymore.

"What do you want, Hud?"

I stare at her with wordless need. "You."

"I'm right here."

"No, you're not. You haven't been for a while."

Her gunmetal grey eyes meet mine, entangled with secrets I can't stand any longer. I wish I could reach into her mind and pull the truth free with my bare hands.

"You gonna tell me who hurt you?"

"I've already told you," she answers too quickly. "That dumb bitch, Megan. She's one of Britt's lackeys. Are you sure you haven't dipped your dick in her too?"

"Stop changing the subject. This isn't about Britt."

Tossing the cigarette, she faces me with such vitriol, I back away from her. There's a caged animal beneath her vulnerable exterior, a slavering beast that matches my own.

Deciding to stand my ground, I let her stalk right up to me. Her fists bunch in my t-shirt, irises flickering with flames that I recognise within myself.

"Tell me what you need," I plead.

"I need you to leave me alone."

"Stop lying to my face."

She leans into my touch as I brush her cheek with my knuckles, tracing dark bruises that can only be inflicted by fists. Someone touched what's mine. That can't go unpunished.

"You can't give me what I need," she whispers.

"Try me. Take whatever it is, don't hold back."

Brooklyn lets out a sigh, her nose brushing against mine. "We can't both be angry. I don't want to hurt you, I want to hurt the entire fucking world. All of it."

Clamping my hand around her bruised throat, I back her up against the wall, spreading her legs with my knee. No matter what she says, I know her better than anyone. She thrives on the thrill of the chase, toeing the line between pain and pleasure.

Who else falls in love with four damaged misfits with more baggage than a goddamn airport? Broken people always band together, hoping to find the missing pieces of themselves in someone else.

"Why can't we burn the entire world? Who the hell says we don't have that right?" I press my lips to her pulse point, loving the way it skips a beat for me. "If that's what you need, we'll march out there and kill every last motherfucker who dares to look at us wrong."

"We can't."

"Like hell we can't. I'll be the judge, jury, and executioner for you, blackbird. I'll be the bad guy if that's what you need. I'll be the monster. As long as it buys me your love."

Her haunted eyes squeeze shut, giving in to me. I kiss my way down the slope of her neck, hating the bruises inflicted by someone else's hands. She's begging for me, dying for the sweet release only my touch can bring.

I love that I have this effect on her, that her body is just as addicted to me as I am to her. She's the goddamn air I breathe, the light at the end of the tunnel and the darkness all at once.

"We're going to die here," she mutters.

"Perhaps."

"I don't suppose we deserve a happy ending."

I bury my fingers in her loose hair and tug sharply, relishing her intake of breath. "Maybe we don't. Hell, I know I don't. But there is one thing I do know for sure."

"What's that?"

I offer her a cruel smirk.

"We'll die together at least."

Our kiss is an inferno of frenzied need. I devour her lips until she's moaning and rubbing against my body, seeking more friction. I loved the innocent girl I used to know, but this sexually confident animal is something else.

Brooklyn spreads her legs, inviting me closer, until I'm pressing my dick right against her crotch. I can feel her heat from here, begging to be unleashed. Just as I prepare to bend her over, a blaring alarm fills the room.

She jumps with fear at the rush of noise, and I smash her to my chest, hating her reaction. It's just a fire alarm, probably another drill. *Why is she so afraid?*

"Let's get outside before the guards break the door down."

"I... I don't think we should."

I frown at her. "We can't stay here."

Her eyes try to plead with me, but I grip hold of her wrist so she can't resist. Grabbing a bleary-eyed Eli from the bed, also on the verge of a breakdown at the overwhelming noise, we bump into Kade in the corridor on his way back down from the roof.

He refuses to look at me, running down the stairs with his eyes swollen and red. For a second, I almost feel bad. The feeling is quickly extinguished. The stupid dick deserved a few home truths for once.

"Where's Phoenix?" Brooklyn searches around.

"Fuck. He's in his room."

"We have to go get him!"

"He's a big boy. I need to get you out," I insist.

"No, we can't leave him!"

"You're my priority, blackbird."

Seeing Brooklyn freak out, Eli comes to a decision. I watch him wrestle with his fear, reluctantly releasing his death grip on Brooklyn to cover his ears. Sparing us both a nod, he rushes back up the stairs. I think it's the bravest thing I've ever seen him do.

Letting the flood of patients pass us, we join the back of the line heading downstairs. Kade's already gone, slipping away to avoid talking to us. *Fucking coward.*

A melee of guards are herding patients outside while the fire alarm continues to blare, lining them up for count.

"We have to wait for them," Brooklyn begs.

Finding her tear-filled eyes staring up at me, I curse. "Fine. Two minutes."

We hang back on the staircase, the dorms emptying around us. Beneath the scream of the alarm, shouting echoes from out front. I count down in my head, ready to drag her out as soon as the two minutes are up. Eli is probably losing his shit, but he has Phoenix.

"Time to go," I announce.

"No! I'm going back."

Brooklyn breaks my hold, racing back up the stairs. *Goddammit.* Before we can get to our level, she freezes on the expensive carpet, rooted to the spot. A figure blocks our path, clearly waiting for us.

"Don't move or we're gonna have a problem," Jack shouts over the alarm, knife in hand. "That includes you, Brooklyn."

He glances up towards the CCTV camera positioned in the corner of the staircase, giving the briefest of nods. In an instant, the alarm cuts out. I knew it. They all called me crazy, but I fucking knew it. Brooklyn squeezes my hand, warning me to stay calm.

"We have a score to settle, Hudson. I don't like disrespect," Jack heckles.

I push Brooklyn behind me, shielding her with my body. "And I don't like assholes supplying my friends with drugs to kill themselves with. Yet here we are."

He flicks the wickedly sharp knife in his hand, catching it with practised expertise. I'm all too aware that he could bury it in me at any moment. Somehow, I need to get close enough to disarm him.

"You've beat on every single person in here and fucked everything up. Did you keep the stolen drugs for yourself too, dickhead? No one will buy from me anymore," he lashes out.

"What a damn shame."

"Despite all the warnings, you forgot your place. Don't think it hasn't gone unnoticed. We all know what you did to Rio."

I stop breathing.

Brooklyn stares, unblinking.

"You really think we didn't know?" Jack laughs.

"We?" I repeat.

Stumbling backwards, I fight to remain calm. He follows, taking the bait and getting closer. A few more steps and I can sink his own knife in his gut.

"He's under my protection. You can't do this," Brooklyn blurts.

I gape at her without understanding as Jack continues to grin, enjoying the entertainment. "Fuck the protection. Augustus can find a new pet to play with."

"You don't want to do this," she attempts.

"Oh, I think I do."

Stepping out from behind me, Brooklyn refuses to stay hidden. The fear that was quaking her bones is gone, replaced by calm instead. I try to pin her in place, but she shoves me aside, determined to face Jack alone.

"He'll make you pay for betraying him."

What the hell is she talking about?

Jack shakes his head with amusement. "Tell me one thing. What did Rio say to you that night? I'm sure he relished the kill before leaving you to your fate."

"Someone better tell me what the fuck is going on," I growl.

"You've been stumbling around the edges of this for quite some time," Jack says, making me even angrier. "I thought you were smart, but maybe I'm wrong."

Sneaking a worried look at Brooklyn, I find her face slack. She trembles at his words, like the mere mention of Rio's final act terrifies her.

"He said it's all an illusion," she mutters.

Jack's laugh makes my skin crawl. "You took out our best man, shocked the hell out of us all, I'll admit. That wasn't the plan. But turns out, you're far more fun alive than you are dead. Lazlo never got his picture, did he? The idiot miscalculated, but boy did he pay for that mistake."

Losing patience, I launch myself at Jack and attempt to tackle him down the stairs as a last resort. He's fast with his blade, swiping it through the air and slicing my thin t-shirt.

I grit my teeth, burying the pain while shoving him away. He stumbles before regaining his balance, waving the weapon in warning.

"Another move and I'll gut you."

"Try it. I dare you," I goad.

"You still don't get it, do you? I'm in control here!"

"You're fucking insane."

Brooklyn presses a hand against my bleeding chest, filled with murderous rage. Before I can stop her from getting involved, footsteps echo above us. I'm terrified it'll be Eli and Phoenix. I can't protect them all. With the alarm out, hopefully they've stayed put.

It isn't them.

Someone far worse.

A bag of skin and bone joins Jack, twining her hand around his bicep and pressing a kiss to his lips. Once they break apart, Britt offers me a hateful look.

"Are you familiar with the concept of a stooge?" Jack asks.

Neither of us answers.

Britt flicks her hair over her shoulder, smile lit with glee. "A stooge is a fake participant. The holder of real power in an experiment."

Brooklyn steps forward, dodging my grabbing hands. I feel like I'm free falling as the implications hit me, each realisation another seismic shock.

"You work for him," Brooklyn spits.

Britt giggles. "Don't worry, we aren't here to kill you. He's far too enamoured with his precious little guinea pig." She holds her hand out for Jack to slap the blade into. "But we've been ever so good, so a little treat is in order. Step aside, bitch."

Brooklyn stands firm. "Touch him and you'll die."

"You gonna push us down the stairs like you did that nurse?" Jack taunts.

Before Brooklyn can punch their lights out, Jack dodges her and makes a run at me. I topple down the first few stairs, scrambling to find my feet.

Brooklyn leaps on Jack from behind, but he turns the tables and smacks her into the wall. My vision tinges red when he straddles her body, pinning her wrists above her head.

"You look best weak and vulnerable," he leers.

Intending to snap his fucking neck for touching her, I'm unprepared for Britt to take the next chance to come at me with Jack's knife. I move to block the blow, but at the last second, she slips through my grasp, slashing the blade deep into my left arm.

Taken off guard, I stumble again and attempt to stop the blood pouring between my fingers. She's cut something bad based on the heavy flow. I've got no time to waste.

"You were supposed to love me," Britt yells, delivering another slash—this time to my right hand so I lose grip of the banister. "You've fucked me and discarded me, treated me like a worthless toy. I took it all, whatever you needed because I loved you. Within a week of her arrival, you tossed me aside."

Crimson gushes through my grip, staining the carpet red. Dizzy from blood loss, I can't move or protect Brooklyn from the blow Jack delivers to her temple, causing her to fall unconscious on the stairs.

"Britt, p-please," I say, raising a bloodied hand.

She swipes the blade straight across my palm, cutting so deep it scrapes along bone and I almost lose the contents of my stomach.

"You underestimated me, Hudson. Others see my potential. When they approached me, I knew this would be my revenge. I couldn't say no."

Her body collides with mine, hanging above me with an unhinged smile. Britt swings the blade back again, preparing for a fatal blow. I'm entirely exposed and unable to defend myself.

"All I had to do was play the game, follow orders. Easy peasy."

Kissing her fingertips and placing them against my lips, she smiles.

"Goodbye, Hudson."

Trapped beneath her, awaiting the final strike of the knife, I begin to lose consciousness. I don't see Britt. I don't see the familiar walls of Blackwood. I don't see the weeping wounds debilitating me. One haunting image takes centre stage.

Brooklyn.

Clambering to her feet, unsteady and weak, her forehead bleeding from the recent blow. She snatches a nearby fire extinguisher and manages to raise it high, letting out a scream before it connects with Jack's unsuspecting head.

The world blurs again, fading fast.

Next thing I know, hot blood sprays across my face.

I blink through a curtain of red, gagging on coppery death. Where Britt stood mere seconds before, horror waits instead. She stares at me with empty eyes as

Brooklyn finishes dragging the knife across her throat, connective tissue and muscle exposed by the slash.

Britt falls in slow motion, collapsing on the empty staircase with a thud of finality. Brooklyn still clutches the bloody knife, her breathing heavy. Wiping red-dipped hands on her jeans, she offers me a decisive nod.

"You were right. Let's burn the whole fucking world."

CHAPTER 28
BROOKLYN

THROUGH ASH - MOON TOOTH

DARKNESS. *Screaming. Terror.*

Our nightly routine of horror begins.

"Shhhh, it's okay. I've got you."

"I'm s-scared," *I whimper, snuggling my bunny rabbit.*

"Don't be, I'm here. I'll always be here. Close your eyes and listen to my voice. Nothing else."

My brother's comforting weight settles behind me in the bed, his arms ensconcing my body. He strokes my sweaty hair, singing under his breath. I'm sure no eighteen-year-old wants to spend his Friday night in bed with his baby sister, but he does it regardless.

"I can still hear her," *I admit.*

"She won't touch you, I won't let her. Try to go to sleep."

"How?"

"Counting sheep, remember? Let's do it together."

Her furious screaming continues as we count imaginary sheep together in hushed tones, barely fitting in my twin-sized bed with baby pink sheets. Mum came home a couple of weeks ago.

Now she's sick again.

Worse than ever before.

We fled upstairs when she started smashing all the photographs, accusing us of awful things. She thinks we stole her children and took their place. I hid under the kitchen table when she split my lip with her fist for the second time this week.

"I thought the doctor was going to make her better," *I cry.*

"Me too, kiddo. Maybe it will take some time."

"But she was gone forever. Why didn't it work?"

Tightening his arms around me, I hear my brother sigh. "Try not to worry. Everything will be fine. She'll come back to us eventually."

It doesn't stop the tears from flowing. Of grief and pain, terror and uncertainty. What happens when he leaves for college? Who will protect me then? I'm so afraid of being alone in this house with her. Mum is gone, perhaps for good. I don't know who this remaining person is.

"Will she ever get better?"

"I don't know, Brooke. But no matter what happens, we're still a family. We always will be, through thick and thin." His breath stirs my hair, laced with the scent of roll-ups he smokes from his bedroom window.

"What happens when you're gone?"

"Don't think about that."

Somehow, my lids grow heavy. With the strength and protection of my brother keeping me safe, I can dare to sleep. He won't let her get to me again, not tonight at least. As long as I have him, everything will be fine.

I can't imagine a world without him in it.

———

Dream and reality have become one.

After countless sessions of this torture, the relentless pounding of the hose ceases to register. The water is freezing, blasted at me with such ferocity it steals all rational thought and leaves me numb. I can't remember the last time I felt my body.

At first, I accepted my fate willingly—the sheer agony of being plastered to the wall with a relentless spray of water while the guards laugh. I slipped into a semi-conscious state, tormented by dreams and unearthed memories. It was a relief to mentally check out.

"That's enough, Jefferson."

"Sir?"

"Turn it off. We want her conscious for this evening."

The water abruptly stops, the bulging hose slumping as it empties. I collapse to my bruised knees, gasping for air and puking up all the water I've swallowed. My body is exhausted from the exertion of remaining awake, despite Augustus's latest cruel game.

A pair of expensive loafers sidles up to me and Augustus sinks to his haunches, a slender finger sliding under my chin. He looks like an avenging angel, so beautiful and deadly all at once.

"Do you know why you're being punished, Miss West?"

"Fuck you," I spit.

"Watch it. Untameable beasts get put down regardless of their value."

Dropping his grip on my chin, I slide bonelessly to the floor. Augustus's lip curls, taking in my weakened state. Even as my body fails me, my mind remains strong. There are no more dark corners to scare me anymore, I know what I've become.

I slit Britt's throat and bathed in her blood with pleasure. No matter how long he tortures me for doing it and risking everything, I refuse to apologise for being the monster he made.

"Our work here is important, but so is control. You broke the rules," he informs me.

"There are plenty more desperate whores in this place who you can recruit to your sadistic regime." I shove dripping hair from my face. "Plenty more stooges, right? You've got your pick of the weak and vulnerable to manipulate."

"Not everyone has the appropriate… *resilience*, to withstand the truth."

I laugh, my throat raw and painful.

"And what exactly is that truth?"

Augustus contemplates me for a moment, fiddling with his diamond cufflinks like usual. I realise the doctor himself has an anxious habit, beyond his control. We're all slaves to our minds, even him.

"It takes help at all levels to run an operation of this scale," he answers. "While my projects are my priority, those who enable the smooth running of this process are crucial. The stooges answer to me. You killed one of mine without permission, thus there are consequences."

"Maybe you should've given me permission then," I retort.

Delivering a swift backhand, Augustus's eyes flare with anger. I fall on to my back, laughing hysterically at the pain. It's a welcome comfort after days of numbness.

"You're lucky everyone was out," he snarls, like I should be grateful. "No one is looking for Brittany Matthews. She will disappear and you will pay for the inconvenience it cost me."

"Put it on my fucking tab."

What's another worthless stooge to him anyway? There are plenty more where she came from. The truth was there all along, I just didn't want to face it. Blocked it out, concealed the memories and lied to myself for convenience. Rio was just a pawn, a symptom of a broken system. So was Jack, and Britt too.

Spitting blood, I face Augustus without fear. "Why did you send Rio to kill me? He was another of your minions, just like Lazlo. Hell, the asshole bragged about his damn promotion."

"Rio did as he was told."

I shake my head. "We both know that Lazlo stepped out of line, got too cocky. Did you punish him for it? Early retirement, my ass. Keep killing your employees and you'll run out of loyal subjects."

Augustus sneers at me. "Lazlo has been dealt with for his insolence. Miss White too, the stupid bitch. I don't tolerate disloyalty. You would do well to learn that lesson."

Managing to wrestle my broken body against the wall, I fight the violent shivers. Every ounce of warmth is leeched from this room, removing any sense of comfort. It's a clever mind game, another tactic.

"I still don't understand what this is all for."

"This is the biggest, most elaborate scientific endeavour in human history," Augustus boasts. "Every minute of footage we gather is crucial. Every single patient belongs to me. You live your pathetic lives, and we study you, intervening where necessary… pushing and encouraging where needed."

"To what end?"

His lips curl in a satisfied smile, as if he's enjoying his pet monkey jumping through hoops and finally coming to her senses.

"To find those suitable for induction to the Z Wing. Eliminate the worthless and find the potential. We have an obligation to provide, Blackwood is merely a sorting system. We give you purpose, transform you into something new. A valuable commodity that many will pay handsomely for."

"Who? Pay for what?" I demand.

Disregarding me, he stalks from the room despite my shouting. Now the floodgates are open, I want to know it all. We've been so fucking stupid. It was there all along, every warning sign and red flag. The sense that something was incredibly wrong.

I just didn't realise how wrong.

Rio was right—it's all an illusion.

"Oh, Miss West." Augustus pauses in the doorway. "We will be attending an important event this evening. Disobey me again and I'll be the one shedding blood this time, though I'll let you choose which boy to surrender to me. Sound fair?"

I blanch at his threat, and he grins.

"Don't let me down again."

Despite everything, a desperate, dependent part of me wants to please him. It wants to follow orders and reap the benefits. Months of careful planning and he's seized control of a traitorous piece of my mind, through intimidation and control.

The slam of the door reverberates throughout the chamber, and I slump. Every instinct wants to defy Augustus, but the threat against my guys leaves me exposed. He claims that Hudson is alive, recovering in the medical wing. I want to believe him, but this man is a snake whose only agenda is to serve himself.

In the oppressive silence, I realise that I can hear the odd gasp of pain. Glancing around the empty chamber, I find no one there. Not even Logan. I miss his presence, the funny comments, and his protective gaze.

As the sound persists, I creep along the stained floor until I find a tiny metal grate built into the wall.

"Hello?"

Silence.

"Is anyone there? Please..." I trail off.

I'm so fucking scared, I want to add. I can't shut my eyes without hearing my brother's voice, the whole twisted ball of trauma rising to the surface in my endless solitude.

"You should listen to him. He won't warn you again," someone whispers.

Latching my fingers into the rusted metal, I tug hard, but it refuses to budge. There's nothing but darkness on the other side, laced with a sharp, coppery scent. Freshly spilled blood.

"Who are you?"

"You beat the shit out of me, so you should know."

"Seven?" I gasp.

"Bingo."

Collapsing against the wall, I tune into the sound of his breathing. I wonder which Seven I'm talking to—the empty, brutal machine that Augustus has created, or the deeply buried person within who longs to escape.

"How are you feeling?"

"Like shit. For Augustus's new princess, you have a mean swing."

"I'm not his goddamn princess."

Seven snorts, before hissing in pain.

"Sure you're not... *princess*."

Wringing out my dripping wet hair, I take a moment to gather myself. Talking to Seven is like looking in a terrifying mirror, reflecting back the inevitable. I'm terrified of becoming him, despite the resemblance growing with each passing day.

"What's your name?" I sigh.

"Seven."

"No. Your real name."

"Seven."

"That isn't your name."

"It's the only name I have left."

A sudden wail pierces the air, coming from outside the chamber. It sounds like a wounded animal struggling to escape and sets my teeth on edge. We're not alone down here.

"Who is that?"

Seven's voice is exasperated. "Probably five. She's a screamer."

I feel the sudden urge to make myself sick and remove the infection Augustus has implanted inside of me, even though I haven't eaten in so long.

"There are more?" I whisper.

"Only two others are still alive," Seven replies, his voice almost emotional. "One, three, four, and six are dead."

Unable to stop myself this time, I retch water and stomach bile until nothing remains, my throat shredded raw. Seven remains silent as I sob, uncaring of my mental implosion. He's as heartless as Augustus intended.

"No point crying about it, you'll be dead soon too."

"Jesus Christ... shut the hell up."

"Just making conversation, princess. I should have killed you when I had the chance." Lowering his voice, I only just catch his next muttered words. "Would've been kinder."

Before I can argue back, the clank of the door's lock turning sends fear running down my spine. I wipe my mouth in time for Jefferson to stride in, twirling my favourite pair of handcuffs. *Not.*

He frowns at me by the metal grate, and I rush to stand, feeling this alien need to protect Seven from punishment after nearly killing him myself.

"Come along, inmate. We've got places to be."

"Where?" I ask.

Grabbing a fistful of my hair, Jefferson dashes my skull against the wall until I see stars. Disorientated, he snaps the cuffs on tight and drags me from the room.

"Come on. We leave in ten minutes."

"To go where?"

His grin glints with malice. "You'll see. It's party time."

Dragging me back down the gloomy corridor, I can hear the wailing more clearly out here from behind another locked door. It's guttural, inhuman. I'd rather slit my wrists again than become that person.

"What is that?" I manage to ask.

Jefferson stops in front of the door, sliding open a little hatch. Something screams at me not to look, but I can't stifle the need to know what fate awaits me.

"Meet Patient Two. She got too cosy with another patient. See what happens when you misbehave?" His breath is hot and sticky against my ear. "Best learn from this, else you'll end up the same."

Tucked into the corner of a rank cell, bolted and chained in a straitjacket, is a girl. Or what remains of her, leaving nothing but a vacant ghost behind. A thick, bloodstained bandage loops around her head, covering where her eyes should be.

"Oh my God," I whisper in horror.

"Can't get distracted by pleasures of the flesh without any eyes." Jefferson sneers. "Patient Two forgot who she belongs to. She fell in love. Pathetic. Take note, Brooklyn. You'll be next."

CHAPTER 29
BROOKLYN

SHED MY SKIN - WITHIN TEMPTATION

"YOU'VE GOT to be kidding me," I mutter.

Staring down at the black silk dress buried in tissue paper, I fight the urge to rip the delicate material into shreds. The expensive hotel bathroom feels so wrong, like I'm intruding somehow.

I've never been in a hotel room before; I don't belong in this world of normality and rule abiding. To this uncaring society, I'm nothing more than a taxpayer's inconvenience.

There's a bang on the bathroom door that makes me jump, with Jefferson lingering right outside, waiting for me.

"Hurry up, inmate. I ain't got all day."

I did not expect my night to go this way. As soon as I was escorted from Blackwood under the cover of night, bundled into a waiting limousine, I knew I was screwed.

The trip to the city took a couple of hours and the two guards up front refused to answer my questions. We parked outside a glitzy, boutique hotel crowded with expensive cars and glamour, only to find Jefferson waiting for my arrival.

Apparently, I have a job to do.

I'm too afraid to ask what.

Sighing, I drag the dress from its wrapping, eyeing it with disgust. The spaghetti straps are almost non-existent and will leave every inch of my scars on display. I have no doubt it's a deliberate choice; another of Augustus's games to make me feel more vulnerable.

Stripping down to my underwear, I turn to look in the mirror, not recognising the person staring back at me. Avoiding mirrors is self-preservation at this point.

Who am I?

Who will I be when Augustus is done?

My body is stick-thin, devoid of any weight I managed to gain after arriving at Blackwood six months ago. Both of my arms are warped and disfigured with endless marks, the thick scars overlapping, and screaming insanity to the outside world.

Gritting my teeth, I slide the dress on and study my reflection. The material clings to my protruding bones, but I'm thankful for the floor-length. At least I look the part.

Another bang on the door makes me flinch and I slip my feet into the matching heels, leaving my ash-white hair to spill over my shoulders. It offers little comfort, but I'll take what I can get.

My thoughts drift to the guys.

Are they okay?

Do they miss me as much as I miss them?

Will I ever see them again?

"Move it, Brooklyn. Don't make me come in there."

Fighting a growl, I emerge into the hotel room. Jefferson sweeps his eyes over me, nodding with satisfaction before gesturing for my wrists. Once I'm cuffed, he drapes a sheer scarf around my body to hide them from sight.

"Let's move. Augustus is waiting."

"You gonna tell me why the hell I'm here?"

He snorts, sparing me a cold look. "Shut your mouth and maybe you'll survive the night. Cause any trouble, and I'll make the isolation chamber look like a goddamn fairy-tale. We clear?"

Suppressing a shudder, I nod once. Perhaps for the first time in my life, I should keep my attitude to myself. Something tells me Augustus won't forgive and forget this time, should I overstep.

Jefferson takes my compliance with glee, pinning me against the wall. His hand slides through the slit in my dress, brushing right against my panties in a deliberate move.

"Touch me and you'll lose your fingers," I warn.

"Shut it. You'll be needing this."

Flourishing the key card to the room, I gulp hard as he slides it into the elastic of my panties before retreating with a wink.

I'm still lightheaded with fear as we leave and emerge into the bustling foyer downstairs, surrounded by glinting chandeliers and finery. A steady stream of guests mill about, sipping champagne and conversing in low voices.

After a minute of studying them, I realise each exit is protected by armed guards. They aren't even bothering to conceal the weapons on them, watching us all with professional masks.

Yet nobody seems afraid.

In fact, most of the guests are packing too.

Guided into the grand ballroom, we head for a circular table in the top corner. Two seats are already occupied, and I hesitate when I see who is sitting beside Augustus, dressed in a matching tuxedo.

Holy fucking hell.

Seven looks so different, I almost didn't recognise him. His wild hair has been tamed and cut short, revealing his bruised, beaten face while leaving his dead eyes front and centre. I stare a little too long at his lips, eventually tearing my gaze away.

Augustus looks his usual well-groomed self, brushing off his black silk shirt that perfectly matches my dress. When he sees us approaching, he knocks back a measure of amber liquid, offering me a pleased smirk.

"You certainly clean up well, Miss West."

Fighting the urge to break his damn nose, I keep my mouth shut. Augustus raises an eyebrow, ready for a smartass retort that never comes. I hate how pleased he looks at my newfound compliancy.

Jefferson passes me off, retreating to his own seat. I'm tugged to Augustus's front by the painful cuffs around my wrists, which he flourishes the key for.

"Are you going to behave?"

I consider spitting in his face, but refrain.

"Why am I here?"

"Still full of questions I see. Do you never learn?"

"Nope. I'm afraid not."

Unlocking the handcuffs, Augustus tucks them into his pocket and touches his lips to my ear. "This gathering has a whole roster of potential investors who are interested in Blackwood's work. Several members of the board are also in attendance to network and take on new clients."

"Clients?"

Augustus deposits me right next to Seven. I'd rather spend the night being tortured with the hose than between these two sadists. Taking his place, Augustus glances around the room and studies the occupants for potential exploitation.

"What would be the point in creating the perfect supply of ruthless, brutal killing machines if there are no buyers lined up to purchase said machines?" He chuckles. "I told you... valuable commodity."

Holy shit.

I'm going to be fucking sold.

As more guests begin to take their seats, the gentle caress of violins in the background is drowned out by the intense ringing in my head. I lose control of my breathing, and just when I think I'm going to pass out, a sudden weight settles on the bare skin of my left leg, exposed by the slit in my dress.

Warm, steady... calming.

Then I realise who's touching me.

Out of the corner of my eye, I find Seven's eyes burning a hole into my head. Where the usual vacuum of emotion lies, there's a glimmer of recognition instead.

The hope is back, a buried persona in a hardened shell. He gives me the subtlest head shake, his thumb grazing over my inner thigh as I shudder.

Then the hand is gone.

His soft lips meet my ear instead.

"Keep it together, I don't want to kill you. He'll make me if you fuck this up, princess."

"Maybe you should."

"Is that really what you want?"

"You can't give me what I really want."

Seven scowls before wiping his expression back to practised emptiness. I glance at Augustus, who's looking away just long enough for me to palm the silver dinner knife from the table. I'll jam it in his neck and get myself arrested if that's what it takes. I will not be sold like an animal.

Before I can act, a hand forces me to release the knife, which falls to the floor. I look up to find Logan waiting for me, silently communicating before skulking back to his place in the corner, watching the room.

I'm stunned to silence by his surprise presence, but of course there's no explanation. Augustus doesn't seem to notice, straightening his tuxedo and smoothing his hair back, preparing to go into battle.

"Come along now, Miss West. Show us all that pretty smile."

With his hand clamped on my arm, we leave Seven and Jefferson behind. Augustus refuses to release me, even as we situate ourselves at the end of the nearby bar, far from the glare of watching gazes. He pitches his voice low, his demeanour deliberately relaxed.

"There is a gentleman attending tonight who has caused significant problems for our operation. He has a senior position in the corporation and remains protected by his allegiances, thus you must complete your task... *quietly*. I can't have other members of the board catching wind of this."

Catching a glass of champagne before the waiter takes off, I ignore Augustus's disapproving look and knock it back in three gulps. Fucking hell, I'll take a stiff shot of tequila over this fancy shit anyway.

"This hardly seems like a quiet place," I comment.

"It's the only public event Martin is attending."

"And what exactly is my job?"

Augustus faces me so there is no mistaking his command. "I want you to eliminate the threat by any means necessary. Prove your worth to me and perhaps, I will let your friends live."

"How am I supposed to do that without anyone noticing?"

Augustus smirks. "Trust me, he'll find you."

Chewing on my lip, I consider his orders. He's given me no reason to believe that he won't hurt Hudson, Kade, Phoenix, or Eli. Perhaps he will anyway, just to spite me.

"Why should I believe anything you say?"

Augustus slides his phone out and taps the screen, before passing it off to me. My blood runs cold as I watch the CCTV feed from inside the medical wing back at Blackwood.

Hudson lies unconscious in the bed, swathed in blankets and wires. He's hooked up to a bag of fluids as he recovers from a transfusion. On his left, Halbert stands guard.

"If you don't comply, Halbert has instructions to tear open Hudson's stitches and let him bleed out. It will be slow and painful, and I will make you watch every last second of it," Augustus states calmly.

"You wouldn't dare."

Eyes burning, Augustus turns and nods to Jefferson who makes a call. On the screen clutched in my death grip, Halbert saunters over to Hudson and grabs his arm, ripping the thick bandages free. He slides a penknife from his cargo pants, digging it right into Hudson's flesh.

Even without sound, I can hear his screams.

The wide, agonised 'O' shape of his mouth tells me all I need to know as he cries out in his unconscious state, fighting his sedation. Halbert plucks the stitches like he's playing a goddamn violin, slicing the first one and parting flesh. I slam the phone down and refuse to watch anymore.

"I'll do it," I concede.

"Good. Let us begin."

Taking my arm, I'm guided over to another table. I clear my face of all emotion and slide a cold mask into place, one that would rival even Seven's dead gaze. Augustus greets several of the smartly dressed men with handshakes, before pulling out a chair for me.

"And who is this fine beauty you have on your arm?"

"My latest acquisition," Augustus answers.

"Of course, I've been waiting to see her for myself. What a fine specimen."

Forcing a smile to the creepy, middle-aged men studying me, I keep my lips safely sealed. They talk and share drinks, leaving me to watch in silence. All I can think about is Halbert sitting inches from Hudson, who is unable to defend himself.

Augustus turns to me with his charming smile firmly in place. "You look a little pale, dear. Why don't you return to your room? Let the men talk business."

Just as I'm about to politely decline, I spot the warning in his eyes and nod. Fleeing the ballroom, I ignore Logan as he pushes off from the wall and trails behind me. Jefferson has his hands full with Seven who appears to be drowning himself in free alcohol.

Unable to stomach Logan right now, I throw myself into the elevator and hit the button before he can follow. The ride up is blessedly silent, and I take several calming breaths now I'm free from the lion's den.

My relief is short-lived.

When I emerge, a man is waiting for me.

"Took you long enough," he calls out.

I freeze on the spot as he approaches. Also middle-aged and portly, he wears a fine designer suit that covers his generous gut. But his smile is all teeth and predatory hunger. When he seizes hold of my hair and drags me over to the door, I realise who I'm dealing with. My target.

"Come on, stop wasting my time. I've paid a handsome fee for you," Martin warns, tugging my hair hard enough to hurt. "Off the books, of course. Quite unethical for me to dip into the company supply, but you were far too tempting to resist."

It's already happened.

Augustus fucking sold me.

"Be a lamb and open the door. I'm growing impatient," he orders.

Stuffing my fear down, I slide the key card from between my legs and ignore the sharp exhale from next to me, his whiskey-tainted breath making my skin crawl.

Once inside, the door shuts behind us and I'm left to dance with the devil alone. Little does he know, I'm no lamb.

"For a nutcase, you sure scrub up well. What are you in for, petal?"

"Wouldn't you like to know," I reply, eliciting a deep laugh.

"I heard you're a fiery one. My favourite."

My first mistake is giving him my back. I'm completely unprepared for the harsh blow to the side of my head. Stumbling on my feet, Martin punches me in the stomach, letting me collapse on the nearby bed.

"You think I'm stupid, kid? Augustus just let me buy his newest pet psychopath without any complaint. Fucking fool."

Martin discards his suit jacket, rolling up his shirt sleeves.

"He ain't got shit on the people I deal with, selling his projects for profit. He sits in his ivory tower, ruling over us all like he has a clue what it takes to be part of Incendia. Pathetic."

Incendia.

I grab on to the knowledge with both hands.

With a fistful of my hair, Martin hits me again and again. I don't put up a fight, willingly taking the beating. He has to think he's winning. Blood pours from my mouth and nose, smearing across the pristine bedsheets, which only seems to excite him further.

Pouncing on me, Martin pins my legs wide open with his considerable weight. I nearly scream out loud when he drags his tongue up the left side of my face, licking every drop of blood from my skin.

"Delicious. Nothing quite like the taste of the insane."

He rips the spaghetti straps of my dress in one move, exposing my bare breasts. I make myself go limp, pretending to be compliant as his lips wrap around my nipple.

"Scream, petal. I love the sound of it."

"Please stop," I beg, making my voice desperate.

"I still paid for you, so I'm gonna get my money's worth. You ain't gonna kill me."

My mind begins to shut down, numbing out to deal with the inevitable. I can feel his throbbing erection between my legs, grinding against me. It makes me want to peel my skin off with a knife just to remove the feel of him.

I focus over his shoulder, trying to tune his moans out. He's fallen for the act— hook, line, and sinker. All I need is an opening, and what I see offers me the chance.

A holster around his shoulders.

He's armed. *Bingo, asshole.*

I make myself raise my hips to rub against him with a breathy sigh that I hope sounds convincing. Martin releases my nipple, pausing to glance up at me.

"Fucking slut. You're loving this. Want to taste my cock, psycho?"

Biting the inside of my cheeks, I nod.

His nostrils flare and he releases my arms long enough to reach for his zipper, already stroking his erection. With a handful of his tiny shaft, he's powerless to stop my next moves.

I draw my knee up, smashing it right into his face and waiting for the crunch. By the time he's flopped sideways on the bed, I've stolen his gun. The weight feels so goddamn good in my hands.

I press it to his forehead, grinning.

"Not much cock to taste, frankly."

"Come on now, sweetheart. I was just fooling around."

"Spare me the bullshit," I hiss, savouring the sense of power. "It changes nothing. You're a pervert."

His eyes shine with literal tears, the big man is quaking in his boots at the presence of a gun to his head. It'll be my pleasure to spray his brains across the wall.

"I'm a father, I have kids. You can't do this," he begs helplessly.

Snorting, I click the safety off. "You think I care about your kids? They're better off without you."

"Whatever Augustus wants, I'll do it. I won't tell anyone what happened here, not even the rest of the board. Please."

With his life in my hands, the weight of the moment threatens to crush me. Caught on a track between two moving trains, I'm out of viable options. Sacrificing myself to this unholy deed is the last move I have left.

There's a brush of chilly air over my shoulder and I know what I'll find. A rapidly expanding shadow, curling around my limbs. The ultimate face of all my demons crouches beside Martin's cowering body, drenched in blood and decay.

His skin is peeled back from his bones, eyes still infecting me with poisonous anger. He always finds me in my worst moments. Vic is dead, but his memory will forever haunt me.

Come on now, Brooke.

Don't be shy. Finish the job.

"You again? Leave me alone," I shout.

Martin flinches, his eyes darting around the room and searching for someone else. When he realises we're alone, his face pales even further.

"Who are you talking to?"

Pull the trigger.

It's clean, mess-free. Easy.

Vic disappears before reforming on the other side of the bed, cloaked in darkness. I swallow hard, avoiding looking directly at him. Even in my hallucinations, I can see the brain tissue exposed through his broken skull.

He wanted to rape you.

Just like I did. Make him pay.

You're not alone. Let's do it together.

I've crossed the point of no return. The people I love could be killed at any moment and the memory of man I murdered is taunting me. I can't do this shit anymore.

Vic saunters over to me, his bloodied hands forming over mine on the gun. I know it's in my imagination. He isn't real, but his control is all-powerful.

He makes me the monster that I truly am.

Together, we unleash hell.

My guttural scream reverberates around us, bullets piercing Martin's flesh and spraying red death across the walls. His eyes are blown wide, empty of all presence as his slack, lifeless body hits the floor before I'm done unloading the gun.

In the aftermath, I hold my ripped dress up to cover my chest and sink into the corner, clutching my aching head. Vic's laughter echoes inside of me, morphing into the terrible screams that never seem far away.

I can almost feel my mother's ghost staring down at me, proud of the abomination she's created. We're both children of Blackwood now. Lost to my own mind, time ceases to exist, and I dip out of the world until a noise brings me back.

"You were right. She was definitely worth the investment."

"I told you. We're fortunate that plans changed for the better."

"I'll sort clean-up, but you need to dispose of the body."

"It won't be a problem. We're equipped for such things at Blackwood. Leave it to me."

The two conversing voices startle me from my numb, semi-conscious state and I find Augustus has appeared in the bedroom, inspecting Martin's cooling corpse with pride. I've passed his clever little test.

Behind him, another man from the table stands with his attention firmly on me. He sinks down on one knee, his expensive cologne turning my stomach. Running a hand over my arm, his lips curl in a satisfied smile.

"I can see why my son has fallen so hard for you."

Certain I misheard, I stare into his soulless eyes.

"W-what d-did you just say to me?"

Gripping my chin so hard I can't pull away, he laughs.

"Or should I say, technically speaking, *sons*. Leroy Knight—it's a pleasure to meet you."

CHAPTER 30
KADE

THE LIGHTHOUSE - HALSEY

TEARING THE ROOM APART, I stuff clothes into my bag almost at random. I'm paying no attention to the tornado of destruction around me, drawers pulled out and stacks of books upended.

The past few months have been hell. Pure, unadulterated hell. I didn't think it could get any worse. Then the call came in, Cece screaming and crying down the phone, yelling for me to get my ass out of here.

I'm a goddamn idiot.

I never belonged in Blackwood.

The door to the bedroom slams open as Hudson storms in, wobbling on his feet. He's barely dressed, still wearing his hospital tag and bandages, but determined to stop me.

"I heard you on the phone," he growls.

"Jesus, Hud. Go back to bed."

Launching across the room, he attempts to rip the bag from my grasp. "You're not leaving. We have no idea where Brooklyn is, shit is going down and you belong here."

"Back off. I can't stay and you know it."

He shoves me into the wall with surprising strength, considering he followed me all the way from the medical wing where he's been for over a week now. I took the call in the corner of the room, thinking he was asleep. Clearly, I'm a moron.

Hudson glares, white as a ghost. "We need you here."

I laugh bitterly, beyond done with everything.

"Why? Britt's dead, Brooklyn is gone. Phoenix and Eli are out of danger. You're alive. I'm needed elsewhere right now, and you can't stop me from leaving."

Hudson stumbles as I push him away, overpowering him in his weakened state. My real family needs me now. I knew leaving Mum behind was bad, but I never thought the threat would come from her. She's always been so strong.

"What happened?" he demands.

Sinking to the bed, I bury my face in my hands. "Mum took an overdose. Cece is in the hospital with her, but she's scared and alone. Dad's away at a business event, but when he gets back…"

I trail off, not needing to fill in the blanks. No doubt there will be further punishment for our mother.

"Fuck! Is she… okay?"

I shrug numbly. "I have no idea. I've got to go."

"You can't leave." Hudson shakes his head. "They're going to let Brooklyn rot in the hole if we don't do something. You're the only one who can get her out, Kade. Don't give up on her."

"She slit Britt's throat in front of witnesses, without remorse. I can't do shit with that."

"Bullshit!" Phoenix yells, running in with Eli hot on his heels.

The door slams shut behind them and they both face us, wearing matching expressions of weariness.

"The entire institute thinks Britt was transferred," Phoenix rushes to explain. "We all know it's been covered up by management. Jack is gone too. Hell, they even ripped the goddamn carpet out. She's in the clear."

"I fucking told you," Hudson hisses. "Jack and Britt were working for Augustus, the same as Rio. They're all in on it, that's why it's been covered up. He's a lunatic and he's got our girl in his clutches."

"You were half-dead from blood loss and delirious!" I insist.

This place can get beneath your skin and make you question everything, but there's no way the entire institute is a lie. I can't accept that. Not after all I've given up to be here, by his side. My entire life was put on hold. I refuse to believe that it was all for nothing.

"Open your fucking eyes," Hudson shouts.

Ignoring him, I stuff my final belongings in the bag. The old-me would have thrown himself in at the deep end, sorted this for them and taken all the validation that entailed. All for the chance of finding some scrap of self-worth. *Pathetic.*

I'm no longer that person, not since Hudson made me realise just how shallow I've been. The last two years have been a huge waste of time; I'm as worthless as ever and the people I care about have suffered in the meantime.

"Wait," Phoenix pleads, blocking the doorway. "We found something that you both need to see." He spares Eli an uncertain look. "Out in the woods."

"I don't have time for this!" I exclaim.

"Trust me, make time. Seriously."

With a huff, I gesture for him to take the lead. Hudson still glowers at my luggage, but even he can't sway me. I've tried to fix the most broken of human beings, neglecting the very people who needed me most. I'm done.

We follow Phoenix out into the crisp morning air, skipping through the crowds going to breakfast and making a beeline for the perimeter. As we slink through the grounds, I realise where we're headed and draw to a halt.

"I've seen the damn chapel before. You're wasting my time."

"It's not the chapel," Phoenix mutters.

We head for the loose section of fence and all slip beneath it one by one, taking it in turns to watch out for patrolling guards before blending into the greenery.

I hesitate when we pass the chapel, heading into the wilderness beyond. This is way too far out to be safe. If we get caught out here, that'll be it. Attempted escapes are viewed as on par with the most serious transgressions.

It's a one-way ticket to an adjoining cell with Brooklyn.

If she's even still in Blackwood.

The thought pains me and I stuff it down. That girl has four men chasing her and zero regard for any of them. As much as part of me hates to admit it, I can't do it anymore—be her shining knight in armour. I know the truth now. She can't be fixed.

"Where are we going?" Hudson bellows.

"This is all private land," Phoenix answers, ducking beneath a thick willow tree. "We were on the roof last night for some fresh air and noticed smoke in the distance, barely visible. It was coming from this way, so we followed it."

"Private land owned by Blackwood," I supply. "And what the fuck are you doing skulking around out here? Are you trying to get yourself in trouble?"

Both still ignoring me, we emerge into a clearing. The caustic scent of smoke invades my lungs and I cough, peering through the murky haze. We're surrounded by so many trees, the outside world is completely obscured, making it the perfect hiding spot. In front of what appears to be a garage, the ashes of what must have been a huge bonfire remain.

"We found the guards out here last night," Phoenix explains.

"Doing what?"

His Adam's apple bobs as he gestures for me to approach the towering pile of ash and debris. I poke at it with my toe, stirring still-lit embers. A sickly sweet, cloying scent hangs in the air, and I can't put my finger on what it is, unlike anything I've ever smelled before.

"They came in vans, unloading these... bags. Long, thick bags." Phoenix shudders, reaching for Eli's hand. "We figured they were just burning trash. Standard, right?"

I make a non-committal hum while Hudson remains silent. Phoenix crouches down, reaching into the still-smoking ash. We all seem to take a collective breath as he wraps his fingers around a long, curved item.

I don't have a clue what it is until he offers it to me, my stomach suddenly twisting. Hudson claps my back as I try not to throw up, but his retort is cut off when he also gets a look at what's in Phoenix's hand.

A bone.

A fucking *human bone.*

"We saw who was in the bag, before they fed him to the flames."

Neither of us speaks for several loaded seconds, too shocked.

"Who?" I manage to ask.

Eli's soft rasp answers my question. "L-Leon."

The world grinds to a halt as we all stare down at the charred bone, lost for words. Hudson turns and walks away, fisting his hair before spinning back to face us. He seems completely lost, unable to tear his gaze from the bone Phoenix still holds.

"Leon was transferred."

"Officially," I comment.

"The same as Britt," he finishes.

This time, I puke my guts up until there's nothing left in me but regret. I allowed myself to believe that Rio was working alone, and the drugs were smuggled in like all places, through hidden channels. Unable to admit that I've helped my father invest in a conspiracy, which kills the sickest people in society for the past two years.

Fucking fool.

"They're killing patients and burning the bodies. Leon asked too many questions and he disappeared. Coincidence?" Phoenix looks between us all. "I think not. It's wakeup call time."

Hudson vocalises my worst fear.

"Do you think... they've killed her?"

None of us can answer that. Phoenix looks devastated while Eli's hands ball into fists, probably itching to cut. Hudson punches a tree and I barely hold on to my damn head.

We did this.

We didn't protect her.

"She's alive," Phoenix pleads to the universe.

"She has to be," Hudson adds.

Before we can all lose our shit, the hum of an approaching engine breaks the silence. I tackle Hudson back into the forest while Phoenix drags Eli to safety, the four of us watching as a convoy of blacked-out SUVs emerge from a dirt track and pull up in front of the garage.

All holding our breaths, none of us pay attention to our surroundings. The click of a gun directly behind us rings out like a bullet. I swallow hard, preparing to attack a guard if necessary, but I turn to find a familiar scowl instead.

"Someone want to tell me what you're all doing here?"

Sadie cocks the gun, not yet lowering it. Dressed in dark, stealthy clothing, she waits for our answer as I raise my hands.

"Want to answer that question yourself, huh?"

"You're the ones out of bounds," she retorts. "I have every right to be here, believe it or not."

"You have the right to threaten patients with that thing too?"

"You shouldn't be here." Sadie flashes me a warning look. "This is beyond you. Go back to the institute and forget everything you've seen here. You hear me?"

"That's not happening. Explain yourself," Phoenix snaps.

Just as she begins to offer another half-assed excuse, shouting has us all turning back to the unfolding scene. The doors to the cars are slamming shut, various armed guards flooding out.

We all watch in disbelief as the trunk is opened and something is thrown out with a heavy thud. Another thick, body-shaped bag that leaves little to the imagination.

"What the fuck?" I hiss.

"Shut your mouth or we'll all be dead," Sadie whispers.

When Jefferson's boots hit the ground, I see red. That slimy fuck has been bad news since day one. He unzips the bag, revealing the horror to us all.

The man inside is full of blood-stained bullet holes, his chest practically shredded. I study his slack face, something nudging at the back of my mind.

I know him.

I think… he works with my father.

Double fuck.

"Dispose of the body. We can't have word of this getting out."

Augustus's voice precedes him sliding from the back of the SUV, flicking invisible lint from his coat. Jefferson nods, beckoning for his boys to come and drag the corpse away to be burned.

"As far as the board is concerned, Martin retired and relocated to South America," Jefferson states.

"Make it all legitimate. No loose ends," Augustus instructs.

"Yes, sir. What about her?"

The other rear door opens and when a pale, scarred arm falls out, I'm scared half to death. Hudson curses up a storm and receives a warning smack from Phoenix, silencing him.

We all watch with bated breath as the rest of a bloody, limp Brooklyn is shoved from the car. Searching for signs of life, I study the rise and fall of her chest.

She's alive.

The sheer relief of our group is palpable.

"Return her to the Z Wing before the drugs wear off," Augustus says, studying her prone form. "Take Seven too. I'll need to do some reconditioning, set up the machines. He's become… emotional. Compromised."

In tandem with his words, another person exits the car, this one standing unassisted. I frown at the gangly man, his tuxedo failing to hide his obvious malnutrition and recent beating.

With his face hidden, none of us can determine his identity. Probably another poor bastard under Augustus's almighty thumb. He kneels beside our fucking girl, cradling her to his chest.

"I'll kill him for touching her," Hudson vows.

"Tell your inner alpha-hole to calm down already."

"Shut it, Kade. Else I'll break your neck too."

"Just look. He isn't the one hurting her."

We all watch as the skeletal man tucks loose hair behind Brooklyn's ear, almost tenderly. They're both bundled into another car, this one not stained with a dead man's blood, and driven back to the institute.

It takes a while for the remaining guards to finish up and once everyone is gone, corpse and all, we face each other. Unblinking and astonished.

"I have to go," Sadie declares.

"Hold up. You need to explain yourself."

She glares at me. "Not now. Go back to the dorms and keep your stupid heads down for once. Stay out of trouble and leave this to me."

Pocketing her weapon, she races back through the trees before I can ask what the hell she's talking about. The others don't even bother to watch her go, staring at the place where Brooklyn's battered body fell to the ground.

"What have they done to her?" Phoenix snarls.

I'm caught off guard by a sudden blow as Hudson delivers one of his classic right hooks, sending my glasses flying. He boots me in the ribs for good measure and I fall to the forest floor, cradling my stomach.

"I told you!" he shouts. "You laughed in my goddamn face and called me crazy. *Delirious.* I've been telling you all for months that Augustus is bad news. He pulled the strings behind Rio, Jack, fucking Lazlo. All of it."

Offering me a hand up, Phoenix shoots him an exasperated look. "Is this really the time to start turning on each other? We've all made mistakes, including you."

Before Hudson can give him a matching black eye to mine, I clamber to my feet and wipe the blood from my mouth.

"You're right. I was wrong. Shit, I was so stupid."

"Music to my fucking ears," Hudson thunders.

Peering around the deserted clearing, Eli remains silent. Somehow, he seems less shocked by all this. Like he somehow knew the darkness of Blackwood runs far deeper than any of us could have ever anticipated. He's learned to see the absolute worst in people after all he's been through.

Phoenix bites his lip. "What do we do now?"

Facing the family that a mere hour ago, I intended to abandon and leave behind, I realise what must be done. It won't be easy. It won't be legal. I'm not even sure if it's possible.

But it is necessary, for myself and those I love, to survive whatever nightmare this place has in store. Hudson was right—I can't leave. The work isn't done. I'm not ready to go.

Not without them.

"We prepare," I state with conviction.

They all turn to look at me.

"For what?"

Meeting each of their eyes, my decision is sealed.

"To leave Blackwood Institute. All of us. For good."

CHAPTER 31
BROOKLYN

WHAT YOU NEED - BRING ME THE HORIZON

THE SOUND of the cell door slamming open startles me awake. My head pounds from the drug-hangover of whatever they used to knock me out, bitter acid weighing heavy on my tongue.

Vision clearing, I squint and realise I'm back in the isolation chamber. Curled up in the furthest corner, every inch of skin on show, covered in bruises and dried blood. I blink and find Jefferson grinning at me.

"There she is."

"What... how... how did I get here?"

He snorts. "Rough night? You did good. I saw what they brought back, you must've unloaded the whole clip into that asshole. Impressive work."

His words spark understanding, the rush of memories making me even more dizzy. Martin pinning me down. The finger-shaped bruises on my inner thighs. His leer as he palmed his cock. Tears and begging. Blood and bullets and shattered bone. Two awaiting clowns, smiling with the pride of sadistic parents.

Oh my God.

Kade's father.

Kade's motherfucking father.

"I'm going to be sick," I declare.

Jefferson rolls his eyes, waiting for me to finish heaving. My stomach is cramping hard from not eating for so long, and when I'm done losing my mind, he disappears before returning with a bowl of soup. I greedily gulp it down, accepting a bottle of water too.

"You'll be pleased to learn that it's your lucky day."

I rub my temples. "Tell that to my head."

"Quit moaning. I checked your dose myself. You're fine."

Tossing a random bundle of clothes at me, Jefferson's impassive face gives nothing away. Even as I stare and wait for him to turn his back, he continues to watch me with that damned grin.

The blood-stained silk dress hangs from my body, and I refuse to break eye contact as I pull it off, tossing the balled-up fabric aside. I'm tossed another water bottle and use this one to clean off as much skin as possible, the water trails coming away bright red.

"A shower would be nice," I mutter.

"I ain't waiting around for you to get yourself all dolled up, inmate."

"Fuck you, Jefferson. Even prisoners get basic human rights."

"You're not a prisoner."

"Then what am I?"

He drags his filthy gaze down my body. "You're nothing. You don't exist."

Yanking the oversized shirt over my head, I manage to get my legs beneath me and draw up the faded jeans, pooling around my ankles. I'm sure I could rival Seven with my skeletal body at this point, but I feel physically ill after eating only a bowl of soup.

As quickly as I'm up, my legs give out and I nearly fall flat on my face. Jefferson has to hold me by the waist to steady me, much to his amusement. The entire room lies crooked and wobbly, with the after-effects of the drugs still to wear off.

"You're wrong," I gasp.

"How's that?"

"I exist. You can't take that away from me."

Laughing some more, Jefferson drags me from the isolation chamber, out into the corridor of the Z Wing. "You belong to Blackwood. Property—that's all you're allowed to be now."

Before I can attempt to summon the strength to argue, the most harrowing scream rattles the doors of each cell along the corridor. The level of pain and misery in that cry for help doesn't bear thinking about.

"See what happens when you let sentiment get the best of you?" Jefferson sneers.

"You took Patient Two's eyes. What else could you possibly do to her?" I ask, almost afraid to hear the answer.

"That isn't her screaming."

"What?"

"Shut it. No more talking."

I'm escorted down the winding corridors and back up to the main basement level. Deposited in Augustus's empty office, the screaming still echoes in my head. I pace the thick carpet, my strength slowly coming back to me, itching to escape far from this hellish place.

It was Seven screaming. I want to claw my way out of here and take him with me. The thought of them hurting Seven... hurts me.

I'm fucking screwed.

Halting beside the framed photograph on the wall, I stare at the grainy version of Lazlo, surrounded by his loyal nurses. Seeing him in the flesh, not some twisted hallucination... it's surreal.

I remember the day I ran from this very office, convinced that I'd conjured the entire nightmare. He took the time to destabilise me. Lie to me. Twist my mind into whatever he saw fit. I hope that whatever Augustus did to him, it hurt.

"Miss West?"

Augustus leans against his desk, watching me carefully. I don't return to my usual place, needing the distance as he takes his seat. His claws are so deep in my mind, I'm no longer in control.

"I just wanted to thank you for your work before you return upstairs."

My eyes snap to his in shock. "You're letting me out?"

He watches me closely, fingers laced. "You did as required. That deserves a reward, don't you think? You may return upstairs and see your friends again."

"What's the catch?"

"No catch, Miss West."

Hugging myself, I wait for him to laugh and throw me back in a cell. It's a game. He's doing it again; fucking with my head, dangling false hope to break my spirit just a little more. He waits, watching and smiling, for me to thank him. I'd rather die. I know what this is—a distraction.

"Why does Kade's father work with you?"

Augustus sighs, leaning back in his seat. "Don't ask questions when you aren't ready for the answers. Get out of my sight before I change my mind. You don't want to insult my generosity now, do you?"

Despite being tempted to fight it out to the ugly end, demand the truth no matter what it costs me... I'm so goddamn tired. I want to see the sun and sleep in an actual bed. To wear my own clothes and have a hot, uninterrupted shower.

But most of all, I want to see the guys. Even if they need to shout and scream at me for all I've done, tell me they hate me and never want to see my face again. I'll take it. I'll take whatever the hell I can get.

"Needless to say, I'm counting on your discretion," Augustus adds.

"What does that mean?"

"Our work is to be treated with the utmost confidentiality. You are not to breathe a word to anyone about the events of the past few months, up to and including last night."

"You want me to lie to the people I love," I supply.

"Alternatively, they may take your place in the Z Wing if you prefer. Seven's cell has some extra space while he's..." Catching himself, Augustus chuckles. "Back in treatment."

Unable to begin to unravel that statement, I glance towards the door, too nervous to move. Augustus watches to see if I dare take his dangled gift.

"Go ahead," he encourages.

Reluctantly, I lay my hand on the door handle and attempt to find some courage. Once open, I peer out into the corridor, my heart battering my rib cage. Freedom is right there.

"Miss West," Augustus calls.

Here it comes. The inevitable laughter, dragging me back to my cell and rolling in the hose. More starvation and mind games. Videos from my childhood and evil taunting.

"Enjoy your day," he finishes.

Blinking, I wait for the punchline. It never comes. Seizing hold of the single, solitary scrap of hope that remains, I run. Feet pounding against the floor, followed closely by my escort back to the world of the living.

As I emerge into the reception, Jefferson hot on my heels, I have to squint against the bright sunlight. This is a hollow victory.

All I can think about is Lazlo releasing my mother back into the world after 'fixing her', testing his work and how much control he had over her from afar. Look how that turned out. This isn't a reward. I'm a guinea pig, a ticking time bomb.

"Off you go then." Jefferson sighs, seemingly disappointed to lose his plaything.

"What day of the week is it?"

"Sunday. Your friends are eating breakfast."

Looking down at my borrowed clothes, blood-stained skin, and wrists lined with obvious bruises, I feel utterly exposed.

"I can't walk in there like this."

Jefferson digs his fingers into my arm. "We took care of your accident with Britt. You're going to play along and act normal. Just remember, we have eyes everywhere. One step out of line and I'll know."

I hate to even think it, but I feel completely alone as Jefferson leaves me to face the music. There's comfort in repeated, brutal torture and humiliation. You learn how to close yourself off, make yourself small and insignificant enough to survive. Dealing with the consequences of my actions is far more terrifying.

I can't face them.

They can never know what I've become.

Stuck on the threshold of the cafeteria, I make myself peek inside at the crowd of patients fuelling up for the day. Guards watching them all, more sinister now than ever before.

How many know what happens here? Who else has come under Augustus's scrutiny, ready for admittance to the Z Wing? Are there more stooges ensuring his experiment continues uninterrupted?

Shaking all over and entirely overwhelmed, tears begin to fall down my cheeks. Looking over to our table is worse torture than the chamber ever could be. My heart seizes at the sight of all four guys, eating and talking, like their world continues to exist without me—while I'm nothing without them.

I can't move.

I'm stuck. Trapped behind glass.

They're eating. Breathing. Living.

"You should go to them."

Jumping out of my skin, I clutch my chest and find Logan there, as always, ready with some more words of wisdom. Like he never even left.

"I c-can't."

"Please, Brooke. Don't be alone, family is important. Go be part of it."

I shake my head. "I'm not part of it anymore."

He watches me with such sadness, like he wants to say more but can't. I manage an awful smile, looking back at the table. I've been gone for who knows how long. Of course, they had to carry on living. So why does it hurt so goddamn badly?

Leaving me in peace, Logan melts into the crowd as patients leave the cafeteria, heading for classes. It almost seems real, this illusion. Cleverly constructed to hide the truth. I can't lie to all four of them, protecting Augustus and his madness.

Sudden heat flushes through me as I realise that I've been spotted. Managing to meet his haunted, emerald gaze, I watch Eli filter through the stages of shock. He's so fucking beautiful. Cheekbones sharp enough to slice my flesh and lips begging to clean my bloodied wounds.

His mouth drops open slightly, like he isn't convinced I'm not a ghost. Lamely, I raise my hand and offer him a dejected wave.

That's all he needs.

My mind has always been his wonderland.

Without disturbing the others, Eli deposits his tray and makes a beeline for me. I turn and run away before anyone else can follow, not ready to face them all at once. Waiting outside for him to catch up, soft footsteps join me.

I wait for his rejection.

It doesn't come.

His fingers link with mine, like they were made to be.

"You didn't have to follow," I say defeatedly.

The light squeeze of Eli's hand signals his disagreement.

"I shouldn't have come back. You're safer far away from me."

Eli hugs me tight enough to make my ribs creak. It's all I need. A hello and goodbye wrapped into one tragic moment. His soft curls rub against my cheek, and I bathe in his scent that smells more like home than any building ever could. He's my safe place. My twin flame. My fucking partner in darkness.

I wonder if I'm his.

I wonder what my insanity tastes like to him.

"Missed... y-you," he manages to whisper.

"Fuck, Eli. I missed you too," I croak.

Drinking me in with his eyes, he smiles. I'm tugged along, through the quad, without looking to see where we're going. I don't need to know. Eli is my guiding light. He always has been.

Passing the deserted dorms and guards that now seem to know exactly who I am, we reach the perimeter. Eli wrestles with an older, rotting section of the security fence, creating a new hole.

I don't worry about the cameras.

Augustus can't do anything worse to me.

Wading through shrubbery and billowing trees, we're soaked to the bone from the drizzling clouds. I greedily gulp in the scent of fresh rainfall, thankful for the first time in my life for such a small thing.

We eventually reach the graveyard, overgrown and abandoned, just as I remember it. It feels like forever ago since our first time on those steps, interrupted by guards who knew exactly where we were.

This is Augustus.

Bring the asset back in range or pack your bags.

It was his first appearance in my life before I even knew it, ordering the guards to track us down. The devil was at the door all along.

We collapse before the mausoleum.

I try to find words and fail.

Both of our tongues have been stolen.

Letting my head fall to his shoulder, Eli's hand refuses to leave mine. We cling to each other for safety, and the horrors of the basement slip away. It's just us—two broken souls, finding a semblance of peace in one another.

Eli squeezes my fingers again, and I know he wants an explanation. I have nothing to offer. Even if Augustus covered my actions up, the guys know. Hudson saw the whole thing. They've seen for themselves who I truly am.

"I'm so fucking sorry," I stutter.

Eli lets out a long exhale. "No."

"Don't make excuses for me."

"No."

"Stop saying no. Christ, I shouldn't be here."

Grabbing me by the chin, Eli makes me look at him. So many words brim in his forest green eyes; there's a fountain of emotion waiting to be released from his frozen lips.

Instead, I kiss him. A pure, simple kiss. An apology. He guides my head down to his lap, letting me lay across him while holding me close. My eyes fall shut as tears continue to burn my skin.

"Sometimes, I wonder if the world outside Blackwood really exists," I say, not bothering to hide my broken pieces any longer. "There has to be more to life than this. Else what would be the point in living? I don't want to if this is it."

"This... isn't l-living," Eli struggles out, his body quaking with anxiety. "But... one d-day..." Ducking his head low to meet me, he guides my lips to his again. "We w-will."

Without opening my eyes, we drink each other in like desperate lovers, separated by a chasm of death. His tongue claims every inch of my mouth, and I tug on his hair, taking every ounce of his mind, body, and soul for my own. I bury the stolen pieces of him deep inside, locked down tight where no one can ever take them away.

Opening my eyes, I offer a pathetic smile. "You will. I'll never leave this place. Not now."

Pressing a gentle kiss to the tip of my nose, Eli shakes his head. "T-together... or n-not at all." His grip on my chin tightens as his lips sweep across my cheeks, kissing tears away. "W-won't leave y-you behind. R-rather d-die... than live... without y-you."

I can't help but let out a watery laugh.

"I love you too damn much to drag you down with me."

"Don't... c-care. Together... n-not at all."

The stubborn, incredible son of a bitch rests his forehead against mine. Breathing each other's air, we make two halves of one damaged whole.

I stare deep into his irises. "Swear it."

He cocks an eyebrow in question.

"Swear that you'll always be mine, and you won't ever forget me. Swear that no matter what happens, you'll still be my monster. I love you and I need you to swear on your goddamn life that you love me too, because I'm an unstable, fucked-up murderer who can't live without you."

The confession exhausts me.

I prepare for him to leave.

Instead, Eli's face lights up with a soul-destroying grin.

"Yes," he whispers.

"Yes?"

"I s-swear."

"Then it's a deal."

With nothing but the whispered promises that bind us, I could die happy with no regrets. Eli's smile doesn't fade, and I know what's coming. His penknife glints in the spring sunshine and I bite my lip, anticipating his next moves.

This is how we began.

Sealed in blood and sickness.

It's only fitting, this should be our end.

I leave the comfort of his lap, laying back on the cold stone of the mausoleum where six months earlier, he sliced me open when I couldn't cut myself. This time, it's different. I'm offering my body for slaughter.

Eli lifts the borrowed shirt, disregarding blood and bruises, kissing across the scarred expanse of my stomach. He rolls the jeans down low enough to expose my hip, casting me a final look for confirmation.

"Trust... m-me?"

I nod, savouring his gruff voice. "Always."

Holding the penknife in his practised grip, I stifle a hiss of pain as the blade meets my skin. At first, I think he's just cutting me, but the tip of his knife glides further across my flesh. I don't need to look, I trust him with my entire life.

With his careful work complete, Eli sits back on his heels and brings the bloodied blade to his lips. This time, I watch with fascination as he carefully licks along the edge, lapping up every drop of my warm blood.

His jeans bulge from the sheer pressure of his erection and he looks back down at me with indescribable need. I peer down my body, burning with curiosity.

When I find his handiwork, I can't help but grin at the macabre pronouncement of love. *Perfect*. Eli settles on his back beside me, holding the penknife out for me to take.

He lifts his shirt, exposing washboard abs and that mouth-watering trail of hair heading straight down. I straddle his body with ease and accept the blade, ready to copy his design.

When I'm done, we match perfectly.

Donec mors nos separavit.

Both claimed by the other, each sentence cut deep enough to scar perfectly, leaking sweet crimson droplets on to the desecrated stone beneath us.

"What does it mean?"

"Until d-death... do us p-part," he whispers.

I smile, shaking my head. It's enough. Eli will always be enough. No matter the cost, or how much of myself I have to tear off in strips and sacrifice to ensure his continued safety.

I'll protect the heart he's been brave enough to gift me until my last fucking breath. No matter what it takes, he will watch the sun rise outside of this damned place. He will see the world and *live*.

I'll ensure it.

Even if it's the last thing I do.

"Get over here and fuck me," I beg shamelessly. "Make me forget, just for a minute. I'm too scared to face them."

Without complaint, Eli rips his shirt off completely, pausing to admire his new, bloodied brand for a moment. The words are a little wonky from my shaking hand but he grins regardless.

"Babygirl," he manages to say.

"Yeah?"

Spreading my legs and settling between them, he crushes his lips to mine, stealing the air straight from my lungs. When we break apart, there's courage in his voice.

"I… l-love you."

I blink away tears. "I love you too, Eli."

CHAPTER 32
HUDSON
FUCK IT - GLASS TIDES

IT TAKES every single ounce of control I possess not to break her door down. Self-growth, I know. This girl is making me fucking soft.

Lungs seizing from sprinting all the way back to Oakridge, a single text message burning a hole through my mind, I finally reach my destination. Phoenix and Kade won't be far behind, it went out to all of us.

Our lighthouse beckoning us home.

She's back.

Eli finds me first, legs crossed as he sits smoking in her window. Raising a hand to warn me from ripping the bathroom door off its hinges, he gestures for me to sit down. I can hear the shower running inside. My blackbird is inches away, the closest she's been for so goddamn long.

"When?" I demand.

He shrugs.

"Why did she come to you first?"

Eli gestures again for me to sit.

"You should have called sooner."

"Sit," he whispers hoarsely.

Too shocked to yell further, I sink on to Brooklyn's mattress. It isn't long before the door opens again, Phoenix near-falling across the threshold in his rush to get inside. Kade follows much more subdued, his face betraying his nerves.

He feels responsible.

None of us were prepared for the truth.

There's plenty of blame to go around.

"Where is she?" Phoenix snaps.

Eli points towards the bathroom, warning him with his eyes. It speaks to how much we've changed, seeing Eli dish out the orders for once. She's changed us. Made us more than we were, softer around the edges. Something has come out of all this pain.

Hope.

Goddamn motherfucking hope.

Kade rests against the wall, arms crossed. He still won't look at me fully. Janet is alive, discharged from hospital and begrudgingly staying with her sister while Kade's father is away on business.

Surrendering control has been hard for him, I know that. But there's a little too much bad blood between us right now for me to do any comforting. I can't think about him or his father without needing to punch something.

"How is she?" Phoenix asks.

Accepting Eli into his embrace, I watch the pair exchange a kiss.

"Any idea how she got out?" I add.

Eli doesn't answer either of us, shrugging again. We'll have to wait and find out. The shower seems to run forever, a soundtrack to our anxious wait.

Kade jiggles his leg, and Phoenix smokes two cigarettes, physically twitching with anticipation. When it shuts off, we all stand a little taller—ready to finally step up to the plate, once and for all.

The door opens and I lose all rational ability to remain calm. She emerges like a rabbit in a snowstorm, near-invisible skin on a skeleton, so far from the beautiful creature I've loved for near-on six fucking years.

Squeezing water from her straggly ash hair, Brooklyn freezes, wrapped in a towel that fails to hide all she's endured.

"Blackbird," I whisper reverently.

Grey pinpoints of devastation find me.

"Hudson."

With everyone else frozen on the spot, I inch closer. We're all drinking her in, unsure of how to respond. Brooklyn's light on her feet, ready to run at any given moment. I study her black eye, bruised face and arms, ghostly complexion, and marked weight loss.

They've taken everything from her.

But they haven't taken us.

"Can I…" I clear my throat. "Hold you?"

Retrieving yoga pants and a white shirt from her wardrobe—one of mine, which makes my heart fucking flip like a dewy-eyed virgin—she nods.

I cross the room, careful to take it slow. I've never taken anything slow in my entire life, but for her… I do.

Opening my arms, I let her close the final metre separating us. She's reluctant at first, before colliding into me so hard, I almost lose my balance. Sweeping her off her feet, her face buried in my neck, I feel myself deflate at last.

"You feel so fucking good in my arms," I admit.

"Don't let go. Please… fuck. Just don't."

Her voice breaks as she trails off. Distantly, I realise that she's crying. Awful, ugly sobs that are completely unlike the person I know. The emotion shocks the shit out of me, but I cling on tighter, somehow hoping she will slip beneath my skin like a phantom and stay there, where I can keep her safe.

Phoenix coughs behind us. "Firecracker?"

Brooklyn's head lifts and I know the moment she locks eyes with him, braving a smile. "Hey trouble."

"Can I get in on the action?"

Releasing her, she pads over to Phoenix and engulfs him in a desperate hug. Kade decides to stop being a spineless shit and pushes off from the wall, waiting his turn. The last bit of tension drains out of her at his reassurance.

I'm her protector.

Phoenix, her reason to smile.

Kade is her certainty.

And Eli... her equal in the dark.

"Back together." She sighs.

"And nothing will change that ever again," I vow.

———

Amongst the pain, separation, and carnage, there's a final afternoon of something resembling actual living.

We don't talk about Augustus or the bloody, bullet-filled body. Britt's death or the burnt remains of countless bodies in the woods. We don't even acknowledge that the ground is preparing to open and swallow us whole.

We all sense it—that our time in Blackwood will come to an end soon, one way or another. So, instead, we do the one logical thing in the face of impending doom.

We go swimming.

By some miracle, the guards are preoccupied with a nasty fight kicking off outside the cafeteria, leaving the five of us to head for the gym. We choose a time to sneak in when it will be deserted for an hour, while the rest of the institute eats lunch.

The pool, in typical Blackwood style, is a glimmering jewel of polished marble. Olympic-sized with high, gothic windows and touches of stained glass, it undoubtedly features on the slick marketing campaign dished out to executives looking to invest in Augustus's madness.

For good measure, we barricade the door.

Fuck Blackwood.

We owe them nothing now.

Phoenix quickly strips down to his boxers, and cannonballs into the water, letting out a scream as he soaks us all.

"Last one in is a loser!" he calls.

"You're the only loser here, Nix," I shout back.

Retreating to the safety of a bench in the corner, Eli keeps his clothes in place and watches us all instead, this huge grin splitting his mouth.

I hold Brooklyn's hand as she leans heavily on me, begging me with her eyes not to hound her with the million questions waiting to be answered.

It can all wait.

For now, we're alive.

"Coming in?"

Biting her lip, she nods. "In a minute."

Testing my new-found control even further, I leave her by the side of the pool and strip off my own t-shirt and jeans. Her eyes swallow me whole, lingering on the inked bird I so proudly boast below my heart.

I still remember getting it, three years after the last time we spoke. She owned my heart, even then. I thought of her every fucking day, and no matter what she believes, I did look for her.

Our girl.

My fucking blackbird.

"You just gonna stand there?" Phoenix jeers.

"Be careful watch you wish for, motherfucker."

I cannonball into the pool, near drowning him on purpose. Gliding along the bottom, he doesn't see me coming until I leap on his back, tackling him back underwater. We fight, coughing and spluttering, both vying to drown the other.

Naturally, I win.

"Okay, okay. Truce!" he splutters.

I grin, wiping water from my eyes. "Pussy."

"Some of us aren't built like a goddamn truck."

"Fine, pick a game. I'll still beat your scrawny ass."

Phoenix narrows his eyes, climbing out to search for a ball to play with. While waiting, I look back to the side of the pool. Kade has braved to sit down next to Brooklyn, and after half an hour of awkward silence, he's finally talking.

Based on the way their hands clutch one another while exchanging whispers, it's an apology. Perhaps now, he can heal. Don't we all deserve to be forgiven? Perhaps not. I'm not certain that I do. But Kade... he does.

One day, I'll tell him myself.

After punching the stupid idiot.

Many, many times.

Phoenix leaps back in, engaging me in a game of volleyball, while Kade strips off and joins us. He's wearing a smile for the first time in weeks, and I can't help but return it, even while aiming the ball at his head a little too hard.

"Sorry, didn't see you there." I smirk.

He plucks the ball from the water, flexing his biceps. "That's it, game on. You know I was the school champion, right?"

"Yeah, yeah. I remember the fucking medals."

Phoenix swims over to me, teaming up against Kade. "I think we can take him, Hud. Medals be damned."

"Bring it." Kade laughs.

We play until we can barely move, bruised and battered from the world's most aggressive game of volleyball. Phoenix reluctantly declares Kade the winner, climbing out to find Eli and cover him in water while snuggling him to death.

Even I'll admit, they're cute.

Brooklyn watches them with contentment, and they watch right back, both fucking enamoured with her like the rest of us.

"Blackbird?" I call out.

She sits at the edge, yoga pants rolled up high on her calves so she can dip her feet in the water. Glancing up at me, the corner of her mouth turns up in a brief smile.

"What's up?"

"Are you just gonna sit there?"

"I'm not getting in. It's too cold."

"Don't be a wimp, it soon warms up."

Rolling her eyes, Brooklyn flips me off.

"It's pretty cold," Kade chimes in.

"Shut it, champ. I want a rematch."

Diving back under, I yank him into the water as I pass, swimming over to Brooklyn. Her legs part to let me between them and before she can protest, I grab her by the waist and hoist her in, relishing her adorable squeal.

With her ethereal white hair slicked back, Brooklyn faces me with some of her usual fire. "You're an asshole."

I nearly choke on my relief.

"Say it again."

"Hudson Knight. You're a fucking asshole."

Goddammit, that's my girl. I press her against the side of the pool, letting her feel my hard dick that soon stands to attention. She gasps a little, staring at me through her lashes like a goddamn avenging angel.

I've never been a fan of this sharing shit. We've made a hell of a mess of it, a little too broken to manage something so complex without making mistakes. But right now, I'd like nothing more than to fuck her pussy in front of all my brothers— let them hear her scream for me in person.

"Hudson," she repeats breathily.

"I love it when you say my name."

"That's because you're an egotist."

"Ouch. Well, doc. What treatment would you advise for a self-obsessed prick like me?"

Wrapping her legs around my waist, her t-shirt completely see-through in the water, Brooklyn purses her lips into a pout. "I have many suggestions. None of them PG-rated or safe for public."

Glancing around the room, I find Kade watching us intently from the other side of the pool, while Eli and Phoenix canoodle in the corner. I want her. We all do. My blackbird and all her ugly, shattered pieces are worth sharing.

"Something tells me they won't mind," I whisper conspiratorially.

"What about you?"

"Put it this way, I'm curious."

Letting my lips trail around to her ear lobe, Brooklyn is free to look over my shoulder and see for herself. Everyone is entranced. She throws her head back, letting me slip my hand around her throat. Even as they all watch, I make it clear that she's still mine.

Dragging my hand over her soaked t-shirt, I pinch her nipple visible through the fabric, rolling the bud between my fingers. Brooklyn grinds against me, torturing my rock-hard dick that wants nothing more than to be buried inside of her. But if we're gonna do this, then I'm sure as hell doing it properly.

Holding her to my chest, I climb out of the pool and grab one of the guys' towels, spreading it across the floor. Brooklyn lets me lay her down, stripping the t-shirt from her body.

I find her lips and ravage her, leaving any trace of my previous gentleness behind. She takes it all, biting back with teeth clashing and hips grinding, losing all control.

When we break apart, I find Kade has climbed out to inch closer. He watches—fascinated, intrigued… hungry.

"Care for a taste, brother?"

Kade swipes his golden hair back, gulping hard. Phoenix and Eli haven't moved from their spot, still wrapped around each other, both looking at Brooklyn spread out beneath me. I smirk and Phoenix grins, grabbing a handful of Eli's hair before slamming his lips against his.

"Kade," Brooklyn whimpers. "Come."

Deliberating for a split-second, Kade sinks down beside her, sparing me a nervous look.

"Don't worry, I won't kill you this time."

"How reassuring." He sighs.

True to my word, I give him enough space to gather Brooklyn into a whirlwind kiss. The whole time, my hands remain secured to her hips. As Kade ravishes our girl, I slowly peel the wet yoga pants from her legs, finding her pantiless and soaked for me.

Placing soft kisses along her inner thigh, ignoring the fresh cuts that I'm certain Eli had something to do with, another mark makes me freeze. Black bruises. *Fucking fingerprints.*

"What the fuck?" I bellow.

Kade takes a look for himself, blanching, while Brooklyn attempts to push my worried hands away. There's no excuse to offer. Someone had their fucking hands on her.

"It's okay," she offers.

"Nothing about this is okay. I want a name."

"There isn't one. You don't need to worry about this."

Grabbing her by the hair, I drag her lips to mine and bite down, waiting for the blood to flow. She writhes in my grip, whimpering as I lick the copper flow straight from her mouth. Like I can find the truth she so desperately wants to hide entwined in her blood.

"Hudson…" Kade begins.

I silence him with a single look.

Dragging Brooklyn's legs open, I run my index finger between her pussy lips, drenched and begging for my cock. Pinching her clit before sliding a finger inside her, she moans in pleasure.

"You like that, baby?"

"Yes."

I'll torture the answer out of her if I have to. Adding another finger, I watch as she grinds against my hand, so quickly entranced by a single touch. Then I rip my hand away, right before she can come.

"Fuck!" she hisses.

"I said, answer the goddamn question."

"We're not playing this game, Hudson."

"Then answer. Simple as that."

Brooklyn glares, turning to Kade. Punishing me, she drags his lips to hers. *Fucker*. Then with her foot, she kicks me aside and climbs into Kade's lap, straddling his wet boxer shorts.

I should kill them both.

No one disregards me.

Reaching into his boxers, she frees Kade's cock and strokes, making him hiss. Even if she's touching him, it's so hot to watch her take control. Kade soon gets comfortable, regardless of his audience. She repositions herself, lining him up to her entrance.

"Wait—"

Ignoring Kade, she sinks down on him before any of us can get a word in. We all watch him groan, his head falling back as he grabs hold of her hips. Phoenix and Eli have paused to observe, both mesmerised while touching the other.

"You wanted me to wait?"

"Hell no," Kade grunts.

"I can play games too," she throws at me.

Chuckling, Kade shoots me a smug grin. He meets Brooklyn thrust for thrust, finding his rhythm. He's loving this—watching her bring me to my goddamn knees for the whole group to see.

I'll show them. Spotting my chance, I toss all reservations aside, needing to feel her around me before I lose my mind.

"Fine. Let's play," I declare.

Looming behind Brooklyn, I run a hand over the soft curve of her ass. Kade slows to spare me a look, a question in his eyes. I expect him to back out when he realises what I'm planning, but he just continues fucking my blackbird right in front of me.

With my fingers on Brooklyn's lips, I whisper in her ear.

"Suck, now."

Her smile grows dark. "Yes... *Daddy*."

"Say that again and I ain't fucking sharing."

Acting all innocent, she obediently swirls her tongue over my fingers. Once they're lubed up, I kiss my way down her spine, bringing my fingers to her tight asshole.

She tenses, still riding Kade's cock as I gently slide one finger inside. Hissing out a breath, she clings even tighter to Kade.

"You still want my brother more than me?" I demand.

"Dickhead," she gasps.

After working it in and out to prepare her, I add another slick finger, stretching her back entrance wider. She isn't fighting me, which makes me wonder what she and the two dickheads in the corner have been up to.

Right on cue, Phoenix grins at me.

Bastard.

I try not to get jealous at the thought, but find myself fantasising instead about what it would be like to pass her around the entire group. Clearly, that game of volleyball gave me a concussion.

Brooklyn begins to tremble as Kade thrusts into her, while I continue to play with her asshole. Knowing that she's done this already helps, even if it was with the smug pair in the corner.

Fisting my aching cock, I drop more saliva on to myself and work my shaft, spreading the moisture. I've never done this with someone else, let alone with my adoptive brother already inside her perfect pink cunt.

Extricating my fingers now that she's nice and relaxed, I press the head of my cock against her asshole in warning.

"Hudson..." she whimpers.

"Shhhh. Just relax, I'll take it easy."

Kade draws her in for an open-mouthed kiss, giving me time to spread more moisture over my length and her back entrance, getting her dripping and ready.

It takes all of my self-control to go slow, pushing into her inch by inch, even when she feels so heavenly around me. She gasps and holds on to Kade tight, gradually adjusting to the fullness.

It feels fucking incredible.

Who knew sharing her would be so goddamn hot?

"Okay?" I check in.

Looking over her shoulder, her hooded eyes meet mine.

"Are you going to fuck me now too?"

"Hell yeah, I am. Hold on, baby."

With measured strokes, I begin to move. Keeping it controlled, giving her time to shift if needed. Kade finds his rhythm and we work around each other in a sweaty, frantic tangle. It doesn't take long for Brooklyn to find what works.

Fucking Phoenix and Eli.

I'll kill them when I'm done here.

Shifting her hips to meet us both, she soon falls apart in an intense, blistering orgasm. I savour the incredible sight, biting down on her neck, sucking the soft flesh to leave a mark of my own.

"You're fucking mine, blackbird."

Kade breaks the kiss to say, "And mine."

"Don't forget about us!" Phoenix yells.

She garbles a response, too alight with sensation as we both fuck her into oblivion. Phoenix and Eli watch the performance, and I think they're touching each other too. Both turned on by the sight of our girl, filled to the brim.

The fantasy hits me again, and I wonder what it would be like for all of us to fuck her—one by one, after another. I'm surprised to realise the thought turns me on a hell of a lot.

Kade finishes first, grabbing Brooklyn by the throat as he climaxes. She can't hold her scream in, still holding on to him for balance as I pick up my pace, thrusting into her with more speed. I can't hold it for long, her asshole is so tight.

"Tell me who left the bruises," I command.

Cracking a hand on her butt cheek, she hisses out a breath.

"No... one..."

"You're lying to me."

Brooklyn tosses me a filthy look over her shoulder, gasping when I spank her again, jolting my cock still buried deep inside of her.

"Answer me."

"I'm trying... to protect you," she groans.

"We don't need your protection, blackbird."

Unable to hold back any longer, I grunt through my release, and she clenches around me, coming for a third time.

We all collapse together, warmth spilling between us. Brooklyn ends up half laying across Kade's chest while pooled in my lap, panting for air.

Phoenix hoots, making us all laugh.

"Fuck off, man." I grin at him.

"That was hot, you guys. And more than a little unexpected."

"You're telling me," Brooklyn grumbles.

Kade extricates himself from her arms, blushing now the moment is over. He's retreating inwards again, hiding from us. Grabbing his bicep, Brooklyn makes him look at her.

"Kade... please. You don't have to go."

He looks so uncertain, briefly glancing at me.

That's what this is about.

"It's fine," he mutters.

Brooklyn shoots me a glare that screams *fix this.* I've barely spoken to Kade in weeks, far too angry after our shouting match on the roof. Perhaps it's time I grew the hell up.

"Look, I'm fucking sorry," I concede, hating that damned pain in his eyes. "I shouldn't have said what I did. It was cruel, but I was so angry with you for what happened. But I guess... it isn't your fault."

"But it is," he replies sadly.

"All of us are guilty as hell. Let's call it even?"

Brooklyn smiles at me, proud of my shitty but heartfelt apology. Before I met her, I didn't know the meaning of the word *sorry.* Now I'm dishing it out left, right, and centre. She's a fucking vixen.

"I'm sorry too," Kade offers.

"That wasn't so hard, was it?" Brooklyn says.

Both tugging our clothes back into place and leaving her on the towel, we face each other. Kade claps me on the back, and I draw him in for a man-hug, squeezing him tight.

This is what we needed. Someone to bring us back together. It isn't the first time we've fallen out, and it won't be the last, but Brooklyn glues us together even when we can't do it ourselves.

She studies us both, her expression turning sad as she glances between us all, including where Phoenix and Eli remain in the corner.

It's almost like she's memorising this scene, like any moment could be her last on this godforsaken earth.

I won't allow that to happen.

Not this time.

CHAPTER 33
BROOKLYN

NOT JUST BREATHING - THE PLOT
IN YOU

HAMMERING on the door startles me awake.

I knew it was coming. Nothing good lasts.

Entangled in Phoenix's arms with Eli's head pooled on my chest, I'm trapped. Both are still asleep on the shared mattress we created by shoving the two beds together like usual.

We all piled back into the bedroom after dinner last night, creating a warm nest in which we could watch movies and cuddle.

Phoenix and Eli were very touchy-feely after my little performance with the Knight brothers, needing their own slice of the action. Not that I'm complaining. I could get used to this man-meat sandwich lifestyle.

"Door," Hudson moans from beneath the blankets.

Phoenix tightens his grip on my thigh which is drawn across his body, rubbing right up against his morning wood. I look over the rest of the dark room, finding Kade upright in bed.

"What time is it?"

"Seven o'clock," he groans.

"Fuck. I'll get it."

Disentangling myself from the guys, I fall out of bed and faceplant, much to Kade's amusement. Flipping him off, I yank my borrowed shirt down lower to cover my bare legs, stomping over to throw the door open.

"Miss West," Jefferson leers.

I consider slamming it, but settle on a glare instead.

"Fuck off, Jefferson."

"My my, aren't we brave in front of our little friends?" His grin turns serious. "You know the drill. I say jump, bitch. You say how high. Get your shit and move it."

"Blackbird? What's going on?"

Hudson joins me in the doorway, barely containing his snarl. Dressed in tight boxers that leave nothing to the imagination, his hair is a messy, nuclear bomb site that says far too much about what we spent the night doing.

"What the fuck do you want?" he growls.

Hand resting over his baton, Jefferson takes a menacing step forward. "Back away, inmate. Your girlfriend and I are going for a little walk."

"She's not going anywhere with you. We know our rights, asshole. You can't continue to detain her, not anymore."

This amuses Jefferson even more, his near-hysterical laughter far too loud for this early. "Your rights? Listen up, pal. You have the right to shut the fuck up while I take your girl back where she belongs—if you're done passing her ass around like a goddamn smoke, hmm?"

I should feel ashamed, I knew Augustus had to be watching us in the pool, keeping his eye out for any sign that I was going to break our deal. But somehow, knowing he was watching made it even sweeter. I hope the son of a bitch watched until the very end and saw just how much I enjoyed breaking his stupid rules.

Before Hudson can punch his lights out, Jefferson pins him up against the wall with his arm twisted behind his back, sparing me a cold look that screams of boredom.

"You ready? I can bring this loser too, if you'd like. Keep him company while the bossman deals with your delinquent ass."

When I don't answer, Jefferson yanks Hudson's arm higher until he groans in pain. It takes a lot to make my blue-eyed psychopath hurt, so I quickly back down.

"Jesus, stop. Give me two minutes, alright?"

"You have thirty seconds."

Releasing Hudson, Jefferson smirks at me and backtracks to wait outside. I take advantage and slam the door in his face, seized by a rush of fear. I don't want to go back down into the basement and face the devil in his designer suit.

"We're not doing this," Hudson yells, rounding on me. "I'm done pandering to these people like we have no choice. We can still fight back, they haven't taken that from us yet."

"I can't just ignore him. Augustus won't tolerate that."

"I don't give a fuck what he will tolerate. Look at yourself! Look at what he's done to you!" Hudson pushes me against the wall, gripping my arms hard enough to hurt. "I won't let you do this to yourself anymore. We can deal with his threats."

"You think I want to go?" I shout.

Having thrown a pair of sweats on, Kade rests his hand on Hudson's shoulder, ever the peacemaker.

"She's right. Until we can get the hell out of here, we have to play along. If they begin to suspect anything, we're all in trouble."

I gape at him. "What? Get out of here?"

Both ignoring me, the brothers are locked in an intense stare-off. The mere idea of leaving Blackwood has me too floored to question their silent conversation.

Escape.

A life outside of this place.

I take the brief, foolish flutter of hope and lock it away, dismissing the idea. It won't work, there's no running from this nightmare. It's too late.

Wherever we go, Augustus will always find me. He's too well-connected and I'm too valuable for him to simply let go. He will hurt those I care about just to get to me, and I can't let that happen.

Breaking free from Hudson's hold, I start pulling clothes on. Phoenix and Eli are now awake, watching me with matching expressions of fear. I offer them both a smile, knowing there's no point attempting to hide the truth anymore.

While I kept the details to a careful minimum when they grilled me the night before, they inevitably filled in a lot of the blanks.

Taking both of their hands, I let them draw me into their arms. Phoenix breathes me in, his heartbeat fast enough for me to feel, while Eli shakes all over. It feels inconceivable to me now that I chose to walk away from them before.

If nothing else, it taught me one thing—that when you find something worth fighting for, you hold the fuck on and don't let go. If I have to sacrifice myself to protect these four men, the pieces of my heart that I didn't even know I was missing, then so be it.

I'll walk away, even if it kills me inside.

I have no fucking choice.

I can't protect them from six feet under.

"Look after each other," I murmur.

Phoenix holds me tighter. "You're coming back."

"I know. But still, watch each other's backs. Please."

I squeeze Phoenix one last time before releasing him and turning to Eli. He looks terrified, full of uncertainty and rage. The scared boy hiding from the world I met so many months ago is creeping back in.

"Stop worrying. I made a promise, remember?" Glancing down at my hip, the throbbing engraving covered by my jeans, I tease a smile on to Eli's lips. "Til' death parts us. I'll be back, keep my side of the bed warm."

He nods once.

We sealed our promise in blood.

There's no breaking that.

Before I lose my shit, I follow Jefferson out into the corridor. I can't look at Hudson or Kade, both sharing furious whispers about what to do next. They try to follow, but Jefferson slams the door shut in their angry faces.

Rather than let him cuff me and enjoy my humiliation, I walk downstairs willingly. Head held high, back straight with determination.

All that matters now is keeping them safe. And if they can somehow get out, then I need to buy them enough time to burn this hellhole to the ground and run.

Even if I'm still inside.

I'll happily go down in flames... for them.

———

The familiar scratch of the needle provides a sharp burst of pain, as ice cold drugs rush into my bloodstream in what feels like a much-larger dose than usual. Peering down at me, Augustus slides the needle from my vein and smiles.

"Enjoy yourself, did you?"

With the numbness spreading like spilt blood, removing all feeling from my trembling body, I manage to throw him a filthy look before my facial muscles succumb.

"Screw you."

"Quite the performance." He chuckles. "I'll admit, it is fascinating to me. You five have banded together in the past six months beyond anything I've ever seen before. Creating a pseudo family unit, with all its necessary components. Perhaps it's something I should research further."

I'm unable to threaten him, too busy clinging to the vestiges of lucidity. Rather than remain in his office, Augustus escorts me down into the depths of the Z Wing, passing countless cells and their nameless inhabits.

My previous courage soon evaporates, and Jefferson slings me over his shoulder when I try to run. Instead of tossing me back into the chamber of death, we reach the end of the final corridor, entering a cavernous room that drips with darkness.

The damp walls permeate the air with mould and decay, with two single chairs placed in the exact centre. Handcuffed in place, I slowly lose grip of reality while facing the other empty seat.

Augustus checks his watch. "Bring them in."

Jefferson leaves his post in the corner, sparing me a lecherous look. Finding Logan in the other corner, watching over his boss like usual, he offers me a steadying look. Reminding me to keep my shit together, but it's no use. I'm too far gone, the voices whip through me against my will.

You've always been alone.

Unlovable.

Broken.

Monster.

Gathering around Augustus's ankles, the shadows twist and swirl in the dim light, gaining speed. I shake my head, trying to disperse the images that threaten to drown me. The drugs are fuelling whatever sickness rests ready and waiting within me, eager to obey.

"It's time for you to prove yourself worthy of continuing on my program," Augustus declares. "You've shown great potential, but *Brooklyn* cannot continue to work with me. She's too... human."

"I am a human being," I garble.

"You don't have to be," he corrects. "I won't kill you yet. Prove yourself to me and I will guarantee the safety of your family. Permanently. They won't be harmed for as long as you remain under my care... as Patient Eight."

A ghoulish figure strides from the shadows, as if spawning from Augustus's madness. His hair slick with fresh blood, body shredded by the frantic path of a blade that I know all too well. Vic crosses the dungeon, crouching down beside my chair with his sadistic smile in place.

Don't you see, baby?

We're inevitable.

Your life is worthless without me.

"Get away from me," I plead, the cuffs slicing into my wrists.

Then let him kill you.

Be mine, forever.

Parting the shadows engulfing me in terror, Augustus comes closer to examine me. He looks so desperate to reach into the deepest pits of my mind and study every last bit of damage he's inflicted. They blur together—Vic and Augustus, one real and one a horrifying ghost.

"You will comply, Patient Eight. You have no other choice."

Tearing my gaze away from the storm of shadows infecting every inch of this prison, I look past Vic's evil smile to Augustus.

He wants me to break. Bend. Shatter and implode. Become something else. Something new. Something inhuman.

Instead, I spit right in his handsome face.

"I don't belong to you. I never will."

Vic smirks, like he's proud of me.

There's my girl.

Still mine.

Wiping the sticky globules from his eyes with a look of disgust, Augustus backhands me hard enough to split my lip.

"Disobedient child. No is not an option."

The door to the room opens and shuts again a few seconds later. With my head hanging, blood dripping down my chin, I fight to clear the brain fog trying to pull me under. The scrape of the chair opposite forces me to lift my head.

What I find changes everything.

The entire world fucking stops.

"I believe you two know each other." Augustus smirks.

Also handcuffed in place, looking far too real to be another twisted hallucination, her chestnut hair hangs limp and tangled. Clothing ripped in places, indicating a recent struggle. Knuckles scraped and eyes wild with so much fear, it consumes the anger and grief I would expect.

"Jesus... Brooklyn?!"

"Allison," I whisper in horror.

She's here. Flesh and blood. This is Augustus's trump card. I'm staring at Vic's goddamn fucking *sister*. The author of countless letters I tortured myself with on the roof. She looks at me like I'm a demon from hell that's clawed its way up to ensure her eternal damnation.

"Please... let me go," she begs Augustus. "I have money, name your price. I don't know what this is... but please, I'm begging you."

Drinking in her vulnerability, Augustus grins and clicks his fingers in the air. Seven crawls forward from the darkest corner of the room, near unrecognisable from another beating that's left him limping badly.

Our eyes connect, and the window to his soul is empty.

Devoid.

Perfectly inhuman.

"Unlock her cuffs," Augustus orders.

Hope flares in Allison's eyes, but she begins to sob as Seven hobbles straight past her, kneeling beside my chair instead. His fingertips linger on my bleeding wrists as he does as instructed, so fast I think I must have imagined it. Once free, I stumble from the seat and stand on legs that feel like liquified jelly.

"Allison has been running a hate campaign against you for the past eighteen months," Augustus informs me, circling her chair like the predator he is. "She's dragged your name through every newspaper in the country, ensuring the entire world knows what you did. Even after we wiped your social media presence when you were admitted to the program. She's made it very difficult for you to disappear."

His confession barely registers. I'm too busy staring into Allison's eyes, brimming with tears and silently begging me. For what, I don't know. I can't help her. I can't help myself.

"Tomorrow morning, Allison Brunel will be found dead. Grief, it seems, was inevitable. The newspapers will mourn the loss of such a young life, before burying her name—and yours, by extension—into the depths of the archives where my team will ensure every last trace of this tale vanishes forever."

Allison sobs even harder and I look beyond her to Augustus, proudly boasting his masterplan, his smile razor sharp. Every inch the monster I know him to be.

"Now is your moment, Patient Eight. We both know what her brother did to you. The damage it left behind. He hurt you. Degraded you. *Raped you.* Did he not deserve to die?"

"My brother was innocent. She murdered him!" Allison screams.

Before I know what I'm doing, I've slammed my fist straight into her face to silence her vicious lies. Blood gushes from her nose, slick against my skin. I stare at it with fascination, laughter echoing in my ears like a blade to the skull. Of course, Vic's waiting for me.

You're a murderer, babygirl.

Did Martin deserve to die?

Did Britt?

I was just the beginning.

Augustus breathes down my neck, brushing hair over my shoulder so that his lips meet my ear. "Do it. She deserves it, doesn't she? Protecting that piece of scum, making you into the bad guy. The world thinks you're a monster because of her. Take your revenge."

Unlocking her cuffs, Seven grabs Allison by the hair and tosses her across the room. She collides with the stone wall, the crunch of broken bone punctuating her screams. I step towards her, and the shadows follow, my companions in this hell.

Kill her.

Make her pay.

Make her hurt.

She's the monster.

Touching the back of her head, fingers coming away stained red, Allison shuffles as far from me as her sluggish body will allow. I follow every step; menacing, overcome with primal need. Augustus watches intently, practically bouncing with excitement.

Every single part of me that I hate… it all leads back to her. She turned the world against me. Poisoned the narrative and protected the evil at the heart of what led me to Blackwood. Sold a lie, that her brother was an innocent victim and not the demon I knew him to be.

"Please... Brooklyn. Don't do this," she weeps.

"Why?" I remark coldly.

"I know you're hurting, but this won't make it better. I'm begging you for mercy."

I laugh in her petrified face. "Mercy? Your brother showed no mercy when he forced himself on me, even as I begged him not to. Nor did the police officers that stopped me from killing myself. Or the doctors that put me in a straitjacket and labelled me a cold-blooded killer. The newspapers too, although I suppose I have you to thank for that."

Kicking her in the stomach, she chokes before coughing blood. I boot her in the face next, watching with satisfaction as she spits a ragged tooth torn straight from the gum. It isn't enough.

I can't punish those who hurt me. I can't make them take it back. But I can hurt her, in every single way I've been hurt. She will know what it feels like to fucking *ache*.

"On your knees," I order.

Allison cries even harder, losing all control as she struggles to get to her knees. Wiping snot, tears, and blood aside, her haunting eyes meet mine. Filled with regret and pain, a festering wound that binds us together.

"P-Please..."

"Your brother ruined my life. I'm not the person I used to be." Hands curling into fists, I hold myself back with a shoestring of control. "Killing you won't bring that girl back. She's gone forever."

My own tears spill over as I stare into her frightened eyes. It would be so easy. Over in seconds, with little more than the slice of a blade. I could claim her life for my own.

"But sparing your life... will stop me from becoming something worse," I whisper brokenly, letting my hands fall limp by my sides.

In the corner, watching as always with his steadying presence, Logan nods once —his smile proud of my decision.

Allison gasps, sucking in a deep breath. The click of Augustus's shoes betrays him before he strikes me, sending me stumbling. I clutch my throbbing head, laughing hard.

"You disappoint me," he lashes out.

"Good. Better than pleasing you, asshole."

Clicking his fingers again, Seven follows like a trained dog. The perfect monster, more obedient than I'll ever be. His gaze flicks over me, something akin to recognition in his cold stare before it's quickly smothered.

"Finish the job," Augustus demands.

I stare at Seven, forcing him to look at me. His blank mask has been practised to perfection, concealing anything that remains beneath. But I know he's in there. Somewhere, a human being exists. The world has given up on him, but not me.

"You don't have to do this," I implore.

His nostrils flare, the only indication that he can hear me. Augustus looks fucking incandescent, grabbing me by the throat and slamming his fist into my jaw.

"Shut it, Miss West. Final warning. Seven, if you will."

I collapse on the verge of unconsciousness, my mouth full of hot blood. Seven advances, a deadly blur as he pins Allison against the wall by her throat. He begins to choke the life out of her, and she thrashes, jerking like a dying animal.

"Seven!" I shout, frantically trying to stand. "You don't have to do this, you can be more than the person he's made you. No one can give you your life back, you have to take it!"

Those devastating eyes meet mine again and he's there. I allow myself a fleeting moment of relief as awareness floods across Seven's expression and his grip loosens, affording Allison her first gasp of air.

We're fucking fools.

Death is the only certainty in life.

The deafening blast of a gunshot slices across the room, and in the final second, Allison's petrified eyes meet mine, searching for something.

Forgiveness?

Salvation?

It doesn't matter.

The bullet rips through her skull and sprays the wall with sticky matter. Her limp body falls into Seven's arms, and he holds her close, storm clouds rolling across his face.

"You see how it's done?" Augustus chuckles.

Behind him, Jefferson joins in the laughter as he blows smoke from his revolver, tucking it back into his waistband. I let my forehead crash to the floor, drained of all fight.

"Poor, helpless Brooklyn."

The brush of Augustus's hand on my head doesn't even make me flinch as he strokes my bloodied hair.

"You know what your problem is? You make villains into heroes and wonder why they disappoint you. Game over, kid."

Slapping his hand away, I lift my head and let Augustus see every ounce of fury steeling my spine. He frowns, inching back as I climb to my feet. Seven drops Allison's corpse, sliding his icy mask right into place.

"And you take broken, innocent children and make them into monsters," I spit at him. "We all know who the real villain is here, doctor. Don't kid yourself."

Silent and brutal, Seven flies across the room, ploughing straight into Jefferson. The pair wrestle and beat the shit out of each other in a blur of fists, until the gun skids just out of reach. Grabbing the nearest chair and flinging it at Augustus, I skid across the floor and get my hands on the gun just as Jefferson drops Seven.

"Give me the goddamn gun," he hisses.

Instead, I point it right in his ugly face.

"Why shouldn't I blow your fucking head off, huh?"

With my finger dancing on the trigger, ready to wipe this motherfucker's miserable existence from the earth, the stab of a needle deep in my neck has me screeching.

Augustus plunges another huge dose straight into my vein and prises the gun from my grip, smashing it into my temple.

Powerless little Brooke.

Always one step behind.

It doesn't take long for the drugs to strip back the final layers of pathetic control left inside of me. I lay in a pool of my own blood, the shadows dancing across the stained cell to entomb me in a coffin of my own making. Vic kneels beside me, dragging a hallucinatory finger along my jawline.

No more running.

Just give in.

Your fight is over.

"No," I murmur, closing my eyes.

All I see is them. Their faces. Their smiles. The men who I love, and who love me back. With my body near convulsing from the force of drugs flooding my system, I get my feet beneath me.

Logan stands by my side, a certain presence in the face of so much madness. At least with him, I'm never alone. He looks after me the only way he can in this land of impossible choices.

The next few seconds pass in slow motion as I look away from Logan's reassuring smile, finding Seven also climbing to his feet. He wipes blood from his brow and throws himself at Augustus with his remaining strength, seizing control of the gun.

Another gunshot blasts my eardrums, and I watch enraptured as Jefferson stumbles, screaming in glorious pain.

One word follows Seven's final move.

"RUN!"

CHAPTER 34
BROOKLYN

HEART OF GLASS (CRABTREE REMIX) BY BLONDIE, PHILIP GLASS & JONAS CRABTREE

BELIEVE IT OR NOT, I used to read a lot. Don't fucking laugh. Before the pills and shots made it impossible upon arrival at Clearview, and I became this broken version of myself.

I read somewhere that the present is nothing more than a fantasy, an illusion we're fed to believe that life could ever be anything more than what came before. Funny how true that feels now, chased by hauntings of my own mind.

You better run, little girl.

I want to hear you scream.

The army of the damned follow the frantic slap of my feet, beating on polished hardwood floors and thick, Persian carpets. All I have to do is get back to the guys. So, I run for my life.

Just like I ran from Mum.

From Vic.

From Hudson's dealer.

From the foster carers.

From Lazlo.

From *myself*.

I can hear the alarm ringing, alerting the guards to suit up and chase after me with their weapons, drag me back into the dark. I didn't hesitate when leaving Seven behind. Whatever Augustus has done to us... it's too late. We're beyond redemption.

Every step I take, Logan follows, encouraging me on and never once leaving my side. "Keep going, Brooke. Don't stop."

Bursting out into the reception, I startle several patients and guards who gape at my bloodied, bruised state. My legs threaten to give out, so I lean against the doorframe, slapping myself to try and regain control. They're after me.

The shadows.

The monsters.

Ghosts with far too much to say.

"You have to run," Logan orders.

"I c-can't…"

"You can. Run and don't look back, do it!"

Stumbling on numb legs, I leave the comfort of his presence behind and follow orders. Before throwing myself outside, I make the fatal mistake of looking back into the mouth of hell.

Behind Logan shouting me on, where previously Vic chased me, a new hallucination takes his place. The original sin, tearing its way into the terrifying present. My past has been a long time coming, and the devil's knocking on my fucking door.

"Mummy?" I whimper.

Her gaunt, skeletal face grins at me beneath the spray of blood and bone left from my brother's destroyed body. Shadows carry her on a crashing wave of grief, fuelling her every step.

Stumbling outside and straight on to my scraped knees, I shred my hands in my desperation to get up. When I look back again, the hallucination of my mother has gone.

In her place, a familiar sick grin beneath delicate wire spectacles invites my fear. Lazlo gives me a three-fingered wave.

Don't you want to see your family again?

Tell me how you'd do it.

Clapping him on the shoulder, exchanging matching sneers, my stomach revolts at the sight of Rio with his head caved in. He winks at me, my brain conjuring every last disgusting detail of how his splattered corpse would have looked.

Nothing about this place is real.

Don't you see that yet?

It's all an illusion.

With sunshine beating down on me, I don't stop at the shouts and screams around me. More guards flood out of a nearby building, yelling into their radios as they lay eyes on me.

Ducking through buildings and empty corridors, I run from a threat no one else can see. Their tasers and batons mean nothing to me. I'm more afraid of what happens when my demons catch up to me.

Somehow, I find myself outside of Oakridge. Ploughing into an unsuspecting patient, we both end up sprawled across the grass, gasping for air. I fist handfuls of dirt and drag my battered body upright, searching for salvation.

Crowded around a nearby bench, I find it. My reasons for existing. Plotting with their heads together, they all turn to see the source of the commotion and blanch at the sight of me.

"Brooklyn?" Kade shouts.

Hudson vaults over the bench, ready to rush to my side. I hold up a bloodied hand, screaming at the top of my lungs for him to stop. His expression split wide open with fear, he draws to a halt.

"Blackbird? What… are you okay?"

"Stay back!"

Pain lances through my head like the crack of a whip and he goes wobbly, blurring around the edges. When my vision clears, I don't see Hudson anymore. His predecessor stands in his place, cracking his knuckles in anticipation of my punishment.

End of the road, babygirl.

We're all here for you.

No escaping.

Vic crouches in the grass, still certain in his undying possession of my soul. I can't live while he haunts me. I'll never be free of the man who took the final part of me and smashed it into unrecognisable pieces. Teeth gritted on a scream, I grab him by the throat and attack.

It's kill or be killed.

I'll murder him again if I have to.

Fists blurring, my knuckles breaking under the ferocity of my desperation, I pummel Vic into the ground. Real or not, his blood is warm and victorious. I let myself dance in it, throttling the living death out of him.

When my body refuses to fight anymore, I wrap my hands around his neck and squeeze with everything I have left. The chorus of screams and whispers rips through me; a lethal hurricane adding fuel to the fire.

Kill him. Kill him. Kill him.

Kill him. Kill him. Kill him.

The past plays on a ceaseless, inescapable loop. I'm back in that apartment, blood slick between my thighs and knife clutched in my hand. Nothing else matters. Not the guys watching. Not the patients. Not the guards. Not even Augustus and what this means.

Brooklyn, Patient Eight.

We're one and the same.

Human and inhuman.

Victim and abuser.

"Leave me the fuck alone, Vic!" I scream.

Dashing his skull with a rock, I watch the life drain from his eyes for a second time. The satisfaction is even sweeter this time. Victory is mine. He can't haunt me now, never again. I've killed the ghost rattling its chains inside my head.

No.

Not quite so easy.

Not in this world.

Slowly, irrevocably... the world filters back in. Yelling, panicked voices and begging. Arms latching around me like steel bands and dragging me backwards, pinning me to the cold ground. Threats and crying, pain and suffering.

As the shadows peel back, retreating into the corners of my mind, the real world is finally revealed. I find the truth waiting. Vic isn't dead. He isn't real. It was all in my head.

"Firecracker..." Phoenix weeps, holding my face to his chest. "Baby, what have you done? Oh, fucking Christ..."

Hudson is being held back by a guard, handcuffed to hold him at bay and away from me. His eyes collide with mine and I can't fathom what's there.

Beyond fear.

Beyond worry.

The abyss looks back at me.

I should thank whatever God remains that Eli is hidden from sight behind us. His disgust would gut me. I couldn't take that final, devastating blow.

"I d-didn't... I thought... I..."

Phoenix holds me even tighter. "Don't speak. Not now."

Sprawled out on the crimson stained grass, hands pumping a lifeless chest, I watch in disbelief as Kade presses his lips to a beaten pulp of face, shouting for help from the guards standing frozen. He holds the lifeless body in his arms, his shirt rapidly turning from white to red.

You thought you could get rid of me that easily?

I'm inside of you.

There's no digging me out.

Vic's laughter snaps the threads of control keeping me conscious and the tears come. An almighty tsunami in the face of a mindless bloodbath.

As Phoenix holds me upright, I stare down at the innocent life added to my already weighty conscience. The patient I collided with and was too out of my goddamn mind to recognise. All I saw were the shadows.

Not reality.

Not her face.

Not my friend.

Not... *Teegan.*

"What have I done?!" I scream uselessly.

No one can answer me.

Not this time.

By the time I'm dragged away from the scene, shot with a sedative and body-slammed by multiple guards, there's no fight left in me. All I can see is the bloodied shell of my first real friend, strewn across the grass and unresponsive to emergency first-aid.

I let them take me away from her corpse, uncaring of where I'll end up. The darkness awaits and I enter it with open arms. It's where I belong. What I deserve. Not even the guys protest.

They all watch me go.

Empty and heartbroken.

CHAPTER 35
KADE

CHEMICAL - THE DEVIL WEARS PRADA

THE HOT, relentless summer sun beats down on me as I smoke outside the library. Crushing my finished cigarette beneath my shoe, I watch the dying embers disappear from the world.

I should feel something, knowing that mere metres away, Halbert and his buddies are guarding my filthy dealings. Guilt, shame even. But I don't feel it anymore. I don't feel anything.

"Can I pay the rest next week? I'm waiting for my commissary to come in," Todd bargains, his face hollow and drawn from months of heavy drug use. "Please, man."

"You know the deal."

"Please... I n-need this. I c-can't... I can't sleep. Every night, I see her face. She's fucking haunting me, I can't sleep!"

His words make me sick to my stomach, but I don't let it show. I see Teegan's face too, every night when I close my eyes. Beaten and slack as I pumped her chest, begging for a heartbeat.

But I can't be weak. Not anymore. The institute has to be afraid of me now, I command respect and authority everywhere I go. It's the role of the stooge and I play my part to fucking perfection.

Palming a wrapper of pills, I subtly inch backwards to duck out the path of the watching CCTV cameras, indicating for Todd to follow me. With no one watching, I pass him the dose.

"Not a word."

He nods gratefully. "Thank you."

"Be ready. Wait for the signal, like we discussed."

"Got it. Soon?"

I squeeze his arm. "Soon. We'll get far away from here."

The hope blooming in his bloodshot eyes twists my gut. I glance away, shutting back down. He knows what's coming—I've been laying tracks for a long time now, getting others onside to stage our grand escape.

Ensuring he's ready, I take a deep breath and draw my fist back, ploughing it into his face. It has to be realistic, no one can suspect that my heart's not in it. We're all playing the game now.

"You heard me, inmate. No payment, no deal!" I bellow.

Shoving him away where the camera can see, Todd plasters a pained expression on, clutching his bleeding face. The fake tears are impressive. I let him run, imprisoning any sense of guilt in the depths of my mind where it can shut the fuck up and leave me alone.

I'm not Rio, but I get the job done.

That's all Augustus wanted.

Emerging back into the scorching afternoon, I find Halbert studying the groups of patients sunbathing and eating lunch outside, no doubt calculating his next victim to harass for entertainment. When he sees me, he notes my scraped knuckles and grins like the sadist he is.

"You know, I never would've thought you'd have the stomach for this, Kade."

"People can surprise you."

"Mr Straight-Laced, Daddy's Pet. It's actually funny how far you've fallen. I'm almost proud."

I battle the urge to strangle the living daylights out of this asshole, while Halbert sneers in my face.

"Little Miss Brooklyn would be so fucking proud if she were still here. Hell, I doubt she's even alive. Probably slit her wrists the minute they returned her to Clearview."

I almost stumble, quickly smothering any emotion before he can take advantage. It's a trick I've learned by necessity in recent months. Her name is like a curse, the incarnation of evil that cannot be spoken aloud. Not anymore. Not without consequences.

"When's the next shipment?" I drone.

Halbert looks annoyed that his words didn't meet their target.

"Tomorrow evening."

"Tomorrow then. Feel free to fuck off in the meantime."

He tries to grab my crisp white shirt, but I shove him instead, watching with satisfaction as he falls into a nearby bench. Halbert scrambles to his feet, hand resting above his baton in a clear warning.

"Watch it, Knight. Just because you're the boss's newest slave, don't mean I can't beat your ass for insubordination," he hisses.

"Take it up with Augustus. I have places to be."

Dismissing him, I straighten my glasses and stomp away, leaving Halbert to fume. He's nothing more than a brainless foot soldier, he can't do shit to me. Not after all my careful work to get to this point and earn the trust of the institute.

Becoming Blackwood's bitch is the hardest thing I've ever done, and it cost me everything.

My friends.

My family.

My entire fucking life.

I had to leave the person I was behind, become someone else. Someone I hate, and who makes me sick when I look in the mirror every night. But it will be worth it.

I will watch this place burn.

Weaving my way back through the crowd, patients avert their eyes and clear themselves from my path. Most view me with equal parts fear and confusion. I command the respect of all those around me, patients and guards alike. Just like Rio did.

It took a lot to earn my new reputation, painstaking work and a complete abandonment of my morals. It was a task to focus on in the gut-wrenching emptiness left in her wake.

She's been gone for four months.

Four endless, torturous months.

Back in Oakridge, I let myself into my room and prepare for whatever state I'll find Phoenix in. I refuse to sell to him, so his now-regular manic episodes are managed with medication alone—no drugs or booze to grant him mercy.

I refuse to do that to him, no matter how much he screams and threatens me with death. She isn't here to bring him back from the edge, and none of us have the remaining strength to do it either.

"Phoenix?"

"Back so soon?" he retorts.

Finding him curled up in the corner of his bed, a cigarette hanging from his lips, Phoenix scowls at me. I remove my shoes, tucking my second phone away in its discreet hiding spot.

That's for business matters only, nothing for the guys to concern themselves with. Only one of us needs to be getting our hands dirty.

"Are you planning on getting up today?" I sigh.

"Why should I? And since when do you even care?"

"Knock it off, Nix. I'm the one who kept you out of solitary when you beat the shit out of that jock the other day. Just take your fucking meds and do what the therapists say, alright? This has to stop."

Flopping on to his back, Phoenix crushes the cigarette against the wall and laughs; a cold, empty sound so far from the friend I once knew.

"The meds don't work anymore. Nothing does."

I swallow hard, trying to loosen the tendrils of shame strangling the life out of me. This is all my fault. Searching the lifeless room, my gaze lingers on the bag of belongings stashed under my bed. I make myself look away. No one can stomach to open it and see what remains of the girl we lost.

"Where's Eli?" I ask tiredly.

If possible, his voice turns even colder.

"You know full well that he refuses to see anyone, even me. There's no reaching him now." Phoenix chews his lip, his pain clear to see. "He isn't ever coming back to us."

Covering my face with my hands, I rub my temples to ease the constant ache. I thought we were broken before. She put us back together; our blackbird, our firecracker. The fucking light in the dark who came out of nowhere and became our entire goddamn world without realising it.

Now… we're nothing.

Without her, I've lost the only family I had.

"I'm trying to fix this," I mutter, chancing a look at him. "I'll get us out of here, Nix. All of us. The pieces are there, we're ready. I'm waiting for the right moment."

Phoenix scoffs hatefully. "And what did it cost you, huh?"

Patience expiring, I slam my fist into the wall.

"I've done this for our fucking family. You think I wanted to sell my damn soul to Blackwood? To become the one thing I hate?" I shout. "Convincing Augustus and his band of psychopaths that my allegiances lie with them is our ticket out of here. I'll do whatever it bloody well costs to see this through."

Abandoning his bed, Phoenix scrapes a hand through his washed-out brown hair. The blue has long since faded and he never bothered to replenish it. Not for this half-life, caught between living and dying. He isn't willing to accept that she's gone, but we have to move on. Even if that means leaving her ghost behind.

"You make me sick," he accuses.

"I'm doing what's necessary. Someone has to."

"Tell yourself that if it makes it easier. Meanwhile, the people you sell to suffer at your hands and Blackwood makes a profit."

Surging to my feet, we end up nose to nose.

"I'm trying to save us all." I seethe.

Phoenix loses control, his fist sailing into my face.

"This place is a fucking cancer! Preying on the sick and making them worse for their own damn benefit. Nothing is worth helping them. *Nothing.*"

Leaving me to remove my glasses and wipe my bleeding nose, he grabs his leather jacket, sparing me a final disgusted look before exiting the room. I stare at the door that smashes shut in his wake, desperate to chase after him and make things right.

I can't stop, not yet. No matter how much they hate me for it, I have to get the guys out. It's what Brooklyn would have wanted. It's what I promised her. And it's what I'm damn well going to do, no matter how much of myself I must lose in the process.

———

Carrying the final box down from the loading bay, I jerk my head towards the back entrance. Taggert follows, dumping his boxes on the trolley before signing off on the delivery.

Tony tucks the paperwork away and turns to me, grin pulled tight with pleasure. I'm sure my father gets a kick out of sending him to do these deliveries; the days of me reporting simple day-to-day business are long gone. I know the truth now, the real reason behind his investments and interest in Blackwood Institute.

Dad's in on it.

They all are—the board of directors.

A shadowy, nameless corporation bankrolling Augustus and his madness, feeding drugs and contraband back into the system and watching it all play out in real-time for scientific curiosity. A self-sustaining social experiment on the country's most unstable and bloodthirsty delinquents.

And I'm helping them.

Oh, how the mighty have fucking fallen.

"Evening, Kade. Your Ma says hello," Tony greets.

I try not to focus on the obvious swelling across his bruised knuckles and what that may entail. Breathing through my nose, I plaster an unaffected smile into place.

"Tell Dad the money will be with him by nightfall."

"Good job. He's pleased with your work."

My skin crawls at the insinuation. Talk about keeping it in the family. Why manipulate and bankroll random patients when your very own son can do the dirty business required to keep this experiment ticking over?

"Transfer it into the offshore account. I'll text you the details," Tony instructs, glancing at his phone. "He wants an update on Hudson too. Best be keeping him in line, kid."

I glare back. "Hudson is under control. Tell my fucking father to stop worrying about him and leave it to me, I'm capable of looking after my stupid brother."

"He's been in solitary six times in the past month alone."

Fuck. I tried to keep it as quiet as possible, but Augustus must have ratted us out. Hudson is as volatile as an erupting volcano right now, and not to mention unpredictable.

"I've got it under control," I repeat.

Tony looks unconvinced, drawing back his jacket to flash his gun at me. "You better. Else I'll have to intervene and deal with him myself. Your father doesn't want any more trouble, least of all from that street rat."

Climbing back into his truck, Tony offers me a final wave before driving off into the waning sun. I stand there with my fists clenched, vibrating with anger.

After all I've done to prove myself, the piece of shit who calls himself my father still holds Hudson's life over my head as bait.

I'm so sick of losing the people I love. I hate being the bad guy and want nothing more than to be back on the right side of this mess.

All my plans are laid, the pawns are in place and paid off. We're ready to give Blackwood a taste of its own medicine. If I'm going to act, then now's the time. Before I lose my brothers for good.

Dragging my phone to my ear, I hit Hudson's name. He picks up on the first ring, the sound of pained grunts and a clear scuffle echoing down the line.

"Bit busy here," he snaps.

"Finish up. Get the others and meet me in the ruined chapel."

The sound of a final, punishing blow has my teeth grinding together. Where I'm working from the inside, Hudson's taken the other direction. He's waging his own war against Augustus, breaking every rule in the book, and causing havoc in his grief.

"What's this about?" Hudson growls.

"It's time. I'm fucking done."

Silence.

"Hud?"

"Tonight?" he utters.

The shred of hope in his voice is a blade in my gut, twisting and slicing until I'm near doubled over with emotional anguish.

"I'm sorry it couldn't be sooner," I whisper shamefully.

"We can't leave, Kade. Not without her."

Tipping my head up to curse at the sunset, I lose patience. "Jesus Christ, how many times are we going to rehash the same argument? She's gone. Brooklyn isn't coming back. We can't stay here waiting for a ghost, Hud. It's time to worry about ourselves."

"They didn't send her back to Clearview," he argues hotly.

We've been going around in circles for months, ever since that day. The official story was that she transferred back to Clearview, losing her place at Blackwood. Our girl is lost in the system, far from our reach now. But I'm the only one who will admit it.

"She's probably dead." I sigh, hating to say it aloud. "Pull your head out of your ass and look around you for once. We're done, our lives here aren't worth living. I've already lost Brooklyn and I won't lose you three as well."

My voice breaks, choked with emotion.

"We can't leave," he mutters.

"Stop, Hud. Just stop. Think about the others."

Hesitating, he lets out a pained noise. "What's the plan?"

"Get the guys, I don't care what you have to do to convince them. Meet me at the chapel with your bags in one hour."

Pausing, I allow myself a sliver of anticipation.

"We're leaving Blackwood Institute. Tonight."

CHAPTER 36
BROOKLYN
NUMB - LINKIN PARK

THIS ISN'T LIVING.

Existing… perhaps.

But even that seems a stretch for this eternal state of purgatory. I suppose it's all I deserve, after everything I've done to get here. The innocent blood staining my hands.

Propped up in the corner of the room, I watch as Seven beats on the male target. He has already broken the poor bastard's arm, which hangs limp and twisted at an unnatural angle.

"I'm going to ask you one more time," Jefferson drones.

Walking with an obvious hobble, the asshole doesn't get his hands dirty anymore. Not since Seven shattered his leg with a well-placed bullet and earned himself a terrible punishment. Patient Two thought she had it bad, blind and broken.

Favouring his left side, Seven cracks his fist against the man's face again, shattering his jaw. The bastard near pisses himself with fear, barely able to speak.

It doesn't stop Seven, nothing does at this point. Even after Augustus's grey-faced doctors removed the hand that fired the shot, he's as ruthless as ever.

"Who leaked the data, Roberts?"

Weeping uncontrollably, the man shakes his head.

"It wasn't me!"

Jefferson laughs, indicating for Seven to hit him again. "The leak contained years' worth of material. Enough to bring this entire operation to its knees in the wrong hands. Someone wiped the damn CCTV and covered their tracks. I'm going to need you to do better than that."

"I s-swear… I d-don't know," he sobs.

"Stand down," Jefferson instructs Seven.

Dropping the dying man in a puddle of his own urine, Seven curls his lip in disgust and wipes off his remaining hand, coated in blood. After nearly an hour of this, he doesn't yet seem sated.

"You're up, Eight."

Stepping forwards, I spare Jefferson a glance and he nods, indicating for me to have a go. I roll my neck, preparing for what needs to be done.

We're a lethal duo. Seven breaks them down and I take the kill, by any means necessary. Augustus's prized weapons of mass fucking destruction.

Kneeling beside the pathetic worm, I slide a finger under his chin to raise his eyes to mine. Wide, terrified, and laced with secrets. He knows the truth. I can see his lies, taste the desperation on my tongue.

"The truth," I instruct.

"Please… I d-dont know!"

Sliding a sharp knife from one of the pockets in my cargo trousers, I hold it up to the single lightbulb hanging from the ceiling. With Roberts watching, I drag my tongue right along the edge, tasting cold steel and death.

"The truth," I repeat.

"I t-told you… I don't fucking know!"

I brush my lips against his ear, keeping my voice feather light. "Every time you lie, I'll cut something off. We'll keep going until nothing remains. Any preference where I start?"

I drink in the feeling of power, allow it to fill my veins, soak beneath my skin, and repair the pain that shreds me down with every waking moment.

Dragging the tip of my blade along his jawline, circling his eye socket, I dig it in just deep enough to elicit a thin stream of blood.

"Time's up. I want an answer."

Holding the blade mere inches from his eyeball, Roberts finally screams for me to wait. The slimy worm held up better than I thought, I'll give him that.

"It wasn't me… but I know who did it. Some woman. She came into the office with a visitor's ID, said she was under instruction from Augustus himself. She had the right paperwork! All I did was follow orders, I d-didn't know… I thought she was legit!"

"I want a name." I grin, ready to cut him. "Or your eye. Choose."

"I d-didn't know her… I'm begging you…"

I love it when they beg. It makes it more satisfying when I silence their pathetic, traitorous tongues for good. These people are maggots. The lowest of the low, working for Augustus and keeping his enterprise above reproach. They don't deserve to live after all they've enabled.

Jefferson makes an impatient noise, stomping across the room to take a phone call. I don't move, still holding Roberts' life in the palm of my hand. With Jefferson out of earshot, I lean in to whisper again.

"Tell me and I swear, I'll make Augustus pay for doing this to you."

I widen my eyes to implore this idiot to keep quiet. He may work for the devil, but allegiances only run so deep. A fatal beating will change priorities for people very quick.

"I swear to you, I d-don't know her name," he mutters, blood spilling from his mouth. "But… she h-had pink hair and hippy clothes. All l-loud and shit."

His breaths are turning wet and rattly, a sure sign that his lungs have collapsed. Broken ribs will do that to you. Nodding quickly, I release my grip on his shirt and let Roberts drop.

Just as he looks relieved, like he'll be spared somehow, I grip my knife and slash it across his throat in a single move. The gaping, bloody smile exposes muscle and nerve, ending his life in a split-second.

"Nothing?" Jefferson hisses.

Glancing across the room, I find that he's finished his phone call. I clamber to my feet, tucking my knife away and wiping stained hands off on my clothing.

"He's a pencil pusher. He didn't know shit."

"Goddammit. Augustus is going to have my balls."

I glare at Jefferson. "Like you have any."

He flashes across the room, even with his shitty, impaired leg. Pinning me against the wall with a crushing grip on my throat, Jefferson punches me in the stomach, knocking the air from my lungs.

"Watch it, Eight. I can still hurt you."

"And I can still shoot you. Oh, wait. Already been done."

Using his knee to spread my legs open, his entire disgusting bodyweight pinning me against the wall, Jefferson touches his tongue to my ear, dragging it all the way along my jawline.

"I prefer you like this, whore. Empty and devoid. Do you even remember what you did, huh? Whose blood stains your filthy hands?"

His words expand the black hole festering inside of me, a gaping chasm that deepens more with each day. I can't think about *her*. I refuse to.

Surviving this hell means burying my head in the sand and blocking out the person I used to be, leaving nothing but an animal in my place. If she didn't get to live, then neither do I.

"What about those you left behind?"

"Get the fuck off me," I warn.

Jefferson's sick laugh reverberates around me, slipping beneath my skin and pulling at those damned memories again.

"Poor Eight, alone in the world. They shared your pussy like a fucking meal. But who's screwing you now, girlie?"

I let my eyes fall shut, the sharp burn of tears surprising me. I don't cry anymore, I haven't done so in a very long time. Yet somehow, he pulls the unwanted emotion free.

I don't even know why I'm crying, nor do I recognise the faces that bubble up through my subconscious and demand to be acknowledged. They're strangers to me now. A distant memory, beyond my reach.

"I'm sure they all forgot about you. You're just another worthless piece of trash to be discarded. And one day, when Augustus is done… I'll be the one to fuck you until you scream and beg for mercy," Jefferson whispers. "Only then are you allowed to die."

With his hand still gripping my throat, he crashes my skull into the wall until I lose grip of the world and slip into unconsciousness, grateful for the relief.

When I finally come to again, it feels like an eternity has passed. I'm strapped in a straitjacket that pins me to my cot, staring up at the ceiling. Cracked, faded, barely lit by the light leaking beneath the door to my cell. Not a single other piece of furniture, beside the metal toilet bowl in the corner.

"Seven?" I whimper.

His silence presses into my skull with too much dread for me to hold inside. Augustus knows I hate being pinned down, so he makes a point of putting the straitjacket on me now. Keeping me subjugated and afraid, under his control.

"Sev? You there?" I repeat desperately.

"I'm here, princess."

I glance at the metal grate tucked into the nearby corner. On the other side, my only slice of human comfort in this hellish plane of existence. Alone in my insanity but for the one monster who understands what it's like to lose everything.

"How long was I out?"

"Few hours."

I slump back on the rock-solid cot.

"You okay?"

No answer.

"Please... talk to me, Sev."

My whimpered plea sounds pathetic, but I can't afford to be strong in front of him. Maintaining it in front of everyone else is draining enough, the marks that Augustus sends us to beat and kill.

Seven is the only one who knows what it's like to be unmade; your entire mind deconstructed brick by brick, re-laid into a new construction. One of Augustus's choosing, a new person and identity, removing all reminders of what came before.

What was my name?

Who was I?

Did... someone, anyone, love me?

Am I missed?

Does anyone fucking care?

More tears soak my bruised face. I haven't allowed myself the luxury of crying for a long time, it only invites more pain by removing the locks of every box inside my head so the darkness can run free.

Something has stirred it.

The whispered words of a dying man, and a description that sounded so familiar, but I can't remember the person I once knew.

"You should rest," Seven eventually responds.

"I don't want to. Tell me something good."

"There is nothing good."

We share the silence, revelling in the reprieve from Augustus's relentless abuse. Conditioning, he calls it. When we slip up, we're beaten. Ruthlessly. That's the least of it. I'll take a whip and a steel-capped boot over the psychological torment any day.

"What did Roberts tell you?" Seven asks.

Biting down hard on my lip to break the skin, I latch on to the pain and use it to focus my mind, clearing shadows and ghosts threatening to creep back into the driver's seat.

"Nothing."

"I thought we didn't keep secrets," he says sadly.

"And I thought we didn't talk about the truth."

I can hear Seven's sigh from here, even with inches of concrete between us. "There's no getting out, princess. May as well tell me. Right now, I'm all you've got left."

"He... described someone," I admit. "The woman who stole the information. I don't know who she is, but she sounded familiar."

"How so?"

Conjuring the image that finds its way through my mental barriers, I see the face of a woman. Soft and rounded, smile lines and bright, untainted hope. Hair cotton-candy pink and dressed in multi-coloured linens, every inch the comforting therapist.

"I think she was from... *before*."

Seven knows what I mean without having to explain—we both skirt around that deep, disturbing chasm that joins us together. An endless void with no bottom.

We had lives, once upon a time. I'm sure of it. The pain in my chest that refuses to ease tells me that much.

"Do you remember your life?" I ask gently.

"Flashes. I remember helping people. The rest... it's like watching a storm roll in on the horizon," Seven reveals.

He's having a good day today. Most of the time, Seven doesn't exist. After re-conditioning or a particularly bad job, he's nothing but an empty machine. The person that I know comes and goes like the rising tide, glimpses of humanity that soon vanish again.

"What about you?"

"Nothing. Just people, feelings. Scents I can't place and faces with no names. I think we're broken, Sev."

"Princess... we were never whole."

The sound of approaching footsteps has my heart threatening to explode, a familiar walk and universal sign of dread. I wait, expecting my own cell door to be flung open. The click of the lock in the neighbouring cell rings out instead.

"Bring the machine," Augustus orders, his voice faraway.

I battle against the straitjacket, even if it's futile. "Leave him the fuck alone! Hey, asshole. Come here and face me yourself!"

Augustus ignores my baiting, he's used to my bullshit by now. I've grown protective of Seven, the man who lost a hand to give me a shot at running.

I can't remember how it ended that day. All that remains is the scent of death and the sound of screaming. I know it ended badly. She still comes to me when I pass out, the nameless girl leaking blood across the grass.

Just thinking about her has agony lancing through me, such intense heartache that I stuff it back into the box and disregard any hope of ever remembering.

"You're up next, Eight." Augustus cackles.

I shout and rave, demanding freedom from the restraints pinning me helpless. As they begin to hurt Seven, Logan enters my cell to make his regular reappearance. My only other company in this place, another anomaly that I don't care to question.

"Calm down. You can't help him."

"Seven!" I scream.

He screams right back, but it's not at me. The pain is so awful, he can't help but react. His monster pales in comparison to those who keep us here, broken and battered. I thrash and buck in the cot, ignoring Logan's continued pleas to relax.

I'm alone down here. I've lost everyone and everything that once mattered to me. Seven is all I have left. Without him, or even his disembodied voice through the grate, I may as well be dead.

Perhaps, I already am.

I should've known I'd go to hell.

CHAPTER 37
ELI

I FEEL IT TOO - DREAM STATE

SITTING ATOP THE ALTAR, my legs crossed beneath me, I stare out through the smashed stained glass. Hot, sticky rivulets of blood run down my inner arm from the deep slashes I inflicted, teeth bared, and movements frenzied.

Cutting has always been about control for me. Taking back what others have stolen; my body, my tongue, my mind. I've always been the one in control, not the blade.

All the progress I made, it's gone. Futile and irrelevant. Now, I'm beholden to a force greater than myself. The ingrained need to self-destruct. It's always been there, even when I was a kid.

She helped me tame it.

Lock it away, become something more than a victim.

I can't do it without Brooklyn. Before, I was playing at this game called living. Crushing on one of my best friends when I wasn't plotting my next suicide attempt. She gave me something—recognition. Understanding. Company in my own personal form of hell.

For the first time in my life, I felt seen.

The thought of her alone in Clearview, locked away from humanity for the rest of her days... hurts me more than I can ever vocalise. But there are no flavours to drown me in anxiety and despair.

Not anymore.

That's what life without Brooklyn tastes like. Fucking nothing. Endless, immeasurable, inhumane nothingness. Ever since we were told about the transfer, I've seen the world in tasteless shades of grey and I fucking hate it.

The sound of footsteps outside has me rolling down the sleeve of my hoodie, stashing the penknife away from sight. I haven't spent time with the guys, or anyone for that matter, in months.

I hoped that alone, I could fade away undisturbed. But Phoenix's desperate text message led me here, a single bag packed, and a tentative lifeline dangling in the air.

"Eli?"

Glancing up, I find all three members of our splintered family walking towards me, slotting the rotten door back into place. Hudson and Kade look the same, but gaunter and marked by clear exhaustion.

I almost don't recognise the person beside them. Lips I've tasted and lines of muscle I've traced with my tongue. Phoenix stops metres away. "You came."

I take in his shaggy brown hair, hollow eyes, and painfully sharp cheekbones, indicative of the constant onslaught of mania I've witnessed from afar. We're both adrift and out of control without our anchor to weigh us down. The blue-haired man I love is far away now, maybe gone forever.

I nod once.

"I'm glad you're here. Thank you… for coming," he offers.

Shrugging, I turn and find Kade smiling at me. Exchanging awkward greetings, like we're nothing more than strangers, I hop down from the altar, and we all crowd around as Kade lays out a stack of papers. I stand at a distance, feeling wary. I know who he is now—Augustus's stooge and Blackwood's bitch.

Can he be trusted?

Do I have a choice?

"Four months ago, I promised you all that I'd get us out of here," Kade begins, his voice laced with sadness. "I'm sorry it took us losing everything to get here. I have a plan, but it will take all of us to pull this off."

"What kind of plan?" Phoenix prompts.

Hudson lights a cigarette, wincing as he flexes his bruised hands. I'm surprised to see him out of the hole, he hasn't made it a day without fighting for a long time. I've heard the whispers and rumours even in my solitude.

"Everything is in place. My clients are ready, we make our move at dinner," Kade confirms.

Hudson stares. "Our move?"

Kade's smile is triumphant, even a little proud. "We're not the only ones done with Augustus's bullshit. It's taken months of planning and pretending to be his fucking pet, but now the entire institute is on our side. Everyone I've sold contraband to is ready to go. Tonight, gentlemen… *we riot.*"

Dumping his backpack on the altar, he tips it up and out falls a stash of sharp knives, enough for two each. Phoenix lets out a surprised laugh, but quickly grows serious as he inspects one of the weapons, a slow grin spreading across his lips.

"For real?"

Kade claps him on the shoulder. "For real. We're busting the hell out of here and taking down as many bastards as we can on the way out. Damn them all. We have enough people to stand a real chance. Worst case scenario, we burn this hellhole to ash."

Exchanging back slaps and hugs, the pair practically bounce with excitement. I lock eyes with Hudson, expecting him to be doing the same. But instead, he's solemn, staring at the knives.

"What is it?" Kade frowns.

Hudson takes one, weighing it in his hands. "We can't leave without clearing the basement. Every poor motherfucker in there has had their life ruined by Augustus. We're not leaving them behind to die alone, the world needs to know what happened here."

"There isn't time..."

"Make time," Hudson snaps. "Unless you want to be responsible for the deaths of however many innocent lives rest beneath our feet. We need proof."

Phoenix looks crestfallen. "Look, Hud... she isn't in there."

Refusing to meet anyone's eyes, Hudson shakes his head. "Believe what you want, I haven't given up hope. That transfer was bullshit. You take out the guards, give me some patients who know how to throw a punch, and I'll clear the basement."

"There are too many guards," Phoenix argues.

"We outnumber them three to one," Kade supplies, like he's actually considering it. "With enough of us fighting back, it will catch on and spread. We can ignite the entire patient population if we do this right. That's enough of a distraction... it could buy you some time."

"Count me in," a voice chimes in.

All turning to look over to the now-open door, Sadie stands in the crumbling aisle dressed in all-black. She reaches into her coat pocket, pulling out two guns that are slammed down on to the altar. Hudson immediately takes one, while Kade seizes the other.

"You got my message then."

She spares Kade an assessing look. "Didn't think you'd actually pull this off. I'm impressed. I spoke to your contact on the outside, they're ready and waiting with the escape plan. Don't miss your window, you hear me? I'll cover your exit."

Kade nods, offering Sadie a hand to shake. The puzzle pieces click into place, and I realise that I was right all along, she is on our side. More than we knew.

"I'll come with you," she tells Hudson.

"Why?"

"Because I'm here to make sure Blackwood is brought down. The basement is the key to achieving that. Last week, I stole data from a secure server associated with Blackwood's parent company."

"You did what?" Kade exclaims.

She briefly meets his gaze. "I came here for a reason. Hudson's right, we can't leave them down there. This goes so much deeper than any of us ever realised."

"Is she down there?" Hudson hisses.

We all stand to attention, desperate for her answer.

"I don't know," Sadie admits, though I spot the doubt on her face. "I've seen files from what Augustus has been doing, whoever is down there needs our help. You do your job and I'll do mine. This place is primed to blow... we just need to ignite the flames."

Phoenix throws his arm around my shoulders, touching me for the first time in many long months, like nothing has changed between us. He takes the time to look around our rag-tag group, fuelled by sheer determination to bring this place to its knees.

"Let's go fuck shit up." He grins.

Hudson smirks with confidence. "Amen to that."

All taking our weapons and sliding them into discreet hiding places, Kade stashes our bags of meagre possessions in the shrubbery outside of the chapel, within easy reach.

When our work is done, we'll run into the woods to meet his contact. Then, we will escape into reality. A world that rejected me and cast me out a decade earlier. I'm fucking terrified, but nothing could convince me to stay here.

Passing under the cover of night as we troop back to the institute, preparing to shed life as we know it and step into the unknown, I grab Phoenix's arm and haul him to a stop.

"You good?"

I stare into his eyes. "N-No."

Obliterating the distance between us, he cups my cheek and pulls me against his body. It feels so fucking good. Too good for me to refuse, despite pushing him far away in recent times. I couldn't be with him without her. It didn't feel right, just a reminder of all that we'd lost.

Licking my lips, I force out the words.

"I'm... s-sorry."

Phoenix's face crumples with pain and he presses his forehead to mine, holding me in place. Our breath mingles as we drink each other in, taking a moment to reconnect.

"You don't have to apologise to me."

"D-do," I stutter.

"No. You don't. Losing Brooklyn..." His voice cracks and he shudders. "It's changed us all. I don't know what the future holds, Eli. Whether she's even still alive or within reach. But I fucking swear to you, I'm going nowhere. Friends, lovers, I don't care. You're mine and I'm yours."

Our lips meet in a sweet, tender kiss which eases the wounds that have kept us apart. Sceptical or not, I know Phoenix is still hopeful that she's out there. Praying that our firecracker, our babygirl, will come back to us.

Perhaps we will have a future once more.

But not without her in it.

CHAPTER 38
HUDSON

ANARCHY - LILITH CZAR

THE ATMOSPHERE in the cafeteria is laden with thick, palpable tension. Even the guards look on edge, like they can sense that something is coming. The fall of a fucking empire.

In turn, each of Kade's allies meets our eyes, subtly nodding. It's a good third of the room that have been bought off with drugs, contraband, and the promise of revenge.

I'll admit, Kade's done it this time.

I'm reluctantly impressed.

Phoenix sits taut and ready, his arm around Eli's shoulders, who he seems determined to protect. I have a sneaking suspicion that Eli will surprise us all with his thirst for violence. There's danger flickering in his irises, anger and unmatched fury.

"Thirty seconds," Kade murmurs.

Staring down at his watch, we hold our breath as the silver hands tick down to the hour. The scrape of cutlery and low mutterings of conversation fade into the background in those final moments; the calm before the storm.

At exactly six o'clock, the fire alarm explodes in a violent riot of noise. Several patients scream and jump up, panicking already. Guards look around in shock, unprepared for the sudden noise. Quickly realising this isn't a drill.

Thick, heady smoke begins to seep down the corridor from around the corner, precluding the spread of glorious flames that will cause enough mayhem for us to stage our escape.

"Todd did it." I laugh, equally surprised.

"Doesn't take much to burn a library," Kade returns.

At the sight of the rising haze infecting the corridor, the anxiety in the room increases tenfold. It's a dangerous cocktail that we will use to our advantage. Kade smooths his shirt, mirroring his father in so many ways, before climbing up on to the table.

This is it. His moment.

Countless faces look up, ready at his mark.

"For months, we've been pushed around and treated like nothing more than animals," he shouts above the alarm. "We're human beings, not cattle to be herded and slaughtered. This isn't a hospital anymore, it's a prison. Well, I say, *enough is enough!*"

Reaching into his pocket, Kade pulls Sadie's gun and holds it in the air. Dozens of guards quickly stand to attention, yelling for back-up and marching towards our table.

Pulling our own weapons, we crowd around Kade, giving the signal for everyone to follow. In turn, each table unveils its tribute. Spread throughout the room, armed by the very system of contraband that Blackwood has used to manipulate its victims.

Homemade shanks, knives, even loose bricks. Every creative weapon imaginable. We're armed like savages and more than angry enough.

Bursting into the room, Halbert skids to a halt and spots Kade, his expression set in hard lines. He retrieves his baton and taser, like that could ever rival our stolen firepower.

"Everyone on the ground!" he orders.

Nobody moves an inch.

Where patients would have previously cowered and surrendered control, they now hesitate. Something's changed. Empower a few, and the rest will follow.

We all stare at Halbert with defiance, no matter how loudly he shouts again for everyone to bow to him. Kade ensures the entire room is watching as he raises the gun and points it straight at Halbert.

"You first!" he yells.

The deafening blast of his gunshot cuts through the blaring alarm, and we all watch as the bullet flies into Halbert's exposed chest, a perfect bullseye shot. Kade was always the better hunter. Ruthless and precise in equal measure.

With Halbert collapsing in a puddle of blood, all hell breaks loose in predictable fashion. The dozens of guards surrounding the perimeter arm themselves and charge, ready to beat us all into submission if necessary.

Every single patient that has been paid off with Kade's system throws themselves into the melee; stabbing, slicing, and screaming their way through the black-clad wall of authority intending to steamroll us all.

Before Phoenix can make his first move with the knife clenched in his fist, Eli streams past him, tossing his entire body weight at a nearby guard in a blur of fists and serrated steel. Blood sprays across the linoleum and they both drop, but one comes out victorious.

Eli pulls himself to his feet, covered in crimson with the biggest goddamn smile on his face. He grabs hold of Phoenix and kisses him roughly, before shoving him away again.

Phoenix whistles. "Let's party then."

Leaving the pair to embrace their depravity, I give Kade a final nod and he covers me as I race through the madness, dropping anyone not on our side with a swift punch or kick, keeping my gun stashed for later use.

It doesn't take long to break through—as predicted, the patients who haven't fled out into the smoke-filled corridor have been overcome by the crowd, drawn into the riot spirit. I pass two of Rio's ex-buddies strangling a particularly brutish guard and pummelling his face into mush.

"Hudson! Over here!"

Sadie shouts me down through the war zone, barely recognisable through the smoke growing hotter by the second. Dozens of sprinklers burst into action, flooding the cafeteria and reception with water that only increases the frenzy of confusion and fury.

Taking advantage of the distraction, we link hands and vault over the welcome desk, heading for the corridor beyond. Both pulling our guns, we drop the three guards racing up the staircase before they even have a chance to react.

Sadie's shots hit the exact centre of their foreheads with well-trained precision, and she stops briefly to steal their security swipe cards, passing one to me.

"Who the hell are you?" I yell.

She flashes me a grin. "Your guardian angel."

Taking the stairs two at a time, encountering even more guards rushing to the surface to help, we're both sweaty and drenched in blood by the time we enter Augustus's dreaded basement.

An echoing corridor stretches out before me, lined with familiar solitary cells, all marked with occupied signs. Two nurses wait in the corner with... *Mariam*? She offers me a brief smile in greeting.

"What the fuck?"

Sadie stops me from advancing. "They're with me. We're gonna get these patients out."

With no time to question it, I nod. "What about the rest?"

"I'll catch up, go sweep the next level!" Sadie orders.

Leaving them to break the cells open, I follow the signs for the infamous Z Wing. I've been down here enough to hear the rumours, after spending months deliberately breaking the rules to get myself locked up, searching for any sign of Brooklyn.

Keeping my gun trained upright, just as Kade's dad taught me when hunting, I inch through the freezing basement with light footsteps.

It's too quiet, something isn't right. The deeper I go, the darker it gets. Older concrete turns to slick stone and cells become empty, blood-stained chambers.

The first few doors I throw open are a bust, albeit stomach-churning. A rusted, crimson-soaked bathtub boasting shackles has rage nearly blinding me, but I stuff it down. The next room holds nothing but a wooden chair in the centre, marked with the scars of whip strikes.

The goddamn evidence down here.

It's enough to bring Blackwood down.

Pausing to snap a few hurried photos on my phone, the sound of screaming and shouting has a chill running straight down my spine.

Multiple voices and crying comes from far off, the final level of the Z Wing. With a deep breath, I head into the darkness, prepared to face the devil himself if needed. Whatever it takes to find my girl. I refuse to leave without her, not this time.

I'm coming, baby.

This time, I'll fucking save you.

CHAPTER 39
BROOKLYN

WORST PART OF ME - I PREVAIL

"COME ON. TALK TO ME."

I ignore Logan's desperate pleading and focus instead on the screams coming from Seven's neighbouring cell. They've been in there for over an hour, working their magic on my friend. All because I dared to speak to him and reveal his humanity.

Augustus bought my silence by agreeing to remove the straitjacket, so now I must obediently listen to Seven endure the torture and keep my cowardly mouth shut.

"He'll be fine," Logan reassures.

"Will you shut the fuck up already? You're not helping."

"Panicking will solve nothing."

"Gee, thanks. Like I didn't know that already."

His sympathetic eyes strip me down to my core. Despite everything, his presence in my cell is reassuring. Logan's been the one constant, never once hurting me, maintaining his silence.

I trust him in ways I cannot explain with mere words alone, and he always appears at the right moment, exactly when I need a voice of reason to offer some shred of hope.

"This isn't your fault."

"Everything is my fault," I sob, fisting my hair.

Crossing the cell, he shocks the hell out of me by drawing me into his arms. The simple embrace obliterates any remaining control and I fall apart, clinging to his strangely familiar scent.

Logan strokes my hair. "You've always done your best. We don't blame the prey for falling victim to the jaws of a predator."

"This is my fault." I break down. "Everything that's happened, my entire fucking life... I brought it all on myself. I deserve to be punished, not Seven."

"You're wrong. You were just a kid, and she was a monster. There was nothing you could have done. I know that. Stop blaming yourself for the entire world and all its evil."

"Wait, what?"

His voice filters through my mind, pulling at something unfathomable. That snarled, tangled ball of yarn reaching back into the past, drenched in tears and spilt blood.

I stare into Logan's gunmetal gaze, his irises cast in storm clouds so similar to my own. He offers me a smile that unnerves me even more. It's the smile I dream about every night.

"Who was a monster?" I whisper.

The crack of fists on flesh punctuates my words, followed by more screaming from next door as Seven takes his punishment. I can't help him, the floor falling out beneath me too.

With the cell melting away around me, collapsing under the weight of gathering shadows and darkness, I stare at Logan.

My friend.

My captor.

My abuser's protector.

"You were just a kid," he repeats.

Clutching my throbbing temples, I let out a wail as the images hit me, just like my brain has been trained to do. Augustus has fanned the flames of insanity, encouraging the permeation of past and present. Seven's screams have pulled the trigger, sending me spiralling back into the clutches of my memories.

And Logan's here.

Like he always is.

Losing myself to the onslaught of hallucinations, the dark staircase stretches out before me. I creep downstairs like always, inching towards the inevitable discovery of just how cursed my family blood is.

Only this time, it's Seven screaming as Mum relentlessly beats on him. He has infected my dream, taking my brother's place in the twisted memory.

The two familiar voices bend and blur as I push the kitchen door open several inches to peer inside. Over my shoulder, following in my wake, Logan watches.

"Don't look," he begs.

"Why?"

A crimson kaleidoscope spreading across white tiles, the wet thump of a saw slicing through flesh and bone echoes around us. They're dismembering the body into easily disposable parts. Mum and Dad working in harmony, bound by the sickest of love.

"There's nothing you could have done," Logan whispers.

"I should have stopped them."

"Nobody blames you."

"I fucking blame me, alright?" I snap.

Sighing heavily, with more pain than makes sense, Logan steps away from the kitchen. Like he already knows what horror lays inside and doesn't need the reminder.

"You need to forgive yourself. It's the only way out of here."

Looking back up at him, it finally fucking clicks. The piece of this damaged puzzle that has evaded me for so long. Augustus may have unwound that ball of yarn, used it to tie me up in knots and choke me to death, but he couldn't control everything.

Letting the horrified tears soak my cheeks, I back away, hands covering my mouth. Logan doesn't follow, watching me inch away from him with anguish.

"No. It can't be!"

"Time to wake up," he implores.

Turning on my heel, I run for my life. Back up the staircase, into my teddy bear filled bedroom. Under the covers of the twin-sized bed and screaming back into the present, emerging like a reborn phoenix from ruin and damnation.

I'm not in that house, drenched in death. Not anymore. My cell surrounds me instead, now shadowless. Where the locked door was bolted, imprisoning me in hell, it now stands open. The lock has been blown out by what looks like a gunshot.

There's a voice.

A whispered, hopeful prayer.

"Come on, blackbird."

Who is that?

Is this a dream?

Am I fucking real?

Forcing my fuzzy mind to focus, I blink and find someone kneeling in the corner with me, where I've cowered in a tight ball.

"That's it, baby. Open those eyes."

Sharp pain lances across my cheek where the person strikes me, snapping me out of it. My vision clearing, I focus on their outline, waiting for the details to become clear.

Devastating, aquamarine eyes.

Messy black hair.

Weeks of unshaved stubble.

Swirls of countless dark tattoos.

"Please come back to me," he pleads.

The man seizes my body, pinning me to his hammering chest. I latch on to the sound of his frantic heartbeat, blocking out everything else. The steady beat feels like shockwaves penetrating my skull, the aftershocks of a catastrophic earthquake.

"I've got you and I swear on my damned life, I'm never letting go. I found you… I knew you were here, and I fucking found you. Just like I said I would," he declares.

The realisation comes slow and painful. Like congealed blood scrubbed from a stained kitchen floor, washed with bleach and lies to hide horrors most wouldn't even dream of.

I know him.

This is real, not a dream.

For the first time in so long, the shadows aren't clouding my vision and whispering their violent delights in my ear—I'm being held in his strong, very much *real* arms.

"Hudson?" I test his name.

"Fuck... it's me, blackbird."

Reaching up to graze his cheek with my fingertips, rough to touch, I search his familiar face. Letting every last detail wash over me, allowing the invisible threads I've fought so hard against to guide me home. A glimmering North Star in the darkness.

"You know me. Remember me."

The rusted locks on their mental boxes are blown to pieces and it all comes rushing back, everything I have compartmentalised and allowed Augustus to crush into insignificance.

Hudson.

Eli.

Phoenix.

Kade.

I'm... Brooklyn.

"You didn't forget about me," I whimper.

"I left you behind once before, and I took an oath to make that right. I didn't save you then, baby. But I bloody well will now." He presses his lips to mine, desperate and frenzied. "Always and forever."

Lifting my malnourished body into his arms, Hudson tries to stand, intending to lift me from the cell of death with his head held high. I shout for him to stop, the invisible shackles sliding back into place.

"What is it?"

"You can't take me with you."

"Fucking bullshit! We're getting out of here."

Staring into his crystalline gaze, I shake my head. "I can't leave this place, I'm so sorry. This cell is where I belong. The things I've done—"

My voice abandons me, too overwhelmed to go on. Grabbing my jaw tight and forcing me to look at him, Hudson's determined gaze seizes hold of me and refuses to let go.

"You are more than the things you've done."

"No," I insist. "I hurt people."

"You're a fucking human being. We've all harmed, and we've all been harmed. That's called life."

In my lowest moment, *she* comes racing back to me. Her memory. Slack, lifeless face covered in blood the same violent shade of red as her hair. All signs of joy and hope drained away, leaving nothing but a wasted life behind. A shining light and innocence that I snuffed out with my bare hands.

"I k-killed her. Teegan!"

Of all reactions, I don't expect Hudson to laugh.

"You foolish, beautiful fucking lunatic." Tilting my chin so I can't look away, he grins. "Teegan's alive."

"What?"

"She's alive, Brooke. Spent weeks in intensive care, three surgeries and a hellish recovery. Augustus gave her early release to avoid a lawsuit. She's back home, collecting records and dying her hair crazy colours. I spoke to her last week."

Releasing a pent-up breath that I feel like I've been holding for many, many months… I manage to smile. "She's alive?"

"Hell yeah, she is."

"Oh my God. She's alive."

Hudson nods. "Can we get out of here now?"

It doesn't change anything, nor does it take back all the evil I've inflicted at Augustus's command. But that meagre, tiny scrap of hope is enough. Something to hold on to in a land of misery.

I let Hudson carry me from the cell, pausing in the doorway so I can slide down his body to stand on my own two feet. Turning back, I look into the dark corner behind me, searching for him.

Logan waits.

Smiling proudly.

Ready for me to leave him behind.

"Please come with me," I beg.

Hudson looks at me with concern, glancing around the empty cell. I ignore him, taking a few stuttered steps back inside, freezing when Logan raises his hand to warn me off.

"You don't belong here. Time to leave."

He smooths his bright blonde ponytail, the exact same shade as my own hair. Just like our mother. And our eyes, deep grey pits of hopelessness, inherited from our father.

Logan never belonged to Blackwood. He isn't Augustus's guard, part of the game, or a patrol sent to watch over me. All these months… he lived in me.

Logan isn't real.

He's my brother.

"All along, it was you," I whisper to thin air.

The memory of how he looked ten long years ago stares back at me, wearing his smartass grin with pride. He never intervened or spoke. He never existed. But all this time, I had my brother with me. I wasn't alone. He was there to hold my hand, like he always did in my darkest moments.

"I promised you I'd remain by your side," he explains.

"That was years ago, before she killed you."

"Doesn't matter. I told you, reality can be whatever you want."

Hudson gives me the most bemused stare as I talk to myself. I must look insane, addressing an empty cell and sobbing my fucking eyes out. It's fine. Crazy suits me anyway.

"Thank you for staying with me."

Logan winks. "You got it, kiddo."

I lift my fingers to my lips, pressing a gentle kiss before blowing it into the air. From across the cell, Logan catches it and presses his own fingers to his lips.

"Please don't leave me again."

"I'm sorry, Brooke. It's time."

The shadows gather at his ankles and crawl their way over his body, pulling my hallucination back into the darkness from which he spawned. Where Logan once stood, nothing but an empty torture chamber remains. His work is complete.

I'm right here, kiddo.

I'll never leave you.

I'm so proud of you, Brooke.

Covering my thudding heart with my hand, I turn my back on the hell I've come to recognise as home. Hudson waits for me, unnerved but accepting, gun at the ready to defend us until his last breath.

With his strength, I leave the past behind. We break out into the gloomy corridor and the endless screams are silent at last.

"Brooklyn?"

Waiting for us, an exact replica of the description I received from Roberts but couldn't place, Sadie smiles before throwing her arms around me.

"We got you, girl. I knew we would," she says triumphantly.

Before they can drag me from the Z Wing, I gesture to the three locked doors around me. Each with more horrors waiting.

"We have to take them with us. All of them."

"Who?" Hudson frowns.

"Augustus's projects. We're the only ones left."

Sadie nods, facing the two cells opposite us. I've never seen Patient Five before, only a glimpse of Two. Though I heard their awful stories through Jefferson's taunts.

"I'll get these open," Sadie offers.

"We have to get Seven." I gesture to the next cell.

Hudson raises his gun, pushing me behind him. With perfect aim, he shoots the lock off in one smooth hit and wrenches the heavy metal door open.

I follow him in, catching his whirlwind of movement rushing at whoever waits inside. When the dust settles, Hudson has Jefferson in a headlock with the gun pressed right up against his temple.

"Move and you're dead," he hisses.

Jefferson snarls. "You're an idiot!"

In retaliation, Hudson pistol-whips him to the ground. I take the chance to step inside, expecting to find Augustus and finding nothing but a broken, unconscious body instead.

Seven is strapped to his cot with dozens of wires stuck against his bare chest to pass their painful electrical current. He's finally passed out, unable to endure any more.

"This is Seven. He's coming," I explain quickly.

Hudson seems unconvinced. "Why?"

Refusing to back down or feel ashamed of our connection, I begin to rip the wires free and battle with Seven's restraints.

"He's a friend. I'm not leaving him!"

The edge of delirium in my voice spurs Hudson into action, and he punches Jefferson between the eyes, knocking his ass to the floor. Leaving him to choke on his own blood, Hudson takes over and gets Seven free in seconds.

"He's only got one hand," he growls, noting the stump.

"Augustus cut it off."

"You're kidding me?"

"I'm not. Let's go!"

Throwing Seven's skeletal body over his shoulder, Hudson tries to shove me towards the door, but I don't move. Jefferson is still breathing. This sadist is partially responsible for all I've endured.

Before I even have to ask, Hudson slaps a knife into my hand. "All yours, baby."

I steal a mind-melting kiss, clutching the weapon tight. With tingling lips, I crouch down and meet Jefferson's weakened gaze.

"You told me that I wasn't allowed to be a person."

Attempting to scramble away from me, I press my knee against his chest, pinning him in place as he gasps for breath.

"News flash, Jefferson. *You're not allowed to be alive.*"

With the memory of Patient Two's desperate cries in my mind, I raise the knife high and before he can react, stab it straight into Jefferson's left eye socket.

Blood and fluid spray across my face, but I don't flinch. Carving his flesh is a messy task, but I savour every last second as I finish with the left socket and move to the right.

When I'm done, Jefferson finally lies still. Not even a twitch. Nothing remains of his eyes, deftly removed by my blade before I cut his throat for good measure. I leave the bloody lumps beside his head as a warning.

We will never be blinded to the truth.

"That was so fucking hot," Hudson groans.

"Seriously?"

"Don't toy with me, blackbird. I don't have time to fuck you next to this asshole's corpse. Move your sexy ass before I change my mind."

His gaze burns with desire, despite the blood drenching my entire body. Admiring the lethally sharp knife, I keep it for myself by stashing it up my sleeve.

"You're a damn psychopath, Hud."

"Says the girl carving eyes out." He laughs.

We share a fast, intense kiss that leaves us both gasping and begging for more. I make myself step away from him, glancing one last time at Jefferson's remains before leaving him to rot in hell. He will never leave this place again; the site of all the pain and misery he inflicted, now his final resting place.

Sadie waits for us in the corridor, unaware of what took us so long. Her eyes bug out when she spots me, but she doesn't question the heavy dousing of blood. I doubt she'd approve of my revenge, no matter how angry she is.

Two patients hang off each other behind Sadie, both female and thinner than starving children, covered in dirt and blood. One, I assume Patient Five, holds the other in a close embrace. Patient Two looks different than the last time I saw her, then newly blinded and writhing in pain. Thick scar tissue lies where her eyes used to be.

Before we can say anything, a gasp from Sadie has me spinning on the spot. She stands frozen, mouth slack and hands raised in utter shock. Like she's seen a ghost in real life and can't quite decide if she's losing her mind or not.

"Jude?" she calls out.

Eyes bouncing between Hudson and Sadie, I realise that she's addressing the unconscious body slumped over his shoulder. Sadie takes two halting steps forwards and cups Seven's slack face, searching his features like he's the holy damn grail.

"It's him. Jesus Christ, it's really him."

Her story comes rushing back to me all at once, told months prior in a hurried exchange of heartbreak. The brother she lost to Blackwood's brutality and assumed dead, leading to a cold case and wild-goose chase across the decades.

Jude. Seven.

One and the same.

"You're sure?"

Tears stain her cheeks pink. "He's alive. After all these years... I just assumed I was looking for a body. But I swear to God, Brooke, that's him. It's Jude."

Hudson hefts Seven's weight, bouncing on his feet. "Look, I don't give a shit if this is Santa fucking Claus or the goddamn tooth fairy. Can we move?"

Suitably chastised, we break into a run to escape the Z Wing before our luck runs out. Hudson takes the lead, ducking through corridors and empty doorways, while Sadie covers him and the precious cargo with her own gun raised high.

The blare of a distant alarm spurs us on, and the closer we get to the surface levels, the louder it grows. I take the rear, shoving Two and Five forwards, urging them on despite their terror.

Five has to guide every step that Two takes into the unknown, clinging to her for safety and guidance. I don't know how long they've been locked away down here, but staying is riskier than leaving this life behind.

"Patient Eight! Hold it right there!"

Our bloodied, exhausted group draws to a halt back on the main level of the basement. Blocking our exit, the inevitable stands.

My nemesis himself, owner of the keys that imprison my broken mind. He awaits with a gun in hand, trained on me along with three others that are clasped in the guards' hands.

"Augustus."

"Patient Eight. I should have known," he thunders.

Hudson cocks his gun in warning, gaining Augustus's attention and angering him even more.

"Your friends have pulled the plug on the most expensive social experiment in living history. I'll make you pay for this."

Hudson can't help but laugh. "Poor doc. That's the problem when you fuck with so-called criminals. We're notoriously hot-headed and don't like to be screwed with. You didn't figure that out yet, genius? Get out of the way or they'll be dissecting your corpse next."

His weapon dangling threateningly in the air, we're too slow to react as Augustus points it straight at Hudson. Time slows to a crawl as his finger dances on the trigger. Then, with the bullet mirroring the deafening crack of a whip, Augustus surprises us all by firing off a shot.

The crash of Hudson's gun hitting the floor precludes him falling to his knees, blood pouring between his fingertips, clasped over his left shoulder. I scream his name but freeze on the spot, unable to move an inch as Augustus trains his gun on me next.

"Listen to me very closely, Patient Eight."

Hudson remains conscious, writhing in pain as he fights to stem the bleeding. Facing Augustus, I note the hateful smirk twisting his lips, and mentally vow to wipe it from his fucking face.

"I won't punish you for your disobedience if you walk over to me," he commands. "Leave these delinquents to their fate. Come back to me and all will be forgiven. You have my word, Eight."

"Your word?" I utter.

"Have I ever given you reason to doubt me? Are your friends not alive and well, just as our deal entailed?"

Hudson's hiss of pain underscores Augustus's words. He sways on the verge of unconsciousness, crimson pooling on the ground beneath him.

Piping hot rage races through my veins, obliterating all remaining emotion. Embracing the welcome emptiness, I let myself slide back into Patient Eight's skin, wearing her persona like a wolf in sheep's clothing.

"Brooklyn... stop," Hudson groans.

I disregard his pleading, taking careful steps to return to my master. Augustus offers me a lazy grin as he watches me approach, full of confidence. Like he never doubted his ability to regain control over my mind.

Hudson shouts my name again, attempting to draw me back, but I lock him out. There is no room for sentiment or emotion. Not in this world.

I learned that quickly in the dark, shutting out the weakness of my feelings to survive each day of torture. But I see it now, the undeniable truth. As long as Augustus lives, I can never be free. His control will remain absolute, regained with words alone.

I stop mere inches from where he waits, allowing him to sweep a hand over my face, his satisfaction palpable.

"Back where you belong," he preens.

"Doctor Augustus?"

"Yes, Eight?"

The urge to submit to him is all-consuming, like his voice has become entwined within the fabric of my soul. It takes every ounce of will I have left to palm the knife stashed up my sleeve, still slick with Jefferson's blood.

"My name is Brooklyn West."

Augustus's eyes flare with delicious shock right before I jam the knife straight into his chest. The rush of hot blood soaks my hand, and I lean close, lips against his ear.

"*Not* Patient Eight."

Savouring the cry that slips from his lips, Augustus stumbles and falls. His weight crashes into me and I twist the knife for good measure, digging it in even deeper.

The blast of gunfire from Sadie and the remaining guards doesn't distract me from enjoying a moment I've dreamed about for months.

"You could have been... so m-much more," Augustus gurgles.

Examining the crimson rivulets soaking his shirt, I let a desolate smile spread my lips.

"I'm enough. I always was."

How inevitable the fragility of human life is, even for those who twist it into something unrecognisable, creating a parasitic monster inside the body of a man.

Augustus collapses in a lifeless heap, his empty orbs staring back at me. Crouching down, I drag the knife free from his chest to keep as a memento. Sadie drops the final guard with a well-placed bullet and the corridor falls silent.

"Blackbird?"

His voice draws me back, peeling away layers of numbness and brutality. Hudson has struggled to his feet, still clutching his shoulder to stem the bleeding. When he looks at me, his expression is full of twisted pride.

"Come back to us, little heathen."

I force out the voice of Patient Eight, chaining her in the darkest corner of my mind. Hudson takes careful steps towards me until I'm bundled in his arms, the unsteady roar of his heartbeat anchoring me in the present.

"He's dead and can't hurt you anymore."

Unable to speak, I nod against his chest.

"Come on, let's go home."

"Home?" I repeat.

"The guys. They're all waiting."

As we separate, Sadie disappears into Augustus's nearby office. She emerges seconds later with a laptop stashed under her arm, her grin triumphant.

"Evidence. We're gonna take this toxic waste apart."

Limping and badly injured, but still alive, we leave the Zimbardo Wing as a group. We make it back to the reception, barely able to see through the thick cloud of smoke and smothering flames.

"We have to get to the woods," Sadie yells.

Hudson grimaces. "Follow me!"

Ducking through the smouldering building, we run from wild, angry flames. All around us, the unmoving bodies of guards and patients alike are left in the aftermath, burning to ash. A complete bloodbath has taken place.

What the hell happened here?

The carnage outside the main building conceals our tracks, with the few remaining guards failing to maintain order. Patients swarm them, wielding shanks, and stolen batons, beating them into a pulp even as the scream of approaching sirens warns of their impending doom.

Hudson shouts at me to run and we take off. Desperation and pure determination to survive chase us through the darkness. I'm barely able to put one foot in front of the other, fuelled by adrenaline.

Looking back over my shoulder, I watch as Blackwood Institute crumbles to ruin behind us, an unrecognisable hulk of burning hell. The sight spurs me on to keep running, even as my body fails me.

The hole in the fence has become an entire break, clipped with wire cutters, and ripped apart. Letting Sadie and the girls go first, Hudson takes the rear with Seven draped over his back, his entire shirt soaked with blood from the bullet wound. He waves me off when I frown at the mess, urging me forwards.

We race through the woods, following the beam of light flashing into the sky in a rhythmic pattern. I spot the chapel in the distance, a small group gathered outside.

Dangerous hope chokes me.

Several figures stand to attention when they spot us, gaping in shock, before one person breaks into a run.

I realise who it is.

Legs pumping like a steam engine.

Arms outstretched and frantic.

"Eli!" I scream at the top of my lungs.

The others falter in disbelief, before shaking themselves out of it and following in a sprint. Surrounded by thick woods and darkness, the distant light of out-of-control flames lights the path of our reunion.

"Kade! Phoenix!"

As Blackwood falls, I find my way home.

"Brooklyn!"

"Firecracker!"

The person I used to be ceases to exist until I'm back in their arms, crushed between four familiar bodies. Patient Eight slips away, and Brooklyn West takes her place. Everyone is shouting and sobbing, lost to the carnage.

But one voice raises above the others.

Strong and unwavering, for the first time ever.

"Are you real?" Eli asks desperately.

I hesitate, before grinning at him.

"Yeah. I'm fucking real."

EPILOGUE

KADE

STARING OUT AT THE CALM, breezeless ocean, I inhale a deep lungful of salty sea air. Letting it wash over me, stripping back the grip of every dark moment the past four months have entailed.

Scrap that, the past year.

So much suffering and unnecessary pain. All of it endured just to get to this point—freedom. Not only with my brothers, but my whole family intact. Our girl as well, alive and breathing.

It isn't over yet.

But this is the start of a new chapter.

"Kade?"

Turning my back on the English Channel, I find Mum waiting for me. I walk into her arms, accepting the warm embrace. I'm grateful she survived her own form of hell. It's been so long since we even hugged.

"You did it, son. You did it."

"Not without your help."

"Nonsense. This is your victory, Kade."

She meets my eyes with such pride radiating from her, it knocks me for six. After we escaped Blackwood, using the chaos of the war zone behind us for cover, getting to our rendezvous point was relatively easy.

Mum awaited, a car and supplies in tow, just as we planned after so many months apart to avoid Dad's suspicion. Eighteen hours of exhausted driving later, we stand at the furthermost edge of Northern Scotland, far from civilisation.

"How's Hudson?"

Her teeth worry her lip. "We got the bullet out, he'll be fine. Though I'm sure we will have to listen to his moaning for a while."

I snort. "That I can live with."

Mum nudges my shoulder. "Come inside, Sadie wants to show us something."

"I'm coming. We need to make a plan."

"It's all ready for you, son. As we agreed. I'll drop you off and return home, Cece still needs me."

"What about Dad? I can't let him hurt you again."

She pinches my cheeks, her signature motherly smile in place. "He's too busy dealing with the fallout of Blackwood burning to the ground. Doesn't even know I'm gone. I'll be home and packed up before he knows it. I can't run with you, Kade. I'm sorry."

I draw her close for another hug. "I know. One day, we won't have to run anymore. Then we can be a family again, all together."

Mum wipes her tears, smiling.

"We will. Until then, use the burner phone. I'll keep you updated on our location. Tomorrow, I'll sign the divorce papers and move with Cece, off the books. He won't be able to find us."

Satisfied with the plan in place, we trudge back up the cobbled path, hand in hand. Tomorrow, we will also set off. Retreat to a designated safe place, off the grid and paid for with cash.

Somewhere for our exhausted group to rest, heal, and recuperate. Plan our next moves. Find ourselves again. Whatever needs to be done to fix the damage inflicted by Blackwood.

Back in the tiny, rented house we crammed in for the night, I find the bare kitchen packed tight as Hudson and Phoenix gobble sandwiches. Clearly, he isn't on death's door, based on the way he practically inhales the meal.

"Glad to see you're feeling better." I laugh.

He shrugs, before wincing in pain.

"Sorry, bro. Can't get rid of me that easily."

"Dammit. I'll have to shoot you myself."

Mum throws her arms around him, mindful of his bandaged shoulder. She's loved being a parent again, however briefly. And I've never seen Hudson smile so much as the past day, even if we're running for our lives.

In the cramped sitting area, passed out and curled around each other like sloths, Brooklyn and Eli are joined at the hip. He hasn't detached himself from her yet, but that's okay.

Our Eli has come back to us in the past few hours alone, alive and kicking after months of silence. He even spoke to me to offer his thanks.

I did it.

After selling my soul to the devil, I did it.

We're free.

Dragging a chair out to join Sadie at the kitchen table, she's surrounded by stolen paperwork and pouring over Augustus's laptop. She barely stirs, knocking back a cold cup of coffee and shuddering in disgust.

"How's... Seven? Jude?" I ask awkwardly.

Her haunted eyes meet mine. "I had to tie him down with sheets. The sedatives I managed to steal won't last for long, but it's a temporary solution for now."

Nodding, I file that away for a later discussion. The beginning of a long list of pressing issues, along with the additional passengers we weren't expecting. The girls that Brooklyn refers to as Two and Five haven't spoken either, holed up in the bathroom, asleep together in the empty tub.

"I need to show you all something," Sadie announces.

Waking up Eli and Brooklyn, we all crowd around the kitchen table. Hudson folds Brooklyn into his good arm, his face buried in her hair. She glances up at me and I can't help but grin at the thrill of seeing her with us, after so long thinking she was gone for good.

Mouthing, I hope she can read my words.

You're beautiful.

An adorable blush stains her cheeks, and she gives me a wink, promising retaliation. Managing to drag my gaze from her, heat already pumping through my veins, I refocus on the laptop sat before Sadie.

It contains countless classified documents. A treasure trove of information and a twisted rabbit hole that will undoubtedly drag us all down it for a whole new rollercoaster ride.

"What is it?" I prompt.

"Take a look at this."

Sadie pulls up an odd-looking map of the country, bathed in shades of black and white, almost military style. The crossed lines form a grid, with several red markers spread throughout the entirety of the UK. In the bottom corner, the map is watermarked with a logo, proudly proclaiming the company name.

Incendia Corporation.

"What's going on?" Hudson asks.

Opening her notebook, Sadie clears her throat.

"Hazelthorn House, Compton Hall, Kirkwood Lodge, Priory Lane, Harrowdean Manor, Blackwood Institute."

Finishing reciting the list, she faces us all with wide, terrified eyes. "These are the six psychiatric inpatient facilities under the jurisdiction of Incendia—the parent company that Augustus worked for. All still operational to this day."

Stunned silence follows in which you could hear a pin drop, despite seven of us packed into mere metres of cramped space.

I snatch up her notebook, scanning the list again and comparing it to the satellite images on Augustus's laptop.

Six markers. Six institutes.

"What does it mean?" Brooklyn whispers.

Glancing between our bedraggled group, the matching expressions of horror and realisation as we all stare at the undeniable list, I vocalise the fear that everyone is feeling.

"It means Blackwood was just the beginning."

BONUS SCENE

BROOKLYN

Time ceases to exist in the darkness of the Z Wing.

Reality punches through our numb shields like morse code—a blip, a dash, a flash of comprehension in the gaps between where confusion lies. We have to piece it together and sort it into a haphazard quilt with sheer will alone.

Punch. Punch. Punch.

The drip of stale water.

Screams echoing around me.

Whip. Whip. Whip.

Wind whistling through my cell.

The barest whisper of his hoarse voice.

Slash. Slash. Slash.

"Eight? You awake?"

Curled into a tight ball, I squeeze my eyes shut. The constant pain is no longer an accurate measurement of time passing. Broken bones and beaten flesh are the new normal.

"Go away, Sev," I croak back.

"Sure. I'll just step outside and give you some privacy, shall I?"

He's a sarcastic son of a bitch. But deep down, I know I'd rather be trapped in this hell with a soulless psychopath than with nothing but the demons in my head.

"Just because we're stuck here together, doesn't mean we have to talk."

His resultant silence is deafening. All I can hear is the erratic hammering of my heart beat. It's a bold-faced lie. I can admit that to myself down here, with nothing left but my own bitter truth.

I want him to talk to me. Fuck, I want him to keep me alive when the whole world is determined to snuff out the last spark of light left inside my broken chest.

Seven has become my last glimmer of hope in a fucking hopeless world.

"Talk to me," he pleads. "Tell me something that I don't know about you."

Shifting closer to the air vent that separates our two cells, I search for an answer and come up empty. I can feel it at the edges of my mind—the dregs of the person I once was. Embers floating amongst the ash of a ruined life.

"There's nothing," I rasp. "What about you?"

He's silent for a pregnant pause. "I had a friend. Once."

"A friend?"

"In the last institute," he adds. "There was this other patient. Just a kid. He was in the cell next to mine for a while and we talked a lot, until one day, they took him. He never came back."

"What happened to him?"

"Couldn't handle Augustus's torture."

Fuck. I wish I could say that fear is coiling around my vital organs and slowly choking the life from my veins, but my lies are futile. I'm not afraid. Not anymore.

The darkness is my home now.

My armageddon.

The battlefield for my sanity.

"His favourite food was coconut-flavoured frozen yoghurt. I remember that clearly." Seven's voice is a mournful whisper. "He enjoyed playing sports in school, before he was admitted. Badminton and rugby."

"Do you remember his name?"

"No. Just the sound of his screaming."

Down here, that's as good as it gets.

"What's the first thing you'd do if we got out?"

Seven scoffs through the air vent. "We're never getting out."

The flow of escaping tears stings my cheeks. I didn't realise I could still cry. It's been a long time since I've felt enough to let the tears flow, but something in his voice has teased the despair out of me.

"Please. I need something to hold on to," I beg him.

When there's another silent beat of hesitation, I wrap my fingers around the metal grate of the air vent. It's ancient and rusted to hell from the dampness. There's nothing but darkness on the other side.

Until a finger brushes mine.

The faintest, barest whisper.

"I would hold you," Seven responds in a strained voice. "And never let go."

Our fingers can hardly touch through the obstruction, but the tiniest flicker of his skin touching mine is like a defibrillator to the heart. I'm shocked to the point of near unconsciousness, my soul reignited and set alight.

"What about you?" he asks.

I curl my index finger so it hooks around his.

"I've spent my whole life praying for it to end," I admit. "More than once, I've tried to speed up the process myself. Death is all I've ever wanted in this world."

Seven's breathing hitches.

"And now?"

"Now," I echo uncertainly. "Now… I want you to hold me too."

"Fuck, Eight. If that isn't something to live for, then I don't know what is."

"You can't live for me. It's too late for us now."

"I refuse to believe that. I can't."

His finger still strokes mine, a reverent hymn that calls to the depths of my damnation. He isn't my lighthouse in the dark. No.

Seven is pure darkness that's creeping its way across the fallen earth. He's the inevitability of night swallowing day. Death stealing life. Hatred consuming hope.

He will never be my saviour.

We're too ensnared in the devil's clutches for that.

"If we were out there, in the real world," he says, "I would press my lips to yours and fucking devour you, Eight."

My heart beat skitters. I can't help but want more.

"And then?"

"Then... I'd touch every inch of you that I've dreamt of tasting since we met."

It physically pains me how much I want that.

"Where?" I ask breathlessly.

He shifts on the other side of the vent, and his raspy voice sounds closer. The rustle of fabric moving causes my pulse to spike again.

"I'd trace your collarbones with my tongue," he murmurs. "And kiss my way down to your gorgeous tits."

Curling closer to the vent, I trail a hand up my leg. We were allowed to rinse off after our last job, and I was left in an oversized shirt, now ratty and bloodstained from the ulcers on my back.

"I'd take each of your rosy nipples in my mouth and bite down," Seven continues huskily. "They'd be so hard for me, Eight. Just like my cock is right now."

Hand slipping beneath my t-shirt, I find the ragged cotton of the boy shorts I was provided. My hand dips between my thighs to find the slick heat gathering at my core.

"While sucking on your tits, I would push your legs open to expose your pussy. You'd be dripping and begging for my cock to fill you."

Thumb circling my clit, I slide a finger between my folds. Screw this fantasy future. I'm soaked right here, right now. If I could, I'd take a sledgehammer to the wall just to let him fuck me in front of Augustus's cameras.

"Would you taste me?" I wonder.

"Fuck yes, I would." Seven chuckles. "I bet you taste like a dream. I'd make you come all over my tongue first."

Pushing a finger into my slit, I moan quietly. I know he can hear me. The soft *thwack* of him touching himself accompanies my breathy pants for more attention. His voice alone is driving me wild.

"What next?" I urge him.

"Once your juices are smeared over my lips, I'd kiss you again and make you taste yourself."

Needing more, I press another finger into my cunt, tweaking my clit with each rotation. Just imagining his hand down there instead of my own has my muscles clenching with anticipation.

In the darkness, I can let our bleak surroundings melt away. We're not in the Z Wing, chained, beaten and starved. It's just us. Patient Seven and his Eight. No one else. We're the last two survivors on a barren earth.

"Would you beg for my cock, Eight?"

"Yes," I mewl.

"I'd make you crawl on your knees and plead for me to fuck your pussy. Even then, I wouldn't fill you. Not until I'd fucked your perfect mouth first."

Spreading my legs wider so I can thrust into myself at a deeper angle, I don't give a fuck if Augustus or one of the guards is watching our little show. The cell is dark enough to conceal us.

Even if it weren't, it wouldn't stop me from doing this. Down here, Seven is the one breathing life back into my lungs. No one else. He's the only one holding my hand through this hellish torture.

"I want to hear the sound of you choking on my cock as I fuck your throat," he croons. "Would you take it all? Every inch?"

"I would," I admit.

"But I wouldn't finish in your mouth. I want to feel your cunt clenching around me when that happens."

Swirling my fingers, I stroke the tender spot deep inside my cunt that sets off fireworks beneath the shell of my skin. In my mind, he's poised above me, playing my body like his favourite instrument.

"Imagine your fingers are my cock buried inside you," Seven instructs. "Feel me slamming into you, Eight. I wouldn't be able to hold myself back."

I follow his whispered commands, stroking my pussy until it feels like I'm going to explode. The pressure of two fingers buried inside me has morphed into a different fantasy, one where my hips are pinned beneath his.

"That's it, princess," he encourages. "I'm going to fuck you so hard, you won't be able to walk straight. Imagine that."

"Please," I garble.

"Please, what?"

"I need you to touch me, Sev. Fuck."

His voice lowers into a pained scoff.

"Trust me, I would if I could. Keep touching yourself, Eight. I want to hear you come all over your fingers for me."

Stray tears squeeze out the corners of my eyes. Even on the verge of falling apart, it doesn't stop the grief from overwhelming me; the knowledge of all we've lost, our lives stolen by a master puppeteer.

"Stop," Seven admonishes. "It's just us here. No one else. Feel my arms around you. Let go, princess. We can come together."

Pinching my clit to drive my release to the edge of a precipice, I feel the tears drying on my cheeks as the wave finally crests. Seven's dirty words are drowned out by the roar in my ears.

He's holding himself up above me in my mind as his hips drive into me in a pounding, relentless rhythm. Our bodies are slick amidst a frantic tangle. When his lips wrap around my nipple, simulated by a twist of my fingers, I let go.

My whole body tenses as the orgasm washes over me. Seven grunts on the other side of the air vent, relishing his own climax. For a brief, glorious moment, I can almost picture the thick concrete barrier between us crumbling.

Letting my head slump against the floor, I fight to catch my breath. Aftershocks are still sending twinges through my system.

"Eight?" he whispers.

"I'm here."

"We're not done yet. You still need to clean your mess up."

"What?" I frown into the darkness.

"Your fingers are wet. Tell me how they taste."

Pressing my thighs together, I bring my hand up to my face. Seven's silent as I suck my fingers into my mouth and lick the salty fluid from them. My heart damn near stops when I imagine him doing this instead.

"There's a good patient," he praises.

With the taste of come weighing on my tongue, I curl back into my previous position, almost hugging the wall. It's freezing cold and hard as a rock, but with enough brain power, I can picture his heat curled around me.

We lapse into our usual comfortable silence until it's broken by the harsh lash of someone screaming in the distance. The hairs on my skin stand on end as I break out in terrified gooseflesh.

"Sev," I squeak.

"Shhh," he soothes. "It's okay, princess. Focus on the sound of my voice."

But it's drowned out again by screaming. Over and over the sound echoes, like someone's skin is being peeled from their bones without anaesthetic. I grind my teeth together to hold a choked sob inside.

The screaming doesn't usually bother me, but my emotions are high on the surface tonight. Seven does that to me. I can't always keep my soulless mask in place around him.

"Tell me something I don't know about you," he asks again. "Anything, Eight. I just want to feel close to you."

While my eyes clamped shut to staunch the flow of tears, I sneak my finger through the air vent again, and the tip of his index finger meets mine.

"I can't remember," I choke out. "It's all gone."

With our fingers interlinked, he whispers a promise into the darkness. "Then that's the first thing we'll do when we get out."

"What is?"

I can almost taste the smile in his words.

"Make new memories."

PLAYLIST

LISTEN HERE:
BIT.LY/SACRIFICIALSINNERS

Secrets - Written By Wolves
Nightmare - The Veer Union
Face Me - The Plot In You
Why you gotta kick me when I'm down? - Bring Me The Horizon
Lonely - Palaye Royale
Careful What You Wish For - Bad Omens
I Think I'm OKAY - Machine Gun Kelly, YUNGBLUD & Travis Barker
Montreal - The White Noise
No Answers - Amber Run
Animal In Me - Solence
Carry On - Falling In Reverse
Hospital For Souls - Bring Me The Horizon
Thousand Eyes - Of Monsters And Men
Designer Drugs - FNKHOUSER
Impersona - What Haunts You
Smells Like Teen Spirit - Malia J
High Water - Sleep Token
Madness - Ruelle
Violent Pictures - Dream On Dreamer
Save Me - Omri
Saint - Echos
15 Missed Calls - Mouth Culture
Higher - Sleep Token
If I Say - Mumford & Sons
My Body Is A Cage - Arcade Fire
Adrenaline - Zero 9:36
Destroyer - Of Monsters and Men
Deathbeds - Bring Me The Horizon

Through Ash - Moon Tooth
Shed My Skin - Within Temptation
The Lighthouse - Halsey
What You Need - Bring Me The Horizon
Fuck It - Glass Tides
NOT JUST BREATHING - The Plot In You
Heart of Glass (Crabtree Remix) - Blondie, Philip Glass & Jonas Crabtree
Chemical - The Devil Wears Prada
Numb - Linkin Park
I Feel It Too - Dream State
Anarchy - Lilith Czar
Worst Part Of Me - I Prevail
If I Were You - Nothing But Thieves

DESECRATED SAINTS

BLACKWOOD INSTITUTE #3

Blackwood Institute

TRIGGER WARNING

Desecrated Saints is a why choose, reverse harem romance, so the main character will have multiple love interests that she will not have to choose between.

This book is very dark and contains scenes that may be triggering for some readers. This includes self-harm, graphic violence, psychological torture, and strong mental health themes including psychosis, trauma and suicidal ideation.

There is also explicit language used throughout and sexual scenes involving blood play, breath play, knife play, asphyxiation and mutual self-harming.

If you are triggered by any of this content, please do not read this book. This is a dark romance, and therefore not for the faint of heart. Additionally, this book is written for entertainment and not intended to accurately represent the treatment of mental health issues.

PROLOGUE
SEVEN - 2016

STRAIGHTENING my pressed blue shirt and matching pinstripe tie, I give my reflection a decisive nod. It's time. No more skulking around, stealing the odd stack of papers or eavesdropping behind locked doors.

I need proof.

The world has to know what goes on in here.

Leaving the safety of my comfortable office behind, I slip down the thickly carpeted corridor of the prestigious Blackwood Institute. This is my place of employment, and a source of constant worry for the past six months. It's far from the romanticised dream I'd built up in my head.

"Doctor Farlow?"

Freezing, I plaster an impassive mask in place.

For fuck's sake.

Miss White's designer pumps sink into the soft carpet as she joins me, dragging her eyes over my muscled chest. Her flirtation has only increased in the time I've worked here, reaching unprofessional levels that make me uncomfortable.

"What can I do for you, Warden?" I smile politely.

"Please, Jude. How many times must we discuss this?" Her red-painted nails scrape over my bicep. "Call me Elizabeth. I just wanted to see how you're getting on. I heard you had a difficult time last week."

I match her smile. "Naturally, working in an environment like this poses its challenges. But don't worry about me. I can look after myself... Elizabeth."

Her tinkling laughter grates against my skull.

"Oh, Jude. You do amuse me. I'll leave you to continue with your day, but should you need anything... you know where to find me. No matter the hour."

With a final lingering look, she retreats in a cloud of sickly sweet perfume. I watch her return to her office down the corridor. I have no doubt that her thick lashes and pouty lips hide a multitude of sins.

The incident she's referencing involved a patient who had a complete psychotic breakdown in the group session I was facilitating, and it drew a lot of attention to my traineeship. I can fend off their questions and pretend to be unfazed, but truthfully, that session was the final nail in the coffin.

I knew the patient, Lucia, had been struggling for some time. Her regular clinician is a dinosaur who refuses to discuss his treatment methods with me, but he also happens to be my boss. I've had to tread very carefully as a result.

There are a lot of unusual things about Blackwood.

And many unanswered questions.

Scanning my ID badge, I let myself into the gloomier corridor that leads down the winding staircase. The solitary wing is my least favourite place in this gothic museum of insanity. I avoid it by necessity. My work does not concern those incarcerated in Professor Lazlo's basement, but Lucia has been missing all week.

I'm done lying to myself about Blackwood's involvement in her deterioration. Inching past locked cells and occupied signs, I pause to read the names printed across the paperwork attached to each door. By the end of the corridor, I've yet to find Lucia's name.

She isn't fucking here.

What now? Think!

With a glance at the ever-present CCTV cameras, I throw caution to the wind. I won't unravel this mystery by playing it safe. Passing Lazlo's office door, I take the next staircase down. This one is lit by faint bulbs that cast the entire world in uncomfortable shadows.

The temperature drops even further as I emerge on the lowest level of the basement. Expecting more solitary confinement, I'm unnerved by what I find instead. These aren't the padded cells equipped to handle the sickest of patients I've seen in Manchester and Clearview.

I'm staring at torture chambers, blood-stained and windowless.

With my heart threatening to shatter into terrified shards, I inch inside the closest room. The door is ajar to air out the scent of industrial bleach. A rusted bathtub sits in the centre, boasting medieval-style shackles that make my stomach turn. I have to cover my mouth to ensure I don't throw up.

The bathtub is full of crimson, bloody water, as if the occupant sliced a vein, exposing them to the cruel justice of death. Peering around the chamber, I note the scratch marks and dents scattered across the concrete walls. Someone was locked in here.

No, not someone. An animal.

Whatever remains of a person when you strip the humanity away.

"Doctor Farlow. Fancy seeing you down here, son."

Jumping out of my skin, I turn to find Professor Lazlo lingering in the doorway. With his arms crossed and wire-framed spectacles hanging around his neck, he grins at me.

"Finally opened your eyes, did you?"

"What is this place? Where is Lucia?" I demand.

"No need to raise your voice. We're both professionals, are we not?"

Gesturing around the chamber, I laugh. "You call this professional? Where is my patient?"

"Lucia is my patient, Jude."

"I have the right to enquire about her welfare!"

Lazlo sighs. "Fine. You want to see Lucia? Be my guest."

Turning on his heel, he stalks off down the murky corridor. I follow, shivering from the sub-zero temperature and something far worse—real, tangible fear. I suspected foul play, but nothing like this. I'm out of my depth.

Lazlo pauses outside the final locked door, rust-spotted and made from thick, impenetrable metal. Retrieving a black swipe card, he waves it over the hidden scanner and the squeal of old hinges fills my ears.

In those brief seconds before the interior is revealed, I consider running. Actually running. But it's no use, as two of his personal guards have joined us and now box me in on both sides. My unease triples.

"Five? You have a visitor," Lazlo singsongs.

Choking on my panic, I glance into the damp cell. An old-style cot rests in the corner, boasting a familiar bag of bones, strapped down with heavy restraints. Blinking at me with no recognition, Lucia's mouth opens and shuts without a word.

"Holy shit," I breathe.

"As you can see, she is acutely unwell and must remain here."

"What on earth are you doing to her?"

Lazlo chuckles behind me. "Reconditioning."

Before I can defend myself, sharp pain blooms in the back of my head. I fall to my knees, my vision blurring. I'm surrounded by brutes with tasers. I scream at the electrical current, jerking and thrashing until the torture ceases.

"You should have stayed upstairs," Lazlo says simply.

"You w-won't… get a-away… with this!"

Peering down at me with his spectacles replaced, his dead orbs of sick human curiosity scare the living daylights out of me. Lazlo smirks, taking in my still-twitching form, before turning to his two guards.

"Call Augustus on the private line. Tell him to come and collect; I have two new acquisitions. Bring the sedatives too. Let's prep them."

Sparing me a final glance, Lazlo shakes his head.

"You'll wish you never stepped foot in Blackwood Institute."

CHAPTER 1
BROOKLYN

DIED ENOUGH FOR YOU - BLIND
CHANNEL

STRETCHED out on the sandy hill, a steep slope leads straight down to the thunderous crash of waves. Part of me is tempted to throw myself over the edge rather than face the people behind me. Instead, I watch the sun sink on the horizon.

On all sides, nothing but ravenous ocean waves surround us. The nearest town is miles away, with a total population of fifty this far up north. We arrived a few days ago, moving under the cover of night. The plan was executed to utter perfection.

I spent the first couple of days unconscious. My body had shut down on me. I wish I could go back to that oblivion now. As I turn my back on the sea, the deep hole I created with my bare hands waits for me. It took me almost an hour to dig. I'm weak from months of imprisonment.

According to Kade, it's been four months.

I hardly believed him at first.

Humans are fucking resilient. Our bodies kick in and keep us alive, even when our minds have checked out. The last few months are a blur to me, punctuated by regular doses of horror. The devastating stares of all four of the men I left behind affirm the truth.

I was Patient Eight for a long, long time. Now, I don't know who I am. Brooklyn West is gone, Patient Eight too. Someone else remains. A broken creature, born of blood and pain.

"Blackbird?"

Glancing back, I find my family waiting for me. All of them look at me with equal parts relief and guilt. I fucking hate it. Crouching down, I retrieve the journal from my discarded leather jacket.

"You don't have to be here for this," I mutter.

Tentative footsteps approach.

"We want to be," Kade says gently.

"You don't. None of you can stand to look at me."

I catch Phoenix's flinch as he runs a hand over his odd, natural-brown hair. He doesn't look like the person I remember. Fuck, none of them do. My guys are gone, just like their girl is. We're drowning in the unknown, lost at sea without hope of rescue.

Stepping forward to join his brother, Hudson's gaze is too intense to bear. It's like staring into the sun, full of fire and brimstone, fury and devotion in equal measure. He holds the entire group's strength now.

"That's not true and you know it," he insists.

"We had to get here before the authorities could catch up to us," Kade adds. "It wasn't for any other reason, Brooke. You were exhausted too. We wanted to let you rest."

I look away from them all, returning to the journal that's somehow followed me for all these years. I was surprised to find they brought a bag of my belongings with them when we escaped Blackwood. Identifying the items that used to mean the world to me is an impossible task.

I cared so much back then, before my entire being was deconstructed, piece by fucking piece. Now, my memory is bruised and scarred from months of abuse. Flicking through the journal, countless dark entries assault me, along with the names of my lost family, immortalised by ink.

The battered polaroid photos that I entered Blackwood with are still tucked away in my bag. I can't stand to look at them. With a final glance at the heavily laden pages, I drop the journal into the hole in the ground. There are no words to be recited at this funeral, no eulogy or emotional speech.

I'm the only one left alive to mourn Logan's ghost.

I feel so alone without him by my side.

With his blonde ponytail and warm, humoured eyes, he was always ready with some retort to take my mind off the onslaught of torture. It feels wrong to mourn the dead. Why should we? It's the living who suffer, the ones left behind to wade through the fallout.

"I'm sorry I forgot about you. I couldn't have asked for a better big brother. I hope that wherever you are... you're at peace. I know I won't be until I see you again."

Eyes closing, I find Logan's imaginary face waiting.

You have nothing to be sorry for.

Forgive yourself, kiddo. Let go.

You have my permission to move on.

I crouch down, shoving wet sand back into the hole. Wild, desperate sobs wrack my entire body. Hudson quietly joins me on his knees. I instinctively dodge the arm he tries to wind around my shoulders, letting out a low growl.

"It's just me, baby," he murmurs.

"Please... I can't be touched right now."

Nodding, he silently helps me fill the hole in. By the time we're done, my journal has vanished from sight and Logan disappears too. He's just another ghost now, one of many that haunt my life. I find my feet and turn to face the guys, scrubbing away my tears.

"He died protecting me," I admit roughly. "When our mum's delusions and paranoia got worse, she would beat on me and smash shit. Logan always stood between us, until he didn't."

"What happened?" Kade asks carefully.

There's no point in sugarcoating it.

I have far worse to tell them.

"She murdered him when I was ten years old. My father helped to cover it up. Even then, he was afraid of losing her. They were both victims of her sickness, one way or another."

No one knows quite what to say to that. I tried to explain my hallucination to Hudson, the phantom that kept me company for many lonely months. A person I'd erased from my memory until Augustus pulled him from the depths of my traumatised brain.

"What was he like? Your brother?" Phoenix asks.

"He was alive."

There's nothing else to say. I can't delve into the toxic waste of the past yet. It's too painful, the knowledge of all I've lost along the way. It feels like Logan has died all over again, leaving me alone in the world.

"Come inside," Hudson orders, his hand outstretched. "We all have questions. I'm sure you do as well. No sense avoiding them any longer."

"I can't. I need… space."

His arm drapes around my shoulders. I can't help but fall into his warm embrace. Hudson winces as he jolts his injured shoulder in the process, another reminder that the last few days really happened.

"You've had enough space. We need you now."

"No. You don't."

He stares deep into my eyes. "I fucking need you, alright? Stop arguing. I'll throw you over my damn shoulder if I have to, fuck the gunshot wound."

Studying the other three, they all seem equally desperate for something from me. I'll tear strips off myself without blinking an eye if they need something to hold on to, even if the girl they're in love with is long dead. Yet somehow, I'm still here.

The breath I've been holding since leaving Blackwood whooshes out of me. It isn't a trick, we actually escaped. Left our lives and convictions behind to begin again. But it isn't that easy—our demons have followed us. The unresolved suffering of many months apart won't be ignored.

"That won't be necessary," I concede.

Phoenix visibly deflates, leaning on Eli by his side. My curly-haired twin flame stares at me with such intensity, I feel like my skin will peel back from my bones and reveal my darkest secrets. He's barely left me alone since our reunion, trapped in his own terrified bubble. We've returned to a world he hasn't seen for a decade.

When I woke up here, he was there.

Watching. Studying. Waiting.

I've seen the deep, vicious slashes across his arms. Much like Kade's weight loss, Phoenix's brown hair, and Hudson's newly scarred knuckles, it's undeniable proof that time has passed while I dwelled in Augustus's mental prison. Their lives continued in my absence, however painfully.

"Hudson?"

"Yeah, blackbird?"

Cupping his unshaven jaw, I force myself to smile.

"Thank you for saving my life."

My monstrous sinner sacrificed everything to save me from the darkness, to atone for all his inhuman deeds in the past. Despite everything, I owe him my life. What remains of it, at least.

"You're the one who saved us, baby."

CHAPTER 2
BROOKLYN

OUT OF THE BLACK - ROYAL BLOOD

HANDS CLUTCHING A MUG OF TEA, I settle into the sofa beside the empty fireplace. It's late summer, but the temperature is cold up here. Soon, we will need thicker clothing and logs to burn. If we are to remain here for the rest of our days, we have to prepare.

There's nowhere else for us to go. We're outlaws now. Even more than we were before, far beyond the constraints of society. As I look around the cottage that Kade's mum organised for us, I realise it can't last. We've been missing for almost a week already.

They will come for us.

What we did to escape won't go unpunished.

In the kitchen, Kade and Sadie chat in low, urgent tones. She accompanied us up north with no preparation. The presence of Seven—or Jude, as she calls him— changed everything. I have a feeling the temporary peace is about to explode.

"Firecracker?"

Hesitating with a beer in hand, Phoenix looks longingly at the empty space beside me. I sigh and pat the cushion for him to sit.

"You don't have to ask."

"I didn't want to assume."

"I'm not made of glass, Nix. Just sit the fuck down."

He curls up by my side, tentatively resting his head in my lap. I hesitate before stroking his brown locks, sifting the strange hair with my fingertips. It looks so wrong, this colour. Like the person I knew has also faded away.

It doesn't take long for Eli to approach like a silent sentry. He doesn't bother asking permission, burrowing into Phoenix's side so the three of us are curled up in a dog pile. Their familiar scents wrap around me, slipping beneath my skin and warming the empty shell of my heart.

"You feel so fucking good," Phoenix whispers.

I swallow the lump in my throat. "You do too."

"I didn't think I would ever see you again. None of us did."

Eli lets out a rumble of agreement, but no words. He hasn't spoken since we found each other in the ashes, communicating with little looks and deep frowns.

"Yeah," I say lamely.

"Did you miss us, Brooke? As much as we missed you?"

I flex my spasming fingers, fighting to regain control of my extremities. His question has me feeling all kinds of fucked up. Eli grabs my hand. I meet his green gaze, shining brightly beneath the nasty bruises he gained in the riot.

"I had to... put you guys aside to survive," I admit.

"What does that mean?"

"There's stuff you don't know. If I remembered you, I wouldn't have survived what Augustus made me do. Losing myself was the only way to make it through."

"What did he make you do?"

"Christ, Nix. Lay off."

His head lifts from my lap to pin me with a glare. "We deserve to know. Do you have any idea what we've been through in the last four months? Fuck, Brooke. You're not the only one that barely made it through."

I find the entire room listening to our argument. We're a sorry sight, all covered in bruises and lacerations, bandages and pained grimaces. Kade and Sadie are seated at the cluttered kitchen table, while Hudson rests against the countertop. Every single one of them is staring at me.

"Don't shut us out again," Phoenix begs.

"I can't do this right now."

I shove him off my lap and retreat to an empty corner. I can't have any of them touching me while I still have one foot in that basement. There's a slither of Patient Eight alive and kicking inside of me. She's below the surface, a violent force pumping through my veins.

"Show them the pictures," Hudson orders.

Kade's hazel eyes bore into me, already seeking forgiveness. The entire room falls away as he turns his laptop around so everyone can see. Each hazy photograph shows a different slice of hell. My blood freezes as I watch.

The Z Wing.

Solitary confinement.

Isolation chambers.

Bathtubs and shackles.

Empty syringes and straitjackets.

"What the actual fuck?" Phoenix walks over for a closer look. "I don't remember seeing all this shit when I was in the hole."

"This isn't the hole, it's something else entirely," Kade surmises.

He doesn't break eye contact with me, not once. It's unnerving. He's demanding the truth without mercy. I don't have to confirm it. He can see the photos are real from the way my body shakes.

"I took these on my way down to find her." Hudson knocks back his beer. "It was like a fucking horror show down there. Mariam helped us to free some of the patients being held."

"We turned them over to the authorities for protection," Sadie speaks up for the first time. "I don't know if they made it out alive. Incendia's reach is further than we can comprehend."

Approaching the safety of my corner, Hudson's footsteps ring out like gunshots. The tension carved on his face warns me of what's to come. His gentle handling is about to expire.

"Tell us what we need to know," he demands, hands on his hips. "We've danced around each other for well over a year now. None of us have walked away. Tell the truth and don't you dare leave anything out."

"Hud," Kade warns, frowning.

"Stay out of this. We need to know what we're dealing with."

"Are you sure you're ready for it?" I counter.

Hudson's expression hardens. "You can't scare us off."

"What if I told you that I deserved to be left in that basement? I've done things these past few months... things I can never tell you. Some I can't remember. We were Augustus's... brute force. Me and Seven."

"What does that mean?" Sadie interjects.

Sinking further into the corner, I wrap my arms around my bony legs. "He needed people that he could control. We had no choice but to obey, no matter what he ordered. Refusal resulted in punishment."

Phoenix fists his brown hair. "Like in these pictures?"

All I can muster is a nod.

Turning his back, he seethes through gritted teeth, angrier than I've ever seen him. My head is spinning with confusion. They're all so different. I feel like I don't know them anymore and it's killing me inside to think that. I can't get back all of the lost time.

The fact is, none of us survived Blackwood.

We all died in that riot.

Only scraps of our souls escaped.

"Let's all just cool off a bit." Kade closes his laptop. "We've got a lot of evidence to trawl through and we haven't managed to access Augustus's hard drive. This is going to be a long process."

I shiver, not cold, but fearful of the invisible threads in my mind that pull taut at the mere mention of Augustus. Dead or not, his sharp claws remain inside of me.

"Plus, the data I stole from Incendia's headquarters," Sadie supplies.

The mental image of the security guard's final moments jumps into my mind. Sadie doesn't need to know what me and her brother did to the poor motherfucker. I can still see his throat gaping open in a red, dripping smiley face. Worst thing is, I enjoyed it.

"What did you get?" I ask neutrally.

"Mostly records of stakeholders and shares, basic corporate stuff. It'll take time to decode it all."

"I have copies of my father's files. We should collate the evidence and start from there." Kade absently cleans his glasses. "If we can trace Incendia back to him and Augustus, we're in business."

"I, uh, met him."

I fight the urge to slap my hands over my mouth. I didn't mean to say it out loud. Kade looks at me with confusion creasing his brows, like he's piecing together a puzzle that's fighting him at every turn.

"My father?"

I manage a jerky nod. An odd kind of darkness passes over Kade, his expression morphing and changing. There are shadows in his eyes that never used to be there.

"When?" he barks. "Why didn't you tell me?"

"It's... complicated. I was on a job."

His next words become a jumbled blur as ringing fills my mind. All I can do is stare at Kade while acid churns my stomach, noting all the similarities between him and his father. I can almost taste Martin's warm, sticky blood in my mouth. It soaked my entire body after my bullets tore him to shreds.

I don't realise I'm hyperventilating until Sadie approaches me. I read the words on her lips. *Breathe. In for four, out for four.* My nails dig into my skin as I scrub my face, trying to remove the awful feeling. I'm still covered in blood. I can fucking feel it.

The guys helplessly watch me fall apart. It sickens me to leave myself so vulnerable. I've maintained my thick shields for months, pushing the hysteria down to stay alive. It won't stay buried anymore. Sadie's words finally begin to resonate, and I grab hold of the distraction.

"Repeat after me... what day is it?"

"Tuesday," I bite out.

"What time?"

Checking the clock above the fireplace, I recite the time.

Sadie tries a calming smile. "Good. What's your name?"

"I... I... I don't know."

Her warm hand slips into mine, squeezing so hard it hurts. I try to ground myself with the feeling, working on taking the smallest breaths to relieve my lungs.

"I know," she replies. "You're Brooklyn. Okay? Nobody else."

"Nobody else," I whisper in a small voice.

"Brooke, I need to know. Jude... was he with you? On these jobs?"

"We worked as a team."

"Doing what, exactly?"

I finally meet her bleak gaze. "Whatever Augustus wanted."

The tension in the room reaches a breaking point. Kade tosses his glasses aside to rub his temples, while Hudson curses and storms into the kitchen. Phoenix is bouncing on his feet like a live wire, in complete opposition to Eli, who silently shuts down in the corner.

I know it must hurt them, the fact I blocked them all out while relying on another man. Desperation is a cruel mistress. It doesn't bargain or leave you with easy options, only the impossibility of putting one foot in front of the other.

"What happened to him?" Sadie whispers.

There's a sudden chorus of loud banging, like explosions are destroying our temporary home. We all look at the partition door, where the bedrooms lay beyond. The sound of a struggle filters through and something tells me it isn't Two or Five making such a racket.

We all knew it was coming.

He's awake.

"You didn't tie him down again?" Hudson bellows.

Sadie's face contorts with pain. "I just... I want to talk to him, even if it's just for a moment. We can't keep him sedated and locked up like an animal."

The door crashes open. Tall, gangly, and wild-eyed, Seven stands unsteadily on his feet. He's dressed in a borrowed pair of Hudson's sweats, leaving his scarred, bruise-laden chest bare. I can still see the healing marks from the electrocution that nearly killed him.

He takes one look at us and goes on the offensive. A blur of bare feet and tangled brown hair, the animal that kept me company launches himself across the kitchen. Hudson intercepts him before he can attack anyone. The pair tumble to the floor, exchanging powerful blows.

"Stop! Let him go!" Sadie shouts.

With the pair wrestling and snarling like wolves, I don't think anyone expects Seven to come out on top. Hudson's the burliest of the group, carved from muscle and bad decisions. But they don't know Seven like I do. Even with one hand, he's a ruthless killing machine.

I quickly grab a knife from the kitchen block, dancing past Kade. I don't need his protection. Seven slams his one remaining fist into Hudson's face, becoming frenzied at the sight of fresh blood. Before he can kill the man I love, I throw myself at him.

We collide and roll across the hardwood floor, the sharp press of the blade trapped between us. One wrong move and we'll both bleed out. Seven's still weak from being half-starved to death, so despite his adrenaline rush, I manage to gain the advantage. I end up straddling his chest.

Hudson swipes blood from his mouth. "Grab her!"

"Wait! I can calm him down!"

Seven growls gutturally, but his eyes are wild with terror. Underneath the rage, he recognises me. His movements slow slightly. I press the knife to his throat, my teeth bared. He almost smiles before bucking and slicing his own skin without caring. He wants me to kill him.

"Seven! Stop it! You're safe!"

The pain doesn't register in his expression as his throat begins to bleed. Hudson looks ready to drag me away by my hair, so I throw the knife across the room and watch it embed in the floor right next to his left foot. He jumps back, giving me several precious seconds.

I grab Seven's bleeding throat and begin to squeeze, easily crushing his windpipe. He stops fighting, succumbing to my bruising grip without complaint. His inherent trust in me is dizzying.

"Sev?" I repeat, softer. "You don't need to be afraid."

"His name is Jude," Sadie barks.

"Is that really relevant right now?"

Staring into Seven's eyes, my nails dig deep into his flesh. Blood begins to weep from the wounds. He'll pass out soon. I wait for a trickle of awareness to return, keeping him on the edge of consciousness. I won't abandon the man who kept me company when we had nothing but endless screams for comfort.

"It's me, Eight. I'm not leaving you."

When I loosen my grip a little, Seven gasps. His head crashes against the floor, his entire body going limp. He's drained of the rage consuming him and surrenders completely. When his amber eyes meet mine, there's a tiny flicker of awareness.

"Where are we?" he rasps.

"You're free, Sev. No more Augustus. Consider us even now."

The thinnest smile dances across his lips before it fades.

"We're never free, princess. He's in our heads."

Too far gone to stay awake, Seven passes out. I quickly let go of his rapidly bruising throat, brushing a strand of limp hair from his forehead. Shoved aside in a split second, I'm replaced by Sadie, who cradles his body and checks his pulse.

"What was that for? You hurt him!"

I struggle to stand, wrestling with my urge to punch her indignant face. Violence has become my default, so turning it off is harder than anticipated. Grimacing, I let her see the fury beneath my human mask.

"Hurting is the only thing we understand."

She flinches, holding her brother tight, but I'm not done.

"Augustus starved us, beat us, broke us into pathetic pieces, and sent us to fight a war against our will. If we didn't kill in his name, he sent guards with whips and fists."

"Brooke..."

"I'm not done. Seven—fucking Jude, if you insist—was electrocuted at least once a day, usually when they caught him talking to me. That was before they took his hand too."

Hudson tries to put his arm around me again. I shove him hard, ignoring the pain that lances across his face when he collides with the kitchen cupboards. I'm far too angry to be touched, even by him.

"Blackbird, please—"

"Stay back!"

I want to hurt them all. My fucking family, but the sight of them is just another reminder of the person I've become. I want to beat them, bruise them. Drench us all in innocent blood. It used to be us against the world. Now, I'm locked in my own hellish purgatory and not even they can reach me.

"Augustus wanted to take our humanity, and he succeeded."

"We need to talk ab—"

"Fuck off, Sadie. You have no clue. None."

I storm back outside and let the front door slam behind me. I can't look at any of them right now, not while Augustus's ghost is breathing down my neck. He lives on in my head, reminding me that no matter how far I run... my mind will always belong to him.

CHAPTER 3
KADE

GIVE - YOU ME AT SIX

STANDING on the wraparound porch that surrounds our rural retreat, I finish smoking my cigarette and pull the burner phone from my pocket.

Mum called last night, reassuring me she had packed her things, ready to move to a safe location with Cece. She's filed for divorce from my father. Once she realised his involvement in Blackwood's operation, it was a done deal. Even though we both had to play along for months, plastering on fake smiles to give us the faintest hope of escape.

The door clicks open behind me, disturbing the early morning. Brooklyn is shoving her ash-white hair up in a ponytail. Dressed in one of Hudson's t-shirts, she looks too fucking perfect. I want to say something, anything, but she takes off to begin her jog.

I watch her go, struggling with the exercise. Her legs are like pins, dangerously thin and weak. There's no ignoring all she's been through. It's a constant reminder of my failure. I may have gotten us out, but by then, it was too late. The damage had been done.

Now, I don't know how to fix it.

When Brooklyn returns, she leans against the porch, gasping for breath. I study her silently for several seconds, hating the way she seems too afraid to meet my eyes. Her secrets are suffocating us.

"What do you want, Kade?"

"You should be asleep. It's six o'clock."

"I can't fucking sleep. Get off my case," she snaps.

"You want something useful to do?"

I'm rewarded by a flicker of the person I used to know, her grey eyes dragging over my body. Uncrossing my arms, I inch closer, itching with the need to touch her. Even if she screams bloody murder.

"What did you have in mind?"

"We need supplies. I'm going to drive into town." I drag a single fingertip along her bare arm. "I could use a hand with making a list and shopping for everything we need."

Her smile turns me to pathetic mush. Seeing her again, alive and breathing, fuck. It will never get old after being left in the dark for so long. I could watch her forever and die a happy man.

"I'll throw some clothes on," Brooklyn decides. "Don't leave without me."

"Ten minutes. Try not to wake anyone else up."

She cuts me a small grin. "Yes, sir."

Leaving her to head for the room she's sharing with Two and Five, I return to the bedroom I'm bunking in with Hudson. The girls are still out of it. Sadie gave them some more stolen meds in the middle of the night. Their screaming could wake up the Devil when their nightmares hit.

I throw on some sweats, leaving the two shirts I managed to flee Blackwood with untouched. I don't need to be that person here. Hudson shifts in his twin-sized bed, moaning in his sleep. He passed out after polishing off a bottle of vodka with Phoenix.

I should establish some house rules.

Too much freedom could be a bad thing.

Returning to the country-style kitchen, complete with a farmhouse stove and huge bay window with a view of the surrounding woods, I listen for any other signs of movement. Phoenix and Eli are asleep in their own room, while Sadie and Seven share another.

"You ready?"

Emerging from the hallway, Brooklyn's located a pair of yoga pants to go with Hudson's stolen t-shirt. She flicks her gaze over my outfit, humming with appreciation.

"Can I help you with something?" I ask cheekily.

"Nope. You look good, all casual and shit."

"Well, there's no one to impress out here in the woods."

Grabbing her leather jacket from the back of a chair, Brooklyn snorts. "Maybe this bullshit has taught us something after all. You never needed to impress anyone."

"Only you."

Pausing to take a deep inhale of the worn leather, I catch the faint smile that graces her lips. Before I can, she picks up the notepad and pen I left on the counter to scribble things down.

"Do the girls need anything?"

Brooklyn shrugs. "More clothes, I guess."

"Have they spoken to you?"

"Barely. We should sit them down and talk."

"Are you sure that's a good idea?" I frown.

"I probably have a better shot than anyone else at getting something out of them." Brooklyn scans an empty cupboard. "Seven knows them better than me, but he isn't capable of talking to anyone. Sadie has him sedated again."

"She's going to run out soon."

"He'll come around."

"Do you really believe that?"

Her gunmetal-grey eyes meet mine, carrying a heavy burden that I can't hope to understand. None of us can undo all the damage that's been done, no matter the control freak in me demanding that I try.

"I have to believe that," she admits. "If I don't, then what would be the point? If Seven can get better, so can I. We can leave the people we became behind."

I capture Brooklyn's hand as she heads for the door, pulling her close. She comes reluctantly at first, still struggling to accept comfort, but eventually relaxes against my chest.

"You're still you, love."

"I'm far from me. I don't know what's left, after everything..." Her voice trails off. "He didn't leave me with much. I'm just grateful to be alive, I suppose."

"It's ironic, don't you think?"

"What is?" Brooklyn sighs.

"A year ago, would you have thought you'd ever be grateful to be alive?"

She surprises me with a chuckle. "I suppose not. If you're trying some gratitude therapy, I'd advise you to give up. I'm never gonna be grateful for all we've suffered."

"Neither am I. But we're alive, Brooke. That's something."

"You're right. It's something."

Scribbling a note for the others, we head for the Jeep that Mum left for us to use. Brooklyn hops into the passenger seat and I fire up the engine, pulling out onto the forest-lined dirt track that leads back to civilisation. We travel in comfortable silence, both lost in our thoughts.

By the time we reach the quaint, cobbled streets of the nearest Scottish town an hour later, the sun has risen. I can hear Brooklyn's stomach rumbling from here. We'll both be chewed out for leaving when we return, so I'm going to make the most of this moment.

"Wanna get breakfast?" I waggle my eyebrows.

"I thought we were keeping a low profile."

"Doesn't mean we can't have some fun. How long has it been since you were out in the real world, unsupervised? The Christmas trip doesn't count."

Brooklyn studies her bruised knuckles. "Two years, I guess. I can't remember, it's been so long."

"Exactly. What do you want to do?"

"I don't know, Kade. Anything."

"You have a choice for the first time in your life. We can do anything, be anything." Pulling into a parking space, I face her sad smile. "Come on, love. There must be something."

Biting her lip, Brooklyn nods to herself.

"I want to cut my hair."

"Your hair?"

"It's too long. I hate it. When I look in the mirror, I don't want to recognise the person looking back at me. I want to be someone else."

"That can be arranged, but I happen to like who you are."

I draw her lips to mine in a gentle kiss. Brooklyn reciprocates, her tongue sliding into my mouth, reclaiming my damned soul for her own. I'd forgotten what she tastes like, hatred and rage in a softened shell. The kiss deepens, and she grabs a handful of my t-shirt, seeking more contact.

To hell with it.

I grab her by the hips and drag her over the console, uncaring about the public street around us. It's deserted at this hour. Straddling my lap, her delicious weight presses against my erection. I surrender control to her frantic lips, content to lose myself. All that exists is the feel of her skin on mine.

"Kade," Brooklyn breathes.

"Yeah?"

"I need you, right now."

I brush my nose against hers. "We're in a car park."

"Nothing makes any sense. I can't look at the others without feeling like the worst person on the planet." Her eyes scour over me. "I need to know why I'm here, and not six feet under."

Skating my hands under Hudson's t-shirt, I find her bare breasts. Underwear is on the long list of essentials to buy, but I'm not complaining. Her nipples are rock hard and begging to be touched.

"Are you not wearing panties either?" I murmur.

"Why don't you find out?"

Lifting from my lap, her hand dips inside my sweats to find my hardened cock. I hiss out a breath as she takes a handful, stroking my length. When her hand cups my balls, I let my eyes roll back in my head. Nobody's laid a finger on me since we last slept together and it shows.

"Fuck, love. You better stop before I blow my load like a damn kid."

"I want to see you come for me," she goads.

Checking to make sure the coast is still clear, I snatch her hand from my sweats and pin it to the steering wheel. Brooklyn's eyes widen in surprise. She doesn't fight back as I work her yoga pants down to expose her bare cunt, begging for my attention.

"You're not the one in charge here," I growl at her. "Did you forget that you're my dirty little slut, huh? Do I need to remind you how this works?"

She bites her juicy bottom lip. "I need reminding."

Sliding my hand between her legs, I find her soaked pussy. She's wet for me already, so easily wound up. I push a finger inside of her before swirling my thumb over her sensitive nub. Adding another finger, I lean in to bite her lip myself.

The steering wheel at her back traps us close together, with no room to escape. Losing patience with my toying, Brooklyn shifts and removes my fingers from her wet heat. Her cunt is pressed up against my dick, inches from salvation. As I wait for her to make the final move, she hesitates.

"What is it?"

Insecurity flashes across her expression. "Has there... been anyone else?"

"You're kidding me, right?"

"It's fine if there has been... hell, I don't know why I'm asking. It's been months. I don't expect you guys to have waited. Forget I said anything."

Stroking her painfully sharp jawline, I force Brooklyn to look at me again. She's anxious and uncertain, the vulnerable girl beneath all her icy layers stripped bare for the world to see. Her many personas are dizzying, but I love that I can tease this version of her out.

"Not even for a second," I answer without hesitating. "None of us. Not even Phoenix and Eli were together. We don't work without you, love. You're our centre."

Brooklyn looks pleased with my answer on a primal level. Before I can offer more assurances, she guides my cock inside of herself. I groan, seizing her by the hips to guide her movements. Shoving my hands aside, she pins me with a fierce look, reaffirming her control.

"I'm disappointed I don't get to kill anyone who's touched you."

"You sadistic little bitch."

The corner of her mouth lifts up. "*Your* sadistic little bitch."

Moving to meet her thrust for thrust, I'm barely able to speak as heat burns through me. She's hugging my cock so tight. After months of taking very long showers with nothing but the memory of her scent, I'm not going to last long.

Brooklyn doesn't care, taking every frantic thrust. We can hardly get enough of each other, our tongues battling and teeth clashing like animals. When a car drives past, she ducks down low but continues to grind on me despite the possibility of getting caught.

I hold her head to my chest, plastering on a neutral expression for anyone passing. If anything, it makes this even hotter, marking my property for the whole world to see. Maybe I should take a leaf out of Eli's book and carve my initials into her ass. It'd certainly teach the rest of our fucked up family a lesson.

With an evil laugh, Brooklyn cups my balls again.

"Fucking hell, love," I grind out.

"Let them catch us. Why not?"

"This isn't Blackwood. We're breaking the law."

"You care about that?"

"Like hell I care. Fall apart for me, Brooke. Show me how pretty you are when I pour my come inside of your tight cunt. I want to see it dripping out of you."

"Goddammit, Kade."

Coaxing my release to the very edge, she slams herself down on me and I'm shoved into the awaiting abyss. I can feel her walls clenching around me as our orgasms collide. Biting down on her lip to silence her mewling, I let her milk every last drop from me.

In the sweaty aftermath, she slumps against my chest. We both fight to catch our breath before bursting into near-hysterical laughter. We're literally in a public car park, getting off like horny teenagers.

"Did we just fuck in your mum's car?"

"She technically did buy it. So, I suppose we did."

"Well, what she doesn't know won't hurt her."

Stroking loose blonde hair from her face, I trace the seam of her mouth. "I'd forgotten how incredible you look while falling apart. I want to fuck you again later, where everyone else can hear how much you love my cock."

Her eyes widen. "Jesus, Kade. You're a filthy son of a bitch."

"Hey, I've been celibate for four months. Prepare for more of this."

Lifting Brooklyn back into the passenger seat, I give her some privacy to clean up. By the time we climb out of the Jeep and begin walking into town, she seems content for the first time since we escaped. We walk with our arms wrapped around each other, studying the perfect, early morning scenery.

"What do we need to get?"

I glance at the scribbled list. "Clothes, fresh food, and long-life cupboard shit that will last. Medicines, first aid kit. Toiletries. Booze. Cigarettes."

"Booze and cigarettes?" She laughs.

"We can't get any medication without being discovered. At least three quarters of our group takes it for various reasons. Booze is my short-term solution."

"So Phoenix can drink himself out of a manic episode?"

"If necessary."

"We're totally fucked, aren't we?"

I peck her cheek. "Totally fucked, but free."

We lapse into silence as the town centre approaches. The closer we get to civilisation, the more Brooklyn's good mood evaporates. Her eyes bounce about anxiously, and I can feel the fine tremor creeping over her. It's worsening by the second.

"You good?" I ask worriedly.

"Fine."

Surrounded by the high street, countless shops are starting to open. More cars park as people begin their weekend chores. The cacophony of noise blurs together, a slice of normality amidst the carnage we've been conditioned to. It's unnerving.

When a young man throws open the window to his cafe, the loud blaring of his radio is the final straw. Brooklyn's hand is ripped from mine as she abruptly stops. Crouching down in the middle of the pavement, her hands slam over her ears.

She tries to make herself as small as possible, curling up in a tight ball. It nearly breaks my heart in two. I wave off the concerned cafe owner and kneel beside her.

"Love? You're safe. I'm here with you."

"I c-can't do this, Kade."

"Talk me through it. Tell me what's happening."

"It's too much! I can't fucking breathe."

She battles against the panic attack, following my quiet instructions. We sit here for ages while the world wakes up around us. Several bystanders offer to help, but I quickly make excuses and tow her away before we arouse more suspicion.

We flee into the cafe, sliding into an empty booth. The owner immediately turns off the radio when I throw him a thunderous look, retreating back to the kitchen. With the safety of cracked plastic seats surrounding us, Brooklyn finally opens her eyes.

My heart stops dead in my chest. She isn't looking back at me with those devastating grey eyes. My girl is gone. Her face is slack and emotionless. Before I can react, she pounces on me. Her hands clench around my throat with surprising strength.

I grab her wrists, trying to prise her hands away from my windpipe. Brooklyn shoves me from the booth, and we go tumbling to the hardwood floor. I manage to roll us before her fist connects with my jaw and knocks me off balance.

"Brooklyn! Stop!"

Without responding to her name, she dropkicks me into a nearby table, which smashes. I gape in shock as she grabs a broken table leg, snarling at me again. Yelling her name does nothing to prevent her from striking me with it until blood is pouring from my forehead.

"It's me! Brooklyn, please—"

Snarling like a rabid animal, I have to grab a handful of her platinum hair to regain the upper hand. She lands beside me, and I crack her head against the floor for good measure.

"Stop fighting me, dammit!"

The pain barely registers. She's like an empty shell. Her nails rake down my cheek, narrowly missing my eye. Bleeding and running out of steam, I go for the nuclear option. Pain isn't getting the message across. I need to force out whatever monster is running riot in her head.

Managing to scramble back and grab another barstool, I test the weight of solid wood. If I can knock her insane ass out, I'll have time to formulate a plan that doesn't involve us both landing in a prison cell for assault and criminal damage.

"I'm sorry, Brooke. Forgive me."

Running at full speed, I smash the barstool into the side of her head. Brooklyn drops in an instant, clinging to consciousness. She's still writhing and beholden to invisible voices. I pin her arms down with my spread legs, cupping both of her cheeks to force her to look at me.

"Patient Eight."

In an instant, Brooklyn goes limp.

"You will stop fighting me."

Like a mindless machine with the plug pulled out, staring up at me is an empty vessel ready for its next command. I'm terrified by the gaping void inside of her; it's so clearly visible. The person I know was gone in an instant when this beast seized full control.

Before she can attack me again, I mutter another apology and punch Brooklyn straight in the face. Her head smacks into the floor as she's knocked out cold. Keeping her pinned down, I take stock of the destruction around us just as the cafe owner reappears with a phone at his ear.

"Please don't call the police," I blurt.

CHAPTER 4
BROOKLYN

CRAZY - ECHOS

HANDS BRACED on the bathroom sink, I stare at myself in the mirror. I'm sporting a colourful black eye and swollen face. Kade didn't pull his punch yesterday. I let my fingers trail over the sore flesh, proof of what he claims happened. I can't remember a fucking thing.

I lost my shit and the world disappeared from sight. She took over. Patient Eight. I'm inhabiting this body with another person now. The result of careful calculation and experimentation. She's made her home in the desolate wasteland of my sanity.

Ignoring the sound of Hudson and Kade bickering about another supply run, I turn the shower on. Neither of them is willing to leave me after my performance in town. I've refused to come out of my room since, unable to look at Kade now that he's had a glimpse of the real me.

The girls kept their silence, and I didn't bother to break it last night. None of us have the answers we need; talking about all the shit still to resolve feels futile. Under the beat of scorching water, I let the frustrated tears flow.

I must stand beneath the spray for an hour without moving, trying to scrape some control together. I still feel freezing cold, despite the hot water. The chill of my basement cell refuses to thaw, no matter how far from Blackwood I am.

When the shower door slides open, I flinch.

"Kade, I swear to God—"

Peering over my shoulder, I find someone else waiting. Eli stands with his acid-wash t-shirt dangling from his hands. Adorable, chocolatey ringlets frame perceptive eyes that are full of questions he can't vocalise.

"Not now, Eli. I need to be alone."

He doesn't budge.

"Are you just going to stand there until I say yes?"

Eli nods, smirking.

"Fuck's sake. Just get in."

I turn away as the door clicks shut, then his heat is at my back. Slender, heavily scarred arms wrap around my waist. We stand in silence for the longest time, surrounded by steam and the scent of fruity body wash.

"Did they send you in here to sort me out?"

Eli bites down on my shoulder in response.

"I'm fine. You should all stop worrying so much."

Spinning me around to face him, Eli's eyes bore into me. I wonder if he can taste my lies, if they weigh on his tongue like the acrid flavour of smoke. I study his body, weirdly relieved to find it the same. Some things haven't changed.

The burn scars still cover his entire torso, thick and gnarly like tree bark. Running my hand over the fresh cuts on his bicep instead, I ask a silent question. They can't be more than a week old and they're deep; brutally so. His dark eyes answer me, laden with secrets.

"Phoenix says you haven't spoken to him in months."

A head tilt, as if to say *so what?*

"You had a life before me. Why did you shut down and walk away when I was gone? You were all alone. Hurting yourself. Struggling. I want to know why."

With water clinging to his impossibly thick eyelashes, his eyes scrape all the way down my skeletal frame. With the briefest whisper of his fingertips, Eli traces the shiny, healed scars that mark my left hip. Remnants of a time long passed, and the eternal promise we sealed in blood.

Donec mors nos separaverit.

"Until death do us part," I whisper.

Eli offers me a sinister smile, his thumb caressing the precise knife marks made by his hand. I find his own matching scars, tracing each word to answer my question.

I get it, better than anyone. Existing is not the same thing as living. We've survived without each other, but lost all that we had in the chasm that separated us. Death didn't part us. Life did.

"The girl you loved is gone, Eli. She didn't make it out alive."

Cupping my cheeks, he wipes the curtain of falling tears aside. His raspy voice still refuses to make an appearance, but he doesn't need to speak for me to know exactly what he's thinking.

"We can't play this game. I'm not worth it."

Turning off the shower, Eli raises his eyebrows and steps out for me to follow. I'm engulfed in a thick towel, disappointed that he didn't bend me over and show me exactly what he's thinking in that complicated brain of his. My core clenches at the thought.

Jesus, Brooke.

Chill the fuck out.

After so long apart, my sex drive is going crazy. Drying off with the soft cloud of brushed cotton, I wrestle with my libido and emerge to find Eli waiting with an electric razor in his hand.

"What are you doing?"

He gestures towards my soaking wet hair.

"Oh, the haircut. We didn't get a chance to do it before my brain decided to go cuckoo." I fist handfuls of long, blonde hair. "Just get rid of it all."

Taking a seat on the closed toilet lid, Eli grabs me by the hips and deposits me in his lap. He plugs the razor in and frowns while attaching the correct blades. Excitement runs down my spine at his crooked smile.

"Do your worst."

Eli sends his agreement in a toe-curling kiss that has me slick between the legs all over again. I close my eyes, holding my breath as the razor meets my scalp. He works slowly and methodically, his fingers tilting my head every few seconds. His throbbing erection presses up against me the entire time.

It feels like an eternity has passed by the time Eli finishes. He clicks off the soft vibrating of the razor and presses a kiss to my temple, signalling his approval. I find him watching me with so much intelligence it makes me want to run away screaming.

"Please don't look at me like that."

His brows furrow with confusion.

"I don't want you to see inside of me anymore. It's pretty fucking dark in here, Eli. Too dark even for you to handle. I'm scared of losing myself again."

Lips skating down the expanse of my throat, he answers me in featherlight kisses, reaching the swell of my breasts. Teeth tugging on my hard nipple, heat gathers in my core. I can feel his dick beneath me. Wriggling on his lap, I can almost get in the right position to—

A loud bang on the door has us jumping like guilty teenagers.

"Fuck off," I shout.

"Family meeting!" Hudson hits the door again.

"We're busy, you wanker."

"Stop canoodling and get your asses out here. It's an order, not a fucking invitation."

Eli's forehead falls to my chest, his curls tickling my skin.

"We should go before he breaks the door down."

Running a hand over my freshly shorn head, Eli nods reluctantly. We stand and face the foggy mirror together. With the moisture wiped aside, I gape at my new look.

"Well... you left some hair."

Eli studies my short, platinum-blonde pixie cut, hair shaved high on the sides with the top section left messy. He turns me around, tucking a wet strand behind my ear while his raspy voice threatens to stop my heart for good.

"Beautiful."

I scoff. "Hardly."

"Y-Yes."

I twirl my arms around his neck, bringing our lips together for a kiss. "I wondered why I made it out alive. I understand now. It was so I could hear that perfect voice every day for the rest of my life."

Eli's lips twitch, an almost smile.

I grab my towel and flee before he can argue back. We dry off and get dressed in matching *Highly Suspect* t-shirts from his collection, exchanging grins before heading for the kitchen. The entire group has gathered in tense silence, Two and Five included.

Hudson spots me first, lingering in the kitchen with another beer in hand. His lips part on a sharp inhale as he takes in my new look. He's staring at me like he's a starving man and I'm his dinner. The thought of him fucking me against the countertop while everyone watches briefly crosses my mind.

"Damn, blackbird."

At his words, the other two turn and their mouths fall open.

"Looking good, firecracker."

Kade grins. "Agreed."

"I needed a change."

I steal Hudson's half-empty beer and deposit myself in one of the armchairs. Sadie spares me a look as I pass, but doesn't say a word. I'm still fuming after our argument about Seven. Curled up on the nearby plaid sofa, Two and Five are clutching each other tight.

I meet Five's timid gaze, offering her a nod of greeting. Her mousy-brown hair is so long, it must brush her butt. She's pretty, beneath the emaciation and bruises. Meanwhile, Two's hair has been buzzed to the scalp, showing off the misshapen lumps of her skull.

"Thank you for getting us out, Eight."

The guys all scowl at the use of that name.

I return Five's shy smile. "I wasn't going to leave you there after everything that happened. Seven either."

"Where is he?"

"Sleeping," Sadie answers.

Five presses a kiss to Two's shaking hand to try to calm her. The guys relax enough to take seats around the room, all nursing their beers despite it being barely lunchtime. Alcohol is needed for this conversation, even if Kade is glaring at Phoenix for drinking.

"Do you both have names?" I finally ask.

Two tilts her head at the sound of my voice, giving me a direct view of her scarred eye sockets. "Not that I can remember. I was one of Augustus's first projects."

It's the first time I've heard her speak.

I'm surprised by the vitriol in her voice.

"It took him a while to figure out what worked," she continues. "He put me in the tub first and electrified the water. Then sensory overload, just like you. I used to listen to you scream at night from my cell. I'm guessing you learned to follow orders like I did."

All of the oxygen seems to leave the room.

I fight to clear my throat. "Something like that."

"Sensory overload?" Kade frowns.

"Using waves of noise to torture compliance out of you," Two supplies. "No rest or sleep. You just lay there and let your ears bleed. There's no running from it."

The heat of all their gazes has sweat beading on my forehead.

"We've seen pictures of the tubs," Hudson hedges.

Two swallows. "Electricity was his favourite, after freezing, sub-zero water. There was another patient, but I can't remember his name. He lost several toes from being submerged for too long."

"Seven told me that Three, Four, and Six are dead," I manage to whisper.

Kade writes that down in his notebook, his gaze wary behind his glasses. This is just the tip of the nightmare iceberg. I don't want them to know what happened in the dark. Pictures are one thing, the truth is another.

Fishing for a change in topic, I glance at Five. "What about you? Got a name?"

"I remember," she answers reluctantly.

Releasing Two's hand, she wraps her arms around herself for comfort.

"My name is Lucia. I was a model patient at first. Anything to keep him happy and avoid the punishment if I didn't follow orders. When I first met Two, I was broken. Alone in the dark. She gave me hope."

Two smiles at Lucia's words, wrapping an arm around her shoulders to pull her in close. When their fingers interlink, I realise what Jefferson meant by his words in the basement. They rebelled by simply living the only way they knew how.

"Can't get distracted by pleasures of the flesh without any eyes," I vocalise the threat Jefferson levelled me with months ago.

Lucia snorts. "Jefferson rolled that bullshit out to you too?"

Ignoring the looks the guys all throw at me, I reach out and take Two's hand, careful not to startle her. Lucia watches me closely, still on full alert. I get it now. Two's her girl to worry about.

"You should know, I removed Jefferson's eyes before I cut his throat," I inform them. "He screamed and begged for death in the end. He won't hurt anyone ever again. I made sure of it."

"A-fucking-men to that," Two declares.

Hudson grins at me, the sadistic fuck. The memory of jamming my blade into Jefferson's eye sockets offers me some satisfaction. I would've preferred to skin his sorry ass alive and stretch it out over several hours, cutting his body away piece by piece.

A girl can dream, right?

"How long were you both under Augustus's program?" Kade asks, all business.

Two shrugs again, unable to provide an exact answer. Judging by what she's told us, several years at a bare minimum. She was Augustus's guinea pig from the very beginning. He afforded her zero privileges for that honour, taking her eyes instead.

Lucia fiddles with her long hair. "I was admitted to Blackwood in 2016 for attempted assault while off my medication. That's the last date I remember."

"Six years?" Sadie exclaims.

"Within a few months, I caught Lazlo's eye and he began the sessions. Once his work was complete, I lost all control and never left the Z Wing again."

I begin to pace the room, ignoring the weight of apprehensive gazes watching me. Despite all I endured at the hands of Blackwood's demons, the mention of Lazlo is enough to set me on edge. He was where it all began, this dark and winding path descending to my own personal hell.

While Augustus was the architect, Lazlo was the pioneer.

I hope his corpse is rotting at the bottom of a fucking lake.

"There's something else you should know," Lucia begins nervously.

Kade offers her a reassuring smile. "Go ahead."

"I worked on many jobs for Augustus. Sometimes alone, sometimes not. Patient Seven... well, he was Augustus's favourite. We were inducted around the same time, but he was more successful than the rest of us. Pure, unadulterated evil."

Ignoring Sadie's sudden fascination with her shoes, I wait for the punchline. Lucia clenches her hands into fists, bashing one against her forehead to blow the cobwebs free. Her next words are forced out.

"Before I was taken to the basement, I met another clinician."

Sadie quickly perks up. "You knew him before?"

"Yeah. Doctor Farlow was nice, genuinely interested in helping patients. He did his best to make life at the institute more bearable."

I watch the tears fall down Sadie's cheeks.

"I did a job for Augustus a while back... an employee was leaking information to the outside," Lucia explains. "I was instructed to execute him. Seven, he was there too. He pummelled the poor man to death with his bare hands, didn't even break a sweat."

"How did Doctor Farlow become... that?" Phoenix inserts.

"Lazlo gave him to Augustus. We were taken together, drugged and tied up."

"To another facility?" Kade prompts.

"I guess so," she answers. "We came back to Blackwood a while ago, although the institutes all look the same. A prison is a prison, no matter where you go. That's when I met Two. Our cells were next to each other. Her voice kept me alive."

Digesting the new information, we fall silent. Everyone looks equally unnerved and sickened. Sadie is worst of all, silently sobbing as she's forced to reconcile Jude's fate with the birth of the man I know—Seven. It can't be easy for her childhood memories to be so thoroughly desecrated.

"Sadie, is it?" Lucia asks softly. "I know you're his sister."

"What about it?"

"I just wanted to say... I'm sorry for what happened. Your brother was a good person, but Seven has killed more people than the entire Z Wing program combined. Augustus loved to boast while prepping me for treatment. I did a fraction of jobs compared to him."

"They told me he went away," Sadie hiccups. "Even produced a fake letter, travel documents, the lot. Nobody believed me. All along, he was there, being slowly chipped away."

"I know it's hard," Lucia offers kindly. "But the truth is, Jude... Doctor Farlow, is gone. If any of us are going to survive, we should lock Seven away for good and throw away the key."

CHAPTER 5
PHOENIX

TIME CHANGES EVERYTHING -
THE PLOT IN YOU

AFTER UNPACKING the food and shoving it into every available space, I declare the job done. Kade is scowling at my messy organisation from behind his laptop. I offered to make the run, leaving him and Sadie to continue working on Augustus's hard drive.

"Did you really have to buy that much alcohol?" Kade sighs.

"Well, it is an essential."

"Just watch it, Nix. This is a small house with a lot of people in it. We don't need any more issues than we already have because your drunk ass can't help but pick a fight."

Slamming a beer down in front of the miserable asshole, I help myself to a bottle of rum. We've been incarcerated for over a year, some of us for several years. It's time to live our lives and figure out who the fuck we are outside of Blackwood.

"I'm not trying to be a dictator," he adds. "We both know things have been… delicate, the past few months. Without meds, it's only going to get worse. Just be careful. I'm not running a rehab centre."

I brace my hands on the cluttered kitchen table. "The meds never worked anyway. I've scraped by since Brooklyn was taken away, no thanks to you. So if I want a drink, I'm going to have one. Got it?"

"Just don't expect me to pick up the pieces."

"No one but you ever does."

I head outside to hunt down Brooklyn and Hudson. It's been a tense week living in close quarters with so much shit going on. I'm not sure any of us have stopped to take a breath yet. She's been avoiding us too, still stuck in her stubborn ways. I'm determined to bring my girl back.

In the generous garden that stretches all the way back to the nearby woods, the late summer sun is sinking on the horizon. It bathes the overgrown jungle of a lawn in brilliant, warm light. The sound of an axe splitting wood draws my attention to Brooklyn.

Working on a pile of firewood, I watch her grab a small log and violently rip it apart with her bare hands. I can see her fingers are bloodied and splintered from here. Hudson watches helplessly, still nursing a bandaged shoulder from the gunshot.

I trail over, a peace offering of rum in hand. "Need any help?"

"Nope," Brooklyn snaps.

"Well, I come bearing gifts."

Sinking down on the grass next to Hudson, I deposit the huge bottle of rum in front of him. He lets out a grunt of appreciation and takes a much-needed swig.

"That's good shit."

"Tastes like freedom, my friend."

He rolls his eyes. "I'll go grab some food. Watch her?"

"Don't need a fucking babysitter," Brooklyn grumbles.

I offer Hudson a salute. "Go, I got this."

Reclaiming the rum, I watch Brooklyn finish her angry, lumberjack routine. Her bad mood clearly hasn't dissipated as she glowers at the campfire, lighting some old newspapers to ignite the wood. She finally collapses beside me and stretches her legs out.

"Nice shorts," I compliment.

She shoots me an unimpressed look. "Your choice, I presume?"

"Hell yeah. I should've been a personal shopper instead of a junkie."

"Hilarious. You realise it's cold here?"

"Don't worry, I'll keep you warm."

"Gee, my hero."

Brushing my fingertips over her ripped denim cut-offs, I caress her inner thigh, determined to coax a smile out of her. Since we're planning to hole up here for the foreseeable future, I picked up enough basics for the whole group and other essentials, using the stash of cash Kade's mum left us with.

Brooklyn steals the bottle of rum and takes a swig, cringing at the taste. "For future reference, I like tequila. You should know that."

"I remembered. It's inside."

"Wait, you did?"

"How could I forget? Jesus, Brooke."

We fall into uncomfortable silence, passing the bottle back and forth while watching the fire grow. I fucking hate that I don't know what to say to her anymore. Hudson eventually returns with armfuls of biscuits, chocolate bars and marshmallows, chucking the bags at Brooklyn.

"What are these for?"

"S'mores, obviously," he deadpans.

"What the hell is a s'more?"

We both gape at her. "You don't know?"

Hudson seizes a bag of marshmallows and loads up three skewers with giant bites of yumminess. He hands them out before sticking his in the fire, carefully turning to avoid burning it. Brooklyn copies, watching with open-mouthed fascination.

It's fucking adorable. When we're done, we sandwich the marshmallows with chocolate and biscuits. Hudson watches Brooklyn with a cheesy grin, counting down from five before we all stuff them in our mouths.

"Holy shit," she groans.

"See? S'mores!"

Hudson is already loading another one up, looking calmer than I've seen him in a long time. While Eli hid himself away and I battled with Kade for any drugs, Hudson spent the past four months beating on anything and anyone. He's got the new scars to prove it.

"So, what's the plan?" Brooklyn pipes up.

My good mood evaporates in an instant.

"There isn't really one."

"Surviving," Hudson supplies.

"And when Incendia comes looking for us?"

I stare into the fire, turning another marshmallow over while deep in thought. Those six institutes have left us in hot water. We all thought we were running off into the sunset, when realistically, we've just pissed off our captors by wiping out one of their prime locations.

"They won't," I answer, but it doesn't ring true.

Brooklyn scoffs. "Denial isn't going to help us, Nix."

"Neither is worrying about something that hasn't happened yet."

"Burying your head in the sand as usual, huh? Real smart."

"Enough," Hudson chastises. "I have spent months doing nothing but worrying about Blackwood. Scrap that, the past two years. We are going to eat s'mores, drink rum, and get pissed. Tomorrow, we figure all this shit out. Got it?"

I spread my hands in surrender. "Loud and clear, sarge."

Hudson pins Brooklyn with a look. "You going to cheer the hell up?"

She smirks. "Come over here and make me, *daddy.*"

I'm gonna finish in my goddamn pants if she says that again. Hudson tosses her a heated look, full of dark promise. Hell, I'd pay to watch that shit. Even if he's the one fucking her before finishing all over her gorgeous face for the world to see.

"Truth or dare?" I suggest with a wink.

I half expect Hudson to punch me in the face. We all know he struggles the most with our unconventional relationship, despite the show he put on with Kade all that time ago. Instead, he passes me the bottle and silently lights a cigarette.

"You first," she pushes.

"You're mean, firecracker. Fine, truth."

"Kade said that none of you have been with anyone else."

I choke on a mouthful of rum. "No messing around, huh?"

"Is that a question or a statement?" Hudson adds tightly.

Brooklyn ignores him, watching me. "A question."

Rather than answer, I grab her wrist and drag her closer. Slamming my lips against hers, she soon gets over the shock and melts into the kiss. My teeth sink into her bottom lip, seeking the promise of fresh blood. By the time we separate, I'm hard and she's gasping for air.

"Does that answer your question?"

Brooklyn makes a non-committal noise.

"For fuck's sake," Hudson grunts. "None of us fucked anyone else. Of course, we didn't. Now take the bloody bottle and say truth, because I have questions too. I'm sick of waiting."

Chastised by the grumpy dickhead, Brooklyn snuggles up to my side and retakes the bottle. Hudson's stare is full of anticipation and barely restrained annoyance. Something serious is eating away at him. I have a feeling our playful game is about to be hijacked.

"Truth," Brooklyn concedes.

"I want to know what the deal with Seven is. No lies."

The crackling fire is the only sound in the silence his question brings. We're trapped in an infinite moment as everything rests on her answer. Brooklyn takes a swig from the bottle, which should indicate that she's passing. Instead, she pulls up her t-shirt to reveal her back.

I stare without blinking, sickness churning in my stomach. Hudson's string of curses would make the most hardened criminals wince. On the expanse of her milky skin, there are rows of vivid, striped scars. All the way down her visible spine, every inch of flesh is viciously marked.

"Who did this to you?" Hudson spits out. "I'll tear them apart and make a fucking hat out of their broken skull."

"You've never seen a whip mark before?" Brooklyn attempts at humour. "Beat you to it. I wonder what Incendia did with Jefferson's eyeballs. I sure hope they didn't put them back in."

Hudson traces a finger over a nasty scar, causing Brooklyn to shiver. She soon pushes him away, dropping the t-shirt back down before he loses his shit for real. I watch the shutters fall over Hudson's face at her rejection.

"Augustus was recruiting a new technician," she explains. "I later found out it was a trap, and this idiot was a mole sent looking for information. I refused to cut off his finger to mail back to his wife as leverage."

I try to drag her into my arms, but Brooklyn shuffles even further away. Neither of us are allowed anywhere close. She clearly can't stand to be touched while recanting this tale.

"Augustus didn't like my disobedience. He ordered Jefferson to beat me until I agreed to do as told."

"Fuck, firecracker."

"By the time I broke, the job was already done. Seven cut the son of a bitch's whole head off to send to the wife instead. He slept in his blood-stained clothes for a week. Augustus loved to dehumanise him even more."

Hudson looks set to explode in a torrent of rage. I watch him stand and promptly punch a tree. If he could go back and murder Augustus's psychopathic ass all over again, I have no doubt that he would. Brooklyn watches him with resignation.

"I was put back in my cell," she continues. "What they didn't know was that I'd slipped a knife into my sock, stolen from Jefferson's belt. I got it back without being discovered. I could barely move after the beating; my back was shredded, and I hadn't eaten in days. I couldn't go on any longer."

Flashbacks threaten to overwhelm me, still raw in my memory despite the time that's elapsed since I found her half-dead. The thought of her alone, back in that awful place, threatens to finish me off. I feel like a fucking failure for giving up on her.

"Firecracker—"

"No," Brooklyn interrupts. "Don't give me all that pitying bullshit. Hudson asked a question. The answer is this: when I had no one, Seven was there in the pitch black—a complete stranger who owed me nothing. He spoke to me through the air vent, talked me down. I could've slit my wrists, but I didn't."

Hudson stares at his bleeding fists, listening but not really present. The tree has matching dents in the rough bark now. He's slipped back into his angry, volatile haze, and can't be reached. I watch as he takes off, stalking into the nearby woods without a word.

"Probably just needs to clear his head." I wince.

"It's fine. I get it."

"He loves you. That's why he's upset that he couldn't be there."

"I know you all think that Seven is the bad guy." She sighs. "I'm not blind. He is the bad guy, but he's also the reason I'm alive. It's down to him that Hudson found someone resembling a person in the basement, not a rotting corpse."

I have so many pointless one-liners to roll out, but none of them will fix anything. He was there and we weren't. For that reason alone, Seven can remain alive. I don't like the guy, but I can accept his existence if it's inextricably tied to my girl. He's earned that much.

"Dance with me," I blurt.

"What?"

Scrambling to my feet, I wobble and realise I'm drunker than I thought. Freedom is doing my sobriety no favours. Offering Brooklyn a hand, she stares at me before letting me drag her up.

"There's no music," she complains.

"Do you need it?"

Hesitating, her arms twine around my shoulders until we're flush together. I gently rest my hands on her hips, teasing the sliver of exposed skin from her low-rise shorts. I can feel her heart hammering against mine, two racing engines set to implode.

"I guess not. Although we look like lunatics."

I grin at her. "Firecracker, we are fucking lunatics."

Beginning to sway my hips, I ease Brooklyn into it by holding her against my body. When she begins to relax at my touch, I twirl her in a slow, romantic waltz. I meant to lighten the mood and make her laugh, but I wasn't expecting this thick, intense atmosphere between us.

It feels like an ash cloud is raining on us both, sucking the very air from our lungs. I'm suddenly nervous. Shoving my insecurities aside, I take Brooklyn's hand and spin her outwards. She ducks beneath my arm before twirling back and colliding with my chest.

"You can dance!" she gasps.

"I'm full of surprises, didn't you know? I'll add dancer to my growing resume."

There's no space between us. I can almost feel the razor-sharp edges of her soul slicing my skin like barbed wire. We're magnetised together, an asteroid on a collision course, set on destruction. Her lips seal on mine and I kiss her slowly, gently, with all the emotion I've never been able to express.

"I'm glad you're still alive," I admit in a low whisper. "Even if another man had to hold you together when I couldn't. I don't give a fuck if he's what you need. I'll take whatever portion of you I can get."

"Phoenix…"

"No buts. If that means sharing, I'll share. Whatever it takes."

"It's not like that," she rushes out.

I slide a finger under her chin. "Isn't it?"

Brooklyn flushes. "I don't know, Nix."

Swaying in the light of the fire, we dance to no music. In all the madness, this is the first time I've been alone with Brooklyn. Anxiety wraps around my lungs as I realise exactly what I want to say, something I regretted never telling her in those long, lonely months.

"Brooke?"

"Yeah?"

Running a hand over her short hair, my thumb brushes her bottom lip. I silently curse my nerves. What's wrong with me? I've seen the world without her, and it isn't worth sticking around for. Tomorrow isn't guaranteed. I want to live for today and spend every second worshipping her.

"I'm in love with you. I want you to know that."

I don't look away or back down. I've spent my entire life running from commitment and emotions. I'm done. She's it for me—every step I take from this day out, it's with her by my side. Brooklyn bites her lip, looking oddly innocent as she mulls my declaration over.

"What about Eli?" she finally says.

I stare into her irises, lit by the flames. "What about him?"

"You love him, Nix."

"So do you."

The corner of her mouth lifts. "How does this work? I love all of you. I'm not afraid to say it anymore; it's time I grew up. I'm in love with every single one of you. I can't exist in this world without you guys. I refuse to."

"No one ever expected you to choose," I offer. "From day one, we fell into this messy, fucked up family without coming up for air. We need each other to survive. It's that simple."

"But how is this fair?"

"We get you. That's enough. We get you, and you have us in return. None of us want to live without this family. We've all been lost and this… this is what it feels like to be found. I love you, and Eli and my brothers."

Despite everything, Brooklyn manages a laugh.

"Generous."

"Shut the fuck up, firecracker."

"You started it."

I bend my knees, dipping her low to the ground, before I sweep her back onto her feet. Brooklyn squeals, a brilliant smile blossoming on her lips for the first time in days. It takes my fucking breath away.

"I'll prove it to you," I whisper in her ear.

"How?"

"We'll burn the whole world and every last motherfucker in it to ashes if that's what it takes to get our revenge. I don't care anymore. Fuck everyone else. They will hurt like we do."

"You promise?"

"I promise. We'll take Incendia down or die trying."

Before she can say anything else, I seal the promise with a final, heart-stopping kiss. Everything I have is poured into the declaration, a goddamn irreversible stamp on my heart that I will proudly boast for the rest of my life.

Somehow, I'm grateful for Blackwood.

It taught us to grow up, and it showed me the truth. While the pain is temporary, family is forever. No matter what happens next, we'll go down in flames... together.

CHAPTER 6
BROOKLYN

DOOMED - BRING ME THE HORIZON

LEAVING Phoenix and Eli spooning in the double bed, I throw a discarded shirt over my head. Watching them as they sleep for a moment, I smile to myself at the sight.

Phoenix is stretched out on his back, chest bare and arms folded behind his head. Eli is curled up by his side, head splayed across his pectorals and leg hitched high on his waist. He still sleeps in a t-shirt to hide his scars, even from us, but they both look so at peace with each other.

Padding into the kitchen, I hit the switch on the coffee machine. The sun has risen, but no one else has stirred. Kade is asleep at the kitchen table, drooling on his stacks of paperwork. He and Sadie were up late again last night.

Going to grab a blanket from the living room to drape over him, I startle when I realise someone else is awake. In one of the armchairs, huddled in a quilt and staring out the window, I find a pale, skeletal shadow of a man.

Conscious.

Blinking.

Breathing.

I stop dead, startled.

"Morning, princess," Seven mumbles absently.

"Jesus... Sev. You're awake."

"You lot have run out of drugs to use on me."

"Us lot?"

He spares me a blank look. "The pink-haired woman."

I sure as hell am not starting that deep dive into family history without being caffeinated. Instead, I watch him while returning to the open plan kitchen and filling two mugs with coffee. His intense gaze doesn't tear from me as I linger over the sugar pot.

"How do you take your coffee?"

"I have no idea," he answers.

Fixing it the same as mine, I tread carefully around Kade so as not to wake him. Taking the armchair next to Seven, I offer him the steaming mug. He wraps his one scarred hand around it. The healed stump on his right arm is tucked into the pocket of his sweats.

I have no idea what to say to him in the cold light of day. Our conversations were reserved for the shadows, a land beyond this world where labels didn't apply. At the mercy of demons and death on a daily basis, we clung together to survive.

Where the fuck does that leave us?

I don't know what we are in the real world.

Seven swallows a sip of coffee. "This is good."

"You remember it?"

"Just the taste. No idea where it's from."

"Anything else?"

Uncertain caramel eyes meeting mine, I'm taken aback to find a person resting there. Glimpses of the man he used to be stare back at me, someone who whispered to me in the dark and coaxed the knife from my grasp with mere words alone.

"Flashes. It comes and goes," Seven admits in his gruff voice. "I heard what they've been calling me. Jude. Was that my name? Before… everything?"

I don't answer at first. His calm exterior begins to falter, the cracks showing a hint of the madness that's battling to break free. I watch his gaze harden.

"Don't lie to me, Eight. We agreed to always tell each other the truth."

"Your name was Jude. Before Augustus. Before everything."

Placing the mug down, Seven brushes his unruly brown hair back to reveal his sharp, angular features and strong jawline. The mop on his head has fully grown out and touches his shoulders. He almost looks like a pirate, in a rugged, sexy-as-hell way.

"I see."

"What do you want us to call you?" I ask softly.

"My name isn't Jude."

"It was."

We follow the voice to where Sadie has emerged from the bedroom. Her sweetheart face and gentle gaze are full of exhaustion. She helps herself to a coffee, pausing to kick Kade's chair. It's like she needs backup while facing us unstable patients. I fight the urge to bare my teeth at her.

Breathe, Brooke.

No killing today. Yet.

"Care to take over, Sadie?" I ask tiredly.

"If you're going to drug me again, I'd advise against it," Seven adds.

We both tense as she passes us, taking a seat on the sofa. I inadvertently shift closer to Seven, driven by an unconscious need to protect him. Sadie doesn't miss a trick as she glances over to Kade for guidance. He's barely awake, sliding his glasses into place and stumbling towards the coffee pot.

"I'm not going to sedate you."

"Only because you ran out." I scoff.

"No." Sadie shoots me an exasperated look. "Because we can't dance around this any longer."

"Dance around what?" Seven utters.

Looking him in the eye, she declares, "I'm your sister."

Preparing myself for Seven to flip out and lose his shit, I'm even more surprised when he remains silent. He just stares at her like she's an alien invader, a crease marring his thick eyebrows. Sadie stares right back. I hate the way she seems almost afraid of him.

"Do you remember me?"

"Your hair used to be dark blonde."

Her mouth drops open. "A long time ago."

"Why did you dye it?"

Wiping away tears that spring free, she takes a breath. "Every time I looked in the mirror, I saw your eyes staring back at me. I wanted to see my reflection without being reminded of my dead family."

I'm sitting on the edge of my seat, prepared for things to change at a pin drop. I know just how volatile Seven can be. Despite everything, he seems to trust Sadie on an unconscious level, even if he doesn't know why.

"Do you remember our parents?"

He draws to his full height, a towering six foot three that dwarfs my small frame. I can still take him down if needed. My lessons in brutality were taught by his violence and bloodthirst. He walks over to the window and stares outside.

"No, I don't remember them."

"They both died," Sadie blurts.

"How?"

Taking a gulp of her coffee, she uses it as an excuse to wipe more tears aside.

"A plane crash when we were young. Grandma took us in, but she died a couple of years before you vanished. The last time I saw you was a week before my seventeenth birthday. We had dinner in the city to celebrate. After that... nothing."

Seven's forehead collides with the fogged-up glass. I watch his eyes slide shut, blocking the whole world out. His shoulders slump beneath the heavy weight of realisation, and my dead heart almost breaks for him.

"How long?"

"Six years. I've been looking for you ever since. It took me a long time to track your movements. I studied before applying to the first place you worked at. The rest is history."

"I don't understand," Seven murmurs.

Kade interrupts by stepping into the living room, looking much more awake. "Maybe we should take a break. We don't want to overwhelm him with too much, too soon."

"Wait, Jude—"

Seven spins, his expression shutting down into familiar, breathtaking anger. I step between him and Sadie on instinct, watching the way she quickly backtracks towards Kade.

"That isn't my fucking name!" Seven yells. "Eight, tell them."

"That isn't her name either," Kade combats.

"You wanna bet, asshole? Maybe I know her better than you think."

Kade pumps up his chest. "Try it, Seven. I was here first."

Fighting the urge to facepalm, I swim through their metaphorical lake of testosterone and stand in the middle with my hands outstretched.

"Can we compare dick sizes another time, please? Sadie, call him whatever the fuck he wants. And Kade, does it really matter if he calls me Eight? Really?"

"Yes! It does."

"Princess, step aside," Seven hisses. "Let me break this bastard's fucking skull."

"She's not your princess," Kade hits back.

Marching up to Kade, I glare until he grudgingly backs off. Unlike Hudson, Kade's anger usually has an off switch. Though I wouldn't be opposed to smashing their heads together for good measure.

"We're on the same side, so let's discuss this like adults." I look between the two infuriating men. "None of this possessive, alphahole bullshit. You both hear me?"

"He started it," Seven objects.

Kade glowers at him. "I should've left you to burn in that damn institute."

"You know, I once skinned a man alive. Want me to demonstrate?"

"Seven!" I bellow. "Cut it out. I'm going to strangle you both."

Sadie shakes her head at us. "We're doomed."

Needing some air, I storm back to my bedroom. The girls are still asleep, bundled together into one cramped bed. They've been quiet since the family meeting, but no longer look at us with bone-deep terror.

By the time I get dressed and have regained a sense of calm, the argument has broken up. Kade is outside talking on the burner phone, while Seven and Sadie sit in silence. Rather than dive back into that cesspit of complications, I step outside to check on Kade as he hangs up.

"Everything okay with your mum?"

His expression is bleak. "Get everyone up. Right now."

"Trouble? Are we safe?"

"For now, but we need another family meeting."

Cursing the universe for hating our delinquent asses, I head for Phoenix and Eli's room and force them out of bed. I'm much gentler with the girls, coaxing them to come out for coffee. My lungs are being squeezed by an impending panic attack when I reach the final bedroom.

"Hud, get up. Kade wants to speak to everyone."

He throws a pillow at me. I dodge and jump on the bed instead. Grabbing me by the ankles, Hudson yanks until I fall into his tattooed arms. He traps me beneath him, his eyes half shut. He's looking too grumpy and hot for my libido to take.

"Is it urgent?" he grunts. "I was dreaming about having your sweet pussy wrapped around my cock. I'd rather skip the meeting and go back to that, please."

My mouth is suddenly dry. "I, uh, have no idea."

"Then he can wait while I fuck you until you scream my name for the whole house to hear, right?" Hudson paws at my clothes. "I want to paint your body in my come, blackbird."

"What is it with you guys acting like animals today?"

"You don't usually mind."

"I've had one cup of coffee and already broken up a pissing contest. Don't make me even crankier, Hud. I'll stab you for my own satisfaction and dance in your blood to celebrate."

"Sounds hot," he purrs. "I'm yours to kill, baby."

Smashing a pillow into his face, I extricate myself from his body and escape before he can tempt me further. In the kitchen, the room has filled up with more sleepy, disgruntled men. I consider my options carefully, taking the space next to Seven on the sofa. I don't miss the way Kade's glare intensifies.

"You good?" I whisper under my breath.

Seven's nostrils flare. "Fucking peachy. When can we go home?"

"This is your home now. Not that cell."

"The cell was bloody quieter, princess."

"Just keep it together, ignore everyone else."

"You mean your boyfriends?" Seven says acerbically.

I rub between my eyes, a headache brewing. "I'm the only one in this room capable of beating the shit out of you. He broke us together, side by side. So don't underestimate me. I'm running very low on fucks to give this morning and my coffee has run out."

Seven sinks back into the sofa, carefully studying the room. He's every inch the violent, mindless soldier that Augustus trained him to be. Kade paces in the kitchen, his fingers flying across his phone while yelling at Hudson to hurry up. My stomach flips pathetically when Eli brings me a fresh coffee.

I catch his hand. "Thank you."

He shrugs, returning to stand by Phoenix's side. Lucia and Two have set themselves up in a safe corner, leaving Hudson to stumble out, dressed only in a pair of skin-tight, black boxers that leave little to the imagination. My mouth falls open before I wrench it shut again.

Kade grabs the TV remote. "You all need to see this."

"What's this about?" Hudson drawls. "Some of us had a crappy night's sleep with all the nightmares and screaming going on in this is fucking cottage." His eyes pointedly stray to me.

"Just shut up and listen."

Flicking over to a national news channel, we all fall silent as breaking news flashes across the screen. There's a familiar video playing that chills my blood. CCTV footage of the main building in Blackwood, burning to the ground. Several headlines run beneath the video, emblazoned for the entire world to see.

Prestigious Institute Suffers Mass Riot & Escape.

Tragic Night At Secure Mental Institution.

Blaze Claims The Lives Of Twenty Patients & Staff.

I reach for Seven's hand as the screen changes, showing fire trucks dousing the flames. Police escort shell-shocked patients into awaiting vehicles to be transferred, dosing them up with medication and restraining a few too freaked out to comply. The sight of body bags has acid burning my throat.

"Why are we watching this?" Phoenix demands.

"Because of this," Kade answers grimly.

Switching to a live conference, the newscaster falls silent. The camera shot is somewhere in London, framed by the famous skyline. Surrounded by glass monoliths and decadent high-rises, the opulence of a wealthier district is clear. I can see Kade clocking all the details.

There must be dozens of reporters lined up. They all stand and begin shouting when the doors to a grand, blacked-out skyscraper slide open. Flanked by security guards, an elderly man takes a stand behind the microphone, tapping it for their attention.

Smoothing his perfectly fitting, pinstripe designer suit with matching diamond cufflinks, his cold, expressionless face is wrinkled and worn beneath a smooth coiffe of silvery hair. His eyes are the most unnerving thing. I feel like he's staring straight into the windows of my soul.

"Who the hell is this prick?" Phoenix grumbles.

I gasp while reading the caption.

Sir Joseph Bancroft II.

Founder & President of Incendia Corporation.

"Motherfucker," Hudson curses.

"A fucking sir?" I exclaim. "You see that?"

Everyone falls silent when Kade waves for us to shut up. The well-bred asshole on the screen clears his throat, smoothing the snake-like expression off his face and plastering on a smile that screams of grief and sadness. I want to fucking puke.

"Twelve days ago, my beloved son and head of our clinical division, Doctor Warren Augustus, passed away. In an act of malice, he was attacked by the very patients he so passionately fought for. My son was murdered by those he swore to protect."

Son?

What the living fuck?!

The clicking of cameras and journalists scribbling notes punctuates Bancroft's words. His identity has shocked everyone here into silence. I swear the son of a bitch fakes a tear that he brushes aside with an embroidered, silken handkerchief worth more than my life.

"This act of violence will not go unpunished. We have been treating the mentally unwell in our private institutes for thirty years. Blackwood Institute will be rebuilt, and we will bring those responsible to justice. Several patients escaped during the riot and remain at large."

Seven's grip on my hand tightens involuntarily, creaking my bones. All of the guys have moved closer, unconsciously closing ranks around us.

Bancroft stares into the camera. "We are working with the police to track down the escapees. I came here today to warn the public and ask for your assistance in locating these criminals. They should be considered extremely dangerous."

Several photographs are plastered across the screen, taken straight from our ID badges. All of my guys are there, bar Seven. He's supposed to be dead, so they can hardly broadcast his picture. The final image that fills the screen stops my heart. My chest burns from holding my breath for too long as I study it.

"Son of a fucking bitch," Kade utters.

Plastered across the screen in merciless, high-definition horror, is my police mugshot. I have no doubt they chose this on purpose to scare the public. I'm blood-splattered and gaunt after the police caught up to me, before I could throw myself in front of a train. I barely recognise the ghost staring back at me.

"That's me alright," I grit out.

Bancroft flashes back on the screen. "Their ringleader, Brooklyn West, was one of Blackwood's most infamous patients. While she may have escaped our care, we endeavour to recapture her and bring her to justice for the atrocities committed. Miss West is a criminal and an inhumane monster."

The corner of his mouth tilts up in the tiniest way. He's staring straight through the camera, into the pits of my murderous soul. His direct eye contact is no mistake. Bancroft knows I'm watching; this conference is for our benefit.

"It is clear her rehabilitation has failed. We will not rest until she is back behind bars, where she belongs for the rest of her life. I will not be taking questions at this time."

Striding away from the roar of frantic voices demanding more information, Bancroft is followed by security before climbing into a blacked-out SUV. I catch the flash of two people waiting inside, but the cameras can't capture their faces.

Kade relaxes ever so slightly. "At least my father didn't make an appearance. He's getting butchered by a media shitstorm for our involvement in this, so that's something."

Hudson snorts. "That'll keep him busy."

I sit unblinking, the conversation around me melting into insignificance. All I can hear is white noise, growing louder and louder as the broken part of my brain unfurls. Stretching its limbs as if awakening from a long nap, thick, tar-like shadows begin to leak down the walls.

Inky droplets swallow the TV screen whole, blotting the room out. I can feel the cold from the basement around me, leaching into my bones, and the bite of handcuffs searing my wrists. Augustus's sound machine blares in my head, leaving nothing but terror behind.

I start to tremble, a heady current coursing through me. Something flickers to life in the corner of the darkened room, birthed from the shadows. A ghost has risen from the dead to walk amongst the living.

"Please no," I whisper, but it's too late.

The bloodied, hallucinatory face of Doctor Augustus stares back at me, his charming smile spread wide. He rests against the TV console, grinning while smoothing his crimson, brain-splattered suit. Even his glossy black hair is clumped with blood and deathly fluids.

Thought you'd gotten away with it, Patient Eight?

I told you before.

Blackwood is your destiny. It's inescapable.

I escape the hallucination by running at full pelt. Voices try to sneak into my stuttering mind, but I shove them all out, flying past the guys without stopping for a breath. Running until I trip over myself, I stumble into the garden, cutting my hands on thorny bushes.

The Devil follows me, guided by the invisible cord that binds us together. No matter how much I scream and beg to be left alone, he lives in that gaping chasm in my chest, carved by his sick will alone. Augustus kneels beside me, studying my state of distress.

Why do you run from me?

You never learn, Patient Eight.

Your mind belongs to me. It always will.

"Leave me alone. You're dead!"

Squeezing my eyes shut, I will him to go away. A cold breeze on the back of my neck answers my plea for mercy, sending more suffering instead. I'm too scared to look, but force myself to anyway. The swarming shadows twist through the air and give way to another skeletal figure.

"Not you," I whimper uselessly.

Logan isn't here to protect me from her anymore. Beautiful face burned from the air bags that did nothing to save her life, Mum's tumbling blonde hair is drenched in blood. Her smile is still the same beneath her soft exterior, predatory and ice cold.

Come home, Brooke.

Back to Blackwood.

You were born for the program, and you'll die for it.

Staring into the empty eyes of my hallucination, I'm trapped. Frozen by fear that I was stupid to think I could outrun. I've held them at bay since escaping, stuffing the voices deeper and deeper into oblivion. Despite everything, I knew I couldn't run forever.

Someone wraps their arms around me, attempting to shake me from my stupor. I think someone else is shouting, but it's no use. I still can't breathe. Can't think. Can't exist on this hellish plane, where ghosts walk in the skin of the living and haunt me even when I'm not asleep. I should've died in that basement.

"Brooklyn—"

"Get out of the way. She needs me."

"Fuck off."

"I'm the only one that can pull her back!"

Their voices sneak through the constraints of my fading lucidity. My traumatised brain recognises the gruff, pained tenor of my lone saviour. He's whispered to me many times in my darkest moments.

A rough hand cups my jaw and I stare into a pair of molten eyes, burning like wildfire. Matching horror and suffering stares right back at me.

"Breathe, Eight. Just breathe for me."

Seven grips my face until it hurts, demanding my brain to follow orders. Even with his best intentions, it's no use. I can still see her over his shoulder. She crooks her index finger at me. Mum won't go back to her shallow grave, content to continue ruining my life.

Devil child.

Couldn't even protect your brother from me.

You should have died a long time ago.

"You killed him, not me," I yell at her.

Seven looks over his shoulder to follow my gaze. I take the opportunity to punch him in the face. If I can get into the woods, maybe the hallucinations will leave me alone. Attempting to run, my feet are quickly swept out from underneath me. I end up with a face full of dirt as Seven pins me down.

"Jesus, princess. You're making me look sane!"

"Fuck you," I spit. "Let me go, Augustus!"

"It's me! He can't hurt you. Come back."

"Please… l-let me go. Mum's after me."

"She isn't real," Seven shouts. "Look into my eyes, Eight. Nowhere else."

He strikes me so hard, my lip splits in the process. I hear someone raging in the distance, but nothing exists beyond my line of sight. Only Seven's wide, burnished eyes, coaxing me back to reality. I taste the hot, metallic flow of blood slipping between my lips. It helps to latch on to the pain.

"That's it, Eight. Just us, no one else."

"Augustus—"

"Is dead," Seven finishes.

"And we'll be next."

He strokes my sweaty hair as I greedily suck in air. I can see the guys gathered on the porch, none of them daring to take a step closer. Kade is holding a seething Hudson back, while Phoenix and Eli cling to each other for strength, both looking terrified.

"Don't look at them," Seven orders. "Do as you're told for once."

"I c-can't do this, they're going to come for me…"

"You think any of us would let them?"

Seven offers me a tiny, threatening smile. I peer around apprehensively, but the shadows have abated. He's holding me in this plane of existence, keeping the madness in my veins from poisoning the world again.

"You got me out of Blackwood. I'm going to keep us out."

"How?" I whisper brokenly.

His grin turns savage, dripping with violent rage.

"I'll kill them all, princess, and bring you their heads on fucking stakes."

CHAPTER 7
BROOKLYN

LEFT ALONE - ZERO 9:36

DUCKING THROUGH THE OPPRESSIVE WOODLAND, I feel myself relax. I'm more at home in the darkness than anywhere else. I need the space to gather my thoughts. We've been hiding out here for another week, ever since Incendia decided to drop a nuclear bomb on our heads.

With few options, we had nowhere else to run. The guys have been worse than ever, refusing to leave me unaccompanied. It only got worse when I wouldn't discuss the whole losing my mind and becoming a complete fruit cake thing. I've been drowning myself in our dwindling supply of liquor instead.

"Blackbird! Jesus, slow down."

I run to escape Hudson chasing me through the forest. After two weeks of forcing myself to eat, I'm still weak and unable to get far before his long, powerful limbs catch up.

"Leave me alone, Hud."

"Can't a guy go for a harmless run?"

I shove him away and brace my hands on my knees. I can feel him glaring beneath his shock of unruly black hair and shining eyebrow piercing, his angled jaw clenched. Every inch of well-honed muscle is on display in his running shorts and tank top.

"What do you want?"

He shrugs. "Just jogging, that's all."

"Run somewhere else."

"You really think you should be out here alone right now?"

I fix him with a cold stare. "I don't need a babysitter. Least of all you."

"What's that supposed to mean?"

With rage steeling my spine, I prowl forward until he's backed against a nearby willow tree. It's still weird to see Hudson surrender to me after so much pain and misery inflicted by his hands. His aquamarine eyes are lit with amusement, like he's enjoying the show I'm putting on.

"You, of all people, know I can handle myself," I explain angrily.

"That doesn't mean you have to. We're all just trying to help you get through this, but you're pushing us away and trying to hide from what's happening back out in the real world."

"I am not!"

"Lies. You're being a fucking pussy, Brooke."

Before my fist can connect with his jaw, Hudson snatches my hand. I wrench it from his grasp, snarling like an animal. No one will find his body out here, right? I'll be doing the world a favour by slitting his throat.

"I'm a pussy? You've barely spoken to me since you stormed off like a baby last week. I'm not the only one in denial here. If I'm a pussy, you're a coward."

"You take that back," he utters.

"You first, dickhead. Don't start a fight if you aren't prepared for the truth."

Hudson tries to grab me by the throat, but I block him and slam my fist into his gut instead. Doubling over, he grabs my waist and pulls me with him. We both tumble to the moss-covered ground. Writhing and attempting to claw his face, I let out a hiss as he straddles my body.

"We're dropping the pretence then, yeah?"

"Fuck you," I growl. "Let me go before I really hurt you."

"I'm not done." Hudson grips my throat. "Yes, I have a problem with the way Seven looks at you. You're my fucking blackbird, you hear me? Mine. I share your ass with three other men already, and you want to add a fourth into the mix?"

Managing to get a punch to the face in, Hudson barely reacts as he's knocked off balance. I take advantage of his surprise and turn the tables. With my legs wrapped around his torso, I hold him captive beneath me and headbutt him straight in the nose.

"Fight me all you want." He glowers through the blood streaming down his chin. "I'm not afraid to put your infuriating ass in the ground. Try another punch, see what happens."

Curiously, I dip my index finger in the stream of hot blood coating his face. Hudson watches as I swirl the moisture around my finger, before bringing it to my mouth and consuming every last drop.

"Nobody said anything about adding a fourth person or whatever you're insinuating, you controlling, egotistical bastard. I spent months watching Britt trail around after you like a bitch in heat. Now you know how it felt."

Staring up at me, Hudson lets loose a laugh.

"Jesus Christ. What are we doing?"

"You missed this, admit it."

"I missed you. Not your temper."

Leaning close, I peck his lips. "Who did I learn my temper from, Hud?"

He grabs a handful of my short hair and drags my lips back to his. Teeth clashing, I forget how to exist while Hudson makes it his mission to invade every inch of my mind. He forces everything out, kissing me like the sky is falling down around us and this is our last moment on this earth.

The steady stream of blood running between our lips makes everything messy as hell. Like a red flag to a bull, my remaining self-control is obliterated. Seizing his sweaty tank top, I break the kiss to rip it over his head, revealing his inked torso and healing shoulder. The bullet wound is still swollen and inflamed.

"I used to dream about killing you myself, after you left me behind at St Anne's." I trace the injury with my finger. "Never thought I'd be the one standing between you and death when the time came."

Hudson chuckles. "Clearly, you're the only one allowed to take me out. If I'm to die, the least I can do is give you the satisfaction of taking my pitiful life."

"What would the fun be in that?"

I bite his plump, inviting bottom lip. Hudson retaliates by gripping the hem of my loose t-shirt. Tearing it over my head, he makes short work of tossing my sports bra aside too. My breasts are exposed to the damp air, contrasting the heat of his mouth securing over my hardened nipple.

Gasping, I grind myself on his lap. His erection is pressing up into me, demanding attention. Rolling the other bud between his fingers, Hudson pauses to glance up at me.

"You know, I've been thinking. Since you slit Britt's throat, it's only fair that I put a bullet between the one-handed psycho's eyes. Equality and all that shit."

"Seven isn't a psycho, and don't pretend like you're doing me a favour by hating him."

"You're seriously defending him?" he replies incredulously. "The man who decapitates people, skins them alive, and broke Phoenix's fingers yesterday for changing the TV channel? He can barely move his hand."

"So what? Seven likes the Discovery Channel. It calms him. Phoenix should've minded his own business."

"Stop deflecting," Hudson snarls.

"That man saved my life. He's far from perfect, but I owe him a debt that I intend to repay. I'm not going to break my promise just because your fragile ego can't handle a little competition."

"Competition?!"

Curling his hand back around my throat, Hudson squeezes right above my pulse point. His eyes look like two shards of ice, ready to slice me open and spear my heart with their rage. I can't fight back as he flips us so I'm back beneath him, slamming me down on the forest floor.

"There is no competition," he hisses. "I love your infuriating, crazy ass. I'll kill you myself before letting anyone steal your attention from our family. Strangle you until you're blue and make you watch as I break that son of a bitch's neck. Maybe I'll even fuck you next to his cold, dead corpse."

"What the fuck is wrong with you?" I choke out.

"As we've established, a lot. Don't believe me? I'll prove it to you."

He rips my yoga pants off before seizing my panties. I suppress a shiver when he brings the damp material to his nose, breathing deeply. When the first droplets of rain hit my bare skin, I try to escape again. It's getting heavier, penetrating the thick canopy of trees to soak the ground.

Hudson growls at my movement, shoving my legs open even wider until my pussy is exposed to the elements. I feel utterly vulnerable, hating the way his gaze eats up every last inch of my most private place. With a hand splayed across my lower belly, he drops between my legs. My back arches as his tongue meets my folds.

"Keep still or I won't let you come."

"Lay one more finger on me and I'll break it," I warn, hating the way my body betrays me. He's always held this invisible power over me, even in the darkest days of our relationship.

"You don't wanna be my little whore, hmm?"

"Nope. I'm done."

Hudson ignores me like usual. I groan against the back of my hand as he slides a practised finger into my slit. I'm worried that someone is going to stumble across our secret tryst and see how toxic this shit is.

"What about now? Still don't want your daddy to touch you?"

"God fucking damn you to hell, Hudson Knight."

Curling his finger deep inside my pussy, my orgasm explodes out of me. We're both getting soaked in the storm, but it doesn't stop Hudson. He flips me over so I'm lying face down on the wet earth. His hand cracks across my butt cheek.

"Hud!" I attempt to claw myself free. "We're done here."

"We're not leaving until we get a few things straight."

"We can't—"

"Shut the fuck up, blackbird, or I'll make you."

"You're not listening—"

"I said shut it, you disobedient slut."

He spanks me so hard, I can't help crying out. I'm forced into a doggy position like a puppet on strings, beholden to the cruelty of its master. We're drowning in the heavy summer rain and my hands dig into the wet mud, covering myself in dirt as I battle to escape.

Hudson refuses to let me go. He knows exactly what he's doing to me. Trailing a wet digit over my asshole, I bite back a groan of pleasure. My body is betraying me all over again, ready to submit to his every possessive demand, whether my brain wants it or not.

"You pretend like you don't want to be owned and fucked like an object." Hudson buries two fingers back in my pussy. "But you thrive on having your choice taken away. You love it when I fuck you like the whore you are. Don't you?"

"You're a fucking asshole."

"*Your* fucking asshole, blackbird. Forever and always."

"Fuck your forever. I'll kill you long before then."

Hudson's fingers disappear and the tip of his cock presses against my tight opening. I'm caught between trying to escape and letting him fuck me. He's right; I grew up in pain and sickness, and now it gets me wetter than a fucking nun with her crucifix. The sadistic son of a bitch knows me too well.

Trapped amidst the storm that surrounds us, Hudson's thrusts mirror the beat of my traitorous heart. He fucks me just like he used to, all raw aggression and hatred, lost in our mutual need to hurt one another. Pummelling my pussy, he growls his annoyance at the lack of hair on my head to wrench.

"Tell me you're mine and I'll let you finish," he commands.

"Is that what you want to hear? That you still have your sick, twisted claws stuck so deep inside of me, I couldn't walk away even if I wanted to?"

"Yes."

"Well, I guess that means I'm yours."

Delivering another bruising smack to my ass, Hudson's tempo increases until I feel like I'm going to explode. Alight with sensation, the tension in my belly twists into a rising crescendo. I decide there and then that he can't get the last word. Not this time.

We can both play dirty.

I'm done being his victim.

"Plus Eli's and Phoenix's," I add, savouring his sharp inhale. "Kade's too. I've fucked them all, you know. Every single one of your friends has had their cock inside of me. How does that feel, Hud?"

"You're digging your own grave," he warns.

"Maybe I could be Seven's too. I'll make you watch while he bends me over and takes me for the first time, just to prove my point. You saved my life in that basement, but that doesn't mean it belongs to you alone."

Hudson's too far gone to withhold my release for pissing him off. The coiled spring deep within me snaps, pushing me off the deep end. I moan through the orgasm that threatens to swallow me whole. He manages another thrust before grunting his release, his heat spilling into me.

I shove Hudson away before he can collapse on me. We both sprawl out, covered head to toe in gelatinous mud and fallen leaves. Panting for every breath, my gaze collides with the two sparkling, oceanic jewels greedily taking me in. I'm surprised by the reluctant acceptance I find there.

"I dragged you out of that basement for myself." He flashes me a warning look. "But also for my family. Don't underestimate what I'll do for them, Brooke. I've given up the one person I care about to make them happy."

Hudson throws my sodden clothes at me, watching without shame as I quickly cover up. Now that we've both said our piece, the electric tension between us feels calmer, more settled. Before my brain kicks in, I tuck myself into his arms.

"I'm glad you found your home, Hud."

His fingers tilt my chin up to meet his eyes. "You're our home, blackbird."

Vulnerability shouldn't scare me anymore. I've lost everything, but I've also regained the most precious thing in the world to me. A family. Hiding from them isn't helping anyone. I can't spend the rest of my life running away from my feelings.

I watch rain cascade down Hudson's face. "I love you."

He offers me a crooked, satisfied smile. "I love you too. So much it scares me."

Dragging a finger over his bloodied nose, already bruising from where I headbutted him, I feel a matching smile play across my lips.

"Even when you're a masochistic dickhead who should be locked up for the rest of his days."

Hudson smirks. "At least I'm consistent."

"Consistently aggravating, sure."

"That's probably the nicest thing you've ever said to me."

With an eye roll, I take his hand. We set off in a slow jog, my energy sapped by our frantic fuck fest. By the time we reach the cottage, my teeth are chattering. We thud up the carved wooden steps to the wraparound porch, listening to the sound of shouting inside.

My clothes are completely ruined. I'm only wearing my stained yoga pants and sports bra, covered head to toe in dirt and swirls of blood. Hudson doesn't look much better, bruised, bleeding, and shirtless. The moment we step inside, Phoenix's and Eli's eyes land on us.

"Fucking dammit!" Kade yells. "It's gone."

"What's wrong?"

He slams the lid of a laptop shut hard enough to send papers flying. "Augustus's hard drive was wiped by remote override. I've been trying to get it back, but there's nothing I can do. Incendia are on to us."

Hudson grabs a bottle of water from the fridge. "Not to point out the obvious, but we know they're on to us. Our fucking faces play every night on the news."

Kade glances at his brother and spots our state of disarray. His eyes widen, trailing over us both in a comical way. "What the hell happened to you? Did you get mauled by a bear out there?"

"I fell over," I lie easily.

Snuggled up on the sofa with a movie, Phoenix throws an arm around Eli's shoulders. He's staring intently at my bare skin on display while trying not to laugh. Eli's grinning at the pair of us, his shoulders shaking with silent laughter. It's painfully obvious why we're both covered in mud.

Kade looks exasperated. "Why is your nose bleeding?"

"We both fell." Hudson grins ear to ear.

Phoenix waves his two broken fingers that are strapped together. "I fell too, right into some asshole's fist. Funny how often that happens around here, isn't it? Very coincidental."

"You should know better than to mess with Seven's television schedule." I dump my ruined running shoes. "He's now obsessed with the cooking channel. I think he got bored of the nature shows. Wait until he finds the porn."

"Are we moving on from the fact our one lead has been destroyed?" Kade exclaims.

Ignoring him, all three guys stare at me.

"What? Six years in a locked basement makes for a lot of curiosity," I say innocently. "Who can blame him?"

Kade dismisses us all with a colourful curse. I catch the dusting of pink across his cheeks. He's got the dirtiest mouth of them all, and somehow, he maintains this innocent-as-fuck exterior.

"Is there really no way to get the hard drive back?" Hudson returns to the topic at hand.

"Nope, I tried everything. We're toast."

"We'll figure something out. That wasn't our only lead."

Tossing my wrecked t-shirt in the bin, I'm intent on a hot shower to ease the ache between my legs. The pair of jungle cats cuddling on the sofa are watching me closely. I don't break eye contact as Phoenix whispers something in Eli's ear.

Before we have a chance to investigate how many people can fit in the shower, the partition door slams open. Sadie struggles out with a duffel bag, her shock of pink hair tucked into a dark beanie. She startles when she sees us all.

"Going somewhere?" I break the silence.

"I'm leaving while Seven is asleep."

"We've discussed this, we're not ready," Kade rushes out. "There's still too much we don't know. We lost Augustus's laptop, but I'm working on a profile for Bancroft and..."

Sadie raises a palm to halt him. "This is precisely why I have to leave. The sooner, the better. Incendia will catch up to me when they find out I'm related to Jude. We're all in the firing line."

"But why are you leaving?" I demand.

Sadie seizes the remaining stacks of paperwork from the table to avoid answering my question. I grab her arm before she can turn away. There was a time when I considered us something akin to friends. Now, I'm not sure where her true loyalties lie.

"I'm sorry, Brooke. I have a job to do."

"What job? Who are you really?"

"I vowed to bring Jude's killers down. Augustus is dead, but the real monsters are still out there. Five more institutes. Incendia didn't build itself. They killed my brother and I want justice."

"Your brother is here. Alive. He needs you."

She shakes her head. "Jude isn't coming back. I belong out there, doing what I was trained for. I trust that you'll take care of him. Hell, you know him better than I do now."

"Trained for?" Hudson chips in.

"I've come to understand that Sadie was assisted in her search for answers," Kade answers for her. "Her employer enabled her to hide her true reason for being in Blackwood."

"Employer?" I repeat.

"She already blew her cover during the riot," Kade continues to fill in the blanks. "Now, she's planning to infiltrate Harrowdean Manor under a whole new identity to find more evidence to corroborate our stories."

The room explodes with disbelief and countless questions. Sadie seems uncomfortable, avoiding looking at us now that the truth has been revealed. I always found her presence too convenient, but this takes the biscuit. She's a fucking spook.

"Is Sadie your real name?" I blurt out.

"Does it matter?"

"Well, if we don't know you or your employer, who can we trust? Seems rather convenient that they're able to simply slip you inside a secure institution, no questions asked."

"You're suggesting I actually work for Incendia?" Sadie splutters.

"They could be on their way right now."

"So after sneaking into Blackwood under a false name, helping you stage your escape, killing Augustus, breaking out several patients and burning down half the institute, you think I work for the people that did this to you?"

I reluctantly admit defeat and back down. Even if I don't trust her as far as I can throw her, there was no faking her pain when she realised Seven was still alive. All of this is far too elaborate for one of Augustus's lackeys to pull off.

"Who do you work for?" I try again.

"That's classified."

"Why are you going back inside?" Hudson questions.

"Augustus's laptop was linked to an external server that's controlled by Incendia. The information I stole from that server is with my team, but it's heavily encrypted. Without that, all we have is some grainy phone footage and a story that no one will believe."

Her team. I file that information away. She's a lot more than she has let on. I feel like we've been living with a stranger for the past three weeks.

"You're saying no one will believe us," Phoenix surmises.

Sadie nods. "We can't bring Incendia down with our stories alone. They have more connections than you know. Investors, private sponsors, government authorities protecting them."

"If the government is protecting Incendia, who's your employer?"

"I'm sorry. You already know too much. This is for your safety, as well as mine. I'm under strict orders."

Kade rubs his temples, looking defeated. He isn't accustomed to not being in control. Weeks of work have yielded no results and we're back to square one.

"Incendia is looking for us. We're public enemy number one," I point out.

"Which is why I have to do this alone."

"Not exactly," Kade speaks up.

Sadie rounds on him. "Absolutely not. It's too dangerous! We just got you guys out. There's no way I'm letting you go to London. I'm handling this alone."

"We lost our one lead. Let us help."

"No!"

"That's not your decision to make."

"What's in London?" I interrupt.

"I've been speaking to someone on the dark web," Kade answers. "Blackwood is a hot topic right now. They claim to have evidence about what went on inside. I proposed we meet to discuss."

He stares at me with defiance, daring me to protest. The thought of diving back into this toxic wasteland of secrets and subterfuge holds zero appeal, but we're sitting ducks here. Freedom means nothing when we're still running for our lives.

"Who exactly is this contact?"

"We have no clue! That's why it's too dangerous," Sadie snaps.

"You're playing your part, let us do ours," Kade insists. "We can't hide forever. I want us to live. That can't happen until our names are cleared."

"You're wading into a war you don't understand."

"If Sadie can get into Harrowdean Manor under an alias and prove what's going on, we have a chance at bringing Incendia down." I look at her. "Let us help. Tell your employer to draft us in."

There's a chorus of nods from the guys. They're all on board with my plan. I don't trust Sadie or the people that she represents, but that doesn't mean we can't use her.

"How can I trust that you're safe to be out in the real world?" she asks acidly. "Or that neither you nor Jude will start butchering people? I can't take that risk."

She seems to regret her words immediately, lips parting on an apology that never quite makes it out. I stare, letting her see all of the agony and self-hatred that's been building beneath the surface, choking me to death.

"I can't sleep," I reveal in a harsh whisper.

"Brooke—"

"When I close my eyes, I see their faces. The people he made me hurt." I look away, shame burning my cheeks. "Not even killing Augustus fixed what he did to me. But watching his empire burn to ashes, ensuring nobody will ever go through what we did... that's worth risking it all for."

"You're gambling with your lives," she says grimly.

"And that's our fucking choice. Make the call."

With a curse, Sadie pulls out a basic burner phone. She taps on one of three names in her contacts. The name begins with H. Her voice is resigned.

"Wait here. This isn't my decision. If you wind up dead, that's your responsibility. I hope you know what you're doing, Brooke."

I swallow hard. "Yeah, me too."

CHAPTER 8
ELI

YOU ARE EVERYTHING - HOLDING
ABSENCE

KADE AND HUDSON sit up front in the Jeep, watching Brooklyn yell at Sadie. They're standing outside the second-hand car we picked up on the way out of town.

Seven is sleeping off his vodka-induced hangover in the other car. Phoenix keeps a wary eye from the passenger seat, blowing cigarette smoke out the window.

"We should level with her, she'll understand," Kade insists. "This is the safest option."

Hudson glares daggers at Seven's sleeping form in the back of the car. "She'll kick our asses in the blink of an eye when it comes to that bastard."

"Look at what happened on the supply run. Separating them is just a precaution, in case something goes wrong on the way down south."

Kade's words enrage me, but I swallow it down. Treating Brooklyn differently will further alienate her from the group. She's pulled away from us as it is. Seven was the only one who could talk sense into her last time she had a breakdown. Whether they like it or not, he's part of this now.

"The further she is from that freak, the better," Hudson growls. "We need to keep them apart."

"While we're travelling, I agree it's best to ride separately. But you can't kick him out of her life forever. She needs him too."

"Fuck off, Kade."

"Just saying, brother. Time to face facts."

Hudson exits the car, which rocks from the force of him slamming the door shut. He marches over and stands between the shouting pair, ending the fight with a few brief words. Grabbing Brooklyn by the scruff of her shirt, he drags her back and throws her in.

"Brooke—"

"Shut the hell up," she barks.

Casting me a despairing look, Kade fires the engine and waits for Sadie to pull out onto the main road. Phoenix gives me a three-fingered wave as they pass, leaving us to follow into the fading light.

"Whatever game you're all playing, it's childish," Brooklyn says acerbically. "This is either some bullshit pissing contest or plain jealousy. Both are unnecessary."

"Sadie can handle her brother without your assistance, blackbird."

"Did you put her up to this?"

Hudson draws an invisible halo over his head, attempting to lighten the mood. With a sour look, Brooklyn crosses her arms and stares resolutely out the window. He isn't going to win this fight with her.

We've all been on a knife's edge while preparing to leave the safe, woodland retreat in Northern Scotland. After three weeks of something resembling peace, all too soon we're back in at the deep end, desperately trying not to drown.

"Have you heard from Lucia and Two?" Brooklyn asks.

"They checked in an hour ago, back at the cottage," Kade answers while turning onto the motorway. "They'll be okay. You guys should get some sleep. We have a long drive ahead."

Hudson shakes his head. "I don't feel good about this."

"We have no choice. Can't hide in the woods forever."

"Enough already! Quit being all wise and shit."

Kade suppresses a snort. "Maybe we should've left your miserable ass behind too."

We had no choice but to drive to London. With no passports and the entire country looking for us, flying wasn't an option. I can't help but feel like we're retracing our steps back into the lion's den. The aim of the game is to keep a low profile, pass under the radar and not get killed. *Easy peasy.*

"You good?" Brooklyn breaks the silence.

I ignore her searching gaze, attempting to control my breathing. I'm doing a crappy job of pretending like I'm good with this plan. The world passes in a blur of motion on the busy road, every mile back to civilisation serving to increase my anxiety. I haven't been outside in a decade, even longer than Seven.

"Shut your eyes, Eli," she murmurs. "I've got you. Lay down."

Reluctantly, I rest my head on Brooklyn's shoulder, and she entwines our fingers together. I don't belong in this strange world and want nothing more than to slice, stab, and punch my way out of the limelight, back into the safety of society's trash heap.

We drive through the night, the bleak stars our only companions on this road trip to hell. Kade and Hudson swap over somewhere around Sheffield, not bothering to disturb our tangle of limbs in the back. I don't sleep at all. I'm content to listen to Brooklyn's breathing while trying to keep my shit together.

As the dawn glow spreads across the darkened sky, the fuel light flicks on. Kade lets out a curse. We pull up at a petrol station ten minutes later and Brooklyn unravels herself from me. There are only two other cars—a red truck and a transit van. We study the vehicles, weighing our options.

Kade sighs. "I think it looks quiet enough."

"We're too exposed out here," Hudson argues.

"I agree." He switches off the engine. "But we're out of good options. Help me fill some canisters, then we can avoid stopping again. I'll text Sadie and get her to meet us."

Leaving the brothers to deal with the fuel, Brooklyn climbs out and stretches. We passed Sadie and the others a while back. I can see the worry on her face as she urgently scans the passing road for the other car. Separating the group was a shitty idea in my opinion, made worse by Hudson's insistence on being an asshole.

"Come with me to get food?" she offers.

I stare at her, unblinking.

"We should stick together."

She's right, but that doesn't stop the panic swarming through my limbs. The taste of ashes and battery acid is so intense as it crowds my mind, I nearly double over from the intrusion. The flavours have been calmer for a while, but everything about this situation is triggering me. Old habits die hard.

"I'll be with you the whole time," Brooklyn reassures. "You should ease back into the world, Eli. Hiding won't make it any easier."

Her outstretched hand beckons me. Those storm-cloud eyes are filled with hope that threatens to devastate me worse than any panic attack. Making my numb legs move, I climb out and flip my hood up to cover my face.

"Stick with me," she mutters.

"Okay."

Her grin is worth the pain of speaking aloud. My throat aches from just one word. Brooklyn tows me towards the shop after accepting a stack of cash from Kade. I survey our surroundings, clocking the young couple exiting their truck. Nobody is paying us any attention.

Get a fucking grip, Eli.

Can't be scared of the world forever.

The shop bell dings as we step inside, keeping our heads tucked down. I don't look where I'm going, following the thump of Brooklyn's Chucks. I'm fighting to remain conscious, my lungs constricted tight. She draws to a halt in the snack aisle, cupping my cheek.

"There. Not so hard, was it?"

I offer her a look of pure fear.

"I'm here, Eli. I'll always be here to hold your hand." Brooklyn's smile would bring whole armies to their knees. "Choose your snacks and let's get the hell out of here."

Gulping my terror down, I face the endless rows of crisps, sweets, and junk food. Too many choices. Too many unknowns. I haven't chosen a meal in a fucking decade. It's all too much.

"Salt and vinegar is my favourite," Brooklyn muses.

Dread coats my tongue, tart and bitter. My heart explodes in a frenzied rush, and I smash my fist against my forehead, savouring the sweet release of pain. Her grip on my hand tightens as she watches me unravel.

"Come on, stay with me. You can do this."

"Don't... m-make me..." I stutter.

"You can do this. There's nothing to be afraid of."

"No!"

Cursing under her breath, Brooklyn drags me away from the prying eyes of the cashiers. I'm shoved into a low-lit bathroom out back, the stench of bleach and cheap cleaning products turning my stomach. She slams the door behind us and twists the lock.

Before she can say a single word, my control snaps. The crappy bathroom melts away, lost to the fear that battles to consume me. By the time my vision clears, I have Brooklyn pinned against the tiled wall by her throat, her nails scratching at my hands.

The air between us is electrified as I hold her captive. Vulnerable. Pinned. Mine. Burying my face in the crook of her neck, I let the emotions and flavours wash over me in a deadly tidal wave. She's been my life raft since day one, keeping me afloat as I squeeze the life out of her.

"Fuck you," I croak.

Brooklyn slumps against the wall when I find the willpower to let go. She eyes me warily while rubbing her throat, where red crescents mark my fingertips digging into her.

"I deserved that."

"N-No."

"I fucking forgot you, Eli. I forgot you all," she shouts at me. "It makes me so mad, I can't take it. I don't know what the fuck I'm doing anymore. Nothing makes sense."

I speak the only language I know how. Securing my lips to hers, Brooklyn surrenders herself to me. I'm still furious with her. Myself. The monsters that tore us apart. The world that cast me out and refuses to take me back. The scared, stupid child inside me who can't speak for himself.

Brooklyn groans against my mouth, our tongues violently battling each other. She takes the chance to wrap her legs around my waist, pinned against the bathroom wall by sheer rage alone. I rub my rock-hard cock into her, seeking absolution.

"Talk to me," she pants.

I bite the soft flesh of her neck. "T-Talk?"

"Tell me what you need. I wasn't there. I'm sorry that you had no choice but to isolate yourself from everyone just to survive. I'm sorry that I couldn't hold your broken pieces together."

Tracing my tongue over the dark bruise blooming on her skin, I take a deep inhale of her scent, a combination of all our essences in one. Hudson's musky aftershave. Phoenix's flowery, apple-blossom shampoo. Kade's citrusy deodorant. Even Seven, with his newfound love for freshly ground coffee.

It brings sweet relief, the scents of home she carries, suffused in her skin. Like warm apple pie and fresh linens, the flavours unfurling from the deepest pits of my mind. I've tasted nothing but despair for so long, I forgot what it feels like to belong.

"Please," I whisper, lost for words.

Brooklyn presses her forehead to mine. "Speak, Eli."

Clearing my throat, I summon the spark of courage buried deep in my mind and breathe in the comfort of her scent again, a reminder of family and home that's been lost to me for so long. It gives me the strength to force out the words that have haunted all my years of silence.

One question.

"Tell m-me… how t-to… exist."

I can feel her hot, relentless tears against my cheeks as the boundaries between us melt into insignificance. She's curled around my heart like a cancer, poisoning my cells and twisting my entire persona into something unrecognisable.

"You have to be here with me," she murmurs, lips ghosting over mine. "Live in this moment, no matter how shit it is. Not in that house fire. Not in Blackwood. Here, right now, in this bathroom. Destitute fugitives on the run. Losing our minds and cast out from society. But fuck, we exist."

A hateful laugh breaks free. "H-How?"

Her sigh glides over me, a soothing balm on frayed nerves.

"Like this."

Reaching into the pocket of her leather jacket, she slides a wickedly sharp knife free. The exact same one she used to claim Jefferson's and Augustus's lives. My mouth waters as she studies the blade, holding it in her palms.

"Why?" I struggle out.

"Because you don't have to hide from me or pretend to be something you're not. Hurt yourself, Eli. Cut, bleed, scream and rage, if that's what it takes. Do whatever you need to until you can exist too."

Clasping the knife in shaking hands, I shove my shame and resentment far out of reach. She's seen me, the real me. Time and time again. I don't have to hide the broken parts of myself that need to hurt just to get through the day. Rolling up my sleeve, I expose healed cuts and countless scars.

Her gaze burns a hole into me, but I focus on the pearlescent veins begging to be sliced. My hand is trembling so badly, I can barely hold the blade, let alone press it deep enough to bring relief. The need to laugh bubbles up at the irony of it. Now, I'm the one asking for help, not her.

"Fucking h-hand."

Brooklyn bites her lip. "Been there. Let me."

She takes the knife to my inner arm, below the healed cuts from a few weeks back. The bite of pain follows her precise cutting, dragging the serrated metal over porcelain skin. Brooklyn slices me six times with the precision of a surgeon expunging a deadly infection.

Crushing her lips against mine, she claims my heathen soul while painting her name in blood and sickness. The anxiety gushes out of me with the crimson flow, leaving me weak at the knees. I draw my first easy breath since leaving the safety of the cottage.

"Welcome back," she murmurs. "Better?"

Feeling unsteady, I manage a nod. I'm too busy studying the fascinating artwork painted by my blood. Each trail drips on the bleached floor, blooming red against dirty white. The need is still there. More. I'll always want to cross that line just one more time, no matter the risk.

"We should go. The others will be worried."

Rinsing the knife off in the sink, Brooklyn slips it back inside her pocket. My fingers twitch with the urge to steal it from her, sink the tip deep into my wrist and slice my way far from this place. Even if that means leaving her, Phoenix, and my whole family behind. The temptation is so strong.

"W-Wait—"

She stares, unnerved by the sound of my voice.

"Thank y-you," I rush out.

"You don't need to thank me."

I bury my fingers in her short locks, exposing her lips to me again. I can't get enough of her, ravenous and unable to control myself. Brooklyn melts into me like ice cream on a summer's day. I bend her over the small, built-in sink, regardless of the guys waiting for us.

"Eli—"

Her protests are silenced as I peel her jeans and panties down, enough to expose her bare ass. My fingers find the slick heat gathered between her thighs. She can't pretend she isn't turned on right now.

"We don't have time."

Pressing her lower back to position her, I race to undo my belt. I don't give a fuck where we are. I need to be inside of her before I lose my mind. She's the only thing that brings me back from the edge. Her words dissolve into breathy sighs as I push inside of her.

Brooklyn's hands grip the sink. She's so goddamn tight and wet, even with minimal prep. I surge in and out of her with impatience, each stroke forcing the demons in my head to retreat. I need more. With every second, breathing becomes easier, and the world grows more bearable.

I don't stop even as there's a loud knock on the door. Desire and panic clash, serving to speed up my frantic thrusting. Brooklyn finds her knife, holding it at the ready as someone pounds on the wood again.

"Who is it?" she yells.

"Get your asses out of there, kids. This ain't a damn brothel!"

Before she can answer, I wrap my hand back around her throat from behind. She squeaks before falling silent. I'm so close to the edge. This is the first time I've fucked her in months, and I can't control myself like I usually would. She's taken over, leaving me to trail in her blaze of glory.

When I finish, Brooklyn lets out a groan of sheer bliss. I release her throat so she can suck in air, fighting to catch her breath. Her walls clench around me as I ride the relentless waves of my release.

"Jesus, Eli. Talk about bad timing."

Fighting a laugh, I reluctantly slide out of her and grab a handful of toilet tissue. Brooklyn turns and blanches when she sees what I'm doing. Her cheeks are stained red with embarrassment when I bring the tissues between her legs, cleaning up the mess I've left behind.

We both find intimacy terrifying.

That's exactly why I'm doing this.

Flushing the toilet, I tug my jeans back up and fasten my belt. Brooklyn's avoiding looking at me while straightening herself out. Before she can unlock the door, I snatch her hand. Her fierce grey eyes scrape over me with uncertainty.

We're still trapped in the safe bubble that allowed our darkness to unfurl, but the terror of reality is knocking on the door. We can't stay in this moment forever, even if we want to. Digging deep, I clear my throat.

"Baby g-girl... I l-love... you."

Brooklyn's mouth splits in a grin of devastating pride. My throat hurts like hell, but for the first time, I don't feel anxious when speaking. I'm not afraid of her. She's my safe haven. I catch the stray tear that tracks down her cheek, a precious pearl of pure emotion. It tastes salty on my tongue.

"Fuck, Eli. I love you so goddamn much."

I let her drag me back out into the world, this time keeping my hood back and my head held high without fear. I have nothing to be afraid of with Brooklyn by my side.

I can face the world.

I'm not alone anymore.

CHAPTER 9
BROOKLYN
PSYCHO - AVIVA

STICKING close to Sadie's car, we pass through the outskirts of London. The roads are packed with weekend traffic, shoppers and tourists going about their business. I desperately drink it all in. Every last face, smiling and laughing, enjoying the last of the summer sun.

"Where is she taking us?" Hudson grumbles.

Kade checks the rearview mirror for a fifth time. "I have no idea."

"Are we meeting her team soon?" I ask instead.

"Maybe. I think we can trust her. She wants the same thing as us."

Hudson snorts. "What is that exactly?"

"To see Incendia burn," Kade answers solemnly.

Leaning between their seats, I watch Sadie's car. Seven must be lying down in the back, probably still asleep. Phoenix appears to be smoking and chattering away while Sadie drives. The separation from my men is killing me—Seven fucking included.

"I only trust our family, nobody else," Hudson says. "First sign that something's off, we're getting the hell out of here."

I sit back in my seat. "Seconded."

He looks over his shoulder to shoot me a possessive grin. It's rare that we agree these days, but I'm far from comfortable endangering our family. Nothing about this situation is controllable or safe. We've only just discovered freedom; I won't go back to living our lives in a prison.

"Relax, Brooke. You trust me?" Kade smiles.

"Trusting you isn't the problem."

We don't speak again until nearly an hour later, when Sadie turns off the busier central streets and heads into London's seedy underbelly. Passing through an industrial area, the roads are paved with cracked concrete and shadowed by abandoned warehouses. There are no signs of life.

She parks outside a deserted, faded blue warehouse that looks tightly sealed from the outside. There isn't another soul on the street, far from the nearest suburb. Kade pulls up and I'm flying out of the car before it even stops, itching to set eyes on Phoenix and Seven.

"Any problems?"

Sadie stretches her arms above her head. "Of course not."

The car door opens before I can get to it. Seven slides out, stretching his long legs and surveying the street. His shoulder-length brown hair is mussed and tangled from sleep, framing attentive eyes and lips that are pressed together. Every inch of his body is pulled taut with tension.

"Sev?"

His hand grasps mine on instinct. "Princess."

"You good?"

"Just haven't been outside in a while, that's all."

I squeeze his hand before releasing, preparing for the incoming blur of motion. I'm scooped into Phoenix's arms and spun around so fast I think I may throw up. When he puts me back on my feet, I balance myself on his broad shoulders.

"Was that really necessary?"

"It was a long drive, firecracker. Did the chatterbox keep you company?"

Eli's hand appears out of nowhere to whack him around the head. Phoenix plasters on an innocent smile, dragging him close. I'm sandwiched between the two of them with zero complaints, fascinated by the sight of them kissing in front of our entire group. It's intoxicating.

"Can we save the public orgy for another time?" Hudson grunts.

I meet his icy blue eyes. "Jealous?"

"You're playing with fire, blackbird."

"My favourite. Care to join us?"

Hudson hesitates. "Perhaps."

Sadie unlocks the rusted grate that covers the entrance to the warehouse. The scream of old metal makes us all wince. She drags it up, exposing multiple heavy-duty padlocks across the entrance. After unlocking each one, she disappears inside and indicates for us to follow. With a final look around, we all step into the darkness.

Inside, the scent of mould and decay has me gagging. Kade shines the light on his phone to guide our steps deeper into the disused warehouse. It looks like an old workshop, with the burned-out remains of a car at the very centre, surrounded by countless tools and broken machines.

"Sadie? What is this place?" I call out.

Pulling a squeaky lever built into the cinderblock wall, gloomy yellow lights slam on. Sadie faces the group, barely sparing her surroundings a glance. She looks far from happy to be here.

"Home."

The warehouse is split into two levels, with the workshop on the ground floor hiding a grubby break area behind a thick, plastic sheet. Two sofas are pushed up against the walls, with old, peeling movie posters from a time long gone. A metal staircase leads upwards to a mezzanine level, the floor constructed from metal sheets and lit by bare filament bulbs.

"There's a bedroom of sorts upstairs, bathroom too. It's dirty and basic, but it'll do." Sadie grabs a new duffel bag from a locker. "You need to stay alert. London is too exposed."

"What do you mean, home?" Seven asks angrily.

Sadie doesn't even look at him, rifling through the bag of old clothing. When she pulls a gun from the locker, everyone tenses. She checks the chamber and tucks it into her waistband.

"I lived here for a few years," she admits. "Dad owned the workshop before he died. I should've sold it, but I couldn't bring myself to do it. When Grandma died, I had nowhere else to go."

Seven stands frozen, his entire, furious posture carved from marble. A thunderous expression is written across his face, but I can see the truth in his eyes. Guilt. When he tries to lay a hand on Sadie's shoulder, she flinches.

"I'm not going to hurt you," he utters in disbelief.

"I didn't mean... that's not..." Her gaze falls to her hands. "I'm sorry, Ju— I mean, Seven. I get this is hard for you. I didn't expect things to pan out like this either."

"You didn't think you'd find me alive, you mean."

"Something like that."

"Would you rather I was dead?" he hedges.

Nervously smoothing her bright-pink hair, Sadie looks unnerved by his question. She doesn't deny it, still focusing on her feet instead. Seven waits for a few awkward seconds before stalking off. He slams through the plastic sheet to escape into the break room.

"What about you?" Kade studies the warehouse.

Sadie shakes herself out of it, throwing the duffel bag on a nearby table and scraping her hair back. "I have to get to Harrowdean by Monday. They're expecting me. I'll keep in touch on the burner phone."

"When will your employer contact us?"

"When he's ready to," she says ominously.

"We need a bit more to go on than that."

An echoing rattle cuts off our conversation. Hudson and Kade both pull guns they kept after our escape, while I palm my knife. Phoenix follows suit, holding his own knife at the ready. We all stand prone as footsteps near.

The tension explodes when a figure emerges through the gloom. Standing with obvious trepidation, the man has a head full of tight, dirty-blonde ringlets that hang messily across his face. Piercing blue eyes several shades lighter than Hudson's scour over us, hidden behind wire-rimmed glasses. His bottom lip is caught between his teeth.

"Theo," Sadie gasps. "What are you doing here?"

His eyes land on her, guarded expression transforming into one of sheer happiness. Adjusting his dark flannel shirt and denim jacket, he prepares for incoming as Sadie runs at full speed. I don't miss the way Hudson and Kade keep their weapons raised.

"Long time, no see." Theo laughs. "I had to see you."

Embracing him, we all gape as Sadie secures their lips together. The pair exchange a blistering kiss despite their audience. When Kade pointedly clears his throat, they finally jump apart.

"Come on, I'll introduce you." Sadie drags him to our circle, shooting us a deliberate look of warning. "Everyone, this is Theodore. He's a… uh. Well. A co-worker, shall we say."

His smile is extremely awkward. "Nice to meet you all."

"Who exactly are you?" Hudson tucks his gun away.

"Um, Theo. I'm… tech support?"

"Tech support?" I repeat incredulously. "You don't sound so sure."

Theo clears his throat. "Among other things. I'm the techie."

He releases Sadie's hand and pulls a heavy backpack from his shoulders. We follow him to a table, remaining at a wary distance. Reaching inside his packed bag, Theo slides a laptop free, along with a zippered pouch. He casts Sadie a smile before tipping the contents out.

"It's all here for you, like we discussed. Figured I'd hand deliver it."

I gape at the pristine fake passport and ID that Sadie looks over, along with other forged documents that will grant her a whole new persona. She slowly checks the items, nodding her approval. Theo relaxes a little, his entire body geared towards her.

"Other things like forgery?" Kade enquires, his gun lowered for now.

Theo nods. "Perhaps."

"He's the best around." Sadie stuffs the items into her duffel bag. "Theo joined the team around the same time as me. Three years ago. He's the gearhead of the operation."

"What precisely does this team do?"

"You haven't told them?" Theo frowns.

Sadie avoids his gaze. "I thought I'd leave it to Hunter."

"They need to be debriefed before then."

Theo opens his laptop, and his fingers fly in a blur of movement, even faster than Kade's impressive speed. When he turns the screen to face us, we study a terrifying slab of architecture. Carved from huge steel beams and slices of solid, tinted glass, the building is truly huge. I'm certain I've seen it in the news or on TV.

"I work for Sabre. We both do."

The name is unfamiliar, but judging by Kade's sharp intake of breath, it's a big deal. Theo rubs the back of his neck, flustered from all the attention on him. I get the impression he doesn't step into fieldwork that often.

"The private security firm?" Hudson guesses.

"My employer and his business partner started it seven years ago," Theo answers. "We're now one of the biggest security firms in England. We take on the most challenging cases. Serial killers, assassinations, corruption, conspiracies. You name it."

"Conspiracies like Blackwood?" I suggest.

Theo spares me a curious look. "Sometimes."

"Where do you fit into all of this?" Kade directs to Sadie.

"I was investigating alone," Sadie says reluctantly. "I got sloppy and ended up in hot water. Hunter's team found me. They took me in, trained me, gave me the chance to do things the right way. To find justice for"—she glances at the back room where Seven fled—"everything."

Theo takes her hand and squeezes it, the pair sharing small smiles. My brain is struggling to keep up with this latest development. First, we learn that Sadie's not only a double agent, but a mole inside of Blackwood via this mysterious firm. Now she's screwing one of them? *Colour me confused.*

"I hear you're meeting a dark-web contact?" Theo asks, anxiously fiddling with his shirt sleeve.

Kade nods, itching to pick the techie's brain.

"Can I take a look at your firewalls, make sure it's safe? I've had some dealings with online crooks."

"Sure," Kade agrees enthusiastically.

Theo beckons him over. They begin exchanging far too many overcomplicated words for me to keep up with. I bypass Sadie and head out back to where Seven disappeared. Beyond the thick, plastic sheet lies another low-lit room.

This one is a makeshift kitchen filled with several stained lunch tables. Seven's lanky, scar-strewn body is hunched over at one. He's breathing hard, a fine tremble seeming to run over him. I approach with tentative steps.

"Sev?"

"Go away, princess. I'm in no mood to talk."

I collapse on the bench seat next to him, bumping our shoulders together. "Come on, don't shut me out. We've played that game before."

"You're stubborn, aren't you?"

I scoff. "Are you only just realising that?"

Lifting his head, golden-caramel eyes pierce my skin. He has this unique ability to slip deep into my veins and poison my thoughts. There's barely a breath between us and the air is charged with sudden anticipation. Seven licks his lips, watching me intently.

When he dares to brush the back of his knuckles against my cheek, a tiny sigh of pleasure escapes my lips. His dark smile widens. I should be ashamed, but I'm quivering with need at his touch. I want more.

"Sadie—"

"I don't want to talk about her," he snaps.

"What do you want to talk about?"

"Are you screwing all four of them?"

His question takes me aback. I feel the instinctive need to hide my unusual relationship with the guys. Love is weakness, but I don't need to protect them from Seven. He isn't the enemy, even if he seems like it at times.

"Yeah, I am."

"And they're okay with that?"

"Depends who you ask."

His thumb glides over my bottom lip, tender and gentle. This person is unlike the violent monster that lives within his human shell, a terrifying beast that matches my own. I bury the urge to bite his finger, knowing it will only encourage this thing growing between us.

There's something burning low in my belly, a carnal need I can't ignore. It's been there for a while, smouldering into a roaring inferno. I just wasn't ready to acknowledge it until now.

"What if I told you that I can't stop thinking about kissing you?" Seven's voice is dangerously soft. "Every time I close my eyes, I picture myself tracing every last mark on your body with my tongue, and making you fall apart with my cock buried deep inside of you."

Clenching my thighs, I fight to take an even breath.

"I'll have you screaming my name for the world to hear," he adds darkly.

"Which name?"

Seven grins, full of promise. "My name isn't Jude anymore."

"Then I'd happily scream for you and the whole world to hear, Sev."

"Even your boyfriends?"

Narrowing my eyes, I level a challenge. "Even them."

With the sound of voices playing behind the plastic sheet, this isn't the moment to delve into things. But as I inhale Seven's scent, still unfamiliar after all our time spent separated in the basement, I struggle to maintain my grip on the situation. I shouldn't, but I want him. Just like I want all of them.

"This is a bad idea," I breathe.

"Most definitely."

"Someone will get hurt."

Seven smirks. "I'll do all the hurting. You'd look better naked and stained with fresh blood when we fuck, princess."

"I've warned you about killing the guys approximately nine times now."

His little eye roll makes my heart flip, the traitorous organ. Cupping my cheek, Seven strokes my skin, and I try to remember every reason why I can't do this. None of them stop me from staring into his pained eyes, begging him to take the final step that I'm too cowardly to make myself.

"I don't care what you want. I'll kill them and take you for myself," he warns.

"Then we're going to have a problem, aren't we?"

"Even better."

Closing the gap between us, the lightest brush of lips has me combusting from sexual tension. It's all I need to grab hold of Seven's shoulders and crush my mouth against his, stealing the kiss I've long dreamed of. His tongue seeks access that I quickly grant.

We dissolve into a frenzy. He's devouring me like we could be dragged apart at any moment. I can taste the coffee he's developed an obsession with on his tongue. When his hand sneaks beneath my shirt to stroke the underside of my braless breasts, I gasp against his lips.

"Brooke? You good back there?" Phoenix calls.

I break the kiss. "Yeah… all good!"

Retreating footsteps slow my panicked heartbeat. I sigh with relief, looking up to find Seven glaring at me. He quickly grabs my wrist so tight, I yelp. He's grinding the bones together. The softness in him has dissipated, replaced with animalistic rage.

"Are you ashamed of me?"

"No, of course not."

"You think I won't break the necks of your men if that's what it takes to have you? I'll kill them, Eight. One by one. You can watch as I choke the life from their broken corpses. Will you still yearn for me then?"

Before Seven can react, I slam my fist into his face. He topples off the bench, spitting blood from his split lip. Advancing without mercy, I straddle his body and punch him again. The sight of his blood spreading across the floor has my entire body humming with satisfaction.

"You don't have to kill your way through life, Sev! There are people who care about you. I care about you. But nobody threatens the lives of those I love, not even you."

"You kissed me," he accuses.

"You kissed me first!"

Dipping a finger in his warm, slick blood, I draw it across my lips until I'm coated in his vitality. Claimed. Tainted. Owned. His blood sinks beneath my skin and ties our souls together with an unbreakable bond forged in the darkest depths of Augustus's basement.

Seven watches with wide eyes. I resist licking my lips, leaning in to press them against his. Grabbing handfuls of his untameable hair, I tug until he hisses with pain. His hand wraps around my throat, caressing my vein, ready and ripe for the taking.

"Do it," I command. "I dare you."

"If I kill you, I will never know what your pussy tastes like."

He releases his grip on my throat and shoves me aside. I roll and manage to find my feet, preparing for a blow that never comes. Seven stares at me like I'm a puzzle he can't fathom, confusion marked across his expression. He wipes his lips before fleeing the room like his life depends on it.

"Sev, wait!"

He ignores me and disappears back under the plastic sheet. I'm left alone, gaping at the blood-stained place where he laid, wondering how the fuck I'm going to convince four men that barely manage to share, to add a fifth.

That, or Seven kills them.

Blackwood was fucking simpler than this.

CHAPTER 10
BROOKLYN

LOST - OLLIE

THE SAND IS *soft beneath my feet, grains of cheap amusement for the child version of me sitting several metres away. With white-blonde hair scraped up into pigtails, my dad scoops her up before spinning her around in a circle.*

"Broooke! The best princess in the realm."

"Daddy, stop!" she screams.

"Ready to go in the water? Let's wake up Mummy, come on."

I hug myself tight while watching my dad leading child-me back up the beach, where an umbrella has been hammered into the sand. Mum's staring up at the cloudless sky with a blank expression, lost in her thoughts. My mouth dries up when I see who sits next to her.

He's far younger than I remember him, his blonde hair short and well-trimmed. He grew a ponytail later in his rebellious youth. With a bright smile and dimples, the sight of my brother makes my heart seize with agony.

"Who's ready to go for a swim?" Dad cheers.

Logan shoves the rest of his ice cream in his mouth. "Me, me, me!"

Ruffling his hair, Dad kneels beside Mum and gives her a shake. "Mel? You okay?"

"Yes, of course."

Reaching into his backpack, Dad retrieves a camera and starts rolling. Mum forces herself to stand, wiping the dark shadows from her face. By the time he turns the lens on us, she's cuddling child-me from behind, tugging on my platinum pigtails.

"Smile for the camera! Show us your big teeth."

The words have me clutching my head, the awful reminder threatening to tear me to shreds. I watch the memory play out, trapped behind an invisible barrier. It's the exact same one that Augustus threw in my face in the dungeon, using it to break my remaining sanity down to its last atom.

"My beautiful wife." Dad sighs happily.

"Don't get all soppy on me now, Ian. Come on, let's take her to the sea."

I scream through the hands I have clenched over my mouth. Watching from afar, Logan films them skipping through the sand, swinging child-me between them. Seeing it from this angle reopens the festering wounds that want nothing more than to rip me open.

"Brooke?"

Glancing up, I find the younger version of Logan looking right at me. I've infected this happy memory with the inevitability of the future, and he's staring with accusations buried in his grey irises.

"You shouldn't be here, kiddo. I told you to forget, move on."

"I c-can't. Every time I close my eyes, I see you."

Thick trails of blood begin to weep from his eyes, gushing down his cheeks and staining the white sand beneath his feet. Logan becomes a grotesque painting of human suffering. I rush to help him, but my hands pass through his body like they're parting shadows, unable to grab hold of something that doesn't exist.

"Devil child. You're next, Brooke."

Her voice sends a chill down my spine. Mum now stands mere inches away. At her feet, two twisted and broken bodies lay, no longer smiling as they enjoy the seaside. Dad's neck is cracked and misshapen, while bloodied handprints mark the strangled throat of my childhood self.

"Blackwood is inevitable. Return or face the consequences."

"No! I can't go back. Not now, not ever."

Her lips brush my ear, laced with the stench of rotting flesh. "You're nothing more than a monster, Brooke. A lying, remorseless murderer. Exactly what I birthed you to be."

Letting out a bloodcurdling scream, the last thing I see is her cruel gaze burning my insides, an undeniable figment of the inevitable. She is my past, my present, and my future.

I'll never be anything more than a child of insanity.

A child... of Blackwood.

———

Lighting the cigarette with trembling hands, I blow smoke out. The cold workshop beneath me is silent as the rest of the guys sleep. I made sure to swallow my screams rather than wake everyone up.

Still kidding yourself, Miss West?

Gulping hard, I stare resolutely ahead. I won't entertain the smirking, shadowy version of Augustus lingering behind me.

Can't outrun your own mind.

Our work isn't done yet.

"You're fucking dead," I whisper.

As you will be too.

This path only ends one way.

You can never live a normal life.

"I'm doing a hell of a lot better than you. The guys got me out. I have a chance with them."

Still looking for a family, are you?

They'll die soon enough.

You're poison. Just ask Vic.

"Enough! Get out of my head!"

Phoenix groans in his sleep, startled by my voice. Crushing the cigarette, I silently curse. He's spooning Eli from behind as they both sleep on the threadbare mattress that fills the mezzanine level.

Glancing around with my breath held, I find Augustus's snarky ghost gone. Thank fuck for that. I don't want the guys to know I'm still hallucinating. They worry enough as it is.

Dressing in a loose, acid-wash t-shirt from my backpack and a pair of old blue jeans, I sneak back down the wobbly stairs. Hudson and Seven are both still out of it, opting to take the two downstairs sofas. I quietly sneak past and slip into the break room.

"Morning, love."

Nearly jumping out of my skin, I find a bedraggled Kade working on his laptop at a table. He eyes me with his glasses tucked up in his shaggy, overgrown blonde hair, a steaming mug of coffee in his hand.

"You're awake?"

He shrugs. "Evidently, so are you."

"Couldn't sleep."

"More bad dreams? I didn't hear you."

I make a non-committal noise, peering into the coffee pot before deciding to brave a cup of sludge. My head feels like it's ready to explode and the sun isn't even up. Grabbing a stale granola bar from the cupboard, I pad up to Kade.

His arms wrap around me as I deposit myself in his lap. He smells like the cheap shampoo we found in Sadie's basic bathroom, complete with a camping shower and cracked mirror. I can't help but stroke his messy hair. He looks so different from the slick, polished man I once met.

"Have you heard from the girls yet?"

"They're fine. You didn't answer my question. Bad dream?"

"Nope," I mutter. "Not going there."

Closing his laptop with a sigh, Kade grips my chin. I'm unable to look away from him and the demands brewing in his hazel eyes. Our lips brush in a brief, tender whisper.

"You can talk to me," he urges. "I know I don't understand what you went through like Seven or Hudson do, but that doesn't mean I'm not here for you. We all are."

"I know."

"Do you?" Kade kisses the corner of my mouth.

When he pulls away, I gulp down some crappy coffee to buy some time. I'm wrestling with my ingrained need to hide from him. All I've done since the day we met is run at full speed, away from intimacy, emotions, everything. I'm not that person anymore, but her claws are still buried deep.

"Lazlo treated my mother a long time ago," I finally say.

Kade stills. "Professor Lazlo? In Blackwood?"

"She had her first admission after giving birth to my brother, then another when we were young."

"Fuck, Brooke. Why didn't you tell us?"

I squeeze my eyes shut. "He broke her, Kade. Blackwood is the reason she lost her mind. That's why she murdered Logan and crashed the car. Incendia is the reason my entire family is dead."

Kade's soft fingertips glide over my cheeks, wiping the traitorous moisture away. Beneath the shampoo, I can smell his familiar, squeaky-clean scent. Everything about him is solid, steadying. I can trust him with this secret.

"We'll make them pay," Kade proclaims. "I swear on my life, they will all burn for what they've done to us. We won't rest until Incendia is dead and buried in the ground."

"It won't bring them back," I whisper roughly.

"Open your eyes, Brooke."

I shake my head. "I can't."

"It's just us. Let me see those beautiful eyes."

Forcing myself to obey, I meet Kade's kind, loving gaze. Even after all the pain he's endured for us, goodness still shines within him. He replaces his glasses, his expression steeling with determination.

"Nothing will bring your family back. But the family you have now? Nobody will ever take it away from you."

"You promise?"

"I promise. Always and forever."

I roll my eyes. "Did Hudson give you that line?"

"What? It's probably the most poetic shit he's ever come out with."

My mouth is magnetised back to his. I drink in the pure, unshakeable essence of Kade. Our protector and leader, the man who secured our family's freedom from those who tore us apart. As long as we have him by our side, I know we'll always be safe. I can't protect those I love from the demons of this world alone.

"Are we ready for tonight?" I sigh.

"As ready as we'll ever be. The contact wants to meet us at ten o'clock. I've got the location scouted out. Once we've exchanged information, we'll get out of here. I still owe you that breakfast date."

The thought of our warm, cosy cottage in the middle of nowhere makes my heart sigh with happiness. It was a slice of peace and calm amongst the carnage of our lives. I'm ready to run away all over again.

"I'll hold you to it, mister."

His smile is infectious, warming the fabric of my dead soul. "You got it, love. I'm a man of my word. When the dust settles and Incendia is no more, I intend to spend every second of my life proving that to you."

"I think I can live with that."

Sharing another lingering kiss that leaves me breathless, we break apart when Sadie and Theo emerge from the locker room. They slept there for the night, and I definitely heard them hooking up when they thought we were all asleep. Her cheeks are flushed, their hands linked as they enter the kitchen.

"Morning campers," she chirps.

I climb off Kade's lap. "Ouch, Clearview flashback."

Sadie sticks her tongue out at me. "I was an excellent counsellor. I have no idea what you mean. No one else let you raid the vending machine before group therapy."

"To buy our cooperation, I'm sure."

"It worked though, didn't it?"

Theo listens to our conversation while fixing two mugs of coffee. He blushes when our eyes connect for a brief second. He's got some major social anxiety going on, but I can't help but like him in an odd sort of way. Wearing another flannel shirt, this one covers a vintage superhero t-shirt.

"When are you two planning to leave?" Kade queries.

Taking seats on the opposite side of us, Theo opens his laptop and sets to work. He pushes his silver, wire-rimmed glasses up his nose when they slip down. I have enough men in my life, but even I can admit he's adorable.

"Alyssa will enter Harrowdean tomorrow. I'll be returning to HQ to report back. We'll be in touch. Hunter will want to meet you all and obtain your evidence."

"Alyssa?" I splutter.

Theo's face pales. "I, ah… um. I didn't say that."

Kade exchanges a look with me. "You definitely did."

Sadie glowers at Theo, causing him to blush even harder. He looks like a literal beetroot, hiding behind his laptop for safety. You wouldn't believe this skinny, timid geek works for a huge security firm.

"Your name is Alyssa?"

"I really didn't mean to let that slip," Theo curses.

Punching him on the arm, Sadie returns her attention to her phone, dismissing the conversation. Kade subtly shakes his head, ordering me to drop it. We've all had to make sacrifices in order to survive. Her life has been put on hold too, I suppose.

"When are we meeting the infamous Hunter and his team?"

Theo meets Kade's eyes. "He will dictate that. You'll be contacted."

"You're not going to tell us anything? Seriously?"

"Classified, I'm afraid. Keep your heads down and eyes open, that's my advice. This contact appears to be on your side, but loyalties change. Good people don't sell information for no reason."

"We're capable of taking care of ourselves," Kade defends hotly.

"More than you pretentious assholes know," I add.

Theo winces. "This is why I don't do fieldwork, for Christ's sake. I need to report to the bossman." Scooping up his laptop, he flees the room before we can pry him with more hard questions.

"Sabre is on your side." Sadie grabs her own stale breakfast from the cupboard. "You'll see. Hunter's going to kill me for not sticking around to see them all."

I grab her arm before she can pass, hit by a wave of anger so strong, it feels like my insides are on fire. Her eyebrows raise and I squeeze until she's wincing in pain, fighting to break my grip.

"You knew, all along."

"What the hell are you talking about, Brooke?"

"All those months in Blackwood, you pretended like you had no idea what was happening. Dropping your hints and lecturing me about breaking the rules, when all along, you knew what was happening."

"I didn't know for sure." Sadie manages to wrench her arm free. "I was searching for answers, like you. If I'd known the truth, do you really think I would've left you at Augustus's mercy? Do you think that little of me?"

I level her with a challenging stare. "You've given no evidence to the contrary. We didn't even know your real name until now. I thought you were my friend."

"It isn't that simple and you know it," she hits back. "You love to stand on your pedestal, but the truth is, there's only one person in this room who deserved to be in Blackwood. Look in the fucking mirror, Brooke."

Sadie doesn't flinch when I slap her across the face. I can't stop myself. A bright-red handprint blooms on her cheek. She touches the marked skin with her fingertips, lips parted in disbelief.

"You once told me that no matter what the newspapers print, I'm not a monster." I fight back tears that she doesn't deserve. "Thank you for being another disappointment. I'm sure your dead parents are proud of what their kids became."

Sadie slams her coffee cup down so hard, it shatters and breaks into pathetic pieces. Kade watches us both with trepidation. I wonder if she'll hit me, and whether I'll actually enjoy the punishment.

"Fuck you, Brooklyn. You and Seven deserve each other. My brother died in that place, and so did the girl I used to be friends with."

"We're still alive! You need to let go of who you thought we were."

"I'm not the problem here. When this is over, I never want to see either of you again."

Her declaration lashes me like the strike of a whip. I can see the pain in her eyes, but Sadie doesn't take it back. I've pushed her too far this time.

"You got that?"

"With pleasure," I hiss back.

Sadie freezes when she realises we're not alone. In the plastic-covered doorway that Theo fled through, Seven stands with an open wound of grief on his face. Golden eyes filled with so much pain watch his sister.

"Jude—"

"You're right," he interrupts in a deep, dangerous voice. "That person did die, long before you bothered to look for me. Feel free to leave, sister. I have a real family here."

"That's it?"

"That's it," he confirms. "We don't need you."

Wiping her wet cheeks with the back of her sleeve, Sadie strides from the room without another word. I can hear her yelling at Theo to get his things. In a matter of minutes, the sound of the grate lifting fills the warehouse, followed by silence. None of us know quite what to say in the wake of their departure.

"I'm sorry, Sev," I offer.

He simply shakes his head. "She doesn't see me, just the person she lost. I can't be her ghost. Not anymore. I have to live as well."

With that pearl of wisdom, Seven storms off too.

"Jesus Christ." Kade sighs.

My thoughts precisely.

CHAPTER 11
HUDSON

KEROSENE - VANISH

WITH MY ARM tucked around Brooklyn's waist, we join the queue outside the bustling nightclub. Bright neon lights and thumping bass music fill the street, with a winding trail of bodies waiting to be admitted into its sweaty depths.

After trekking across London, armed and debriefed by dictator Kade, I feel like we're about to walk into the jaws of death. Every face I spot looks like a potential threat. Incendia could be anywhere. Anyone. We're just sitting ducks waiting to be taken out here.

"I don't like this one bit," I grumble.

Brooklyn peers up at me through thick eyelashes, pouting her red-painted lips. Her short hair is messily tousled, paired with a black tank that shows off her cleavage, ripped jeans, and her leather jacket. She looks good, more like herself than she has in a long time.

"When was the last time you went clubbing?"

"We're not here to party, blackbird."

"We can multitask." Her smile is devious. "It's been a long time since we danced together."

I huff, recalling the school prom that I took her to many years ago. She looked like a dream in this pale-pink dress from a thrift store, all floaty and shit. Like a ballerina sent from heaven above to rescue my soul from damnation. She admitted to stealing cash just to buy it for our date.

Even though we lived in the same foster home, I met her on the doorstep and offered her a single rose that I swiped from a nearby market. That was before the head carer and resident voice of doom, Mrs Dane, crushed it beneath her shoe. She called me a son-of-a-bitch thief. I've never seen Brooklyn laugh so hard.

"I still think about that night, you know."

Sliding a finger underneath her chin, I raise her grey eyes to meet mine. "It was the best night of my entire fucking life. Even when you mixed weed and booze, then puked out of your eyeballs."

Brooklyn snorts. "I was an amateur."

"And still hot with your head in the toilet all night."

"It feels like a lifetime ago. We were so different back then, but at the same time, not. Sometimes I can't believe I'm here with you, after all this time. It's still us, huh?"

"It's always been us, baby. And it always will be."

"You're becoming a soppy bastard, Hud."

I grip her chin hard, digging my nails in slightly. "Don't mention it. I'll still take you over my knee and hit you until you beg for mercy, which naturally, I won't give."

The queue finally begins to move. I glance over my shoulder, finding Kade ready and waiting. He's keeping a close eye on Seven by his side, while Eli and Phoenix bring up the rear. We've all freshened up for the occasion, wearing clean clothes and matching grim expressions.

My expectations for this meeting are pretty low as it could easily be a bust. We have to try though, especially now that Sadie has fucked off to get herself killed. We can't sit and do nothing while Incendia hunts our asses like wild dogs that have escaped the pound.

"Eyes sharp, we don't know who is watching," I instruct.

Seven scowls at me. "Shouldn't I go in first?"

"Why, fuckface?"

"Because one of us has the best chance of dealing with any trouble that arises. I'm not sure you can handle yourself, pretty boy, should the time come."

"Want me to knock you out to double check?"

Seven glares, but makes the smart decision to back down. I fight the urge to slam him against the brick wall and break his nose anyway. The fresh bruises on his face tell me Brooklyn's already kicked his ass enough recently. He seems to enjoy antagonising me as much as I enjoy plotting his death.

I step up to the bouncer, palming him a roll of cash to slip inside without having IDs checked. The nightclub is a riot of glistening bodies, spilled drinks, and drunken idiots snorting cocaine off every available surface. Definitely not one of London's finer drinking establishments.

Kade used to take me to all the hotspots when I was first adopted. This place is firmly outside of the law, and the perfect place to meet our dark-web contact. We won't be interrupted by the authorities. I have no doubt Incendia would kill them to keep things under wraps.

"Stay off the party powder. We don't need any slip-ups tonight." Kade takes charge as he steals Brooklyn from my arms. "Beer only, no shots."

Phoenix eyes up the white powder. "You're no fun."

"You can stick to water."

"No fair! Why does everyone else get to have fun but me?"

"Because last time we were out in public, you scaled a Ferris wheel and someone plummeted to their death," Brooklyn replies flatly. "No drugs, Nix. I mean it."

Glowering at us all, Phoenix takes Eli's hand and guides him to the dance floor. Eli wears a mask of crippling anxiety, and I'm surprised he's still standing. His jaw clenches as the loud music overwhelms him. I watch Phoenix slam their lips together, stealing his attention from a panic attack.

Lately, I've been fascinated by watching them.

And admittedly, a little intrigued.

"You know who we're looking for?" I force myself to look away from the pair.

"Not a clue. We're supposed to wait for the signal," Kade answers.

"In that case, let's get a drink."

Heading for the bar, I keep an eye on Seven as he situates himself in a lookout position. He screams of danger with his unkempt hair, stony face and unyielding scowl. Everyone gives him a very wide berth as he glares at them like it's his day job.

Kade orders a round of beers then disappears to set himself up next to our sadistic guard dog. It annoys me how easily he's accepted Seven into our midst. The guy's a fucking nut job. Kade should be more careful, but we all know he's a bleeding heart.

"Stop staring at Seven," Brooklyn orders.

I take a swig of beer. "Please just let me kill him. I'll make it quick. No charge for body disposal."

"You're not funny."

"It's not a joke."

"What's the time?" She sighs.

"Quarter to ten. Nearly time."

I'm itching to hold her close and far away from danger, but coddling Brooklyn West isn't a mistake I'm going to make again. She'll have my balls before letting me shield her from harm, and I most definitely don't want to give them up.

"Fancy a dance?"

Her lips tilt up in a smile. "Thought you'd never ask."

We head for the cramped dance floor, passing Phoenix and Eli, who shoot her heated looks. Brooklyn pauses to kiss them both, still clinging to my hand while pleasuring my friends. The act has my dick standing to attention. Once she's done, we move to the steady beat of music.

Before long, we're drenched in sweat and screaming along to a Black Sabbath song, losing sight of our surroundings. Just being here, with her sexy body writhing against me, makes all the bullshit worth it. She's my blackbird again, just for a moment.

"If you don't stop, I'm going to fuck you right here, in front of all these stoned lowlifes," I warn under my breath.

Brooklyn sinks her teeth into my neck, marking me for the entire club to see. "Would that be such a bad thing? Could be kinda fun."

"While I can just about tolerate sharing you with the assholes I call my brothers, I'm not comfortable with an entire nightclub seeing what's mine. I may get stabby."

She smirks. "Spoilsport."

"Come on, let's go find our guy."

We grab Phoenix and Eli, following Kade and Seven further into the shadows of the packed nightclub. Some drunken idiot stumbles into me and spills beer all over my shoes, earning himself a black eye in the process. Brooklyn grins at me, thriving on the thrill of violence.

Before the night is out, I'll have her screaming my goddamn name for everyone to hear. Especially Seven. I no longer give a fuck about subtly. Losing her has taught me to savour every last moment.

In the smoking area, we pass a pack of cigarettes around. Kade and Seven don't accept, too busy surveying the group of friends drinking at the table next to us. Their rowdy voices betray their inebriation. Clearly, they aren't here to assassinate us.

"What now?"

"We wait," Kade replies.

The minutes trickle by until it's nearly half past and our contact is more than late. We down another round of beers and reluctantly call the night a bust, preparing to get the hell out of this sweatbox. Before I can drag Brooklyn back to the warehouse and settle between her luscious legs, the blare of a fire alarm cracks through the night.

Kade stiffens. "That's our signal."

We watch the punters escape through a fire exit. The smoking area empties, while security focuses on the crowd inside the club, leaving us alone. I grasp the gun tucked into my jacket, unease trickling down my spine.

"I should've known it would be you lot."

All turning, we find a hooded figure sliding through a concealed back entrance. Her voice sounds chillingly familiar, almost a little smug. I don't bother to hide my weapon while aiming it straight at the stranger.

"Who the fuck are you?" I shout.

"Drop the weapon or this meeting is over."

Settling on a nearby bench, she gestures for us to follow suit. We advance as a group, maintaining a safe distance. I place my gun on the table but keep it within reach. I won't put it away until I know who exactly we're dealing with.

"You're late," Kade barks.

"I have to be very cautious these days. Incendia is crawling all over this city, looking for the likes of you. They would gladly put a bullet in my brain if they catch up to me."

She reaches up to push back her hood. Straggly, grown-out blonde hair and an exhausted face are revealed, far from the perfectly put together facade of the person we knew. Life on the run has done her no favours.

"Miss White."

"In the flesh," she drawls.

We all gape at the ex-warden, looking so rough and unlike herself. She puffs on a cigarette, taking the time to inspect each and every one of us. When her gaze lands on Seven, the cigarette falls straight from her fingertips.

"Doctor Farlow? Jude?"

Dammit, I really hope he breaks her jaw for using that name.

"Who are you?" he hits back.

Miss White stares, open-mouthed. "You... don't remember me?"

"I wouldn't take it personally." I snicker.

Brooklyn rests her palms on the table, commanding Miss White's attention back from the ghost in our midst. "We arranged this meeting to discuss an exchange of information."

"Brooklyn West. I hear you've gotten yourself into quite the pickle."

"We're not here to talk about me, Warden. Where have you been?"

Miss White lights a fresh cigarette while eyeing Seven. "When Augustus took over Blackwood, I knew my days were numbered. Nobody was permitted to hold more authority than him. I was just an obstacle for him to eliminate. I had to run, before it was too late."

"You've escaped Incendia's clutches for nearly nine months." Kade glances back to the nightclub still in disarray. "We don't have much time. If they're searching for you, it's because you know something."

Miss White appears nervous. "I have information about Blackwood, Incendia Corporation, and all of their dirty dealings. Names, dates, the lot. All of it can be yours."

"For what price?" Brooklyn deadpans.

"A fresh start." Miss White gnaws her lip. "Since your escape, Bancroft has tripled his presence on the streets. I'm running out of assets and time. I want my safety guaranteed."

Kade laughs in her face. "We can't guarantee our own safety. How exactly do you propose we do this for you? We know nothing about Bancroft."

"He has enough power to rally the support of the entire country and ensure our deaths. That's all you need to know. Don't play games with me, Kade. You're all working with Sabre Security."

My hand inches closer to the gun on instinct. I'd love nothing more than to put a bullet between her eyes. Brooklyn lays a reassuring palm on my leg, urging me to remain calm.

"I have no idea what you're talking about," Kade lies easily.

"You think I didn't know what that pink-haired fool was doing at Blackwood all along? I ran that place for seven years and had extra hidden cameras in all of my staff's offices. Alyssa Farlow, tut tut."

Seven's hands curl into tight fists, resentment clouding his face. Kade once mentioned the concealed camera in Mike's office, uncertain of what the warden's intentions were. She's a slippery fucking snake.

"I couldn't get rid of her without incurring the wrath of Sabre," Miss White continues. "I was there when she campaigned for information about her brother. I never forget a face. Tell your annoying friend that I want to make a deal with her employer."

Before anyone else can say anything, there's a blur of movement. Phoenix seizes hold of Miss White by her faded shirt and dangles her in the air. I've never seen him look so enraged.

"You protected Rio. He nearly killed Eli and Brooke! You helped them run the system. Smuggling in contraband, making sick patients worse for your own amusement. Playing us all like puppets and reaping the rewards. How do you sleep at night?"

Miss White scratches at his hands, attempting to break free. Before Phoenix can actually kill her, I lay a hand on his shoulder, easing him off. She hits the bench with a thud, rubbing her chest and spluttering.

"I was just doing my job. Augustus was the mastermind!"

"You turned a blind eye while the rest of us suffered," Brooklyn snaps.

"But I didn't profit from it."

"So you were just getting paid to be a ray of fucking sunshine for us all?" I point out, ready to blow this entire shitshow off. "Cry me a damn river."

Miss White cuts me a cold look, but doesn't refute my argument. We all know that she's a piece of work, there's no point denying it. She reaches into her coat pocket and places a slim thumb drive on the table.

"It's all on there. I'm just asking for a second chance, that's all."

"Who says that you deserve it?" Brooklyn laughs.

"Are you really one to talk? Call me a monster if you want, I've probably earned it. But it takes one to know one, Miss West. Don't forget what brought you to my institute."

I throw an arm around Brooklyn's shoulders, attempting to stop her from creating a bloodbath, but the next growl of anger comes from behind us.

"You knew."

Seven rounds on Miss White. Rather than hold her in the air, he tosses her thin frame across the courtyard without a second thought. She screams and smacks into a brick wall with a crunch. Blood spreads from the back of her head as she fights to get to her feet and falls.

"Jude, please—"

"You knew. All those months, you knew exactly what Lazlo was doing. You knew about Lucia, the Z Wing, everything. Do you know what they did to me, Elizabeth?"

Judging by the look on Miss White's face, she knows she's in trouble.

"Please... I didn't know what they were going to do to you. You have to believe me."

He punches her straight between the eyes. Miss White sobs as she clutches her bleeding, swollen face. I feel zero need to intervene. The bitch deserves a good beating for all she's enabled.

"Six years, Elizabeth. Six goddamn years. You did nothing."

"I didn't know you were alive..."

"Don't lie to me!"

The fire alarm cuts off, indicating our time is running out. I pocket my gun and help Brooklyn stand, catching sight of her swiping the thumb drive. Miss White's a fool. We could simply leave her for dead and escape with her bargaining chip right now.

Too easy, a mental voice whispers.

Raised voices coming from inside of the club have us all glued to the spot. Backing my family into the corner of the smoking area, myself and Kade train our weapons on the empty doorway. The beat of heavy footsteps approaches.

"Whatever happens, get Brooklyn out," I instruct the group.

She fires a curse straight at me. "I'm not leaving without you, motherfucker."

Shouting and barked orders rip through the air, with a rush of bodies entering the smoking area. Faces cloaked by thick balaclavas, the assailants carry scarily professional assault rifles. In a matter of seconds, we have six of them trained on us.

"Drop your weapons!"

None of us move, aiming straight for their heads.

"You're outnumbered. Back down, kids."

Surrounding us in a tightly packed circle, one figure steps forward and tears the balaclava from his face. I'm not even surprised to find Taggert, one of the less-than-friendly guards who made our lives miserable in Blackwood.

"Where's your buddy, Jackson?" I sneer.

"Burned to ashes by you fucking psychos," Taggert shouts.

"Don't worry. You can join him soon enough."

"That's not how this is going to go. We've already found your little warehouse hideout. There's no running. We can do this the easy way or the hard way."

While we face the group of thugs, Miss White sneaks around us with her head tucked low. When she reaches Taggert and accepts his outstretched hand, it becomes clear that we've been played. Her grin confirms my fears. Looks like Incendia needed her after all.

Miss White spares us a derisive look. "Here they are, as we agreed."

"Then the deal is done." Taggert gives her a nod before turning to us. "The boss only wants patients Seven and Eight alive. The rest of you are disposable."

Seeing red, I fire off a quick shot before anyone can react. It catches the man to Miss White's left, who screams and clutches his shoulder. Chaos descends as our two groups collide. I take out another bastard with a kick to the groin, crushing his throat beneath my foot.

Shooting the next one in the kneecap, I prepare for collision as the tough motherfucker carries on coming at me. Knocked straight off my feet, my head hits the ground and I see stars for a sickening second. The tip of his steel-capped boot connects with my ribs next.

We end up wrestling, his balaclava ripped off to expose his face to my fists. He's got several pounds of muscle on me and returns every hit. Panic begins to inch in as a blast rattles my eardrums. With matter splattering my face, I push the lifeless body aside.

"Need a hand, pretty boy?"

Seven is grinning down at me like the deranged lunatic he is, discarding a stolen gun to offer me a hand up. Taking it, I shoot him a scowl.

"This doesn't make us even, you piece of shit. I ain't no pretty boy."

"Whatever you say. I won't save your stupid ass next time."

The sound of fists meeting flesh draws us both to Brooklyn. She's kneeling nearby, beating the absolute shit out of Taggert with her bare fists. She looks too damn good covered in fresh blood. I don't intervene; my girl can handle herself.

I'm here to enjoy the show.

My dick is aching just watching her.

"Stay down. Final warning," she yells.

"We're just... the b-beginning." Taggert coughs up blood. "He w-won't stop coming for you."

"I'll kill the next people Incendia sends too. Say hello to Jackson for me."

Pulling out the knife stashed in her jacket, Brooklyn lifts her eyes to mine. Ensuring I'm watching, she brutally slashes the blade across Taggert's throat. He drowns in a geyser of blood, also covering her head to toe in crimson rain. Brooklyn doesn't even flinch, wiping her eyes.

"Like what you see?" She quirks an eyebrow.

"More than like, baby."

"Help me kill the rest of these assholes and you can show me how much you like it."

Seven clears his throat. "Touch her and you'll die next."

I stifle the urge to shoot him. "Whatever, man."

We catch the moment Phoenix cracks someone's skull, letting the body hit the ground with a satisfying thud. He winces and cradles his broken fingers. We're not all accustomed to fighting, but I've seen what he can do when he really loses control.

With the advantage of anger on our side, we obliterate the hired skins that Incendia sent. Kade and Eli hang back, letting the rest of us clean up. When the bloodbath is over, it leaves shell-shocked silence and six dead bodies.

"Time to go," Kade declares.

"What about her?" Brooklyn gestures to where Miss White is attempting to hide from us. "We can't leave her alive. She knows Sadie's real identity."

I offer Seven my gun. "It should be you."

He studies it for a moment before rolling up his sleeve instead. My kinda guy, I'll admit. We all step back to give him room to work, drinking in the blissful terror eating away at Miss White.

"Please, Jude... I beg you. Don't do this."

"That person is gone, Elizabeth. He isn't coming to save you."

"I d-didn't mean to... please have mercy..."

"Silence!" Seven spits in her tear-stained face. "There is no mercy in this world."

Weeping and begging for her life, Blackwood Institute's prestigious warden dies a pitiful death. Seven kicks her in the face so he can straddle her dying corpse. Her fighting is futile. His wrath is inescapable.

"Jude..."

"Goodbye, Elizabeth. I'll see you in hell someday."

Leaning in close to press their foreheads together, Seven drinks in her fear while wrapping a single hand around her throat. One is all this animalistic man needs.

"We should stop him," Kade comments.

"No." I shake my head. "I think he needs this."

Seven slowly, intimately chokes the life out of Elizabeth White. By the time he's done, she's blue and twitching, her legs jerking a final few times. When he lets go, Seven's trembling from exertion. Her throat looks collapsed from the force of his grip.

None of us dare approach. He looks ready to tear us all to shreds. Staring at his single, bloodied hand, the stump on his other arm hangs limp. I don't stop Brooklyn from carefully approaching, trusting her judgement when it comes to this... creature.

"Sev?"

"Stay back," he roars.

She ghosts a hand over his shoulder. "I'm here, Sev. You can come back now. The job's done. It's time to go."

"Eight?"

"Yeah, it's me. We're a team, aren't we?"

Managing to look up, the look on Seven's face scares even me. It's raw and brutal, far beyond anything that could be classified as human. He's a predator and a hunter wrapped up in a lethal tornado of rage. My instincts are telling me to keep Brooklyn as far away from him as possible.

"I'm sorry, princess," he apologises.

"What for?"

The pair exchange a long, hard look.

"I should've given you a go on the bitch. We kill together, not apart."

Brooklyn grins. "I'll let you off on this occasion."

I can't suppress my laughter. Everyone looks at me like I'm mad. We're surrounded by bodies, now is not the moment to lose it. Grabbing the pair of maniacs, we take one final glance at the bloody scene.

There are no CCTV cameras in a shitty place like this, but it wouldn't matter either way. We're already being hunted. Now, we've fired our first shot. Let the war commence.

"What now? We can't go back to the warehouse." Brooklyn leans on Seven, wiping blood from her nose. "We need somewhere to clean up and lay low."

Phoenix steps forward with a nervous smile.

"I have an idea."

CHAPTER 12
BROOKLYN

LUST - SAINT JHN & JANELLE KROLL

STEALING through the dimly lit suburbs of London, I stare at the back of Phoenix's head. It's taken us all night to sneak across the city, dodging CCTV cameras, screaming sirens, and even a police helicopter. We couldn't exactly hop on the underground.

"Any idea where we're going?" I whisper to Eli.

He shrugs, sparing me an exhausted smile.

I'm beginning to miss my comfortable bed, sandwiched between my guys, with the safety of four walls and no prying eyes nearby. Kade checked in with Lucia and Two a couple of hours ago, exchanging brief words. They're still holed up in Scotland.

"You heard from Sadie since she left?"

Kade sighs. "She isn't answering her phone."

"You think her cover is blown?"

"It doesn't look like Miss White exchanged information yet."

He spares Seven a nervous look, limping and deadly silent by my side. We need to know what happens next. Our so-called contact was a trap this whole time, and the thumb drive is worthless. We're back to square one.

Passing several street corners crowded with teenagers on skateboards, I tighten my leather jacket around me, hoping to conceal the blood beneath it. This is as rough as London gets, but Phoenix stalks down the street like he owns the place.

I hardly recognise the persona he's constructing before our very eyes. He stands taller and more confident with every step towards our destination. Turning a corner, we run straight into a huge crowd. The blare of music accompanies the youths, all drinking beer and smoking.

"Stay frosty," Hudson orders.

Phoenix glances back at us. "That won't be necessary. Stick behind me."

The crowd parts to allow someone to step forward. A glinting switchblade in the kid's hand makes my heart speed up. Phoenix is going to get himself killed by some scrawny little shit on a power trip at this rate.

"You ain't welcome here!"

Authority imbues every inch of Phoenix's bruised and battered frame. "Tell Travis that Phoenix has come home. Run along now, kid."

The teenager spares us a frown, but follows orders. We gather as Phoenix glares at the others, all watching us like we're aliens. I palm my knife, ready to stab my way out of a second fight of the night if necessary. We didn't survive Incendia's cunts just to die now.

"Home?" Kade echoes.

Phoenix shrugs. "We needed somewhere safe."

"You've never spoken about your home before," I chime in.

"Never had a reason to. I didn't leave here under good circumstances."

We fall into tense silence until the roar of an engine comes racing around the corner. The sea of people parts, admitting a modified truck painted in a violent shade of green. It's complete with painted flames, tinted windows, and a huge rear spoiler.

Several men hop out of the truck. Fierce scowls, lip piercings, and visible tattoos mark each person. Every single one of them is armed to the teeth with sawed-off guns and switchblades. I even spot some knuckledusters.

"Stay quiet, leave this to me," Phoenix warns.

Transforming from the happy-go-lucky person I know, his spine straightens and his shoulders roll back. He paces over to the truck, where the men exchange scandalised whispers. When the driver's door slams open, a pair of bright purple, buckled stomper boots hit the ground.

"As I fuckin' live and breathe... Phoenix Kent."

"Hey, Travis."

Flicking aside a joint and scraping back his red mohawk, Travis bundles him into a hug. They slap each other's backs, with the remaining men seeming to relax. We tentatively surround Phoenix, still on high alert.

"Where the hell have ya been?"

Phoenix shrugs. "I've been around."

"Two bloody years, Nix. You were gone for a long time."

"Tell me about it. You miss me?"

Travis punches him in the shoulder. "This place ain't the same without ya. Are these friends of yours, or do I need to set my boys on them?"

Phoenix circles his arm around my waist. "They're with me. Listen, Trav. We're in trouble and need somewhere to lay low for a bit."

"You got it, Nix. Anything for you."

Whistling to the nearby kids, Travis rattles off his orders. The group converges around us, concealing us from sight. We head off down the street, bathed in dawn light. Travis falls into step beside Phoenix, his pierced face lit with a grin.

"Charlie's gonna freak when she hears you're back, bro."

Phoenix tenses. "Perhaps hold off on telling her. It should be me."

"Nah. She'll be over the moon. She's missed her brother. It's good to have ya back, Nix. Too fuckin' good."

"It's only temporary, until we're out of trouble."

"I never got a chance to thank you for—"

"Don't mention it," Phoenix interrupts. "It's in the past."

Approaching a run-down house with bass music rattling the bricks, Travis gestures for us to enter. Inside, the stench of smoke and acid burns my throat. Marijuana plants bake under heat lamps, while giant vats of chemicals lay abandoned. Looks like they're cooking meth.

"Classy," Hudson comments.

Travis frowns at him before clearing his throat. "There are some spare rooms upstairs. I'll track down some clean clothes. You all look rough as hell."

"Do you have a shower?" I cringe at the sight of myself.

He gives me a slow, perusing look. "For you? Sure thing, sugar. My room's free if you wanna help yourself. Need a hand with all that blood?"

"Want me to break your legs?" Hudson casually leans against a stained wall. "Or your neck, perhaps? I really have no preference. Loser's choice."

Travis raises his hands. "No trouble here, mate."

Phoenix tugs me to his side and kisses my cheek. Travis looks even more intrigued, glancing between us all. Before he can ask questions I don't have the answers to, I leave the guys to their bickering and testosterone. I've had more than enough of people's bullshit for one day.

Up the sagging staircase, there's a sea of discarded drug paraphernalia. More marijuana plants fill several of the bedrooms, leaving an earthy stench in the air. Sweat drips down my neck from the industrial setup. Thick electrical cables feed into lights and heaters.

I locate Travis's room by the writing that's burned on the door by a cigarette. His space is pretty disgusting. Piles of unwashed clothes and empty liquor bottles litter the threadbare carpet. By some miracle, his en-suite bathroom is permissible, beyond the used condoms and knock-off aftershave bottles.

There's no lock, so I take my knife into the shower with me after stripping off clothing that reeks of death. The water is barely warm, but it feels amazing against my bruised body. I brace my hands against the cracked tiles and let my gritty eyes slide shut.

I'm suddenly exhausted. The adrenaline that kept us running across the city has deserted me. As the events of the night run through my mind, a whisper creeps in, emboldened by violence and bloodthirst.

How many people have you killed now, Brooke?

You've become everything you hate.

Vic would be so proud of you.

"Vic is gone," I recite, clutching my knife tight.

As you should be too.

This is just the beginning.

Blackwood is calling your name.

I wash the crimson stains from my knife, entranced by the serrated steel. I'm not sure how many people I killed last night. Their empty, lifeless stares all blur into one. It shouldn't be so easy, but I've spent months running from one kill to the next.

Patient Eight never had a conscience.

I'm not sure Brooklyn West does either.

Pressing the blade to my stomach, I make five neat, parallel cuts. It still isn't enough to calm down. Cutting myself again, I feel my lungs constrict. I have to stop right now. I can't afford to black out from blood loss here. As my panic increases, Sadie's advice rings in my head—list what you know.

My name is Brooklyn West.

I am twenty-two years old.

My family is dead.

I'm a murderer.

There's a monster inside of me.

I deserve to be alone.

"Shut the fuck up," I berate myself.

I haven't hallucinated Vic since I killed Augustus. I thought I'd expunged the whole mess from my mind in that moment, but he's still in there. His voice lives on in everything I hate about myself.

"Brooke? You okay?"

Phoenix lets himself into the steam-filled room. I'm shocked to find Hudson following him. They both pull off dirty clothes to start cleaning themselves in the sink. Down to their boxers, I study the countless bruises and injuries from our firefight.

Poking his tender ribs, Phoenix curses. "I'd like to go a week without someone breaking part of me. You nearly done in there, firecracker?"

Turning off the shower, I don't trust myself to speak. The minute I step out, I realise my mistake. There are no towels and my clothes lay in a sticky, ruined puddle. Shifting on my feet, the weight of two burning gazes has heat flooding between my thighs.

"What the fuck are those?" Hudson barks at me.

I back up against the shower door as he advances. His fingers coast over the fresh cuts without permission, catching the blood that leaks down my stomach. His brows furrow, fingertips digging into the wounds until I'm hissing between clenched teeth.

"Take your hands off me," I grit out.

"You're still doing this?"

"When the need arises. It's none of your business."

Hudson yanks me forward until our chests meet. Completing the trap, Phoenix slots in behind me and grabs hold of my hips. These are the last two people I'd expect to be sandwiched between. I can barely stand from the blistering wave of need that wracks me. Whether it's to cut again or fuck, I really don't care.

"You did good tonight." Hudson kisses his way along my jaw to meet my lips. "Watching you kill those fuckers had me hard all goddamn night, blackbird."

"And me," Phoenix adds.

"We lost our one lead. We're all battered and lost in the middle of London. Sadie's in danger. This entire thing was a waste of time and we're going to be killed."

Hudson scoffs. "Well, when you put it like that…"

I suppress a shudder as Phoenix bites my ear lobe. His cock is pressing right up against my bare ass, with only a pair of boxers separating us.

"...but I'm sure we can improve the situation," he finishes.

Quickly ditching his underwear, Hudson takes a seat on the closed toilet lid. I'm tugged into his awaiting lap, still trapped and unable to run. His healing bullet wound looks inflamed, surrounded by black bruises, scratches and lacerations.

"You promised me no more cutting," he murmurs.

"When?"

"Don't be a fucking smart-ass, Brooke. Talk to me."

I duck my gaze. "I don't want to become Patient Eight again. I want to stay with you guys, my family. Not in the past. This is the only way I know how."

"Then let us help you," Phoenix pleads.

Hudson nods. "You don't need to do this alone."

Studying the fresh cuts again, Hudson's tongue darts out to wet his lips. I watch as he coats his fingers in my blood, something dark and smouldering in his icy-blue irises. Without shame, he spreads the wetness over his dick and pumps it several times.

"If you're gonna do this, we may as well make the most of it," he says darkly.

My mouth goes dry as Hudson's thumb swipes over my clit, painting my sensitive flesh red. With the flick of a switch, I'm overcome by desire. All I want is to feel the beat of his heart. I want proof that we're still alive and this is real.

My eyes slide shut as doubt takes root. How do I know my brain isn't conjuring this entire reality? I'll shut my eyes and wake up in the Z Wing again, longing for a life beyond my imprisonment. Perhaps I'm dead already. This could all be a cruel dream.

"Eyes on me," Hudson demands.

Startled by his gruff voice, I force myself to look at him again. The rest of my blood disappears in his mouth as he sucks his fingers dry.

"You're not allowed to hide from me, blackbird. I want to see your pain. All of it. You keep running and hiding this shit from us, and it ends now."

Before I can shake my head, he grabs my nipple and pinches it hard.

"Fuck, okay," I submit.

"Okay what? Answer me, bitch. I can't hear you."

Riled up by his taunts, I grind down on Hudson's lap. His velvet-soft head is pushing into my slit, spearing me on his length without filling me. With another wriggle, he's buried deep in my pussy.

"Okay, daddy."

I punctuate my words with a thrust. Hudson growls, his fingertips digging deep into my hips. From this angle, he's filling me to the brim, but I'm still the one in charge. All he can do is sit there and let me take control.

Slamming down on his length, I can feel my core clenching. He pinches my sore nipple, swallowing my grunt of pain with another kiss.

"You look so perfect riding my dick," he compliments. "Such a dirty whore, aren't you? Letting us both watch you like this. One of us was never enough for you."

"Fuck off, Hud."

"I knew there had to be a benefit to this sharing crap," Phoenix hoots. "Live porno."

Hudson glowers at him. "Shut up."

Grabbing his shoulders for balance, I set a bruising pace. I need to fuck the darkness away before it consumes me. Sweat beads across my forehead as my core begins to tighten. Hudson groans with each thrust, his lips inflicting a dark mark on my neck.

It must take a lot of self-control for him to let me lead. Even when we were lovesick kids, he'd take charge and fuck me, regardless of my feelings. I've spent my life being used and abused by Hudson Knight, but I wouldn't change a goddamn thing.

"Thought you didn't share?" I tease him.

"Rules are made to be broken, Brooke."

"You've fucked me at the same time as Kade before."

"He's my brother. I ain't rubbing dicks with Phoenix."

I grab Hudson by the throat, mirroring his own domineering move. His eyes widen, but he doesn't fight me. Toying with his pulse, I revel in the feeling of complete control. His life is in my hands. I own his black soul, and if I wanted to, I could take it all away.

"I'm getting a bit jealous here," Phoenix says.

I toss him a heated look. "Be right with you, baby."

Chasing my release to the very edge, glorious tension unravels in my lower belly. Hudson is staring at me like I'm a precious piece of artwork that he can't tear his eyes from. The feeling is heady—being adored.

My days of hating this monstrous, complicated man are long over, but the intensity of our obsession remains. He's the air I breathe and the choking grip on my windpipe at the same fucking time.

"Take it," he demands, meeting my strokes. "Show me how you fall apart for me, blackbird. Let Phoenix hear you moan my name."

With a final few pumps, I watch with pleasure as Hudson's eyes roll back in his head. My own release crests and overwhelms me, an all-consuming tidal wave of sensation. Heat spreads through my body, spilling across his lap when I slide off.

"Dammit," Phoenix curses. "I should've filmed that shit."

"When I can give you the live show anytime?"

His lips spread in a cheeky grin. "I ain't gonna say no to that. Bring your ass here and let me spank that gorgeous fucking skin for teasing me like this."

I push my lips against Hudson's for a final time, swiping wild black hair from his forehead. He grabs my chin and forces me to deepen the kiss, stealing one last slither of submission. Phoenix clears his throat, but that doesn't stop Hudson. He's more than happy making him wait.

"I'm letting you fuck him," he whispers fiercely. "But you're still mine. Don't forget it."

"Whatever you say, Hud."

"Go on. Show him a good time."

Approaching Phoenix with the caution of a stalked deer, my newfound confidence suddenly dissipates. The roles have reversed in mere seconds, leaving me dizzy. Phoenix's gaze burns with authority and defiance. He won't surrender to me like Hudson did.

Lifting a single eyebrow, he doesn't have to say a word for me to know exactly what to do. On instinct, I sink to my knees on the bathroom floor. My eyes stare downwards, waiting for permission to look up.

"Good girl," Phoenix praises. "So obedient for me, aren't you?"

I hear Hudson's sharp intake of breath, but all of my attention is fixed on Phoenix as he finishes stripping. I'm a little nervous about touching him in front of our captive audience. I don't want Hudson to change his mind and chicken out.

"Suck it, firecracker."

Obeying his command, I wrap my lips around Phoenix's cock. He grunts as I hollow my cheeks out, taking him deep into my mouth. This isn't my first rodeo with Phoenix. I know exactly how he likes it. In no time, I have him thrusting into my mouth until my eyes tear up.

The perfect blend of rough and attentive, he toes that dangerous line with precision. Before he can finish, Phoenix pulls out and drags me up. I'm shoved into the bathroom counter, having to brace my hands on the sink. His palm cracks across my butt cheek, making me gasp.

"Such a naughty slut, Brooke. You like that?"

"Yes Nix," I answer obediently.

"How come that asshole is called daddy, and not me?"

Peering over my shoulder, I find his smug grin in place.

"Don't push your luck," Hudson warns while climbing in the shower. "I'm not above drowning you in that sink and fucking our girl over your corpse instead."

Phoenix spanks me several more times, each harder than the last. Pain and pleasure blur into one confusing maelstrom within me. I'm so wet, made worse by the sight of us in the mirror. Phoenix leans over me like a Greek god, playing my body with fine-tuned precision.

He finally slips inside of me, ending my torturous wait. Each collision sets my soul on fire as his body worships mine, already warm from the recent orgasm. When he presses a finger into my mouth, I swirl my tongue to moisten it.

"Easy baby," he encourages, pushing it inside of my asshole. "Such a good girl, aren't you? It's been so long since I fucked this sweet, perfect pussy."

It doesn't take long for Phoenix to have me crying out his name. I have no doubt the entire house can hear us, even his drug dealer friends. Let them listen. I'm proud of our relationship, no matter how complicated or crazy it may seem to the outside world.

Phoenix bites down on my shoulder before spinning me around. I hop up on the bathroom counter so he can settle back between my legs. Filling me once more, I now have a perfect view of Hudson in the shower. He smirks while watching us, wrapping a hand back around his cock.

"We have an audience."

"Let him watch. This is my turn," Phoenix grunts.

Throwing my head back, I savour every stroke of his body. It's been so long since I've felt this close to Phoenix. For the longest time, I thought I'd never see him again. I'm glad to be proven wrong.

When he finishes, the idea of his juices mixing with Hudson's has me climaxing again. I nearly slide off the counter in a boneless heap before he catches me. I'm carried back to the shower and passed to Hudson, who starts washing me with shower gel.

It feels weird, letting someone be this close to me. Trusting them enough to be vulnerable. Between all of my guys, I'm being looked after. Loved. Cherished. I don't know how I survived four months without that, but there's no way in hell it will ever happen again.

"That was fucking hot, blackbird."

I wink at Hudson. "You're full of surprises."

"Perhaps I'll share you with someone else next time," he muses.

Hot damn, sign me the hell up.

CHAPTER 13
PHOENIX

SUMMER SET FIRE TO THE RAIN - THRICE

STARING out at the crowded street, I watch the throng of teenagers pass roll-up cigarettes back and forth. The whole scene is a reminder of the person I used to be. There was a time when the mean streets of London feared my name.

Travis used to work for me, not the other way around. He was my best runner and number two, helping me execute my grandmother's vision. Then our entire lives blew up in our faces after a big drug bust. I had to face the consequences of my dirty dealings.

I paid the price instead of them.

Blackwood was my punishment.

I don't miss that life, and I certainly don't belong here anymore. My addiction was born from this toxic waste pit of a life. I can't wait to leave as soon as the coast is clear. We've camped out for a few days, resting our broken bodies while letting the commotion die down.

Kade's been watching the news obsessively. Somehow, they've managed to locate surveillance footage of us fleeing the south side of the city on foot. It isn't safe to move again while the whole city is looking for us.

Incendia is still hot on our heels.

If I'm honest, I don't think it will ever be safe.

"Nix? You got a minute?"

Travis waits in the doorway to the filthy living room. I let the net curtain fall shut, irritation already boiling beneath my skin. Brooklyn is snoring on the sofa, staying within sight at my request. I'm not having any of these lowlifes bothering her.

"What is it, Trav?"

"She's asked to see you again. Third time today."

"Not now. I can't."

"She's the boss," he points out. "It's been two years since you got taken away by the coppers. Charlie has questions too. She's all grown up now."

In a matter of seconds, I have Travis pinned against the peeling wallpaper by his throat. He chokes out an apology when my fist meets his annoying face. It should have been him who got locked away, not me. How dare he lecture me? He doesn't deserve the empire he's inherited, even if I don't want it.

"I've been away, but don't for a second think that I'm not still in charge here. I took the hit for my nana's whole organisation. Dozens of you could've done time if it wasn't for me. You owe me. Capiche, fucker?"

"Yes, N-Nix."

"Tell her that I'm busy. I don't care what you have to say, just get her off my back. I am not endangering her life by bringing her into this mess."

Tossing him aside, Travis swipes blood from the corner of his mouth before fleeing from the room. I haven't dipped into my dark side in a while, but it's very much still there. It was bred into me by the fearsome woman who raised me and Charlie when my piece-of-shit mum bailed on us.

You'd think being related to a gang leader would be hard going, but Nana loves fucking fiercely. I wouldn't be alive without her, even if she made me into the deadbeat, asshole addict I truly am. I grew up on these streets. I took the fall for them. This is my kingdom, whether it makes me sick or not.

"You can't avoid her forever."

Brooklyn's hoarse whisper draws me back from my anger. I find her sitting up, rubbing her bleary, tired eyes. She lets me collapse in her lap and strokes my newly re-dyed blue hair. Eli stayed up with me last night to do it. The memory of his blue-stained hands and tentative smile makes my chest warm.

"I have to keep Nana safe." I sigh heavily. "Charlie too."

"I get it, we're bad news. But she's family, Nix. Two years is a long time. Say goodbye before we have to run again. Give her some closure in case we don't come back."

I roughly grab Brooklyn by the chin. "Don't give me that bullshit, firecracker. We have no choice but to survive. I refuse to lose you again. Incendia can kiss my ass before I let that happen."

Her smile is so sad, it stabs me right in the damn heart.

"I fucking love you. Perhaps too much."

"I love you, Brooke. Quit it with the sad talk. Shit's depressing enough."

"Ain't that the truth. Let's find the others."

We head for the kitchen together, hand in hand. Kade has taken over the scarred table in the corner, sweeping used needles and empty liquor bottles aside to pour over more printed documents. He looks frantic, circling and highlighting anything he can find.

He's attempting to profile Bancroft, but so far, the man's squeaky clean. He was honoured for services to the medical industry several years back, as Incendia's empire of institutes grew. The millions of images a quick search brought up made me sick. He's well-loved and protected by his reputation.

"Anything?" I ask tiredly.

Kade shoves his glasses into his hair. "Fucking nothing. He's worth millions and has shares in just about every public stock going. I've counted three political parties funded by his donations. Don't get me started on this stupid knighthood. The media loves this bastard."

Hudson takes a gulp from an open bottle of vodka. "What about your dad?"

"Bancroft's been on the campaign trail with him three years in a row, along with a lot of financial endorsement. Dad's piggybacking on his reputation by sitting on Blackwood's board of directors."

"Chummy, huh?" I snort.

Brooklyn shakes her head. "That's one word for it."

Releasing her hand, I approach Eli. He's standing at the back of the kitchen, staring out at the falling rain. Running a hand over his arm, he startles at first before nuzzling into my side. I kiss his mop of ringlets, wrapping an arm around his shoulders.

"Where's Seven?" Brooklyn asks behind us.

"He's been outside for four hours now," Hudson answers. "Won't say a word to any of us, same as yesterday. He just keeps on hitting that bag and pacing."

We stare into the overgrown chaos of the garden that hasn't been tended to in decades. Buried amongst the billowing trees and weeds, Seven has found an old punching bag. He's methodically beating the shit out of it without breaking a sweat. It's a mesmerising sight, watching his fury play out in real time.

Brooklyn comes to stand next to us, frowning. "This isn't good."

"What? It's a healthy outlet," I argue.

"It always took him a while to come back after jobs. Sometimes weeks would pass before he returned to being himself again, not just… Patient Seven. I should go out there and help."

"Give him some space to cool off. You can't coddle him forever," Hudson says without his usual vitriol. Seems like the ice man is beginning to thaw after all.

The sound of the front door smashing open interrupts our conversation, sending us all into fighting mode. Kade and Hudson both pull weapons, while Brooklyn wields her knife like it's an extra limb. I shove Eli behind me before he can protest and square my shoulders. Heavy footsteps are approaching.

If Incendia has found us, we won't go down without a fight.

I refuse to die here, of all places.

"On my count," Kade instructs, gun cocked.

Before he can offload a round, a shrill, furious voice lances through the kitchen. The door smacks against the wall as it flies open, ending my short-lived relief. Enraged, crystal-clear blue eyes land on me.

"Phoenix motherfuckin' Kent. I'm gonna have your hide, boy!"

Before I can hide from her wrath, Eli helpfully shoves me forward. Nana approaches and smacks me around the head, cursing like a drunken sailor thrown overboard.

"Nana, calm down!"

"Don't tell me to fuckin' calm down! Jesus H Christ." She yanks me into a suffocating hug. "Come here, you little toerag. Let me get a good look at you, at least. Two years!"

"Stop swearing! I'm here, aren't I?"

My nana, Pearl, is a short and stout woman, all wrinkled skin and old-age charm. Her silver hair is styled in a slick bouffant, matching her skirt and pressed shirt. Despite her charming, grandmotherly appearance, there's a terrifying woman beneath the surface.

It takes a certain kind of person to run an entire criminal empire in their retirement. Nana handles the front of the business, a shady strip bar called Mamacita's in Tottenham. An army of subordinates does the rest of the dirty work —myself included, once upon a time.

"What in the holy hell are you doing here? How long?" she demands, ignoring everyone staring at us like we're insane. She takes a lot of getting used to.

"Only a couple of days or so, we ran into trouble."

"Trouble!" She smacks me upside the head again. "I know all about your damn trouble. The news is showing your stupid grin every night! My entire fuckin' knitting circle thinks my grandson is a mass murderer!"

"You go to a knitting circle?" I stare in disbelief.

Her eyes narrow on me. "Ain't I allowed to have a fuckin' hobby? I've been dealing with these morons on my own since you got put away. Sometimes I gotta cool off too. I knitted a holster for my revolver."

Before she can wring my neck, I dance backwards. Nana seems to realise that we're not alone. Her steely gaze bounces between the entire ragged group before landing on Brooklyn. She studies every bruised and scarred inch on display, her lips pressed into an unflinching line.

"You the girl that got my boy in trouble?"

Brooklyn winces. "I guess I am, ma'am."

"Don't ma'am me, missus. The name's Pearl."

Depositing herself in a chair, Nana pulls out a cigar and lights up.

"Someone better get me a drink while my grandson here explains why the pigs are knocking on my door every day. I ain't slept a wink all week! It's bad for business."

Everyone watches her with bemusement. I should have warned them; she's a fucking tough nut to crack. Hudson obediently surrenders his bottle of vodka, looking more than a little intimidated. Nana glares until he produces a glass, then she knocks back a stiff measure.

"We had to leave Blackwood. Our lives were in danger there," I explain, earning myself the stink eye. "The corporation behind the institute is very powerful and wants to silence us. That's why we ran, Nana."

"You do the things the news is accusing?"

"Of course not," Kade asserts. "We're being targeted."

"Innocent people don't get targeted, kid."

"We did burn down Blackwood and kill several guards," Brooklyn interrupts, facing Nana without fear. "Plus the men in the nightclub. That wasn't a lie. We had no choice."

Nana appraises her, puffing out cigar smoke. She respects straight-talkers more than anything. Lying or making excuses in our family usually got you a hell of an ass kicking, if not worse.

"They're saying you're a murderer. I read the news."

Stepping between the two women, I prepare to take Nana down a notch or two.

I won't have her shaming Brooklyn for what the news is peddling. I know exactly how many lives Nana has ended or ruined through the family business. We've all got blood on our hands.

"We were in Blackwood for a reason," Brooklyn offers plainly.

Nana stares at her before a cheeky smile lights up her face. "I could use a girl like you around here. I never liked that institute, pretentious and full of overpaid wankers. They wouldn't let me see my boy for six months, then he didn't want me to come anyway."

Her caustic glower is sent my way instead. *Great.*

"I didn't want you to see me like that." I recoil, avoiding her accusing gaze. "It took me a while to get clean, and it wasn't pretty in the meantime."

"I'm your grandmother, Nix. I've seen you at your best, and I've seen you at your worst. You hurt this old bird's heart, but I'll live. It's your sister who deserves an apology."

At the mention of Charlie, guilt smothers me. I've been gone for so long, I'd convinced myself that my family was better off without me. Charlie was a kid when I got put away. Now, she's fourteen years old. I've missed so much. I'm no better than our waste-of-space mother.

"Guys," Kade interrupts. "Something happened."

He's back at his laptop, looking pale. The room falls into tense silence as he turns it around for us to see. It looks like another news conference has been called. The reporters are back on the steps of luxurious downtown London, surrounded by wealth and carefully concealed lies.

"Son of a bitch," Brooklyn curses. "That's him."

The cameras paint Bancroft's well-groomed exterior in high-definition horror. He's dressed in another fine suit and tie, his diamond-encrusted watch on full display. The conciliatory smile on his face makes me want to punch a fucking wall.

Hudson stills next to me. "Look who it is."

Hanging behind Incendia's perfectly groomed president is a very familiar, unwelcome face. I've seen pictures of Kade's asshole father before. He's staring straight ahead, an impenetrable mask on his middle-aged face, framed by slicked back, salt and pepper hair.

There's a low hum of conversation from the reporters, documenting this alliance. It's a publicity stunt and warning rolled into one. They know Leroy Knight's sons are involved. He's effectively disowning them and painting an even bigger target on their backs by doing this conference.

"Three days ago, law enforcement tracked our missing convicts down to a nightclub in South London," Bancroft recites. "They claimed the lives of six brave men. Today, we praise their heroic efforts and condemn the animals that led them to their slaughter."

"Who's this ugly stuffed shirt?" Nana booms.

Brooklyn's hands brace on the table. "That's who we're running from."

Nana studies the broadcast with a look of murderous rage. She's well accustomed to deciphering bullshit in her line of work. This guy's entire persona is a golden fucking sham.

"The situation is in hand," Bancroft continues grandly. "We're working to bring these monsters to justice. Should anyone have a sighting of the people on your screens, we urge you not to confront them, but to call the authorities with the following number."

Kade's fist slams down on the table. "Paying the public to do his dirty work for him."

"Clearly, the police are in his pocket too," Brooklyn adds. "He owns everyone and everything."

Our pictures flash up on the broadcast in all their harrowing detail, including Brooklyn's infamous mugshot. But this time, a sixth photo has been added. It's an old snap of Seven, dressed in a blue cap and gown at his university graduation. He looks younger and a hell of a lot more… stable.

"I thought they were keeping Seven quiet." I watch the conference draw to a close. Bancroft and Kade's father climb into an SUV and speed off without answering any of the reporter's questions.

"They're getting desperate," Kade hedges, his face red. "Time's running out. They know the minute we start talking, that's it. Game over."

"So why don't we? Talk, that is."

"Who would believe us?" Hudson rages, pacing the small kitchen. "Even with proof, we're just a bunch of mentally ill criminals to the public. We'll be tossed in a cell and fucking executed."

"I could have one of my boys put a bullet in that bastard's skull," Nana says sweetly, crushing her finished cigar. "Just say the word, kids. Quick and easy."

"Stay out of this, Nana. It isn't safe."

"I can protect myself, Nix. I've been in the game for a long time."

"I haven't spent the last two years rotting inside of Blackwood for you to throw it all away!" I shout at her, losing my temper. "Stay out of this. That's an order."

Her crystalline eyes harden, filling with indignation. "Do you think I will listen to you, boy?"

"You fucking will."

"Watch your tone. I'm still in charge here."

"How come you didn't get locked up then, huh? My life got ruined instead."

She blanches, seeming to deflate. I immediately want to take my words back. I did the crime, so I had to do the fucking time. There's no way I would've let Nana go down for all the shit we've done.

"I'm sorry." I pull her into a hug.

She sniffles emotionally. "Me too, kid. Missed your goofy face around here."

"I'll come back, I promise."

Her response is cut off by dirty dishes rattling in the sink. We all stop and stare, noticing the mini earthquake. Liquor bottles and chipped glasses are shaking in the kitchen cupboards.

"What is that?" Kade exclaims.

Nana's glass of vodka vibrates and falls off the table. The house is overcome by a heavy beating sound, and it takes a moment for the penny to drop. It sounds like the spinning rotors of an incoming helicopter.

"Is that what I think it is?"

Kade shoves cables and paperwork into his backpack. "Let's get the fuck out of here. Quickly, move!"

Seven bursts back inside, his caramel eyes wild as he gestures towards the garden. Leaves and branches are flying everywhere in the choppy wind. It must be right above us. Terror and panic sweep over the entire room.

I shove Brooklyn towards the door and grab Eli, directing everyone towards the front of the house. With a bit of luck, we can use the gang to conceal our movements. If we can get to one of the cars, at least we have a slim chance of getting the fuck out of here.

"Nana! Go home," I yell above the noise. "Stay out of this."

She pulls me into a fast, frenzied hug. "Run and don't look back, you hear me? Take this. Call me when you're safe."

Shoving one of the phones we use for dealing into my palm, I press a kiss to her cheek. If I was her obedient leader, she was the empress of us all. Neither a hero nor a saint, but family, nonetheless. That's something I won't ever take for granted again.

"I love you, Nana."

"And you, boy. Get out of here."

She hobbles towards the garden where she can slip out through the back. The others will get her to safety. It pains me to see her go like this, but I don't allow myself the luxury of emotion. We can mourn all that we've lost another time.

We race through the chattering house and onto the street, where the glow of overhead lights sweeps across the concrete to search us out. Travis is lurking nearby in the cab of his truck. My heart stops when I catch sight of the girl in the passenger seat, her long brown hair and chocolate eyes matching mine.

"Phoenix!" Charlie shrieks.

Waving her off, I scream at the top of my lungs. "Char! Run!"

She yells at Travis, gesturing towards me.

"Go!" I shout again.

"Not without you! I'm coming!"

We're all nearly swept off our feet as more ferocious wind whips the street. The helicopter is preparing to land. A sudden rush of fluorescent lights blinds me, and I stumble into the unknown. I'm dragging Eli with me until our hands are viciously ripped apart.

"Eli!"

My family vanishes in the brilliant white light. I can't see a fucking thing, searching around with my hands and tripping on a curb. The world slows to a snail's pace in the blinding unknown. All I can hear are the shouts. Screams. Bellowed orders and begging cries.

Charlie's desperate voice grows ever closer, parting the blazing light. Her strong hand grasps mine before it's torn away again. Blinking hard, I clear my vision long enough to spot her flying through the air, far away from me.

"Phoenix! Help!"

She's tossed across the street by an unknown figure, dressed in the same black uniform the dickheads at the nightclub wore. Swarms of people are invading the street. They all carry guns and radios, scanning the crowd with urgency. When two of the black-clad individuals begin to fight each other, I realise something is amiss.

We're not alone.

They aren't on the same side.

Gunshots and wet, meaty punches writhe through the air in a chorus of violence. My ears ring in the wake of the helicopter that has landed amidst the chaos. Yelling something at the pilot, an enormous mountain of a man leaps onto the street.

I swear the helicopter shakes with the force of his huge, muscled weight exiting it. His hardened gaze sweeps over the messy scene, searching for something. When he spots us cowering and trapped by the fighting, he taps the comms in his ear and speaks.

"What's happening?!" Hudson yells.

Kade finds his feet, bleeding from a gash in his forehead. "I don't know!"

The fighting rages on as the melee of bodies collide and become one. It's impossible to tell who works for who. Someone else is here, and the newbies are gleefully wailing on Bancroft's hired skins. Searching the war zone, I catch sight of Charlie on the other side of the road.

My stomach plummets.

She's trapped by a gun to her back.

"Charlie!" I roar.

Her bleeding face manages to turn in the gravel and two tear-stained eyes meet mine. I shove past Hudson, desperate to get to Charlie before it's too late. Travis and his boys are still lost in the madness, being beaten bloody while others run for their lives.

"Nix!" Brooklyn shouts after me. "Stop!"

Her voice is cut off by a shriek. Kade convulses on the road with a taser jabbed into his side. Hudson's rearranging some fucker's face, as Seven tears apart anyone that dares come close to him. Brooklyn is attempting to drag a semi-unconscious Eli out from underneath a pair of fists.

"Phoenix!"

Charlie's pained begging nearly rips me in half. Caught between my sister and my brawling family, I have to make an impossible decision. My feet move of their own accord as I race towards Charlie. The barrel of a gun nudges the back of her head as she sobs.

Everything stops.

Time ceases to exist.

With the distance between us shortening, I'm so close to tackling the asshole threatening her life. Mere inches away, close enough to taste her terror. Leaping the final few steps, I'm flying through the air when the shot rings out.

That short, controlled blast changes everything in a second.

The light in my sister's eyes winks out of existence.

Blood explodes like a bomb dropped in the ocean, covering me in warmth. I hit the ground and take down the gunman with me, his weapon skidding out of reach. Before he can come up for air, I'm breaking every single bone in his face. An anguished, animalistic cry pours out of me.

Thwack.

Thwack.

Thwack.

Agony races across my knuckles, punctuated by the cracking of shattered bone. The gunman stops moving as I cave his head in, feeling like my entire body is about to explode with rage. Collapsing in a puddle of blood, I finally look at my sister's dead body.

She's gone.

Gone.

Fucking gone!

Someone's calling my name. Over and over again. It doesn't register. Nothing exists but the empty, lifeless orbs staring back at me. I didn't even get to speak to her, let alone say goodbye. I'm her big brother.

It's my job to keep her safe.

It… was my job.

There's nothing left to protect now.

"Phoenix!"

Brooklyn screams like a banshee, pointing at the person heading straight for me. In the riot of warring bodies, a spindly figure slices and stabs at random. She parts the sea of blood with a knife in each hand, cutting countless throats. Her bald head and hollow cheeks are exposed by her lack of balaclava.

She's closing in on me.

I don't run.

There's nothing left in me to feel fear.

My family is stolen away across the street. Tossed over several hulking shoulders, they're packed into the helicopter. I watch the huge guy from before jam a needle into Brooklyn's neck. He drags her away as she bucks and fights, eventually going limp.

The last thing I see is Kade's floppy body being lifted and carried, disappearing with the rest of them. Pain tears through my left thigh as a dart pierces my skin. The approaching woman tucks a tranquilliser gun back in her holster.

Paralysing fear takes over. The world blurs fast, disintegrating at the seams as drugs attack my mind. I can still see Charlie's body staring back at me with accusations in her eyes. All I want is to wrap my arms around her and take the last five minutes back, no matter what price I must pay.

Incendia's foot soldiers circle like vultures.

Then… nothing.

CHAPTER 14
BROOKLYN

BIRDCAGE - HOLDING ABSENCE

TIME TO WAKE UP, *Brooke.*
We're going to go for a little drive.
Far, far away from here.
With a scream lodged in my throat, I shoot upright. A wave of dizziness washes over me. My surroundings are blurred as I blink to clear my vision. Are we back at the cottage? Or... no, we were in London. That's when it hits me.

The nightclub.

Phoenix's Nana.

Helicopters.

Bullets.

Screaming.

As shadows settle around me, I slap a hand to my neck. It's throbbing and tender from the needle stuck in my flesh. All I can remember is seeing Phoenix trapped on the wrong side of the street, covered in his sister's blood, with enemies advancing on all sides.

"Phoenix!" I scream and flail.

Losing my balance, I fall from the soft mattress beneath me and smack into the floor with a groan. It doesn't matter. I need to find Phoenix. Splayed out and gasping for air, fragments of reality begin to filter in, like piecing together smashed glass.

Plain white walls.

Smooth, polished floor.

A single light built into the ceiling.

There's a bed to my left, the sheets disturbed from where I fell. No windows. One door and a serious-looking lock. Pushing up on my hands and knees, I hear a snort from across the room.

"Graceful, Brooke. You mind keeping the screaming down? My head still hurts from when you bashed it in with your bare hands."

Trembling all over, I force myself to meet the wide, expectant eyes of my best friend, Teegan. Framed by flowing, bright-red hair, heavy eyeliner and her usual gothic armour, she stares me down with the corner of her mouth lifted in a grin.

"Tee?" I whisper fearfully.

"The one and only. Long time, no see."

"What are you doing here? Where... where are we?"

"Neverland, obviously. I'm waiting for Peter Pan to come save us."

Sprawled out in the corner, she props her Creepers against the wall. I clutch my chest, feeling like I'm having a heart attack. Did Incendia catch her too? Are we both prisoners now? I have to find the guys. I won't let anyone hurt them just to get to me.

"Where are the others?"

Teegan chuckles. "You're going to get them killed, you know."

"Where the hell are they?"

"Not here," she singsongs.

Getting my jelly legs beneath me, I manage to stand. The room is still swaying with the aftereffects of the drugs, but I make my way to the door without faceplanting. It refuses to budge, no matter how loud I shout and rage. We're trapped in these four walls.

"How long have you been here?"

Teegan sighs. "All I ever wanted was to be your friend, B. That's it. Where did that get me, huh? Three surgeries. Intensive care. They had to wire my jaw shut. All your fault."

Before I can beg on my knees for her forgiveness, a slow, mocking clap fills the room. With my back against the wall, I nearly jump out of my skin. Hudson's glaring at me from the empty bed.

"Landed yourself in more trouble, I see."

"Hud?"

His smile takes a venomous edge. "I never regretted what I did to you all those years ago. You needed breaking in. I wanted to ruin you, watch you scream and suffer, desperate to escape."

Squeezing my eyes shut, I wrench them open again, ready for him to disappear in a cloud of shadows. His sharp gaze remains, digging beneath my skin like a parasite. Each step towards me has my hammering heartbeat racketing even higher.

"You should have died on that roof last year," Hudson spits. "Everything was perfect until you came along and fucked up our lives. Now, we're all dead because of you."

Teegan concurs with a gleeful hoot. "Don't worry, Brooke. She's coming back for you. You escaped fate before, but not this time. Once you're dead, we can all live in peace."

"But... what if... what if I want peace too?" My voice breaks right as my knees give way. "I don't want to be alone anymore. I... I think I want my happy ending."

Frigid cold races down my spine as a pair of lips meet my ear. Rubbery and hard, the brush of the dead is unmistakable. Vic will always live inside of me. I can't dig out his poison wrapped around my bones.

"You don't deserve your happy ending," he taunts. "Thought you'd gotten rid of me, did you, darling? I'm never far away." His skeletal finger taps my temple. "Right here, until the end."

"No! Get me out!" I curl up in the tightest ball imaginable. "Please… please let me out."

My voice deserts me, drying up into oblivion. Tears flow and my body shakes with tremors. I don't know how long I lay there, sobbing and pleading for an escape. The choir of voices breaks my solitude with their taunts and constant barrage of vitriol.

When a hand clasps my shoulder and shakes, I scream again.

"Hey, Brooke! It's me!"

"Theo?" I gasp.

His blue eyes and soft, boyish features peer down at me behind his glasses, framed by dense, blonde curls. He's dressed in another flannel shirt and tee, with an ID badge swinging from his neck. My mouth opens and shuts like a dead fish. I feel like my vocal chords have been severed.

"No need to panic. I won't hurt you."

"W-Where?"

"Somewhere safe," he confirms.

His words ring true, but my panic is too far gone. Moving lightning fast, I throw my entire body weight into him. He yelps and crashes to the floor in a heap. Before he can hurt me, I fall back on months of fighting to survive, and strike him right in the temple.

Theo slumps with a gasp of pain, his skinny limbs hanging limp and useless. Across the room, Hudson resumes his sarcastic clapping. The voice of my abuser has gone, but Teegan still lashes me with her angry stare. My heart stops when two more figures rise from the bed.

"Better run, love," Kade warns. "She's coming."

Eli stares without words, a trail of blood running from the corner of his mouth. I watch in horror as deep stab wounds appear in all of their bodies. Invisible knives shred the people I love, slashing every bit of skin. Throats, arms, wrists. A tsunami of blood approaches.

Run, little Brooke.

Run from Mummy.

I'm going to catch you.

I tear through the ajar door, leaving Theo's unconscious body behind. An endless, dull corridor with thick carpet greets me, lit by corporate lighting. Bearing right, I run like my life depends on it. The ghosts are going to swallow me whole if I don't fucking run.

A warren of corridors and empty offices beckons me deeper into the building, with the fires of insanity licking at my heels. I think I can hear someone shouting in the distance, but they're trapped in another dimension and unable to reach me.

I'm too distracted by the ghosts hunting me down to notice the person waiting to capture me. My entire body smacks into something tall, hard, and terrifying. Thick, trunk-like legs give way to an impossibly huge, barrel chest and arms with enough muscle to lift a truck single-handedly.

Two hands clamp down on my arms.

The low, throaty grumble of a beast makes me freeze.

"Stop right there, kiddo."

"No! Let me go, Logan!" I scream.

"What are you talking about?"

I'm too disorientated to stop the onslaught of memories from overwhelming me in quick flashes. Logan standing on that godforsaken beach. His body heat curled around mine. Counting sheep in the dead of night. Standing between me and fists. His blood painting the elusive art of death in red ink.

"Jesus, Brooklyn. Stop fighting me."

"No! Let me go!"

The mountain captures me in his arms like a bloodthirsty spider in its web. I let out another scream and fight back until I'm tossed over his shoulder, with strong arms clamping down on my legs.

"I need a pay rise for this shit," he grumbles.

The world hangs upside down as he angrily stomps down another long corridor, taking several sharp turns before thumping up a flight of stairs. On the next level, he swipes a pass and bursts into what looks like an office. I catch the blur of several bodies all rushing to stand.

"What the hell, Enzo?" Someone exclaims.

"I caught her attempting to flee the building."

"You have to let me go." I smash my fists into his back. "Teegan's coming for me... and Hudson, Kade, Eli. It isn't safe... the ghosts are going to get me. I need to run!"

"Blackbird? We're right here."

Hudson's voice yanks the plug from my body. In an instant, I'm left exhausted and lifeless. My captor pulls me back over his shoulder until I'm cradled in his arms like a tiny baby. Piercing amber eyes bore into me beneath an untamed shock of black hair.

"You going to behave?" he questions.

"Put me down before I gouge your eyes out," I threaten weakly.

A smile spreads his thick, angular lips. "I'd very much like to see you try, wildfire. We can spar this out if you'd prefer. I'll happily beat you into submission."

"Touch her and your eyes won't be the only thing at risk," Hudson warns calmly. "Your choice, pal."

He rolls his eyes. "I'll pass."

I'm placed back on my feet and the carpet rushes to meet me until someone grabs me from behind. Crushed in a back-breaking hug, Hudson's comforting scent wraps around me.

"You were right behind me," I wheeze.

"We've been here all day, waiting for you to wake up." His frown deepens as he studies my face. "What did you see? Who was it?"

"N-Nothing."

"Dammit, Brooke. Don't lie to me. You promised to tell us if you started seeing shit again."

Before I can die of embarrassment, I'm torn out of Hudson's embrace. Two petrified green eyes rake over me. Eli's forehead smashes into mine as he squeezes me hard enough to hurt. I can feel the dangerous hammering of his heart from here.

"You're okay," he murmurs.

His rough voice breaks the last of my composure. I sag into his body, allowing him to hold me up. Another column of warmth meets my back and helps Eli to manoeuvre me into a seat at the long table.

"I've got you, love," Kade whispers.

Hudson quickly takes the seat to my left and grabs my hand in his tight grip. Eli steals the other empty seat, leaving Kade to roll his eyes and find a new place to sit.

"Where are we?" I ask timidly.

"London, Brooklyn West."

The new voice captures my attention and refuses to surrender it. At the other end of the table, beside the annoyed giant that interrupted my fleeing, sits another unfamiliar man.

Tall, well-tanned, and built with the toned gait of a gym addict, he openly stares at me. His features are angular and handsome, though slightly disfigured by a puckered scar that bisects his eyebrow. His chin is covered in a rugged scruff of beard, harshening his model-perfect looks.

Wearing a checked suit and blue tie that complement his coffee-coloured eyes, the stranger's chestnut-brown hair is tied back at the nape of his neck. I suppress a shiver. He looks a little bit too much like Augustus, with his designer garb and palpable authority.

Hudson squeezes my hand. "Brooke, this is Hunter."

"Director of Sabre Security," he supplies.

I gape between the two strangers, my head on a swivel. "This is Sabre? Not Incendia?"

The mountain to Hunter's left steps forward, cracking his scarred knuckles. "I'm Enzo, second in command. Incendia attempted to extract you. We stepped in and brought you here for protection."

"Protection?"

Hunter cocks his head, considering me. "We've been monitoring your movements for a while. Blackwood Institute was the tip of the iceberg for our investigation into Incendia."

"You're Sadie's team, aren't you?"

"Alyssa works for us," Enzo confirms.

Right on time, the door to the office slams open and a very disgruntled-looking Theo storms in. There's a dark bruise forming on his forehead as he limps. His furious gaze crash lands right on me.

"Bit of warning next time you decide to coldcock me."

I lift my chin in defiance. "You should've ducked quicker."

Enzo chuckles, earning himself a sharp look from Theo. Hunter watches us all with steely attention, his chin resting on his laced fingers. I hate the way he's studying us, picking apart our demeanours and filing all the information away for dissection. It's unsettling.

The three men take their seats, maintaining a safe distance from us. I stare down at the smooth surface of the table, noting the two absences from our group. I'm almost too scared to ask, but make myself anyway.

"Where is he?"

With a throat clear, Kade seals my fate.

"Incendia is holding Phoenix hostage."

"Is he okay?"

"They haven't contacted us with a ransom yet," Hunter answers crisply. "So, we don't know."

Willing myself to keep it together, my voice steadies. If I let the cracks show now, I'll never piece myself together again. The neutral expression plastered on my face is flimsy at best.

"And Seven?"

"Out cold," Enzo replies. "He was a bit agitated when he woke up and started damaging our property. Our on-call doctor gave him a muscle-relaxant and a small dose of a sedative."

"I want to see for myself, right now."

"You'll answer our questions first."

"Like hell. Take me to Seven."

Slamming his hands down on the table, Hunter levels me with a stern look. "You have been a huge pain in our ass. We know who you are. We know what you've done. You're in no position to make demands."

"What the fuck is that supposed to mean?"

With his laptop opened, Theo points a remote control at the wall. There's a projector built into the ceiling, casting light on the spotless surface. My stomach twists as a CCTV feed is brought up, dated several months back. I recognise the bustling metropolitan street, surrounded by luxurious hotels.

"Please no," I whimper.

The guys still around me as the feed shifts to a full view of a hotel's foyer. It's draped in glistening lights and crystal chandeliers, with countless armed guards. I watch my skeletal form get dragged down a grand staircase by Jefferson. My handcuffed hands are just visible.

"Where is this?" Kade growls.

"An investor's event held by Incendia several months back," Theo answers. "Here's the main floor of the hotel. We've identified several members of senior management."

Augustus and Seven come into view, seated at the bar and awaiting our arrival. The guys around me remain silent as the tape plays. On the screen, I'm shoved into a seat next to Seven, where I later palm a dinner knife. I can still remember Logan's voice telling me to stop.

It's weird to watch myself wrestle the knife away with my other hand, as if another person inhabited my body. I had no idea Logan wasn't real. When Seven slips his hand under the table to stroke my bare leg, Hudson abruptly stands up.

"Hud—"

"I don't want to hear it, Brooke. Not right now."

Rejection pierces my chest. Hudson paces away and stands by the huge, floor-to-ceiling window for a moment. The tape is paused until he returns, now avoiding my gaze.

"Show them the rest," Hunter instructs.

Just when I think it couldn't get any worse, a grainier feed takes its place. This is tucked away at an odd angle. A hidden camera, then. I begin to shake as two figures enter the hotel bedroom. I don't need to watch the rest.

My hands curl into fists under the table when Theo adds sound. *Fucking thanks for that.* The awful sound of my struggle reverberates around us. On the screen, Martin has ripped my dress and pinned me down, preparing to inflict his disgusting will.

Fighting. Shouting. Begging.

The sound of a zipper being unfastened.

Then, gunfire.

On and on and on.

I can hear myself sobbing on the tape as the bullets tear free, until the clip finally runs out. Eli attempts to rest a hand on my shoulder, and I automatically leap away. Pain scores across his face. I abandon the table, retreating to the safety of a corner, dreading the next moments of the tape.

You were right. She was definitely worth the investment.

I can see why my son has fallen so hard for you.

Or should I say, technically speaking, sons.

"Motherfucker," Kade curses darkly. "He was there?"

I stare down at the office carpet, unable to answer. The sound of Kade's footsteps feels like the approach of doom, until his fingers are clasping my chin. I have no choice but to surrender to him.

"You left this part out," he accuses.

"I'm sorry, Kade."

"Why didn't you tell me he did this to you? Both of them?"

"Does it matter?"

"Yeah, it matters! What else don't we know?"

Hudson lays a hand on Kade's shoulder. "Lay off, brother. This isn't helping."

"All she does is lie, lie, and lie some more. Secrets. Omissions. Half-truths. What else are you hiding from us, Brooke? How many people did they make you kill?"

Kade shakes me hard enough to rattle my teeth. I have half a mind to punch him in the face and run. Anything to avoid facing the reality of my actions. I've only fed them strips, hiding the monstrous truth because I'm selfish. I don't want to lose them again.

"We're aware of twenty-eight targets over the space of four months, all deceased," Hunter interjects. "The actual number is likely a lot higher. We estimate Patient Seven's body count to be in the hundreds."

I peel Kade's bruising fingers from my arm. He's frozen, an unreadable expression written across his face. The flash of judgement beneath his shock feels like a knife in the back.

"Not everyone should be saved," I whisper tearfully. "Some of us can't be brought back over that line once it's been crossed."

"This is such crap!" Hudson explodes, shoving Kade aside. "What you did in

Blackwood doesn't have to fucking define you. We've all been forced to do shit we're not proud of."

"Twenty-eight people," Kade repeats.

Hudson rounds on him. "You killed my fucking mum. I don't give a damn whether you wanted to or not. Her blood will always be on your hands. Who are you to judge Brooklyn?"

The fight drains out of Kade like a pin in a balloon. He scrubs a hand over his tired, bruised face, before managing to look up at me. Shame twists in the depths of his hazel eyes.

"He's right. I'm sorry, Brooke. I had no right to say that stuff."

I lift my shoulder in a shrug. "I did those things. Me."

"Patient Eight did those things."

"What if we're one and the same?"

Closing the distance between us again, Kade takes my face in his hands. Despite our audience, the rest of the office falls away. All I can see is the pain and desperation eating away at him, attempting to tear a new chasm between us.

"I don't give a fuck," Kade whispers roughly. "I'm in love with Brooklyn West. If that means loving Patient Eight too, then that's exactly what I'll fucking do."

"You can't love me. Not like this."

"You don't get to decide that! There's no choice in this, no walking away. I've loved you since the moment we met, and I'll love you until our very last goodbye."

I try to step away from him, but he refuses to let go. We've been two steps forward, one step back, since the very beginning of this fucked up journey. But now... I don't know if I can follow them into the light. This path only ends one way for me.

"Incendia won't stop until I'm dead. Maybe that's what I deserve... but you guys don't. I won't let you throw your lives away for me, even if I love you too."

Behind Kade, Hudson stares at me with possession and rage in equal measure. He looks like he wants to burn the entire world down just so we can walk together through the ashes. If I try to walk away, I have no doubt he'll drag me right back to them, kicking and screaming.

Hunter, Enzo, and Theo sneak out to give us some privacy. When the door clicks shut, Eli joins our little huddle. Fearsome need wars across his expression as he tucks a piece of hair behind my ear.

"It's... our ch-choice," he stutters out.

Hudson nods. "We're choosing you."

"Today, tomorrow, and every day to come," Kade says vehemently. "If Phoenix were here... he'd say the same thing. It's going to take all of us to bring him home."

"All of us?" I repeat.

Eli slides his hand into mine, and Kade releases me into Hudson's strong embrace. Between the three of them, I feel my body begin to relax. They're my foundation. My strength. The force that keeps me going.

"Let's go find Seven," Hudson suggests, seeming shocked by his own words. "Perhaps today will be the day he decides to be a sane human being."

"Unlikely," Kade mutters.

As we step outside the office and back into the brightly lit corridor, Enzo and

Hunter are talking rapidly with their heads together. Theo has vanished. I try not to shiver as their eyes sweep over us.

"We want to see Seven." I try to sound braver than I feel.

Enzo folds his powerful arms, muscles bulging against the tight fit of his black t-shirt. He defers back to his leader with a nod. Hunter scares me the most. It's in the way he looks at me, full of perceptive intelligence. My secrets dance in his eyes like embers from a flame.

"I expect answers to my questions," he says curtly. "Your protection here is only temporary, and it comes at a price. We're putting ourselves at great risk."

"What do you want from us?"

Hunter's fingers drum against his toned arms. "Sworn evidence from all five of you about Blackwood. Plus, the two you've got smuggled away. You're going to help me bring Incendia down."

Kade bites his lip. "The others are... elsewhere."

"Irrelevant. We can retrieve them."

"We're not going to prison," Hudson adds next.

"You will be given our full protection while this is taking place. Your testimonies can be used to negotiate a plea deal with the government. I can't rule out eventual prosecution."

"Where is Seven?" I repeat, losing patience with this asshole. "Right now, I don't give a fuck about the world or Incendia. I need to know that the people I care about are safe. Then we can bargain."

Studying me with that piercing stare, Hunter nods. "Enzo will take you to your friend. We have temporary accommodation for you. After that, we do things my way."

"Are we safe enough to stay here?"

"We're good at what we do," Enzo answers me. "Our staff are all highly trained. Nobody is getting through that front door without a hell of a fight."

Checking with the guys, they all reluctantly nod.

"Take them upstairs," Hunter instructs Enzo, pulling his phone out. "I'll contact the SCU and lay the groundwork. They're not going to believe this."

"Gotcha. Follow me, kids."

Sticking close together, we follow Enzo down the thickly carpeted corridor. Hunter watches us leave with a contemplative look, his phone already pressed to his ear. Our eyes connect at the last second before we step into an elevator.

I'm left wondering exactly whose hands our lives are in... and if we're any safer here than we were in Blackwood.

CHAPTER 15
SEVEN

LOST - THE HUNNA

THEIR VOICES FADE into the background as I stare out at the lurid city lights. My hand is pressed against the glass wall, leading to a generous balcony that hangs high above the rest of the world.

I'm in no state to sit around eating takeout with Eight and her men in our temporary apartment. Watching the ease with which they talk and joke around is torturous. She lights up in their presence, becoming more than the vacant machine I know.

They make her whole.

I'll never be able to give her that.

Unlocking the door, I slip out into the night. At the top of Sabre's formidable skyscraper, the wind encapsulates me in an impenetrable bubble. I've never felt so alone in the weeks since our lives changed forever... but it isn't safe for me to be around other people.

Jude was a good person, I think.

Seven is his opposite in every way.

There's a click behind me as the door reopens, disturbing my solitude. I don't need to look. I know it's her. She's never far behind—the phantom that wrapped herself around what remains of my humanity.

"Sev? Are you hungry?"

"Leave me be, Eight."

With a sigh, she joins me at the edge of the balcony. Our shoulders brush momentarily. I sneak a glimpse of her dangerously short hair, sharp cheekbones, and breathtaking beauty. Everything about her sets my pulse racing. I didn't know I could actually feel anymore. Not until she came along.

"We're all worried about you," Eight murmurs. "Even the guys. I know things are difficult with them, but you don't have to hide out here by yourself. Come and eat something."

Biting my lip, the truth attempts to strangle me. I don't give a flying fuck what her boyfriends think. Whatever this twisted thing is between us, it was forged in the hottest of fires, born of blood and death. Such bonds are unbreakable.

"Do you think the people we used to be are still in us somewhere?"

Hesitating, Eight shakes her head. "They're gone, Sev. That doesn't mean we can't have lives, however imperfect and painful. I just don't know if we deserve to."

"Neither one of us can live a normal life, not now."

"I think you may be right." Eight captures my hand. "But fuck being normal. I know what I have with the guys may seem strange, but we're a family. I want you to be part of our family too."

Something flutters behind my ribcage, reawakening an organ that I long thought dead. I don't know what this unnameable feeling is. Sensations sometimes come over me like waves and I can never label them. Not after so long being stripped of all human emotion.

"What do your men think of this proposal?" I ask pointedly.

She musters a small smile. "They're all in, Sev. It may help if you stop breaking people's fingers and threatening to skin them alive, but somehow, your violent charm has won them over."

I raise an eyebrow. "My charm?"

"Well, I adapted what they said. It was more along the lines of *go fetch the sadistic bastard*, but you get the gist. This whole solo-gunslinger thing is unnecessary."

"Solitude keeps us alive."

"You deserve to be more than just alive," Eight implores me. "I'm not going to watch you fade away. We didn't survive Augustus's hell just to let him win now."

Before I can stop her, she drags me back inside the luxurious apartment. I feel instantly on edge. The soft furnishings and glittering lights are offensive after so long spent in the dark. I can feel her tensing up too, but the moment we step into the large, open plan living area, Eight relaxes.

A cream-coloured sectional sofa dominates the airy space. There's a flat screen television on the wall, along with armchairs and lamps dotted about. Soft, woven blankets and fresh plants soften the stark decor, giving it a comfortable feeling. But I feel even more out of sorts.

The entire room is boxed in by more slabs of glass that make up the walls, giving undisturbed, panoramic views of the city. If this palace is one of Sabre's spare rooms, I dread to think where they actually live.

"Hey," Hudson greets warily.

Their eyes train on me the moment we step inside the room. I slide an arm around Eight's waist in a clear mark of possession, too stubborn to back down. I'm surprised when Hudson takes a deep breath, nods to himself, and looks away without yelling.

"Food?" Kade asks us. "Enzo sent up Chinese takeout."

"Are we sure they didn't poison it?" Eight jokes.

"Erm, negative. It's better than what we've been living off, though."

Eight leads me to a pair of oversized armchairs, gently shoving me into one of them. She grabs a carton of food and drops it into my hand before tending to herself. Chest burning with another odd feeling, I dig into the noodles.

"What's the deal with this place?" Hudson says around a mouthful of food. "Not to be a dick or anything, but we don't take handouts. They have an agenda. Are we going to play into their hands?"

"Since when are you not a dick?" I reply bluntly.

Tense silence is broken by several rounds of raucous laughter. Hudson scowls at me over the Chinese food, but it's without his malice. He's becoming somewhat more amiable as time goes on, though I wouldn't mind finding a shallow grave for his body anyway.

His blonde-haired brother looks amused. Eli, the quietest of Eight's motley crew, is hammering her on the back as she chokes on a wonton. He's the least objectionable of them all. I hate quiet people less.

"Hudson being a dick aside." Kade grins at me. "We most certainly don't take handouts. I want Hunter's protection, sure. But we came here for answers and we're not leaving without them."

"You think they know anything?" Eight asks after gulping water. "They seemed desperate for us to talk. This deal is shady. It doesn't guarantee us anything."

"Sabre knows more about Bancroft than we do."

"You drew up a profile."

Kade shrugs. "Finding information online is one thing. With Sabre's resources, they have access to classified information. I bet they've got a good fix on Bancroft already."

"Why does that matter to us, though?"

Hudson clears his throat. The pair exchange uneasy looks, seeming to communicate without words. Eight slams her carton of food down and crosses her arms.

"You don't have to treat us like invalids."

Despite having enough secrets to sink a damn ship, Eight doesn't like stuff being kept from her. I watch them all stare off in a battle of wills, until Kade sighs and abandons his own food carton.

"While you were both still sedated, we gleaned some other information from Hunter. They've been investigating for several years now. He knows far more about Incendia than we do."

"Why are the institutes still operational? Clearly, he has evidence. Why isn't it enough?"

"Connections," Hudson supplies. "Influential friends. Investors. Government contracts and associations. Incendia is practically state-owned, so many of its shares are held by people in positions of power."

"*Sir* Joseph Bancroft," Eight recites grimly. "Fuck, we're so dead."

"Not exactly."

Eight casts Kade an incredulous look. "Miss White was a bust. Augustus's laptop was fried. Incendia took Phoenix... we don't know what they're doing to him." She gulps and shoves her pain down. "What aren't you telling us?"

Glancing between all of them, we're clearly missing something important. Even Eli is squirming in his seat, succumbing to the mounting pressure. Our tiresome wait is broken when Hudson clears his throat.

"Well, it would seem that Professor Lazlo is alive."

Silence descends like a cloud of fog. Smothering, clinging, unable to be scrubbed from our skin as it sinks deep inside of us. While the three men plead for leniency with their eyes, Eight is set in stone.

"He's willing to meet and wants to exchange information," Kade adds.

"Willing?" I repeat.

Hudson knocks back a mouthful of water. "Sabre have offered him the same deal. Protection in exchange for his sworn evidence and full cooperation in bringing Incendia down."

"And later? Will he be arrested?"

Kade looks uncomfortable. "He will be in a position to argue for a plea deal. Immunity from prosecution if he testifies under oath, kinda thing. Hunter has a government contact who can be trusted when the time comes."

"A plea deal."

Eight's voice is hard as nails and utterly unyielding.

"I'm sorry, love."

"You're telling me that the man who murdered my entire family, imprisoned Seven, tortured Lucia, and arranged for Rio to kill me won't face a single day of punishment for his actions?"

Hudson looks away. "It's a real possibility."

I try to put my hand on Eight's shaking leg, but she stands up, walking away from us all. Hudson pursues her and she yells at him to back off. Her mind is already gone.

"It was all for nothing," Eight says to herself. "Our lives have been destroyed and it was all for fucking nothing! He's going to worm his way out of everything."

"Blackbird—"

"I'm going to kill Hunter and his stupid team."

Hudson blocks her exit, his hands raised. "Just stop. Let's talk about this."

"I don't want to fucking talk!"

Shoving him hard, Hudson stumbles into a glass end table that promptly smashes. Eight stares at him open-mouthed for a second before running from the room. Nobody seems to know what to say.

"Go get her." Hudson stands, wincing at his scraped hands. "She'll listen to you."

His show of faith is a surprise. Nodding, I take off after Eight. The front door to the apartment is wide open. I chase after her ash-white hair, somewhat doubting my ability to calm her down right now.

"What's your plan?" I shout down the darkened corridor.

Even at this hour, the hum of late-night activity fills the skyscraper from the lower levels. Eight has stopped in front of the elevator, her hands braced on her knees as she breathes hard.

"Do I need a fucking plan?!"

"Might do, princess."

"I'm not your goddamn princess! I'm a stone-cold assassin and I've been fucked over for the very last time. Are you going to help me kill their sorry asses or not?"

Eight smashes her finger into the elevator's button, but it's stuck on another level. She batters it over and over again, growing more frustrated. I draw to a halt by her side and chuckle.

"Alright, assassin. No need to take it out on the elevator."

"How are you not more mad about this?" she hisses at me. "Lazlo is the reason you're here. He broke us both and Sabre wants to serve him a brand-new life on a gold fucking platter. Why aren't you angry?"

Reaching out, I tug Eight closer. She smashes against my chest with a faint gasp. Banding my arms around her slim, sexy body, I revel in the feel of her skin on mine. Her eyes are wide and curious, tempting me further. My lips gaze over the exposed slope of her throat, leaving featherlight kisses.

"Because I don't believe in justice," I murmur throatily. "None of us get what we deserve in this life. Otherwise, we would be dead and buried, and Incendia scattered in ashes. Neither has happened."

Eight offers me a desolate look. "I don't want to live in a world where the people that killed my family are free to do as they please. I want my revenge, Sev. I don't give a fuck if I have to pay the ultimate price to achieve that."

"You'd throw away everything just to hurt the people that hurt us?"

She looks down, hiding her darkness from me. With a low growl, I tug her head back up. I want to see the bloodthirst and rage swimming in her eyes. That dark, sordid place inside of her is where I found my home.

"I'm supposed to say no, right? Pretend like I'm happy with what I've got."

"No," I reason. "Maybe this is the way back."

"Back to what? There's nothing left for us in our old lives."

"You said it yourself. Family."

Blinking rapidly, Eight's mouth clicks open. I ease it shut and close the final inches between us. She doesn't move or fight back, content to let our destructive collision play out in real time. When our lips meet, it feels like electricity is flowing through my veins.

I push past her lips with my tongue, desperate to claim every damned inch of her. I want her breath. Her lifeblood. Her thoughts. Her pain. Her hope. All of it belongs to me now, because I can't find it on my own. She needs to show me the way back.

Breaking the mind-melting kiss to glance up and down the deserted corridor, I check that we're still alone. Eight is panting hard, her back now pressed against the elevator doors. Finding the soft elastic of her waistband, I give no warning before pushing my hand into her panties.

"Sev…"

"Shut up, Eight. Let me feel you."

Her back arches as I find the soaked heat between her thighs. Jesus, she's so damn wet for me. Circling her sensitive nub, I give it a sharp tug before seeking her entrance. Eight lets out a mewl for attention, pushing her hips forward to seek more of my touch.

When I shove a finger in her pussy, she moans again. I begin to work it in and out, watching for her reaction. I've dreamed of touching her for so long, staking my claim in blood and desire. I want her to look at me the way she looks at them. I need her to want me back.

"Does the idea of revenge get you all wet and worked up, princess?"

Eight's teeth sink into her bottom lip. "Yes."

"What about slicing the throats of our enemies and fucking each other in a puddle of their spilled blood? Does that make you hot?" I ask curiously.

"Fuck… yes, it makes me hot."

Grazing my lips against her ear, I drop my voice even lower. "What about me bending you over Lazlo's cold, dead corpse, and fucking your tight cunt for the entire world to watch?"

Adding another finger to her slick warmth, I speed up my movements. She's beginning to tremble against my body, trapped in place and unable to run from me this time. Her legs spread wider with each thrust of my fingers, desperate for more. When I curl a digit to touch her sweet spot, she gasps loudly.

"I'm going to come."

"Fall apart for me, princess. I want to see it for myself."

Her forehead crashes into my chest as she orgasms. My cock is aching with desperation, but I won't take her here. Not like this. Pain and suffering brought us together. Seeking vengeance for all we've endured will mark the beginning of our future, however long or short it may be.

"Here's exactly what you're going to do." I slide my fingers from her panties and slowly lick her come from each one. "You're going to put a pretty smile on and play the game with these assholes. I don't give a fuck how, but we must convince them we're the right ones for the job."

"What job?" Eight repeats unsteadily.

Smirking, I push two of my fingers past her lips. Her eyes widen as she's forced to taste her own release, but then her tongue flicks over my digits, cleaning up what remains. I push them further into her mouth, touching the back of her throat until she gags.

"We're going to bring Lazlo in," I whisper, fucking her throat with my fingers. "While they're waiting for his worthless hide, we're going to peel the skin from his bones and enjoy every precious second it takes for him to bleed to death."

She gasps for air as I slip my fingers out. Stray tears mark the soft surface of her cheeks. Leaning in, I consume the salty droplets with a flick of my tongue. Her lips seek mine out with force, our teeth clashing.

When we finally break apart, darkness has unfurled in the grey depths of her eyes. It's a welcome sight, the infection of violence and evil. Like spilled ink tainting everything around it. The person her men know—Brooklyn West—takes a back seat.

I'm left with the soulless demon that Augustus created. My equal in every sense, an extension of the sickness bred too deep into me to dig out. Patient Eight smiles up at me. My partner in darkness.

I don't care if the good part of her has to die. All I want is the monster that dwelled beneath the ground with me. This execution will ensure that.

CHAPTER 16
BROOKLYN

PRETTY TOXIC REVOLVER -
MACHINE GUN KELLY

"NOT IN A MILLION YEARS," Hunter states flatly.

Sitting behind his neatly organised desk, he stares at me with defiance. There isn't a single crack in his facade. Arms crossed over his crisp, white shirt, his lips press into a tight line. Countless muscles bulge through the material, advertising his strength.

"It should be us," I argue back. "We're experienced and capable of handling anything on Lazlo's part. If you send an army of spooks in there, you'll scare him off. Let us handle this."

"Am I not speaking English? I said no. End of discussion."

Swivelling in his leather office chair, he runs a hand over his slicked back, chestnut ponytail. Despite being in his late twenties, he seems far older than his years. I feel like a speck on the radar compared to his wealth and knowledge. Sabre is living proof of it.

His office is far bigger than it needs to be and lit by the sun shining through the tinted glass windows. Packed bookshelves, ring binders, and textbooks make way for cork boards full of photographs, papers, and connecting ribbons of red string. He's mapped out everything in excruciating detail.

Blackwood sits at the centre of Hunter's organised madness. Cut-out news articles featuring Bancroft, Incendia, and several political big fish are pinned in between, connecting the other five institutes that each hold their own place. At the very top, there's a printed alert from law enforcement.

Wanted.

Armed & Extremely Dangerous.

Our faces stare back at me.

"You've spent so long trying to do the impossible." I gesture up at the packed cork board. "You run the risk of losing the best lead you've ever had. Lazlo isn't going to waltz in and start spewing information."

Hunter looks nonchalant. "I will convince him."

"How? Unlike Incendia, you have to follow the law."

"Why do you care?"

"I don't want to see anyone else get hurt!" I snap at him.

"With all due respect, Sabre is well-equipped to handle someone like Lazlo. We've been tackling criminal enterprises since long before you turned up."

"And we're not equipped? You've seen us in action. We know what we're doing."

Standing up, Hunter moves to the window. Hands laced behind his back, he considers the vast city landscape before picking up a framed photograph from his book-covered console. I can spot him in it, along with a younger carbon copy, complete with flowing brown hair and a cheeky grin.

"I'm trying to keep you safe," Hunter spells out, putting it back down with a frown. "You're making my job increasingly difficult."

"Look, I appreciate what you're doing for us, but we have a say in this too. Lazlo is the reason we're here. He started this by taking our lives from us."

"We're attempting to give you them back."

"What lives?!" I throw my hands up.

"Yourself and Jude Farlow are fugitives under temporary house arrest. I have warrants from the government, police and secret service, all demanding I hand you over for re-incarceration. Most of them report to Incendia."

My voice dries up as Hunter focuses on me.

"You'd be dead if we didn't step in. That is what we're giving you, Brooklyn. Your lives. Help us to understand how Incendia did this, and we can secure your futures."

"I can't do anything knowing Lazlo is still out there!"

"You need to let this go. Our team will bring him in."

"This man ruined my life." I march up to the desk and slam my hands down. "I'm willing to accept that he is a valuable asset. All I'm asking for is the chance to get some closure. Then Professor Lazlo is all yours."

Hunter sighs heavily. "You're impossible. The best place for you is here. The moment you step foot outside, I cannot guarantee your safety. The people looking for you won't hesitate to turn you over."

"Bring it on. Someone has to bring Phoenix home."

"You really do have a death wish, don't you?"

"I can't just sit here and do nothing!" My emotions overwhelm me at the thought of Phoenix. "It fucking kills me to know he's alone. We don't know what they're doing to him right now."

"We're trying to find him. Incendia has a lot of boltholes."

Our argument is interrupted by a sharp knock at the door. Theo pokes his head in, looking drained and far too pale in yesterday's rumpled clothing. He briefly glances at me before focusing on his boss.

"We have a problem."

"What is it now?" Hunter growls.

Theo appears nervous. "First contact from Incendia."

I'm following him into the corridor before Hunter's even moved. The steel grip of panic on my lungs is suffocating. Down the hall, Theo's office door is open. It's a glorified Nerd-Vana inside. Wires, cables, and countless monitors clutter the shadowed room.

He keeps the sun blotted out with thick blinds, while every available wall space is covered in surveillance maps, official documents, and the odd superhero poster. Tripping over a haphazard stack of programming books, I nearly fall on my ass before a pair of hands catches me.

"Careful, wildfire. Theo's organisation leaves a lot to be imagined."

Rippling muscles place me back on my feet with ease. Enzo's disarming smile peers down at me underneath an overgrown, messy mop of raven hair. He's back in all black again, finished with a pair of shining army boots.

"Where are the others?" I huff, smoothing my clothes.

Enzo props his huge shoulder against the wall. "On their way, I would imagine. Does my company bother you? Most people are afraid of me around here."

Hands propped on my hips, I hit him with an eye roll. Enzo is the biggest person I've ever met. He looks like the Rock and the Hulk had a fucked up love child. All raw power and rippling muscle, wrapped in a tanned, gruff exterior. Yet there's a softness in his amber eyes, and a playful lilt to his smile.

"Oh, please. You're a teddy bear."

He actually splutters. "I've worked at Sabre for almost a decade. Trust me, kid, I'm not a fucking teddy bear. I bet my kill count is a hell of a lot higher than yours."

"Maybe you can talk some sense into your boss's thick skull, then."

"I doubt that. Hunter's my best friend, but he's also a stubborn son a bitch."

"I have every right to bring Lazlo in! He's mine."

Enzo scoffs at me. "Gambling this opportunity on some misguided sense of personal justice isn't Hunter's style. We have no idea how Lazlo is alive."

There's a bang as someone walks straight into the door. Theo stumbles in, rubbing his red forehead. He ignores us, frowning instead at the new coffee stain down his t-shirt where the liquid has slopped over.

"Late night, brains?" Enzo teases. "You have a bed at home, you know."

Theo dumps his mug at the desk, yawning loudly. "Alyssa made contact at three o'clock this morning. I stayed up to decrypt her message for Hunter. She's still safe."

I don't miss the sheer relief that washes over Enzo before he stuffs it down again. I'm starting to wonder just how close this so-called team really is.

"You've heard from her?" I ask neutrally.

"A couple of days ago," Enzo grumbles, looking unhappy. "She's refusing to be pulled out, despite the risk. As far as we're aware, her cover is intact. She's being cautious."

"Let me get this straight. Sa—um, Alyssa, is allowed to risk her life to infiltrate an institute but I'm not permitted to bring someone in? How is that fair?"

"Because Alyssa works for Sabre," Hunter booms as he enters, flanked closely by all four guys. "She's undergone extensive training for this role. I have faith in her abilities."

"What's going on?" Kade pulls me into his arms.

We all gather around Theo's monster of a computer, with a dozen different monitors hooked up and millions of windows open. It's like staring into a chaotic extension of his brain. Eli takes my hand, holding on tight as a video file is pulled up.

"What is this?" Seven asks warily.

Theo clears his throat. "It's a warning."

Hitting play, there are several sharp intakes of breath. The camera pans across a darkened concrete cell. Unlike the torture chamber where I was held, this one features a wide, two-way window that allows for constant observation. I stare at the balled-up body in the top right corner, shivering all over.

"Let's try this again," Bancroft's regal voice drones.

Phoenix's swollen face is almost unrecognisable. He's been beaten into a pulp. One dislocated arm hangs limp at his side, while his clothing is ripped and blood-stained. He can barely move, and his teeth are gritted in agony.

"Nix," Eli rasps.

I tighten my hold on him. "We'll get him back."

Our entire group watches in horror as a guard enters the cell, dragging a huge hose in with him. I already know what's coming. It seems like a minor punishment, but after long enough being pounded by freezing water, you begin to lose grip of your mind.

This is just the warm-up act.

After ten minutes of relentless water, another beating begins. I have to walk away, bracing my hands on the wall while the group curses at the unfolding scene. Eli eventually joins me, unable to stand it for a second longer. Both of us cling to the other, silently praying for the man that binds us together.

The worst part is, Phoenix still doesn't make a damn sound. Throughout the torture, there isn't a single grunt or cry of pain. It's like he can't feel it anymore. He's already given up.

"There's more," Theo says reluctantly.

I look back in time to see the camera man exiting the cell. In the adjoining room, behind the glass, Bancroft stands ready to deliver his message to us. His hands are casually tucked in the pockets of his tailored trousers, a sinister smile stretching his mouth wide.

"Brooklyn West," he drawls. "You have forty-eight hours to hand yourself and Patient Seven over to the authorities, or Phoenix Kent will suffer the consequences. Don't try to run. I have the resources to hunt down every single person you've ever cared about and bring them back here for the same treatment."

Right on cue, there's a guttural scream.

It seems Phoenix couldn't hold out any longer.

"The clock's ticking, Miss West. I'll be seeing you soon."

The feed cuts out, leaving stunned silence.

"The file has been coded to erase itself after it's been watched," Theo explains with frustration. "Pretty high-level programming, but I suppose Incendia can afford to pay an expert."

My fist sailing into the wall seems to break everyone out of the spell.

Swallowing a scream, I shake out the pain in my bleeding knuckles. All I can hear is Phoenix's scream ringing over and over again in my head.

"Any idea where the video was taken?" Enzo breaks the tension.

"It doesn't match any of the institutes we've infiltrated so far," Hunter replies. "There are two locations we haven't gotten inside. I doubt Incendia would use their headquarters to hold him. It's too obvious."

"Priory Lane? Kirkwood Lodge?"

"Both possibilities, along with Harrowdean. Alyssa hasn't entered the experimental wing yet. They're being extremely cautious after recent events."

"Can we trace the message?" Hudson suggests.

Theo's fingers race over his keyboard. "I've tried tracing the IP address, but it's been rerouted and bounced all over the country. They aren't taking any chances. Everything else has been anonymised and the video itself erased."

"You're saying we have no way of finding him," I choke out.

Hunter's voice is solemn. "Our options are very limited."

Looking around the packed office, I find Seven's steely gaze burning straight into me. He gives me a stern nod, his balled-up fist twitching at his side. That video was just another reminder of everything Lazlo has to account for, past and present.

"Professor Lazlo worked for Incendia for thirty years." I step in front of Hunter so he has to look at me. "If anyone can tell us this video was filmed, it's him. I will get the information we need."

"My decision hasn't changed," Hunter elucidates.

"Neither has mine. I don't give a fuck whether or not I have your permission to leave. If we don't locate Phoenix, I have to hand myself over either way. I won't let him die for me."

Seven steps forward. "I will accompany Eight. We can meet Lazlo at an agreed upon location and deliver him to you, safe and sound. This isn't our first operation together."

"What makes you think that you're going and not one of us?" Hudson challenges him. "I still don't know if we can trust you with Brooklyn's safety."

"I've kept her alive for a hell of a lot longer than you morons," Seven argues flatly. "While you gave up on her, I was out there in the real world, protecting her. I've proven myself more than enough."

Kade rests a hand on Hudson's shoulder. "He's right. None of us are trained in the field. We have to track down where Phoenix is." He looks at me sternly. "Get what we need and come back alive. We're trusting you to do this right."

Guilt embeds itself beneath my skin. I disregard Seven's stare, taking the time to look between the guys. Hudson looks furious with this decision. Eli's eyes are still on Theo's laptop, even though the video has long since disappeared. His expression is distraught.

"We'll bring him in," I answer, wondering if it's the truth. "For Phoenix."

Hunter growls his frustration. "You kids are going to get yourselves killed."

"Let us do this and I'll give you that sworn evidence," I concede, hoping to appease him. "Whatever you want, I'll go on record. Augustus, the Z Wing, everything. It's all yours."

Immediately, he perks up.

"Everything?"

"Everything," I confirm. "Get the other two here and I'll convince them to testify as well, in exchange for protection. Just give me this one fucking thing. That's it."

Lips pursed, Hunter nods once.

"Don't make me regret this, West. You have a deal."

CHAPTER 17
BROOKLYN

ME & MY DEMONS - OMIDO AND SILENT CHILD

MIST AND DARKNESS cloak the abandoned dockyard. High above us, the moon offers a meagre slice of light, paving the way for our cautious footsteps. There isn't a single soul in sight this far out of the city. Nothing but ghosts and invisible demons walk these roads.

I tap the comms tucked in my ear. "Do you copy?"

"Check," Hunter answers. "Eyes up and ears open, West."

"Copy that, team leader."

Next to me, Seven strolls with lethal confidence. "Tell the pencil pusher to butt the hell out. This is our score."

"It's just to keep in contact in case things go south," I rationalise.

"Or to control us with. They don't trust us."

"Would you? We're hardly trustworthy."

Seven grumbles unintelligibly.

"That's what I thought."

Heading further inside, we keep a careful watch. This site was closed over a decade ago and left to disintegrate into the ravages of time. Old, rusted shipping containers and burned-out vehicles mark the post-apocalyptic landscape. It's the perfect place for this meeting.

"Lazlo is due to arrive in five minutes," Hunter informs me. "Remember, use force only if necessary. Bring him back alive, Brooklyn. That's non-negotiable."

"You got it. No asshole piñata today, noted."

"Fucking spoilsport," Seven mutters.

I can hear Kade's worried voice in the background, but Hunter soon tunes him out. The guys were very reluctant to let me do this. Hudson even threatened to tie me up in our fancy-as-fuck apartment. Not that I would mind a little bit of bondage, but this is my moment to own.

I can't be a songbird trapped in its cage forever.

Brooklyn West and Patient Eight have to become one.

In the furthest corner of the dockyard, we gather around the long-dead embers of a bin fire. Theo already scouted the place out with his drone army, ensuring there are no pedestrians to interrupt our task. The minute Lazlo approaches, they'll know about it.

Seven twirls a blade in his hand like a circus performer. "This could easily be a trap. Miss White's bait didn't work. They're taking another shot."

"Not this time. Lazlo was excommunicated for trying to get me killed, despite being hand-selected for Augustus's program. He was removed within seconds of Augustus entering Blackwood."

"Your point being?"

"Incendia doesn't forgive or forget. Miss White was an obstacle to be removed. Lazlo? He was the grand architect of their empire, and he stabbed them in the back. They wouldn't recruit him for this."

"Incoming," Theo's voice whispers in my ear.

"He's here."

Holding out my hand for his knife, I exchange it for the gun Enzo handed me. Seven's a far better shot than me. With our weapons raised, we stare into the gloom, waiting for our ghost to arrive. The crunch of footsteps cuts through the cloying mist.

"Brooklyn West!"

Parting shadows, the short, rounded figure of Professor Lazlo approaches our location. Dressed in worn civilian clothing with an old hat covering his crop of grey hair, he studies me through his smashed, partially sellotaped spectacles. He looks far from the terror that haunts my hallucinations.

I clear my throat. "Professor Lazlo."

"Two of my finest creations. Oh, this is a treat. Pleasure to see you again, Doctor Farlow."

A snarl escapes Seven's gritted teeth. "Professor."

Halting opposite us, Lazlo slides his hands from his pockets to hold them up in surrender. The gleeful smile on his lips is even more deranged than it was during our sessions together. A year in exile has done him no good, even less than it did for Miss White.

"I am here, almighty Sabre. Ready to surrender myself."

Seven cocks his gun. "You're alone?"

"Of course." Lazlo beams at him. "Who do I have left in this world, Jude? Like Frankenstein longing for the embrace of his creation, my life ended the day my work was taken from me. I am all but dead."

"How are you alive?" I ask next.

Chuckling again, Lazlo inches closer. I immediately back up, my body reacting on instinct. Just having him near me has my heart racing and body twitching with barely controlled anger. I want to tear him apart, limb from fucking limb.

"Thirty years at Incendia taught me one or two things, including how to disappear. When Doctor Augustus ordered my immediate removal, I was taken captive by the very corporation I helped to build. My escape took months of planning and a large dose of luck."

"Luck?" Seven scoffs.

"Perhaps God was shining down on me."

"Bullshit," I fire back. "You had help. Who?"

"An interesting question. I'm not certain you'll like the answer."

I ensure Lazlo is watching while I test the sharp tip of my knife. He hasn't stopped smiling for a second, seeming far too pleased with our reunion. I fucking hate the satisfaction we've granted him.

"The plea deal Sabre has cooked up for your pampered ass is conditional on your cooperation," I try to say calmly. "Information, Professor. That's all your life is worth. Prove you're not wasting our time."

Flashing yellowing teeth, Lazlo's grin is triumphant.

"Your mother helped me."

Seven flashes me a warning look, silently ordering me to keep my shit together. This is just another one of his endless mind games. I won't fall for it again.

"Spinning another tall tale?" I laugh. "Nobody is going to protect you or your lying hide. This is a waste of time." Stepping away, I take a second to gather myself.

"She was there, wasn't she? You saw her."

My retreating footsteps are halted by his words.

"I heard the news reports," Lazlo continues. "A deadly firefight in London. Several gang members left dead in the pursuit of England's most sought-after criminals. I have no doubt that Bancroft sent her."

Like falling through cracked ice into the depths of the ocean, my entire body stands frozen. Every word he speaks infects my mind with more of his venom. Despite everything… an image swims into my mind. All I caught was a glimpse from across the street.

Strolling through the flames, the woman headed straight for Phoenix, intent on violence. Her misshapen skull was exposed by her bald head, with two sunken eyes raking over us. A skeleton draped in papery skin, she was more dead than alive. I saw her, but… she wasn't my mum.

It's a lie.

This is just another trick.

Incendia wants to tear me apart.

"You're fucking unhinged!" I scream at Lazlo, whirling around in fury. "My mother is dead. She died! Crashed our car on purpose, nearly killing me in the process. She's been gone for twelve years!"

"Do you still dream about her? I'm sure you do. Does she speak to you too, Brooklyn? I wonder, is her voice whispering in your ear right now?"

"Don't listen to him," Seven barks at me.

Faintly, I can hear Hunter shouting through the earpiece. His voice disappears as I drop it to the ground. In the blessed silence that brings, I stare at Lazlo. He isn't smiling anymore.

"I rewrote the very fabric of her consciousness," Lazlo boasts. "Years of experimentation and research. It was easy enough to issue the right command to harness those threads again, all these years later. I'm certain Bancroft punished her for helping me."

"She's dead," I insist again. "I don't know how you escaped, but my mother is dead."

"Her hair fell out many years ago," Lazlo reveals conversationally. "The body suffers irreparable damage after enough rounds of electroconvulsive therapy. Tissues shrivel and die, brain cells degenerate. Memory slips away. It's difficult to imagine the person she used to be. So full of life."

"You took that from her!"

"Science took it. Can you see her now? Is Mummy going to come back and save you this time? I doubt she remembers she ever had children."

The distance between us melts away. Before I know what I'm doing, Lazlo is trapped beneath me as my fists sail into his face. Blood hits the gravel, teeth shatter and bones break beneath the weight of my fury. When Seven drags me up, Lazlo is covered in blood and cackling like a hyena.

"She was more scar tissue than human when they pulled her from that car wreck," he coughs out. "The trauma of it broke what remained of her mind. It was easy to recreate Patient Delta from the remains."

"No! Let me have him!"

"We can't do this…" Seven says uncertainly.

"This was your fucking idea! Let me go!"

"You made a promise. I want nothing more than to see him dead, but I can't watch you destroy the only family you have left."

"Get the fuck off me!"

Managing to locate my knife, I knee Seven in the gut. He trips and falls, unable to protect himself from the blade I press right to his throat. His chest is heaving much like mine, eyes wild with indecision.

"Phoenix," he blurts out.

I still, imprisoned by his voice.

"We need to find him," Seven reiterates. "I'm sorry, Eight. Lazlo deserves this, but Phoenix doesn't. We can't kill him yet."

The splash of tears on my cheeks almost breaks my resolve. Patient Eight never cries. She is harder than nails and tough as old boots. Brooklyn West is a little more broken. Between the two, I'm falling into fragmented pieces, caught in the middle.

"Damn you, Sev. What a time to gain a fucking conscience."

"I'm sorry, princess."

I spin back around to find Lazlo still laughing his ass off. He's almost as unhinged as his patients now. Seven takes my offered hand up and we approach the piece of shit together.

"You're going to come with us and identify a location." Seven points the gun at Lazlo's head. "Once our friend is located, you'll tell Sabre everything you know. Fail to do this and I'll be the one to cave your head in with my bare hands."

"Hand," Lazlo singsongs.

Bad move.

Seven launches himself at Lazlo in a blur of madness. Bodies tangle and bones break in a chorus of beautiful, explosive rage. Clutching his now shattered right arm, Lazlo stares at the bone protruding through his skin. He's actually crying, the spineless worm.

"You don't need your arms to answer questions." Seven dusts himself off. "Shut your goddamn mouth or I'll break the other one too. I only need one hand to do it."

"Couldn't manage the gun, huh? Come on, break the other one, then!"

"You talk too much," I snap, my booted foot connecting with Lazlo's face.

His head cracks against the ground, knocked unconscious and nearly unrecognisable through the injured mess. He'll be banged up for a while, but he can still talk, even with missing teeth and a broken arm. Hunter should be thankful he's still alive.

Leaving me to stare at our beaten prisoner, Seven retrieves the discarded earpiece. He doesn't bother offering it to me, slotting it in his ear instead.

"It's done. Yeah, he's alive."

Muttering some more, I tune Seven out. All I can see is the rise and fall of Lazlo's chest. Blood flowing from his nose and mouth is evidence of his heart continuing to pump. Each breath is another sick taunt. He was right.

I do dream about her.

I do hear her.

I do see her.

My mother is alive in so many ways. If he's telling the truth, then the human carcass of the person I once loved is still out there. A monster behind the wheel, trapped and unable to die. The last decade of my life has been one long, twisted lie. Like so many other things.

"Eight? Still with me?"

"I saw her," I manage to whisper. "She was there."

Seven's hand lands on my shoulder. "It's just a lie. A distraction. Don't let him hook you in."

"Why would he lie?"

"To unhinge you! Just because you want her to be alive doesn't mean she is. You're fooling yourself, Eight. She's dead and she isn't coming back to play happy fucking families."

His harsh words punch through my chest. Feeling like I can't breathe, the world becomes draped in shades of red. Blood. Anger. Love. Retribution. This colour has so many meanings. For me, all I see is the arterial spray that coated my childhood home's kitchen as it poured from Logan's throat.

"She's alive."

Seven's fierce gaze glares down at me. "Don't let him in your head!"

"I c-can't do this…"

"Goddammit," he curses. "It's taking every ounce of control I have not to put a bullet between this asshole's eyes. I need you, Eight. Come back to me."

Staring up at his savage eyes, I can almost glimpse the surface of the ocean I'm drowning in. We need to pull each other out. Both of us are incapable of managing emotions anymore. Seven stands frozen as I smash into him, already seeking out his lips. Our mouths meet in a hot frenzy.

I don't care if Hunter and the team are on their way. The monster that broke us both is lying mere inches away, somehow still breathing. He doesn't deserve to exist in this world, but if I kill him, I'll lose the only lead we have to finding Phoenix.

Seven is right.

This is the only way.

"How long do we have?" I ask against his lips.

"Ten minutes, max."

Nodding, I take the pair of handcuffs that Hunter issued us with from my coat pocket. It feels like poetic justice to cuff Lazlo's unconscious form, attaching his wrists to a huge metal pipe to keep him trapped.

With our hostage taken care of, I grab Seven's hand. We run side by side, slipping into a nearby abandoned structure. Dodging smashed windows and littered debris, I slam him against a crumbling brick wall.

"You want to do this right now?" Seven asks gruffly.

"Shut the fuck up. It's this or I gut that son of a bitch like a fish. I can't do nothing. I'm losing my mind here."

Eyes darkening, Seven's hand curls around my throat. "You want me to hurt you, princess?"

Fire burns in my lungs from the lack of air as he begins to tighten his grip. I'm shaking all over, two people warring inside of me. One of them is going to win this battle. I can't let it be Patient Eight. If she sneaks back in, I won't ever find myself again.

"Yes," I squeeze out. "Hurt m-me or I'll hurt him."

Flipping us around, Seven crushes me against the wall. My hands meet the hard brick as he bends me over by pushing my lower back. His movements are harsh and hurried, without any gentle introductions. I don't give a damn; I'm happy to be handled roughly.

When my borrowed combat trousers and panties are shoved down my hips, I gasp at the cold, night air kissing my bare pussy. It's freezing in here, even with my entire body flushed. Seven's palm cracks against my ass cheek, sending a flash of pain straight down south.

"Do you think of me when you're fucking them, Eight?"

His fingers slide between my legs, seeking out the wetness gathering at my core. I bite back a response as he shoves two fingers deep inside in an attempt to coax the truth free.

"Answer me," Seven commands.

Gliding in and out, he keeps torturing me with his fingers. I have to bite my lip when he circles my clit and pinches. I won't give it to him. I have enough possessive hotheads in my life without his bullshit too.

"I bet you do," he croons. "I hope you see my face when they make you come. Do you remember the night I whispered to you while you touched yourself for me, princess?"

I can't suppress a gasp when he pulls his fingers from my pussy, hitting my ass again instead. Each touch is like the lash of a fiery whip. We're running out of time, and it makes this even hotter.

"That was one time," I manage to respond.

"I knew you remembered it. The little moans you made while finishing all over your fingers had me so hard. I wanted to break through the concrete and fuck you myself."

The zip of his fly has my heart rate skittering with anticipation. My legs are shaking, even without much foreplay. I don't need him to hold my hand and pretend this is anything but animal lust.

"You look so beautiful, bent over and glistening for me, Eight."

"No time," I groan, feeling the hard press of his cock against my entrance. "Make me forget what that son of a bitch has done to us."

Seven's fingers bury in my crop of hair, wrenching the short strands. Without warning, he surges inside of me. I cry out, full to the brim with his impressive length. It takes some adjustment, but he doesn't give me time to get comfortable before starting to move.

"Scream for me, Patient Eight. Let that bastard hear his failure. We're still here. We're fucking alive."

His thrusts set a relentless pace. Each stroke of his cock adds fuel to the flames, burning all rationality to a crisp and leaving my mind empty. I can't focus on anything but the man worshipping me in every violent way I want. His palm bruises me, hitting my ass over and over.

The beat of a familiar helicopter breaks our gasping tangle. Knowing we could get caught at any moment adds to Seven's urgency. It's like he's hammering his rage into me, expelling the madness in the only way he knows how. Hurting someone.

I let my release build, spiralling higher and higher. Every muscle in my body is quivering and ready to explode. The helicopter touches down outside with a loud whirring sound.

"Sev," I moan. "We have incoming."

"Silence, Eight. I'm not done with you."

Reaching around to tweak my clit again, the sharp burst of sensation sets my body alight. I scream out my orgasm, barely able to hold myself up against the wall. Seven's strokes become more ragged, relentlessly beating into me. Just as I expect him to finish, he pulls out and spins me around.

"On your knees, princess."

"What?"

The sharp slap of his hand against my face sends bolts of electricity down my spine. Not able to process the strike, Seven's hand on my shoulder forces me to kneel before him. The savagery in his molten eyes should scare me. I'm entirely at the mercy of the violent beast that lives within him.

"Open wide. Show me how well you can swallow my come, and I promise not to tell your stupid little boyfriends about our plan to kill Lazlo."

It's like his claws are buried deep in my mind, pulling all the right strings. My mouth falls open, ready and waiting to accept his shaft. With his cock nudging the back of my throat, Seven releases a bellowing grunt.

He fills my mouth with salty warmth. Pumping several more times before sliding his dick from between my lips, Seven watches intently. Without breaking eye contact, I swallow every last drop of come from my tongue, even stopping to lick my lips.

"Did I do a good job?" I ask innocently.

There's awe in his eyes. "You're fucking breathtaking."

"I'll take that as a yes, then."

Finding my feet, I hurry to pull my clothes back into place. Seven doesn't protest as I march back up to him and capture his lips in a fast and furious kiss, ensuring he can taste his own seed in my mouth. His low grumble of approval has me wanting to bend over all over again.

"Jesus, Brooke."

I still, confused. "What did you just call me?"

Seven looks equally unnerved by his own slip-up. Shaking his head, he focuses on fastening his trousers, ignoring my stare.

"Come on." He offers me his hand. "I can't believe I'm doing this. Let's go hand this sack of shit over to Hunter. We can keep what's left when they're done."

Digging my heels in, I don't follow.

Seven stops and looks over his shoulder at me.

"What is it?"

"It's just... I... well, I care about you, Sev. Deep down, you're a better person than you think you are. I just thought you should know that."

The frown on his face deepens. Seven doesn't understand and process feelings like the rest of us, though he's changing with each day spent back in the real world. For a moment, I think I spot a flare of hope in his gaze. It's quickly extinguished.

"You shouldn't care about me," he deadpans without emotion. "I'm not worth caring about. You have your family. You don't need me adding to the burden."

"You're part of that family now."

He finally lifts his eyes to mine. "Perhaps."

Taking the lead this time, I tug his hand so he follows. It's time to get what we need from Lazlo and end this madness. Bancroft's deadline is still ticking down at the back of my mind. If we can locate Phoenix, our next challenge will be getting him out.

We need to do something drastic.

And I have just the idea.

CHAPTER 18
PHOENIX

LYDIA - HIGHLY SUSPECT

SHIVERING VIOLENTLY, I stare up at the cracked ceiling of my cell. They moved me in here several hours ago, needing to scrub the bloodstains from the last place.

The steady throbbing of my right hand has faded into a dull, numb ache as survival instincts kicked in. I held my screams back until they removed the third finger.

Now, my throat is torn and hoarse.

Bancroft wanted everything.

Names. Locations. Plans.

I've never set foot inside of Sabre, so I'm fucking worthless. That only angered him more. Afterwards, the beating worsened out of spite. I allowed myself to mentally check out, picturing Brooklyn's and Eli's faces.

There's an aggressive bang on the door before it swings open. Bancroft's favourite, thick-skulled subordinate, Harrison, peers in at me with palpable glee beneath his military buzz cut and unyielding eyes. The grin on his face can't mean anything good for me.

"Ready to comply, Kent?"

Using my one uninjured arm to sit up, I gather saliva in my mouth and spit directly at him. Harrison's smile transforms into a glower as it lands right at his feet.

"Bite me, dickwipe."

"I'll take that as a no. That's cool, man. More play time for us."

"Want to dislocate my other shoulder? Maybe take another finger?" I snark.

Popping my own socket back in place was one of the most painful things I've endured, but I didn't fancy losing the whole arm.

Harrison smirks. "Nothing quite so pedestrian, don't worry."

I can barely shuffle backwards as he approaches, unable to run from his long, confident strides. A steel-capped boot to the face knocks me unconscious. Lost in a dark haze, I come back around to low conversation and the clank of metal bars being secured.

It takes all of my remaining energy to wrestle my heavy lids open. Days of abuse, zero food, and licking droplets of water from my cell walls have left me broken. As my latest prison settles around me, the last of my courage dissipates. I'm locked in a tiny, oppressive metal cage, surrounded by steel bars.

The odd sense of inertia draws me to look down. My cage isn't screwed into the floor. Instead, I'm dangling several feet in the air. Directly beneath the cage, a vat of murky water awaits. It's wide enough to fit the entire thing, while a foamy scum floats on the top of black, sludge-like water.

Bancroft's voice crackles through a speaker. "I've grown tired of your lies, Mr Kent. This is your final chance to tell us something of use. After that, you will be disposed of."

Wrapping a hand around the bars, I laugh maniacally. "Do whatever the fuck you want. I still won't give you shit. My family won't leave me here. They'll kill you soon."

"Good," Bancroft declares.

My blood chills. "Good?"

"Let them come. I'm aware that you're worthless to me, Mr Kent. When your family comes running to save your pitiful hide, I'll finally have patients Seven and Eight within my grasp. That's your purpose here."

Fuck, fuck, fuck.

I'm the motherfucking bait.

"Why torture me, then?"

Bancroft snorts. "We need some entertainment."

The deep groan of chain links grinding sparks panic within me. The cage is shuddering as it begins to lower into the putrid water. I don't waste any precious energy shouting or fighting, it won't stop them. As my body is lowered into the freezing depths, too many disgusting scents to process assault me.

I'm swallowed by decay and death.

The world disappears into inky darkness.

Clamping my mouth and eyes shut, I float like a dead body. My lungs begin to burn before long, screaming out for relief. No matter how hard I tug on the metal bars, they refuse to budge. The stumps where my fingers used to be burn, and my shoulder is too weak to do much damage.

Fighting is futile, but human instinct doesn't listen to reason. Terror and panic force me to batter the cage regardless. At last, exhaustion pulls me under as my chest screams for oxygen. In the semi-conscious haze, I accidentally open my mouth and swallow a mouthful of water.

Whatever was in this pool before me, it's been left behind to rot. Then, there's light and so much oxygen, I can't even gulp it down. Pulled out of the water, the cage dangles on its heavy chains. I cough up water as Bancroft's laughter reverberates around me.

"Enjoy your swim, Mr Kent?"

"F-Fuck you!"

"Manners. Lower him back in."

Peering through my soaked blue hair, I catch sight of someone on the platform behind the cage. It's another guard, one I've seen hanging around and watching the abuse. I'm submerged again before I can protest, even as someone bursts in and shouts for Bancroft's attention.

Back in the water, I wait without hope of rescue. This time, they leave me in for much longer. Whatever commotion is going on, I've been left and forgotten. Fuck, am I going to die here? I thrash and writhe before being pulled into unconsciousness by oxygen deprivation.

Her face finds me in the dark.

My lighthouse, guiding me back home.

"Firecracker," I whisper.

We're surrounded by packed bookshelves and empty desks in Blackwood's library. She saunters towards me, sprawling out in my lap like a lazy cat seeking attention. I cup the back of her head, letting our lips meet. It doesn't matter if the CCTV cameras and guards are watching.

Her love is worth the punishment.

"Do you dream about the future?" she murmurs, curling her slender limbs around me. "We could have a life after Blackwood. Out there, in the real world."

I tuck sun-kissed hair behind her ear. "I want to see you get out of here and finally get better. We could do anything... be anyone. Live far away from this madness as a real family."

"All of us?"

"We love you," I reply simply. "Your future is our future."

The lightest smile plays across her lips. That's how I know this isn't real. My Brooklyn doesn't look like that when she smiles. It's always underscored by pain and emptiness shining in her eyes, despite the hope tugging at her lips. She never fully smiles. Not really.

"Then you better wake up," Brooklyn says.

"I don't want to let you go. This might be the last time I see you."

Her hand cups my cheek, gently stroking. "Not a chance. You don't have my permission to die yet. Hold on, Nix."

Air is pushed past my numb lips as two firm hands pump my chest. I come screaming back into the real world. Rolling onto my side, pain races through me as I vomit water over and over again, unable to peel my eyes open.

"That's it, get it all up."

"Brooke?" I gasp.

"Afraid not. Just little ole me."

While I'm gulping down air, someone carefully pulls my eyes open and shines a phone's flashlight in them. I flinch back, every single inch of me throbbing with agony. When the light is done burning my retinas, I find the same guard staring down at me.

"Get off me."

"Relax, Nix. It's me."

Glancing around the room that has emptied out, the guard pulls the cap from their head. Beneath that, a short, brown wig is tossed aside, freeing a shock of bright-pink hair. The man becomes a woman right before my eyes, peeling off fake facial hair last.

"A-Alyssa?"

"It's still Sadie to you. Can you sit up?"

Guided upright, I blink and stare at her. Clothed in Incendia's signature black garb, her feminine features have been carefully disguised, but I see it now. She's been here all along, hiding in plain sight.

"Did you get a kick out of watching them beat me up?"

Sadie scoffs. "Hardly. I have an appearance to maintain. As soon as I found you, I alerted the team."

"Brooke? Is she here?"

"They're all coming."

"What about Bancroft?"

"Momentarily distracted. Theo leaked the video Hudson took in Blackwood's Z Wing to the media last night. There are huge protests outside the gates of here and Hazelthorn."

Coughing up more black water that sears my throat, Sadie hammers me on the back. Once the fit is over, I shove dank, wet hair out of my eyes. We're still alone. Bancroft and his cronies have vanished.

"You really went for the nuclear option."

Sadie shrugs. "It won't last long. Incendia will have the video deleted from existence soon enough. But we've caught them off guard. It buys us some time."

Grabbing my bad arm, Sadie tries to pull me to my feet. I hiss and yank it away from her, cradling my aching joint. When she spots the blood leaking from my inflamed, swollen right hand, her eyes widen.

"Uh, Nix?"

"I don't know where my fingers are," I answer for her. "You didn't see that bit, huh?"

She shakes her head. "I'm so sorry."

Taking my other arm instead, Sadie finally gets me on my feet. Everything goes a little wonky, forcing me to lean my entire weight into her. She guides me down the metal platform, my body trembling as filthy water clings to my bloodied clothes.

"Hold on. I'm gonna get you out of here."

Hold on.

Hold on.

Hold on.

Her voice blurs and becomes one with Brooklyn's in my mind. She's walking here with me, pouring her strength into my broken body. Despite popping my shoulder back in, it still throbs, but not as badly as my hand. My feet carry me on instinct while I float on a lake of fire.

"Here, put this on."

Sadie helps to strip the sodden t-shirt from my body and offers me a clean black one. I don't miss the way her eyes linger on my multi-coloured torso. My cracked ribs are black and blue. Stepping out of the boxers that Bancroft permitted me to leave on, she helps me into cargo trousers next.

With a black cap on my hair, I look like one of them. Sadie places her wig and hat back on, minus that fake facial hair. We look pretty shit, but it's better than nothing. Pulling my good arm back over her shoulder, I'm led into the basement's shadows.

"Bancroft will speak to the crowd to try to appease them," she says, winding down a lengthy corridor. "This is his base, while Augustus's territory was Blackwood. He has his own office upstairs."

"What about Kade's dad?"

"Not that I've seen. But there's someone else—"

The thud of footsteps ends our conversation. We're nearly above ground, the signs leading to what seem to be dormitories starting to appear. Many locked and bolted cells surround us in the gloom, although most seem to be unoccupied. This is a smaller operation than Blackwood.

Standing between us and salvation, a human skeleton guards the passageway leading above ground. Protruding limbs and painfully hollow eye sockets stare back at us with palpable misery. The woman's tiny frame is clothed in a black uniform that hangs off her.

I immediately recognise her inhuman gaze.

She was there in London.

This is the evil bitch who sedated me and brought me straight to Bancroft for judgement. The empty shell of a person begins to approach us with measured steps, two long, sharp knives clutched in her hands.

Sadie loosens her grip on me. "It's her. On my mark, run and don't look back."

"Who is she?"

Our feet begin to retreat away from the approaching monster.

"Patient Delta."

CHAPTER 19
BROOKLYN

RIGGED - THE PLOT IN YOU

"DAMN, Theo. You sure know how to make a stir."

His awkward chuckle fills my ear. "Didn't take much. The bloodthirsty press did most of the work. Who doesn't love a good national scandal?"

Tucked into Hudson's side, we stare at the huge crowd of protesters swarming Harrowdean's gates. We're hidden in the forest to the side of the institute, keeping watch while Hunter and his team infiltrate from the rear. The loading bay has been cleared for them to enter through.

This place is a lot smaller than Blackwood, but still intimidating as hell in all its gothic, Victorian beauty. It looks like an asylum of a time long past, all ornate crests and stained windows. It's almost ironic, knowing what cruel practices continue to be performed behind closed doors.

The blare of a new alarm cuts through the crowd's angry shouting and chants. Looking over my shoulder, I check that Theo's van is still parked in the distance, out of sight.

"The patients are going into lockdown," Hudson observes. "Right on cue. That should clear the grounds so Hunter and the team can enter undetected."

"I can't believe Sadie found Phoenix in there."

"We got lucky. This is the hard part."

We both study the swarm of black-clad guards marching down the driveway. They establish a barrier between the protest and the winding road leading to the institute. A convoy is waiting behind the iron bars of the gates, beneath another ornate crest. Bancroft is sandwiched between his bodyguards, preparing to speak.

"We're going in," Hunter announces.

"Be careful," I respond into the comms.

Enzo and Seven are accompanying him, along with two of Sabre's best agents. Their job is to quietly extract Sadie and Phoenix while Bancroft stops this mess from imploding. Despite knowing that Seven can more than hold his own, I can't help but worry. I never wanted to see him inside of an institute again.

Hudson squeezes my arm. "He'll be okay."

"How can you be sure?"

Meeting his oceanic eyes, I find resolution staring back at me. He's always been able to read my mind with a mere look. Hudson traces his thumb along my jawline, each gentle touch revealing a softness to him that I rarely see. Just sweet, loving glimpses amidst the possession and control.

"Because he has something to live for. We all do."

I swallow hard. "I really hope you're right."

"I usually am, baby."

"Arrogant? Sure."

Despite the carnage around us, our lips meet like they simply cannot bear to be parted. I will always long to be the air that Hudson breathes, the reason his shrivelled, black heart continues to pump each day. He owns a broken, twisted piece of me that nobody could ever come close to.

"When this is all over, I'm going to spend every single day of my life proving myself to you," he says above the shouting. "I want to be the man you deserve, blackbird. The person I should have been all along."

Pecking his lips again, I sit back. "You always have been that man, Hud. I never wanted the good parts of you. Your darkness is my home. The rest is just an added bonus."

"I fucking love you."

"Ditto, dickhead."

Our tender exchange is interrupted by the boom of Bancroft's voice through a speaker. We both turn to look from our hiding spot in the trees. He emerges from his swarm of guards, attempting to appease the angry crowd. Placards and pumped fists announce their fury as the protest grows even louder.

"People are really mad," I comment.

"Why wouldn't they be?"

"I just figured nobody would care."

His hand finds mine. "Shit like this gives me hope that there might be a chance for us out there. People need to stay angry; it's the only way the truth will come out."

The spark of flames breaks through the evening gloom. Someone has lit a Molotov cocktail and thrown it straight at Incendia's goons. Bancroft is shoved out of the way, with two terrifying slabs of muscle descending upon the guilty culprit. I can spot the batons and tasers in their hands from here.

We watch for several minutes, each second adding fuel to the flames of indignation. More protesters are getting physical and attempting to assault Bancroft's hired skins. Every snap of a camera infuriates Bancroft as he attempts to shout meaningless platitudes, claiming this is nothing but a smear campaign.

Hudson taps his earpiece. "Status update? Things are getting hairy out here."

Radio silence.

Dread sinks in as we wait, watching the tensions escalate further. Incendia doesn't care if they have the authority or not, resorting to violence to tame the crowd. At the back of the protests, the cameras continue to capture the ordeal. People are finally paying attention.

"Why aren't they answering?" I ask after several minutes.

"Signal may be disrupted in the basement."

"Sadie was supposed to meet them fifteen minutes ago. I don't like this. Something is wrong."

Glancing at Theo's nondescript van in the distance, it remains unmoved from the thick cover of shrubbery. I hate not being able to see my guys inside. Anxiety itches along my skin, causing my fingers to quake.

"We can't just sit here. Come on."

Hudson growls his frustration as I take off, making a beeline for the van. We have to take the long way around to remain concealed in the trees. All three guys inside flinch when I slam the door open. Theo's wired into one of his contraptions, with a dozen different video feeds open.

"Are you okay?" Kade immediately reaches for me.

"Our comms have gone down."

"Us too," Theo grumbles. "I'm boosting the signal, but still nothing. They must be running a blocker inside the institute. I'm trying to hack their system."

I watch as Kade's eyes stray to the rapid lines of computer code racing across the screens. He locates a laptop and digs in, exchanging low whispers with Theo. Eli is sat with his back against the van wall, impatiently flipping his penknife in one hand.

"Anything?" Hudson prompts, hands braced on his knees.

"Just static," Theo confirms. "We're running a malware program to take their systems down, but they've prepared for us. I can't skip over the code before it rewrites itself."

The sounds of increasing shouts and another explosion of fiery glass reach us. Looks like Incendia more than has its hands full. Our plan should be working, but we're still not hearing a damn thing and the clock is ticking. They're beyond late.

"Fuck this," I decide. "I'm going in."

Hudson grabs my arm. "Not a chance."

"Take your hand off me before I break it. Our family is inside that hell hole. Either come with me or stay here, but I'm going in."

Fisting his wild hair, Hudson looks ready to knock me out with his bare hands. I'm prepared to leave him behind when there's a low hissing from our earpieces, followed by the sound of laughter. Unlike Bancroft's pompous drone, the voice is rough and gravelly, like an abused throat after too much screaming.

"Who is this?" I ask shakily.

The rasping chuckle ceases, leaving uneasy silence.

"Where is Phoenix?"

My eyes connect with Eli's wide, emerald orbs. He's clutching the penknife in his white-knuckled grip, waiting for the same thing we both want to hear.

"Where is he?!" I repeat.

Heavy breathing. No words.

"Who the fuck are you?"

There's a sharp slapping sound of a fist meeting flesh, followed by yelping. It's light and feminine, beneath the tinge of pain. Far-off shouting filters through the earpiece, still punctuated by the silent, anticipatory breathing of the attacker.

Something wraps around my throat and squeezes. A tendril of sickness, the weight of family history sinking deep into my bones. I can't escape this drowning pool of blood. It's pulling me down... deeper and deeper.

"Mum?" I whisper softly. "Is that you?"

"Brooke..." Hudson mutters.

I wave him off, my breath still held.

Please don't be real.

You're dead.

My whole life hasn't been a lie.

"Come," the dead voice whispers.

There's a crunch as the line goes dead, like the earpiece has been crushed. My question hangs in the air, unanswered. With the iron grip on my lungs refusing to abate, I'm left staring at Hudson's face.

"Are you with me or without me?"

His eyes harden with determination. "Always with you."

I turn to look at Kade and Eli. "With me?"

Nodding, Eli pockets his penknife and quickly stands. His lips mouth the silent words *with you*. Kade ditches his laptop and joins us outside the van, leaving Theo to continue beating his keyboard into submission.

"Let's go get our boy," he declares.

Theo snatches two guns from the weapons box and slides them across the van's floor without looking up from his laptop.

"Be careful and don't get killed. I am not doing that paperwork."

The riot of noise from the crowd in the distance accompanies our footsteps into the unknown, gradually fading as we pass behind the perimeter of the institute. Much like Blackwood, it's a testament to the wealth and opulence that Incendia wields as a weapon. Another slick, well-funded campaign enabling the abuse and exploitation.

Sliding through the chain-link fence that has been broken with wire cutters, we enter the loading bay. It's spookily deserted, with nothing but empty boxes and parked vehicles. The bay door hangs open ominously, despite the flashing red light above it.

"This doesn't feel right," Kade murmurs.

Hopping up on the brick platform, I peek inside the dark institute. "Whatever Bancroft is doing here, it's nothing we haven't faced before. Come on, we're running out of time."

We sneak inside together. This part of the small institute is ghostly silent, packed with storage rooms and empty cupboards. With my knife clutched in hand, I take the lead. We studied the floor plans meticulously while Theo was busy stirring up a media shitstorm.

Unlike Blackwood, Harrowdean's experimental wing lies beneath a disused dormitory. It's approximately half the size, but features observation rooms along with ancient solitary cells. The architecture is a lot older, keeping the pre-existing design of the asylum.

"Can you hear that?" Hudson asks as we race through the corridors.

Pausing on the threshold of a glamorous, refurbished reception area lit with chandeliers, we all strain to hear the distant roar. Too many voices to count, screaming and shouting, like an almighty brawl is taking place. We're too far from the front gates for it to be the protest.

"Patients?" I hedge.

"They are supposed to be locked down," Hudson observes.

Kade glances out of a window, his face lit by the glow of the quad lights. "Not so much. Take a look at this."

All gathered, we peer out at the disaster. Harrowdean's patients are far from locked down in their rooms. Something obviously went wrong. In the generous space of the tree-lined quad, a mob is forming. Fists fly and patients brawl, spilling blood and tears across the cobbled stone.

Some are yelling and wrestling, while others simply watch the chaos unfold. The few remaining guards not dealing with Theo's pals from the press are attempting to tame the wild animals and failing.

"Where are they?" I scan the crowd.

Kade points across the quad, towards the distant lights. "That's Kingsman dorms. Decommissioned for patient use. Sabre's research indicates the experimental wing is housed beneath it."

"Only a sea of lunatics between us and them," Hudson concurs.

"They aren't lunatics." I glance between them all emphatically. "Hell, these people are us. Trapped by a broken system. Powerless. Bullied. We're better than the world that cast them aside."

Out of them all, I don't expect Eli to speak.

"N-Nobody... g-gets hurt."

I take his trembling hand in mine. "Only Incendia."

Cracking open the heavy doors, we slowly inch outside and stick close to the high stone walls of the main building. Floodlights have been slammed on to reveal the growing brawl, with a few more guards arriving to bring order to the mayhem. Linking hands, we begin to pelt through the crowd.

"Straight ahead, take a left," Kade instructs.

With my gaze trained on the disused dormitory, I'm too late to spot an incoming blur of motion. Someone ploughs straight into my side, tackling me to the wet grass. Eli's hand is ripped from mine as I fall.

"It's too loud! No!"

A fist connects with my jaw, while a tangle of bones attempts to pin me to the ground. Grabbing the young girl by the shoulders, I use my strength to wrestle her aside. She can't put up much of a fight, her stick-thin body soon becoming trapped beneath me.

"No! I'm scared, let me out!"

"Hey, hey," I shout down at her. "It's alright, I'm not one of them. You're okay."

"I want to go home! I want my mum... please..."

With the fight leaving her in an instant, she goes completely limp. Tears streak across her pale cheeks beneath a bush of tangled auburn hair in need of a good wash. Hudson attempts to offer me a hand up, but I shake him off.

"What's your name?" I ask urgently.

The young girl peers up at me with trepidation. "I'm... I... I don't know. I want to go home. It's s-s-so loud..."

"Jesus," Kade curses. "She's out of it."

"Let's get you up, okay?" With a lump in my throat, I help her to stand. "I know you're scared. All you want is your home."

She nods rapidly, like a timid bunny rabbit. "They're f-fighting."

Wrapping an arm around her shoulders, I point to the darkened reception where we came from. "See that old building there? You're going to run inside and find a quiet corner to hide in, okay? Can you do that for me?"

Giving her a shove, I watch her slender limbs scamper into the night. She doesn't look back, hugging herself tight while holding back the tears. Unable to shake the emotion raging through me, I force myself to leave her behind.

"Head around the side." Hudson points ahead. "That was the rendezvous point."

Bearing left, we leave the chaos of the quad and fall into quieter, swaying juniper trees. The abandoned dorms are oddly quiet, lit by faint lights but seemingly deserted. When we reach the entrance doors leading inside, we all stop dead.

"Oh my God," I say under my breath.

Lifeless limbs splayed out before the wide entry steps, one of the agents that accompanied the team lies dead. Wilson. His throat has been brutally slashed open, dripping bright red on to the ground. Kade picks his way around the corpse, looking nauseous.

"They must be inside. Watch each other's backs."

Bancroft's voice cuts through the air from the distance, punctuated by the sounds of patients being battered and subjugated. He's taming the crowd. We're running out of time.

"Hurry," I urge, climbing the stairs. "We need to leave."

Inside the dorms, bare overhead bulbs light the state of disuse. This wing is clearly used for nothing but shady dealings. Old signs point towards the different floors, with one denoting the basement ahead. Taking several sharp turns, we almost trip over another huge body on the ground.

"Enzo!" I screech.

His giant frame is sprawled out, breath hissing between his clenched teeth. He's barely conscious, one hand clamped over a bleeding wound in his leg. Kade drops to his knees, setting to work analysing him.

"Go! I got this!" he urges.

"We can't split up now." Hudson searches around us with his gun raised.

Eli removes his belt before crouching next to Kade. Together, they get Enzo sitting up with his back meeting the wall. The belt wraps around his leg as a tourniquet, hoping to stem the heavy flow of blood.

"D-Downstairs," Enzo grits out. "Ambush."

"Dammit." Hudson glances at the stairs leading down, then back at Kade. "Get him back to Theo. He's lost too much blood. We'll go ahead and find the others."

"Not alone," Kade rebuts.

"We don't have a choice. Take Eli, get Enzo out. We'll find our boy."

Hudson steals my hand, dragging me onwards as Kade protests. I cast them a final, desperate look before we begin our descent, uncertain if we'll ever see the world beyond this basement again. The last time we were somewhere like this, it took everything to leave with our lives.

Loud voices and shouting reverberate around the thick concrete that leaches all heat from our bodies. As we emerge in the subterranean paradise beneath the dorms, the distinct sound of crying fills our ears. It sounds like a grief-stricken animal, mourning a lost cub. Hudson moves in front of me.

"No... p-please... No..."

Someone's pleading guides us into the commotion. Amidst a long corridor of locked cells and bare bulbs, a red-stained crime scene unfolds. I don't know where to begin, there's so much blood. Kneeling in a rapidly spreading puddle, Hunter's face is shielded by his curtain of long hair.

I'm stunned to realise the frenzied begging and soft sound of crying is coming from him. He's knelt over, cradling someone close to his chest. To his right, Seven stands still as stone, staring down at something. Blood is steadily leaking across the parquet floor.

"Nix," I whimper aloud.

On his knees at the end of the corridor, Phoenix's head is lowered, execution style. He dares to lift his eyes to meet mine for a second. Shock and agony race across his heavily beaten face, like he can't quite believe what he's seeing.

"Eight," Seven thunders.

Tentatively stepping into the firing line, I give Hunter a wide berth. When I get to Seven's side, I realise who is cradled in Hunter's arms. Torn apart by violent slashes and numerous deep stab wounds, her eyes are slowly falling shut. They meet mine at the last moment.

"I'm s-s-sorry," she croaks.

"Alyssa." Hunter chokes a sob. "Stay with me, my love. Don't do this. I need you."

He's stroking her stained pink hair, their lips almost touching. She tries to cup his cheek and leaves a bright-red swipe on his skin. It's a devastating sight. Her eyes shut forever as mortality pulls her soul ashore.

"No. Alyssa..."

Seven watches his sister slip away, unable to traverse the distance between them. Not a single emotion crosses his face. The only sign that he feels anything is in his clenched fist.

Hunter's head lowers once she's gone. He looks nothing like the formidable pillar of strength I've come to fear. In this moment, he's another broken victim of Incendia.

"Weapons down!"

Metres ahead, the dead-eyed woman offers her ultimatum. The knife in her hand meets Phoenix's throat, digging in hard enough to break the skin. More blood soaks his pale flesh. I scrape together the courage to meet her stare, searching her face for any hint of recognition.

She doesn't look like my mother. Her hair is gone, leaving her skull exposed to the world. Gnarly scar tissue warps most of her features, shaded by dark circles, as if she hasn't slept a single night in her life. While the burns corroborate Lazlo's story, I can't find the person I knew in her eyes.

"Who are you?" I shout at the ghost.

In answer, she presses the knife against Phoenix's throat even harder. He chokes out his terror, a river of tears soaking into the discoloured skin of his face. One slip and he'll be dead. I think I'll die with him.

"Weapons down," she repeats in a dull voice.

Hudson aims straight at her. "After you."

She pulls the knife from Phoenix's throat. My relief is quickly extinguished as the sharp tip buries into his left thigh. She stabs him so hard, it reaches all the way to the handle. Phoenix's raw scream slices through my head like a razor blade to the wrist, right before he slumps.

"You're going to fucking die for that!"

His attacker simply shrugs. "You didn't listen."

Taking another blade from the belt around her nonexistent waist, she rolls up the sleeves of her black shirt, as if preparing to butcher us all. It exposes the translucent skin stretched across her bones, broken by a single swirl of dark, ancient ink. My heart almost breaks free from my ribcage.

What's this, Mummy? Letters?

A reminder to always love my little miracles, Brooke.

Why would you forget about us?

Sometimes Mummy's head gets loud, baby. But I'll always come back to you.

"No. It isn't true!"

My voice is a lightning strike of disbelief and horror. Hudson tries to say something to me, but it doesn't break through the haze of memories. Everything else falls into insignificance. Unlike the many months I've spent hallucinating my mother, this ghost cannot be returned to my imagination.

Because... she isn't a ghost at all.

Lazlo was right all along.

I'm staring at Melanie West.

My feet move without being instructed. I dodge Hudson's hands, stepping further into no man's land. Neither he nor Seven follow, but they keep their weapons raised. I don't need a weapon. Bullets and blades won't protect me from this hellish truth. It's too late to fight my way out of this.

"Mum?" I vocalise gently.

Her head cocks, two washed-out eyes scraping over me.

"It's... it's me." I inch closer with my empty hands raised. "Brooklyn. I'm your daughter."

Mouth clicking open, she doesn't speak a single word.

"I'm here," I attempt to say through my tears. "Please... Mum. Drop the knife. None of us are going to hurt you. We don't have to do this."

I swear, the smallest spark of humanity lights her irises. Still, the blade remains in her grip, inches from Phoenix's semi-conscious body. He's losing so much blood. I'm almost close enough to pull the knife from his leg and bury it straight in my mother's chest... but I can't.

Despite everything, I fucking can't.

I've lost so much.

Her. Dad. Logan.

My childhood. My innocence.

My freedom. My sanity.

My own mind.

"I can't… I don't want to lose you," I whisper brokenly. "You remember the sun, Mum? Every morning and every night, we climbed up on the roof to watch it. You always said—"

"P-Put yourself… way… b-beauty," she botches, her voice barely audible.

More tears course down my cheeks. "That's right."

"Where is h-h-he?"

Her grip on the knife slackens as she stares, her eyes melting my skin like battery acid.

"Who, Mum?"

"S-Such… good… b-boy…"

My shaking hand raises, close enough to whisper along the tattooed skin of her wrist. Expecting my touch to break that final boundary, I meet her eyes again. The dying embers of the car crash that stole my family from me stare back at me.

Her hand raises, fingers on the verge of wrapping around mine. I can see my mother. She's there. Swimming back up to the surface, battling to find me again. I need to grab her, pull her up, save her…

The blast of gunfire explodes in my eardrums. The bullet tears into my mother's shoulder and she stumbles with a vicious snarl. Blood hits my lips in a light spray before she falls, her mouth hanging open.

"No! Mum!"

"Grab them!" Hunter commands.

I try to reach for my mother. All I want is to cradle her in my arms, stop the blood flowing from her shoulder. She's there, so fucking close. I could have a parent again. When someone's arms band around me like great steel train tracks, I'm cruelly dragged away.

"I'm sorry, princess."

Bucking and thrashing, Seven's lips meet my ear as he orders me to stop fighting. I can see Hudson picking Phoenix's limp body up like a baby before Mum can hurt him again. She's down on the floor, clutching her shoulder and staring straight at me.

Seven tosses me over his shoulder, not giving me the opportunity to escape. All I can do is hammer my fists against his back, screaming for him to put me down. I have to get to her. If we leave her here, I'll never see my mother again. Bancroft will crush what memories she's accessed.

"Let me down! Stop!" I howl.

His arms tighten, pinning me to him. "She killed my sister. I'll spare her life for you, but I won't let you die for her."

"No!"

"We're leaving, Eight."

"MUM! MUM!"

My distraught screams bounce off the concrete walls surrounding us as we flee.

Beyond Sadie's dead body and Phoenix's bloodied form, all I see is the bleak, hopeless gaze of the monster watching us go. She chooses not to pursue, lying and awaiting punishment instead.

In that moment, I don't see Lazlo's empty machine.

All I see is my last remaining parent.

Letting us escape is the only thing she has left to give me.

CHAPTER 20
KADE

RESET ME - NOTHING BUT THIEVES

ARMS FOLDED, I stare through the window into the private hospital room. Phoenix is still out of it, several drips feeding antibiotics and pain relief into his prone form. His hand is resting at his side, ensconced in bandages.

Eli stands next to me, his lips pursed. He's barely moved from this spot in the few days since we got Phoenix back, even when they operated on the remains of his amputated fingers. It was touch and go when an infection took root, but he's finally stabilised.

Sunup to sundown, Eli awaits the day Phoenix's eyes will open.

Until then, we've lost him as well.

"Eli." I rest a hand on his shoulder. "The memorial begins in half an hour. I'm sure Brooke's going to need you there."

He shrugs my hand aside. "N-No."

"What do you mean, no? We're set to start giving evidence tomorrow. Everyone is on edge. We need to stick together right now."

"Together?" he snarls without a stutter.

Turning his furious, green-eyed gaze on me, Eli's face has transformed with anger. It's unnerving to see his usually silent self so worked up and intent on tearing me a new asshole.

"We w-were safe." He points at Phoenix. "Coming h-here... m-mistake."

"We had to do something. This is our lives we're talking about."

"What l-lives?! T-taken everything... look... h-him!"

"And we're taking it all back," I snap while throwing my suit jacket on. "The world is finally listening to us. We have their attention. This will all be over soon."

"What c-cost?"

His simple, sharp question cuts me to the core. It's the same one that Phoenix threw at me several months ago, before we escaped. I've always been the first one to make the hard choices. Sometimes, you must compromise and bend your own morals to defeat the darkest of evils.

To escape, we had to become the bad guys.

But to win this war, we must find ourselves again.

Unable to appease him, I leave Eli to his silent vigil. He returns to staring at Phoenix, his jaw set in a hard, merciless line. I can't give him what he wants. The prospect of peace seems as far away as ever, while each day we suffer more and more losses.

Sabre's medical wing lies on the fourteenth floor of the building, while Sadie's memorial is taking place in a private, local church. Incendia is on the back foot after our performance in Harrowdean and the extensive media coverage, granting Hunter the confidence to honour her with a small service.

Stepping out of the elevator, I emerge into the gleaming foyer. A small group has gathered at the entrance to HQ, decked out in black and surrounded by the newly enhanced security detail. I can't make eye contact with Hunter, who is hiding behind a pair of dark sunglasses. His hunched shoulders tell me enough.

"Over here." Hudson beckons me over.

Joining the others, I find Brooklyn standing alone in the corner, staring outside. She doesn't turn to speak to any of us, her face slack and eyes reddened. I'm not sure she's slept since witnessing Sadie's last moments.

"What's the holdup?" I fish for a topic change.

Looking scarily normal in a dark shirt and jeans, the nerve in Seven's jaw ticks as he stares into space. He's even tied his hair back and had a shave, revealing every dark circle and mark on his skin. The poor son of a bitch looks drained and utterly wiped out.

"Turns out Incendia couldn't firefight our news story at the same time as Harrowdean's mini riot." Hudson gestures outside. "This lot gathered a while ago and won't move."

Glancing out through the tinted glass and layers of security checks that protect Sabre's privacy, I spot a gaggle of reporters. Cameras and news vans dominate the busy London street. Security is attempting to hold them back, setting up a perimeter as they battle for a single picture of what lies within.

"Are we even safe here?"

I shrug at Hudson's question. "We've been given temporary protection. Hunter's contact in government intends to argue for clemency in exchange for our testimony, same as Lazlo and the girls."

"How do we know it isn't another ploy?"

"We don't," Seven states flatly.

"Incendia is everywhere." I watch Theo and Enzo arrive in matching black suits. "Exposing them needs a smoking gun. We hold the leverage to bargain for our lives with these testimonies."

"Once we give our information to them, the government will turn us over to Incendia for execution." Hudson scoffs at us both. "We're being led to slaughter."

"The deal will be signed in black and white."

"You're being fucking stupid."

"What's the alternative? Live out our lives in hiding?" I fire at him.

Hudson's hands ball into fists as he storms away, attempting to approach

Brooklyn instead. We're all on edge and frustrated. The thought of giving evidence to Hunter's team and a room full of complete strangers is uncomfortable as fuck.

Lucia and Two were petrified when they arrived yesterday. Hunter had them flown down from Scotland on a private flight before setting them up in the apartment opposite us. We've drawn them into this pandemonium now. I hope to God we don't regret bargaining with their lives.

"Get this shit locked down!" Enzo yells at two of his agents, gesturing at the madness outside.

He's favouring his right leg after the incident in Harrowdean narrowly missed his femoral artery. Any closer, and the doctor admitted he would be a hell of a lot worse off.

"That's an order. We will not be hounded by a bunch of vampires fishing for a story!"

"Enzo." Hunter's throat bobs as he approaches.

"No! I am not risking anyone else's safety."

Several more agents are sent outside to begin crowd control. The rest of the extensive security team lines up in formation to surround us on all sides. Brooklyn shrugs off Hudson's attempt to put an arm around her, insisting on standing alone. She still won't meet my eyes.

We head out into the heavy rainfall, using thick, black umbrellas to hide our faces. Sabre's foot soldiers keep the convoy moving at high speed. Enzo is barking his orders like a drill sergeant, slipping into full-on scary leader mode. It's unnerving after getting to know the gentle, caring side of him.

Packed into an armoured SUV, we manage to escape the media circus. Nobody knows what to say as the miles tick by. When we pull up outside a quaint chapel with stained glass and intricate limestone carvings, I succeed in grabbing Brooklyn's hand. She's chewing her lip so hard, I can see it bleeding.

"Are you okay?" I ask softly.

"Fine."

"Are we doing the whole lying thing again, love?"

"Fuck, Kade. Nothing about this is okay. Sadie's dead."

"I know. This never should've happened."

"The last thing I said to her was so fucking cruel. I can never take that back. Phoenix nearly died and lost three fingers." Her eyes bounce to Seven's hand. "We've all suffered so much. And for what?"

I thread our fingers together. "Our freedom."

"How can I ever be free while my mother is still imprisoned?"

Seven can't look at her, staring outside at the downpour. I know it killed him to drag her away like that in Harrowdean. He had to choose between his sister's murderer and the girl he loves. Leaving her mother alive was supposed to be a mercy, even if Brooklyn can't see it right now.

"It isn't her anymore." Hudson winces at his words. "I'm sorry, blackbird, but the person you knew is dead. She's too far gone to be saved. Look at what she did to Phoenix."

"And what if I'm not Brooklyn anymore either? What if I'm destined to end up just like her?" She rubs a spot between her knitted brows. "Her sickness is in me. I'm the same as her."

"You're nothing like your mother," I argue hotly.

"Do you really believe that?"

There's a sharp rap on the window from one of our burly escorts. I roll the heavily tinted window down and bark at them to go ahead. I'm not leaving this fucking car until Brooklyn can meet our eyes again. I won't tolerate this doubt and self-hatred for a second longer.

Tugging her hand, I drag Brooklyn into my lap. She ends up straddling me in the spacious car. Ignoring both Hudson's and Seven's interested gazes, I tip her head up with a single finger under her chin.

"You're going to listen to me and listen well," I demand with fire. "This is the last time I'm going to explain this to you."

"Kade—"

"Listen to me, Brooklyn West. You are the most infuriating woman I've ever met. You're fucking crazy, you drink far too much, swear worse than Nix's batshit Nana, and resort to violence far too quickly."

Her lips part, almost reaching a smile.

"I have zero clue how we're going to straighten out the shit in your head." I stroke her cheek with my thumb. "You're fucked up, unstable, and sometimes, you scare the hell out of me. That's the truth nobody wants to tell you."

Tears shine in her eyes. "I told you to let me go. You still can."

"Shut the fuck up. I'm not done."

Unable to help myself, I let my palm slide up her bare leg. She's wearing a short black dress, which exposes her creamy thighs as it rides up. Despite the funeral taking place across the road, my cock hardens beneath her.

"My life hasn't been the same since you walked into it." I graze my lips against hers. "You insisted on trying to kill yourself rather than be saved. I've been terrified of losing you since. Every single one of us is wrapped around your finger. We love the bones of you."

"Damn straight," Hudson reiterates.

Seven is silent, watching us very closely.

"Whatever it takes, we will save you now, and every time in the future," I finish, my own voice faltering. "If you need to be Patient Eight, we will still love you, because you're one and the same. Good and bad. That's the girl I love."

"How can you love someone like me?" she whispers. "I've hurt so many people."

Hudson takes her spare hand. "You were the first one to treat Eli like a human being. You saved Phoenix when he lost his sobriety last year."

"You brought my brother back to me and showed me how to survive after what… what my father made me do." I shudder at the memory. "You wouldn't let me push you away, no matter what."

"You forgave me for the most evil, disgusting thing a person can ever do to someone they love," Hudson adds shamefully. "Despite everything, you chose to give us a future. Together."

On the curb outside the church, hidden in our own private bubble, we offer our heathen souls for judgement. Brooklyn can't look at either of us, her tears hitting my pressed white shirt as she struggles to breathe.

"You taught me... how to be human again."

Seven's voice is so quiet, I almost miss it. He's staring outside at the torrential downpour, frowning at his own distorted reflection. Brooklyn's head finally lifts to seek him out.

"I was dead before I met you." He lets their eyes collide. "You could've left me to rot in that basement. I deserve it more than anyone. I've hurt innocent people, tortured them and taken their lives."

"Sev..."

"You know it's true. I am the least deserving person of redemption."

"I thought the same." Hudson finds a small smile.

I nod in agreement. "You convinced every single one of us otherwise. You've hurt people, Brooke. Just like the rest of us. But I'm willing to bet my life that you've saved just as many."

The smile I've been waiting for blossoms on her lips. She looks too fucking beautiful like that, all shy and furtive, unsure of how to handle being praised for something.

"So the question, love, isn't how we can love someone like you. It's how could we not?"

Brushing her short locks, I meet those silvery, gunmetal eyes that always hold so much pain. Everything rests on her answer.

"I love you," Brooklyn murmurs after a beat. "For longer than I've admitted to."

Her declaration punches me in the chest. I feel like I've waited my whole life to hear those words.

"Me too, love. I'm done letting fear rule my life." I look between the other two. "We face this together. Nobody in this family grieves alone."

Squirming on my lap, Brooklyn attempts to exit the car. I grab her hips, holding her in place. I should let her go, but I'm fucking selfish. Her scent is a mouth-watering, enchanting fog that drapes over me. She's the siren calling my corrupted soul towards eternal damnation.

"Kade," she breathes.

My hand slides further up her dress, a finger hooking under the elastic of her panties. I meet Hudson's eyes over her shoulder while slowly dragging them down. He's staring at her with lust. The windows are so heavily tinted, nobody can see what we're doing from the outside.

Brooklyn lifts from my lap, allowing me to remove her panties. She gasps a little as I toss them over to Seven, embarrassment colouring her cheeks. I love the timid but sensual angel within her that comes out when we fuck.

Hesitating for a second, Seven brings her panties to his nose and inhales deeply. "I can smell your arousal," he tells her with a crooked smile. "Do you like people watching you?"

Undoing my belt and attacking the fly of my trousers, Brooklyn falters at his question. We all know she has a kink for group activities. I think about what we did in Blackwood's swimming pool at least once a day.

"You don't have to watch us," she grinds out.

Sitting back, Seven stares. "I'm curious."

Opposite us, Hudson begins to touch himself. "Me too."

Taking my cock in hand, Brooklyn begins to pump it up and down. I take the opportunity to imprison her in a passionate kiss, exploring every inch of her body that's exposed by the tight dress. She should dress in borrowed hand-me-downs more often if they look like this.

Finding her clit, she's wet and dripping already. I play with her, despite the inappropriateness of our surroundings—in the middle of the street, opposite a church. People walk past our blacked-out car every so often, glancing at the windows without seeing inside. It's fucking hot to know we're breaking the rules.

"Take it, love," I whisper to her. "I want to fill you up."

With a moan, she lowers herself down on my length. At this angle, I'm pushing so deep inside of her, I almost finish before we get started. It's a snug fit, with warmth wrapping around my dick in a welcome embrace. I don't give a damn if what we're doing is wrong.

She's the only thing worth living for on this planet.

Without her, we have nothing.

Beginning to move in a slow, coaxing grind, Brooklyn takes her time. She's letting me thrust deep inside of her, with two steadying hands placed on my shoulders. Our lips find each other again. I can taste the heartache on her tongue. We shouldn't fucking be here, mourning another loss.

"We have to stop," she moans.

Lifting my hips, I meet her movements. "Not a damn chance, love. You don't get to decide that. We own every inch of your soul. I decide when and where I want to fuck you."

"But, Seven—"

She freezes when I grab her throat, forcing her to look at him. Seven's watching our performance and stroking his cock, a delicious darkness swirling in his eyes. He doesn't look uncomfortable in the slightest.

"He belongs with us," I implore her. "Just look at him. None of us can fucking think straight around you. This is the power you hold over us all."

Emboldened by my words, Brooklyn rides my dick faster. She looks like a goddess on top of me, taking every last drop of pleasure I have to offer her. I can feel her walls tightening around me, preparing to fall apart. Swirling my thumb over her nub, she can't hold it in any longer.

"Say my name, Brooke. Let them hear it."

"Fuck, Kade!"

I grab her throat and continue thrusting upwards, ready to spill myself inside of her. Knowing we're being watched and appreciated undoes my self-restraint. I want to see my come stream down her leg, knowing she's covered in me as we enter that church.

Brooklyn slumps against my chest as our releases coincide. Every muscle in my body tenses, drowning in a powerful wave of pure sensation. My fingers run through her messy hair, needing to touch every single part of her to prove that she's all mine.

Before she can catch her breath, she's torn from my lap. Hudson's already unfastened his dark-wash jeans and doesn't waste any time spearing her on his proud length. Brooklyn gasps loudly, filled back up before she's even had a chance to come down from her orgasm.

"My turn," he growls. "I need you too."

They fuck frantically in the back of the SUV, not stopping even as there's another tap on the window. Hudson's too busy pounding his ownership into her, ensuring Seven's watching the entire time. He's getting himself off, studying Brooklyn with quiet intensity.

He can't tear his eyes away.

Like it or not, he's already one of us.

Laying Brooklyn down across the leather seats, Hudson shoves her dress up to her waist and plunges back inside. Her legs spread wider in the space of the car to allow him full, unfettered access. We both watch the show with fascination as Hudson drives her back to the edge.

"Come, blackbird. Coat my dick in your juices," he goads.

The cry of ecstasy she releases sends a shiver down my spine. Both finishing, Hudson's head rests against her breastbone. It's a brief second of panting before they break into raucous laughter. Once again, we find ourselves in another morally fucked situation.

I grab a packet of tissues from Brooklyn's discarded coat pocket and toss it at them. "Clean up, you lunatics. Hunter will come out here and smash the window open if we keep him waiting much longer."

"Worth it." Brooklyn hands Seven a tissue too.

The stormy-faced man actually nods. "Agreed."

CHAPTER 21
BROOKLYN
HURTS LIKE HELL - FLEURIE

KADE RELEASES my hand outside of the car. Taking a deep breath and yanking my dress down, I turn my head up to the sky. Raindrops hit my tongue in a sweet explosion, and I savour each one. This is what it's all been for; beginning to live again.

I have even more of a reason to now. For the people that aren't here, we have to survive.

Seven hangs at the back of our group, his head downturned and defeat laying heavy on his shoulders. Letting Kade and Hudson take the lead, I slide in next to him. He lets me take his empty hand.

"Kade's right," I tell him. "You're not alone."

Releasing a deep breath, he nods. "I guess."

"Come on. I won't let go of you, I promise."

Flanked by our two blank-faced agents, their suits bulging with concealed holsters, we enter the small church. It's a beautiful, mid-century classic, carved from slabs of limestone and lit with flickering flames. Dozens of candles have been lit inside, until it looks like the constellations of a midnight sky.

Down the narrow aisle, we take the empty seats at the front. Hunter, Theo, and Enzo all stand to the right in their expensive, fitted black suits, boxed in by their own security detail. Not a single one has been able to look at us. It's clear that while Sadie was saving our lives, they were protecting the woman they loved.

There's no elaborate service. Scripture and sentiments mean nothing to the people left behind. One by one, the three men take their turn laying a single, long-stemmed rose on her coffin. Enzo's cold mask doesn't break. He stands frozen and desolate, like an abandoned mountain range.

"I love you, beautiful. Remember that."

Theo goes next, his cheeks stained with tears as he presses a kiss to the coffin's surface. He's the most emotional of them all, but the hard set of his jaw betrays the angry torrent battering him from within.

"I'm fucking sorry, Lys."

Hunter goes last, passing Theo in the aisle. His steps are hesitant and afraid, so unlike the powerful force to be reckoned with that he's projected since day one. This is far more terrifying than any threat levelled against him or his team. After laying the rose, he stares down at the inscription.

"I didn't keep you safe. I will never forgive myself for that. You paid the price for my stupidity."

After several long seconds of contemplation, Hunter turns his back on her remains. His gaze is fixed on the cobbled stone of the church, unwilling to reveal his pain to anyone else. Enzo quickly pulls him into a crushing bear hug.

"It's my fault," Hunter croaks.

Enzo holds him tighter. "Stop it, Hunt. This isn't on you."

"We should've pulled her out. I was so desperate for answers, I put her at risk."

"We made the decision together," Theo speaks up, wiping his eyes. "Alyssa was her own person. She wanted the truth more than anything."

Hunter scrubs his face. "No outcome is worth this. I jeopardised a member of the team. That's on me."

"Stop it," Enzo demands. "Alyssa's death isn't on us. It's those evil, corrupt bastards that have to pay."

Taking several deep breaths, Hunter finally manages to look up, and our gazes collide. His picture-perfect, stubbly features are carved in agony. I swallow the lump in my throat, dropping his gaze.

We all know why Sadie is dead.

Our demons aren't so different, after all.

"Fuck," Theo stutters. "I can't believe... this is goodbye. She... I... goddammit."

Enzo tugs them both into a frantic hug, all three men huddling together. It's heartbreaking to see them embracing each other, mourning the one missing person from their family together. I can't imagine losing one of my guys and the pain it would bring. A piece of their souls will forever be missing.

"Go on," Kade instructs us.

With a steadying breath, Seven squeezes past me. I follow him up to the awaiting coffin. He's clinging to me so tight, I fear my bones will break. Miniature quakes rock his entire frame as he battles to keep his emotions under control.

We stop at the side of the coffin.

"I don't know what to say," he admits.

I wrap my arm around his firm bicep. "She's still here, Sev. Say whatever you need to."

"She can't fucking hear us."

"Just get it off your chest."

Sighing, Seven releases my hand to trace his sister's name with his finger. "I shouldn't have said what I did in the warehouse. You'll always be my family. Jude may be gone, but I can still be the person you thought I was."

I hold his long-stemmed rose for him. With bleak eyes meeting mine, he nods once. I step closer and place the rose on the coffin, feeling the weight of the moment bear down on me. My friend is gone. She was the first one to be there for me, to see beyond the thick walls I put up.

Sadie was a good person.

Flawed, imperfect, but undeniably good.

"I hope we make you proud." I swipe beneath my eyes with my coat sleeve. "Thank you for being a far better friend than I ever was. You deserved more than this."

We barely make it back to our seats. The sombre mood feels suffocating. All I want is to escape and mourn in private, let my emotions overcome me where nobody can see. Some things need to be endured alone.

As we line up to file back outside, a shrill ringtone pierces the air. Looking surprised by the noise, Hunter stares down at his screen with a frown. When he answers, his low hiss of greeting would terrify most callers.

"I see," he deadpans. "How did you get this number?"

We all watch with trepidation.

"If this is an attempt to scare us off the case, it's entirely misguided."

"Hunt?" Enzo asks with concern.

Meeting the wide eyes of his best friend, Hunter puts the phone on speaker mode. Every single person inside the church stiffens at the light, conversational tone in Bancroft's voice. He sounds far too fucking happy.

"I do apologise for breaking up this sad, sad affair."

"What do you want?" Enzo blusters.

"It seems you're intent on destroying the hard-earned reputation of your firm by associating with these convicts. I'm willing to offer you a final chance to step aside."

Hunter scoffs bitterly. "You killed one of our own. This is no longer a professional endeavour. Believe me, I will take great delight in demolishing your organisation overnight."

"Well, your confidence is amusing at least." Bancroft laughs sadistically. "Since you're all mourning, I thought I'd offer you a gift. Patient Delta has been punished for her transgressions."

The heat leaches from my body, leaving me cold and empty.

"Punished for letting us escape, you mean," I accuse.

"Ah, Brooklyn. You know better than most what disobedience gets you."

"What do you want?" Kade steps in front of me.

"Mr Knight! I thought I recognised your voice. It's been a long time. There's someone here who would like to speak to you."

With a shuffling sound, a deep throat clear causes my heart to somersault. Hudson rests a hand on his brother's shoulder, staring at the phone with trepidation. I'd recognise Leroy Knight's voice anywhere.

"I expected more loyalty from you, son, after all I've done for you."

"Father," he grits out. "I'm doing what's right."

"I wonder if the authorities will agree when they charge you with first-degree murder. Poor old Stephanie, killed in cold blood. How is my adoptive boy? Gotten over his short-lived grief yet?"

"Fuck you," Hudson shouts.

"Hello, Hudson. In all fairness, she was a whore. The world is well rid of your mother."

His foot connects with several of the chairs, sending them flying across the church in wooden splinters. I attempt to approach him, but Hudson hisses at me in warning.

"What about my mother?" Kade interjects. "You can't keep up this manhunt for long. She won't protect you anymore. You're going down, along with this entire corporation."

"Sentiment," Leroy hums. "It's something I've warned you about. When everyone you love is dead, we will have this conversation again. Perhaps then you will learn your lesson."

"We'll see about that, old man."

"Shall I add harassing my clients to your list of charges?" Hunter intervenes smoothly. "Along with torture, unlawful imprisonment, illegal experimentation, and a million human rights violations?"

"I think you'll find the law to be on our side of this, Mr Rodriguez." Bancroft takes charge from Kade's father. "Turn the fugitives over or I won't be held responsible for my next actions."

Staring ahead at Sadie's coffin, Hunter's face transforms into a mask of terrifying determination. He looks ready to go to war, win or lose.

"Go to hell, *sir*."

"Poor choice, Mr Rodriguez. Let's see who will believe you after this."

The line goes dead.

"What the fuck just happened?" Enzo exclaims.

Just as Hunter's mouth opens to speak, the sound of two gunshots explodes from outside of the small church. The grand, arched doors slam open, leaving two crumpled bodies to collapse inwards. The men are bleeding from smoking bullet holes shot at a perfect, point-blank range.

Too perfect.

Something evil is here.

Everything happens too quickly. Hunter and Enzo pull their weapons with practised ease. They train their aim on the gate-crasher, along with the other two agents boxing us in. Kade roughly shoves me behind him.

"Who are you?" Hunter bellows.

Dressed casually in a thick parka, plain black clothing, and a scruffy baseball cap, the silent, brown-haired man enters the church. His sunken face is covered in stubble, adding to his roughened exterior. He looks homeless. In his eyes, no emotion awaits.

Enzo hobbles into the aisle. "Stop right there."

He keeps walking regardless of the guns facing him. Each step stamps our death certificates. When the man pulls his hand from his pocket, we all spot the small black detonator. Every second is a revolving door of quick-fire developments.

The crash of bullets pierce his chest.

Enzo's gun recoils from the blasts.

The detonator slips for an alarming second.

Bancroft's monster recaptures his prize.

"Who the fuck are you?" Enzo repeats.

Head cocked, he smiles. "Patient Beta."

His thumb collides with the detonator. Survival instincts kick in as a thunderous boom echoes throughout the church. The man explodes in a blinding torrent of light. Bricks, pillars and slabs of stone fly everywhere, propelled by fire and hot ash.

Reality comes in sharp, painful fragments.

All I can hear are the panicked shouts and screams of our group. I'm knocked off my feet by Kade's weight. He takes the full force of the blast, his body shielding me from harm. Pain still sizzles through me as I impact with the stone floor.

My ears ring, obscuring my stunned senses.

I can hear Seven screaming my name.

Darkness is swallowing my vision.

The last thing I remember is the look on Kade's face when I finally told him that I loved him. I want to see that smile every day for the rest of my life. Not just on him, but all of them. Even if I have to die and leave reality to do that.

CHAPTER 22
BROOKLYN
TERESA - YUNGBLUD

IT'S times like these that I miss Blackwood. Don't get me wrong, it was a miserable hellhole. But at least the horrors were predictable. I could steel myself for more torture and bury my vulnerabilities to survive. I can't do that out here.

The blows just keep coming.

Real life is a cruel motherfucker.

Dabbing the swollen lacerations on my face, I grit my teeth through the pain. I'm resolutely ignoring the whispering shadows behind me. Fear and pain bring out the worst parts of my traumatised brain.

The on-call doctor already dug the shrapnel out of the injuries on my body when they wrapped me up a few hours ago. I stuck around until they took Kade into surgery to set his broken arm.

Hudson and Seven are still being treated too, while Hunter and Enzo are holding an emergency meeting with their staff. Sabre is going into full lockdown. Everyone has been informed of our presence and tasked with one priority—no more fuck ups. They lost four agents in the church.

The bathroom door creaks behind me, admitting a headful of dark ringlets and two searching eyes. Eli looks me up and down, his hands raised to take the cotton swab from my grasp.

"I'm fine," I protest as he steals it.

"N-Not."

"It's just a few scrapes and bruises. Kade shielded me."

Pushing me to sit down on the closed toilet, Eli's eyes narrow as he resumes dabbing the nasty slices. I quickly told the doctor to fuck off after enough poking and prodding. My patience for clinicians is very short.

"The others?" I ask worriedly.

"Concussions."

"Both of them? No broken bones?"

"Go… s-see."

I stare at the soft sweats and blue t-shirt that I stole from Phoenix's stuff to wear. He must've worn them already, as his warm, inviting scent clings to the fabric. Inhaling deeply, I let Phoenix's essence wrap around me.

"I needed to get out of there. Too many doctors and nurses, I couldn't fucking think. You know Hunter sent a shrink to talk to us? Some asshole called Doctor Richards."

Nodding, Eli bites his lip.

"I don't want anyone else digging around in my head."

"H-Help... you."

I duck my gaze. "There's no helping me."

My eyes are pulled back up as he strokes a finger over my jawline, cheekbone, nose, eye socket. Cataloguing every inch of my face, his smile is knowing. He can see the swirling shadows inside of me. Sickness and rage demanding retribution, keeping me forever trapped in the past.

I can't let go.

Even if I wanted to, my mind won't let me.

"We were supposed to be safe here." I push Eli's hands away and stand. "How could they attack us like that in the open?"

"Show y-you."

Placing the bloodied cotton swab down, Eli grips my hand. He guides me back into the living room and flicks the TV on to a news channel. I have to hold his arm to steady myself as the world tips on its head.

"You've got to be kidding me."

The reporter is reading a statement from the police, claiming the church explosion was no mere accident. It was an attack by none other than... six mentally unstable criminals, recently escaped from Blackwood Institute. The police investigation is ongoing, but no arrests have been made.

"This can't be happening."

Images of the fiery church ruins are shown. Beneath that, the appeal for information leading to our capture is repeated. The story briefly touches on rumours of medical negligence against the corporation, but it's quickly dismissed and overshadowed by the main story.

"They're spinning it to fit their narrative, burying the story about Harrowdean with this madness."

"Yeah," Eli agrees flatly.

I watch the news story until I can no longer see straight. For someone that generally spends their life pretty angry, I'm beyond livid. This isn't a game. It's a character assassination, one move at a time. They're going to beat us into submission.

"Are those reporters still outside?"

Eli nods uncertainly.

"Good. We're going to give Incendia a taste of their own medicine."

Throwing my leather jacket on to cover my heavily scarred arms, I retake Eli's hand. My heartbeat is roaring in my ears, but I don't allow myself to stop and consider if this is a bad idea. All I know is that I can't stand the fucking injustice any longer.

The grand foyer we departed from hours ago is a hubbub of frenetic energy. There's an even heavier security presence than earlier, blocking every entrance and exit while checking employees' badges and fingerprints for good measure. They aren't taking any chances.

At one of the glass entrance doors, a scowling, bald-headed agent studies the reception. He looks like a terminator, his hand resting on a visible gun in its holster. I wait for him to recognise me and let us pass, but he refuses to budge.

"Carl, step aside."

Theo appears at our side, dressed down in blood-speckled sweats and a tight muscle shirt. Damn, he's hiding some firm pectorals under his usual goofy clothes. His face is marred by a row of stitches and his sprained arm is in a sling.

"Theo?"

Meeting my eyes, exhaustion and grief stare back at me in shades of Antarctic blue. The gentle, caring soul within him has been broken and imprisoned in a cage. He looks done with the world and everything in it.

"Alyssa shouldn't have died like that," he offers bleakly. "We let her down. Now, we don't even have a body to mourn. They've taken that from us too."

"I'm so sorry, Theo."

"The truth doesn't matter to them, but it does to the world."

"What do you want us to do?"

Theo's grimace hardens. "Tell it."

At his order, the reluctant agent scans his thumbprint and opens the huge glass door for us to step outside. Eli moves tentatively, his hand bunched in the material of my leather jacket. We descend the steps until he digs his heels in, rubbing at an invisible pain in his chest.

"What is it?"

"C-Can't... hate m-me..."

Wrapping my arms around his trembling body, I feel his face bury in the crook of my neck. We embrace in the chilly wind, caught between safety and retaking our lives. One misstep and we'll crash into the chasm of death waiting to devour us whole.

"Nobody could ever hate you, Eli," I whisper into his soft, lemon shampoo-scented curls. "The world just doesn't understand people like us. I'll still keep you safe."

"P-Promise?" Eli stutters.

"I promise. Just keep talking to me."

His lips caress my ear. "Anything f-for you... baby girl."

Hearing his raw voice return more every day will never get old. His sweet little smile spears me right in the heart. Hand in hand, wrapped in each other's strength and determination, we approach the horde of reporters. The minute they spot us, the shouts for attention begin.

Our identities are hardly a matter of secrecy after recent events. Every dark and sordid detail of our lives have been printed for the country to read. We're the monsters that burned down Blackwood Institute. That's all the world will ever see when they look at us.

But not today.

This is our chance to take control back.

Eli's grip on my hand becomes crushing as we stop metres from the barrier keeping the crowd of reporters back. Flashing cameras blind us as the shouts and calls for attention grow more frantic. For the first time in so long, we hold the power. They want to hear our voices.

"Brooklyn West!"

"Did you bomb the church?"

"What happened inside Blackwood Institute?"

Keeping Eli by my side, I approach the closest microphone. Everyone falls silent, too many curious gazes to count lasering their attention on my injured face.

"What do you want to tell the world, Brooklyn?" the reporter asks.

Cameras flash.

Shouting falls silent.

The world awaits a single word.

"My friends and I have been subject to a lot of speculation in recent weeks." I take a deep, steadying breath. "Our stories don't make for easy reading. I'm not here to profess our innocence to the world. Nobody ends up in Blackwood Institute for being sane."

Eli's hand squeezes mine, sending a message of strength.

"We entered Blackwood seeking treatment and rehabilitation." I study the huge crowd. "Instead, all we received was abuse, malpractice, and exploitation. These institutes are not designed to help people. The truth is far more terrifying."

"Is this the same institute in which you incited a riot that led to the deaths of patients and staff?" another person shouts above the shocked whispers.

Zeroing in on them, I don't break eye contact. "This is the same institute in which clinicians engaged in illegal experimentation and psychological torture, using society's most vulnerable people as their unwilling subjects."

A roar of noise almost bowls me over. Too many questions to count are hurled at us both. Eli retreats several steps, his teeth gritted. I can practically taste the panic leaking off him in waves.

"Why should we believe you?"

"Where's the evidence?"

"Are you going to surrender to the authorities?"

"No," a rasp of terror replies.

Eli quakes all over while staring ahead for the first time. He returns to my side. More cameras flash, capturing his stormy face and the thick lines of shiny scar tissue covering his arms. He didn't cover up before coming outside. Not even all of the guys have seen his skin, yet here he is.

Living unapologetically.

This Eli... is still afraid.

But he's no longer letting it dictate his future.

Letting his arm envelop me in warmth, I fist the material of his t-shirt and face the cameras with resolution. I want them to see us like this. Together. United. Unbroken. He looks down at me with a hint of a smile, emotion shining in the rolling, grassy hills of his eyes.

"We will fight until every last patient has been freed from Incendia's clutches," I state into the microphone. "The indifference of the world towards people like us has enabled this abuse for too long."

"What are you going to do?" another person shouts.

"We're people. We matter, and we will stand up for our rights until society decides to give a damn. This isn't over."

I let Eli take me away, despite the tsunami of unanswered questions licking at our heels. The silent but steely agent escorts us back to safety, cutting off the shouting as Sabre's entrance door seals tightly shut.

Inside, the packed foyer is spookily silent. All of the enormous screens are tuned in to the local news. They all saw us speak. Every single person standing between us and certain death.

One by one, Hunter's employees begin to clap, led by Theo. It starts slowly, like a gathering storm stretching across the heavens, brewing into an all-consuming tsunami. I feel lightheaded, relying solely on Eli's embrace to hold me up. The applause doesn't stop.

"Why are they clapping?" I whisper to him.

"P-P-Proud," he murmurs back.

If I die at Bancroft's hands tomorrow, I'll take comfort in the knowledge that despite everything I've done, I made somebody proud. Hell, a room of strangers, inspired by a dark tale told by six delinquents. As for the beautiful, broken man at my side... his pride is all I ever wanted.

We escape upstairs, taking the elevator back in stunned silence to decompress. Hunter will no doubt track me down for a bollocking when he sees the news, but I don't give a fuck. All I want is a soft, warm bed and Eli's lips on mine. I step into our borrowed apartment with a sigh.

"Bed?" Eli suggests.

His arms band around me from behind, holding me close.

"What about the others?"

"They... find us."

"Then bed," I decide.

I'm lifted off my feet and spun around in a dizzying circle before Eli cradles me in his arms. My lips find their way to his on instinct as I'm carried towards one of the bedrooms we've been crashing in. Our kiss starts slowly, gently, with repressed emotion and promise.

When his tongue slips inside my mouth, I suppress a growl. Eli kisses me back with fervour, seeking to devour me with his touch. Everywhere his skin is on mine feels like it's on fire. His foot impatiently kicks a bedroom door open, and a sharp squeak has us breaking apart.

"Oh my God, Nix?"

Phoenix's head is stuck in a loose white t-shirt as he wrestles to take it off. Cursing colourfully, he manoeuvres his heavily bandaged hand.

"Firecracker? Eli?"

We rush at Phoenix together, both shouting his name like an answered prayer. My arms snake around his neck in a tight, desperate hug, while Eli snuggles his waist from behind so we're wrapped in a teary sandwich. Phoenix grunts in pain, but he doesn't push us away.

"Nix," I repeat, on the verge of sobbing.

"I'm here, guys."

"H-Hurt?" Eli stammers.

"It's alright. I'm getting better."

There isn't a part of him that isn't bruised or discoloured. Covering his face in light kisses, I feel the relieved tears flow. He's greedily drinking me in with his eyes. When we pull the t-shirt over his head, his torso reveals more abuse and suffering. Hearing Eli curse is a clear indication.

Dark stripe marks meet heavy bruising and endless scabbed-over wounds from a knife. My hands cover my mouth, nausea locking my throat up tight. Knowing what instruments and malice cause these injuries is one thing. I can handle my own pain. The people I fucking love? That's a no-go.

"It's okay," Phoenix offers weakly. "Please don't cry."

"No… it's not."

His one good hand strokes over my hair. "I'm back now. Nothing else matters."

"I'm sorry, your sister… she… I…"

"I can't talk about her," he croaks, cutting me off. "I just want to hold you both."

I carefully guide him over to the unmade bed I slept in last night with Kade and Hudson. Eli fluffs the pillows and tucks the duvet around Phoenix, fussing over him with such adoration, it makes me cry even harder. Fuck, I could win awards for emotional overload as of late.

Phoenix pats the space next to him. "Come on."

"I could leave you both to—"

"Brooke," Eli interrupts in a stern whisper. "C-Come."

Taking the other side, he's careful to avoid Phoenix's bad leg from the stabbing. It's still bandaged and stiff, along with his tightly wrapped hand. Stripping off the sweats I stole, I shove my stupid self-doubt to the back of my mind and slide in next to Phoenix.

He smells like hospital antiseptic and cheap shampoo, but I don't care. Beneath that, he's still my blue-haired maniac. Curling up against his side feels like throwing the doors to our cosy cottage open and running inside with open arms. Next to him, I'm finally home.

"I thought we lost you," I choke out.

"I promised to follow you in this life and the next; conspiracies, assassins and finger-chopping bastards aside. I still have one good hand to do this with."

His fingers bury in my hair, encouraging me to look up. Before I can take a breath, Phoenix is kissing the living daylights out of me. His soft lips move against mine in a passionate dance, demanding every ounce of submission I have left to give.

I'll happily let myself be consumed by him.

Death doesn't scare me, but losing him does.

Phoenix's teeth nip my lip with his usual playfulness, even as my tears leak between us in a salty flow. We end up gasping and laughing together. Everything about this is so fucked. Our happiness at being reunited feels futile in the face of so much tragedy.

"So," Phoenix whispers. "You don't mind another boyfriend with missing body parts, right?"

I kiss the corner of his mouth. "If you don't mind a girlfriend with enough baggage to sink a ship and four other boyfriends, then nope. I can deal."

"We're counting Seven in this shitshow now, huh?"

"Group vote. Nothing to do with me."

He nuzzles my throat. "Damn. I miss out on all the important stuff."

Resting his weary head on Phoenix's chest, Eli releases a contented sigh. I curl up tighter, letting my fingers bury in his ringlets to gently massage his head. He can sleep now for the first time in days, knowing Phoenix is back exactly where he fucking belongs.

With both of us snuggled close, I feel the tension drain out of Phoenix's body.

"Do you need anything? More painkillers? Or we can move to another bed, give you some space."

"You're staying right where you are," he says firmly. "Everything I need is in this room."

As I lay there staring at his face, too many words to count beg to escape my lips. His expression is conflicted. When Eli's light snores fill the room, I feel Phoenix's chest shudder with the first sob. He's biting his lip to keep his crying silent.

"I'm so sorry," I repeat, my own cheeks wet.

"I couldn't keep her safe. Charlie is dead because of me."

"No, she isn't. They did this. It's not your fault."

His tear-logged, chocolatey eyes meet mine. "I didn't get a chance to say goodbye. She was just a kid when I left. Now, I'll never see her again."

"You will. Not on this earth, but one day. I believe that."

"Does it make it easier?" he asks through his agony. "Believing?"

Taking his good hand from my leg, I link our fingers together. His sister is dead. Sadie's gone, lost in spectacular ashes. We've lost our future. Our lives. The freedom that drove us to break our way out of Blackwood's cruel grasp.

It's all far more than we bargained for. But who gets what they deserve in life? None of the guys asked for this. I brought darkness into their lives the day I arrived, but they haven't once blamed me. The least I can do is hold Phoenix in his grief and put his broken pieces back together, just like he did for me.

"Nothing makes this easier. We're here though, Nix."

"Stay with me tonight? Please?"

"I'm not going anywhere. Sleep, I've got you."

It takes a long time for him to drop off, his tears staining the pale-grey pillowcase beneath his head. I hold on tight through every last teardrop, determined to keep him afloat amidst the falling rain of his agony. It's all I can do now. Nothing else will end this torment.

When I fall asleep too, Kade's earlier words echo in my head. He was right all along. We get through shit as a family. Together, not apart.

All we have left in this world is each other, and that alone is worth enduring all this pain and heartache for.

CHAPTER 23
BROOKLYN

FOURTH OF JULY (REMIX) - FALL OUT BOY

SITTING in the bland waiting area, I'm surrounded by comfortable sofas, fake office plants and generic artwork. Being in an unfamiliar environment is making me anxious as hell, but knowing that Enzo and Hunter are taking testimony from Patient Two in the next room gives me some reassurance.

I volunteered to come, as she was the first witness to be called. She looked terrified, holding my hand until the very last second. Being separated from Lucia is hard for her after so long spent protecting one another.

They've holed up in their apartment since arriving, but I had a brief chat with them last night to explain the plan. Honesty in exchange for a chance, but only if we can convince the world it's the truth.

Four stony-faced government agents went in over an hour ago, their slick suits and shiny briefcases paired with glaring ID badges. They insisted on meeting in a neutral location to begin with—a safe house in Central London that's been converted into an office space.

"Hey." Hudson strolls in with two cups in hand. "Brought you a coffee. Want anything to eat? There's a shop down the street. I could get you a peanut butter sandwich. Your favourite."

I accept the steaming drink. "How do you remember that?"

"I made enough of them in the middle of the night. You clearly didn't learn your lesson when Mrs Dane refused to give you dinner. But still, you kept talking back."

"She never learned that hitting me and starving me don't work. How are the others?"

"Kade texted. They're back at HQ. Phoenix is resting while Eli plays nurse to them both. Seven is outside, glaring at anyone walking past the building. He hasn't moved since we got here."

"Nothing out of the ordinary, then," I snort.

"Typical psychotic behaviour. That's Seven, right?"

Studying the rugged lines of Hudson's face over the rim of my cup, I find no resentment there. He's vehemently hated Seven since the beginning, refusing to change his stubborn-ass ways. This nightmare has changed us all in so many ways.

"What about you?"

"Me?" he echoes.

"Are you okay?"

Hudson frowns at me. "Why wouldn't I be?"

"We will have to testify under oath about our pasts. Every last gory, messy detail will be laid out for the entire world to hear and judge when Incendia is exposed. It doesn't make you nervous?"

Draining his cup, Hudson crushes it easily in his scarred fist. When he stands and checks the time instead, I wait for him to fire a typical asshole response.

"How long will she be in there for?" he asks distractedly.

"Uh, probably a few hours."

"Let's get some air."

Reaching out a tattooed arm, I'm offered his hand.

"Come on, blackbird. I won't bite."

"Maybe I wouldn't mind if you did."

Our fingers slot together like puzzle pieces as he softly kisses my lips. Those brief, tender flashes of the sullen boy that made me peanut butter sandwiches never fail to melt me inside. We sneak out before anyone can notice, Hudson's feet skipping down the staircase with an odd sense of excitement.

When we break outside, Seven stiffens. "Problem?"

"Calm down, guard dog." Hudson mock salutes him. "Last time I checked, we're still free citizens. Let's go have some fun. I ain't sitting in that waiting area all morning."

"It isn't safe to be wandering around."

"Hunter's going to kill us one by one," I add.

"Fuck him," Hudson snaps. "We're adults. Let's live a little."

Considering him, Seven nods. "What did you have in mind, pretty boy? Better not get us killed."

Stifling an eye roll, Hudson takes a beanie from his pocket. He slides it over his overgrown black mop before tugging the hood of my jacket up, covering my face. Seven dons a baseball cap and tilts it down for coverage.

"Follow me." Hudson smirks.

Heading into the city's madness, we have no choice but to trust his sense of direction. He knows this place like the back of his hand after being adopted by Kade's family. I've heard the stories of their wild, drunken weekends away from the suffocation of the mansion.

Walking with a skip in his step, Hudson eagerly soaks in the surroundings.

"Did he drink or something?" Seven says in a stage whisper.

"What makes you think that?"

"He's far too happy. I don't recognise him."

"Heard that," Hudson calls back. "Keep your eyes on my girl and your opinions to yourself, dickwipe. I'm tolerating your existence, but that can soon change."

"Charming," Seven responds coolly.

More people start to appear as we rejoin the central strip. London is a riot of activity and endless variety. In the time I've spent here, even hiding for fear of our lives, I've never seen two people alike. I love the chaos.

Seven slings his arm around my shoulders. His amputated hand is tucked away in the pocket of his jeans, hiding it from the world. With our cuts and scrapes concealed, we could be three normal, everyday people. For just a moment, I want to live in that fantasy.

"Can we get food?"

Hudson lights a cigarette. "We can do anything, but there's someone who wants to see us first."

Cutting down a side street to avoid the crowding of bodies on the main roads, he leads us to a quieter borough. Seven looks on edge, acutely aware of every face that passes us.

I have to physically hold him back when a pair of police officers clock us from their patrol car. I hope we're far enough away for them not to see our stupid faces that are plastered all over the news.

"They don't recognise us."

"How can you be sure?" he growls. "Can't I kill them just to be safe?"

"I seem to remember you promising to be a better man not so long ago."

Blanching, his shoulders slump. "Yeah."

Everyone is handling Sadie's death differently. While her dying face has haunted my dreams since, I know that Seven has barely slept. Even when I try to coax him into bed for a few hours, he just stares outside at night, unblinking and silent. It's like he's waiting for her to return and give him another chance.

"You can talk to me," I remind him.

"There's nothing to discuss."

"We used to talk, late at night. No topic was off-limits."

Seven sighs. "I remember, princess."

"Nothing has changed. I'm still... whatever you need me to be."

"What if I don't know what I need? Everything has changed."

"My feelings haven't."

His caramel eyes scrape over me like molten lava. I could lose myself in his gaze, even on the days when it's cold and filled with the icy fires of hatred. Seven sees part of me that I keep hidden from the world, underneath the shame and loathing of what Augustus has made us.

"I'll be here until you know what you want," I promise.

"When this is all over, you'll leave."

His words stop me dead in my tracks. Hudson realises we're having a moment and crosses the road to finish his cigarette. I peer up at Seven, attempting to read the unfathomable look on his face.

"Why?"

"What we have isn't fit for the real world," he says in a matter-of-fact tone. "You said it before. Surviving and living are two very different things. I've kept you alive, but that doesn't mean I'm capable of helping you live."

"You seriously think I'd walk away after all we've been through?"

Seven shoves unkempt hair behind his ears. "I wouldn't blame you. There's no future for me in this world, we both know that. I'm not capable of getting better. They'll lock me up and throw away the key."

I take a shallow breath. "You are exactly who you're supposed to be. Jude, Seven, fucking Santa Claus. I don't give a damn what you are or how you got here. Don't you know how I feel about you?"

Biting his bottom lip, a glimmer of want flashes across his expression. Seven wraps himself in barbed wire and violence to survive the brutality of this world. Life is easier when you wield your pain as a weapon, cutting down all who dare to come close. The torment of staying alive is easier that way.

"You're scared." I grab a handful of his plain t-shirt. "I know what it's like to lose everything that matters to you. When I make a promise, I keep it. You will never have to lose me."

He looks so vulnerable, wracked by indecision.

"I don't want to be a burden to anyone, even you," he finally admits.

"Fuck, Sev. I was a wreck long before Augustus got his hands on me. I can't get through a single day at the moment without crying. I see shit that isn't real, hurt people who don't deserve it and need the strength of five men just to keep me on my feet. If anyone's a burden here, it's me."

"They love you. There's a difference."

I cup his cheek. "What difference? Are you so thickskulled that you can't see I fucking love you too? I'm in love with you, Sev. I have been since that damned basement."

Emotions churn in his irises after so long spent turning off his humanity. He's no longer the gaunt, lifeless man I used to be terrified of. His impenetrable shield is falling down, revealing someone else inside.

"I'm not sure what love means." Seven's brows crease. "But... I think it would feel like this. I can't breathe when I'm around you. All I want is to drink the oxygen from your lungs. Living in a world without your strength at my side is no longer an option. I can't take another step alone."

Brushing my lips against his, I seal the kiss with a sigh of blissful defeat. This isn't a battle I want to win. I'll surrender my weapons and allow myself to fall on Seven's sword. He can take the last remaining shard of my heart and do with it what he pleases... as long as I can stay right here, in his arms.

"That's love," I say against his lips. "You never have to be alone again."

Folded into his strong, scarred arms, I feel myself slump. We melt into each other like rain dissipating on a summer's day. Cars and pedestrians pass us, but the world is insignificant. He's the beginning and the end of my existence in this precious moment.

"Oi, lovebirds!" Hudson heckles us. "Get a fucking move on."

Seven's chuckle brushes over me. "I really can't kill him now, can I?"

"We're a package deal, I'm afraid. You get used to him."

"I think I already have."

We cross the street together to join our disgruntled third member. Hudson studies me first, then Seven, before releasing an exaggerated sigh.

"This asshat is sticking around then, huh?"

Seven's smile is smug. "You'd miss my sunny personality too much, pretty boy."

Hudson gets him in a headlock, and the pair wrestle their way down the street. I'm left to watch and laugh, mentally betting on who will win out. When Hudson prevails, Seven mutters something about breaking his skull and returns to my side.

"Hud? Where are we going? Getting hungry here."

"Nearly there, blackbird."

It's another fifteen minutes before we stop in the middle of a busy, vibrant market borough. Countless stalls and food vans shout their services, a delicious tangle of aromas floating towards us. Businessmen flag down customers to part with their money, while customers gobble street food and fresh doughnuts.

Guided through the traffic, we head for a tiny coffee bar tucked between two thrift stores. Inside, the warm ambience invites comfort. The smell of freshly ground coffee immediately perks Seven up.

Colourful Tiffany lamps and armchairs dipped in rich velvet warm the coffee shop, reminiscent of an old-school Victorian tearoom. Hudson removes his beanie and strolls towards a table tucked into the furthest corner, where two figures are crouched over their cappuccinos.

"Janet?" Hudson asks nervously.

With a headful of pristine blonde hair and deep, kind hazel eyes, Kade's mum is the picture of middle-class charm. She looks vastly different from the last time we saw her, heading off to finalise her divorce and run. Her spotless dress and expensive heels are gone, replaced by worn jeans and a floral blouse.

"Oh, Hudson," she cries out.

He's nearly knocked off his feet by the strength of her hug. She sobs loudly, soaking him with her tears. Behind them, Kade's younger sister watches on with wet cheeks. Cece is also blonde and classically beautiful like her mother, all soft lines and bright smiles.

"Calm down," Hudson grumbles. "You're causing a scene."

"You be quiet. A mother is entitled to hug and kiss her baby."

Seeing something so pure come from such evil warms my chest. Hudson secretly loves her attention; there's no denying the shine of tears in his eyes. Unconditional love isn't something he's experienced a whole lot of.

Seven disappears to order drinks. I laugh at him salivating over the extensive coffee menu. We have a decent stash of cash left over that Kade distributed when we left Scotland. When Janet spots me over Hudson's shoulder, her tears intensify.

"Brooke. You're looking so much better, my dear."

I clear my throat awkwardly. "Thank you, Mrs Knight. I'm getting there."

Bundled into her perfume-scented embrace, she kisses my short hair. "Please, call me Janet. We're beyond such formalities now. Come, sit. We don't have much time."

Crowded around the small table, Cece offers me a quick squeeze before retaking her seat. Janet refuses to release Hudson's hand. He rolls his eyes while pecking Cece's cheek. Seeing him around her is too fucking sweet for me to take. I adore the soft soul within his cruel, hardened shell.

"Do you need anything? More money?" Janet worries. "I can get more for you."

"We're fine," Hudson answers. "Everyone's safe. We're staying with the security firm that Kade told you about."

"Good, good. I needed to know that before we leave."

"Is something wrong?"

Janet grimaces. "We're on our way to the airport. My sister owns a villa in Southern Spain. Leroy is putting pressure on us with the divorce proceedings, and we can't hide here any longer. His threats have become physical. I fear for our lives if we stay."

"How are you getting out of the country?" Hudson frowns.

"Don't worry about us. We have all the right documents. My husband isn't the only one with friends in the right places." She lifts her sombre gaze to Hudson. "We came to say goodbye."

Adam's apple bobbing, he squeezes her hand tight. "As long as you're safe. Things are going to get messier here as the truth comes out. The more distance between us, the better."

Seven returns, already downing his third espresso shot. He stations himself against the wall, his caffeine-fuelled gaze trained on the front entrance.

"What about Kade?" I ask nervously.

"That boy has worried about the world since he was eight years old," Janet says with a wistful smile. "Such a kind child, so full of love. He's borne the responsibility for our family's sins for too long. This worry is mine to carry, and mine alone."

"Mum," Cece pleads.

Janet tucks hair behind her ear. "You'll see him again, Hudson too. When this is all over, we can be a family again."

"May be sooner than you think." Hudson grins at her.

The tinkle of the store bell interrupts our exchange. Seven doesn't move or pull out a weapon, so I let myself relax. Hudson stands up to greet the newest customer entering the coffee shop.

With his broken arm in a plaster cast and face covered in dozens of cuts, Kade awkwardly lumbers up to the table. He offers Hudson a grateful look before facing his family.

"Mum. Cece."

"Oh my God." Janet covers her mouth. "What did they do to you?"

Kade grunts as she slams into him, searching every inch of his body for more wounds. Cece starts to cry all over again, looking lost in her corner. I clear my throat, prompting Hudson to pull her into a hug. She needs her big brother more than anything right now.

"It's okay, we're all being looked after," Kade reassures them both. "Just a few bumps and scratches. I can't believe you were going to leave without saying goodbye."

Still fussing, Janet straightens the sling holding his cast. "You've spent so long looking after everyone else. For once, I wanted to protect you from worrying. It's a mother's job."

Taking a seat, Kade looks pale and even more exhausted than usual. The arm fracture was pretty severe, broken in two places following the blast. His recovery is set to take a while.

"The explosion? You didn't do it?" Janet hazards a guess.

"It was all them," Kade confirms sadly. "We're being framed."

Janet pulls an envelope from her handbag and slides it to Kade. "I was going to give this to your brother. It's sworn statements from us both."

"What?" Hudson exclaims, stealing the envelope.

"I don't know much. You saw more of his business dealings than me, Kade. Everything I have seen is in there. Fundraisers, business partners, investment dinners. If nothing else, it will ruin the last of Leroy's reputation."

Kade manages a tight smile. "I'll get it to the right people."

With the envelope tucked away, Janet gets emotional again. The clock is ticking down. I watch a taxicab pull up outside of the coffee shop and blare its horn. She hugs her two sons, before letting Cece get a squeeze in too. I'm the last person she approaches.

"Brooke." Janet clasps my shoulders. "There's something else. I didn't know for sure until I met you, but you look so much like her. Except for the eyes."

"What are you talking about?"

Her smile is tight, pained. "Early on in my marriage, Leroy worked for an investment bank. He was involved in brokering a multimillion-pound loan to expand a psychiatric institute. Real cutting-edge stuff for the nineties. I was so proud that day, I could barely take my eyes off him."

"Mum," Kade warns.

"She smiled and thanked me for my husband's hard work while her clinician watched on." Janet ignores his deliberate stare. "I was pregnant with Kade at the time. Such an old memory, but you deserve to know."

"You met my mother?"

As the taxi driver hits the horn again, Janet offers me a sad look. "All I wanted was a happy marriage and children to fill the void I couldn't fathom in our life. I didn't know what his involvement would become."

"You couldn't have known," Hudson mutters.

"I wish I could tell you all that he wasn't always such a monster. I have wasted my life fooling myself." Her eyes stray to her boys, then Cece. "My marriage brought me the greatest gifts of my life. For that, I'm thankful."

With a final squeeze, she takes Cece's hand and heads for the waiting taxi. My heart is thundering against my ribcage. I can't help but cringe away when Kade reaches for me. All I see when I look at him is the cold, deadly stare of his father in that hotel room.

"Sorry," I rush out. "It's not you."

"No, I'm sorry. I should have told you. Dad has a lot of secrets. Incendia was one of them for a very long time. I am ashamed to call that piece of shit my father."

I meet his worried gaze. "Whether he's your father or not, when this is done, you will only have one parent left. That's a damn promise."

CHAPTER 24
ELI

CASUAL SABOTAGE - YUNGBLUD

"WHEN WAS the first patient admitted into the Zimbardo wing?"

Hunter's crisp, all-business tone takes no prisoners. He's been grilling Professor Lazlo for the last hour, relentlessly pinning down every last detail. The four government agents are all listening and taking meticulous notes, alternating in turns with the questioning.

It's satisfying to see Lazlo's full, utterly damning confession being recorded for later use, even if the contents turn my stomach. After Patient Two's opening evidence, the agents' attitudes abruptly changed. The wealth of information we've already given them is undeniable and the worst is yet to come.

"This guy is full of shit," Phoenix complains, his hand running up and down my leg. "He's dodging the hard questions and trying to avoid blame. Does he think we're stupid?"

Snuggling closer to him, I let my lips brush over his exposed collarbone. He isn't wearing a shirt, exposing his chiselled chest and many healing bruises. We're sprawled out on the huge sectional sofa beneath the duvet we stole from the bedroom, a massive bowl of popcorn between us.

We haven't been separated since he returned from the medical wing. It's been a full week of late-night testimonies and short tempers from the whole group. We left Brooklyn and Hudson to argue about dinner and controversial pizza toppings an hour ago, retreating to the living room to watch the live feed.

She refuses to watch it, and I don't blame her.

All we have to do is sit here and listen.

She lived through this shit.

None of us know what giving evidence is going to do to Brooklyn's fragile mental health. If her worsening mood and rapid-fire temper leading up to next week are anything to go by, we're in for a bumpy ride. She and Seven are next on the list. Clearly, Hunter is saving the most explosive for last.

"Stick your pineapple crap up your ass, Hudson! It does not belong on pizza!"

The angry slam of a door startles me. Phoenix murmurs for me to breathe, his arm trapping me against his naked chest. I wait for it to pass, accepting the intrusive flavours in my mind. Bitter smoke and harsh chemicals are replaced by sharp, fruity oranges and the sweet tang of freshly picked mint leaves.

Rather than fight against it, I'm trying something new, letting the anxiety and flavours wash over me without diving headfirst into them. We have such little control over our lives at the moment. This is the only thing I can change, and I'm learning to cope with things differently.

I think this is what recovery is supposed to feel like.

After years of fighting, it feels good to let go.

"You two wanna keep it down a bit?" Phoenix calls out. "It's only pizza, firecracker."

"No! I do not want to keep it down!"

Storming into the room, Brooklyn's hands are curled into fists. She looks primed to explode, her platinum pixie cut standing in all directions. Not to mention the visible cuts on her inner arms, revealed by her tank top. Hell, I'm the last person to judge how she decides to cope.

"I am so done with that arrogant, know-it-all, suffocating asshole hanging all over me!" she rages, throwing a decorative cushion at the wall. "If he offers to run through my testimony one more time, I'm going to stick his eyeballs on cocktail sticks and serve them for dinner."

"Can we get a side order of fries with that?" Phoenix deadpans without a smile. "Maybe some dips too, cheeky bit of mayo. Make it a real spread. Eli? Thoughts?"

I nod enthusiastically.

Hands on her hips, Brooklyn pins us both with an exasperated scowl. Phoenix cracks and laughs so hard, it vibrates through my body with the lack of space between us. Even I manage a low chuckle.

"It's like living with five goddamn teenagers!"

"Come sit down before you explode," Phoenix orders while still laughing.

He switches off the television before Brooklyn can spot the live feed. When she watched a mere thirty seconds of evidence earlier in the week, she had a complete meltdown.

We caught her talking to Augustus again. Or rather, the sick, invisible version of him that exists in her head. Enzo intervened when she cut herself with a kitchen knife while screaming at the thin air to leave her alone.

Hunter's overpaid shrink, Doctor Richards, was forced to sedate Brooklyn. He's having a field day medicating us all after weeks of surviving without. Phoenix is back on mood stabilisers too. He's been a lot calmer since.

"Baby girl," I coax in a deep, rasping voice.

That's all it takes to penetrate her enraged fog. My girl can never refuse when I find the strength to gather my crappy voice. With a final annoyed huff, she stretches out on the sofa beside me.

"Why aren't Kade and Lucia back yet?"

"It's only been a few hours," Phoenix reasons. "We can't all be there. Taking it in shifts was the right call. Kade will get her through it."

"It should be me supporting her."

"You… h-hurt enough," I stutter out.

"I'm fine! Jesus Christ."

Phoenix's hand eases under my shirt, stroking the skin of my stomach in a teasing caress. "Do we believe that crock of shit, Eli?"

I shake my head.

Brooklyn groans. "Stop psychoanalysing me. I get that enough with the others."

With Phoenix's skin on mine, I tilt her face towards me. She accepts my palm on her cheek without thinking, her dark eyelashes hiding the anguish I know I'll find in her eyes. When our lips meet, I coax the truth from her soul with each stroke of my tongue.

I can taste her anxiety and fear, sense the visceral terror eating away at her. Recanting all she's been through to us was scary enough—laying it bare for a huge, national investigation, and basically the whole fucking world to hear, is a whole other story.

"You call that a kiss?" Phoenix teases, his fingers tugging at my waistband. "I can't get over there to do it myself. Show her a real kiss, Elijah."

Ignoring his taunts, I let my tongue tangle with Brooklyn's. She's relaxing into the kiss with each hot, heady second, surrendering to the claim we hold on her soul. When I bite down, seeking the slick tang of her blood, she presses her body into me with a mewl.

"Still fine, firecracker?"

"Fuck you, Nix," she growls between kisses.

"Not from there, you can't. Shall we take this into the bedroom?"

"You think I care if someone sees us?"

Brooklyn's challenge is full of sexy confidence, making my cock jolt in my boxers. She's become bolder recently, no longer afraid of taking what she wants. We've come too close to death for caution. I woke up to her lips wrapped around my cock the other night, her pussy wet and begging for my touch.

Taking control of the situation, Brooklyn climbs over me to sit in Phoenix's lap. I shift my leg, allowing me to sit up and watch their performance. Their lips meet in a sizzling collision, with his unbandaged hand wrapping around her slender throat.

She grinds against him while fighting for dominance, his grip appearing to steadily increase. Watching their two opposing forces face off, I dip my hand into my sweats to stroke my length. Blood drips down Brooklyn's chin as Phoenix attacks the nip I inflicted, but he licks it aside with enthusiasm.

"I wonder what your blood would taste like on Eli's cock," Phoenix muses, sending electric bolts down my spine.

She doesn't miss a beat. "Want to play a game with us, Nix?"

"Depends what the prize is."

Brooklyn grabs a coin from the coffee table. "Heads or tails. My pick or yours. Eli gets to play our willing victim."

Fuck, I'm going to come just listening to her dirty mouth.

"The prize?" Phoenix prompts.

"You still want me to be your little slut, Nix? I'll do that and more. Whatever you want. I know you like us submissive."

Looking triumphant, he nods. "Deal."

Brooklyn throws me a heated look before tossing the coin in the air. It lands against the back of her hand, the answer hidden from sight.

"Heads and I get to taste your blood on his cock," she announces.

"Well, then tails and I watch you ride Eli's face."

When she lifts her hand, Phoenix audibly groans. The heads side is facing upwards, marking her victory, but he sure as hell doesn't look like he minds.

"Got a knife, Eli?"

"C-Coat."

Brooklyn gets up and searches in the pocket of my leather jacket that's hanging over a chair. As she saunters back to us, she tears the loose tank top over her head, exposing her bare, perfect breasts. Stepping out of her comfy yoga pants, she's left in nothing but a scrap of soaked cotton.

I continue rubbing my dick as she returns to Phoenix's lap, twirling the penknife in her hands that months ago, I used to inflict the scars on her hip. The same steel blade kisses Phoenix's wrist as he willingly offers it to her, his bottom lip caught between his teeth.

"Ever cut yourself?" Brooklyn asks curiously.

Phoenix smirks. "I prefer to torture myself with Class A drugs. I lack the patience for pain that you two share."

"It doesn't have to hurt." Pressing the penknife to his wrist, Brooklyn pushes the blade in deep. "Feel that sharp sting?" She begins to drag it along, parting his flesh. "It burns, right?"

Phoenix looks both turned on and disturbed as she deftly slices his wrist, deep enough for blood to trail down to his elbow. When she pulls the blade from his arm, the breath whooshes from Phoenix's mouth.

"And now?" Brooklyn raises an eyebrow.

"It feels like sprinting for the finish line and taking your first glorious breath," he wonders. "Fuck, I'm actually turned on by this."

"Told ya. Let's have a taste, shall we?"

Brooklyn takes my blade to her mouth, sliding her tongue along the serrated steel to taste his essence. I fist my cock tighter, trying to relieve the hunger burning up inside me. She's never looked so damn powerful, and Phoenix looks fucking perfect worshipping her sadistic ways.

Her sick lesson continues as she smears his blood all over her hand. Coating her skin in the red lubricant, she turns back to me. I let go of my aching length, allowing her to lather it in the warm, sticky substance.

Her lips wrap around the tip, sliding it deep into the welcoming prison of her mouth. I let my head hit the back of the sofa, gripping her short hair with my spare hand. She bobs on my length, taking it base to tip several times, each one nudging deeper into her throat.

"Hot damn," Phoenix murmurs. "Can you taste me, baby?"

Coming up for air, Brooklyn licks his blood that's smeared all around her mouth. She spots the bead of pre-come gathered on my cock and goes back for that too, her tongue swirling around the tip.

"Why don't you find out for yourself?" she challenges.

Dragging me up by my t-shirt, Brooklyn pushes me along the sofa towards

Phoenix. He's still finding walking difficult while his injuries heal, but the way his gaze devours me leaves no room for hesitation. He looks at us both like we're heaven and hell all in one, trapping him in an infernal battle for his soul.

I straddle his chest before pushing my cock against his lips. Seeing Phoenix Kent surrender to me is something I never thought possible. He's the dominant one in our weird dynamic, but watching him eagerly take my length in his mouth opens a whole new realm of possibilities. I move my hips, savouring the feel of his tongue gliding over my length.

"Why don't you let him see how you taste, Eli?" Brooklyn suggests. "I want to watch you fill his mouth with your come and let Phoenix drink every last drop. He needs to learn to play by our rules too."

"Y-Yes, baby girl," I say obediently.

Increasing my pace, I abuse Phoenix's throat as roughly as he's done to me, time and time again. To his credit, he never once falters. Brooklyn lays back down and gracefully slides off her underwear. When she spreads her legs, two fingers push deep into her pussy. Watching her pleasure herself while I fuck Phoenix's mouth is too much.

I roughly grab a handful of blue hair to steady myself, punishing Phoenix with the fast pace of my thrusts. His hand reaches out to grab a handful of my bare ass when I release a strangled cry. His lips don't relent, milking my release until I'm pouring hot seed directly down his throat.

When I pull out, there's blood and come painted across Phoenix's mouth. I don't give a fuck anymore. Shifting back, my mouth slants against his in a dominant kiss, cementing my new-found kink for taking control. I can taste myself on him, mixing with his blood and fusing our souls together.

Brooklyn's moan of pleasure brings us back to reality. Her head is thrown back as she works herself into a frenzy, her fingers pumping in and out of her slick heat. Climbing off Phoenix, I stand above them both in a position of power.

I'm calling the shots now.

They'll both bow to me tonight.

"No," I command before she can climax.

Her movements halt instantly, even as she releases a frustrated groan. Pointing at the hard lump straining against Phoenix's own sweats, I raise an expectant eyebrow.

"W-Watch... you f-fuck him."

She submits to my order, crawling to Phoenix on her hands and knees. I scoop her discarded panties from the floor as she positions herself above him, inhaling the sweet fragrance of her arousal. Phoenix looks bemused as she frees his dick and sinks down on it. He's not allowed to do anything but submit.

Brooklyn begins to move, grinding on him in confident strokes. Just watching them together has my erection strengthening again, but this isn't about me. This is Phoenix learning to take his own medicine for the first time. As Brooklyn quickens her pace, I move to stand behind her.

She trembles when my fingers dance down the length of her visible spine. I pepper kisses along her lower back, reaching the curve of her pert ass. She gasps in shock when my tongue traces the crack of her asshole, before slowly pushing inside of her.

"Fuck, Eli!"

Removing my tongue, I push a thumb into her moistened back entrance next. She moans again at the intrusion, slowly relaxing as I gently slide a second finger inside. I love watching her squirm.

"Care to join us?" Phoenix lets out a strangled breath.

Even with my fingers fucking her from behind, Brooklyn refuses to relent. Watching them from this position is so hot. I can see Phoenix's glistening sheath gliding straight into her cunt. Feeling the throb of my swollen cock, I know I'm ready to join back in. This shit is too hot to miss.

Transferring saliva to her tight, inviting asshole, I prepare to push inside my baby girl. She's already on the verge of falling apart between us, balancing herself on Phoenix as he watches us perform. The moment I begin to ease inside of her, she screams through a hard, fast release.

I hold her by the hips, biting back a moan of ecstasy. She's so fucking tight, I can feel Phoenix's length pressing up against mine as he fucks her pussy at the same time. We're filling every available space inside of her. Struck by an idea, I pick my penknife back up.

"Keep still, beautiful," I whisper in her ear.

A light sheen of sweat covers Brooklyn's face as she stares down at Phoenix, doing exactly as told. I wrap an arm around her from behind, pressing the stained blade right against her jugular vein. It's juicy and throbbing with blood waiting to be spilled.

"Eli," Phoenix warns, watching us.

Just to punish him, I push the blade deeper into Brooklyn's neck. His mouth closes immediately. This is the status quo now. I'm in charge, and I want to hold her life in the palm of my hand. A single slip or momentary lapse, and she'll bleed out while riding his cock.

"F-Feel that?"

"Yes," Brooklyn hushes.

I move my hips to push into her, and her walls hug my cock. She's gasping and trying not to move, a thin stream of blood spilling down her neck and painting mortality across her breasts. I meet Phoenix's widened eyes.

"Lick," I demand.

Watching him obey me is thrilling. Brooklyn continues to ride him while he brings his tongue to her left nipple, cleaning up the trail of blood swirling across her porcelain skin. When I take the knife from her throat and offer it to Phoenix, he looks at me questioningly.

My girl knows, though.

She's seen the darkest recesses of my broken mind.

"Please," Brooklyn begs.

Offering her scarred and sliced arm for his perusal, Phoenix looks like a deer caught in the headlights. I've never seen him uncertain or afraid in the bedroom. He's usually the alpha male, doling out the humiliation. We've blown his comfort zone to smithereens and left him to pick up the scattered pieces.

"You… want me to cut you?"

"I'm scared, Nix. I don't want to walk into that interview room and forget who I am."

His eyes flick to mine again. I nod encouragingly, still gliding into Brooklyn from behind. She's trembling all over as another orgasm builds. When Phoenix takes a deep breath and brings the knife to her arm, carefully slicing a patch of skin, Brooklyn's release crests for a second time.

Pain and pleasure.

Sickness and sanity.

Love and obsession.

Nothing about our union is so easily categorised. We are made of extremes, testing the boundaries no normal person would dare cross. I grip her hips tighter before pouring myself into her asshole, already exhausted from my second release of the night.

Phoenix tosses the blade on the sofa, his fingers gripping the fresh wounds he's inflicted on the girl he loves. Swirling the blood with his thumb from the leaking cuts, he looks fascinated. His stained digit pushes into Brooklyn's mouth before she can protest, forcing her to clean her own blood from his skin.

"Beautiful," he utters.

She greedily sucks on his thumb, riding the waves of her climax. That pushes Phoenix over the edge. He releases a guttural moan, his forehead resting against her sternum while filling her up. Unable to remain upright, we all collapse in a dog pile.

Limbs, arms, come, and blood spread across the sofa. We fight to catch our breath before erupting back into laughter. The living room is a fucking mess. Cushions and stained fabric surround us, so there's no denying what we've been up to.

Right on time, the door opens to admit a waft of fresh dough and melted cheese. Hudson is carrying a huge stack of pizza boxes, balancing several extra boxes of baked cookies on top. He stops dead in his tracks when he spots us all, naked and laughing at the look on his face.

"I, uh. Pepperoni pizza, extra cheese. No pineapple," he says in bemusement.

Brooklyn props her chin on her hand. "Thanks, baby. That wasn't so hard, was it?"

"I dunno," Phoenix chuckles. "Felt pretty hard to me."

I've never seen Hudson blush before, but fuck me gently, his cheeks are bright pink as he deposits the pizzas and takes a seat in one of the stuffed armchairs. He stares at all of our naked skin on display while grabbing a huge slice of pizza and inhaling it.

"I'm not cleaning this shit up," he says around a mouthful of food. "And you can pay Hunter back for his ruined sofa."

CHAPTER 25
BROOKLYN

DIE4U - BRING ME THE HORIZON

STARING into the dead eye of the camera, I feel a chilling sense of déjà vu. The interview room is dull, with blank white walls and two boarded-up windows. I'm terrified to blink, in case the world melts away and I'm back in that basement, ready for a new experiment to begin.

Are you scared of the truth, Miss West?

Running won't help you.

Let's pick up where we left off.

Clearing my throat, I shove Augustus's sick taunting from my mind. In the corner behind me, Hunter sits with his laptop. He hasn't spoken a single word to me, but I can see the almost-black circles beneath his clear eyes. He's grieving, but still holding up his end of our bargain. I can respect that.

"Here, water." Enzo deposits a plastic cup in front of me.

"Thanks."

Hesitating, he peers down at me. "Just tell the truth, kid. You're not on trial. These people will ask you difficult questions. Don't fight them. It'll only make this worse."

"Not on trial... yet."

Squeezing my shoulder, Enzo retreats to his corner. His huge arms band across his barrel chest, every inch of his towering frame screaming intimidation. It feels good knowing he's here to keep me safe, even if neither of them can fend off the demons within me.

Ten minutes later, there's a sharp rap on the door before it opens. Three men and one woman enter, dressed to the nines in pressed suits and blank, corporate expressions. After coolly greeting Hunter and Enzo, two of them sit in front of me. The others take the chairs behind and pull out their notebooks.

"Brooklyn West?" the woman opposite asks.

"Yeah, that's me."

"My name is Agent Barlow, this is Agent Jonas." She gestures to the man next to her. "We represent the Serious Crimes Unit. We've been assigned to this case to gather the information needed to proceed with an investigation."

Her pale-green gaze is sharp, attentive, framed by perfectly blow-dried, blonde waves. She looks like a spotless piece of artwork, slick and polished in her finery. I feel awkward and entirely insignificant in my ripped jeans and Hudson's *Badflower* t-shirt.

"I understand," I respond.

With their notebooks and thick dossiers of paperwork set up, they adjust the camera on its tripod, so it faces me at a direct angle. The moment it starts to record, sweat begins to trickle down the back of my neck. I hold my shaking hands in my lap, hiding them from sight.

"We have spoken to Professor Lazlo. Are you familiar with this individual?" Agent Barlow asks.

"He was my therapist last year before my care was transferred to Doctor Warren Augustus. He later imprisoned me for several months and began a lengthy period of psychological torture, abuse and manipulation."

Sliding a glossy photograph over to me, I'm faced with the icy, intelligent eyes of my oppressor. Augustus looks slick and well-groomed in the image, dressed in his usual tailored suit and tie. He seems to be leaving a lavish fundraiser event for Incendia, captured climbing into a fancy sports car.

"This man?" Agent Jonas speaks for the first time.

I meet his steely brown gaze beneath a head of thin, silver-grey hair and defined wrinkles. He's older and seems sterner somehow, his entire posture geared towards aggression. My hackles immediately rise.

"That's him."

"Several serious allegations have been levelled against this man by other patients. We have spoken to Lucia Killmore and Patient Two. Both credit their imprisonment to Doctor Augustus."

"Did they tell you what else he did to them?"

"We're not here to discuss them," Agent Barlow interrupts. "Professor Lazlo has admitted to tampering with your medication during solitary confinement and later dosing you with unregulated experimental drugs for a long period of time."

"He tried to have me killed." I watch several hands scribble down notes. "Another patient was on Incendia's payroll in Blackwood, tasked with maintaining a steady supply of contraband into the institute for clinicians to observe and document. It was a social experiment."

Turning to a fresh piece of paper in her overflowing notebook, Agent Barlow offers me a small smile. "Start from the very beginning. The more you tell us, the better equipped we are to offer you a deal."

"How can I trust that you will?"

"We're here for the truth, Brooklyn."

Sparing Enzo a panicked look, he gives me a nod of reassurance. It does nothing to abate the fear wrapping around my vocal cords. I just got my family back; I can't lose them again. We have no way of knowing if a deal can be made. These suits are not taking my guys away from me.

"Mr Rodriguez and his firm have secured your protection from immediate incarceration," Agent Barlow explains, each word like a gut punch. "We have dozens of unconfirmed reports of fatalities and a very small pool of suspects. Actions have consequences."

"I... I was under duress."

"For all of them?" Agent Jonas supplies.

"Do you have any idea what they did to us?" I snarl back.

He crosses his arms, looking unimpressed. I doubt my case will be helped if I break his nose, despite the temptation. We survived by fighting tooth and nail, no matter this asshole's opinions. They will never know what we went through in the dark.

"Brooklyn," Agent Barlow says gently. "I came into this process feeling sceptical. Incendia has a spotless reputation and, as I'm sure you are aware, many connections across the country. I've come to realise there is far more than meets the eye in this case. I want to help you."

"Does your colleague feel the same way?"

Releasing a huff, Agent Jonas nods. "We've been assigned to this task force to find one thing—the truth. If you can give that to us, we can take it back to our superiors. This is the only way to help yourself."

Biting my lip, I glance between them. "What if myself and my friends vanished?"

"We would be forced to pursue and charge you with a very long list of crimes that would ensure your lifelong imprisonment. Until we have enough evidence to the contrary, you remain a convict."

"What the hell happened to innocent until proven guilty, huh?"

"You were guilty long before you stepped foot inside Blackwood Institute," she states plainly. "That much is indisputable. Help us prove that you're a victim here, not the perpetrator."

Fresh out of options, I slump back in my seat. My mind winds all the way back, past late-night kisses and broken-hearted reunions, bloodied hook ups in graveyards, and glimpses of real, tangible hope that were swiftly extinguished. I turn back the clock on the best and worst year of my life.

I'm back in Clearview.

Just another statistic, praying for death to come.

The whole filthy tale takes hours, each revelation of horror dragging onwards. Endless questions meet multiple shocked silences. Notebooks are swapped out, fresh pens are retrieved, and litres of coffee consumed. When the clock strikes on my seventh hour under examination, I'm struggling to hold it together.

"Do you recognise this person?"

Agent Barlow hands me another glossy, printed photograph. Guilt and shame twist my insides until I can barely breathe. Teegan's bright, lively smile stares back at me beneath her red hair and a handful more facial piercings than the last time I saw her. She looks different.

I can't ignore the handful of scars marking her face, along with the slightly crooked tilt of her healed nose. To my horror, she's missing several teeth in the photo too. The phantom pain of them cutting against my knuckles has me jumping up. My chair crashes to the floor behind me.

"When was this taken?"

"Last week," Agent Jonas answers. "We reviewed her files to confirm her discharge as authorised by Doctor Augustus. The records surrounding her injuries mention a patient attack while in custody."

With tears stinging my eyes, I hug her photograph to my chest. I can almost feel her arms around me, demanding a tight, desperate cuddle while laughing through the pain. I'd do anything for one more hug. I've lost the only two friends I've ever had.

That fucking hurts.

"Did you attack Teegan Lopez?"

"She was my best friend." I study her healed, happy face. "People close to me... they get hurt. I hurt them. Everything I touch turns to shit."

I sense Enzo stepping towards me as my crying intensifies. I'm too exhausted and emotionally drained to keep a lid on it any longer. She will forever bear the mark of our friendship. I did that to her. She gave me her love and trust. In return, I nearly took her life from her.

"Brooke," Enzo placates. "Just take a deep breath."

"This is never going away, is it? I thought... I thought I had a chance. All I wanted was a chance to live.".

Agent Barlow stands, her hands raised in a calming manner. "Miss West, we're not done here. Please sit back down and answer our questions or things will get a lot more complicated for you."

"They won't ever let me forget," I whisper to myself. "Augustus was right. I can't escape Blackwood. My past will always follow me. You can't help me."

"This is your chance to avoid prison. You need to earn it."

Still holding the photograph slicing my heart into ribbons, I ignore their voices. The walls are closing in on me like an optical illusion. I'm going to be crushed to death under the weight of their accusations. Just as I curl my hand around the door handle, Enzo's arms attempt to trap me.

"No! Get your hands off me!"

"Brooke," he repeats. "Calm down. We're trying to help."

Jamming my elbow into his ribcage, I take the brief distraction and wrench the door open. Hunter is trying to follow, but he's still sore from the explosion and moving slowly. The government agents don't move a muscle. All they care about is their recording, capturing my madness. Another point against me.

"Brooklyn, stop—"

Ignoring Hunter's growly voice, I sprint into the waiting area. Pacing in front of the door with a stony expression, Seven stops when he spots me running at full speed.

"Eight?"

I throw myself at him. "I can't... can't... breathe!"

Holding me against his firm chest, he cups the back of my head. "I've got you, princess."

He's caught in a heated argument with Hunter and Enzo, who followed me from the interview room. I can't hear a damn word while hanging off him. My ears are ringing loudly, like I'm drowning in electrified water. Each beat feels like a hose pipe of water battering my body, or the sharp sting of a whip cracking against my skin.

Seven scoops me off my feet, cradling me like I'm a lost child relying on him to bring me home. I bury my face in his neck, letting the sobs wash over me. I'm powerless. My surroundings mean nothing as I fight to stay in the driver's seat.

"Hold on, Eight. I'm getting you out of here."

Awash in darkness, I cling to the feel of his skin on mine. He smells like freshly ground coffee from the cup he quickly drained, and Hudson's aftershave. They've been sharing clothes since they're similar in size. My fingers tangle in his soft mane of hair. I grip it tightly, needing to feel something real in my hands.

Seven doesn't say a word as he sprints far away from the building and those seeking to dissect my brain further. My feet hit the ground and cold air washes over me. Propped against a wall, his huge hand shakes my shoulder to try and rouse me. I'm barely holding on.

"Eight? Talk to me. Show me those beautiful eyes."

"They w-won't let me live," I choke out. "I've d-done too much. I'm going to prison."

"You know we would never let that happen."

"We're both going down! We can't win this!"

I'm growing even more hysterical, staring into his pained, caramel orbs looking down at me. I've spent so long trying to spark hope in Seven's dead soul. I can't find it in myself anymore. Every twisted, hateful taunt my hallucinations have thrown at me over the years is coming true.

"I w-won't go back inside." I gulp hard. "I'd rather die."

"That's not an option, Eight. You're better than this."

"Am I? You know what I've done! I should just get it over and done with."

Gripping my chin, his forehead smacks straight into mine. Our souls are trapped together in an inescapable prison. I can smell the cigarettes and coffee on his breath, feel the palpable emotion crackling between us. The days we spent clinging to life are gone. Now, we're waiting for death.

"If you need forgiveness, I'll fucking give it to you," Seven says fiercely. "You are forgiven, Patient Eight. The world broke us once. Don't let it take our future too."

"I can't run… they'll follow me. I don't want to live in a world without you."

"So what? You don't live at all? That's fucking bullshit, Eight!"

His face is carved in devilish fury, a tidal wave of anger simmering beneath the surface. When his hand latches around my wrist, it nearly grinds my bones together. I fight and writhe, but Seven won't let me go.

"You want me to live for you? I expect the same goddamn thing," he hisses.

"I… I c-can't. Not like this."

"I refuse to accept that."

Dragged down the alleyway, I throw every insult under the sun at him. All I want is to get on the first truck heading out of town and hide from the inevitable. The agents don't give a fuck about what Augustus did to us. I'm a monster to them. Someone who deserves to be locked up.

Seven tows me to the very back of the dank alley, where a sketchy fire escape wraps around the tall, run-down tower block. I scream some more as he throws me over his shoulder, trapping my legs with his arm. I have to shut my eyes when he begins to scale the fire escape.

The world is tilted upside down, growing higher and higher. My fists batter Seven's back but yield no results. He keeps me imprisoned until we reach the top of the building. He's panting hard after the gruelling climb. It's abandoned up here, nothing but smashed pallets and a few pigeons.

"Here we are, then," Seven announces darkly. "Nice tall building, nothing stopping you. Wanna give up and die? Be my guest. Off you go."

I'm placed back on my unsteady legs. We're at the very edge of the rooftop, with an unfamiliar London suburb stretching out in all directions. It must be at least two hundred feet high. I can almost taste the clouds on my tongue.

"What are you doing?" I splutter.

Seven grabs my bicep and hauls me even closer to the edge. My battered Chucks involuntarily step up, heaved by his immense strength. I'm mere inches from plummeting and becoming a puddle of matter. One step or the slightest slip, and it's all over.

"This is what you wanted, isn't it?" he bellows. "Your men told me about what happened in Blackwood. I'm not going to stop you like they did. If you want to do this, fucking own it."

"I... I..."

"What is it, Patient Eight? Haven't got the balls to do it?"

"Fuck you, Sev!"

His steadying hand disappears from my arm. I wobble in the cold air, feeling the first patters of autumn rain hit my face. The rumble of an overhead aeroplane fills the excruciating silence between us. Seven stands there, waiting and watching.

"Clock's ticking."

"Why are you doing this?" I scream at him.

"Because you're being a coward! You told me to live, goddammit." His hand is a tight fist, like he wants to deck me. "You gave me a family and showed me what it felt like to belong. Now, you want to bail!"

"I'm fucking scared! That's all!"

"Spare me your excuses. You think I'm not scared? Sitting in that fucking room, dragging up six years of trauma? It's terrifying for me too! I'm doing it for you, for our family. The one you gave me."

Teetering in the air, I stare at him. My saviour. My monster. The keeper of the absolute worst parts of myself. The world wants to bury us alive, regardless of the truth. We're both being sent down to hell.

"We will never matter to them," I spell out. "Our lives are forfeit."

His hand moves like a lightning bolt. One moment, I'm a breath from death. The next, I'm falling into his awaiting arms and swept off my feet. Seven looks at me like I'm his entire fucking world, dead or alive. I can hardly breathe from the intensity of his possession.

"Your life will never be forfeit to me," he whispers roughly. "And certainly not to the others. You stood next to that coffin and promised that I would never be alone. Did you mean it?"

With my fingertip, I trace the shiny scar marking his forehead. I can still hear his screams. Augustus punished us together that day. It was late into our imprisonment, once the boundaries between us melted away. Seven stepped in front of the blow meant for me, taking a whip directly to the face.

"I meant it," I murmur.

"Prove it. Stay with me."

"Why?!"

"Because I can't survive without you!"

"What if they take us away from each other?" I shout through my tears.

Rather than answer, his lips crush against mine, bruisingly hard. I can't kiss him back. This isn't a show of love. There's no tenderness or romance. It's a punishment for daring to toss his fragile heart aside. He steals my breath and bites my lip, taking every bit of proof he needs.

"I swear on what's left of my life, I will always find you," Seven vows, kissing me softer. "I fucking love you, Eight."

"You do?"

"Of course I do, you frustrating creature. I own the final piece of your heart. Nobody will ever take that privilege from me."

We seal our promise in a heavy raincloud, trapped by wind and the uncontrollable power of fate. I don't complain once as Seven bends me over and fucks me on the rooftop, both soaked to the bone but uncaring. The entire city watches us collide, granting us a brief second of solitude.

He repeats that he loves me.

Over and over again.

I whisper it back, silently praying for the strength to be what he needs. I can feel this journey drawing to its close. We've travelled so far, battled for each second of sanity and belonging, yet still we're barrelling towards the edge of a cliff. I can't change that now.

The only way out of our love is death.

I've always loved a tragic ending.

CHAPTER 26
HUDSON

YOUTH - CLEOPATRICK

RIDING the elevator back to the apartment with Kade, we're both far too pleased with ourselves. Brooklyn's surprise is ready to go. The others have kept her distracted all afternoon while we prepared.

We've been granted the rest of the day off from giving evidence after Brooklyn's breakdown yesterday. Eli is the last to be called from our group. After that, we await the next steps. Each day has only brought more questions, so anxiety is at an all-time high.

"You think she'll like it?" Kade worries aloud.

His voice snaps me out of my overthinking.

"Fuck knows. She isn't herself at the moment."

"Are any of us? This whole situation is fucked."

I look at him, noting the lines of exhaustion. "You not sleeping much?"

He shakes his head. "Talking about everything was rough. I handed all of Dad's files over, the lot of them. Four months of working for the bastard taught me a few things, but I'm now an accomplice."

"That's bullshit. You got us out."

Kade scoffs. "I smuggled contraband, sold drugs, incited a riot and supplied weapons to convicted murderers. Oh, not to mention burning the place down and helping several convicts escape. They want my fucking head."

"Everything will work out."

"How can you be so sure?"

We arrive at our floor with a ding and step out of the elevator. I clap Kade on the shoulder as we head for our temporary home, hating the uncertainty in his voice. He's the last one to start doubting himself.

"There's no other option, that's why," I answer easily. "We did the impossible before. We'll do it again."

"Do you remember when I had to beg you to eat a single meal with me in

Blackwood?" Kade asks randomly. "A mere conversation took weeks of pleading. You'd given up."

"People change." I shrug off the shame eating me alive. "I grew up. Getting Brooklyn back changed everything for me. If that was possible, then I could do anything. Even learn to live with myself."

Before we can head inside, Kade's hand grabs my shirt sleeve.

"Hud… no matter what happens, I'm glad I got my brother back."

Jesus, he's determined to kill me off with this emotional shit. We're all going fucking insane in this place.

"Yeah, I love you too, jackass." I get him in a headlock and mess up his styled blonde locks. "Can we move on now? I'm not fucking kissing you."

"I still hate you, bro. You're a pain in my ass."

"And I will be forever. Thanks to you."

Entering the apartment together, we find the others spread across the sectional sofa in the living room. Phoenix and Eli are keeping up their end of the bargain, sandwiching Brooklyn between them while a movie plays. She doesn't appear to be paying attention, anxiously picking at her nails.

"Right, then." Kade claps his hands. "Who's ready for some fun?"

"Fun?" Brooklyn wrinkles her nose.

Draining a bottle of water from the kitchen, I toss her a smirk. "You know, fun? It's when you get off the fucking sofa and join the land of the living. Maybe even crack a smile. Sounds crazy, huh?"

"Does this fun involve alcohol?" Phoenix grins mischievously.

Offering Eli a hand up, Kade moves to grab Brooklyn next. She squeals while being lifted into the air and pushed in my direction. I imprison her in my arms before she can crawl back into bed and hide like she's taken to doing.

"Come and find out."

"Where's Seven?" Brooklyn frowns.

"He's… out," I answer lamely. "Preoccupied."

"I thought he was with you guys. Where did he go?"

Silencing her questions with a kiss, I pillage her mouth until Phoenix starts wolf-whistling. We break apart, both breathing hard. He's hanging off Eli, still needing support with walking.

It's the first time I've seen him look like himself after losing his sister. His latest depressive episode has been rough, even with medication. He'll always suffer from these intense, brutal cycles.

Kade takes Brooklyn's other hand, so we both have a grip on her. She's reluctantly pulled along, leaving the warm bubble of the apartment behind. I won't let her slip back into a detached haze. We have enough to contend with as it is. Whatever Seven did yesterday, it brought her back to us.

We ride the elevator down to the second floor, where Hunter's cleared the training room for us. I cover Brooklyn's eyes as soon as we step out, keeping her blinded. Phoenix and Eli follow Kade into the room, lit by giant windows.

In the centre, a professional boxing ring resides. Various machines and weights are dotted around the perimeter, along with benches and whiteboards. There's a gym upstairs that I located a while ago, but this is for group training more than working out. It's where Enzo puts his spooks through their paces.

"You better not be leading me to the shrink, Hud."

"Do you really think I'd do that to you?" I chuckle.

"Fuck knows. Kade spent an hour trying to convince me to talk to him."

"Well, there's no crazy talk tonight."

In the top corner of the room, we've set up a hell of a party. Fold-up tables full of snacks, beers and bottles of liquor await. Kade even managed to find some cheesy birthday decorations, hanging streamers and banners off the walls to complete the surprise. He looks damn pleased with himself.

Phoenix looks around. "Nice. You two should be party planners."

"Shut it," Kade orders, smiling. "Alright, she can look now."

Kissing Brooklyn's soft neck, I remove my hands from her eyes. She blinks several times while looking around, taking in every last detail. She seems confused more than anything.

"Are we having a birthday party? For who?"

"All of us," I whisper in her ear.

Kade smooths his loose, white t-shirt, appearing nervous. "We were talking the other night and realised we have never celebrated our birthdays. Not in Blackwood, that's for sure. So, we're having a joint party."

Helping himself to a beer before Kade can yell at him, Phoenix wrenches the cap off with his teeth like an animal. "Ahh, alcohol. My old friend. Happy fucking birthday, kids."

After a long moment of hesitation, a wide, brilliant smile blossoms across Brooklyn's face. It takes my breath away. For a moment, she looks like my blackbird. Not the jaded woman I know now, but the innocent, lively kid I used to know. Sometimes, I catch myself missing that person. Even if I did kill her.

"Hunter actually allowed this?" she asks excitedly.

To answer her question, the door to the training room opens again. Enzo steps in with a loud whoop, carrying a huge cardboard box in his arms. I've never seen him in anything but all-black cargo trousers and a form-fitting t-shirt, like he's permanently ready to kick some ass.

Behind him, Hunter is following in casual jeans and a polo shirt, looking slightly more subdued. His usually sleek hair is rumpled and loose, framing downcast eyes. His grief is still painfully obvious, but he agreed to this plan with minimal argument. He cares a lot, deep down.

"Did someone say party?" Enzo grins.

Depositing the cardboard box and opening it, he unveils a huge, glistening chocolate cake. It's made of several tiers, each boasting fudge frosting and white chocolate drizzle. The smile on Enzo's face widens as he steals a truffle off the top and sticks it in his mouth.

Hunter pointedly clears his throat.

"What?" Enzo shrugs. "It looked tasty."

Brooklyn leaves my embrace to approach them both. Enzo looks slightly surprised when she throws her arms around his neck, placing a kiss on his stubbly cheek. It's like she's hugging a mountain lion.

"Thank you for this."

His cheeks turn pink. "I didn't do shit, wildfire. Just cleared the room for your entourage."

Leaving him, Brooklyn approaches Hunter next. He looks positively unnerved by the prospect of her hugging him. I've never seen him give out affection, even with his team members. I doubt many people see beyond the professional armour he coats himself in.

She pulls him into a hug and also gives him a peck on the cheek. "Thanks, Hunter. This is exactly what we needed."

"You're welcome," he says gruffly. "Just keep it down, alright?"

Everyone converges around the drinks table, filling up plastic cups with all manner of hard liquor. Kade doesn't even protest as Phoenix drains his first two cups with enthusiasm. Theo chooses that moment to sneak in, skirting around the back with a set of speakers and his laptop.

When the heavy beat of music fills the room, everyone looks up at him. Theo appears startled by all of the attention, sheepishly rubbing the back of his neck while finding the right playlist.

"What's a party without music?"

Already looking a little glassy-eyed, Phoenix shrugs off Eli's overprotectiveness and begins an awkward dance. His leg is still stiff and healing, but that doesn't stop him from shaking his ass while everyone laughs at the sight. When he crooks a finger at Brooklyn, she shakes her head.

"Don't be a spoilsport, firecracker. Come show me those moves."

"You're such a dumbass."

"And a hell of a dancer."

Before she can protest, Eli shoves her in Phoenix's direction with a devious glint in his eye. He follows and the trio dance to the music like idiots, pretending the huge training room is a downtown nightclub. I nearly choke on a mouthful of vodka lemonade when Enzo joins in, busting out his retro dance moves.

"Well, she's smiling." Kade watches them with palpable happiness.

I knock our cups together in a toast. "Good call, brother."

Theo joins us in the corner, quietly helping himself to a drink. He props himself against the wall, watching everyone else with sadness in his eyes. Like Hunter, he seems flat, drained, a shadow of the sweet and socially awkward person we met.

Incendia has taken everything from them.

Yet, they still showed up for us.

"She seems better today," Hunter observes.

I pass him a beer. "Sounds like they grilled her pretty hard."

"Seven hours straight. I should have called it off sooner."

"You're trying to help us," Kade answers. "That's already more than we could've asked for."

Looking thoughtful, Hunter watches Enzo dance and drink with the other three. It must be something to reach such success with your best friend at your side. They've been running Sabre for seven years now, growing it from the ground up with nothing but their determination to help those who can't do it themselves.

"You kids ever think about putting your experience to good use?"

I consider Hunter's question. "What were you thinking?"

He takes another pull of his beer. "I could use some new blood around here. People who know how to handle themselves and don't scare easily. We often take on recruits with chequered pasts."

Kade looks intrigued. "You're offering us jobs?"

"Something to think about. Gotta do something with your lives, right?"

With that, Hunter puts his beer down and disappears from the room. His party spirit didn't last long, but he still made an effort to show his face. That's far more meaningful than any empty words he could offer. We watch him leave, and I can already see the cogs in Kade's oversized brain turning.

"Let's get through the shitstorm heading our way first," I speak up. "With the stuff we've had to go on the record about, we'll be lucky to walk away from this."

Kade's smile dims. "There's still a chance, Hud. Don't we deserve that?"

"Fuck knows, man. The world ain't fair like that."

We watch the rest of our group enjoy the makeshift party. Brooklyn's ditched the oversized sweater she was wearing, twirling in Enzo's expert arms as he swoops her low to the ground. Phoenix and Eli are waltzing, their bodies moulded together like star-crossed lovers.

I watch my family, whole and content.

Kade's fucking right.

We deserve our second chance.

A couple of hours in, the music has shifted to gentle, coaxing guitar strokes and crooning vocals. Kade is playing cards with Theo and Eli on a workout bench, while Phoenix sleeps off his eighth vodka shot with a power nap. Enzo's eating his body weight in snacks, stealing more cake when he thinks nobody is looking.

At the edge of the boxing ring, Brooklyn stands alone with her arms resting on the bungee cords. She's staring out at the moon, shining through the high ceiling windows. I stop at her side, content to watch her seemingly at peace after so much turmoil.

"You think we'll have another party next year?"

Pulling her back against my chest, I nuzzle her short hair. "Every damn year, blackbird. We have lots to make up for. Remember your seventeenth? The carer screamed at you for puking on her clean carpet."

She huffs a laugh. "I didn't even know you then."

"We lived together for weeks in the foster home before our paths crossed. I knew you long before you ever said a word to me in that nurse's office."

"I didn't stand a chance, did I?"

"Not if I had anything to do with it. I watched her slap you on my first afternoon. You'd skipped out on chores to patch up one of the younger kids. She hit you hard, and you didn't flinch once."

Brooklyn shakes her head. "I hated that bitch so much."

"That's when I knew I had to talk to you. I'd never seen such courage, especially after watching Ma get her ass kicked for so long. You stood up for the younger kids when nobody ever asked you to."

Turning in my arms, Brooklyn peers up at me with those silvery eyes. I could lose myself in the mesmerising constellation. Even after years of memorising every inch of her, each day still brings new discoveries. I don't think I'll ever stop falling in love with her.

For so long, all I had were my ruined memories and a lifetime of regret. Holding her in my arms again is something I never deserved. If nothing else, the world has granted me one miracle. That's all I need.

"I should've followed you when I had the chance," she whispers sadly. "I still remember the day you left. You begged me to say something, anything. All I could feel was my broken heart thumping."

Agony spears me in the chest. I have to forcibly shut the lid on a box of awful memories. If I could go back in time and kill my younger self for being so fucking cowardly, I'd do it without hesitating.

"My life went wrong when you left it."

"I'm the one that fucked things up," I remind her. "I had no right to demand your love after what I did. Running felt simpler, easier. Looking at you was like looking in the mirror."

Her hand strokes the rough stubble covering my jawline. I lean in to her gentle, loving touch, so unlike the cruel lash of her hatred that I accepted for so long.

"I'm glad I had the chance to go back and make a different decision." Brooklyn's smile is heartbreaking. "I think we had to break apart to fall together again. I needed to see a world without you in it."

"How was it?"

She runs a thumb over my bottom lip. "It was fucking empty."

Taking her hand, I drop it on my shoulder. My hands find her hips, drawing her closer to me. Ignoring the room and all of its inhabitants, we begin to sway to the gentle music. Our surroundings fall away. I'm a love-struck, obsessed teenager again, staring at the sun after so long in the dark.

I spot the door opening over her shoulder and bring our gentle dance to a close. This is the moment I've been waiting for since we left Blackwood. Cupping Brooklyn's face before she can look, I ensure her eyes are only on me.

"I know I missed your birthday, but here's your present. I love you, blackbird. It's time to let go of the past, and I hope this helps."

Seeming confused, she kisses my lips before turning to look. Seven has arrived, tugging his baseball cap off to release his unruly, chestnut hair. He's dressed to blend in, wearing a hoodie and loose jeans. I specifically asked him to retrieve our guest. Even I'll admit that the asshole is good at protecting people.

"Oh my God," Brooklyn breathes.

Behind Seven, our guest of honour arrives. Teegan enters the room with obvious anxiety. She walks slowly, hesitantly, clocking all of her surroundings and the familiar faces with a tiny smile. Dressed in ripped jeans and a silky, black shirt, her bright-red hair pops against her rice-powdered skin.

She looks good, healthy. Alive.

"Tee?"

We all watch on in slow motion. Brooklyn's steps are filled with trepidation, but she can't help inching closer to her long-lost best friend. Teegan looks her up and down, leading me to panic for a split second. She seemed game on the phone.

"Brooke," she responds, a smile blooming.

That's all it takes. Friendship is a weird concept, even to the most adept of humans. It can break and bend so many times, but some bonds survive the test of time. The two girls meet in the middle of the training room, smacking into each other so hard, it must hurt.

I can hear Brooklyn crying from here, but the usual sorrow isn't there. She sounds happy for the first time in so long. Teegan has her in the tightest hug imaginable while stroking her short hair, whispering something to her. Seven comes to my side, looking like the cat that got the fucking cream.

"You don't get all the credit for this," I point out.

"Sure thing, pretty boy. See whose bed she crawls into tonight."

"I'll stuff your corpse beneath mine. Problem solved."

We circle around Brooklyn and Teegan while still giving them some space. Eli's arm is hugging Phoenix's waist as they watch the reunion, both smiling. Kade looks emotional at seeing the two girls reconnect. Everyone is happy to finally have the band back together.

"Girl, where did your hair go?" Teegan laughs.

Face soaked in tears, Brooklyn beams. "I thought I'd steal your edgy style."

"It suits you." Teegan looks her up and down. "Damn, I fucking missed your voice. You never called me back." She glances at me pointedly. "I left so many messages for you."

Smile dropping, Brooklyn stares down at her feet. "I... didn't know what to say. An apology didn't feel like enough. I'm sorry, Tee. I should've called after we escaped."

"I had to hear the gory details from this charming asshole instead."

"Hey," I protest hotly. "I kept my word, didn't I? You wanted a reunion."

"You did?" Brooklyn blurts.

Teegan still holds her tight. "Now I am offended. I haven't seen you in over six months. That's too long for any friend to take. You look so different."

"I didn't think you'd want to see me after..."

She trails off, staring at her feet.

"Brooke—"

"We don't need to talk about this."

"It wasn't your fault," Teegan insists, ignoring the shutter falling over Brooklyn's face. "I never blamed you for what you did. Not once."

"You should. I hurt you."

"Blackwood hurt us both."

Gripping her shoulders, Teegan forces Brooklyn to look up and meet her eyes. Shame is devouring her whole, leaving nothing but pain behind.

"The first time we met, I said you'd be better off sitting somewhere else. Even when I explained about my condition, you refused to move."

Brooklyn manages a tiny smile.

"Nobody has ever accepted me so unconditionally," Teegan continues firmly. "Not even my family. They try, but they're still embarrassed by my compulsions."

"Please," she croaks. "Don't forgive me."

"Why the hell not?"

"Because I don't deserve it."

Teegan shakes her head. "We all deserve to be forgiven, Brooke. Even the monsters. That's what makes this life beautiful. The ability to love, no matter what."

Like hugging an immovable, stone statue, Teegan refuses to let Brooklyn escape her forgiveness. She snatches her hand and drags her to a quieter corner to continue talking.

I never knew Teegan well in Blackwood. Months of keeping her posted on Brooklyn and our whereabouts has allowed me to befriend her. More than anything, she has a good heart.

This will prove, once and for all, that Brooklyn can be forgiven. I'll slay every single demon left tormenting her until the work is done.

CHAPTER 27
BROOKLYN

HEAT WAVES - OUR LAST NIGHT

AGENT BARLOW SITS BACK in her seat, appearing mildly stunned. On her other side, Agent Jonas is staring at his notebook with a heavy frown. Neither of them seems to know what to say to me now that the story is complete. Even told in stages, it's a grim and horrid journey to the depths of human suffering.

"I killed Jefferson," I repeat, looking between them both. "I'm not going to deny it. He spent months torturing me and Seven. I also killed Augustus. He took everything from us."

"Bancroft is aware of this?" Agent Jonas confirms.

"Yes. He wants revenge for his son's death, and the damage we caused to Incendia's reputation. Blackwood Institute was their crown jewel. The entire operation grew from there."

"With Lazlo at the helm."

Taking a sip of water, I nod. "He was the architect of the entire Z Wing program. Me, Seven, Two and Lucia are the only ones left. One, Three, Four and Six are all dead. I learned that early on."

"Do you have names?"

"Not a single one. Patient Two has completely forgotten her old identity."

Clicking her pen, Agent Barlow looks thoughtful. "With a little digging, we can track down that information. I'm sure her family will appreciate knowing she's alive."

"I doubt she has any. Incendia doesn't like loose ends."

The setting sun slants through the tinted window. I've been here all day, forced to endure the rest of my bloody tale. Somehow, I feel oddly lighter. I've spoken it all aloud, every last detail, even the ones I haven't admitted to the guys. It must be real if it's written down in black and white.

"You mentioned your mother." Agent Jonas's jaw clenches. "Professor Lazlo has admitted to establishing the first round of Z Wing recruits, in which your mother was a victim. Patients Alpha, Beta, Gamma, Delta and Kappa are all confirmed to have entered Blackwood in the late nineties."

"Patient Beta attacked the church. He's dead."

They note that down, processing the new information.

"We have a death certificate confirming Melanie West's death twelve years ago," Agent Barlow highlights. "A car crash of which you were the sole survivor."

"She's alive as Patient Delta." I wring my hands in my lap. "You don't have to believe me. I've seen it for myself, as have Hunter and Enzo. She stabbed Phoenix and killed Alyssa Farlow, another Sabre agent."

I sit still as stone while Hunter quickly excuses himself from the back of the room. Hearing her name is too much for his icy composure to take. Watching him go, a frown creases Enzo's brows. I offer him a nod, indicating he can leave too, but he stays put.

"Brooke... you understand that if we find your mother, she won't be shown any mercy." Agent Jonas seems to soften for the first time. "She's too valuable to let slip through the net."

"What are you telling me?"

Glancing around the interview room, Agent Barlow clicks off the camera with an audible sigh. Everyone stops taking notes.

"In this line of work, sometimes the kindest act is to end things early. She'll be picked apart by the SCU, her mind documented and studied by government shrinks. We've never seen anything like her before."

"She's sick," I say in a raw whisper.

"I know that, but others won't care. Once they've learned everything they can, she'll be disposed of, quickly and quietly. There's no prison or hospital that could hope to contain her."

"I... I understand."

Enzo's meaty palm lands on my shoulder. "Brooklyn has given you everything. What now? Each day that passes only increases their risk here. Incendia will lose patience and come for them."

"We're concluding our interviews with Patient Seven and Elijah Woods in the morning." Agent Barlow closes her notebook. "We are due to report back to our superiors on Friday. A decision will be made then."

"What about our protection with Sabre?" I bite my lip.

"For now, it remains. We will do our best to ensure a deal is made."

They begin to pack up their supplies, leaving me staring at the blank white wall. I'm still walking away empty-handed. We've spilled our souls and received nothing but empty words in return.

"Hey," Enzo says under his breath. "It's going to be okay, Brooke. We will always keep you and the others safe. That won't change."

"Until they come knocking with handcuffs and straitjackets."

His smile is tight, unhappy. In the many tiring weeks we've hidden out here, I never expected to make friends. Especially with the people we once saw as threats. They welcomed us into their home and gave us hope. This new world we've re-entered has been devastating and surprising in equal measure.

Before the agents can finish packing up their paperwork, our meeting is interrupted by a blaring alarm. Our sessions moved to Sabre HQ last week, once the threat from Incendia became clear to the task force. They quickly changed their tune and wanted the assurance of Hunter's team on hand.

"What's that?" I shield my ears.

Enzo presses the comms in his ear, listening to someone speaking on the end of the line. His face transforms, overcome with concern and urgency. He briefly looks at me before turning to the agents.

"We have a security breach. It could be a false alert, but I don't want to risk Incendia catching wind of your presence. They can never know about this investigation."

The two men sitting behind Agent Barlow and Agent Jonas both step forward, unveiling holsters beneath their pristine grey suits. Their quiet attention becomes determination in a split second. Once packed up, all four agents move in a practised formation towards the exit.

"Stay here," Enzo commands me.

"I can't just sit here! Let me help."

"If Incendia are here, they're here for you. Don't move. I'll get Hunter to send a team up to retrieve you."

Ignoring my protests, he pulls his own gun out and leads the way for the others to follow. Hunter has already vanished from outside the door. I'm left standing in the middle of the interview room like a fucking lemon. I'm not going to sit here and wait for rescue.

Sneaking the opposite way down the corridor, I find the exit door to the stairwell. The fluorescent lights have all switched to dark red, indicating the emergency alert. Blaring drills into my head, but I easily tune it out. After months of white-noise torture, a stupid alarm won't slow me down.

My legs race up the concrete-lined stairwell, all the way up to the level with the temporary apartments. I'm breathing hard by the time I get to the top. The hallway seems undisturbed despite the alarm. Reaching Lucia and Two's door, I hammer on it with both fists until my hands ache.

I nearly fall inwards when it opens.

"Eight?" Lucia's eyes peek around the door.

"It's me. Are you both okay?"

She sags from relief. "We're both here. Two's freaking out. What's happening? Are we under attack?"

"I don't know. Keep the door locked and get in the bathtub. Don't open it for anyone. You still have that gun Hudson stole for you?"

Lucia nods frantically.

"Good. I'll come find you when I know it's safe."

Letting her slam the door in my face, I move to our apartment next. My voice bounces off the walls as I scream for the guys, flying between each empty room like a bat out of hell. Nobody is here. I think Kade mentioned something about a boxing match with the new recruits this evening in the training room.

Fisting my short hair, I try to gain control of my spiralling fear. There's no way Incendia could breach this fortress. It would take an army to get past Hunter's precautions and countless employees, all sworn to defend us. A team of well-paid thugs wouldn't stand a chance.

But a sole person?

That's a possibility.

My heart seizes at the thought. I'm moving fast before I realise it. Instinct is driving me towards the eighth floor, where the detention cells reside. I first woke up in one such prison. These days, it's home to our favourite psychopath, the affable Professor Lazlo.

Stumbling down the freezing stairwell, I'm sweaty and panting as I get to the detention block. It's eerily quiet on this level, the offices cleared out and abandoned. Nobody comes here. Around several twisting corners, I reach the long stretch of corridor that holds the cells.

I release a breath when I find it also undisturbed. Checking each cell door in turn, nothing looks amiss. It isn't until I reach the final handful of holding cells that the horror reveals itself. One door is busted wide open, the hinges blackened and twisted from the rotors of a spinning saw.

"Lazlo?" I yell inside. "Show yourself!"

Heaving the broken steel slab all the way open, I tentatively step into the room. My vision is dipped in red from the emergency lighting, but that doesn't conceal the message scrawled across the concrete wall in giant, dripping letters. I can taste the metallic tang of blood in the air.

COME HOME, BROOKE.

WE CAN BE A FAMILY AGAIN.

On the other side of the room, a tiny bed is tucked into the corner. An ocean of fresh, sticky blood separates the space. It's everywhere. Enough to fill the world and spill over in a portrait of death.

Well, the saw had two purposes.

This isn't a murder.

It's an execution.

Lazlo lies dismembered in a pool of his own mortality. Flaps of torn skin, muscle and tissue shed more blood, adding to the expanding spill. His arms and legs have been viciously torn from his torso, the bone shattered and jagged.

I suppress a scream as I slide through the cooling liquid, accidentally nudging the remains of his left leg. He's been cut up like meat and methodically ripped apart. It's like fucking artwork. Close enough to study his glassy eyes, they're trapped in an eternal display of agony. I feel oddly relieved.

Nothing looks back at me.

He's as empty as the monsters he created.

Above the remains of his butchered body, another message awaits, written in the same spilled blood. Fitting, really. I do enjoy poetic justice.

YOU TOOK MY CHILDREN FROM ME.

THE PRICE HAS BEEN PAID.

This message isn't for me. Lazlo's corpse stares up at the dripping words with eyes devoid of any life. It would have been the last thing he saw as his pitiful life was stolen, much like he stole so many of our childhoods and futures.

Blind instinct drives me to the barred window. Hunter granted him some daylight, despite the heavy iron cage over the glass that would block any futile attempt to escape. Lazlo still had the privilege of sunshine for his cooperation, which is far more than he ever deserved.

We're high in the sky, with darkness descending upon the evening horizon. I search the ground beneath us, seeing nothing but people going about their business. The world continues to turn as ours grinds to a halt. Glancing at the smaller tower opposite Sabre's monstrosity, the empty roof is laid bare.

Someone awaits, watching for me.

A blood-stained hand offers a slow wave.

"Mum," I whisper against the glass.

She's staring straight back at me, her entire focus trained on the window—almost like she was waiting for me to come and find her. Like a robot, my right hand lifts in a wave. I can't help it. Watching her sick, twisted smile appear still feels like coming home at last.

Her existence is proof that my family was real.

I didn't imagine them, or the happiness I once had.

With an outstretched hand, she points to my left. I let my eyes stray back to the wall, where the message she left for me is gradually becoming obscured as the wet blood spreads.

Come home, Brooke.

Her familiar, coaxing voice whispers through my mind. Only this time, it's real. When I look back, she's gone. I stare at the empty rooftop, her voice in my ears.

We can be a family again.

CHAPTER 28
SEVEN

SOMEBODY ELSE - CIRCA WAVES

MY FIST SAILS straight into Hudson's face before he can duck and avoid it. I savour his yelp of pain, watching him fall to his knees in the boxing ring. We decided to forgo headgear, so he only has himself to blame for the black eye. I never agreed to pull my punches.

"Dammit, Sev!"

"Too slow," I drone. "Your reflexes are shit."

Spitting blood on the mat, he finds his feet again. "I'm not some psychotic trained killer, so excuse me for taking a hit. You could go a bit easier on me."

"Nobody else will. I'm preparing you for the real world, pretty boy. Patient Delta killed that piece of shit right under our noses. You need to be ready to fight."

"She has a name. That's Brooklyn's mum you're talking about."

"No," I growl at him. "That's the piece of shit who killed my sister. Next time I see her, you best take our girl away, because I'm gonna cave her fucking head in. Sentiment be damned."

"Good luck breaking Brooke's heart, you moron."

"She has enough people to pick up the pieces."

With a curse, Hudson crouches back in position. This time, his boxing glove manages to connect with my stomach. I barely feel the burst of pain. We've been beating on each other for several hours now; I doubt there's a part of me that isn't bruised from his fists.

"How did she even get in?" Hudson wipes his forehead.

I manage to strike him in the ribs. "We were trained to blend in. Invisible, like phantoms passing through shadows. We didn't exist. Only Augustus's machines were allowed to walk this earth."

"Nobody is that good, not even Lazlo's prized patient."

"You're too cocky. It'll be the death of you out there."

With a snarl, his forehead smashes into mine. I see stars for a moment, shaking my head to clear the haze. The smug son of a bitch looks far too pleased with his headbutt. In retaliation, I deliver a roundhouse kick to his midsection.

"Motherfucker! I need a break," Hudson wheezes.

"You wanna sit around and wait for news like the rest of them?"

Before I can react, his foot sweeps out and catches my ankles. I go down hard and fast, my back smacking into the floor. Breathing becomes difficult as I stare up at his smug grin.

"Not a chance," he fires back. "I'd rather beat the shit out of you."

Offering me a hand up, we return to our vicious sparring. It's another sweaty, bruising hour before our solitude is disturbed. Eight saunters into the training room, wearing her workout gear—a pair of yoga pants and a tight, revealing sports bra. I clip Hudson around the ear when he gets distracted.

"Fuck off!" he bellows.

"Pay attention. I'm not playing a game here."

We beat on each other until Eight slides through the bungee cords, not bothering to wrap her hands or put gloves on. She's eyeing us both with violent anticipation, her body seeming to thrum all over. I haven't heard her speak a single word since Lazlo's body was found.

"Can we help you?" Hudson smarts.

She stretches her arms above her head. "Hunter, Enzo and Theo are in a meeting with the SCU. Kade is doing his obsessive-cleaning thing while Phoenix and Eli finish a bottle of rum. I need a distraction."

"I'm guessing one that doesn't involve talking about what happened."

"Definitely not," Eight retorts.

Undoing the Velcro on my glove with my teeth, I toss it aside. "Come spar with us. But if you step inside this ring, you can't leave, princess. Don't expect us to go easy on you."

"I wouldn't want it any other way."

Hudson frowns at us both. "I can't hit a girl, especially not her."

Eight catches him off guard with a karate chop to the throat. His knees meet the floor for a second time as he coughs and tries not to throw his guts up. She's a fucking savage, especially when angry.

"Feel free to sit it out," Eight offers.

While her most insufferable boyfriend recovers, I box her in with my fist raised in anticipation. I'm glad she doesn't treat me differently for only having one hand. The best thing about Eight is that she embraces every messy, imperfect aspect of us all. Especially the darker parts.

"First to tap out loses?"

I nod at her suggestion. "Hope you're prepared to go down."

In response, she dances towards me on light feet. It's like watching a bloodthirsty ballerina encircling her hopeless prey. I duck and weave, landing a few quick blows to her torso. As I'm bringing my leg up for another kick, someone shoves me from behind, causing me to faceplant.

"Nobody said anything about not playing dirty," Hudson taunts.

I roll onto my back. "Fucking bastard."

"Nice to know our friendship is mutual, asshole."

"Will you two stop flirting already?" Eight complains. "Either fuck each other or quit messing around. You can't expect me to watch this shit and not get ideas."

I catch the hopeful glint in her eye. She looks at us both like we're her fucking dinner. Hudson helps me back up again, but this time, his hand lingers on my back. I lost my shirt a couple of hours ago, and his fingertips seem to caress the hard muscles of my deltoids for a brief second.

"You're playing with fire, blackbird."

Eight leans against the edge of the ring to catch her breath. "I've seen the way you look at each other. Friendship, my ass. Don't act like you're not curious, Hud."

"I'm straight," he splutters.

"Why does that have to come into it? I'm sure Eli thought the same thing. Sometimes people's energies connect. Doesn't mean it has to be labelled or pinned down."

Sauntering towards us, Eight runs a hand down Hudson's defined chest, exposed by the sweaty material of his blue tank top. I watch his throat bob. His eyes are trying to stray over to me as he battles against it.

"You don't even want one little taste?" she taunts.

"Brooke..."

"What if I helped?"

Leaning in, her mouth meets Hudson's without mercy. I stand rock still, his thumb rubbing tiny circles into my back. I don't think he knows that he's doing it. Eight controls their kiss with confidence, taking every ounce of control without giving a single bit back.

When they break apart, Hudson's lips are parted and he's breathing hard. She grabs a handful of his top and uses it to wrench him towards me. We end up chest to chest, with her excited eyes skipping between us both. I duck my head close to hers, stealing my own kiss from her sweet lips.

Hudson watches our tongues duel, heat entering his gaze. When Eight pulls away from me, his fear is obliterated by burning need. I let him come to me, our noses brushing before I can feel the hesitant whisper of his lips on mine. He's waiting for me to cross the finish line.

"Kiss him back," Eight orders me.

I've never been one to deny her darkest desires.

My mouth attacks Hudson's in a furious frenzy. With that final barrier laid bare, he doesn't hesitate to give as good as he gets. There's nothing gentle or tender about our first kiss. It's violent and aggressive, a testament to our loving hatred for the bond tying us together.

Eight's hand strokes my arm, her familiar scent washing between us both. This is still about her. Releasing Hudson's swollen lips, I roughly drag her between us so her tight ass is pressed right up against my cock. Trapped in place, she doesn't protest as we kiss again over her writhing body.

If she doesn't stop moving, I'm going to blow my load long before I'm buried inside her cunt. Hudson's hand twines in my hair, roughly tugging on the long strands. I release a low hiss, biting his bottom lip in retaliation. The taste of his blood in my mouth turns me on even more.

A hand snakes over my hip and down into the soft material of my sweats.

Eight's playing a very dangerous game as she slides into my boxers, taking hold of my erect length. Her strokes begin light and teasing, before she's working my shaft from base to tip.

Hudson breaks the kiss to gulp down air. "I've never... uh, you know. Been with a guy."

Swiping the leaking blood from his chin with my index finger, I clean the crimson droplet off with my tongue. He watches every move, his own tongue darting out to lick his lips.

I run a hand over Eight's head. "On your knees, princess. Pretty boy here is shy."

Eight chuckles. "Hudson, shy? Ha. We'll see about that."

She bows before us both, her knees meeting the floor of the boxing ring. Hudson gulps as she unties the drawstring on his workout shorts, dragging them down and freeing the bulge in his boxers. His dick disappears inside her mouth as she greedily takes his full length.

"Fuck, blackbird."

With my hand still on Eight's head, I take control of her movements. She's sucking his cock, but I'm the one in charge. Each pump of her mouth is on my terms. When she gags a little, I push her even further, forcing her to swallow every last inch. I love the way it makes Hudson shudder with pleasure.

Before he can finish inside her mouth, I pull Eight back by her pixie cut. She wipes stray tears from her eyes, still managing to look fucking perfect with a glaze of pre-come on her lips. If there's one thing our girl can do, it's give one hell of a blowjob.

Hudson spares me a look before placing his hands on my shoulders. "Down. You take it now."

Just this once, I'll give him what he wants. Kicking off my remaining clothes without shame, I sit down on the spongy floor of the boxing ring. Eight watches me stroke my length as she peels off her yoga pants, revealing her lack of underwear.

Goddammit, she's too fucking dangerous.

Perfect for a pair of hotheads like us.

Throwing her sports bra aside, she crawls back on her reddened knees. Hudson strips his remaining clothes off and helps guide her forward, so she's kneeling with her face inches from my dick.

"Suck his cock, baby. I want to watch you pleasure him."

"Yes, daddy," Eight echoes, too quick for it to be the first time.

I look between them. Is this a thing? If so, it's fucking hot. Hudson grins, the cocky son of a bitch. I'm about to insult him when Eight's mouth wraps around my length, and all sense leaves my mind. She cups a handful of my balls while going to work, determined to drive me wild.

Kneeling behind her, Hudson buries his face between her legs from behind. Eight's spine arches as he finds her bare pussy. She's trying hard not to get distracted while servicing me, but Hudson's sensual attack is pushing her limits. He licks his glistening lips when he comes up for air.

"Is our girl sweet?" I smirk.

To my surprise, he doesn't back down from the challenge.

"Want a taste, Sev? You only have to ask."

Leaning over Eight's bobbing head, he pulls me back in for another hard kiss. I can taste her salty juices on his tongue as it sweeps through my mouth. Hudson's earlier shyness has long since left the building. We break apart and he winks, looking all too satisfied with this turn of events.

"Now you have to watch me fuck our girl."

I sit back and lift my chin with defiance. "Go right ahead."

Eight's lips tighten around my cock as Hudson surges inside of her. She's barely suppressing a moan, her hands gripping my muscled thighs deep enough to leave nail marks. It's interesting, watching their dynamic. Hudson fucks our girl much like I do, every thrust scarring an irreversible brand into her skin.

My dick hits the back of her throat, and I can't help but growl. Every time Hudson pounds into her, she bites down slightly. The light graze of her teeth against my sensitive flesh is sweet torture. I'm moving my hips in time with her movements, seeking more and more of her compliance.

Unable to hold it in any longer, I feel my climax rise. I want to finish with her tight walls clenching around me, but I'll settle for staking my claim in front of this stubborn asshole. Right before I can finish in her mouth, I pull Eight back by her hair and her eyes widen with surprise.

Fisting my cock, I finish all over her face, covering her in my seed for the entire world to see. Glistening droplets of come drip down her cheeks and lips. She's gasping still, her mouth slightly parted, letting my juices flow into her mouth. I watch with satisfaction as she licks her lips clean.

"Jesus." Hudson watches us both. "That was messed up."

I quirk an eyebrow. "Jealous?"

He can't reach me, so he delivers a punishing spank to Eight's ass instead. She squeals, flashing me an annoyed look. My big mouth is going to get her in some serious trouble now. I can't help but want to punish her more for the shit she pulled the other day.

"Did your girlfriend tell you about the rooftop last week?"

"Seven," she warns.

"What?" I act all innocent.

Hudson's still slamming into her, his grip bruising her scarred hips. Determined to win this fucked up game of ours, I sit back, stark bollock naked and not embarrassed in the slightest.

"I told her that if she wanted to jump, she could go ahead."

That causes his movements to still, right on the verge of finishing. Eight gasps in pain and frustration, her nails drawing blood from my thighs. He's left her hanging on the edge while his face darkens with anger.

"What?" Hudson utters.

I watch them, far too pleased with myself.

"Ignore him," Eight insists.

"What the hell is he talking about, Brooke?!"

She's ripped from my lap and flipped over by his rough hands. Eight's head lands in my naked lap. Settling between her spread, vulnerable legs, Hudson is free to stare directly into her wide eyes.

"Go ahead," I encourage with a grin. "Tell your boyfriend how you wanted to give up. Tell him that I took you to the edge of a rooftop, and you actually considered jumping off."

"I did not!"

"Stop lying, Eight."

She glowers up at me. "Shut the fuck up, Seven. Last warning."

Her gaze is wrenched back to Hudson by his grip on her chin. There's real anger there, burning in slow, destructive embers. I'm quite pleased with my handiwork. He's even hotter while enraged. Hell, they both are.

"Are we doing this shit again?" Hudson hisses at her. "I've dragged you off a fucking roof once. I won't do it again. We've spent enough of our lives worrying about your death."

"I was never going to jump." Eight bites her lip, but it sounds like the truth. "I just… it's the unknown. I've never feared it before. Now, I have something to lose. I'm terrified of not knowing the future."

Bringing their foreheads together, Hudson's hands move to her exposed throat. Their noses are touching as he inhales every breath she takes. I spot the moment oxygen ceases to enter her lungs. Eight's hands curl into fists as she fights to remain calm, despite being choked.

"My future has meant nothing to me since the day we met," Hudson growls in her face. "I didn't give a damn about anything but you. We belong together, in this world and the next. Where you go, I go."

Eight begins to claw at his crushing hands. Human instinct is a tough nut to crack. To punish her further, Hudson pushes back inside her slick cunt. Her back arches again at the lack of warning. He sets a bruising pace, gliding into her like she's his property—his to hurt and break into pathetic pieces.

"You think death will part us?"

Eight can't answer, her nails tearing his hands to shreds.

"There's no way out of this, blackbird. The Devil wouldn't dare challenge my claim on your soul. Hell will spit you out and back into my arms, where you fucking belong."

I can feel her muscles beginning to tense where our bare skin is touching. She's on the verge of falling apart, even if every instinct is screaming at her to escape and find air to breathe. Hudson won't give it to her without payment. Her complete submission to his will is the price of her release.

"You wanna come, little whore?" he teases her. "Then let's get this straight, once and for all. If we're a motherfucking family, that means we live and die together. No easy exits. No shortcuts."

Her eyelids begin to flutter as her hands tremble. She's going to pass out if he's not careful. At the absolute last second, Hudson releases his hands from Eight's neck. Her next breath sounds excruciating, like breathing underwater. Her skin is already tarnished, turning a nasty shade of purple.

"Come," he demands with a final pump.

The sound that escapes her lips is caught between relief and agony. Hudson's head slumps against her breasts, every taut muscle in his back moving with his rapid breathing. Neither seems able to move as they ride out the waves of their climaxes.

We don't say anything for a long time. Our bodies are wrapped up in each other, spreadeagled across the boxing ring. Eight is staring up at the ceiling, rubbing her sore neck and wincing at the pain. I note that Hudson doesn't bother apologising, nor does she demand he does so.

A throat clearing breaks our post-sex bubble.

"Uh, guys?" Theo stands in the doorway, his eyes averted away from us.

I immediately shove Eight behind me, gritting my teeth against a snarl. If Theo saw even an inch of her bare skin, I'll happily barbecue his eyeballs for dinner.

"What?" Hudson growls, equally annoyed.

"You need to come upstairs." Theo awkwardly rubs the back of his neck. "Hunter wants to speak to you all. It's urgent. Clothes may be a good idea."

CHAPTER 29
BROOKLYN

IT'S OKAY TO BE AFRAID - SAINT SLUMBER

I YANK one of Eli's oversized hoodies over my head, covering the necklace of bruises on my throat. When I spotted them in the bathroom mirror, I couldn't help but stroke the aching flesh with a sick sense of satisfaction.

The voices in my head can't convince me otherwise when I have physical proof of my family's love and twisted devotion.

The walk to Hunter's office is marked by tense, impenetrable silence. Hudson and Seven follow behind me and Theo, both hastily changed into fresh clothing after our... uh, fuck fest. No other word for that toxic fiasco.

"What's the news?" I rasp.

Theo casts me an apprehensive look. "The SCU have made their decision."

"Do you know what it is?"

Rather than answer, he pushes open the huge glass door and beckons for us to enter. I can't help but feel like the hangman is offering us a nice, convenient noose to hang ourselves with. Entering Hunter's office, I take Hudson's and Seven's hands to ground myself.

The others wait inside, all appearing nervous. Kade is propped in the corner, his foot tapping a staccato rhythm. Eli and Phoenix sit next to each other, their entwined hands displayed on the conference table. I kiss both of their cheeks as we pass and find our own seats.

Hunter stands at the head of the table, his arms folded over his perfectly pressed blue shirt. I glance up at his hair. It's loose and untied again. I've come to realise it's a pretty good indicator of his mental state. Right now, he looks ready to burn the entire fucking world down. It's terrifying.

"Now that we're all here, will you answer my question?" Kade sighs.

"Yes, the decision came from above," Hunter concedes. "The task force answers to a higher authority within the Serious Crimes Unit. I'm not familiar with the director, but I've heard he's pretty formidable."

"That wasn't my question. Does Incendia have the SCU in its pocket?!"

"What's happened?" I interrupt with my heart in my mouth.

Releasing his own sigh, Hunter takes the empty seat between Theo and Enzo. None of them can look at us, studying the table instead. I feel the balloon of hope in my chest explode into spectacular pieces.

"The SCU has decided not to proceed with an investigation at this time." Hunter's voice is laden with defeat. "Agent Barlow has handed in her resignation in protest of this decision, along with Agent Jonas."

"They're quitting?" Hudson exclaims. "What the fuck?"

"From what I gather, their superior officer did not agree with the evidence collected. The decision was not theirs to make. After spending three weeks with you all, both felt very strongly that an immediate investigation was needed."

"So why the hell aren't they doing it?" I shout.

"They intend to prosecute." Hunter shakes his head in disgust. "Just not Incendia."

We all fall silent at that bombshell.

"Charges have been filed against Brooklyn for multiple first-degree murders, including Brittany Matthews, Jack Potter, Officer Jefferson and Doctor Augustus. That's without the four-month killing spree. Rio Gonzalez's death is still up for dispute."

"Do I even want to know mine?" Seven drones.

"The list is too long to count."

"Naturally. I'll skip the summary, thanks."

"Kade is facing numerous narcotics charges," Hunter continues. "Along with destruction of private property and charges for inciting the riot. Hudson, Phoenix and Eli stand accused of absconding from custody and participating in the riot. Potentially more if they link guard or patient deaths back to you six."

You could hear a penny drop in the office. I've never seen everyone so equally horrified and stunned into silence, even after all we've been through. Enzo slams his hands down on the table, his face scrunched up. He's turning a brighter shade of red than Hudson did earlier.

"As of tonight, our protection will be rendered illegal and classed as obstruction of justice." Hunter ignores Enzo smashing his chair into the wall. "You will be forcibly removed from the premises, arrested by the SCU, and prosecuted to the full extent of the law."

Kade is the first to find his voice, shaky and uncertain. "What does that mean?"

"Best case? Prison time. Release or parole will be out of the question. For some of you, a psychiatric sentence may be deemed more beneficial. You will be returned to Incendia's care for the rest of your lives."

"Do we get a trial?" Hudson asks.

Hunter shakes his head. "The SCU are in possession of emergency powers granted by the government. High-profile offenders can be dealt with at their discretion, without public involvement. The records will reflect otherwise, but your fates will be sealed the moment they slap the cuffs on."

"That's illegal," Kade argues.

Closing his laptop, Theo removes his glasses to rub his eyes. "So is running a privately funded conspiracy to experiment on and torture the mentally unwell.

Doesn't stop Incendia from taking politicians' money and passing their financial endorsement back to our lawmakers."

"You're saying the SCU has been compromised," I summarise.

Hunter meets my eyes. "I'm saying there's nothing else to be done."

"You made promises."

"We all did," Enzo shouts, rounding on his best friend. "This is fucking bullshit, Hunt. We have the resources to take on whatever jackasses the SCU sends here, their warrants be damned. I won't let these kids go without a fight."

"Then we end up in matching cells with them."

"So be it! This isn't right!"

Theo watches his team members argue, his expression beyond bleak. He lost the one thing he cared about in this fight, the person that gave his life meaning and put a smile on his face. It was all for nothing.

"Eight," Seven murmurs behind me. "We need to leave, right now."

"And go where?" Phoenix responds before I can. "They will follow us everywhere. We can't run away, not this time. This is the end of the road."

"You'd give up so fucking easily?" Seven argues.

"You can't punch your way out of this one!"

The crash of a chair hitting the floor interrupts their argument. Eli has backed up into a corner, his hands slammed over his ears. His green eyes are clouded over and far from the strong man he's grown into recently—one brave enough to live, breathe and speak without fear.

"Eli?" I whisper softly.

"W-Won't... b-back... won't g-go... back."

Sliding down the wall, he buries his face in his knees. I'm powerless to stop his dissolution into a trembling wreck, like the scared little boy I found cutting himself in that graveyard last year. It's fucking devastating.

"Nix," I force out. "I can't..."

Taking over from me, Phoenix crouches in front of Eli. I have to look away from their whispered conversation. It hurts far too much to watch him try to pull Eli back from the edge of insanity. Instead, I let rage steel my spine as I face Hunter again.

"Tell us what to do. Give us something."

Hands braced on the table, Hunter hesitates. We stare at each other for several long seconds, locked in our own private conversation. I leave all of my emotions on display. Terror. Hope. Defeat. Exhaustion. Desperation. Fury. Grief. Hatred. I can barely see through the force of them wracking me.

"Hunter," Theo says uncertainly.

"No," he snaps back. "It's a suicide mission."

Standing tall for the first time, Theo replaces his glasses. I've never seen him butt heads with his boss. He's always the obedient lap dog, but not today. This is the final, backbreaking straw. He's had enough.

"The moment they enter the SCU's custody, they're as good as dead," Theo states simply. "That's a suicide mission. You are sending every single one of them to their deaths."

"What else would you have me do?" Hunter throws his hands up.

Theo refuses to back down. "Let them choose their own fates for once."

With his throat bobbing, Hunter's nod signals his defeat. He reaches inside his suit jacket, pulling out a shiny, embossed slice of paper. It looks like an invitation, dipped in luxurious gold ink and calligraphy.

"This arrived a week ago."

He tosses it down the table for me to pick up. Staring at the invitation, I trace the words with my index finger, each letter punching a hole through my numbness. It's addressed to me in handwritten ink.

Incendia Corporation Invites You To Celebrate The Grand Reopening Of Blackwood Institute - An Exclusive Event For Investors And Sponsors.

I can feel the weight of my crimes pressing down on me like an ash cloud after a volcanic eruption. Beneath the grandiose declaration, the same handwriting has left a private message just for me. Bancroft must have written it, but Augustus's dead voice reads the words out.

Brooklyn.

It's time to return home.

Your mother is waiting for her little girl.

Nobody complains as I run for the nearest bin and throw up until my chest burns. With my hands braced on the plastic edges, I watch my tears drip into the rubbish. I know if I turn around, I'll find Augustus waiting for me. I can feel his presence at the edges of my broken mind.

"He wants to draw you out in the open." Hunter stops next to me, a tissue in hand. "I'm sure they have a cover story ready to be printed, the heroic efforts of the SCU praised for stopping a bloodthirsty criminal. The public will celebrate your death and the safety it brings them."

"But we told the truth!" I shout after wiping my mouth. "We fucking told them. It's all a lie, every single, poisonous word they print."

"Money is the truth for people like Bancroft."

"Then what?"

Stepping up next to me, Seven's face is hard. "We end things our way."

I feel the warmth of the others at my back. Kade takes my hand and squeezes his agreement. The gentle caress of Hudson's breath at my neck is all I need from him. Phoenix and Eli come last, stumbling to complete our bruised and battered group.

Eli's barely able to stand, but there's still fierce determination in his emerald eyes. He manages a single, jerky nod that seals our decision. We're all in agreement on one fundamental fact.

Our lives are forfeit right now.

None of us are surrendering willingly.

Incendia has signed our death certificates already; this is just extra time in the eternal playoff for our souls. Hudson was right about one thing—we live and die together, not ripped apart and locked in cells to await the hangman's noose.

"Can you get us to Wales?" I direct my question to Hunter.

Instead, Enzo answers from across the room.

"I'll show you to the damn gates myself. I'm coming with you." He silences

Hunter's protests before they can begin. "We made a promise and I never, ever go back on my word."

The two men stare at each other until Hunter breaks. He scrubs his exhausted face several times, savouring a deep, fortifying breath. When he unveils his face again, defeat has been replaced by resolution.

"Alyssa died fighting the system. She believed in the truth."

Theo steps up next, his shoulders set firm. "We honour her wishes by fighting for what's right. I refuse to live in a world where evil wins. If Bancroft goes down, Incendia is weakened."

"We have hours of interviews and evidence to strike the killer blow," Hunter concurs. "The SCU has no idea we had our own cameras rolling. Let's release it to the entire world right now."

The idea of three weeks of evidence being released into the public domain has a clinging chill covering my entire body. I feel fucking sick at the thought of reporters, doctors, pundits, and political commentators hearing about the darkest parts of my life.

"Is there another way?" I ask, defeated.

Hunter shakes his head. "We have to force their hand now. I'm sorry, Brooke."

The others all meet my eyes. Their lives are spelled out in those tapes too, but they are leaving the decision up to me. I don't know if we'll ever know peace again once we do this. But if we don't, our lives will end in the most brutal way imaginable. Incendia will win. I can't let that happen.

"Do it," I command.

Theo nods once, disappearing from the room.

"They didn't believe us before." Phoenix looks fearful. "What's changed?"

"Who would believe the ramblings of a psych patient and some blurry iPhone footage?" Enzo laughs bitterly. "But the sworn testimony of several grown adults, backed up by two SCU ex-employees, and buried by the very people the public trust to defend the law?"

"Nobody can ignore that," I affirm, trying to comfort myself.

Hunter actually smiles. "All we need is one head to turn. The rest will follow. There are good people left in government. We're going above the SCU with this footage, and it will blow them to pieces."

In the office of a man I didn't know two months ago, we seal a pact in the only way we know how. Each person spits into the palm of their hand, like criminals agreeing to a truce. Each handshake is exchanged in turn. When I reach Enzo, he pulls me into a bear hug.

"You'll get that second chance, wildfire," he murmurs into my hair. "I had a sister once. She was full of life and never gave me a moment's rest. I couldn't stop the cancer that ate away at her organs, but I can fight until my dying breath to kill every last son of a bitch that comes for you."

Tears prick my eyes. "You can't give up everything for us."

He holds me at arm's length and scowls. "If one person's life isn't worth risking everything for, then none of this matters. We vowed to fight for justice the day we opened Sabre. I'm doing exactly that."

With another bone-creaking hug, he pushes me back towards the guys. I pretend not to notice the way he clears his throat and subtly wipes under his eyes. The lion-hearted boulder of muscle has a heart of fucking gold, and I love him for it. All of them have done their best by us.

Facing all five guys waiting for my direction—the individual pieces of my heart, my motherfucking family—I say the words I never dreamed of uttering aloud.

"Time to go back to Blackwood Institute."

CHAPTER 30
BROOKLYN

WONDERFUL LIFE - BRING ME
THE HORIZON & DANI FILTH

THERE'S something very wrong about driving into Blackwood's car park like normal, law-abiding citizens. No undercover sneaking or clever disguises this time. There's no point in hiding. The SCU's deadline has passed, and Theo offered our lives to the vultures in the media twelve hours ago.

We're fair game now.

There are no more dark corners to hide in.

Hudson pulls the handbrake on the dark, tinted SUV. I'm sitting in the passenger seat, while the other four are crammed in the back. Hunter, Enzo and Theo pull up next to us in a matching armoured company car, giving us a moment to share some final words of wisdom.

I meet Kade's eyes in the mirror. "You look good."

He runs a hand over his perfectly knotted tie, which complements his shirt and trousers. His broken arm is still strapped against his chest. It figures he'd return to his preppy roots for our final trip to hell. This time, he isn't here to impress anyone but himself.

The rest of us wear our battle armour—ripped jeans and band t-shirts, leather jackets and bad attitudes. There's no point in pretending to fit in with the high-society vampires inside. We're not here for them.

I entered Blackwood as myself.

I intend to return exactly the same way.

"You know, I first came here to prove myself." Kade scoffs at himself. "I was chasing after Hudson's ass like a dog with a bone. All I wanted was to compensate for every shortcoming my father threw in my face."

"You saved us all, Kade. Don't forget that."

"I've brought us right back to our deaths. This is my biggest failure."

"You kept us alive," Hudson grumbles from the driver's seat. "We're not going to second-guess the progress we've all made since leaving this place. Not to get emotional and shit, but I'm proud of us all."

Phoenix savours a final cigarette out the window. "Blackwood broke our spirits, but it couldn't break our family. Two years ago, I never expected to find a life worth living without drugs."

Hudson snorts. "I had no intentions of ever leaving this place, three-year program or not. There was nothing in the world that was worth living for." His eyes meet mine. "Or so I thought."

Staring at Blackwood in the distance, Seven's voice is filled with a warmth that I never thought possible. "Jude came here looking for his life's purpose. I lost myself along the way, but after six years, I think I've found it at last."

The last member of our group is listening in thoughtful silence. Eli's wrapped in the same *Bring Me The Horizon* hoodie he wore when we first met. Then, it was shielding his face from the world and all its terrors. Now, the hood lies back. He has no headphones in. His gaze is clear, firm, unafraid.

"T-Twelve years," he stutters, his voice evening out. "I couldn't s-speak when… came here. Not fucking perfect, but… seen outside w-world now." He smiles to himself. "Scary… but b-beautiful."

Our hands link over the console. I take a moment to meet each of their eyes. My guys. My family. There was a time when I was determined to run far, far away from them. Fear and hatred ruled my life, leaving no room for hope.

"I came here to die," I say with a headshake. "Blackwood was supposed to be my way out. I never expected to find a reason to live, let alone five fucking reasons."

Another hand lays on top of mine, then another. One by one, we all link up, holding on to that final scrap of rebellious hope. None of us will leave this place in cuffs. It's always been ride or die with us—get on the train before it runs you the hell over. I can't love any other way.

This is our last stand, together.

Six misfits against the whole fucking world.

Regardless of what happens, what a tale it will be.

"Nobody gets separated," I remind them all. "We go in together and we leave together, even if it's in body bags. I won't see any of you behind bars. We take Bancroft out, no matter what."

Checking weapons and smoothing our casual outfits, the moment of judgement comes. Hunter, Enzo and Theo wait outside in all black, looking far too much like the spooks they relentlessly train. We're going to stand out, but none of us give a flying fuck.

"Wait," Phoenix blurts. "I, uh. Shit, I'm not gonna beat around the bush. I fucking love you guys." His grin is so much like the cocky bastard that first greeted me. "That's all. We can go now."

Hudson wraps an arm around his neck and messes up his bright-blue hair. "Naw, Nix is getting all soft and weepy. Shall we feed him to Incendia first? Get it over and done with?"

"Dammit," Seven curses. "I was planning that for you, pretty boy. Quit stealing my ideas."

The look Hudson sends him is full of challenging heat.

I stifle an eye roll. "Come on, horny assholes. Let's go die in style."

The car park is packed full of expensive sports cars and far too much money for me to stand. We've arrived fashionably late, so the event should already be in full swing. I can't help but feel slightly sick as we begin the long walk up to Blackwood's gates. I never thought I'd come back here.

By the time we reach the grandiose reception building, cloaked in thick ivy and lit by the full moon hanging overhead, my nausea has been replaced by stone-cold fury. Hunter flashes the invitation and we're barely given a second glance by the security detail.

They've been briefed to expect us.

Bancroft wants his crown jewels back.

Inside, I glance around the familiar reception area. The smell of fresh paint permeates the air from the recent reconstruction. New brocade wallpaper meets identical mahogany panelling to the old entrance. Tasteful artwork, antique vases and gilded mirrors add to the opulence that once turned my stomach.

I feel no different now.

It will be my pleasure to watch it burn all over again.

Kade's gaze is locked on the darkened reception desk, behind a closed shutter. I uncurl his fist to let our fingers entwine. The memories are so close to the surface, I can see them bubbling in his hazel eyes.

"You looked so lost the day you arrived," he whispers. "All I wanted was to hold you."

"I'm glad you latched on and wouldn't let go."

He offers me a crooked smile. "I love you."

"Ditto, Mr Knight."

None of us can stand to look at the repaired offices and treatment rooms down the low-lit corridor. I hate to think of what lies below us. Smouldering ruins have been reborn in a new vision of depravity. No matter what, I won't allow any more lives to be ruined in these hallowed halls.

"Sounds like the party is outside." Hunter checks his gun holster. "I'd say stick to the plan, but at this point, I'm not sure there is one. So, I'll say this. Don't get caught alive."

Enzo chuckles. "Cheery."

Their shoulders bump together.

"We're screwed too, old friend." Hunter shakes his head. "I won't let Alyssa down again."

"The SCU can chase us here and see for themselves what they're enabling," Theo agrees, smoothing his bouncy curls. "Let's go kick some corrupt ass and hope to hell this stupid plan works."

We pass another two guards who note our presence and murmur something into their earpieces. The moment they open the doors for us without a second glance, I know our doom awaits. Outside, bright lights reveal the party in full swing. The once quiet, peaceful quad is bustling with activity.

Benches and picnic tables have been cleared to make way for two huge marquees, the pure-white fabric rustling in the cool breeze. Glimmering lights have been strung to provide a warm ambiance for the circulation of champagne and appetisers on polished, golden plates.

There's even a string quartet, the gentle croon of violins accompanying the hum of laughter and conversation. Guests mill about in floor-length gowns and tailored tuxedos, admiring the grand architecture and impressive surroundings. There isn't a speck of evidence from the fire.

"Stick together." Hunter eyes the crowd. "We're going to check the place out, look for any big fish. The more of Incendia's corrupt officials we document, the easier our jobs will be."

"Be safe," I beg them.

Enzo offers me a dazzling smile. "Don't get into trouble without us."

"Somehow, I think they will," Theo jokes.

Sandwiched between slabs of muscle and defiance, we leave them and head for the upper crusts of society. It isn't long before I start recognising people in the melee. Several familiar faces spot me in turn. I remember the middle-aged, pot-bellied men that Augustus introduced me to at his fundraiser.

"Investors," Kade mutters. "I know a few of them."

"Me too. Keep moving."

Grabbing a glass of champagne from the nearest waiter, I down it in three fast gulps. There's a buzz of whispers around us as we enter the nearest marquee, our hardened expressions and casual clothing betraying us to the stuck-up wankers attending Bancroft's power trip.

Kade guides us towards the pop-up bar at the back, helping himself to a bottle of whiskey before the attendant can say a word. He fills several crystal glasses, and we knock them back, needing the liquid courage. It won't be long before someone finds us.

We wait even less time than expected. This entire parade of wealth and power has been laid out for our benefit. A deliberate throat clear has Kade's unsteady hand hesitating over his glass. I recognise the smug, brutish voice before he says a word.

"Care to pour your father a drink, son?"

The bottle hits the bar with a thud.

"My days of tending to your demands are over," Kade responds coolly.

"Your time in the real world has given you a backbone, has it?"

Huddled together for strength, we turn as a united front to face the infamous Leroy Knight. He's standing a few metres away, dressed in an impeccable suit and blood-red bow tie. His salt and pepper hair has been slicked back to highlight his handsome, ageing face.

There's a willowy blonde woman hanging off his arm, too busy eyeing up the waiter to listen to our conversation. Her satin dress and designer handbag betray her shallow motives. She's just another exploit, one in a long line of people to be controlled.

"Hudson," Leroy greets with a smile. "It's been a long time."

"Not long enough," he grits out.

"Keeping my son on his toes, are you? Only now, he isn't paid to make excuses for you."

"Enough," Kade thunders, stepping forward. "This is between me and you."

Leroy laughs in his face, so loud it's actually unnerving. His date frowns at us all before snagging a fresh drink and making a hasty exit. She's probably off to snort some cocaine in the bathroom before she gets paid for pretending to like this sack of shit.

"Think you're a big man now, do you?"

Kade refuses to cower. "I'm more than the person you taught me to be."

The depraved man I know begins to peek through Leroy's glossy, paparazzi-perfect exterior. He wraps himself in finery and lies, but there's a slavering monster rotting him from the inside out.

"You had one job," he sneers at his son. "Make sure the street rat didn't jeopardise my reputation further. That's it. Eighteen more months and you would've been free to do as you please."

Hudson moves to stand by his brother. "Sorry we derailed your plans. How inconsiderate of us. If you want, I can kiss your ass and pretend I don't want to slit your throat? I did it enough back then."

"That won't be necessary. I've come to realise my efforts have been misguided. Thankfully, I have another child. Once I track your traitorous mother down, I will ensure your sister doesn't repeat your mistakes."

Kade's teeth are bared in a threatening snarl. He looks ready to snap his own father's neck, with or without our help. I doubt he'd hesitate over taking this asshole's life, morals or not.

"Cece won't have to experience your poison," Kade elucidates. "They're never coming back here. You're going to die exactly as you should—humiliated and alone. Then my job here is done."

The crowd parts as a handful of grey-faced, heavily armed guards make their entrance. Leroy taps his concealed earpiece with glee. I'm sure he's being well-compensated for his role in this pantomime. We're surrounded, but not one of us cowers in the face of aggression.

The nearest guard points a gun straight at Kade's face. No tasers or batons, they all pull deadly weapons and train them on every single one of my guys. I'm the only one left without a target on me, so I step forward.

"Why don't you come and give me a proper hello, Patient Eight." Leroy eyes me with interest. "You're looking a little cleaner than the last time I saw you."

"I don't make it a habit to execute wayward employees these days."

"Ah, she speaks! Augustus should've removed your acid tongue when he had the chance. Come along, I tire of your childish games."

Glancing between Kade and Hudson, they both give subtle head shakes. The closest armed guard notices and strides forward, smashing the barrel of his gun into Hudson's temple. I stare at his finger on the trigger, my feet carrying me further forward.

"There we go," Leroy croons. "That wasn't so hard, was it?"

Mentally checking out, I make myself walk straight into his open arms. I can smell the liquor and cigars on his breath as his lips graze my cheek.

"Care to dance, my dear? It is a party, after all."

I lower my voice to a low, sensual croon. "I'd rather cut your dick off with a rusty knife and make you swallow it."

"Such fire, Patient Eight. I am glad your spark hasn't dulled."

His hand clamps around my wrist. He doesn't give me a chance to even say goodbye. I'm dragged through the circular tables and away from the others. Fighting back will only ensure their deaths. I allow my mind to completely empty like it used to, sliding back into the safety of numbness.

When we reach the polished parquet of the dance floor, Leroy pulls me into position. We spin around beneath the light of a chandelier built into the marquee. Champagne and whiskey sour in my stomach at the scent of his aftershave washing over me, laced with imaginary blood.

When I glance at the guys, I find them unmoved.

That's when I realise Seven isn't with them.

"Am I boring you already?" Leroy grips my chin.

"I've had better dancing partners."

He spins us around so we're facing the other way. My lack of submission is beginning to grind his gears; I can see the flames of fury in his eyes. Bancroft still hasn't made an appearance, and I'm beginning to feel antsy.

"You know, impulsivity is your greatest weakness. Not many people would accept an invitation to their own demise, Patient Eight. Things would've been a lot less complicated if we did this a month ago."

I curl my lip at him. "I'm here for Bancroft, not your sleazy fucking ass."

Leroy grunts as he slaps me across the face, hard enough for my head to snap to the side. Licking a bead of blood from my lip, I stare back at him with defiance.

"That all you got, old man?"

"Oh, I have plenty more. I'm on strict orders to be a good boy, though."

"The big, powerful Leroy Knight is on a leash?" I cackle. "How mighty of you."

He merely shrugs. "Like with all good plans, preparation is key. Are you ready for your prize? We can't have a treasure hunt without one."

Leroy roughly turns me around. I'm relieved to see the guys are where I left them, though Seven is still missing. Where the fuck is he? I can't see Enzo, Hunter or Theo either. My heartbeat roars in my ears as Leroy grabs my wrist again, towing me out of the marquee.

Nobody blinks an eye as we're escorted at gunpoint. They all watch with morbid satisfaction. It's like they're trapped in a parallel reality, ignoring the real world slapping them in the face. Many people here will be making millions from Incendia's shady dealings, including the Z Wing program and its valuable recruits.

Humans with no humanity.

We're truly on our own in this theatre of death.

Taken away from the party, darkness invades our surroundings. There are no lights on inside the classrooms. Spooky, seemingly vacant buildings block us on all sides. I realise where we're headed as Leroy's nails dig into my skin. Oakridge dorms await at the end of a cobbled path.

This is where it all began.

It's fitting this should be our end.

Floodlights slam on, momentarily blinding me. As my vision clears, the awaiting scene is a terrifying sight. In front of the carved stone steps that my hallucinations once chased me up, a giant wooden stage has been erected. Great beams stretch upwards, running parallel to the platform raised several feet in the air.

Hanging from the beam, I count five nooses.

Perfectly tied and awaiting a sacrificial neck.

Standing next to his macabre construction, Bancroft watches our arrival with visible joy. He's dressed to the nines in a navy-blue suit and matching velvet bow tie. In the harsh light, I can see Augustus in his features. Sharp and cruel, his entire persona drips with intelligence and authority.

"Good job, Leroy. You might want to make a hasty exit. I have no doubt their reinforcements will be arriving soon. I intend to finish this quickly."

"Indeed," Leroy agrees with a chuckle. "I'll be seeing you soon, old friend. We have another election to win."

Bancroft smiles widely. "Who wouldn't vote for the man that brought these convicts to their doom?"

Leroy's grip on me loosens as his hot, sticky breath meets my ear. "Have fun in hell, darling. He's going to tear you apart. It's been a pleasure."

"Run away," I smart. "Like the coward you are."

Delivering his parting blow, Leroy's eyes narrow as he shoves me hard. I stumble and hit the ground right in front of Bancroft. By the time I crawl onto my knees, Kade's father has scuttled away like the pathetic worm he is, and fascinated investors are crowding around to watch the drama play out.

"Brooklyn West," Bancroft greets. "Or should I say, Patient Eight? We do live in extraordinary times when one body can hold two people. Quite fascinating."

The butt of a gun meets my head, forcing me to cower at his almighty altar of undeserved power. Instead of looking at Bancroft, I watch my guys get escorted up the stairs to the wooden platform. None of them betray any fear in the face of death.

"What is this?" I growl.

"Presumably, you accepted my invitation with some vague notion of ending my life. Can't kill a man at the end of the phone, right? I understand. Vengeance is a powerful motivator."

Forever the fearless leader, Kade takes the first noose. The guard loops it around his neck and tightens the thick rope until he's trapped. My horror increases as each noose is filled with its victim. I never underestimated the risk of coming here, but Bancroft's insanity is far greater than I'd predicted.

"Are you going to murder five wanted criminals in front of hundreds of witnesses?" I ask, playing down my panic. "Even for you, that's a gamble. Loyalties change. People talk. You're being reckless."

"Reckless?" Bancroft laughs loudly. "I've always been a gambling man."

"Your son was too." I let the full force of my hatred shine through my tiny, satisfied smile. "His gamble didn't pay off in the end. I enjoyed watching the blood pour as I twisted the knife in his gut."

Before Bancroft can strike me, my hand snaps up and captures his mid-movement. Rather than scaring him, he looks down at my skin on his with amusement. His grin is seriously unhinged.

"Yet, his legacy lives on," he states with conviction. "You are his greatest creation. I honour my son's hard work by finishing what he started. That begins with removing all temptations from your life."

The nearest guard rests his hand on a built-in lever that holds my entire attention. Bancroft is frowning at the empty fifth noose when the harsh bark of another dickhead foot soldier distracts him. Wherever Seven is, I hope to fuck he has a plan to get us out of this.

"Ah, the final piece of the puzzle." Bancroft claps his hands together in mock excitement. "I believe you two have been reacquainted. Sloppy work at Harrowdean, Miss West. Not your finest hour."

Escorted with a gun at her temple, I feel my world implode as Bancroft's final taunt arrives. Her bald head and gaunt face haven't changed since our silent conversation through blood-stained messages and distant waves. Mum doesn't look at me as she's dragged to Bancroft's side.

"Ah, Patient Delta. Did you find her accomplices?"

"No, sir," her dull voice drones.

"Of course not. While I appreciate Lazlo's impressive work, all things must die. The old is replaced with the new. I no longer have a use for you, Patient Delta, as I have your daughter here now."

That's the exact moment when Mum's eyes snap to mine. Her gaze burns like the air bags that hit my skin in the car crash. Still, she betrays no recognition. I can see the same armour I wrap myself in staring back at me. I've seen proof that she lives within it, a tiny, flickering flame determined to burn bright.

"She will take your place."

Her voice remains flat, complacent. "I understand, sir."

Leaving her standing there, Bancroft returns to me. There's another gun now clasped in his hand. I swallow a bubble of acid as he wraps an arm around my waist, his breath licking against my skin.

"Do you enjoy games, Miss West?"

I refuse to answer.

"I do," Bancroft continues. "So, here's one for you. It's rather simple. I will place this gun in your hand. See? Here we go. Get ready now."

He forcibly uncurls my fingers, positioning the weapon in my hand.

"Your choice is rather simple. On the count of three, a lever will be pulled. Four lives will end. You get to watch the ones you love swing on the end of a noose. Sounds thrilling, doesn't it?"

My eyes connect with Eli's.

His mouth forms the words he cannot say.

Until death do us part.

"You have a chance to save their lives." Bancroft raises my hand until the gun is pointed at my mother. "Kill Patient Delta, and I will let them walk away, unharmed. You will take her place by my side, but they will live. I'll have all charges against them dropped."

His words cause my heart to stop dead.

"Tempting, huh?" he purrs in my ear. "Fail to kill her and I'll gladly take their lives. Your mother will live on. Call it a family reunion. You get to have a parent again, but not without paying the price."

The guard standing behind Hudson kicks his left leg out to illustrate Bancroft's threat. I almost scream as Hudson slips for a brief, horrifying second, the noose tightening around his neck with an awful choking sound. He manages to find his feet again after a scramble, looking blue in the face.

"What will it be, Brooklyn? Your mother or the men who saved your life?"

Bancroft's hands leave mine. I'm left holding the gun alone. It wavers in the air, but I don't lower it. One shot between the eyes and my last remaining parent will return to the grave she should have inhabited twelve years ago. I'll lose her all over again.

If I don't, my family dies.

Either way, the choice rests on my shoulders.

"Tick tock, tick tock," Bancroft leers.

I look over to the guys. I'm on the precipice of that rooftop all over again, despite the passing of time that's bound our souls together. It all comes back to this —death holding us apart. I have nothing to offer this world, but they do. Saving their lives is the only good thing I have left to give.

My finger rests on the trigger.

That's when Mum's mouth opens.

"It's okay," she says softly.

Her voice drags me back into the sordid past, but I'm no longer kicking and screaming. The years melt away in the chasm separating us. We're back on the roof of our crappy, suburban house in rural England. Every morning, we climbed the trellis together, praying it wouldn't break.

Here comes the sun, baby.

Close your eyes and pray for something good.

Why do we pray, Mummy?

For the strength to do good in this life, Brooke.

That's why we put ourselves in the way of beauty.

I can feel the hot sting of tears on my cheeks. Despite the years of torture, conditioning, abuse and neglect, Mum's sunken cheeks are wet too. She touches the tears with wonderment, looking surprised at her own reaction.

She has emotions.

She can feel.

She isn't fucking dead.

The slight upturn of her lips severs my final heartstrings.

"Come on!" Bancroft roars behind me.

For a second, I consider raising the gun to my own head. The familiar crop of shadows that spawns beside my mother halts that thought. Broad shoulders, long legs, and a boyish grin form in my hallucination. Brushing his blonde hair aside, Logan stands next to his murderer.

He glances up at her, even if she can't see him.

"No," I breathe out.

Without a single word, Logan meets my eyes. His strength and devotion pour into me, the warmth in my chest expanding and chasing out the darkness. Standing by our mother's side, I take comfort in the knowledge that she isn't alone. He's waiting to catch her on the other side, where peace awaits.

"I'm sorry, Mummy."

Her lips move in a silent message.

I want to see my boy again.

Let go, Brooke.

Bancroft is screaming at me, but I can't hear him. The threats wash over me like the rolling waves of the ocean. Little details enter my awareness and float away again. The guard's hand is pushing the lever a tiny, warning inch as the countdown begins.

Distant voices and laughter echo from our cruel enablers as they watch the show, like it's some twisted performance displaying what their money created. A flash of chestnut hair enters my periphery before it disappears, leaping back into the dark shadows.

"Please," Mum whimpers quietly.

That's when I realise her plan. The empty shell of my mother wanted me to come tonight. She knew this was the only way to be family again. This cruel world won't give us our happy ending, but perhaps the promise of the next will. After years of torment, she has a chance to escape.

I have to give her that.

I'm the only one who can set her free.

The bullet travels faster than the speed of light. Death is such a quick act for a permanent end. My shot is imperfect from my shaking hand, but it catches her right in the forehead. I squeeze my eyes shut to avoid watching the result. Logan vanishes from sight the moment my mother dies by my hand.

He's waiting somewhere, arms outstretched.

I hope she hugs him and never, ever lets go.

Ears still ringing, it takes a moment for Bancroft's unhinged laughter to register. It's a deep, maniacal cackle that mirrors the sheer insanity of his deceased son. I check the chamber of the gun and find it empty. The sick bastard only gave me a single execution shot. I'll have to do it myself.

The whizz of another bullet cuts off his celebration, slicing through the air with deadly precision. The laughter grating against my skull ceases as the guard holding four lives in his hand is struck, wavering in the air before he plummets in a spray of blood.

Reality shatters and reforms in an instant. The doors to Oakridge slam open, releasing a spray of bullets. Two more guards are caught and fall. When Hunter and Enzo emerge with battle cries, closely followed by Theo, I feel a glimmer of hope. Seven isn't far behind, dropping from a nearby oak tree.

Leaves and branches stir in the wind as it suddenly picks up. My senses are awash with the heavy beat of a helicopter, nearly blowing the marquees over. Bright letters spell out its designation—*SCU.* That's when Bancroft realises he's absolutely screwed.

Two hands latch around my neck, attempting to snap the bone. Sliding back into the welcoming arms of Patient Eight, I break free from Bancroft's hold with practised ease. He stumbles, attempting to regain purchase, but I've already rounded on him. His time has run out.

Terrified eyes meet mine.

Augustus is looking at me through his gaze.

"The game is over," I tell him.

My blow is sharp, brutal. Bancroft's knees crash into the grass as he clutches his head, looking dazed. I could walk away right now. I could spare his life. It will do my future prospects a lot of good. But Augustus taught me a valuable lesson when he ordered the murder of Allison Brunel in the Z Wing.

Fuck the moral high ground.

Never leave a job unfinished.

I can hear Hunter's deep boom over the helicopter as help arrives, but I'm not done. Ignoring them all, I sink my teeth deep into Bancroft's exposed neck. He's powerless to push me away. It takes a decade of hatred and rage to tear into his throat, my mouth filling with hot, coppery blood.

Patient Eight doesn't flinch.

She works in calm, collected silence.

He crashes before me with a thud, jerking as arterial spray paints the grass, along with my entire body. I watch the show with warmth running down my chin. Lazlo, Augustus, Jefferson and Bancroft die together in one body. A monster with many faces bleeds to death in the presence of his crumbling empire.

Voices try to break the violent haze that's descended over me. Enzo is staring down at Bancroft's corpse with a look of triumph, while figures jump from the helicopter and swarm all over us. My brain recognises agents Barlow and Jonas back in their uniforms, where they belong.

I feel absolutely nothing. Not until a hand takes mine, regardless of the blood.

"Brooklyn?" Seven asks warily.

That name is like a hot poker in the chest. It tears a hole in my suffocating shields, letting love and light pour in; so much that my knees buckle and he has no choice but to catch me. I'm enveloped in his coffee scent.

"Brooklyn," he repeats. "Come back, Brooke. The work is done. Patient Eight can rest now. She's finished her last job."

The world is filtering back in with loud noises and frantic shouts. Too many people to count are swarming like ants, including government agents with bright-yellow SCU letters printed across their backs.

They aren't arresting us.

We're not being sedated or trapped in cuffs.

Sponsors and investors are trying to run where they can, but they don't get very far. Designer high heels are tossed aside, and perfect dresses yanked up. I spot a couple of the men from Augustus's fundraiser being pinned to the ground. Our eyes collide briefly. Their fear makes my mouth water.

Guns are pulled and panicked phone calls made, but it does nothing to prevent the inevitable. Agent Barlow is the first one to slap cuffs on a man, yelling into the radio strapped to her chest. I recognise the white-haired dickhead she's arresting. He was there that night at the table, when Augustus boasted about his newest acquisition.

I catch the word *boss* being thrown in for good measure.

She's enjoying every last second of arresting her employer.

"Love!"

"Firecracker!"

"Blackbird!"

Their voices shove that last, clinging tendril of sickness back where it belongs. I blink and take a deep breath, standing back on my own feet. Seven is grinning down at me, his thumb swiping the blood from my bottom lip.

"Nice throat-tearing skills, princess."

I press my lips to his, letting him taste our revenge. "Learned from the best."

He holds my hand as the rest of our family converges in the middle of a war zone. In the light of the helicopter and perfect chaos, our reunion is near delirious. I'm passed around, hugged and kissed, touched and worshipped. Four men saved my life on the rooftop hanging over us.

My debt to them is repaid.

Seven has his revenge, served cold and bloody.

There's no fire and death this time. Incendia's ruin comes in the form of real, tangible justice. For the first time in our lives, the world has sided with us. The truth isn't something that many can afford, but when you're stripped of everything, sometimes it's all you have left.

We told ours.

We braved the world's hatred and judgement.

We won.

CHAPTER 31
ELI

HOPE FOR THE UNDERRATED
YOUTH - YUNGBLUD

I ENTERED Blackwood with one certainty—once I stepped through those gates, I would never leave. Each psychiatric unit I inhabited over the years promised recovery and hope after what my father did to me. It took years to find the courage to even be around other people again.

Blackwood was supposed to be my last chance, a final shot at rehabilitation. I was tired. Broken. Scarred. Defeated. A lost, lonely little boy, trapped in the past and unable to move on with the life I had left.

Finding a new family was not on the agenda. I know what families do to you. I still bear the scars to prove it. Those sworn to love and protect us are often the ones most equipped to tear us to shreds, piece by fucking piece.

You never expect to be built up again.

In the darkest of times, light finds its way back in.

We stand as a united front while the cameras flash on our third news conference of the week. Brooklyn's hand is gripping mine tight. In the month since Bancroft's death set the world alight, our private lives have become public property; every last intimate detail unpicked and printed for the world to read.

Sending our sworn testimonies out into the world was a bold move. It's tossed us all from the frying pan and into the fire. Yet, if we hadn't braved that final move, we'd be dead. It was the truth that forced the government to act and realise the SCU was dirty all along.

"This is the final time we will be here before the public," Hunter tells the reporters. "My clients have spent the last month cooperating with law enforcement. They have provided new sworn testimony to investigators. We are grateful to the SCU for reconsidering their position."

"Is it true that you're going to be the new head of service?" a woman asks.

He stifles an eye roll. "That is false. Sabre will be working closely with the SCU following the recent arrest and prosecution of its director. Incendia has many assets that need to be thoroughly investigated for corruption and money laundering."

"Will you volunteer to lead that investigation?"

"Sabre remains my priority. I'm sure the government will choose an appropriate successor. We look forward to working with them for years to come."

Sitting next to him, agents Barlow and Jonas look solemn. Their resignations were quickly halted when news of our stories spread like wildfire. They were the ones who raised the alert and went above the blanket decision made by their director. Now, they're lauded as heroes.

Bancroft knew exactly where to place his own stooge.

Turns out, the director was an old family friend.

One of many in positions of extreme power.

"As the work to dismantle Incendia and the six institutes continues, my team will dedicate all of our resources to seeking justice for the victims." Hunter casts us all a look. "I am requesting privacy for my clients to rest and recuperate. That is all."

Phoenix is squeezing my other hand ferociously tight. We're all connected, needing the reassurance of each other's touch. Enzo stands off to the side, his beefy arms crossed and scowl firmly in place. Nobody would dare go through him to get to us.

We're led from the conference room, blinded by flashing cameras. I rip the microphone off my t-shirt as soon as we're out of sight behind the scenes. This was our final round of questions with the press. The SCU have cancelled all future requests as they officially take over from Sabre.

It will take time, but Incendia is on fire.

The legacy of sorrow is no more.

Each day reveals new levels of corruption—politicians, police officers, members of parliament, the secret service and other turncoats within the SCU. Like dominoes, once one fell, the rest quickly followed. The footage of many public figures and investors watching Bancroft's failed execution was a strong condemnation.

"Head for Theo's office," Enzo instructs.

We gather upstairs in the messy, disorganised space. Theo's sat at his desk, slurping a cup of ramen and watching the live stream far from prying eyes. As we enter, he startles and nearly knocks a cup of coffee over.

"Too slow." Hudson catches the cup easily.

Theo takes it from him with a wince. "It's been a long week. Our public appeal for information has been inundated with ex-patients and detainees coming forward to assist with the investigation."

"From Blackwood?" Brooklyn leans against his desk.

"Harrowdean Manor, Compton Hall, and Priory Lane so far." He frowns at his piece of paper. "More will follow. Incendia's been abusing their privilege for thirty years. Now that the truth is out, people aren't afraid to speak up."

Phoenix snorts. "Snowball effect."

"Not to mention three other facilities decommissioned during the late nineties. Incendia tightened the purse strings, but that didn't erase the evidence. We have hundreds of witnesses ready to go on record."

Hunter strolls in with the two proud agents at his back, finally escaping the reporters. There's something very weird going on with his mouth. I think it's an attempted smile. I had no idea he could do that. The grief that's stained his entire being for so long is absent today.

Agent Barlow deposits her briefcase on one of Theo's cluttered tables. We all gather around as she pulls out thick stacks of paperwork and several ring-bound packets. Each one is placed down in front of us with a meaningful look. I count six legal packets in total.

"Andy, can you take these to Lucia and Patient Two for their signatures?"

Accepting the papers, Agent Jonas offers us all a final smile. The unshakeable government bot has become one of our strongest supporters in the absolute chaos of the last few weeks. All that time spent spilling our guts has earned us something —loyalty and respect. All it took was telling the truth.

Once he's gone to visit the girls in their apartment, Agent Barlow returns her attention to us all. "Are we ready?"

"Everyone's here," Hunter confirms.

One by one, we're each handed a packet of paperwork and a pen. Kade glances between us, a smile tugging at his lips. We've all got one, even Seven. He's frowning at the pen like it's a snake ready to bite his hand off.

"The SCU has been authorised by the prime minister himself to issue a full and unreserved public apology." Agent Barlow meets our eyes. "You have all lost years of your life and suffered irreparable damage. For that, the government takes full responsibility."

Hudson gasps as he scans his packet. "You're dropping all charges?"

"Every single one. No prosecutions will be pursued against you. Any and all crimes committed in Incendia's custody and in recent weeks are being classified as under duress. Nobody is going to prison."

Kade and his brother immediately throw their arms around each other. I'm swept off my feet by Phoenix, his squeal of relief breaking through the shock. We did it. This nightmare is over. Our lives have been given back to us. I've never felt hope like this.

But two of us aren't celebrating.

Seven and Brooklyn stare at each other, clasping identical paperwork.

"Brooke?" Kade frowns at them. "What is it?"

Enzo's head falls as our excitement fades. He can't look at us, nor can Theo. The only one staring straight ahead is Hunter, like he knew this was coming. Tension is rolling off him in waves.

"What Augustus did to you both will go down in history as a heinous violation of human rights." Agent Barlow's smile is tight. "Brooklyn, Seven, the charges against you make for grim reading. We acknowledge the role Incendia had to play in your actions. You're victims, not perpetrators."

"When?" Brooklyn interrupts.

We all glance between them, completely bemused.

"Forty-eight hours. The SCU will release your mother's body. You can bury her before you go."

"What... h-happening?!" I demand.

Everyone startles at the harsh lash of my voice. Brooklyn's eyes slam shut, like she's trying to will herself from this room. It's Seven who answers my question, the papers bunched in his one hand.

"We're being sent to Clearview."

Enzo has to hold Hudson back as he shouts his head off, fists flying. The others filter through expressions of outrage and shock. While they spiral, I approach Brooklyn and cup her cheeks until her eyes open.

"Baby girl?"

"It's okay," she whispers to me. "We aren't safe out there."

"This isn't a prison sentence," Hunter chips in. "You've both been to hell and back. This is your chance to get better. Doctor Richards is taking over as the new head of clinical operations. He wants to help you."

Brooklyn tears her gaze from mine. "What about Zimmerman?"

"He's on his way to a lifelong prison sentence for aiding and abetting the Z Wing program for over a decade. We've connected over thirty transfers into Augustus's care from Clearview, under his direction, for the purposes of human experimentation."

"And you want to send her back to that fucking place?" Hudson rages.

"The facility is being repurposed to support victims of Incendia's institutes. They will be receiving state-of-the-art, real psychiatric care."

"That's exactly the sales pitch we all received," Phoenix adds angrily. "We've heard it all before."

A heated argument breaks out. None of them are paying attention to the determination that's brewing like storm clouds on Brooklyn's face. She lays her hands on top of mine, savouring the tiny glimpse of the lives we could have. It's floating away again, but not out of sight.

"I need to sort myself out before I can be the woman you all deserve." Her eyes beg me to understand. "There's still so much rage inside of me. So much hurt. I can't start a new life until I fix what's broken."

She slips from my grasp before I can attempt to protest. I don't need to scream and rave though. This is her decision, on her terms, for the first time in her entire life. She's choosing to face this sickness head-on. I think that's fucking brave.

"I'll do it," Brooklyn declares.

Agent Barlow nods, offering her the papers again. "Clearview will help those affected by Incendia's Z Wing program. You're not a prisoner there. These people want to help you. I suggest you let them."

Ignoring the continued shouting, Brooklyn signs her life back over to the state with a sigh. Freedom is postponed, and our separation is now set in stone. Hudson turns his back before he hurts someone, fisting his black hair. Brooklyn doesn't approach him, looking to Seven instead.

"I'm not going to leave you on your own," he submits. "We can't live out in the real world like this. I want to be the man Alyssa died searching for. Not just... Patient Seven."

Brooklyn touches his arm. "We'll do it together. Our family will wait for us."

Nodding, Seven takes the pen and signs on the dotted line. That's when the arguing and shouting stops. Kade looks on with bleak acceptance, seeming to realise he can't take this decision away from them. Phoenix holds my hand for strength, his gaze stuck on Brooklyn's face.

Hudson is the last one to turn around. "You can't do this."

"I have to," Brooklyn responds gently. "For us."

Unable to stay away, Hudson walks straight into her arms. His face buries in her neck to hide his despair from us. Kade and Phoenix circle around them in a huge group hug, leaving me to hang back.

I'm too busy staring at the name Seven has signed in black and white, sealing an eternal promise to the one person who deserved to see this day. His eyes connect with mine before he offers me a tiny, hopeful smile.

Jude Farlow.

CHAPTER 32
BROOKLYN

HURRICANE - DREAM ON DREAMER

THIS JOURNEY ENDS where it began—on a sandy hill in Northern Scotland, far from the world.

I stare at the blazing rays of the autumn sunset. The light washes over me in a comforting cloud, pink and orange hues painting a perfect picture. I'm standing here on my last night of freedom, doing what Mum would've wanted me to.

Deep down, I know she's here too.

They all are. My dead family.

Next to me, a six-foot hole has been dug deep into the sand. Hudson insisted on doing it for me. I wanted to bury her next to the spot where, months ago, I put Logan's ghost to rest. I couldn't let go of the polaroid photos then. They've followed me through years of pain, death, and turmoil.

Standing at my mother's peaceful graveside, I clasp those photos in my hands now. My tears splash against the faded, creased faces staring back at me from the past. Clearview, Blackwood, Sabre, here. They've lived through it all with me.

The beautiful, tragic memory captured in permanent ink has haunted me for so long. The beach stretched out in summer sunshine. My small body was being swung between my parents while Logan captured the candid photos. Their smiles were bright and full of love. There were no dark shadows in my eyes.

We were happy. Free.

Untainted by sickness and evil.

Swallowing my grief, I kiss my father's face first. His soft, grey eyes radiate love back at me. With his family in his arms, he was at his happiest. Even if that was his undoing in the end.

"I forgive you, Daddy. You can rest now."

With an arm slung around her husband's neck, the unbroken version of my mother looks vastly different to the person I killed. She was beginning to disintegrate then, but the shell that returned to me was truly broken.

"I'm so fucking sorry," I whisper to her. "Pulling that trigger was the hardest thing I've ever done. I wanted you to rest, Mummy. You deserve to rest."

"Brooklyn? You ready?" Hudson prompts.

Nodding through my tears, I kiss her face. "I have to get better for my family now. They need me, Mum. I can't join you. I have to find a way to live. One day, I'll see you all again."

That should be it, but there's one more person I have to kiss goodbye. I can't let go of all my pain until one final corpse is laid to rest. The little blonde girl swinging between her parents had no clue what was coming her way. She died, too.

"So many people hurt you," I admit, studying my childhood self. "Nobody kept us safe. I've spent so many years trying to kill myself, I forgot to live. I may not be the same person I used to be, but I promise to live for both of us now."

With my final goodbye complete, I watch the polaroids flutter in the air. Sinking down into the sandy hole, they hit the wooden coffin that Kade sourced from the local town.

With a fortifying breath, I turn to face the family I found in the darkness. I lost the people I loved. Not everyone is lucky enough to have a second chance to belong, but I am. All five of them gave that to me.

Hudson's standing next to the grave, a shovel in hand. Behind him, Phoenix and Eli are wrapped up in each other. I drink in the reassurance of their presence. Lastly, Kade and Teegan stand at the back. He's holding her arm while she offers me an encouraging smile.

They're all here. Back at the rented cottage we found our temporary peace in, Hunter, Enzo and Theo are waiting for us. I appreciate their respect for my privacy. All my vulnerabilities are on display right now.

"Brooke?"

I feel Seven's hand slide into mine. He was standing on the cliff's edge, studying the violent sea. With him by my side, I am complete. Every single person I care about is here. Safe. Healthy. Whole. Fucking free.

"I'm ready," I say calmly.

Pressing a kiss to my hair, Seven joins Hudson, shoving sand in the hole with one hand. I stand at the edge of the grave until it's filled all the way in. They smooth the sand over together, concealing my mother's empty body in the rugged beauty of the coastline.

I was prepared for a shadowy figure to appear, but my mind conjures no such horror. Hunter's well-paid shrink started me back on medication. Doctor Richards is actually very kind and amicable, content to sit in silence for hours until I'm ready to talk.

He's preparing for our arrival at Clearview tomorrow morning. Then, our long road to recovery will begin. It promises to be a hell of a bumpy ride.

Clearing her throat, Teegan approaches me next. I let her arms wind around me in one of her signature tight hugs. She penetrated my lonely bubble from day one with her quirks and awkward charm. I couldn't imagine a world without her in it as my best friend.

"I'm gonna come see you all the time," she whispers in my ear. "I'll bring you old records and band t-shirts. Maybe the odd cigarette if I can hide them in my bra."

My laugh is wet, teary. "You have a life to live too."

"Friends don't bail when one of them gets locked in the loony bin. Been there, done that. Got the fucking t-shirt." She pulls back to hit me with a dazzling smile. "When you get out, we'll drink beer and put the whole goddamn world to rights."

"Promise?"

She sticks out her pinky finger. "I promise, crazy bitch. I'll give you guys a minute. See you inside?"

Our fingers link and seal our promise. With a final wink, she begins the long walk back to the cottage. I'm left with the intense stares of five broken, defiant men. Four don't want me to go. One is as batshit crazy as I am. We have to be the most fucked up family on this earth.

"I don't know what to say to you all."

Despite everything, their strangled laughs match mine until we're all gasping and fighting tears. Kade takes the lead and approaches me, a knowing smile on his lips. I happily walk into his embrace, avoiding his broken arm.

"We told you, love. You're ours, in this life and the next."

Hudson clears his throat, his eyes shining. "Always and forever, blackbird."

"You couldn't get rid of us even if you tried," Phoenix says proudly.

Emerald eyes meeting mine, Eli points to his jean-covered hip. His lips move silently, reserving our macabre promise for the intimacy of silence. Some things shouldn't be said aloud.

"Until death do us part," I mouth back.

A gentle hand lands on my shoulder.

"This is our last night outside for a while," Seven points out. "What do you want to do, princess?"

I watch Hudson approach him, their shoulders brushing. Despite everything, he's still being fucking shy. Seven rolls his eyes before taking his hand from my shoulder and snatching Hudson's instead. Kade smothers a laugh at their antics.

"I want a happy memory to hold on to."

Phoenix's face lights up with a devious idea. He tears his sweatshirt over his head, despite the freezing, almost wintery temperature. We all watch in bemusement as his shoes go flying next.

"Last one in the ocean has to wash the dishes."

Then he's gone, sprinting down the steep sandbank and yelling his head off. It's a split second before Eli follows, unable to be parted from his blue-haired soulmate. I watch the pair of idiots go, shedding even more clothes on their way down to the water.

"I fucking hate washing up," Hudson blurts.

He shoves his lips against Seven's briefly before kissing me with feverish need. We're both left standing there as he takes off after the other two, his black t-shirt landing in a nearby shrub.

"He is quite possibly the laziest human on this planet," Seven grumbles, toeing off his shoes. "We can't let them win, princess. It sets a dangerous precedent."

In a blur of long hair and bared teeth, he gives chase. Hudson's fast, but Seven is a whole other breed. They collide halfway down the sandbank and end up wrestling all the way to the bottom, landing in a steamy tangle. I watch four naked blurs head for the crashing waves.

Kade sighs. "Seeing my brother's naked ass wasn't on my list of priorities for today."

"Looks like we're the sore losers."

He grips my chin, exposing my lips to his. "I don't mind washing up. I'll take the forfeit. It's worth it, so I can do this."

Mouth slanting against mine, I melt into the kiss. Kade doesn't fight to consume me like the others; his battle for my soul has long since ended. I belong to him in every single fucking way a person can be owned. Breaking the kiss, his hazel eyes bore into mine.

"Come back to us, love. I have far too many plans for you to let this sickness win."

I stroke his cheek with my thumb. "I promise, I'll come back to you. I lost my entire family to the darkness buried inside of us. You have too, in your own way. That ends right now."

"I don't care how long it takes, Brooke. Let me worry about tracking my piece-of-shit father down. By the time you come back, I'll have his head mounted on a spike."

"Be careful, Kade. He's dangerous."

"So am I. Enough about him. This is our last night together."

Our foreheads meet as our souls collide. I rest my hand over his thudding heartbeat, and Kade does the same. The organ in his chest is thumping steadily, with the certainty he's always exuded.

Kade can't be my safe place anymore.

I have to find that within myself now.

"Take care of them," I murmur. "Keep my family safe."

"Until my dying breath. We'll be here waiting when you're ready."

Our fingers entwined, we slip and slide down the sandbank. The other morons are already naked and in the sea, whining about cold water. I let Kade run in first, sticking to the shallow water to avoid getting his plaster-cast arm wet. He barely dodges Hudson's attempt to dunk his head underwater.

On the shoreline, I look up at the night's sky. The sun has given way to clear stars and sparkling constellations, unburdened by pollution or clouds. My heart thuds in my chest. Once, twice, three times. Reminding me once and for all that I stayed alive for a reason.

"Watch over them, Logan. Lord knows, they need it."

I don't need his ghost to respond to me. My brother has always been there, even when I can't see him. He'll protect my guys until Brooklyn West can return, alone in her body.

HUDSON'S LETTER

Hey, blackbird.

Bear with me. I'm new to this letter-writing shit, but you made us all promise to do it. I want you to have something to hold on to outside of visitation and phone calls. I'm writing this from the cottage. You've been gone for approximately twelve hours. I tried to hold out for longer, but I need to feel close to you.

I know why you had to do this.

It fucking hurts, but I want you to be happy and healthy. This is the only way to do that.

When I met you, my life was spiralling out of control. I was so fucking lonely, Brooke. The world is big and empty when you're sixteen, homeless and abandoned by those who are supposed to love you unconditionally. You were exactly the same as me.

But you gave my life back to me.

I hurt you, baby. I hurt you so fucking much.

Yet, you stayed until the very last second, until not even our love could hold the remains of our relationship together. I had to leave, Brooke. It killed us both, but now, I'm glad. I finally understand why it happened. You said it yourself. We had to break apart to fall together.

I wanted a second chance.

Blackwood gave that to us.

The world looks different now. Hope isn't something I'm familiar with. We've been sitting around since you left, talking about what happens next. I don't know if we have the answer to that question yet. Kade's father is still out there. The world will be chewing over our stories for a very long time. You're gone.

The one thing I do know for certain?

I'm yours.

Irrevocably.

Forever.

Settle in and write me back, baby. I'll be there at the first chance I get to hold you again.

I love you more than life. You're my blackbird, but our girl.

Hud xx

PHOENIX'S LETTER

Firecracker.

Happy six months inside!

That shouldn't be something to celebrate, but after seeing the change in you recently, I'm inclined to think we should mark the occasion. Thanks for the origami paper crane you gave me last visitation. It hangs from the ceiling in our bedroom now. I'm still recovering from the shock of discovering you doing art therapy. Thanks for that heart attack.

The apartment back at Sabre is empty without you.

You should fucking be here.

I started my volunteer program last week. Took a few months to straighten it out given our newfound fame, but the rehab manager is a decent bloke. I'm going to be talking to the kids about gang-related crime and addiction, apparently. The two things I know better than drugs themselves. Ironic, huh?

I'm trying to right the wrong I've inflicted.

I need a new purpose in this world.

Eli got accepted to study remotely at King's College, London. He was over the fucking moon, Brooke. I wish you could've seen his face. All those history essays of mine he wrote have paid off.

The scholarship is pretty generous too. He's talking as well. Little bits here and there. His new speech therapist is a fucking saint.

What else?

I haven't seen Nana. She knows I love her, but I can't go back there. I don't want that life anymore. The day she steps down and retires properly, perhaps we can have a relationship again. Until then, this is the right thing to do for me.

Charlie's grave is peaceful.

She's beneath an apple tree.

Got another formal apology from the government for her death. They just keep on coming as more information leaks out. The case is still developing, even six months later. Each week there's a new arrest. More evidence. Victims coming forward. Hunter, Theo and Enzo are still working around the clock to get that justice they promised Alyssa.

She would be proud of them, I think.

I'll be there next week, firecracker. Until then, I'm enclosing a kiss in this letter.

Forever yours,

Nix

KADE'S LETTER

Hi love,

Happy birthday, Brooklyn.

I hope Seven's spoiling you in there today. We tried to get visitation, but Richards is insistent on not bending the rules. After eighteen months of this, you would think he'd lighten up. I know you had a relapse and things were rough for a while, but still.

You don't need to be afraid of telling us this stuff.

This road you're on isn't easy.

But you're not on it alone.

We've officially been working at Sabre for ten months. It's gone so quickly. Hudson's slotted right into Enzo's new division. He's been in Priory Lane and Compton Hall, documenting any last bits of evidence before the demolition begins. It's given him purpose, I think. Protecting others like you and Seven.

I'm still searching for my father.

We had a hit on one of his offshore accounts a few weeks back. The information Mum provided has left no dark corners for him to hide in. It'll take some time, but we will find him. In the meantime, she's started working again. Opened an art gallery down south in the village she moved to. She sends her love.

Cece graduated from university after taking a break.

She's off to law school in the US next month.

We're all okay. Still here. Nothing's the same without you. I thought we'd get used to it, but your absence never leaves us. We moved into the new house, just outside of the city. Hunter's fortress with the guys is a few miles away. They got a dog too. Adorable little thing. Should we get one? I think we will when you get out.

Your room is ready for when you come home. Phoenix and Eli decorated it in all sorts of ridiculous colours, just forewarning you.

I'm not rushing you. I know you need more time to get better, and this isn't an overnight fix. It's important for you both to be in there, getting the help you need. I'm still holding you to that promise, though.

Come back to us, love.

Our family isn't complete without you here.

Until next time our lips will meet.

I love you.

Yours,

Kade x

ELI'S LETTER

To Brooke,

This is the first letter I've written to you. This feels scarier than speaking—putting pen to paper. I can't hide behind closed lips in a letter. But today marks two years since you left. I figured it's time I put my fears aside and do this.

So, hi, baby girl.

It's me. Your Eli.

I miss you so fucking much. It hurts most at night. Phoenix is usually snoring while I stay up, unable to sleep. When I look at the sky, I wonder if you're watching the stars too. It makes me feel close to you, knowing we're looking at the same constellations.

I'll take whatever scraps I can get.

I passed my exam last week. The uni course is going really well. I love history, but the political science minor is becoming my favourite. I know, sad.

Watching Incendia being pulled apart and its illegal anatomy examined has inspired me to understand the world around me. I didn't see it for so long. This is the longest I've been out in the world since... well, you know when.

It's still weird writing my own essays, instead of Phoenix's or yours. He likes to poke me or blare loud music when I'm working, just for old times' sake. But without you, our smiles don't last. Our relationship is empty without you in the middle.

I'm going to call you this week. When I first started speech therapy last year, Karen made me write a list of goals. It felt stupid at the time. Calling you for a long, meaningless chat about everything and nothing at the same time was number one. I've been practising in the mirror like a fucking dork ever since.

I think I'm ready now.

Get ready, beautiful.

We'll be back in a couple of weeks to see you again. You looked so tired last time. Get some sleep, baby girl. I know it's fucking hard, this recovery bullshit. I'm going through it with you from the outside world. We can compare notes soon.

The first time we met, you said that having a quirky brain isn't a bad thing.

Remember that now.

You took this scared little boy and made him whole again. I'll love you until my very last breath, and even that won't stop me. Donec mors nos separavit. Touch your scars right now. I'll do it too. Can you feel me there?

I can feel you.

Fuck, Brooke. Come back soon.

I love you.

Your Elijah. X

EPILOGUE

JUDE

3 Years Later

HEFTING the duffel bag over my shoulder, I take a final glance around the small bedroom. Plain walls and linoleum floors meet anti-ligature bed sheets and a distorted, plastic mirror. Even after all this time, the precautions of a standard psych ward remain. It's been a hell of a ride to get here.

Today is a special day.

After 1095 days, I am being discharged.

Flicking off the fluorescent overhead light, I turn my back on the four walls that have listened to my fears, hopes, nightmares and sobs for the last three years. Endless nights when I felt like giving up, throwing in the towel and letting death take me to peace at last.

So many times, I wanted to succumb to the person inside my head that kept us both alive for all this time. It was a constant battle to remain in the driver's seat of my own life. Nobody could reconstruct my identity for me. I had to do it all myself, piece by painstaking piece.

I owe my life to Patient Seven.

But Jude Farlow is walking out of here, tall and fucking proud.

Strolling down the quiet corridor of Clearview's mixed ward, I make a beeline for the nurses' desk. The other patients are eating lunch, giving us some time to say our goodbyes. Living with the same doctors, nurses, and orderlies for three years grants you a certain bond.

"Jude!"

Behind the desk, Nurse Holly waves me over. She's bouncing up and down on her toes, clutching a piece of paper in her hands. I drop my bag and steal it from her.

"Is this what I think it is?"

"Yes!" she shouts. "I passed the interview. I'm off to medical school."

We exchange high fives as I scan the confirmation letter again. It looks a lot like the one I received a decade earlier, starting me on a path that I never would've believed at the time. I even helped her prep for the interview, happy to be doing something useful.

"Congratulations. Told you!" I grin at her.

Her smile drops slightly. "I know I should be happy to see the back of you, but I'm gonna miss your handsome face around here. It's been a long three years, eh?"

"Careful," a voice interrupts. "She'll be asking for your number next. I don't have time to go back to art therapy instead of beating her up for trying to steal you."

I don't have to turn around to know Brooklyn is approaching. She smells like oil paint and the cheap soap the hospital provides to wash paintbrushes with. Scarred arms wrap around me from behind as her lips graze my neck.

"Damn, busted." Nurse Holly snickers. "I'm old enough to be his mother, Brooke. But I'm flattered you think I could pull such a charming gentleman."

The two women embrace, squeezing each other tight. I watch Brooklyn subtly wipe her eyes when they break apart again. Nurse Holly doesn't bother hiding her emotions. She's played the maternal role since our first day, even as the ward matron. Despite her big heart, she runs a tight ship here.

"Got everything, kids? Doctor Richards should be here to escort you out in a moment. He's just signing off the discharge papers and checking your travel arrangements."

Brooklyn double checks her suitcase before throwing her old leather jacket on. We're granted a moment of privacy as Nurse Holly bustles off to track the doctor down. Nestling herself into my side, Brooklyn lets out a contented sigh that obliterates three years of tedious therapy and painful separation.

"Your sister used to let us raid that vending machine before group therapy." She points towards the machine at the end of the corridor. "The least disruptive patient was awarded with a snack of their choice."

"Isn't that blackmail?"

"Or good crowd management."

I scan the empty recreation room where each night, patients gather to watch the approved selection of movies. We never ended up there often. There's a courtyard outside, protected by a high-security fence, not unlike Blackwood.

Beneath the floodlights and thick cloud coverage, we spent many nights planning our future. Not just mine and Brooklyn's though. There are four other lives caught in this spider's web. After a long time apart, their lives are about to begin too.

"Will you miss it here?" she hums.

"No," I answer easily. "I can be grateful for surviving Clearview without missing it. This place was my first posting when I qualified. I was never supposed to live within these walls."

"I'll miss the sedatives." Brooklyn snorts at her shitty joke. "The real world is a hell of a lot more complicated than this place. We're jumping from a fishbowl into a giant fucking ocean."

With nobody watching, I press my lips to hers. "I won't let you drown, princess.

We're gonna swim as far from the past as we possibly can. This is the beginning of the rest of our lives."

"No kissing in my ward, you hooligans!"

We break apart at the sound of Doctor Richards' voice. He's a grey-haired, stout man with an acid-tongue and fierce devotion to his work. Not to mention the world's most eclectic fashion taste.

Today, he's wearing his pink slip trousers—bright, lurid fuchsia. All discharge orders are printed on pink hospital paper. It's his little way of celebrating each life that he's saved.

Doctor Richards claps his hands together. "Let's get this show on the road, shall we? I have four very impatient men camped out in my car park. Anyone would think I'm running a B&B in here."

"A B&B would have better food," Brooklyn teases.

He grins at her, pulling his well-worn smile lines taut. "You can eat everything you want now, Brooke. Do think of us poor, tortured souls surviving off beans on toast when you're living the high life."

With an eccentric flourish that matches his wacky personality, Doctor Richards officially signs our lives back over to... us. I hold the discharge papers in my hand, needing to verify they're real. His smile is understanding.

"Are you ready to face the big, bad world?"

Both picking up our belongings, we follow him through the ward's complex security system. Nurse Holly waves from the back office where she's fixing a cuppa, tears shining in her eyes. I knew she wouldn't wave us off. Saying goodbye is hard for the staff too. People who work in mental health are fucking underrated.

Brooklyn grasps my hand tight as we leave gleaming corridors and treatment rooms behind. The exit awaits, real and terrifying. Life begins on the other side of those doors.

"I understand you're off on a trip." Doctor Richards inspects us both over his spectacles. "I'll be in touch when you return. It's important we keep things up with regular check-ins and continued therapy."

He seems taken aback when Brooklyn drops her bag and throws her arms around him. After a second's hesitation, he hugs her back with a little chuckle. This man has quite literally saved her life these past three years. Mine too, one excruciating step at a time.

"Keep this one in line, Brooke. He's a troublemaker."

"I will, doc. See you soon."

Leaving the man that pieced our minds back together behind, I hold the door open for Brooklyn. She ducks beneath my arm, tears already soaking her cheeks. At the bottom of the wide marble steps that lead to Clearview Psychiatric Unit, a huddle of misfits impatiently waits.

Eli is the first to spot us. Beneath his trimmed head of curls, he removes a pair of sunglasses to reveal his incandescent happiness. Tugging on Phoenix's shirt sleeve, he points up at us. His strong, unwavering shout is the biggest change.

"Brooke! Jude!"

That's all it takes to free Brooklyn from her startled daze. She flies down the steps and drops her suitcase in a frenzied blur. Phoenix moves so fast, his chin-length, green hair waves in the autumn air. They collide somewhere in the middle, a tangle of limbs and gasping cries.

Watching them with a pleased smile, Hudson picks up her discarded suitcase. I meet him at the bottom of the marble steps, my own heart exploding with anticipation. He grabs a handful of my grey t-shirt and drags me close until our chests collide.

"Could've got my bag for me too," I say with a smirk.

"Hey, ladies first. I ain't your damn butler."

Then his mouth smashes into mine. We reunite in a battle of teeth and tongue, fuelled by the unquenchable thirst that drives our intense connection. My relationship with Hudson isn't like Phoenix and Eli's close bond. They adore each other. Hudson loves to hate me. He fucks with the same rage that brought us together.

Kade is the last to join our group. His glasses are long gone after he had laser eye surgery last year. Working at Sabre in the intelligence department has led to far too many accidents, especially smashed lenses during an active operation. He slaps my back, grinning from ear to ear.

"Nice haircut, man."

I run a self-conscious hand over my newly cut hair, buzzed on the sides while leaving some strands for Brooklyn to play with late at night. "Thanks. Figured it's time for a fresh start."

Next to us, Brooklyn is still being suffocated by the terrible twosome. She breaks Phoenix's demanding kiss long enough to shoot us all an apologetic look. He's struggled the most with irregular visitation and forced distance. I doubt he'll be letting her leave his sight any time soon.

"I thought you were working today?"

Phoenix strokes her platinum hair, marvelling at the long length. "Change of plan, firecracker. The kids can live without me for a while. This was too good to miss."

He finally surrenders her to the brothers waiting for their reunion. Hudson picks Brooklyn up in his broad, tattooed arms, twirling her around. He looks happier than I've ever seen him in the four long years of our messed-up family. She studies the new tattoos marking his throat and neck, tracing the dark ink.

"Is Hunter's salary feeding your addiction, Hud?"

"Gotta spend my money on something, blackbird." Hudson places her back down, scanning her from head to toe. "If you think this is a lot, wait until you see my back."

"He's gone full thug life." Kade opens his arms wide. "Come here, love. Why am I always the afterthought?"

She throws herself into his welcoming embrace. "Because I know you'll always be here to catch me, Kade. No matter how long it takes, it's always you. That's why."

"You feel so fucking good. Welcome home."

With our reunion complete, Eli leads the way to the awaiting vehicle parked nearby. Where I expected some slick company car that the brothers pilfered from

Sabre, something else entirely awaits. There's a cherry-red VW camper van in the car park. It's been painstakingly restored to perfection.

Brooklyn stops in her tracks.

"Um, what the fuck is that?"

Hudson steals her, their lips smacking loudly. "That is our home for the next three months."

Reaching inside the vinyl-covered cab, Phoenix pulls a giant paper map from the dashboard. He spreads it out across the bonnet, revealing layers of sharpie marks, pins and post-it notes. An entire route across Europe has been obsessively mapped out and thoroughly researched.

"Did Kade get a boner planning this shit to the last detail?" I whisper to Hudson.

He nods with an eye roll. "Even used Theo's new surveillance drones to check out the local hostels for bad vibes. Enzo had to give him a formal warning, even though he couldn't stop laughing."

Gathered around the crazy map, we all study the route that will guide the next months of our lives. Phoenix is taking a break from the rehabilitation centre, while the brothers are on sabbatical from their jobs back at Sabre. Eli's final year of university doesn't begin until after Christmas, when he'll finish his degree.

There's nothing ahead of us but the open road.

Endless possibilities and, for once, a bright future.

Loading up the camper van, Hudson and Kade flip a coin for the driver's seat. I can already see them butting heads every fucking day on this road trip. Phoenix and Eli crawl in the back, already snuggling and sharing headphones like an old married couple.

I stand next to Brooklyn, waiting for her to move.

She turns to look back at Clearview.

"Sev?"

The old nickname doesn't wound me. It slips out from time to time, and it's a welcome reminder. While Jude has walked free, he's infinitely stronger for the pieces of Seven that he took into his heart forever. I can't erase my past and, in all honesty, I don't want to. I'm alive because of it.

"Yeah, princess?"

"What if she comes back?" Her voice lowers. "Eight?"

Trapping her against my chest, my lips meet her ear. "I will always love Patient Eight. Seven loves her too. But Brooklyn West is my future. Jude's future. We'll face it together with our family at our side."

She bites her lip, still uncertain.

"You love me. Real or not real?"

It's a silly coping strategy, something Doctor Richards taught us both in therapy. Our memories get tangled and confused, blurred by trauma. The past we shared and the pain we endured are important. It led us here, to freedom and salvation. We have to remember that. It all meant something.

"Real," I murmur back. "Always real."

Brooklyn looks up at me, hope shining in her grey eyes.

"Yeah, me too. Let's get the fuck out of here."

BONUS SCENE
ELI

If you had told me ten years ago where I'd end up, I think I would've laughed. Like, out loud. My childhood and adolescence are nothing more than an unremarkable blur of tablets, razor blades and stolen tongues.

She is the one shining light in a sea of uninterrupted darkness. A single point of reference amidst the wilderness of my solitude from the human race. Until her, I didn't exist.

The day I caught sight of her icy-blonde hair and narrowed eyes in Clearview all those years ago, my world ceased to turn. The sun was no longer the single point of gravity constructing my reality.

It became her.

My baby girl.

The centre of my universe.

Startled by the burn of my cigarette reaching its end, I flick it to the ground. All around me, luscious green trees, snaking pathways and the glimmer of sparkling sunshine paint a different picture.

No longer is my life defined by locked cells and sharpened needle points. The acceptance letter I received two years ago to study at King's College, London, was the start of my forever.

For the first time in my life, I was granted the chance to choose my own future. I've always loved academia and learning. Now, my day-to-day life is spent immersed in the pages of research papers and books.

Hopping down from the stone wall I've been sitting cross-legged on, I begin the long walk to the nearby bus station. Phoenix drove me for the first few months before he straightened his own shit out and was offered a job at the rehab centre.

"Hey, Eli."

Waving at me from the steps leaving the geography building, Samuel hefts his heavy bag full of books higher on his shirt-clad shoulder. I slow my steps to let him catch up to me and offer him a nod.

He falls into step next to me. "Still up for a study session? I have a summative assignment due next week."

"I've got somewhere to be."

"With the speech therapist?"

"Phone call."

I feel his green eyes slide over to me behind horn-rimmed glasses. "You're going for it this time?"

Shrugging, I focus on the paved path. "I sent that letter last week, but I haven't worked up the courage to call yet."

Samuel remains silent, even as he heaves his heavy load of atlases back up from where the strap keeps sliding down his arm. We became friends a little over a year ago, and his comfort with long, uninterrupted silences is what allowed us to bond back then. Verbally conversing with him is still very new.

I have a friend.

Now, there's a surprising twist of fate.

My phone rings in my pocket, and I offer him a tight smile before hanging back to answer. Samuel waves, nudging his glasses higher up his nose as he lopes off towards the library to dive into another endless essay.

"Nix?" I answer the incoming call.

"Stop talking to that four-eyed fucker and come get in the car before I run him over for stealing your attention."

Spinning around on the spot, I search the nearby surroundings for Phoenix's familiar blue Subaru. He drives the impractical, fast-as-hell sports car like he's fucking invincible.

"Where are you?"

"In my car," he coos in a playful voice.

"Not helpful. Where's the car?"

"Come on, Elijah. I'm getting old over here waiting for you."

Spotting the gleam of a bright-blue bumper peeking through a thicket of trees, I make a beeline for his position.

"Why aren't you at work?"

"Finished early," he quips. "It's date night. Your choice this time."

Shitting hell. Is it Tuesday already? We take the time to go on a date every few weeks, when our crazy schedules will allow. The first Monday of the month is reserved for visitation.

Brooklyn and Jude await our monthly visits, even though we exchange regular phone calls and letters in between. Phoenix protested the most against Doctor Richards' rigid schedule, attempting to blackmail him into bending the rules.

But this is how it has to be.

While we may be their family, we're also painful reminders of the trauma that has led them both to live out the last two years inside Clearview's clinical walls. I see it in Brooklyn's silver-grey eyes every time we embrace.

When she looks at us, she sees everything that we sacrificed and all the pain, grief and heartbreak we endured. Sometimes, love isn't enough. They need the time and space to get better before they can return to us, whole again.

"Can we try that new dessert place on Main Street?"

"I'll never say no to anything sugar related." Phoenix chuckles. "Want to catch a movie after? Hudson's decorating the kitchen. Best to avoid the house until he's done."

"Again?"

"You know he's restless waiting for Brooklyn to come home," he says tightly. "The constant decorating makes him feel better, I think. He likes preparing."

"He's gonna be waiting for a long time for her to see it."

Phoenix is silent. I can practically taste his despair leaking through the speaker. The more months that pass, the harder he's finding this situation. The other two adjusted with time, and I've learned to busy myself to make the separation easier.

But not Phoenix.

He needs her constant reassurance the most. Without Brooklyn here to prop him up, his own demons come out to play. The job at the rehab centre keeps him out of trouble, but we've had a few close calls in the last two years.

Ending the call, I throw the car door open and plonk into the bucket seat. Phoenix is staring ahead, his hands clenched on the steering wheel. I lean over the console to grab his chin.

"Come back," I whisper throatily.

His eyes slide shut, hiding from me. "We've waited for so long. I don't know how much longer I can do this."

Stroking my hand along his jawline before burying it in the bright-red tresses piled haphazardly on his head, I drag his lips to mine. He's hesitant at first, but with my mouth slanted against his, he relents.

Phoenix's pierced tongue slides into my mouth, smashing against mine as he deepens the kiss into a frenzied collision. His hand moves to cup the back of my neck, preventing me from escaping the onslaught.

When I break the kiss, my lips feeling hot and swollen, his breath tangles with mine. What I wouldn't give to throw myself across the gear stick and straddle the hardened bulge pushing against his faded-black jeans.

"We will wait for another two years if that's what she needs," I remind him. "We made a promise, Nix. No matter the cost. She's gonna come back to us when she's ready."

Widened eyes framed by thick, black lashes skate upwards to meet mine. Beyond the bravado and brave-face tactics, there's a scared little kid inside of Phoenix, terrified of losing someone else he loves. Charlie's death fucked him up.

"I hate this," he murmurs.

"Yeah, me too. That doesn't mean we're going to stop being strong for her."

"I know that. Shit's just hard. I didn't think it would be this long."

I wish I could say that none of us did, but truthfully, I knew the day we said goodbye to Brooklyn and Jude that it wasn't going to be a quick fix. I've spent enough time under the glare of shrinks' attention to know how this rodeo works.

"Date night?" I prompt.

Phoenix summons a grin. "You know, hearing you talk to me like this is still weird. I fucking love the sound of your voice though."

Kissing me again, he releases a low growl before forcibly dragging his lips from mine. The fire burning in his irises matches the unfurling desire racing through my veins.

Brooklyn gave us permission to be together in her absence—now that was an awkward-as-fuck conversation—but we aren't the same without her caught in the middle. There's something fundamental missing.

"You have something to do first," Phoenix interrupts with a smarmy grin. "I'm not letting you chicken out again."

"I didn't chicken out."

He narrows his eyes. "She's been waiting for you to call her since you sent that damned letter. Stop being a bloody pussy and pick up the phone."

"It isn't that simple and you know it."

"I know shit, Elijah. It is that simple. Your girl needs you. Step up."

Switching off the engine, he offers me a final, stern look before hopping out and slamming the door. I watch him light up a cigarette and lean against the car's bonnet, leaving me alone in solitude.

My heart pounds so hard against my ribcage, it feels like it's going to tear free from my skin and fall at my feet in a bloodied lump. This shouldn't be a big deal. I go to the monthly visits with the others. It's not like she hasn't heard from me.

But this will be the first time we've properly spoken, alone. Previously, I've always been too scared to speak. Anxiety holds my tongue prisoner and the flavours that still plague my existence make it hard to form a single coherent sentence.

I can taste them now.

Fear. Burned ashes.

Anxiety. Bitter, acrid lemons.

Doubt. Overripe fruit.

But beneath the cacophony of hateful whispers telling me this isn't a good idea, there's something else. Another undertone. The sweet, fresh taste of a flavour I've only ever tasted around my baby girl.

Hope.

It tastes like bottled sunshine.

I made a goal in my first speech therapy session. It's time to complete it. I've made huge progress in the last few weeks, and I can talk to the guys more easily than ever. Brooklyn deserves to be included in that.

Pulling out my phone, I bring the contact number up for Richards' office line. Neither of them are allowed mobile phones inside the unit. Hospital rules. He does allow us to communicate with Brooklyn over the phone during office hours though.

"Richards," he picks up my phone call.

Clearing my throat, I swallow the bubble of terror crawling its way up.

"D-Doctor Richards."

"Yes. Who is this?"

"It's Elijah W-Woods."

There's a brief pause.

"Eli?" he repeats.

"Yeah."

"Never thought I'd hear your voice on the other end of this phone. I see that speech therapist recommendation I made for you is working out well."

My clenched fist collides against my forehead. "I'm calling for Brooke."

"She'll be very happy to hear from you, I'm sure. Let me put you on hold."

The tinkle of ear-aching elevator music echoes down the line. A fine tremble runs over my whole body, head to toe. I shouldn't be this afraid. It's just her. No one else.

But this moment represents something more. An irrevocable step in the right direction, towards a future where I'm no longer defined by the ghosts of my past. I set this goal for a reason.

Now that I have my voice again, all I want is to hear Brooklyn replying back to me for the rest of my fucking life, long or short. That's what it has all been about. Getting better for her. For our family. For our future, just like she's doing.

I watch the time on the dashboard tick away. Minute after minute. Each passing second increases the nervous sweat across my forehead. What if she's mad at me for not calling sooner? Have I completely fucked this?

Then the phone line clicks, and my heart leaps into my mouth. Unsteady breathing rattles through the speaker, like she ran at full speed to answer the phone call.

"Eli."

Her voice tastes like sweet cotton candy and the tartness of freshly squeezed orange juice bursting on my tongue. Relief. Happiness. Safety. Home. It's Brooklyn.

"Hey, baby girl," I whisper back.

"Took you long enough to call. I was starting to wonder if you ever would."

"I'm sorry."

"Don't be," Brooklyn scolds. "I can't tell you how fucking good it is to hear your voice. I've missed it."

My eyes squeeze shut as pain wrings my neck.

"I miss you so goddamn much," I say hoarsely.

"Hell, Eli, I miss you too. Every day."

With darkness saturating my vision, I can almost picture her sitting next to me in the driver's seat. Her voice sounds close enough for that vision to become a reality.

"Are you all okay?" she asks.

"We're surviving," I admit. "I stay busy. It helps."

"Me too. This place is no fun without you though."

I can't help but laugh. "I wish I were in there with you to hold your hand through this."

"It's okay," she offers. "I'm not alone. I just wish you had someone out there too. Is Phoenix keeping you out of trouble?"

"More like keeping himself *in* trouble."

"Sounds about right." Brooklyn snorts. "How's university going? Did you get the grade for your midterm paper back?"

"I passed. Kade cooked tacos to celebrate."

"Sweet. Chicken or pork?"

"Both. Homemade salsa too."

"I would literally stab myself in the eye to eat a taco right now," she replies agonisingly. "The food here sucks so bad, it isn't even funny."

We share a laugh. I remember the lifeless grey sludge that's served behind Clearview's fancy security system well. I ate it for enough years.

"What are you doing tonight? Isn't it date night?"

"You know about that?" I ask, surprised.

"Phoenix swore to me that he'd look after you while I'm stuck here. It was my idea for him to suggest a regular date night with you."

"Why didn't I know that before?"

"We haven't exactly had a conversation in a while." Brooklyn hesitates. "I love talking to you like this. I'm so fucking proud of you."

"Thanks, baby. I... I'm sorry it took me so long."

I can hear the tears clogging up her voice. Emotion overwhelms me in a blistering tidal wave, and tears sear the backs of my eyeballs, threatening to spill.

The last two years have passed in both a blip and a slow, painful crawl. Sometimes, I wonder how we've survived this long. If it weren't for the promise of her one day returning to us, I don't know if we could've done it.

"You never, ever have to apologise to me," she says fiercely. "Not for a second. I'm sorry that I haven't been there to help you through getting your voice back."

"Brooke," I interrupt her. "You *have* been here. Every session, every step of the way. I wasn't alone for a single second of it. I'm never alone when I'm with you."

"I want to exist in your life beyond a figment of your imagination."

"You do, baby girl. You always have."

Sniffling, she clears her throat. "Fuck. I wasn't ready to cry like a bloody baby in Richards' office today. Jude's going to laugh at me."

"You can blame me."

"I intend to."

She gulps hard, and I picture her in my head, cradling the receiver in her hands like a precious lifeline. My grip on the phone increases. If I squeeze tightly enough, it'll be like she's sitting here holding my hand again.

"I love you," I tell her.

"I fucking love you, Elijah Woods. Wait for me?"

"Always, baby girl. I'll see you next week for visitation."

"Wait," she rushes to stop me. "Where are you going for date night? I want something to imagine while I'm eating my disgusting gruel tonight."

I bite my lip to hold back a sob. It's weak and stupid, but she's unhooked the hinges fastened tightly on the emotions I usually hold back. I feel lost without her in my arms.

"There's a new dessert place that's opened up in Greenwich. I heard the waffles are good. Phoenix wants to catch a movie after."

"Anything good playing?"

"Knowing Nix?" I scoff. "He'll choose the cheesiest shit out there, or a horror flick. There's no in between. I'm just going for a slushy and nachos."

"A slushy and nachos," she echoes. "That sounds like heaven."

"We'll go for a date night when you come home. All three of us."

"I'd like that." Her voice catches. "Eli... fuck, whatever you do... just please don't forget about me."

Clasping the phone tighter, I scrub a hand over my damp face. "Brooklyn West, I couldn't forget you even if I fucking tried. You are scarred across my skin... and my heart."

"I love you," she says again.

When the click of the call ending stabs into me, I let my hand drop to my lap. She's gone, but I could hear the happiness in her final three words. If nothing else, I've put that damned smile on her lips. I'll live the rest of my life for that sole purpose.

Ensuring my stray tears have been swiped away, I knock on the window and gesture for Phoenix to climb back in. After his cigarette is discarded, he slides into the driver's seat with a strained smile that doesn't quite reach his eyes.

"Is she... doing alright?" he worries.

Reaching over, I tangle our fingers together and squeeze tight.

"Yeah. I think she is."

He breathes out a sigh of relief.

"It's hard to tell when we go for visitation. Do you feel better?"

My automatic response is to say no, given the steady ache of my broken heart in my chest, but deep down... I do feel better. Our shared anxiety goes both ways.

She's terrified of losing us out here, in the real world, but I'm equally as afraid that she'll do exactly what she's worried about. She'll forget about us.

Something tells me that's never going to happen. But I needed to hear it for myself. Now, I know those words we carved into each other with tears and blood still stand. Our promises to one another have never been broken.

"I do," I respond. "I just needed to hear her voice. She makes all of this bullshit distance worth it, doesn't she?"

Phoenix nods, his frown easing. "She really does."

Releasing his hand, I tuck bright red-hair behind his ear. "Date night? I'm ready to try those famous waffles if you are."

"I sure as fuck am. Buckle up."

EXTENDED EPILOGUE
BROOKLYN

Warm spring sunshine beats down on the cobbled Parisian streets beneath our feet. While families toss pancakes and consume their body weight in syrup back in England, the French celebrate Shrove Tuesday in style.

"Ta-da!" Kade gestures around at the mayhem. "Mardi Gras in Paris. We can check that off the travel list."

"You and your fucking lists," Hudson curses.

"Hey, I'm organised. Suck it up, asshole."

"There's a difference between being organised and obsessive. You should look into that, brother."

Dressed in an open-collared polo shirt and smart jeans, this is as casual as my hazel-eyed control freak gets. I'm still not used to seeing Kade without his glasses on. Part of me wishes he didn't get laser eye surgery while I was gone.

"Jesus Christ." Hudson surveys our surroundings with a frown. "I thought Brits liked to party, but this is something else."

Next to him, Phoenix watches the unfolding carnival with excited fire in his eyes. This is his scene. Alcohol, music and debauchery—minus the drugs.

Immersed in a crowd of enthused onlookers, I feel a pair of wiry arms wrap around me from behind. With his missing hand covered up, Jude snuggles against my spine as his lips trail up the back of my neck.

"You good, princess?" he murmurs. "It's loud."

"Yeah. I'm fine."

"I think Eli's having a hard time with the noise."

I glance to my left where Eli's mass of tight, brown curls are resting on Phoenix's shoulder. His eyes are squeezed tightly shut, and I can see the veins popping against his hands as he wrings his black hoodie.

Despite overcoming his speech impediment in the three years I spent inside Clearview's walls, overstimulation, crowds and loud noises still trigger Eli. Some damage is too severe to ever fully heal.

"Kade." I tap his shirt-clad shoulder. "Can we find a bar or something? Preferably with a quiet corner."

Looking over at Eli's pre-breakdown state, Kade begins to scan the melee for a hideout. The whole main road is swamped with carnival goers—sequins, feathers and brightly painted faces all blurred by colourful smoke bombs.

"Follow me." He begins to walk. "I can see somewhere."

Fisting my hand in the back of his polo shirt, I take Jude's spare hand. Hudson is gripping his bicep, while Phoenix tosses his arm around Eli's shoulders. Together, we form a human train through the crowd.

Music thumps so loud, my teeth rattle from the deep bass. Drunken singing and chanting permeates the thicket of swarming bodies, all dancing and grinding amidst the other costumed celebrators.

I thought the teeming, wild streets of Barcelona were crazy, but this is a whole other ball game. We're at the end of our three-month trip across Europe. The bright-red VW camper the guys restored is officially on its last legs.

Three months isn't long, but it came at the perfect time. When we left England, I was fresh out of a three-year psychiatric stay. I had no idea what kind of life I'd be returning to, let alone how my relationships might have changed in that time.

I never should've doubted my guys.

It feels like Jude and I never left them.

Finally shoving his way through the chaos, Kade guides us into a nearby bar. Most revellers are out on the streets, so there are a few tables to spare. We take the circular booth in the furthest corner, doused in shadows from the low lighting and dark-panelled walls.

All wriggling into the tight space, Eli's forehead immediately collides with the table as he releases a relieved sigh. He turns his head and mouths *thanks* with a tense smile. I blow him a quick kiss.

"Drinks?" Kade suggests.

Studying him with suspicion, Hudson raises an eyebrow. "Since when are you a big drinker?"

Kade shrugs. "We go home next week. I'm just enjoying the moment."

He disappears to locate some alcohol, leaving me trapped between our two resident hard-faced assholes. Jude is staring at the other customers along with Hudson, both on high alert as usual.

I can see that Jude is assessing our surroundings for danger by the tight set of his carved jawline. It screams of tension and suspicion. I touch his muscled leg under the table.

"We're safe. Real or not real?"

His caramel eyes collide with mine. "Real."

"Take a breath then. We're supposed to be celebrating."

"I preferred the empty streets of Krakow last month. This place is insane."

"Seconded," I echo. "I miss the Polish dumplings. You know the ones with potato in them?"

"Those were so fucking good."

Shaking his head to clear the cobwebs, Jude makes himself relax into the booth.

Old habits die hard. Even after countless months of therapy, he sometimes needs a helping hand to keep the demons in their box.

Hell, we all do.

Our real-or-not-real game comes in handy for moments like this. Doctor Richards told us to look out for each other's warning signs. As a result, we've survived our travels with only a handful of incidents.

"Do you think the van will be alright where we parked it?" Phoenix worries, his leg slung over Eli's. "If it gets trashed or stolen, we're screwed."

"It'll be fine," Hudson replies, fishing out his phone. "I checked the hotel car park before we left. There's CCTV."

Returning with a heavy tray in his hands, Kade slides back into his seat with a wide grin. Four huge carafes full of red wine are plonked down in front of us with glasses.

"Are you feeling alright?" Phoenix barks a laugh. "This is enough alcohol for ten people."

"I spent years picking this one up off the pavement after a night out." He gestures towards Hudson, who's smirking to himself. "I figured it's time he pays me back for that."

Hudson snorts. "I will happily scoop you off the floor and find a nice alleyway to abandon you in."

"Try it, and I'll set Enzo on you when we get home."

Mock-shuddering, Hudson spreads his hands in surrender. "He beat the shit out of me enough during our training, thanks. I am not looking forward to going home."

At the mention of home, anxiety spikes through me. We left Clearview and immediately hit the road. It's been healing to check out from the world and reconnect with each other away from our lives, but now, reality is calling.

We can't hide from the future forever. I know the guys all have lives that they've worked hard to establish while I've been gone. Jobs. Bills. Responsibilities. Finding my place amongst that feels intimidating.

"What happens when we leave next week?" I bite my lip.

Kade slides a full glass over to me, his smile patient. "We'll get you guys moved into the house in London. Everything is ready for you."

Jude takes several gulps of wine and stays quiet. I know without looking that he's as apprehensive as I am about this. Nobody tells you how to return home after being through what we have.

It isn't a simple transfer back to ordinary living. We have to find a new normal, a routine, a purpose. This three-month holiday has strengthened our relationships with each other after all that time apart, but the greatest test is yet to come.

"When will you guys go back to work?"

"Probably the week after," Kade answers.

Hudson nods in agreement. "We'll need to be debriefed by the team before we return to active duty. Enzo and Hunter will catch us up then."

I glance over at Phoenix. "And you?"

"I'm in no rush, firecracker. I can help you guys get settled in before going back." He winks at me. "The crazies can wait."

Eli smacks him around the back of his head. "Watch it. You were once a 'crazy' yourself. Hell, you still are most days."

"Sorry, *Elijah*, but you're not so sane either."

Smacking a wet kiss on his cheek, Phoenix fishes his cigarettes from his pocket and sneaks outside to smoke. I'm sure Kade takes it as a personal slight that he hasn't been able to cure Phoenix of all his bad habits.

"School term resumes in a couple of weeks," Eli adds, still looking pale from his near panic attack outside. "I've got a tonne to catch up on."

A tingle runs down my spine, his words ghosting a teasing path across my skin. Every time I hear his voice, steady and unwavering, I get a little thrill.

"I can help, if you want," Jude offers hesitantly. "I've crammed for plenty of assignments and exams in my time."

Eli smiles. "That sounds good, actually."

Chest burning with emotion, I startle when Hudson's phone rings in his hands. He rolls his eyes at the caller ID and answers with a sigh.

"I've got another week before I have to see your ugly face, Enz. Sabbatical means leave me the fuck alone."

"Nice to talk to you too," a familiar voice growls. "This is a social call, so don't get your panties in a twist. You guys alright?"

Already on his second glass of wine, Kade peers over his shoulder to look down at the video call. He lifts his glass in a mock-cheers before necking it back and flinching at the taste.

"Fucking hell," Enzo cusses. "Is he drunk?"

"On his way, I think," Hudson answers with amusement. "You wanna talk to Brooklyn while I deal with my alcoholic brother?"

"Put the troublemaker on, then."

He slides me the phone, and I eagerly accept it. Out of all Sabre's crew, Enzo visited me the most inside Clearview, tagging along to visitation on a regular basis. I saw Hunter occasionally, and Theo only a handful of times.

I don't blame him for avoiding me. Even years later, Alyssa's death is fresh in my mind. She haunts my dreams with her lurid pink hair, sharp tongue and brilliant smile. I know Theo's still grieving her deeply.

"Hey, Enz." I position the phone camera so he can see me clearly. "What's up?"

"Wildfire," he rumbles. "It's good to see your face."

With chaotically messy black hair, rugged-as-hell features and eyes that resemble uncut amber, Enzo hasn't changed beyond a few extra smile lines around his mouth. He's as formidable as the day we met.

"Enjoying your break?"

"It's been good," I answer. "Healing."

His thick eyebrows raise. "You get much healing done with those five oafs there? I'm shocked. Thought you would've killed each other by now."

"Trust me, there've been a few close calls. How's the team?"

Enzo's smile droops. "Oh, you know."

"Yeah... I know."

"We took on a couple of new clients this month. Big clients. It's kept us busy.

Theo's expanding the intelligence department too. We're recruiting two new security analysts to keep up with the demand."

"Damn. You're on your way to world domination then, huh?"

"Something like that." He chuckles. "You know, there's a spot waiting here for you when you're ready. You don't even have to apply."

My heart somersaults. "There is?"

"I can't manage Kade and Hudson alone. Besides, two people can't form a team. We're in need of a third to round them off."

Overcome by conflicting thoughts, I settle for a shrug. "I'll think it over."

"Take all the time you need, and tell Jude the same. We could use a straight shooter like him on the team. You'd both be excellent assets."

Unlike my own indecision, Jude immediately shakes his head in dismissal. He's good at hiding it, but I can see the panic in his eyes. It was painstaking work for him to piece his mind back together.

Working for Sabre would hit a little too close to home after the years he spent under Augustus's thumb. While we bled and broke, side by side, my suffering barely scratched the surface of his. Our recoveries look different.

"I don't think he's interested."

Enzo seems unfazed. "Not a problem. Have a think about it for yourself and come see me when you get home. We can talk then."

"You sure Hunter wants someone like me working for him?"

"Hunter's the one who told me to ask you," he replies. "Trust me, this employment offer is a hell of a lot more generous than what we usually offer new recruits."

I can't help but grin. The stone-cold dictator has a heart in there somewhere, however inaccessible to the outside world. I think I might've cracked the damn enigma code with him.

"Does this mean we get a raise?" Kade slurs.

Enzo scoffs on the screen. "Tell your boyfriend to fuck off for me, wildfire. He's just had a three-month holiday with full bloody pay."

Smirking to himself, Kade smacks Hudson's hands away when he attempts to move the alcohol out of reach. Someone's in a party mood.

"Alright, I have a board meeting to attend." Enzo offers me a wave with his huge paw. "Behave, kids. See you all next week."

With a chorus of goodbyes from around the table, I end the call and stare down at the background on Hudson's phone screen. Shock washes over me, hot and prickly. I hardly recognise the ghosts staring back at me.

"Hud? Where did you get this photo?"

He freezes, caught red-handed. "Uh."

Squinting to make out the two younger faces, their arms are curled around one another, both dressed in second-hand formal wear. I still remember the feel of the cheap, thin dress I stole for that night.

It's me and him.

Nearly... damn, nine whole years ago.

Where did that time go?

"Is that you?" Jude breathes down my neck. "You look so young."

"We went to the academy's crappy equivalent of a prom together," I explain, stroking my thumb over Hudson's scowling face. "I don't remember much of it."

"She was drunk as a skunk," Hudson supplies. "And high, if memory serves. I got someone to snap a picture as evidence."

And he kept it, for all of these years. A treasured, bittersweet secret, buried in the recesses of his phone's storage. The memory endured even when our relationship shattered and life's inevitable cruelty ripped us apart.

Locking the phone, I launch myself at Hudson and throw my arms around his neck. He startles but soon crushes me to his chest, his own heart hammering against my skin. Stupid tears are burning in my eyes.

"It's just a photo, blackbird," he whispers into my hair. "Please don't get upset. I can delete it if you hate it that much."

"No," I rush out. "I'm not upset... I'm actually happy. Don't delete it."

"Happy?" he echoes.

Leaning back, I push my lips against his. "We had no idea back then what we'd end up facing together. I'm fucking glad that despite it all... we're here. Together."

Darkness blooms in his eyes as he smiles, slanting his lips against mine in a tender kiss. "Together."

"Shots! Whoop!"

Phoenix's high-pitched voice interrupts our moment and we break apart. He's carrying another tray towards us, this one laden with miniature glasses filled with a clear liquid.

"Nix," Eli warns.

"Oh, lay off. We're having fun, aren't we?"

"Shots are a great idea," Kade declares, his eyes glassy. "I would like to get so drunk, I forget we have to go back to getting yelled at by Hunter on a daily basis."

"Don't remind me," Hudson mutters. "Pass us some of them."

Dealing out the shots so we each have three, Phoenix only takes one for himself to appease Eli's obvious annoyance. I suppose cigarettes are one thing to be addicted to, but alcohol is a little too close to the hard stuff.

Raising his shot glass, Phoenix looks between us all. "To the future."

We all clink our glasses together and knock back the shot of pure hell. I gag while swallowing it down. *Fuck*. The stuff's like liquid fire. Hudson hammers me on the back before I have a coughing fit.

"Can't hold your liquor anymore, blackbird?"

"I'm a little out of practice," I choke out. "Not many wild, drunken parties in a psych ward."

"That was thoroughly disgusting," Jude complains.

Kade has already seized his next shot and raises it in another toast. "Happy Mardi Gras!"

We all watch him knock it back and gag. He really is on a mission tonight. It's kind of hilarious to watch. I don't think I've ever seen Kade truly let his hair down in all the time we've known each other.

By the third shot, he's turned an interesting shade of green and looks ready to throw up out of his eyeballs. Phoenix tries to cover his mouth to hide his laughter as Kade awkwardly stumbles to his feet.

"Oh my God. I think I'm going to be sick."

"Two glasses of wine and a few shots?" Phoenix exclaims. "That's all it takes to make you throw up?"

"Move out of the way!"

I watch him disappear into the nearby bathroom, presumably to puke his guts up. We all break out in laughter as soon as he's vanished from sight. That was a short and relatively unimpressive drinking session.

"Well, that answers the question of how much it takes to get Kade drunk." Jude snorts into his glass of wine. "Someone should've filmed it to show him tomorrow. He won't believe us."

"His headache will tell him enough," Eli grumbles. "Can we get out of here now? Please?"

The bar is filling up again as the parade passes us, leaving the stragglers to find the nearest watering hole for their own beverages. Hudson shrugs on his coat and stands, offering me a hand up.

"Let's go back to the hotel," he suggests.

Eli looks relieved. "Thank God."

"I'll go scoop the drunkard up." Hudson snorts in derision. "Apparently, it's my turn to be the responsible brother."

———

Head turned upwards, I let the shower's hot spray hit me in the face. It feels heavenly after spending the day winding around Paris's busy streets and getting super sweaty.

In the attached bedroom, I can hear raised voices as they attempt to wrestle Kade into bed. Luckily, the hotel was only a short walk from the bar we'd holed up in. He really can't handle his booze.

Sloughing shower gel off my body, I trail my fingers over the zigzag of silvery scars that disfigure my arms, stomach, hips and thighs. I used to be triggered when I looked at myself; it would make me thirst for more.

More pain.

More blood.

More control.

Now, I've broken the impulse. The thoughts come and go, some days more than others, but they've lost the tantalising power that once dominated me. The darkness has been tamed, boxed and shelved.

If nothing else, I can be proud of that achievement. The last three years of my life have been a challenge unlike anything I ever faced before. Even scarier than torture and death. Facing yourself is the biggest horror of all.

The door clicks open, and footsteps shuffle inside. I brace my hands against the ceramic tiles and lower my head, letting the warm water soothe my muscles. I should've known that I wouldn't be left alone for long.

"I'm going to cave your brother's head in," Jude growls as the bathroom door slams shut. "Bloody idiot."

"I can't believe he threw up on your shoes," Hudson snickers.

"It isn't fucking funny, Hud!"

"Oh, I dunno. I think it's pretty hilarious."

"The bathroom is occupied," I call over my shoulder.

"Sorry, princess. It's an emergency."

The weight of eyes on me is unmistakable. I can feel the sizzle of Hudson's attention from here. He's leaning against the closed bathroom door, arms folded and gaze trained on every inch of my naked skin.

"You just gonna stand there?" I challenge him.

"Is that an invitation?"

Planting my back on the slick tiles, I hold his eyes while skating a hand down the slope of my belly. His lips part as I dance two fingers over my pelvic bone and around to the gathering heat at my core.

Swearing to himself, Jude unbuckles his belt. Hudson is still staring right at me when he steps up behind him. He's struggling to undo his jeans with only one complete limb.

"Need a hand, Sev?" he purrs.

Jude clutches the edge of the sink. "Be my guest."

Reaching around his waist, Hudson unfastens Jude's jeans and pushes them over his hips. I watch with fascination as he drags his teeth along the slope of his neck, nipping and leaving a trail of red marks.

Stroking a thumb over my clit, I swirl my arousal around before sliding a finger inside my pussy. Hudson winks at me as he eases Jude's tight black boxers over his hips next, freeing the proud length of his erect cock.

"You're just begging to be touched, aren't you?" he taunts.

Jude tips his head back. "No. I was just trying to wash up."

"Don't fucking lie to me, Sev."

I watch his caramel eyes slide shut with a hissed breath. Hudson's taken hold of his dick and strokes it from base to tip, teasing his compliance. That nickname is only allowed in these secretive, stolen moments.

Pumping his cock with long strokes, I watch Jude's throat bob. Seeing them battle one another is the sweetest of tortures. Their relationship is equal parts hatred and possession, with a healthy dose of loving violence.

"Blackbird," Hudson summons.

I startle back to attention. "Yes?"

He quirks an eyebrow in my direction. "Yes, what?"

Swirling the finger buried in my slit, I arch my back against the tiles. "Yes, *daddy*?"

"That's better. Open your legs. I want to see my little slut's wet cunt."

Nerves twitching with anticipation, I lift one leg and prop my foot against the shower's frosted glass, giving him direct line of sight between my thighs. Hudson leans closer to bite down on Jude's ear lobe.

"Watch our girl fuck herself for us," he orders in his ear.

Jude shudders, his interested gaze sliding over to me. With two pairs of eyes trained on me, I flush hot from all the attention. They're both silently fascinated by each flick of my thumb across my sensitive bud.

Pulling the finger from my pussy, I raise it to my lips and add a second before sucking them both. The salty tang of my come dances across my tongue. Hudson's smirk expands as I return the two fingers to my core and push them back inside.

"Good girl," Hudson praises. "Give us a good show, and maybe we'll reciprocate."

Head thrown back, I pump my fingers faster, pushing them deep inside myself. Knowing they're watching only adds fuel to the fire spurring me on. I've always loved performing for them—my two lovable psychopaths.

With my spare hand, I grab a handful of my breast and squeeze. It isn't enough. Having them so close, but with only their eyes touching me, is excruciating. I want Hudson to pull my hair while Jude fucks my mouth.

"Please," I whimper.

"Did you hear that?"

His cock still caught in Hudson's grip, Jude shoots me a dark grin. "Sounded like our girl begging for us."

"It sure did. Should we relieve her?"

He considers me for a moment. "No. Make her wait."

Hudson chuckles under his breath. "So be it."

"Assholes," I mutter.

Releasing his handful, Hudson growls as he shoves Jude's shoulder, forcing him to turn around. His back collides with the counter and Hudson drops to his knees. There's only one person on this earth he'd kneel for.

Jude didn't claim that honour first.

No. Patient Seven did.

Lips wrapping back around his thick length, I gape as Hudson hollows out his cheeks to take every last inch. Hell, forget what I wanted. I could watch them fuck each other to death forever. It's a toxic, disastrous sight.

"Look at the infamous Hudson Knight, on his knees with a mouthful of my cock." Jude laughs to himself. "Not so high and mighty now, are you?"

Slipping a hand around his waist, Hudson's palm collides with his ass cheek in a hard slap. Jude hardly bats an eye. He's too busy grinning with satisfaction at the lethal predator kneeling before him.

"You see what I reduce your precious *daddy* to, Eight?" Jude teases me. "Our pretty boy is nothing without us."

"Not your fucking pretty boy," he snarls around his cock..

Patience dissolving, I flick the shower off and saunter out, leaving a trail of water behind me. Hudson halts his movements when I crouch behind him, pressing my wet breasts into his t-shirt covered back.

"Bed," I murmur in his ear.

"The others are in there," Jude points out.

"You think I care?"

Digging my nails into Hudson's biceps, I drag him upwards and shove him towards the door. He begins unbuckling his own jeans with each step. I steal his place and take hold of Jude's erection, squeezing it at the base.

"Walk," I command him.

His eyes widen as I gently tug, guiding him towards the exit while holding his dick like a dog on a leash. Fuck, this is hot. Docile isn't a word I'd use to describe him, but in this moment, he's laying defenceless at my feet.

In the adjacent bedroom, Hudson strips off layers of clothing and leaves them like breadcrumbs. We wrangled three beds. Kade is propped up in one, guzzling a bottle of water, while Phoenix and Eli cuddle in the other.

All three of them startle as we walk in, naked and entangled. The atmosphere in the room shifts in a nanosecond, especially when they note my hand still choking Jude's cock as he stumbles to keep up with me.

"Don't mind us." I grin at them.

Phoenix rests a possessive hand on Eli's thigh. "We don't mind, do we? Always happy to be part of a captive audience."

With an enthusiastic nod, Eli snuggles closer to his human pillow, sneaking a hand under Phoenix's t-shirt to caress his toned stomach muscles.

Still appearing slightly drunk, Kade ducks into the vacated bathroom to freshen up. I take the opportunity to steal his bed and shove Jude onto it, watching with pleasure as he splays out on his back.

"You next, blackbird," Hudson orders, pulling off his t-shirt. "He's all ready for you."

I reach onto my tiptoes to press a kiss to the corner of his mouth. "Thank you for warming him up, *daddy*. How kind of you."

Hand flashing to my neck, Hudson tightly circles my throat and deepens the kiss. His tongue invades my mouth and tangles with mine, demanding every single breath I dare to steal in his presence.

When the kiss breaks, he bites down hard on my bottom lip, lapping up the droplets of fresh blood that rise to the surface. I gulp down a searing breath when his grip on my neck finally relents.

"Go," he murmurs. "Make him come for us, baby."

"Anything for you."

"That's more like it."

Clambering onto the bed, I knee-walk over to Jude's position. His hand tightens on my hip as I position myself above him. I'm already dripping and quivering with need from watching their little performance.

Sinking down on his cock in one possessive move, I throw my head back at the burning intensity. He's buried to the hilt inside me and biting his lip to hold back a groan.

I peck a kiss against his parted lips before beginning to move—gyrating in a teasing, steady rhythm, feeding his cock back into me with each thrust. I can tell he's close. Hudson already drove him to the edge of climaxing.

I'm going to finish the job.

The bed dips behind me, and I feel Hudson's presence before he smacks my raised ass so hard, it sends lightning bolts across my damp skin. He hits me again, harder, urging me to move even faster.

"Who's high and mighty now?" he teases.

Jude bares his teeth. "I'll fuck you raw next, Knight."

"Promises, promises."

To draw his attention back, I crash my palm against Jude's face in a firm slap. He gasps in pain, his wide eyes landing on me in an instant.

"Eyes on me," I snarl at him. "Not that bastard."

"Yes," he breathes. "Sorry, Eight."

"You fucking will be."

Rotating my hips, I take him deep inside before lifting and slamming back down. Jude's eyes roll back in his head, and when they open again, there's an intriguing sliver of darkness flecked through the golden hue.

Hello, old friend.

"You're lucky I haven't slaughtered every last one of them just to have you to myself," he hisses in his old voice. "Don't test me, princess."

Without warning, two hands slide underneath my arms and pluck me from his lap. I slide off his sheath, growling a colourful curse. My back crashes into the mattress as Hudson looms between my spread legs.

He cuts Jude a sharp look. "For that smart-ass comment, you get to watch me fuck our girl instead. Don't forget that she's *ours*, dickhead."

Pinning my legs open, he surges inside me so fast, I almost see stars. The aching emptiness left by his rude interruption is filled back up to the brim. A fog of ecstasy settles over me, expanding with each punishing advance.

"Scream my name for him to hear. Jude clearly needs reminding of how this works. Your cunt will always belong to me, first and foremost."

Vision blackening, I moan through a powerful wave of pleasure that's carrying me to the edge of falling apart. Not even Kade sneaking back into the room and watching our chaotic tangle can distract me from my impending release.

"Now," Hudson dictates. "Scream."

"Fuck, Hud!"

Heat sizzles through me with the onslaught of his cock determined to break me in half. I fall apart with a loud bellow, my hands fisting in the bed sheets. He pulls out before he can finish.

"If you want to come, you'll clean our girl up," Hudson orders sternly. "She's gotten herself all wet and messy."

Chastised, Jude crawls across the bed on his knees to duck his head between my trembling legs. The two swap places with silent ease. I've barely come down from my orgasm when Jude's mouth lands on my soaked pussy.

His tongue spears my slit, lapping at the flow of juices evidencing my climax. When his head lifts, he tilts it to the side and Hudson wastes no time shoving his cock between Jude's open lips, still glistening with my come.

"This will shut your know-it-all mouth up." He pushes into him with quick, frenzied thrusts. "I'll kill you long before you kill me. Remember that."

Hudson rides his mouth for several brutal pumps before yanking a handful of his hair to break the connection. He sneaks around him to settle at his rear. His length now slick, he pushes Jude's lower back to bend him over.

"I'm gonna make your precious princess watch while I fuck you now," Hudson informs him. "She's only yours when I say so."

"What happened to ours?" Jude grunts.

"You had her to yourself for three fucking years. Don't test my damn patience or I'll drive you back to that hospital myself and leave you there."

Like I said… it's a love-hate thing. More often than not, love is hate. We love the very things that destroy us, and show our love in shades of violent destruction. The two extremes will always be inexplicably bound.

I eagerly watch as Hudson gathers saliva in his mouth and spits directly on Jude's asshole, using a thumb to spread the moisture around before pushing the tip of his cock against his back entrance.

"So tight for me," Hudson observes. "Who's in control now, huh?"

Jude can't form a full sentence, settling for an overwhelmed garble of grunts and moans instead. Hudson eases in slowly before shifting his hips and finding his own rhythm. All I can hear is their flesh slapping together.

I actually think watching them fuck the living death out of each other is far hotter than being touched by either one of them. I could watch their angry, loveless tangle of limbs all day long. It's mesmerising.

With the pair wrapped up in each other, I notice a third presence lingering at the edge of the bed. Kade's washed and sobered up, his own erection now clasped in his hands as he watches our performance.

I shuffle further down the bed, giving Jude room to bury his face in the sheets as Hudson continues to pummel his ass. Kade takes the cue and settles next to me, his back meeting the nearby wall.

"Got some energy left for me, love?"

"Plenty," I quip back.

He eyes the nearby pair. "Should we move to the other bed?"

"No need," Hudson interrupts. "I want to watch."

Kade rolls his eyes. "Not sure how I feel about you looking at my dick, Hud. Bit weird."

"Not you," he snaps. "Her. I want to watch her."

With a quick check of the third bed, I find Phoenix and Eli wrapped around each other. They're taking brief, breathless pauses from their tangle of tongues to watch our live show.

No doubt, they'll be demanding my presence next. This was unplanned, but the electricity crackling in the room has eroded any remaining boundaries between us. There's no secrets left to hide.

Straddling Kade's waist, I stroke my hand up and down his hardened length before lining it up with my entrance. After one mind-numbing orgasm, I'm still crazy turned on. I want to fuck every single one of them.

We haven't done this before.

This is a first.

"Wait." Kade grabs hold of my wrists in his iron-clad grip and pins them against my sides. "Slowly. I want to feel how wet you are right now."

"Kade—"

"I said slowly," he scolds. "Be patient."

Moaning in angst, I spear myself on him, letting just the tip of his cock nudge inside. It's a cruel taunt. All I want is his whole length to surge into me and fill every last corner of my pussy with his hot seed.

"Now a little more," he commands.

Sinking further down on him, bit by torturous bit, he controls my descent. I'm kept pinned and compliant on his lap. Not even the shudders of the bed enduring Hudson and Jude's fucking can break his hold on me.

"Such a perfect pussy," he praises, his eyes dark with desire. "Did they make you come already?"

"Yes," I mewl.

"Let's see if we can top that, shall we?"

Pulling on my wrists, Kade allows me to sink down fully on his cock. With his whole girth filling me, I writhe on his lap. Just seeing the other two screwing each other senseless mere inches away is eroding my patience.

"Ride me, baby. I want to see your tits bouncing in my face."

With my wrists released, I brace my hands on his muscular shoulders. Kade's face disappears in the swell of my chest before his mouth finds the stiffened peak of one of my nipples. I groan while beginning to ride him.

His teeth bite down, marking a path of dark marks across to my left breast. Taking that nipple between his lips, Kade sucks my mound into his mouth, his other hand still holding my hip.

"You're so fucking perfect," he groans.

My legs feel like jelly as I raise and lower myself on him in quick succession. I'm chasing something—a release, a high, the irretrievable sense of completion that only he can give me. It feels just out of reach.

When the bite of his nails cuts into my throat, that goal inches ever closer. Kade clasps my throat, replacing the bruising necklace his brother first laid on me, and I feel my lungs seize.

"Keep going," he whispers. "You can breathe when you come, love."

Without a steady flow of oxygen into my starved veins, each thrust of his dick up into my slit is another step towards oblivion. I want to melt into him, our essences suffusing into a single elixir.

Dragging my own nails against the flushed skin of his shoulders and chest, I leave a trail of jagged, blood-flecked scratches. My chest is burning. I need a breath. Just one. A single sliver of air.

But not even the injuries I inflict on his flesh grant me that privilege. All I'm allowed is the hard pump of his cock in my cunt. Over and over. Bruising. Breaking. Imprinting his ownership deep inside of me.

I'm clenched around him, my walls tightening with each second. It's close. The inevitable implosion frays the edges of my brain. At the last second, Kade reads it on my face and releases his harsh restraint on my windpipe.

"There's my girl," he encourages. "Fall apart for me."

With the flow of sweet, glorious air entering my lungs, another release hits me in a well-timed avalanche. Fireworks erupt everywhere beneath my skin in a series of successive explosions.

Forehead colliding with his chest, my entire body quakes and trembles. Each breath burns fiercely in my organs. He's still inside me, but I can feel the warmth of his own release spreading through the space between us.

"Fucking hell, Brooke."

I release an exhausted laugh. "Yeah."

Hudson's grunting has fallen quiet too as he slumps behind Jude, his dark eyes locked on me even as his brother's release drips from my cunt. We're all immersed in the same seductive dance of devils and death.

When Hudson pulls out of him, Jude sits upright, panting for air. His dick is still harder than polished steel. I have no idea how he's held on until now. He ignores Kade gasping beneath me and shuffles closer, until his length is eye level with my face.

"Open your mouth," he growls. "I'm close."

I sneak a glance down at Kade. He isn't protesting, watching us both with an intrigued look in his hazel eyes. I'm not sure quite when we crossed the line from individual sex to all fucking in a lawless pile.

Parting my lips, I let Jude shove his cock inside my mouth. It only takes two hard sucks for his muscles to clench. He pulls out and bellows loudly as a hot burst of come lands on my cheeks and lips.

Dripping in salty droplets, I lick the fluid from around my mouth, feeling more warm liquid soaking into my face. Jude grins at the mess he's made and lets himself collapse backwards into Hudson's open arms.

Huh. Being covered in their seed at the same time wasn't on my European bucket list. I'm not even sure what belongs to who anymore. The greedy voice inside my head preens at that realisation.

"Ahem." A throat clears. "You're not done, firecracker."

I'm too tired to even lift my head, but that doesn't stop a fresh spike of arousal from seeping through me. There must be something irreparably broken inside me if I still want more after all that.

When someone's hand slips into my mane of ashy-blonde hair and gently tugs to lift my head, a burst of energy gives me the strength to sit upright.

Kade is relaxed beneath me, his eyes semi-shut, still floating in his own satisfied, post-sex bubble. The softness of a pair of plush lips brushes against my earlobe.

"Baby girl," Eli purrs throatily.

Hell, I could come for a third time from his low, growling voice alone. Still covered in stickiness, I let him pull me off Kade's lap. A pair of heavily scarred arms band around my naked waist, dragging me across the room.

"Good, Elijah," Phoenix praises. "Bring her to me."

With a view of Hudson, Jude and Kade all watching me be manhandled away from them, the supple fabric of another bed meets my spine. I'm tossed on the mattress by Eli as Phoenix appears next to him.

They both stare at me, already undressed from fooling around with each other. In Phoenix's hands, his worn, black-leather belt is held at the ready. His full lips quirk into a sinister, devilish smile, full of dark intentions.

"Wrists. Now."

Without complaint, I offer myself to him. "Yes, Nix."

Stepping closer, he carefully wraps the belt around my two wrists before flipping me over so that I'm resting on my knees. My arms are lifted forwards, and there's a *clank* as the buckle meets the bed frame, securing the length of leather to the polished metal poles.

Happy with his handiwork, Phoenix sits back, staring down at my whole body splayed out for his perusal. I test the restraints and hiss through my clenched teeth. They're tight, and pain is burning across my wrists.

"Does it hurt?" he queries.

"They're a bit tight."

"Good," Eli concludes. "Make them tighter, Nix."

Grinning from ear to ear, Phoenix ignores my curse of pain and reaches for the belt again. He notches the buckle up a hole, until the bite of leather is almost cutting off circulation to my wrists. I can't flex them at all now.

It's agonising, the sense of total vulnerability. In this position, I'm trapped on my knees, with my back curved and bare ass raised high in the air for everyone to see. My aching pussy is on full display to the entire room.

"Better?"

Eli nods, biting his bottom lip. "Perfect."

"Look at that soaking wet cunt all laid out for us," Phoenix says in wonderment. "Are you dripping because everyone's watching you get fucked like the whore you are?"

When I don't answer at first, his hand collides with my exposed pussy lips so hard, tears prickle in the corners of my eyes. I'm so turned on, it actually hurts. My exhaustion has left the building.

"Answer him," Eli adds.

When Phoenix slaps my slit again, harder this time, I scream out in equal parts pain and pleasure.

"Yes. I am!"

"Am what?" he snickers.

"I… I like that they're watching us."

"What if me and little Elijah here fuck you at the same time… while they're watching? Would you still like that?"

Instead of hitting me again, Phoenix swipes a tender hand over my sore ass cheek. My back arches when his index finger travels lower, between my slick thighs, to find my molten core. He flicks my clit in a merciless tease.

"Going by how soaked your pretty cunt is, I'd say you do want that," he concludes. "You'll have to beg for it first, though. You made us wait until last."

"Nix," I groan.

"Yes? Something to say?"

His finger suddenly thrusts inside my entrance, reigniting the sparks firing deep inside my lower belly. I'm embarrassingly wet after coming a few too many times, sandwiched between muscles and demanding bastards.

"Go on, Eli," Phoenix instructs. "She's waiting for you."

A flash of translucent skin slips beneath me, sliding into the space between my prone form and the mattress. Eli grabs my hip, using it to leverage himself into place underneath me.

His thumb strokes over the familiar ridges of discoloured skin that marks the words he carved into me so many agonising, grief-laden years ago. They're still visible, forever scarred in blood and desperate promises.

Raising his head to whisper to me, Eli's voice is a sinful whisper in my ear. "*Donec mors nos separavit.*"

Capturing his lips before he can escape, I repeat the whispered promise through the stroke of my tongue on his. Every time I kiss him, it's like the first time all over again: Nothing but each other and the desolate remains of a mausoleum witnessing our bartered deals with the devil.

His hand on my hip guides me onto his awaiting shaft. I strain against the restraints, needing the pressure of his punishing steel inside me. I straddle him, my legs still trembling, and attempt to find a comfortable position that doesn't twinge my outstretched arms.

His hips surge upwards, invading the depths of being. Moans fall from my lips, panting and breathless. Being held, frozen in a position of their choosing, is just another layer of power and control that I've surrendered to them.

Eli's thumb skates over my open lips, and I can feel him swiping the remaining flecks of Jude's release from my skin. My pussy clenches tight around him as he sucks his thumb into his mouth, savouring another man's come like it's his own.

Overwhelmed by sensations assaulting me in every direction, I almost crumble at the mere touch of Phoenix's fingertips against my spine. The bed dips with his weight settling on it.

His crotch pushes against my raised ass, and our hot flesh brushes together. I can feel how hard he is. Eli's still hammering into me, commanding our collision from underneath.

I submit to every pump he inflicts on my aching cunt. When Phoenix's hand lowers to my asshole, I know he's going to push me right to the edge.

"Reckon you can take another?" he asks.

Despite feeling like I'm on the verge of a meltdown, I can't help but pant a pathetic, desperate *yes please* as his wet finger circles my back entrance. He's spreading saliva and teasing the ring of sensitive muscle with each stroke.

Phoenix's thumb penetrates me, pushing deep into my asshole. I scream out a pleasured grunt. With Eli's cock driving me to the edge of despair, I know I won't last long when Phoenix joins the party.

Removing his thumb, he replaces it with a slick digit, working it in and out to stretch the muscle wider. I pull again on the belt, causing the bed frame to creak ominously.

My hands are grasping the thick belt so tight, I can see the white of my knuckles straining to escape. Every rotation of his fingers causes me to moan, begging for his mercy.

"Eli," Phoenix warns. "Stop."

With the trained obedience that first enticed me into their fascinating relationship, Eli's movements halt. The minute he stills, Phoenix pushes something much bigger into the crack of my asshole and I scream out again.

"Fucking hell," he cusses. "So tight."

Eli grasps my chin, forcing me to look down at him. "That's it, baby girl. Take it all."

With his other hand, he finds the swollen nub of my clit and strums it. Between his fingers playing with me and Phoenix's length easing inside my ass, my orgasm swells on the horizon, threatening to implode.

"Move, Eli," Phoenix grunts.

Without a complaint, my silent attacker surges back into me. With two cocks filling every space I have available to sacrifice, I become nothing but frenzied breaths and hungry moans for more.

Phoenix's hands are clamped on my hips, guiding his steady thrusts into me from behind. He's starting slow, letting his length brush against the other buried deep inside me.

It's fucking thrilling to know that they can feel each other inside my body. When I manage a quick glance to the side, three sets of awe-filled eyes are enraptured by our display.

They can't seem to look away from us—the two evil sons of bitches determined to rip me apart, atom from atom, just to prove that my entire soul belongs to them.

Forever and always.

Until death do us part.

Eli grabs one of my nipples and twists, dragging my eyes back down to him. His luminous green gaze is almost swallowed whole by darkness with how much his pupils are dilated. It soothes me to know that the feeling is mutual.

He might be my drug, but I sure as fuck am his as well. I'd take Eli's rage above main-lining heroin any day of the week and be entirely satisfied with my choice. He's a far better method of self-destruction.

When his thrusts grow unsteady, I know he's ready to spill himself into me. I throw my head back and release the floodgates on my own desire. We can appeal to God's violent wrath together as we climax.

Warmth shoots into me, hot and heady. I watch Eli's eyes fall shut as a deep, lamenting groan escapes his lips. That's all it takes to push me back into the unknown—falling, spiralling, shattering into pieces.

Skin alight with too many sensations to categorise, I can't summon a single protest as Phoenix pulls out from my asshole. He saunters around the bed, still fisting his glistening dick.

The moment he stops holding me up, my body collapses on top of Eli's in a tired slump. I can hardly hold my shoulders in place to stop the still-tied restraints from wrenching my sore muscles.

Phoenix stops at the side of the bed, stroking his dick over and over. I know he's close too from the ragged breaths hissing between his teeth. They'd already been screwing around while I was with the others.

Grabbing Eli by a handful of his curly hair, he pulls his head to the side. Eli's eyes reopen, locked on the generous inches of hard cock right in front of him. Phoenix bends his knees ever so slightly.

"Mouth open, Elijah. I want her to watch you swallow every drop of my come."

Opening his mouth wider, Eli's dark, thick eyelashes dapple across his cheeks as he waits. Silent and pleading. Compliant and vulnerable. We're both servants to Phoenix's need for domination.

With a final pump of his fist, I watch the strands of come shoot from the tip of his cock and land on Eli's outstretched tongue. He greedily laps up every salty bead, letting Phoenix empty himself into the awaiting prison of his mouth.

When he's done, gasping with a hand braced on the bed frame, Phoenix grips Eli's chin to bring their lips together in a hard crash. I watch, wordless and stunned, as their tongues wrestle right in front of me.

He's tasting his own release in Eli's mouth, drinking it down with eagerness. When their kiss breaks, both look up at me, wearing matching smirks.

"Um." I blink, speechless. "Hell."

Phoenix knows exactly what *not* to say, of course.

"Was that a better show than them two?" he replies.

If I had an ounce of energy left, I'd facepalm. Jude bursts out in laughter across the room while Hudson stares daggers at Phoenix's bare back. Fucking morons. The dick-measuring contest will never end.

"For the record"—Kade's voice interrupts our laugher—"if any of you wankers ever wave your dick near me, I'll fucking cut it off. Zero complaints."

Jude snorts. "I'd like to see you try."

————

Shivering in the cool evening air, the glow of my cigarette matches the glimmers of bright lights that paint Paris's nighttime horizon. On the rooftop balcony, I have a panoramic view of the entire city.

In the distance, the structure of the Eiffel Tower is lit with glinting lights, twinkling like a giant, over-polished diamond. It's the central focal point of what's fast becoming one of my favourite cities.

Leaning against the brick wall, I savour the musky smoke that enters my lungs before I exhale. The pleasure of a good cigarette in the silent peace of darkness is something I will never take for granted again.

It's at moments like this that I realise how far I've come. The day I set foot through Blackwood Institute's gates, I had every intention of being dead within three months. Gone. Zip. Nada.

Nearly five years later, I'm still here. Inhaling. Exhaling. Hoping. Healing. Learning to love again. That twisted seed of sickness in my head did its best to take my life from me... but I didn't let it.

No.

That's not right.

They didn't let it.

That's the thing about soulmates. You never intend to find them and, more often than not, they appear in the unlikeliest of places. Friendships. New acquaintances. Enemies. Toxic, mentally unstable inmates locked up against their will.

We're fucking lucky.

I'm grateful to be alive.

Finishing my cigarette with a sigh, I flick the glowing bud aside. Tomorrow morning, we set off for England. Our three-month trip is at a close, and the impatient future is eagerly awaiting our return.

It's time to finally face the music and begin to rebuild my life. No matter how messy, ugly and goddamn painful that will be.

Nothing is linear in this life. Nothing is easy. But that won't stop me from grabbing hold of this opportunity and riding the hell out of whatever rollercoaster is set to come.

The metal exterior door groans as it's forced open. I stifle a laugh. Clearly, showers aren't the only place that I can expect to be interrupted in. One of the five men that wield my heart are never far from reach.

"Love? You good?"

Kade.

Sweet, controlling, brilliant Kade.

"Yeah," I call back. "Just enjoying the view."

His footsteps join me. Two arms band around my torso from behind, and I feel his chin settle on my shoulder. Together, we study the teeming, almost sentient, capital city together. It's so unbelievably beautiful.

"The others are all asleep," he murmurs.

"I know."

"You couldn't?"

"Nope. Worried about tomorrow, I guess."

Snuggling closer, he kisses my tangled hair. "Whatever it brings, we'll face it together. Side by fucking side."

Spinning in his arms, I turn my back on the so-called city of love and face an even more incredible sight; the bottomless hazel orbs of the man that saved my life, even when I didn't want him to.

Thanks to Kade, I have all of this.

He gave me a future.

"Have I ever told you just how much I love you?"

His smile is so damn wide, it splits his mouth wide open.

"Once or twice. I'll hear it again though."

I press my forehead against his. "Kade Knight, I fucking love you."

"Would you mind telling me that every single day for the rest of our lives? If it's not too much trouble."

"Happily." I laugh, my heart almost bursting. "Just don't turn into an egotistical son of a bitch like your brother. We have enough alphaholes in this group. I need you here to keep them grounded."

"I will always be here, Brooke. To keep all of you grounded."

Our lips find each other, slow and tender. We have the rest of our lives to bicker, fight and bruise our twisted brand of love into one another. All I need right now is his word. A solemn oath. The promise of forever.

"I'm going to marry you one day," Kade blurts.

My breath seizes. "What?"

"I know we're messes, and I'm not saying that our lives will always be smooth sailing, but I need you to know that I have every intention of dying with you by my side."

My throat clogs with emotion, and my eyes burn with unshed tears. Part of me is absolutely stunned that he'd want to permanently, legally tie himself to my chaotic shitshow for the rest of his life. A larger part of me is stunned that I actually want that. With all of them.

"You saved my entire family, Brooklyn West. Every last worthless one of us. And for that, my gorgeous girl, I promise you forever."

"Forever?" I echo, my cheeks soaked now.

His nose nudges mine as a breathtaking smile blossoms on his lips.

"Yeah, love. Fucking forever."

And that right there is why I stayed alive.

For them.

My fucking forevers.

PLAYLIST

LISTEN HERE:
BIT.LY/DESECRATEDSAINTS

Be Invited - The Twilight Singers
    Died Enough For You - Blind Channel
    Out Of The Black - Royal Blood
    Give - You Me At Six
    Crazy - Echos
    Time Changes Everything - The Plot In You
    Doomed - Bring Me The Horizon
    Left alone - Zero 9:36
    You Are Everything - Holding Absence
    PSYCHO - Aviva
    Lost - Ollie
    Kerosene - Vanish
    Lust - Saint JHN & Janelle Kroll
    Summer Set Fire to the Rain - Thrice
    Birdcage - Holding Absence
    Lost - The Hunna
    Pretty Toxic Revolver - Machine Gun Kelly
    Me & My Demons - Omido and Silent Child
    Lydia - Highly Suspect
    RIGGED - The Plot In You
    Reset Me - Nothing But Thieves
    Hurts Like Hell - Fleurie
    Teresa - YUNGBLUD
    Fourth of July (Remix) - Fall Out Boy
    Casual Sabotage - YUNGBLUD
    DiE4u - Bring Me The Horizon
    Youth - Cleopatrick
    Heat Waves - Our Last Night

Somebody Else - Circa Waves
It's Okay To Be Afraid - Saint Slumber
Wonderful Life - Bring Me The Horizon & Dani Filth
Hope for the Underrated Youth - YUNGBLUD
Hurricane - Dream on Dreamer
Bad Life - Sigrid & Bring Me The Horizon

NEWSLETTER

Want more madness? Sign up to J Rose's newsletter for monthly announcements, exclusive content, sneak peeks, giveaways and more!

Sign up here:
www.jroseauthor.com/newsletter

ABOUT THE AUTHOR

J Rose is an independent dark romance author from the United Kingdom. She writes challenging, plot-driven stories packed full of angst, heartbreak and broken characters fighting for their happily ever afters.

She's an introverted bookworm at heart, with a caffeine addiction, penchant for cursing, and an unhealthy attachment to fictional characters.

Feel free to reach out on social media, J Rose loves talking to her readers!

For exclusive insights, updates, and general mayhem, join J Rose's Bleeding Thorns on Facebook.

Business enquiries: j_roseauthor@yahoo.com

Come join the chaos. Stalk J Rose here...
www.jroseauthor.com/socials

ALSO BY J ROSE

Buy Here:

www.jroseauthor.com/books

Reading Order:

www.jroseauthor.com/readingorder

Blackwood Institute

Twisted Heathens

Sacrificial Sinners

Desecrated Saints

Sabre Security

Corpse Roads

Skeletal Hearts

Hollow Veins

Harrowdean Manor

Sin Like The Devil

Burn Like An Angel

Briar Valley

Where Broken Wings Fly

Where Wild Things Grow

Standalones

Forever Ago

Drown in You

A Crimson Carol

Writing as Jessalyn Thorn

Departed Whispers

If You Break

When You Fall

Made in United States
North Haven, CT
28 July 2024

55530795R20441